A Farewell to France

By the same author

NOEL BARBER

A Farewell to France

HODDER AND STOUGHTON
LONDON SYDNEY AUCKLAND TORONTO

British Library Cataloguing in Publication Data
Barber, Noel
  A farewell to France.
  I. Title
  823'.914[F]   PR6052.A623

ISBN 0 340 28732 2

For
Denise Kilmarnock
with love

ACKNOWLEDGMENTS

My most grateful thanks to Anthony Davis for his painstaking help with research both in France and England; to Alan Wykes for his help with the script; to Giorgio Lucich of Florence for his help in arranging my schedule and research on location in Florence and the surrounding countryside; and to Jean Riddell for her patience in typing out the five versions of this novel.

N.B.
London, 1983

CONTENTS

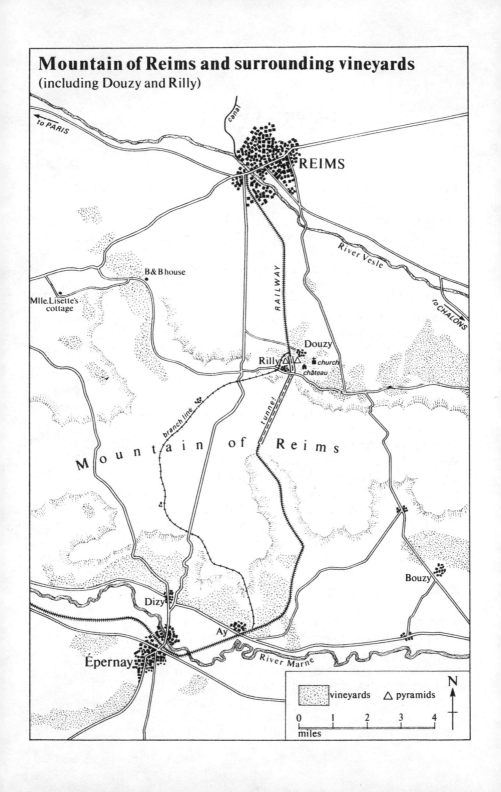

Mountain of Reims and surrounding vineyards
(including Douzy and Rilly)

to PARIS

canal

REIMS

River Vesle

to CHALONS

RAILWAY

B&B house

Mlle. Lisette's cottage

Douzy

Rilly

church

château

branch line

tunnel

M o u n t a i n   o f   R e i m s

Bouzy

Dizy

Ay

Épernay

River Marne

vineyards   △ pyramids

N

0   1   2   3   4
miles

PROLOGUE

For all our youth the Astell family had lived in and out of Douzy, the small château named after the village, hidden by vineyards lining the gentle, sloping hills of Champagne. My American father and mother, his father's father, my French grandmother, my brother and his twin sister, our friends, our lovers – all had made up a patchwork of happiness that none believed would ever end.

Douzy in those days was the warm and friendly heart not only of our home but the village, the orchard where we stole apples, the lake on which we rowed, the fields in which we picked wild flowers, the vineyards, the cellars, the Home Farm with its smell of freshly baked bread, the horses, the cows, the cars. Though never gasping with opulence we were never poor, and it seemed to us, in those far-off days, when I first fell in love with Sonia, impossible that our secure world would ever disintegrate.

Why should it? Even after 1939, Douzy remained unique, an American enclave in a war that gave every indication of petering out through boredom. And if we caught glimpses of gun emplacements in the Champagne area, or read about the Maginot Line, we hardly noticed them in a French world guarded by an army unsurpassed in valour and fighting skills. To us – to thousands like us – we regarded all this with an aloof air, almost flaunting our unconcern as though Americans, even in France, would always remain neutral, closing a collective eye to the dangers surrounding them.

That was before. But then the serenity of life at Douzy was changed for lives that tore us apart, of death and torture for some, despite neutrality, and eventually, after America entered the war, for me a life spent in ditches and barns, hunting the enemy or being hunted – to protect or to kill.

For though I was an American I was also as French as the

11

Resistance leaders with whom I worked. Most of my life had been spent a few hundred yards from the ditches into which I slid, hiding from the Germans, from the house where my father had vanished, and which had been turned into an officers' mess for the *Wehrmacht*. Only my French grand-mother had been permitted on sufferance to occupy a couple of rooms apart from the rest of the house, while I learned, too, that my father, more French in many ways than American, had remained in Reims.

Then, after we had blown up the tunnel in 1944, and the lethal cargo inside it, Patton's armour – drinking four hundred thousand gallons of petrol a day – had thundered in, past Le Mans, Chartres, past Paris itself, scything eastwards in terrifying sweeps, brushing aside the enemy Germans like maggots. By the end of August Patton himself drove into Reims, and for the first time in months we walked freely in the streets, surrounded by thousands of exulting American G.I.s thronging the cafés, the sidewalks, stopping the traffic in the streets itself.

No wonder that at first it was impossible to realise that the nightmare was over – that the sunny skies of the summer of 1944 really did exist, that the air was free to breathe. I remember that moment so well. A Frenchman in the Resistance had joined me for a celebration drink – a beer first in the Bar Central in the rue de Chanzy, and after that a glass of local red Bouzy wine – very rare now – in the rue Gambetta.

Yet though it was a moment for rejoicing both of us felt shy. Despite the backslapping, the free drinks, there was almost a sense of nervousness. After years on the run, I had become instinctively furtive, almost afraid to announce, even to a barman, who I really was.

I was frightened of something else – ironically, the future – and what peace might bring. The war had provided a hiatus in which all our family questions had remained unanswered, like dusty letters accumulating through the letter box when the house is empty. One day soon I would arrive home – and have to sort out the pile of unanswered questions.

Certainly the changes that had washed across France had affected my father and mother. My brother Guy was a different person, as was my sister Anna, tortured. Nor could I forget Olivia, who, with Anna, had been tortured by the Gestapo such a long time ago. But most of all I thought of Sonia. Beautiful Sonia, married to an Italian, an 'enemy' but still the woman I had always loved, always would.

The wonderful youth we had enjoyed together had been sliced away from us in Douzy, where Sonia had been almost a member of the family before she married, where without warning unseen hands drew closed the curtains of time.

Of course I had to report eventually and, late that evening, with the city of Reims erupting in song and dance, and the champagne spilling over every café pavement, I stopped the first military policeman I saw. He looked me up and down – my blue blouse, my uncut dirty blond hair, my scruffy face fringed with beard. Then leaning out of his Jeep he asked me, chewing gum, 'What's the trouble, buddy?'

I swallowed hard. There was no need now for subterfuge, but when I said, 'Corporal, I'm Major Astell of the U.S. Army,' I felt the sudden grip of panic that comes to the hunted; terrified the corporal would disbelieve me.

Hastily I added, 'I've been told to report to Colonel Nolan of Com. Z. I'm from Department Q.J.' 'Com. Z.' might mean nothing more than a gigantic communications network, but the magic Letters 'Q.J.' signified much more – a magical formula commanding instant respect. Still, I felt an odd quiver of apprehension. I had never tried out the secret letters – after all, you were only supposed to use them once in your life, and now I was half afraid they wouldn't work – that after one look at my filthy clothes, my gaunt, dirty face, someone would snarl, 'Beat it!'

'Okay, sir,' said the M.P. 'Jump in.'

Colonel Nolan was very agreeable if a little fussy. He had sandy hair and large horn-rimmed glasses. An armchair soldier, but none the worse for that, he was intrigued by the secret nature of my work, by my unkempt appearance. But he immediately asked an orderly to bring me my first cup of good American coffee for months, made me welcome in a building in the northern suburbs which had been commandeered in his name, and promised me some clean civilian clothes. He also had a tendency to feeble jokes.

'I won't ask you about your work, Major,' he smiled, 'except to say that if you want to take a bath we've got unlimited hot water right here – though I expect you've been in plenty of hot water yourself lately.'

I laughed politely.

'I've been told to give you any help I can,' he added. 'I guess you know that General Patton has established his headquarters in Châlons-sur-Marne – about twenty miles south-east of Reims. We've established our Div. headquarters – the 90th – here at Reims.'

I nodded. 'What I would really appreciate is a little personal help.'

'Anything I can do for you, Major.'

'Well, it sounds crazy, but I used to live near here. Only a few miles from Reims. I've learned that my grandmother was allowed to keep a couple of rooms, but then the Germans kicked her out. I'll soon find out where she is, but I'd like to see the house again, if you could provide transport.'

'Why, sure. But you mean you actually used to *live* here? An American family?'

I nodded again. 'What's left of them.'

'Anything I can do, Major,' he repeated. 'I don't know what you've been up to' – again he looked at me hopefully – 'but I've been told by Div. headquarters to give you top priority. Though you look kinda young for . . .'

'Early thirties,' I grinned, 'but I feel sixty. I'll wear better when I've taken you up on that bath. And Colonel – do my orders say that after I'm debriefed I can have a furlough? I haven't had leave in months.'

'For Chrissakes! You're due for a long, long leave – and you can go where you want. Paris? Back home Stateside? You name it.'

'Switzerland – to see my girl.'

'*Switzerland!* Hold up, Major. I'm willing to do everything I can – but hell, I don't know whether I'm *permitted* to send army property into a foreign country. And then there's the problem of gas. There's none left. Even Patton's run out of fuel. Getting a gas ration for you will be like . . .'

'Don't worry, Colonel. I've got all the gas I need – and my own car. I hid it before the Germans took over. I'll tell you about it after that bath.'

In the end Colonel Nolan offered to drive me himself to our home. Like all Com. Z. officers he had a big car, a driver and an armed G.I. ('In case we need assistance,' he explained.)

'That's too much trouble, Colonel,' I murmured.

'Feel free,' he said. 'It's in a town or a village or what?'

'Well – actually,' I hadn't thought about explanations. 'It's by itself. Rather isolated.'

Most of Colonel Nolan's Com. Z. sector in the 90th Division was centred north of Reims where the N44 highway straggled through the undistinguished suburb of La Neuvillette, a drab series of apartments and shops in busy streets; though soon we reached the busier, wider avenues of the sprawling city centre.

As we edged our way through streets jammed with excited French men and women trying to shake hands with the colonel, some offered flowers, others kisses each time the traffic slowed down. In the streets the girls threw their arms round the G.I.s and kissed them as though their love would never die. They were not in love with any one man, I thought, but with life itself. How could anyone *not* fall in love with liberty and freedom?

Nolan was enjoying himself. He waved paternally, local leader of an army of liberation. He loved the cheers, they loved the handwaves, so everyone was happy. And I too began to catch the frenzy of excitement, though not in the way Nolan did. For though I was an American officer, we were at this moment driving through one of the most historic cities in France, the ancient citadel of Reims, where French kings had been crowned throughout the ages, where in the 1914 war only eighty houses and buildings had escaped damage; and I was an integral part of this city. Here was the first school I attended as a child, the first football games I had played, a whole life spent away from America.

The heart that beat with patriotic fervour was a hundred-and-fifty per cent American. I was willing to die for my country – yet I had reservations. I was ready to *die* for America, yes, but I would rather not live in it. I would also hate to *die* for France – yet I would always be content to live in it.

As I looked out of the window of the car, the wildly enthusiastic crowds actually stopped the traffic at the place Aristide Briand, where the boulevard Lundy runs into the boulevard de la Paix and the nearby champagne houses. As I looked at the people, the surroundings, pangs of youthful memories tugged at me. Behind the *place* was a great open square where on market days – in the heart of a bustling cathedral city – the busy peasants set up their stalls, selling everything from vests to vegetables.

'And behind that,' confided Nolan, 'is the best restaurant in town, the Brasserie Boulingrin. Best French fries in France.'

I had eaten half a life's worth of *pommes frites* at the Boulingrin, its bustling waiters darting between small square tables with their red and white checked paper tablecloths. How many times had Monsieur Leleu, founder of the brasserie, slipped us extra French fries after Papa had said, 'Enough children!'

'I agree with you about the chips – I know the place well,' I smiled. 'Ever thought why its called the "Boulingrin" – odd name, isn't it?'

Colonel Nolan shook his head.

'Years back, an old lady gave the ground where the market now stands to the city of Reims, as a place where the locals could play *boule*. And "boulingrin" is a perfectly proper word – it means a bowling green. And that's where the first Monsieur Leleu founded his brasserie.'

'I'll be damned,' said the colonel.

'Now the *marché* has taken over.' I was looking at the peasants bringing in their produce from the villages that studded the surrounding countryside. The vegetable and fruit stalls were not always filled, but they still displayed an assortment of spotlessly clean endives, celeriac, bundles of *mâché* and a score of other vegetables and herbs. Each unwrapped bundle was examined thoroughly. We could see thrifty, knowledgeable housewives handle tomatoes and peaches carefully, testing one after the other, discarding the unwanted against a noisy background of drama – as though the fate of a French wife's stew depended finally on the one single bunch of onions she had chosen above all the others.

'All this handling of food – it looks darned unhygienic to me,' Nolan said, looking at the mounds of vegetables with distaste.

I almost laughed. 'The French don't *like* their vegetables wrapped, Colonel. They like to pick and choose, handle everything. They like the smell of fresh earth on a bunch of radishes.'

After we had passed the *marché*, I showed the driver the way. We crossed the place Royale – an exquisite miniature version of the place Vendôme in Paris – and then past the cathedral with its smiling angel to the left of the main entrance. After that it was easy. We bore right until we reached the broad avenue d'Épernay, the main road leading straight as a ruler to Champagne's second most important city, Épernay, south of the Marne.

We didn't have far to go. Soon the open road on either side was flanked by never-ending rows of vineyards that spread like a carpet across the great Plain of Reims, fashioned by a beneficent nature to produce a heaven-sent storehouse of riches. Yet the same nature, by a devilish quirk, was able to switch off heaven and switch on hell at will, for this huge flat plain had also from time immemorial provided Europe's greatest natural arena of battle, sitting astride the enemies of a dozen countries anxious to despoil it.

Seven or eight miles further along the straight road, near the edge of the modest Mountain of Reims, we turned left at a signpost, marked 'To Douzy, Rilly, Mailly.' All were famous Champagne names.

'Rilly? That strikes a bell,' said Nolan. 'That's where the Krauts blew up the tunnel sky-high. I heard the Germans were hoarding explosives and blew themselves up by mistake.'

The rumour factory of O.S.S., the Office of Strategic Services, was certainly working efficiently. That was exactly the story which had been deliberately, but inaccurately, started.

'Douzy?' said Colonel Nolan. 'Funny sort of name, isn't it?'

'It *is* an odd name, Douzy. I believe there's another village called Douzy somewhere,' I said as I guided the driver off the road from Mailly, showing him where to turn. 'But we acquired the name by honest-to-God French logic.'

'How come?'

'It was christened Douzy by two families who founded it after leaving two other neighbouring villages,' I explained as our car bumped along. 'The villages are still there. One is called Dizy and the other, a few miles away, is called Bouzy.'

This was a simple and true explanation, but Nolan was much more impressed when we turned off the pale yellow, chalky two-mile private road and he read the weather-worn wooden signpost with its flat statement: '*Vers le Château.*'

'A château?' he exclaimed. He pronounced it Sha-TOH.

'Yes, Colonel. Our home. Hope you like it. Over there! You can just see the roof through the trees.'

'A *château!*'

And that was how, after years of war and waiting, I finally came home to Douzy. As I looked around, driving slowly from the main road, my heart started thumping wildly. I had the curious feeling that I had been catapulted back in time and, struggling inside, was a small boy looking with wonder at what I was doing.

The ground sloped away in a dell where in winter I had sledged down a thousand times as a child, every fold of the long, dipping, tree-studded grass as familiar to me as my own hands. I saw it in memory as carefully tended, but even now the weeds, the thistles, the knee-high grass couldn't rob me of its beauty. I felt a surge of elation, memories stumbling through my brain as we drove past the silhouettes of old barns, derelict buildings, signposts of history along the pathways of my youth, my innocence, my family, my loves, my home.

Through a gap in the trees I saw the distant hills, and beyond them the tree line – where the vines gave way, leaving the higher ground to be ruled by the trees. In the centre stood the black outline of the village church, not in the village of Douzy itself, but outside the cluster of white houses, alone, defiant, in the midst of the vineyards.

As we stopped the car outside the courtyard of the château, I led the colonel through the white stone archway. For all my life the gravel had been free of even the puniest weed, but though it was choked with grass, with more thistles, it still looked beautiful.

The house was deserted, I could see the disapproving frown of closed shutters. But the very fact that it had been occupied by the Germans was an affront. I had a sudden desire to kick the door open, if only to let in the fresh air.

'It's unlocked,' cried Nolan, twisting the knob.

'Saves the cost of a new door,' I said. 'Please – after you.'

Inside the large entrance hall, Colonel Nolan put down his field cap on the ormolu table with its gilded legs which had stood up against the wall – always with a bowl of flowers on it – since before my father was born. From there, double doors led to the main reception room.

'It's magnificent,' the colonel breathed with awe. It *wasn't* magnificent – but the colonel stroked a polished table and muttered, 'Beautiful, beautiful. It was used as a German officers' mess? Thank God nothing was broken.'

In fact most of us had hated this formal room, and I felt I had to apologise for it.

'I'm afraid it's rather pompous,' I explained. 'Grandma only liked stuffy French furniture. Come into the next room, Colonel – you'll find it more comfortable, and I'll get us all a drink.'

But as we moved into what had been our usual, warmer living room, Colonel Nolan exploded with rage. The room was a shambles. Champagne bottles, glasses, plates, many broken, looked as though they had been hurled round the room in an orgy. The striped French wallpaper was stained, remnants of food littered the Aubusson carpet, lumps of chicken, German sausages, were stuck between the cushions of the deep easy chairs. The room reeked of a bar parlour which a careless landlord hadn't bothered to clean up.

'Bloody Krauts!' shouted the colonel. 'Sergeant!' he shouted to his driver. 'Get someone on the R.T. to send in a detail to clear up the place. You've got a map reference?'

Without thinking he picked up an empty champagne bottle from a table, scrutinising the label with a puzzled frown, picked up a second, a third.

'Astell Champagne,' he read out. 'Same name, eh?'

With a sigh I admitted, 'Well, yes, sort of family business. My grandfather founded the mark.'

'Your *grandfather*!'

I said nothing.

'Good God! You make champagne!' He examined a bottle again. 'What does this mean?' He pointed to a second label, '*Reserviert für Angehörige der Deutschen Wehrmacht*'.

My German was good enough to know what *that* meant. 'Reserved for the *Wehrmacht*,' I translated.

'No longer,' cried Colonel Nolan. 'Not now, by God.' Then, as though still unable to grasp the truth, he asked, 'You mean to tell me you lived here for three generations?' He invested the final words with a special awe. 'As it's your home, maybe you could take me on a tour.'

'Sure.'

I led him through the ground floor. It was a tour for me too, a tour of memories, though each door I opened seemed to produce more evidence of the filth left behind by the invaders. In the library, once Papa's pride and joy, all the books had been stolen. In the conservatory most of the plants were dead, some thrown on the ground. It was the same everywhere. In the kitchen I arrived just in time to hear mice scurrying away. The laundry room was six inches deep in water from some broken pipes.

'It's disgusting,' cried the colonel. 'Those bastards will pay for this!'

Trying to cheer me up, he said, 'At least I hope you managed to hide your best champagne. Is that kept in back?'

'No.' I shook my head. 'There's a back entrance some distance away – through the Home Farm, which I showed you, and then there's a main entrance to the champagne cellars about half a mile down the road to Rilly.'

'I remember about Rilly – the tunnel being blown up – and now I'm remembering the name Douzy. Wasn't there something about a huge underground cave?'

'You mean the Douzy and Rilly pyramids?' I knew of course that they were in their way quite famous. I tried to explain briefly the extraordinary phenomenon of the Douzy pyramid, cut deep into the hillside by the Romans nearly two thousand years ago when they were excavating for chalk, which they prized highly as a building material, specially for inside walls.

'I don't get it.' He was puzzled. 'Why underground – and how?'

'The Romans wanted the chalk, but they couldn't use open cast mining because chalk can easily be damaged by frost or rain. So they used to dig a shaft into a convenient hillside, which they could cover at night, then haul the first blocks of chalk from it. As they dug deeper they excavated outwards and deeper from the original shaft, always underground, until eventually the Douzy pyramid was a hundred and twenty feet deep with a base fifty feet wide in each direction. Centuries later, when champagne was invented, someone discovered it was the perfect place to store it.'

'Can we go and see it?' he asked.

'I don't think so. That's the tragedy. When the Germans blew up the Rilly tunnel . . .' I hesitated – I didn't want to let him know that I was the one who had blown it up. '. . . it blew in both the Douzy and Rilly pyramids which were astride the railway line.'

'Pity,' he commented. 'Sounds fabulous. Let's take a look-see upstairs.'

Standing on the main landing, he suddenly asked me, 'How's about your mother and father? They okay?'

'My mother's in America,' I said. 'I'm afraid my father is dead.' I spoke rather shortly; I didn't want to have to elaborate.

'I'm sorry about that. Tell me . . . is the rest of the family safe?'

'I hope so. But my sister married a German . . .'

'Ah! That's bad.' He was almost treating me as an avuncular protégé. 'But don't give up hope.'

'And I have a younger brother. He had a rough time. He had a Jewish girlfriend.' I paused, memories stirring. 'It's a long story.'

At the top of the staircase I showed the colonel my father's room which overlooked the stark outline of the lonely church framed in endless vineyards.

The bedrooms were arranged on either side of the broad, spacious corridor, which was filthy. Some of the pictures had been broken, so had a table. It was wider than a corridor, really, the walls decorated with old French silk, a little faded now, but warmer and more friendly for all that. These were the secret places of our youth, and for a moment I almost forgot the damage the Germans had done, and the other Americans. I hardly realised that I said, 'This was my old room.'

'You'll be wanting to move in after your debriefing,' said the colonel.

'I won't use it,' I said without thinking. 'I prefer this one.' I reached the far end of the corridor and pushed open the door.

The room meant nothing to him, of course – he hardly noticed it – but this was Sonia's old room, the room she used every time she came to stay at the château, first as a schoolgirl on vacation when her diplomat father and mother were posted far away, later as a growing girl. Darling, wonderful, black-haired, impetuous Sonia with those startling cornflower-blue eyes . . . how many times had I made love to her in this room after the house had gone to sleep, tiptoeing to the warmth of her bed, her arms, her kisses?

'Sonia's room', as it was always called, had even been decorated according to Sonia's whim, with matching wall-paper and curtains, even the ceiling papered with the same design of red poppies, so that when only one small lamp glowed dimly it was like making love in a bed of flowers.

I opened the door of the wardrobe. A German uniform hung there, neatly pressed. On the floor lay a pile of dirty linen, shirts, socks, shorts. With a shock reality replaced the phantoms of yesterday. The officer must have left in a hurry. I wondered how long he had lived in this room, if he had ever remotely conjured up a picture of the tender secret nights that had passed in it.

That room had been an echo of our secret lives. All gone, all empty. Revisiting the years of youth, I felt a sudden shiver, as though muffling myself against melancholy, a sense of loss for happy times which had slipped away in carefree days.

I was thinking of the day in 1931 when we first became lovers, when she was only seventeen, long before any of us contemplated an end to the happy days of peace. For that was when it all began, and those were the times I liked to remember, those enchanted days of Douzy. . . .

PART ONE

Summer 1931 – Autumn 1937

As that particular summer's evening drew to a close the white building glowed almost pink, and the west wall – the lower half covered with American Pillar roses – was warm to the touch.

It was a long wall, and in the centre my grandfather had built a conservatory to catch the afternoon and evening sun, a large glass room adorned with flowering plants and white summer furniture. It looked down over the dell, the far end hedged by giant rhododendrons giving a blaze of colour in spring, grassed banks falling away from the other side of the drive, so that as children, when we sledged down in winter snows, we could also skate on the small lake beyond. By the flowering shrubs a wicker gate led to a rough orchard, and beyond that the vineyards stretched in tight, symmetrical rows.

In the pink evening, as one walked up the winding path of the dell, past the shadows of day's end already shrouding the flower beds, the last of the sun shone on the stone and set fire to the window panes of the conservatory.

Here the Astells had lived since 1873 when Richard Astell, the twenty-two-year-old son of a San Francisco real-estate millionaire, set off from Nob Hill to acquire a little 'culture' through the grand tour, and fell in love with Jacqueline de Villebrun, an only daughter whose father owned vineyards both north and south of the Marne, and whose grapes were eagerly bought by the great champagne houses and whose nickname, over the whole area, soon became La Châtelaine.

The château was discreetly hidden. Even from below, from the main road linking Épernay and Reims, you could never catch more than an occasional glimpse of slate roofs glinting like blue-grey steel, for the house lay couched in a wooded park. The curving drive wound from the main road for more than two miles past vineyards, then tree-studded lawns so sloping they could only be trimmed with the scythe, past the kitchen garden – my French grandmother had a fetish for fresh vegetables – and then the long, rectangular flower bed, almost hidden from the gravelled drive, ablaze with every kind of bloom from snapdragons to roses – because this bed was used only for cutting blooms to fill vases in every room.

It was not a pretentious building, not grandiose in the manner of most French châteaux. It had no fountains gurgling, no neatly trimmed box hedges cut in intricate patterns to comprise formal gardens. But all the same, the three-storey building – white stone, with a steep grey slated roof and slender ornate chimneys – was not only impressive, it was beautiful, perhaps because the shape and the way it nestled between trees had been cunningly devised to make Douzy château look smaller, less ostentatious. It gave the impression of being a long low country house, somehow disguising its third floor.

From the top floor, dormer windows peeped out like square eyes in the sharply sloping roof, and here the domestic staff lived: Jean the butler, who had worn a clean white jacket for each meal for twenty years or more; his wife who ran the house; 'Aubergine', a nickname for the chief parlourmaid; Yvette the cook, and sundry others, all related to the vignerons working for my father, and who came and went as they grew up, became pregnant and hastily married. At least, in retrospect, that is what seemed to happen all the time.

The first floor contained what house agents call 'the principal bedrooms', and there were seven grouped on either side of a broad landing, reached from the ground floor by a wide and handsome staircase. For as long as I could remember the décor of the landing had never changed from the dark red silk walls – faded, but no one seemed to notice – and mostly covered with scores of old sepia photographs which had, through the early years, recorded the changing history of Douzy champagne.

No one ever thought of changing the framed photographs, or adding to them, perhaps because Grandma regarded the landing as her own photograph album, and also because she hated change.

How she had shown her shocked disapproval when my parents installed a bathroom in their room, the grandest bedroom in the house, with lovely views beyond the Douzy church. A *private* bathroom connected directly to their bed-room! A bathroom that would be used by only two people! The thrifty men of Champagne sniffed as audibly as Grandma when years ago that bathroom was installed, long before the passing years had allowed modern plumbing to make the bedroom floor of Douzy a warm and comfortable oasis for tired men and women and children.

The ground floor was different: a mixture of Grandma's stiffness and Mama's warmth, largely determined by the layout of the building. The large hall could never be used for any other purpose, for it was bordered by the courtyard which you reached after driving past the cutting flower bed and turning left behind some yew trees, where an arch of white stone in the wall led to the gravelled courtyard.

On the right were the old stables, to the left double front doors led to the hall and an even larger, and very formal, reception room: a *salon*, the French called it – and it still bore the stamp of Grandma's formidable character, for she re-garded all the furniture other than French period pieces as vulgar. So out of deference (and fear?) the *salon* remained as it was in her day. It didn't really matter, for it was used only rarely, when the Astells entertained 'officially'. Behind the salon lay warmer rooms, a sitting-room of low, comfortable armchairs, the walls covered with paintings by artist friends of my father.

Within a few years of my grandfather's marriage to Jacqueline de Villebrun her parents died, and then my grandfather, some years before he died, took a momentous step. Against all the advice of his neighbours and friends, he decided to bottle his own champagne instead of selling the grapes to the big producers. Jacqueline had inherited nearly thirty acres of vineyards – about twelve of them on the Mountain of Reims covered by the famous Pinot Noir red grapes. The rest provided the white Chardonnay grapes which grew south of the Marne near Épernay.

The decision caused a furore. It was an unheard-of step, for the production of champagne, in which several wines of different years are blended, was risky and costly, and most people who were lucky enough to *own* vineyards did much better for themselves by selling instead of making. But since champagne, like port and cognac, is a blended wine, the name of the producer, not the vigneron content to sell his grapes to a big firm, decorates each label.

However, that, it seems, was just what my grandfather wanted – to see his name on the label of every bottle of champagne produced from his own vineyards.

My father did something else. Since two thirds of his vineyards were planted with Chardonnay white grapes, he decided to bottle *blanc de blancs*, produced entirely from white grapes. Other firms had produced small quantities of *blanc de blancs*, which is a lighter champagne than that produced by the traditional blending with red grapes (which have to be pressed more quickly than white ones to prevent the skin staining the juice). But though my grandfather knew that the blend of red and white gave more body, he always believed that *blanc de blancs* was more subtle, was a more delicate champagne. 'The perfect drink,' he always said, 'at midday.'

He designed a special bottle not unlike a Dom Perignon in shape, though with a longer, more slender neck – and so founded Astell champagne; not a big quantity selling brand – he rarely produced more than fifty thousand bottles a year – but both his blended champagne and his *blanc de blancs* were an instantaneous success, a champagne of superb quality in high demand wherever it could be bought.

Since the Astells were never short of money, even after my grandfather died, my father was in the enviable position of never having to compromise. If the vintage was not up to standard then we drank Astell Blanc still wine in place of champagne. Astells produced only the best – or none at all – and so it became as much a hallmark of quality as a French watch by Cartier or a pair of British shoes by Lobb. There just couldn't be anything better.

I was nineteen, and hoping to be a writer, on that eventful day in 1931. I worked three days a week in Paris, learning my trade under the watchful eye of Papa's brother, my uncle Oregon, who was the owner and editor of a weekly newspaper, the *Paris American*. My brother Guy and his twin sister Anna were two years younger, and so was Sonia whose father, Signor

Riccardi, was Italian ambassador to Paraguay. But then Sonia, who even went to the same school in Switzerland as Anna, was like a sister to us, a daughter to our parents. It had always been like this, so that even now in the early summer Sonia customarily joined the family for the half-term break.

During the afternoon I had caught sight of Anna and Sonia vaguely helping Mâma in the garden. Whenever I saw Mama with any gardening implements, even a pair of shears, I hid, or pretended to be deeply immersed in some book. I hated gardening, the more so as there was no need for it. We had plenty of helpers from the vineyards.

But Mama always felt she had green fingers – though her notion of gardening never included onerous chores like weeding or cutting the edge of the lawn; that was a gardener's job. She just enjoyed nipping off dead flowers in the herbaceous border or clipping off overblown roses. She also liked company, and so Sonia or Anna would listen to her chatter.

Mama was adorable. Still under forty, she was as American as apple pie, whereas my father, even though he was half American, was as French as *tarte aux pommes*. And as both our parents knew, these two culinary masterpieces, cooked with more or less the same ingredients, are separated by a common factor – the Atlantic.

That evening, just as I was about to join Mama and Papa in the living room, I paused outside the doorway to admire her, almost surreptitiously. A mother of three teenage children – two of them strapping sons – she had kept her figure as trim as a Chanel model. Her legs were straight and slim, her ankles as good as her wrists, her blonde hair untinted. She was simply, as someone put it at an embassy party in Paris, 'A darned good looker'. I agreed. I was proud to escort Mama anywhere, and I was always suffused with sudden pride when I saw guests eyeing her. She liked it, too – I could tell.

Still unaware of my presence outside the room, Mama picked up a magazine, laughing to herself, enjoying a kind of private joke.

'Can I share it?' Papa asked.

'Share what?'

'The joke that's making you chuckle.'

'It's nothing, really, it's Sonia!'

'But what?'

'Sonia was nipping off dead heads, squatting down. She was wearing a short white skirt and as I looked at her across the flower bed I could see – *well* – I could see *everything*, but I didn't realise it at first, and without thinking asked her, "Why on earth do you wear black panties with a white skirt?" And do you know what she replied? "Oh Auntie, I never wear panties in hot weather. That's *me* you're looking at."'

As Mama added, 'Apart from anything else, it's most unhygienic,' I hardly heard her. My mind was racing, twisting, turning, painting an erotic picture of a beautiful girl squatting on that May afternoon in the garden and, as I imagined Sonia, I writhed with desire.

Even before we became lovers, I had, in the half-formed way of the young, dreamed of Sonia without any clothes on. I had wondered if I could peep at her. I had even had messy and ecstatic dreams about her. But still, it never entered my teenage head – not even in my dreams – that I could ever make love to her. She was like a member of the family. It would be almost like doing it with Anna. Though Sonia *was* different, for she had inherited from her mother, who was half Italian, half Russian, a wild streak as well as a kind of wild beauty.

Mama was still smiling as she added, 'No one's ever going to tame *that* one! When she knows what she wants, nothing will stop her getting it.'

At that moment Sonia came up behind me, unaware that Mama had been talking to Papa about her. Her black hair above the bright blue eyes had been mussed by the wind, and she was laughing with pure happiness.

'Anyone seen Anna?' Sonia rushed unconcernedly into the room while I stood transfixed, thinking of what Mama had been saying, stimulated by such a compound of desire, imagination and frustration it seemed impossible that she could fail to notice the physical change in me. I swore under my breath that I would discover for myself whether or not Sonia wore panties – without ever giving a thought to the long, agonising, ecstatic and at times unhappy trail along which that vow would lead me.

The chance came two days later – chance being engineered

by me. I woke with excitement to a perfect morning, throwing open the windows at exactly the right moment as the sun rose over the rim of the wooded hills then slid effortlessly into another dreamy Douzy day. Only later a storm threatened. It was sultry for May, but I said to Sonia, 'Let's go and pinch some raspberries.'

The kitchen garden, with its netted soft-fruit section, lay beyond the orchard and the Home Farm and, as I well knew, the orchard itself was a secret garden which none could overlook. It was a wild orchard: apple and pear trees, plums, a gnarled crab apple, a couple of twisted old cherry trees, all growing in a sea of untended knee-high grass, studded with poppies like a painting by Bonnard. If you travelled a thousand miles across France you couldn't find a more secluded place.

For a moment, standing at the top of the dell, shading her eyes against the hot sun, Sonia pointed to the gentle scene beyond.

'It's so beautiful,' she said. 'I feel I never want to leave.'

It was. Beyond the long rectangle of the farm buildings, which you could see from this point, the vineyards stretched like rows of orderly soldiers, each acre of land busy with workers. May was turning into June. The first spraying against pests and diseases had almost been completed, though I could see a couple of figures in blue, their metal canisters strapped to their backs, glinting like brass in the sun. They wielded long hosepipes with nozzles, searching out the vital spraying areas.

In the next vineyard, placid, sure-footed horses, tossing their heads against early flies, unerringly trod the yard-wide pathways between the rows of vines, drawing the old-fashioned machine behind them for the first hoeing of the vineyard year. The horses rarely ruined the vines, which were never permitted to grow unhindered, so that the fat round bellies of the horses moved above them. With their legs invisible, they sometimes looked as though they were swimming in green water.

'It's like a painting,' said Sonia.

'You're right.' I repeated her earlier words: 'I, too, never want to leave.' For even though I knew that I had no wish to follow in Papa's business, the vineyards were a way of life to us all, had been since the day we first started to walk. Sonia too. She had known, even as a toddler, how the young vines had to be coddled, as prone to sickness as we were. I had myself learned to use the hoe, to keep the soil loose, never compact. Even when I was ten I had started to learn how the foliage of the vines had to be reduced each year to give the sun more chance to help the grapes on their way – and take care not to remove the wrong branches and leaves which could cause the pollen to fall to the ground instead of blossoming.

And, too, Douzy was 'a family' – one that included all the children of the vignerons. Each one of us was involved. After all, when you own thirty acres, with up to four thousand vines on each acre, there's a lot of work to be done. Wires running the length of the lanes of vines, supported by metal posts three feet high, had to be repaired. Each row had to be inspected regularly; so had the vines themselves – 'Champagne's children' my grandma called them – the shoots about a yard apart with a life-span of around thirty years, and bearing fruit four years after planting.

'Let's go to the farm and get a sandwich,' I suggested. The Home Farm kitchen had always been a haven, for there was no other room like it; it was the headquarters of a multiple organisation, not only the horses, the cows, the pigs and hens, the churns where we made Douzy butter, even Douzy cheese. That was only one end of the farm, for the other end of the farm was like another building, filled with workshops above ground connected with wine making.

'Any chance of a *casse-croûte*?' Sonia knew she could always beg a sandwich from Madame Robert, wife of the farmer, a typical farmer's wife with five children and, like so many farmers in Champagne, with half an acre of vineyards, her badge of independence. She stretched above the huge table, always used to feed the vignerons each harvest, and sorted out strings of garlic and onions and a dozen *saucissons*.

She cut off two thick, slightly moist slices, walked over to the fireplace, which never seemed to die out, and took down from a hook one of a dozen black hams curing in the smoke of its own fire. Slicing a *baguette* longways, she smeared it with home-made butter, then slapped the lot together.

'Madame Robert, you're an angel,' I said and soon we were

sitting down on the roadside behind the farm, munching away until, without warning, Sonia asked, almost too casually, 'What about those raspberries?'

Instantly the image of her which Mama had painted returned. I threw away the rest of the oversized sandwich as she cried, 'Race you to the orchard!'

We dashed off into the dell. I realise now that she knew as well as I did that the orchard, and the chasing, represented the first sensation of an undefined love – not yet to be taken completely – because each time the chase ended we tumbled in the long grass and, just for a moment, with no words spoken, we were locked like wrestlers and, though it hardly entered my head that I could kiss or fondle her, those stirrings were so real, so much of a temptation, that we both experienced a delicious tingle of anticipation. Even then I knew that Sonia wanted to be touched, however briefly. But what she didn't know this time was that I was thinking of Mama's conversation – and that when I caught her (as I always did) I was determined to tip her up.

She was off like a streak. I chased her. We fooled around, dodging round trees, laughing, losing breath, touched by secret excitement before I grabbed her and we fell together, hidden in the grass.

'Got you!' I cried, and in one swift movement I grabbed her ankles and held her legs up. Giggling, she held her skirt between her thighs, screaming but still laughing.

'Stop it, you wretch! Stop it!' she shouted.

I didn't – until suddenly she panted, 'I give up!' As though some invisible force had pulled her arms away, she let go and, all in a matter of seconds, the white skirt fell away from her legs and I knew what Mama had meant when she talked about black panties.

She laughed and kicked out. I loosened my grip, rolled away, and instantly the beautiful triangular black vision became a forbidden mystery, hidden by one thin piece of cloth more impossible to tear away than the bars of a prison.

Sonia wasn't angry, but as I started to reach for her – I think this was the first time I wanted to kiss her secretly – the angry clouds spilled out the first huge drops of rain. They were enormous, the herald of a cloudburst.

33

'Run for it!' I shouted, and grabbed her hand as we raced, panting up the dell, reaching the shelter of the conservatory at the very moment a jagged fork of lightning split the sky. Within two seconds the thunder clapped in a gigantic explosion – the storm was directly overhead – and then a curtain of rain blotted out the end of the dell.

'Just in time,' I gasped. 'You all right?'

'I love thunderstorms,' she nodded. 'I'm going to stay here and watch.'

Papa's two black labradors, which had been chasing us too, slid through the door and lay down panting, pink tongues lolling.

Still breathing hard, I stood facing the back wall with its climbing geraniums. Then Sonia did a strange thing. Almost ostentatiously ignoring the summer chairs, she picked up a flowered cushion and threw it against the back wall. She was directly opposite me. She sat down on the ground facing me, her straight back against the wall, her legs, the skirt above the knee, drawn up until they were almost touching her chin. It was the natural way to sit on the floor; but it was not natural for her to be slightly parted.

All this was done without a word, in a significant silence, broken only by the thunder after each vicious, jagged fork of lightning and the hiss of heavy rain and the noise as it hit the glass roof.

I stood looking at her – everything – and she, pretending to be unaware of the way she was sitting, looked back at me, silent blue eyes unwavering, lips slightly apart.

Had she spoken I might have thought her pose accidental. But she didn't speak. Not a word. She just looked at me steadily.

Two days later Sonia and Anna returned to their Swiss finishing school and I did not see Sonia again until the end of term, July, when I drove down from Douzy to Switzerland to pick the girls up and drive them home.

I had been given my first car, a super-charged T3 M.G., and I longed to drive it on a long run. What fun it would be – or so I argued – for me to drive down to the school and give the girls a treat. Far more exciting for them than taking the stuffy old train from Lausanne to Paris, and *then* having to be met and driven by Gaston, our driver.

Permission to drive to Switzerland faced one stumbling block: my grandma, known to everyone in Champagne as 'La Châtelaine'. My mother might be understanding – at least she hid her apprehension when I drove too fast – but Grandma was a firm believer that no cars were safe unless driven by a chauffeur.

A formidable French lady approaching her seventies, she inspected most of 'her' vineyards daily – by bicycle. La Châtelaine, cycling with determination through sun or rain, was a sight often pointed out proudly to visiting tourists. She symbolised the toughness of a *Champenoise*, for she was a genuine eccentric. Morning or evening, rain or shine, she was always adorned with ostentatious diamonds or other jewellery. And though sometimes in bad weather she would cycle in a pair of corduroys, she always wore her jewels. Everything she did was energetic, perhaps because she used so much of her body in the vineyards, fingers especially, for she could bend down, *feeling* whether something should be done to a particular root of the vine. Her fingers were almost alive with decision; when she wore gloves she never had to work her fingers into them: they slid in with the ease of a second skin.

Once a week La Châtelaine was driven to Reims, the leading centre of Champagne. She always made straight for the Boulingrin, not only because she enjoyed the food there, but because the restaurant was like a club where she could be sure to meet friendly champagne producers. Lunch was only one part of her day; the best part was spent in the hour she gossiped with friends.

In the home she exuded what my brother Guy called 'crinoline sounds'. She *rustled* as she moved from room to room. She wore long starchy dresses that seemed to have been left over from another age, and though she sat comfortably on the horrid French chairs in the *salon* she always perched uneasily on the edge of Mama's American chairs, as though they were made of glass.

'Apart from anything else,' snorted La Châtelaine, 'this dangerous car doesn't seem to have a *top*. It can't be safe.'

'But Grandma,' I implored her, 'the top, as you call it, has nothing to do with the car's safety.'

'In case of accidents, *non*? If there's no top, what's to stop the girls falling out?'

My father said nothing; I think he was terrified of his mother. Even though he was recognised by now as one of the foremost experts in the champagne industry he found it hard to stand up to her. He was tall and thin, though not skinny, very handsome in a lean way, yet somehow – and sadly – slightly remote. Perhaps he spent so much time in the cellars and the vineyards he just didn't have enough time for us.

'It might be better if we waited – these small cars . . .' my father began doubtfully.

'But Papa, this is the finest car in the world. It's an M.G.!' I said, as though that resolved any doubts.

Finally, as so often happened, the day was saved by my father's younger brother, 'Oregon' Astell, so nicknamed because years previously he had worked as a newspaperman in Portland and the name had stuck. He had long since returned to Paris to found his modest weekly paper, The *Paris American*. He would never make a fortune, but he loved the work.

Uncle Oregon was two years younger than my father and, because Grandma insisted on regarding him as beneath saving – '*Un journalist!*' she once said witheringly – he was the only one who cheerfully would tell her not to be so silly.

'Don't be such an old fogy!' Oregon said bluntly. 'You'll be driving with a red flag in front next.'

My American mother had said nothing. She just smiled tolerantly, giving my father time to manoeuvre a few hesitant protests, safe in the knowledge that if Uncle Oregon were present – and he was a visitor to Douzy most weekends – he would overwhelm Grandma. That is just what happened now.

'Of course Larry should be allowed to make the trip,' said Oregon. 'He's old enough to be a soldier – he's old enough to die for his country.'

'Exactly!' shot back Grandma, 'and old enough to die in a car crash! You're a fine one to give advice, I must say. If anything happens' – she crossed herself – 'don't blame me for encouraging such stupidity.'

Everyone finally agreed. I set off in high spirits, spending the night at the Hôtel Richemond in Geneva, where I tried in desultory fashion to pick up a girl, failing through lack of enthusiasm even though the M.G. with its strap across the bonnet, was a great lure when on the prowl.

The next morning, after a large helping of toast and black cherry jam, I drove along the beautiful road bordering Lake Geneva until I reached the small town of Rolle, half-way along the lake. This was the headquarters of St. Agnes, where Anna and Sonia were both boarders. I reached there by half past nine, giving us plenty of time to drive back home to Douzy, and I saw Sonia the moment she stood at the top of the wide staircase – the banisters and stairs a vague picture of shiny, varnished pale brown wood.

Almost demurely, she walked towards the large tiled entrance hall where countless parents usually waited at the end of each term for their equally demure daughters. Only now they had all returned home, for St. Agnes had broken up the previous evening, and that morning I was the only person waiting.

With a sudden constriction, a dry-throat feeling of excitement, I watched as Sonia reached the bottom step and, with a hint of a giggle, gave a mannequin-style turn so that her pleated skirt twirled like a kilt.

I couldn't remember her ever looking more beautiful. Her blue wide-apart eyes set in an oval face were framed by shining black hair, straight, almost down to her shoulders, with a fringe over her forehead. But it was the contrast between the black glossy hair, thick and glorious, the white teeth showing in a smile, and her two-piece linen dress in coral and cherry pink that made me blurt out, 'You look stunning. Like a painting.' And indeed she did. No artist could ever have chosen two more beautiful and contrasting colours. 'To say nothing of that shiny hair,' I added.

'That's my secret,' she smiled. 'I always rinse it in rainwater.'

Standing there smiling, she looked a perfect product of a Swiss finishing school, very 'correct', well brought up, beautifully, but not flashily, dressed – as behoved young ladies of St. Agnes.

'And now let me look at you!' She pretended to study me critically. 'Hm! I see a tall, handsome, loose-limbed young man with rather long blond hair and trusting brown eyes,' she laughed. 'And what looks like a very expensive English sports jacket and a pair of very posh suede shoes.'

And as I walked forward to greet her she added, still laughing, 'I love the way you walk – as though you want to dance. Oh! Larry – it's great to see you again.'

'Term's over,' I laughed in turn, to cover the feeling inside me and, as I kissed her on both cheeks, asked, 'All set? The car's outside. Anna ready?'

For a moment she looked me full in the face, large blue eyes unblinking, then she took a deep breath and said simply, 'Anna's fine. Don't panic, but she's not coming with us. We'll have to drive to Douzy alone. Just the two of us.'

2

Looking at Sonia, standing there radiant and calm, for a moment I was seized with hidden fears, imagining the worst. Not that Anna had been suddenly struck dead, but – oh! anything, that she'd run off with someone, bolted, been expelled even. But then, watching the slow, almost ironic touch of Sonia's smile, I realised with blinding excitement that this was Sonia's doing. She had engineered this sudden vanishing act by Anna . . .

'Not coming?' I cried. 'What on earth do you mean? What's happening?'

'Don't panic. We phoned your mother last night. Take me to Hoffner's for a coffee before we set off and I'll explain.'

Hoffner's, in the lazy main street of Rolle, was a pastry shop and café patronised during term time by the rich and randy boys being educated at Le Rosay, the most expensive school in the world – or so it was said; consequently Hoffner's was out of bounds to the girls of St. Agnes.

'But term's over now, so there's nothing to stop us going,' said Sonia as we sat in a corner. I ordered coffee and assorted cakes. The waitress brought a clean tablecloth with the startling injunction, uttered in the sing-song Vaudois accent, '*Un moment, m'sieur, je vais vous napper!*'

'But what's *happened*?' I asked when the waitress had gone. 'Why? Is Anna in trouble – expelled or something?'

'Nothing's the matter. Anna phoned your mother yesterday that she's twisted her back slightly and felt she couldn't stand the jogging in your silly old car.' Her smile showed she wasn't being rude about my treasured M.G. 'After all, it doesn't have much in the way of back seats. We did phone – but of course, you'd already left.'

'Jeez! If you'd phoned earlier it would have saved me the trip.'

'Very gallant, I must say!'

'Sorry. I didn't mean that. But if Anna has hurt her back shouldn't you be with her on the train? It all seems very sudden, this last-minute attack. What happened?'

The girl arrived with two large *capuccinos*, the tops of the broad cups foaming with hot milk forced out under pressure, the foam sprinkled with splashes of tiny chocolate chips.

Sitting there, overlooking the sunny main street with its baskets of flowers hanging from every lamp-post, I knew even before she started to speak that Sonia and Anna had planned this. They must have done – and for only one reason: Sonia wanted to drive back alone with me. And that meant – well, after that curious incident in May when the storm broke, it could only mean one thing. My first thought, of excitement and desire, was followed by a second one, 'What a girl – and what a nerve! How bloody Russian to plan an adventure like this!'

For it was at times like this – when she couldn't control her sense of devilry – that I remembered how much she had inherited from her Russian grandmother. She might be as Italian as Florence itself, but the Russian ancestry was always lurking beneath the surface. She could not have known what I was thinking, how I was imagining where I would take her, when we could stop, what we would do – if I dared to do anything! She looked at me with those big blue eyes and started finally to speak.

'Darling, beautiful Larry,' she said. 'No, *don't* interrupt – you *are* beautiful – in a manly way, even though you are the world's biggest nitwit! We didn't telephone Douzy earlier, because I didn't *want* to stop you coming to fetch me.' I felt my growing excitement increase. 'And your precious sister is perfectly all right, probably stuffing herself with Toblerone in the train. She might give a realistic twinge or two when she gets to Douzy, but there's nothing the matter with her back. She's as fit as I am.'

I decided to ask only one question. 'But surely Mama said you should go with Anna – and leave a message for me at the school?'

'She *was* starting to say something about that, but then we got cut off – well, don't be cross, Larry. I put the receiver down on the hook.'

'You *what*? The nerve of it!'

'I asked Anna to go by train. I even bought the ticket for her. And' – blue eyes looking steadily into mine, beautiful lips slightly open – 'darling Larry, you *must* know – you *must* realise – that I've always dreamed of being alone with you.'

'Me too.' I was so stunned I felt my legs didn't belong to me as the increasing urge of physical excitement hit me with the force of an expanding iron rod, so that I could only repeat, 'Me too!'

As she rested one pale hand on the back of my brown hand on the table, squeezing it gently, I realised, with blinding excitement, that at this very moment, sipping coffee, the car round the corner, I faced a turning point in my life. Before the day was out I was going to make love to her. Everything about Sonia – from her face and her body, the way she looked, the way she walked, the touch of her hands – radiated the deep-seated physical passion of an Italian, but, too, the equally deep-rooted but longer lasting mental passion of a Russian.

'I hope you don't think I'm' – she hesitated – 'well, making all the running, but . . .' She looked down at the table. 'I felt that – well, you're so *nice*, Larry. I know you feel kind of responsible – you've been told that, so you'd never make the first move and – I know it sounds silly when you're only seventeen, but your mama was only seventeen when she got married – and I'm so *pazza* about you, Larry.'

'*Pazza?*'

'It means crazy – but *nice* crazy, Italian crazy.'

'Russian crazy, more like it.'

'Just *pazza*, darling. I just want – well, to be alone with you for one day. I've been praying for a beautiful day. Maybe we can stop on the way and buy a picnic lunch – a *baguette*, some pâté or ham or something, and a bottle of vino and eat it in a field.'

'Come on,' I said thickly. 'It's a long drive.'

I paid the bill, leaving all the loose Swiss change as a tip, and we walked unsteadily to the M.G. which I had parked in the small square by the lakeside. Across the blue water rose the hills of France. The car was shaded by a row of plane trees, bark peeling, great tufts of summer leaves jutting out from branches pruned back into knobbly stumps the previous autumn.

Then, with neither of us seeming to do anything about it, she was in my arms and I was kissing her, to begin with just our lips closing on each other, soft and gentle, pressed against each other, and then her mouth opened slightly, and mine too, just a little at first, touching almost as though by accident, tips of each other's tongues barely touching, just brushing each other until, almost with a groan, both our mouths opened together and we stood there locked to each other.

Very tenderly, all the teasing, all her mischievous sense vanished. She stroked my cheek and there were the beginnings of two large tears as she whispered, 'That was my first kiss, Larry. It was like sipping each other's love. You'll never be able to leave me now.'

We drove out of Switzerland via Vallorbe, leaving the trim Swiss villages and neat, clean streets at the foot of the long twisting climb over the Juras, the road lined with thick, dark sinister belts of fir trees, reminding me of Gustave Doré's illustrations for *Don Quixote*. The bends of the closed-in forest finally reached the town of Pontarlier, the main street filled as usual with heavy trucks and carts loaded with timber.

Suddenly, driving with one hand, the other resting lightly

on her knee, I said, 'I need a drink – a beer. I've got the most terrible thirst.'

'I wonder why?' she asked innocently.

'Excitement.'

'And love?' she asked.

'For ever.'

Ornate stone gates marked the entrance to the bustling main street, giving the impression of a town fortified with ramparts. And this was true, I thought, as we stopped at a street that actually was called the rue des Remparts. It gave the broad main street, backed by woods and mountains, the flavour of a frontier town. The first café we entered even had a swing door and I almost expected to hear shooting during a poker game, or be greeted by one of those saloon girls who are always called Belle. It *was*, I suppose, the last town before France became Switzerland and it had the busy, unfinished air of a place where only physical labour could earn a decent living. There must have been pale, black-suited clerks somewhere in Pontarlier, but all the brain was hidden by brawn.

The man behind the bar pulled down the porcelain handle, filled a large glass of *bière depression*, half of which I gulped almost before Sonia had time to sip her *café filtre*.

'That's better.' I pressed the palm of my hand on the metal filter section of her coffee, to try to force a few drops through into the cup below, and when she had sipped half of it we set off in the M.G. with a roar – Pontarlier looking like a one-horse western township with me whirling her away across my saddle, saving her from the clutches of the villain.

The country changed soon into a more open landscape as we drove towards Dôle, and my mind was racing at the prospect she had made so clear; unless she had second thoughts . . . Perhaps when it came to the point *she* would say no. Fun, but only necking. Scared, suddenly realising what a momentous step it would be for her to take. Especially as it was her first time. Must be. Or supposing she *did* – and I got her into trouble. The daughter of an ambassador! There'd be hell to play. Yet that kiss at Rolle – that surely was a kiss of promise? I suddenly felt reckless. All at once I didn't give a damn, as we sped along, top down, wind in our hair.

'There!' I cried suddenly, pointing to a glade where the

sunlight dappled through the trees on a rough cart track leading to open fields behind. 'In there!'

For half a second she panicked – and so did I, though mine was a different fear – that we would be lying there and some angry French peasant with a shotgun or a big dog would come charging across the fields and kick us off his property.

'Don't be scared,' I said as we reached the end of the belt of trees and I switched off the ignition. The car was hidden from the road, and ahead of us was a huge field of corn ready for the harvest, acres of waist-high gold in the hot sun, the gold picked out with a sprinkling of red poppies.

'*Are* you scared?' I asked her.

'A bit. I've never done this before.'

'Never?'

'Never.' She looked around nervously. 'So long as no one sees us. I'm scared of that – and everything.'

'Want to drive on?'

She hesitated, then said, 'It seems so easy when you just talk about it.'

I picked up the rug from the back of the car.

'Don't worry,' I reassured her, 'even if anyone sees the car we'll be hidden in this corn.'

We walked hand in hand to the edge of the corn. I somehow managed to hold her away from me, took hold of her shoulders, looked at her full in the face, and said, 'You know I'd never try to force you – but I do want to. Are *you* sure?'

For a moment her lip trembled. I realised she might be going to say no. I had a frantic fear that she was going to say, 'Perhaps we should go back to the car.'

'Don't say it!' I cried.

It wasn't very good the first time – it was all over before she had a chance. It had to be. I mumbled, 'Sorry, darling, I couldn't wait . . .' She stroked my face and there were tears as she whispered, 'I could *feel* you when you – you know' – a little shyly at the use of the word – 'when you came inside me. At school all the girls said it would hurt, but it didn't.'

For perhaps half an hour we waited, lying on each other's arms, and during that time she became excited with the satisfaction of a conspirator.

'Are you all right, darling? Not worried? Shocked?' I asked.

'A bit. But I know I was the one who made the running – though I wasn't sure how far I would dare to go.' She hesitated. 'I've always loved you, Larry. Do you think it was bad of me that day I let you look at me in the orchard? I'm so happy I don't feel guilty – well, not very.'

She sat up, pink linen skirt for the moment decorously over her thighs. Stretching out one slender brown arm, she plucked out some poppies from the golden corn and laid them across my body.

'I shall call you "Monsieur Coquelicot" – Mister Poppy. And that will always be a secret code between us. If *ever* we fight – we never will, of course – and one of us says "Monsieur Coquelicot" we have to stop. And if ever one of us feels like we do now, and there are lots of people around – and we can't do anything, I'll ask you, "How's Monsieur Coquelicot?" and you'll know that I love you.'

As we lay there before the second time, I said, 'You know that all these books about sex which you buy in the Tauchnitz editions – they're full of stories about girls having orgasms a dime a dozen. It's not true.'

'I know. I read Henry Miller – we smuggled it into school. *Tropic of Cancer.*'

'Me too. But I don't want to leave you in the air again – so what I'm trying to say is, darling, before we make love, let me help you while we kiss.'

As I touched her, she shuddered and – eyes closed, mouth open – as I slid inside her effortlessly, she gently pushed my hand away and replaced it with her own and I knew then it would be all right for her, and it was.

Lying there afterwards, with her blouse on but unbuttoned, while I stroked her breasts, her skirt pulled down, my trousers pulled up, she put her hand inside them and caressed me and said, 'That's what I hoped it would be like. That's what I dreamed about in bed at night. But I never thought it would be quite so beautiful. You're not sorry, Larry? Did I please you? Did I make you happy, was I all right?'

'You know you did.'

'Tell me you'll always love me, whatever we do to each other, wherever we are – even if we're apart. Uncle Oregon says there'll be a war one day — tell me you'll always love me.'

'You know I will.'

I lay by her side, hands inside her blouse.

'I'm still vaguely scared of that farmer with a shotgun,' she said, 'but I'll never love anyone else.'

I felt the prick of tears, all the love bursting out of me, and I was thinking, '*I feel the same. There will never, never be another woman in my life. And if there is a war one day, I'll wait for you for ever.*' 'I just adore you,' I said.

'You don't think I was brazen for planning to get rid of Anna — and all this?'

'I would never have dared to do it. I've dreamed about this before — but I never thought you'd go through with it if I asked.'

'I wanted to, so often!'

'Me too. But I was scared to.'

'I nearly didn't go through with it,' she confessed. 'This morning — at Pontarlier, I almost decided to ask you to understand. And then, when I looked at you after we started driving, our hair in the wind, I realised that we were in love, and I didn't feel guilty.' She shivered suddenly.

'Cold?'

'No. I was thinking of the future, looking at you. Those big shoulders, and your chest like warm silk.' She lay her head on it. 'Not hairy,' she laughed. 'I like it better this way.'

'So long as nothing else happens — you know what I mean.'

'A baby.'

'Ever thought of that?'

'I don't care,' she said with the recklessness of someone who doesn't really know what she is saying. 'If anything happens I'll go to a Swiss doctor. I'd never let *you* know.'

'You'd have to find one.'

'Three of the girls at St. Agnes have had abortions. It's quite easy, so don't worry.'

'I might want to worry.'

'Well, it won't happen, I'm sure, but if it does, yes darling Larry, I'd like you to worry. Because the two of us — it is wonderful, really — we've been brought up almost like brother and sister. How many holidays have I spent at Douzy?

And I always swore I would never make love with anyone else but you – so that it would be perfect. And it *has* been perfect. And even my prayers were answered – the sun has never stopped shining, and darling Larry, I love you and I'm *pazza* about you.'

Impulsively she threw her arms round my neck and kissed me and cried, 'Isn't life good to us? I'm starving! Let's forget the picnic idea and have a slap-up lunch.'

We ate at a bistro not far from Arbois where, to the amusement of the patron, she took up a chicken leg in her fingers, pulled off a piece of meat with her teeth, then offered it to me. 'Yes, yes,' she urged me, 'it's like our kisses. This chicken has been in my mouth and now it goes in yours. Then you give me a piece of yours.'

It was not until we were eating our wild strawberries, however, before I had a wild idea. Why couldn't we pretend the car had broken down? Then we could spend the night together.

'Dare you promise me something?' I asked her.

'If I can.' She scooped up a spoonful of the tiny wild strawberries, ate half and gave me the rest.

'Promise? I can be *pazza* too!'

'*Pazzo* for you, darling,' she laughed. 'You're masculine, that I do know. *Pazza* for me, *pazzo* for you. Dare I promise?'

'You dared everything this morning.'

'Well – you know that if I can, I will.'

'It's very simple,' I said a trifle too airily. 'I want to wake up tomorrow morning in a large double bed and have breakfast with you.'

'You're right – you're more crazy than I am.'

'I don't see why it should be so difficult. If my car broke down – we'd be stuck, wouldn't we?'

'Your car break down! Your precious M.G.! You always told me it would *never* break down. Oh Larry! I'd love to. But I'd never sleep a wink!'

'There's nothing to worry about – and it *could* break down. Millions of cars all over the world are breaking down at this very moment.'

'But your mama? What about her? She'd have a fit. She'd suspect the worst.'

'She'll probably never know. And anyway, if she did suspect, she couldn't prove anything.'

It took a great deal of persuasion, but before lunch had ended she agreed. I admit I was nervous. I had never done this sort of thing before but we made a detour on the N1, passing beyond Dijon towards Avallon where I knew a wonderful old inn — a glorified pub really — in the Vallée du Cousin, a wild narrow cleft of land hidden a few miles beyond the main road. The family had spent a night once at the Moulin Blanc, which backed on to a dribbling trout stream. 'I only hope they don't recognise and remember me,' I said as we approached the old courtyard.

'So long as I don't have to appear until everything's fixed,' she made me promise. I jumped out of the car in front of the low, white building. I didn't dare to admit that as I sauntered towards the entrance I was as terrified as she.

I walked into the pretty reception room, smiled at the reception clerk — and then all my nervous fears evaporated, simply because no one seemed remotely interested once I handed over my American passport and completed the police *fiche*. Even I knew that in France, country of discretion, no one ever asks for 'madam's passport'.

'Nothing to it,' I whispered loftily as the porter came to the car and took our luggage up the stairs.

'*Voilà!*' the porter opened the door on to a bedroom with a huge four-poster in the centre, the curtains round the bedposts matching the same blue and white flowered wallpaper.

When I had tipped him and the door was closed, we both jumped on the bed at the same time, almost whooping with pleasure. It wasn't only love — or a teenage crush. It was the *excitement* of our impertinence, so that we were almost giggling at the thought of how we had fooled our parents.

'God! Grandma'd flay me alive if she found out,' I said.

'We've got a secret they'll *never* discover. Even if they find out about us later, they'll never know about the Moulin Blanc.'

But above all it was the gentle intimacy of doing something together for the first time in our lives that touched us. We had our *truite aux amandes* on a small table on the edge of the river: the only light came from candles. And when dinner was over,

and we went to bed, it was knowing that the perfect day in the
sun would end with a night which could never be interrupted
until it was time for breakfast.

We made love all night long, but there were gentle times of
sleep in between and sometimes I woke first and, by a trick of
light, the moon shining through a crack in the curtains, I could
see her sleeping face as she lay there, in the position I would
come to know so well, lying in the crook of my right shoulder,
the sheets half pulled off her bare breasts, her lips in a faint
smile as though she were in the midst of a wonderful dream.

In the middle of the night she suddenly sat up, naked, and
switched on the small light on the right-hand side of the bed.

'What on earth's the matter?' I asked, half asleep. 'You all
right?'

'Yes. But Larry, I just had to know at this moment – *now* –
do you *really* love me? Was this day just for fun – or will you
love me for ever?'

'Forever, you crazy Russian.'

'Russians *do* love people for ever. It comes from inside. I
don't want you to think it's just making love that counts for
you. Being in love does make you do that all the time – but it's
real love . . .'

'My sweet, I adore you, but it's four in the morning.'

'But you *will* love me for ever?'

'I promise.'

'It's a solemn vow. We will love each other for ever. I'll
swear it. Do you?'

'I swear it.' And more awake now, I added laughingly, 'Do
you want me to marry you to prove it?'

'Marry! You're only nineteen. You must be crazy! Marriage? At seventeen? I can't explain what I mean, but – the two
things don't seem to have anything to do with each other.'

'But they *should*,' I retorted rather priggishly, for to my
juvenile, muddled way of thinking, the two *were* inseparable.
It took me many years before I could really accept what she
said.

'But so long as we *love* each other – and you've made a vow,
remember – we'll never be able to leave each other.' And then
she switched off the light, murmured softly, 'Love you,' and
laid her breasts against my shoulder and chest and gently fell

asleep, only waking when the old waiter brought the *café complet* which I had ordered for 8 a.m., and we ate the featherweight croissants sitting naked in that huge double bed, she insisting that we share each piece of the fresh croissant and jam.

We reached Douzy in time for lunch. Papa and Mama and Grandma had not returned from Paris, and there was no reason why they should ever question the time of our arrival. If they did, I would of course tell them that my car had broken down and where we had spent the night – in separate rooms. But why should they ask? The servants probably hadn't the faintest idea where we had come from. We might, for all they knew, have been in Paris with my parents. Anything could happen with crazy Americans. Only Mlle Lisette, our one-time governess and now a fixture, gave me a long, hard look, and pursed her lips. But even her sour stare could not stop me from singing aloud with pure happiness.

The next morning when I came down for breakfast, ravenously hungry, Sonia was nowhere to be seen; only my sister.

'She went for a walk to church,' said Anna.

'At this time of the morning?'

'I know. I was as surprised as you – especially' – with a sidelong glance in my direction – 'when she said she was going to confession.'

Long, long before that I knew, even at nineteen, that the night in Avallon, with all its tenderness and beauty and closeness and warmth, would change my life for ever.

3

It lasted almost twelve months, that idyllic period of love, the love coupled with all the fire and excitement of youth.

After the summer vacation Sonia and Anna returned to Switzerland for their last term and, at the start of the new year, I was not only working full-time for the *Paris American*, but also beginning to write occasional news stories for the *Washington Globe*, whose Paris correspondent, 'Tommy' Tomlinson, rented an office in the P.A. building and called on me for extra help whenever he was too busy to handle the news on his own. I was well paid but, more important to me, I was slowly becoming a cog in a big American newspaper.

During the week I lived at first in the Astell apartment in Paris, driving down to Douzy most weekends. And then, early in 1932, Sonia, her schooling finished, got a job as a translator in Paris. 'Instant translators' were just coming into vogue and Sonia was ideal, she was completely trilingual in English, French and Italian. She was not only stunning to look at, she was highly gifted and was soon taken on by an international agency who hired her out to attend important functions or conferences, so she didn't have to go to a dreary office from nine to five translating dull documents.

Her father, Signor Riccardi, was still *en poste* as ambassador to Paraguay and was delighted when Sonia decided to live in France where the Astells could keep an eye on her. At first she stayed with an Italian friend of the Riccardi family, but this posed a problem: finding places to make love.

Paris in the thirties was made for lovers, yet though we saw each other almost daily we were both anxious when I took her home to the family apartment in the rue des St. Pères, the beautiful, narrow street on the Left Bank, with its antique shops and small galleries linking the *quais* on the banks of the Seine with the boulevard St. Germain.

I *did* take her, of course, often late at night after eating at some small bistro or dancing, but it was a hole-in-the-corner business, for it *was* a family apartment. And though I was the only member of the family who worked regularly in Paris, relatives had a habit of turning up without warning. Papa might have a business trip and elect to stay the night, or Mama might want to do some shopping. One evening Grandma arrived, driven in from Douzy by Gaston the chauffeur, to spend a couple of days seeing old friends. When at midnight I crept in, unsuspicious, with Sonia, only the sound of snoring made me scuttle for the door and take her home, after which I returned to the apartment – alone.

The following morning at breakfast Grandma, a forbidding figure in a long white gown and a kind of loose, linen cap hiding un-made hair, dunked a croissant in her coffee and looked at me reflectively.

After a brisk good morning, she asked, 'I hope you slept well, Larry?'

'Thank you. And you, Grandma?'

'No. I did *not* sleep well.'

'I'm sorry. Did I wake you?'

'Not *you*! But nothing wakes anyone more quickly than the tapping of high heels on a parquet floor. And,' even more drily, 'it's very bad for the parquet.'

As I choked on a mouthful of croissant, she added sardonically, 'If you *must* entertain ladies in our apartment at all hours of the night, perhaps you could ask them to remove their shoes when they enter the front door.' And as I gulped again she added – and I had to hand it to the old girl for her final remark – 'I imagine they would have to take their shoes off eventually anyway.'

Fortunately she didn't seem to have any idea who the visitor had been. Still, we had to do something, and after a few weeks Sonia found the perfect place.

It was a tiny bandbox of an apartment at the corner of the rue des St. Pères and the rue de l'Université. On the entresol, over an antique shop, it was little more than an extra floor squeezed by a rapacious landlord between the ground and first floor, almost a shelf jutting into the dark, cavernous and not too clean entrance hall. It had once been a lodge for a *concierge*, but there was no longer a *concierge* and so we snapped it up, all of two tiny rooms, a small bathroom and a kitchen no bigger than the bathroom. But it had a charm, with windows from both rooms looking out over the street barely twelve feet above the passers-by.

No white paint could ever make the dark living room lighter, but Sonia found some poppy wallpaper identical to that in her room at Douzy and a Spanish painter called Fernandez who decorated both rooms. We furnished it with bargains from the Flea Market. The room was just large enough for a double bed. And this was new, a house present from me, bought at the *Trois Quartiers*.

I also bought another present – this time of a non-lasting nature. I drove down to the flower market on the Ile de la Cité near Notre-Dame and filled the M.G. with a hundred red roses – and one white one.

Then, knowing that Sonia would be out at work, I filled the small bathtub with what looked like a scarlet flower bed, with just the single white rose in the middle.

She hadn't the faintest idea when she arrived home and tugged open the sliding door leading to the tiny bathroom. She shrieked with joy, then a few tears of happiness stained her cheek.

'You are a fool!' I dried her tears on my handkerchief. 'My own Monsieur Coquelicot! Who else in the world would make a surprise like this?'

Soon I more or less moved in. There wasn't enough room for my clothes as well as Sonia's, but that didn't prevent me sleeping there and dashing out each morning to the boulangerie in the rue Jacob for freshly baked croissants.

At first I was worried lest Sonia might have a baby. If only I had realised what a simple solution to our future problems such a quickly forgotten scandal would have been! But as she said, after calling at Geneva on her way back from a trip to Italy, 'The Swiss know how to fix everything. Now I have a diaphragm.'

Sometimes I went late to the office so that we could go to the *marché* at the top of the rue de Seine, the narrow street lined not only with shops selling every kind of food, but in front of them stall after stall, crowding together, the barrows piled high with fruit and vegetables, so spotless it looked as though each apple or leek had been individually polished, each radish personally scrubbed. There was great bargaining in the *marché* – especially among the fat, cheerful, blowzy women, loud-voiced, many still in their cloth slippers, for they had just come down the rickety stairs from their nearby apartments. In their overalls, hair done up in curlers, they examined each piece of merchandise with expertise before opening their small leather purses.

Sometimes we dined at Marcel's, further along the rue Jacob opposite the place Fustenburg where Delacroix had had an atelier in a tiny square with clusters of gas globes on tall straight lamp-posts, that looked like a set from a period movie.

Marcel's was one of the cheapest, smallest restaurants in the *quartier*, and though we could easily have afforded to visit more expensive ones we preferred Marcel's once or twice a week because I think we were eager to be accepted as people who were part of Saint-Germain-des-Prés. I was perhaps envious of the struggling writers and painters who had lived there – men like Hemingway, Joyce and other undiscovered literary giants who had gathered at the feet of Gertrude Stein, or borrowed books from Sylvia Beach at her bookstore, 'Shakespeare and Company', in the rue de l'Odéon.

In those Paris days, Sylvia provided a haven for anyone – rich or poor – who enjoyed books, for she was a warm, generous woman with a happy smile below her brown eyes and wavy brown hair, and she loved gossip, so that when she knew I worked not only for the P.A. but also for the *Globe* she was a valuable source of information.

Occasionally Sylvia came to have a quiet dinner with us at Marcel's, for she hated what she called 'touristy places' and certainly Marcel's never attracted a tourist. Its zinc bar, with hard boiled eggs on the counter and saucers piled up in front of you to keep a tally on the number of drinks served, was tiny. In summer you could sit out on the pavement, in winter inside a glass extension, steamy with heat and the smell of Gauloises.

But the shabbiness of Marcel's was like a welcoming cloak, for it had none of the frostiness of formality. Most of the regulars were lonely men, clerks perhaps, professors or school teachers. They nodded to us gravely, not with familiarity but out of politeness, and we never noticed the off-white walls, the stains on the tablecloths, the one shambling waiter, for he was our friend, *their* friend. When elderly regulars arrived he knew without asking which newspaper, rolled up on its wooden rod, he should take off the wall rack for him. He rarely offered a menu to the regulars like us. We would take the dish of the day because we knew it had been cooked by Marcel himself, good home cooking with no frills, and always marked with chalk on a large slate standing near the cash till where Madame Marcel held sway.

Sometimes, after a good dinner with Sylvia Beach, as on this evening, she walked up with us to the Deux Magots, another haven, where for the price of a drink or a coffee people sat for hours on the terrace watching the crowd saunter along the boulevard St. Germain. At times I caught her regarding us almost quizzically.

'Are you two ever going to get married?' she asked with a smile.

Sonia shook her head.

'Why not?'

I started to speak, but in her 'dark' husky voice Sonia said first, 'We're too happy to spoil it.'

'How Russian!' Sylvia laughed.

That was the way our lives passed by. Unless Sonia went to Florence when her parents were on leave, or if they came to visit her in Paris, we were inseparable and, in those days, when we would dance until the dawn, go to her apartment to make love, and still be ready to face a day's work, there was no city in the world as wonderful.

Paris was one part of our lives but then, as though switching off a film, we shared our other kind of life at weekends: the magic of Douzy. To me, Paris represented fun and work in a wonderful city; but Douzy was home.

And this was a special weekend – the biggest fête day in France and also my twentieth birthday. For I was born on 14 July, the *Quatorze Juillet*, France's equivalent of the Fourth of July. It always meant a double celebration in the Douzy household, for we celebrated birthdays with a few glasses of *blanc de blancs* in the cool white splendour of the Douzy pyramid, one of the showplaces of Champagne.

Luckily none of us knew that within a few hours Sonia and I

would be discovered – and that she would be packed off away from me, from Paris, from our beloved Douzy.

<h1 style="text-align:center">4</h1>

'There's one thing about a drinks party in the pyramid,' my father said to Willi Frankel, a German engineer and a friend of Anna's who had spent several weekends at Douzy. 'It can't last very long. No, it just *can't*.'

Willi looked mystified until I explained that the Douzy pyramid was not only a remarkable natural phenomenon, it was also a working cellar over a hundred feet below ground in which we could store up to a quarter of a million bottles from various years.

'Perfect for keeping champagne,' I said, 'but the temperature always hovers around eleven centigrade. Don't worry! We keep a supply of old Sherlock Holmes-type cloaks for anyone who feels chilly.'

Willi, Guy and I led the way. Papa had gone ahead. Anna, Sonia and a girl called Olivia Jacobsen, who had been invited by Guy for her first visit to Douzy, followed. Grandma had promised to come, but was visiting a vineyard some distance away.

It was a beautiful morning as we walked along in the warm July sunshine, picking the occasional wild flower or blowing the tops off the fluffy 'She loves me, she loves me not' dandelion puff-balls. Everyone was happy. Anna was obviously intrigued with Willi, tall and blond with very correct manners from Düsseldorf. Guy had become friendly with Olivia, at first because she was helping him with his art studies, but I also felt that, though she was several years older than any of us, her creamy complexion, composed face, quiet and serene, attracted Guy as much as her painting.

Midway along the half-mile walk to the pyramid we passed the Home Farm, with its large rectangular buildings, the outer wall of weathered brick enclosing barns, the manure of the farms and horses, the cowsheds, the dairy where we churned butter, even Douzy *fromage*.

'It looks enormous,' said Willi, walking along the never-ending wall that bordered the lane. I explained that only half was a farm proper. The far end housed the buildings of the *cellier*.

'Underground? Is this where we are going down?'

'No, no. Underground are the *caves* – the French word for the cellars, if you like. The *celliers* are not cellars, they're the name given to the champagne workrooms *above* ground – the press, which can handle four tons of grapes at one pressing, the bottling plant, mixing rooms where sugar and sometimes an older vintage of champagne is mixed with the new vintage to pep it up. That's where Papa is a real expert – he's the best in the blending business.'

'Life at your Douzy is very good, is not?' said Willi. 'So why you prefer to live in Paris, hard work as a newspaperman, *nein*?'

'Not easy to explain. I *love* this place, Willi – it's my home – and yet, I don't know why, half of me is always yearning to get out of it.'

I waved a greeting to an old vigneron called Pagniez. One of Pagniez's sons worked in the vineyards with his father – I could see him a few yards away. Pagniez's daughter had worked in the château since she left school – a school paid for with pleasure by Papa who called her, as everyone did, 'Aubergine', a nickname derived from some babytalk mispro-nunciation.

I found Willi's question hard to answer. All I knew was that I found it boring having to listen to 'champagne talk' – my father's friends discussing the influence of supra-cretaceous chalk soil on Chardonnay grapes – to say nothing of produc-tion units, presses, blending, *dégorgement* and a hundred other technicalities. What I *really* wanted was to see my own name on my first novel (if I ever got around to writing it) or else my by-line on Page One of a famous American newspaper.

It would come, I knew it would; I had a complete faith that I would one day succeed. I was lucky in one thing: Papa was understanding, and never tried to force me to follow 'in father's footsteps'. His was a French life, really, more than an American one. He was immersed in a totally French business. He almost always spoke French. He was very quiet and tended to shirk any 'man-to-man' talks as though they embarrassed him, but on the other hand he was tolerant enough to understand that I wanted to make a life of my own. He was gentle, considerate − unless he was so occupied that he hardly noticed our presence. When he was with friends, 'on parade', as his brother Oregon called it, he was good company. But he was the epitome of a man married to his job. At forty-eight he was a handsome man, and had a trick of raising and lowering his voice to accent certain words, as though to give them a special significance that others missed. When he was explaining something, I would hear Papa say in his special voice, 'Oh *really*! I *must* say.'

'I think I understand.' Willi who, after studying at the Sorbonne, had worked for a year in a British engineering works, spoke passable English. 'I lived with my parents in a village for many years and now I get excited living in Düsseldorf. Of course' − his next words didn't sound exactly complimentary − 'I work as an engineer, is different, much more important.'

'Jesus!' I laughed. 'I don't spend all my time in bed waiting for inspiration, you know. I *do* work.'

'Of course. But you do not mind the big change.' And then a little slyly he added, 'You think is different for a woman − someone like − well, Anna, to make a home away from Douzy?'

'Anna? You mean the idea of Anna living in Düsseldorf?'

Willi blushed slightly. 'Maybe one day, who knows?'

'She *is* only eighteen.'

'I know,' said Willi hurriedly, 'If still we are fond of each other, of course I wait.' He almost clicked his heels.

'Papa wouldn't like it.' I kicked some loose pebbles to the edge of the path. 'He's not enthusiastic about the Germans. And what about this Hitler man? Now he has made some sort of alliance with Hugenberg in Harzburg.'

'How you know this?' He looked astonished.

'I *am* a journalist,' I laughed.

'You can forget Hitler. He was only a corporal.'

'Well, I wouldn't ask Papa for permission to marry yet,' I laughed – but I meant it. 'Not until you've got rid of Hitler, anyway.'

Shortly after midday we all reached the Douzy pyramid. I knew Willi would be astonished when he saw it for the first time, though so far he did not seem impressed. The sloping country lane led to large double doors set into the hillside. An old-fashioned sign at the end of the drive announced:

ASTELL & Cie
Negotiants de Champagne

That was all, an almost supercilious sign, as though the product needed no further introduction.

Inside the outer office I could see Willi doubtfully eyeing the bits of furniture, a few charts on the white walls, some sample bottles in an old-fashioned rack. I smiled inwardly. It *looked* ordinary, but I had never met anyone who could resist the sense of shock when they first saw the pyramid.

'This way.' My father led Willi to the far end of the office, where a flight of stone steps dropped still further downwards. They were very broad, a hundred and five of them, but as easy to use as those leading from a dress circle to a theatre foyer.

'Here we are!' My father threw open a second set of doors at the foot of the steps. There was a faint odour of sourness, of damp. And it was chilly. 'After you,' he held open one of the doors politely. 'This is your first visit.'

We stepped on to a white, chalk-stone terrace cut into the wall and illuminated by dim lights. Two butlers in ceremonial white ties and tails, each with his silver tasting dish on a ribbon round his neck, were preparing tulip glasses for the drinks.

'It's a kind of uniform for ceremonial occasions,' I whispered.

Willi gaped in astonishment.

'*O Gott! Oje!*' he cried. 'Is not possible, Larry!'

In front of the observation platform we looked upwards towards the apex, a tiny patch of light far above; then downwards another fifty feet or so to the huge rectangular base below. Everything was blinding white.

'Is incredible,' cried Willi. 'What engineering! How did

anyone build this miracle? Nothing like it in all the world.'

My father, who loved the role of guide, pointed to the apex.

'This pyramid started when the Romans dug that hole.' He pointed upwards. 'As soon as they'd excavated a vertical shaft, rather like a well, they dug downwards, outwards, all underground. Look carefully.' He flashed a torch on to the nearest wall. 'You can see the marks made by men digging out the shaft. Those marks were made by the Romans.'

The balcony on which we were sipping champagne was ringed with railings to form a semi-circular observation platform. On the floor area below a dozen dark and tiny figures scurried round like ants caught in a field of snow.

'Is like a giant crevasse at the South Pole,' said Willi.

As the butler gravely poured out more champagne, my father pointed out the steps built into the sides of the wall, together with other platforms at various heights, and the dark holes of tunnels.

'Give us extra storage space,' he explained. 'We store our best vintages here and in the adjoining tunnels. We use a long chain and pulley on wheels to haul up the bottles, six at a time in special baskets. And in the large tunnel' – he pointed it out – 'there's an ancient truck on rails that leads to the railway at Rilly.'

'This pyramid – is the only one?'

'Good Lord no.' I shook my head. 'There's another one on the other side of the Rilly railroad, and in Reims itself there are forty pyramids, with connecting tunnels.'

'But all this engineering under the ground – I think is very difficult,' said Willi.

'They had no choice if they wanted chalk for building,' said my father. 'Chalk that's exposed immediately to rain or frost cracks or breaks. The Romans *had* to quarry under the ground and cover the whole thing at night with a slab of stone no larger than a table.'

It was the vignerons who discovered that chalk cellars provided the perfect place to store champagne which, unlike most wines, matures in bottles.

After the birthday toasts, my father signalled to the butlers that we were ready to go, explaining, 'There are more than a hundred miles of underground tunnels in the area, like a subterranean city, some broad like avenues, others branching off, some like small city squares; trucks on rails, ventilation shafts – yes, we have everything.'

'Will they ever build more tunnels?'

'Not in my lifetime, if ever.' My father shook his head. 'Apart from anything else, remember that the champagne market is as flat as vinegar. The international market has gone. The Russian trade vanished with the Revolution. The American market vanished with prohibition, while France and Britain are still wallowing in the wake of the 1929 recession.'

This was our home in Champagne, once the bed of an old inland sea which over thousands of years had deposited its thick, chalky sediment and become a vast plain of dry and undulating chalk with only a thin layer of alluvial soil over it. Here stood the mountain of Reims looking down on the valley of the Marne; hardly a mountain, for the highest point of the horseshoe-shaped range of hills was barely six hundred feet above the plains. But different enough for the former to produce 'the wine of the mountain' while the vineyards nearer the Marne were always known as 'the wine of the river'.

And in answer to a question by Willi, I replied, 'No. I'm not going to waste our time taking you to Reims. It's the dreariest, most provincial town in France, filled with priests from the cathedral and colleges.'

To my surprise Willi suddenly announced when we had returned to the house, 'I have bought you a present. Is too difficult to wrap up.' Everyone gave each other gifts at birthdays, but I hardly expected one from Willi. However, he presented me with a thick Malacca walking stick.

'That's great,' I thanked him.

'And useful.'

'Sure, I like walking.'

'No. Look. Let me hold it.' With an almost theatrical flourish he tugged hard at what looked like an ordinary walking stick. It came apart in his hands, revealing a beautiful swordstick which he could slide back into the Malacca cane, using it as a sheath.

'That's terrific.' I examined it with new interest.

'In case Hitler attacks you,' said Willi solemnly – before bursting into laughter.

That evening we held a warm, cosy supper with a few local friends, mostly Americans, after which we drank still more Astell birthday toasts in 'le living room'.

This was Mama's favourite room, long, with a high ceiling in beautiful proportion, and, better still, she had furnished it without regard to Grandma's tight-lipped disapproval of any 'foreign' furniture. Grandma Jacqueline might have the right to keep her family heirlooms in the *salon*; but enough was enough, and behind the stiff, unyielding French furniture Mama, with her American flair for friendly rooms, had her way. Two long deep sofas, coloured in oatmeal, each big enough to seat four people, filled one corner. In front of them was an extraordinary glass-topped coffee table, three yards long, more than a yard wide, with a top made of plate glass an inch thick. Four men could not lift it off the crossed stainless steel legs that supported it. It had been designed years ago by the firm which supplied Papa's champagne bottles. A dozen people could sit round the table for drinks.

In winter a log fire always flickered on the walls. One wall was covered with paintings, many signed personally by Vlaminck, Dufy and (my own favourite) a large picture of some sunflowers, dated 1909 and painted by Gontchorova, the frail Russian lady who lived in the rue de Seine near our Paris apartment. The other wall was lined with bookshelves – something very much against the French tradition, for many people preferred to house their books in a formal library. No doubt this was because newly published French books only had paper covers, so most families had their books specially bound, and that seemed to change them, to clothe the books with a sense of formality, whereas many of our books came from New York or London and had cheerful, bright dust jackets that gave an added warmth to the room. They stretched along the entire forty-foot length of the wall.

The far end of the room offered a tantalising glimpse of the outside world for it was here that the french windows opened on to the conservatory, always filled with plants, ranging from bowls of daffodils and tulips and azaleas in spring to tubs of fuchsias through summer, and barrels of Michaelmas daisies and chrysanthemums in the autumn. Gardeners carried flowers in bloom from hidden greenhouses so that with the changing seasons, the conservatory, overlooking the dell, seemed to be magically endowed with the property of an everlasting summer. And behind them, clinging to the wall, were the scarlet blossoms of climbing geraniums, thrusting up between the rows of wires, and which seemed to bloom even as another winter approached.

Talking to Sonia for a moment I suddenly thought, 'She's right – Douzy is a benediction. If only life – and love – if only all of this could go on for ever.'

Someone else apparently thought the same.

'That's a very beautiful young lady,' said a voice in my ear, 'I think you should introduce me. I just came to Douzy for a pre-dinner drink on my way home, but looking at this vision I'm tempted to invite myself to dinner.'

It was Monsieur Maurice Pol Roger – not only the head of the famous champagne firm, but the mayor of Épernay since the end of the war.

Sonia murmured something polite.

'A picture, sir! Yes, a beautiful picture. *Une photo sans besoin de retoucher.*'

It was a pretty compliment. '*Mais, hélas,*' said the mayor. 'I have to go. Keeping two jobs going is hard work.'

'He keeps *three* jobs going,' I whispered as soon as Papa took the mayor to the front door. 'He's our local eccentric. He goes to the office at eight o'clock every morning and leaves at half past nine, only an hour and a half later.'

'A hard day's work,' Sonia laughed.

'It is. Know what he does? He changes in his car then spends the entire day shooting or fishing. He's already bagged over five hundred wild boar in the woods up on the mountain, and then – believe it or not – sharp at half past five each evening he returns to the office to sign his letters.'

'Larry, darling,' Mama interrupted my thoughts, 'could you be an angel and fill my glass for me.'

Mama looked wonderful. But there were moments when she sat sadly staring into space.

Guy, Anna and Olivia were talking together with my

father, and Jean-Pierre Malherbe, who lived near Reims and automatically came to any party, stood looking at my sister with worshipping eyes. He was openly envious of Willi, who at the Sorbonne had passed every engineering examination that came his way without any apparent effort.

When Anna nearly knocked over my glass, I looked in Willi's direction and said to her, 'Don't become too involved with a German. He might become another Hitler.'

'You're a fine one to talk!' You could never get the better of Anna. 'You and your Sonia. She might become another Mussolini. Yes, she's over there, looking at you.'

I stood watching her. In fact, I was imagining Sonia naked in bed with me – until I caught Mama's eye. Seeing her quizzical look I wondered, did Mama know that I had started my birthday by making love to Sonia before breakfast and that soon, when the party was over, the house darkened, I would creep out of my room to hers and spend the night with her? 'Parents know nothing,' Anna had once declared decisively, but I wasn't so sure at this moment, as Mama looked first at me and then directly at Sonia.

Sonia was sitting in a deep armchair near the french windows, talking now to Jean-Pierre who was learning the skills of champagne production with one of our neighbouring firms; with him were two elderly ladies.

I walked across to them. Sonia had suffered long enough at the hands of Jean-Pierre, an orphan whose American father and mother had been killed in a car crash, but who had lived in France all their lives, so that the only American thing about Jean-Pierre was his passport. He had been brought up by the two delightful American maiden ladies sitting next to Sonia, known all over Champagne as the Misses B and B – Miss Brewer and Miss Barron. Miss Brewer was a distant relative of Jean-Pierre's and had taken him into her care. Miss Barron had originally been engaged as a companion to Miss Brewer, but for many years there had been no boss, no servant. They were now friends who clung to each other with a desperate fear of loneliness. They had a tiny apartment in Paris, and a cottage not far from Douzy.

'It's a fine party, Larry.' Jean-Pierre stood up politely. 'Have you seen Anna?'

'She's with her new boyfriend' – Sonia sometimes had a mischievous streak. 'You've seen him – Willi something.'

Jean-Pierre blushed and immediately Sonia touched his hand, as though asking forgiveness.

'Don't worry,' she smiled. 'He's a German. An engineer or something equally dull. Doesn't sparkle like a true son of champagne – like you and Larry.'

I saw Miss Brewer say something to Jean-Pierre, but he didn't hear her. On purpose, perhaps? The Misses B and B were gentle, kind, nondescript, grey-haired, plump, talkative – and also came to all our parties. Perhaps Jean-Pierre was stifled by their gentle kindness but, even if he tried to escape he failed, for as he crossed the room he was trapped by Grandma who loved to talk to 'a real Frenchman', as she put it acidly, 'instead of listening to all those American accents.'

The fact that none of the Astells had the faintest trace of a foreign accent when speaking French – rather the reverse in fact, when we spoke English – had never convinced Grandma, who believed that we ruined the French language every time we opened our mouths.

'I want a breath of fresh air,' cried Sonia. 'Isn't the café in Douzy village open?'

'It is,' I said. 'Let's pop in for a final nightcap. Maybe we could get some beer as a change from champagne. 'Night, night everyone.' This to the older ones, with a big kiss to Mama and a fervent 'Thank you' for my birthday present.

Looking at me fondly, Mama whispered, 'Don't forget to kiss your Grandma good night – and thank her for the shaving set.'

'Good night, Grandma,' I cried. 'Tomorrow you'll see me with a polished new face – thanks to your new shaving set.'

Grandma's eyes rarely softened, but she stood up, all creases and hidden noises from her stiff dress, and offered two cheeks to be kissed. I obliged and, as the others prepared to leave, Willi bowed stiffly and said formally, '*Bonsoir, madame, et merci beaucoup.*'

It was a polite gesture, for after all it wasn't Grandma's party. But she was unbending, giving poor Willi only a frigid inclination of the head.

'I don't think she likes me,' said Willi.

'Well, you're not Grandma's boyfriend,' Anna said cheerfully, 'so I wouldn't let it worry you. Grandma won't be satisfied until the last German in the world has been buried.'

My father was just behind and, as I walked out of the *salon* into the hall, grabbing my gloves from the ormulu table, I asked him, 'As it's my birthday, Papa, can I borrow the Hisp?'

He nodded almost absently, adding, 'But don't smash it up. We've all had a few drinks tonight. Yes, *indeed*.'

'Promise. And thanks for everything.'

I had my precious M.G., but Papa's family car was much grander, a long, gleaming Hispano-Suiza, driven usually by Gaston the family chauffeur, another of old Pagniez's sons. The 'Hisp.', as we nicknamed it, was like a battleship. The '68' model, it had a nine-litre V12 engine and would hum along at more than a hundred miles an hour.

We all ran out into the warm summer's night, and I shouted to Guy, 'You want to drive my M.G.? Take Olivia with you and follow me.'

Sonia jumped in next to me, while Jean-Pierre and Anna sat in the back with Willi.

There was no short cut by which you could drive from the château to Douzy village, though you could walk there across country in fifteen minutes. But with a car you had to drive almost down to Rilly near the main Reims–Épernay road then double back up a chalky, narrow strip of road, shining pale gold in the moonlight. Not that the detour mattered. July was a benevolent month, it was warm, it was only a couple of miles, and the Hisp purred along like a silky cat. It was a joy to drive her, though I kept the speed down – apart from the Hisp., I didn't want Guy going too fast and smashing up my M.G.

It was not only exhilarating, it was beautiful as we made first for the church with its ugly greyish square tower and squat apology for a spire. At night the church looked abandoned, forbidden, dirty, as if it needed a wash, for the wall had been erected four hundred years ago by mixing big white stone with plaster, giving it a speckled look. But the graveyard, with its horizontal family memorial slabs – ornate and often one on top of the other in French peasant fashion – was neat and tidy, and so was the grey stone plinth bearing the names of local fathers and sons who had died in the Great War.

Silhouetted against the vineyards, the church was an anachronism, nearly a mile from its village, but as we drove on towards Douzy, it wasn't difficult to see the reason why. The village of Douzy might just as well have been built on a switchback.

Anna yelled from the back seat, 'Let's stop at the *mairie* and see if anyone's getting married.'

The *mairie* was an unpretentious house in the steep curving rue Clemenceau, for the village didn't merit a 'mayor's parlour'. The mayor worked in the vineyards, and had a plot of land, and this was his home – despite a front door decorated with special pronouncements: the new revised postal times, but also a discreet notice that the mayor had some potatoes for sale (by the sack only).

Anna struck a match to peer at the only wedding notice.

'It's Anne-Marie Drouet,' she shrieked. 'She's the girl who works in the *épicerie*. I *thought* she was in the family way when I saw her last week.'

'Who's the unlucky man?' someone asked.

'Dunno. One of a dozen, I imagine.'

A few yards down the steep hill stood the Café des Sports, faint lights glowing behind steamy windows, with a sign in bold black lettering, the 'C' and the 'S' picked out in red. Opposite, Madame Roisin's *épicerie* – where the unfortunate Anne-Marie worked – was closed, and so naturally were Douzy's other two shops – the bakery and the butcher. The owners were probably at the Café des Sports celebrating.

Douzy was an integral part of our lives, perhaps because it had grown naturally in the hilly vineyards surrounding it, and so was different from many of the neighbouring villages which often consisted of one long street, straggling and deserted. Douzy clustered rather than straggled, so that our tyres squealed as we twisted and turned through the village streets leading to what the *Guide Bleu* called 'the surprise view' at the corner of Douzy's public washing trough, shaded by a steep roof and surrounded with peeling plane trees. In front of us spread miles of vineyards like black lines of regimental soldiers, black now at night through a trick of the moonlight which robbed us of the green lines of daylight.

Back up the hill, we all trooped into the Café des Sports and ordered cold Slavia beer, while Roland, the *patron*, who knew everyone and everything in the village, said slyly, 'You're twenty today, I hear. *Bonne fête!*' And casting an eye at Sonia sitting at the stained, wooden table – even the way she drank her beer was exciting – he added, 'Soon time to settle down and get married, eh?'

Sonia caught the look, and in her dark throaty voice she just said, 'I'm not ready to get married yet, Monsieur Roland, but, all the same, I'm not going to let Larry marry anyone else.'

The party over, I undressed hurriedly in my bedroom, taking a last look at a pair of cufflinks which I placed on the dressing table. They were beautiful – and Sonia's expensive birthday present to me. I waited a few minutes. The last guests had long since departed; Papa and Mama were in bed.

Gently – the movement born of long experience – I half opened my bedroom door, looking for tell-tale bands of light below other doors. Darkness! I tiptoed the length of the corridor, gently pushed open the last door on the right, and slid into her room.

Sonia was already in bed – well, no, it was a warm summer's night, and she was *on* the bed, lying on her back, hands clasped under the back of her head, legs together, still naked, her black hair tumbling over the white pillow. Only one small bed-light lit up the poppy pattern on the walls, the ceiling, the drapes, turning the small room into a basket of red flowers.

'This is our real present – to each other, *mio adorato*,' she whispered as I snuggled in against her.

I have no idea how my father found out. He must have been suddenly suspicious, because I set my alarm at 5.30 each morning, giving me plenty of time to sneak back to my room before the house awakened.

He couldn't have heard the alarm – I had bought it specially because it gave out a discreet buzz instead of the usual bell. At 5.30 it rang, I turned it off, nestled in Sonia's arms for the best part of half an hour, as I usually did, loving her gently and quietly so that no one would hear any creaking beds.

By six o'clock I carefully pushed open the door which opened into the corridor, peered out to make sure no one was about, then prepared to turn left.

As I gently eased the door shut, my father, who had been quietly standing on my right, hidden by the open door, tapped my shoulder without a word.

I spun round with a cry. I heard a gasp from Sonia. My father, in his dressing gown, looked at me with a kind of cold scorn, then without uttering a single word pointed to my room. The gesture was an order – and one that could not be disobeyed, especially by the twenty-year-old son of the house.

Not until after breakfast did he ask me, quietly, even politely, to go to his study, after an embarrassing meal shared by a silent family, who could sense that something was wrong.

My father asked the usual questions. How could I be so stupid? How long had this been going on? Was I sure she was not pregnant? 'I don't blame you entirely, she's a high flier, but I hope you agree you've been stupid – and worse,' he said. Finally he came to the point.

'Sonia will leave this morning.' The tone of his flat statement horrified me.

'But she works in Paris! She's got a job.'

'I am not interested in her job,' said my father sternly. 'She will resign from it and leave.'

'But you can't force a girl who's independent to give up her job,' I shouted angrily.

'I can – and I will. I'm giving you two damn fools a chance. If you want to save Sonia's' – he hesitated over the word – 'honour, you do it my way. If she goes quietly,' he permitted himself a wintry smile at the allusion to police procedure, 'then we will all keep this despicable skeleton in our own cupboard. And that means that Sonia's mother and father need never know how you've seduced their daughter.'

'And the alternative?'

'If you insist on behaving stupidly, I shall cable Signor Riccardi that you have seduced his daughter and broken up a family friendship that has lasted for years. Then *he* would order Sonia to return.'

'That's blackmail! *That*'s despicable – to use your own word.'

'But I've only got Sonia's welfare in mind. And perhaps you'll remember that your mother is Sonia's godmother. Responsible for a girl's welfare. You're a selfish idiot, thinking of yourself all the time.'

'She still might not go.' I felt a suddenly stubborn streak. 'She might insist on staying.'

'She's a minor. As a newspaperman, you should be a little more intelligent in sizing up people. With his diplomatic powers, Signor Riccardi could have her *permit de séjour* cancelled within twenty-four hours. Don't be so naïve.'

'But I love Sonia. We love each other.'

Until that moment my father had kept himself under control – as he always did. But the word 'love' sparked off a sudden outburst of fury.

'What in hell's name do you know about love!' he cried. 'Is it your idea of love that you cheat a woman like Sonia's mother just because you want to get her daughter into bed? And in my house. God preserve me from modern youth!'

'I don't care what you think – or what you say – we've got nothing to be ashamed of.' And with a sudden rush of anger, I cried, 'I want to see her. Right away. I suppose she knows?'

'See her? In no circumstances. Yes, your mother has spoken to Sonia. And she agrees with me – you will *not* see her. Not alone. You may not be ashamed, but understand this. You've behaved like the worst kind of bastard. The daughter of one of our oldest friends. You may not be ashamed of yourself, but I'm ashamed of you. Yes, I am.'

'I still want to see her,' I muttered.

'Just remember one thing. Italian men don't like their daughters to be – well, soiled. I'm talking about a prospective husband for Sonia. By sending her away, I'm protecting her, protecting her family name. If anyone in Florence ever found out, it'd cause a scandal.'

'They won't find out. You've no right to stop me. And you can't.' Now I began to get really mad, borrowing the temper from my father. 'And if you're so worried about what people think, we'll get married.'

'At your age?'

'Why not? Mama was younger than Sonia when she . . .'

'That's different. You're both too young. You've no career – not yet . . .'

'Well' – with a touch of sarcasm – 'you'll be relieved to know that Sonia doesn't want to get married.'

'More sense than you have.'

'But I *am* going to see her alone and say goodbye.'

'You're not.'

'I am. What are you going to do about it? Try and stop me by force? If you try, I'm off. I'll leave home. And then you can thank yourself for breaking Mama's heart – for that's what'd happen if I left. And I will if I have to. I can be as stubborn as you.'

'Where will you go?'

'Anywhere. I don't give a damn.'

'And live on?'

'I won't ask you for money, if that's what's worrying you.'

He hesitated. 'All right,' he said heavily. 'Arrange the goodbyes with your mother.' Then he left the room without another word.

For the first time, my anger began to diminish, for I knew I had won the small battle. Better – or was it worse? – I realised that my father wasn't really angry. I was the angry son, he the hurt father. Suddenly I was aware that, with his strict code of principles, he was indeed ashamed of me, of what I had done, of the possible disgrace. What a stupid, old-fashioned way for father and son to start a fight! Over a woman, like so many fights in life. He was ashamed as though I had broken a law, almost as if I were guilty of rape. He would probably never believe that it was Sonia who in the first instance had seduced me.

I was still sufficiently angry that before I did anything else – before I even tried to see Sonia – I felt a desperate urge to get out of the house into the fresh air, go for a walk, give myself a chance to cool off. Almost running across the courtyard, I rushed through the arch and almost fell into the arms of Anna and Willi, locked in a torrid embrace behind the yew trees.

'Sorry!' I shouted and prepared to walk down the hill.

'Wait!' cried Anna, gesturing to Willi to leave us alone. 'I'll come back in a minute or two,' she said to him. And to me she asked, 'What happened?'

'Caught in the bloody act.' I kicked some loose gravel savagely. 'Father was actually waiting for me when I walked out of Sonia's room at six this morning. Jesus! Was that one helluva row.'

'What's going to happen to you – and Sonia? She told me she's leaving. Oh! Larry, poor you, poor Sonia.'

'It was too good to last.'

'Willi and I will probably be next,' Anna prophesied gloomily.

'What on earth for?'

'Papa hates the Germans. He's been indoctrinated by Grandma.'

'Silly old cow. Yes, I mean it. But you'll be all right. Get rid of Hitler – he's bound to go – and then . . .'

'Couldn't you bear to wait for Sonia? I mean, let it all blow over.'

'That's the idea, I suppose. But it's so damned stupid – having to wait.'

Suddenly Sonia appeared, walking through the arch, quietly, almost sedately, all the fun gone from those laughing blue eyes. She looked at me a little awkwardly and said, 'Your mother said you'd probably be here.'

'Darling Sonia,' I cried. 'Let's walk down the dell. Though, I suppose,' I added bitterly, 'I'm only allowed to see you if we keep in sight.'

'That's true.' She was very serious but close to tears. 'I did make a sort of vague promise to your mother. She's been very sweet.'

'What's sweet about separating us?'

'Don't let's part like this, darling. It won't be for ever.'

'But why not get married? Run for it, bolt this very minute in the M.G. and get married at the American Embassy?'

'You know it's impossible.' We were walking slowly down towards the bottom of the dell, following the pale ochre path, the green lawns falling away to the bank of rhododendrons and the orchard beyond.

She kicked at some loose stones before repeating, 'You know it's impossible. It's not only *your* parents – it's mine.

I'm only eighteen. There'd be a terrific row if Daddy became involved in a scandal – through me. Specially as Daddy is returning to Europe. If he were to find out what's happened to his only daughter he'd have a fit.'

'But we can't just accept this.' I must have sounded desperate, for she linked her arm in mine so that, unseen by anyone looking at us from the house, she was able to take my hands, lock her fingers through mine.

'We have to – for the time being. It's the only chance – for me to behave – and then we'll try and fix something. I don't know what.'

'We don't even know what'll *happen*. We don't even have any say in anything. Your father could be posted anywhere – Australia, anywhere. And if he took you with him, we'd never meet again.'

'We will.' She continued to hold my hand, squeezing herself close to me as we walked along. 'I was thinking,' she laughed, but not with any happiness, 'here we are holding hands and this is the first time I can remember not feeling excited when you touch me. I feel as though I've been pushed into a cold shower.'

'Me too.'

'But I do believe that if we wait we'll be together again. And in the meantime, here's a little present for you. Don't open it until I've gone. The car's coming to fetch me in less than an hour.'

As soon as I returned to the house I had a talk with Mama. 'But we *love* each other,' I pleaded. 'You of all people must understand, Mama. You were younger than Sonia when you married Papa. I love her,' I added, lapsing into French. '*Je l'ai dans la peau*. What I don't understand is – why can't we just get married?'

She was sitting next to me on one of the large oatmeal-coloured sofas by the big glass coffee table, and suddenly she leaned across and held my hand.

'Believe me, I do understand,' she said. 'But I'm her god-mother. I gave my word to God, in church, that I would look after her. And now, I've failed. Perhaps that's the problem – the way she's been brought up as your sister – it makes me feel that the way you've behaved isn't very' – she was searching for a word that wouldn't hurt – 'very clean.'

'It was the only way,' I said miserably.

'You could have waited, darling.'

'We *love* each other!' As though that excused everything. Then I added, 'Would you like Sonia to marry me?'

'Later, yes. But now, no. You want to be a newspaperman, a writer. Even Uncle Oregon says it's hard work. You shouldn't be tied up at twenty, really darling. You can wait. If Sonia goes to Florence you can write to each other, and then, when you've got rid of all this sneaking business, you'll see her for what she is – a future wife, a wonderful girl. Then perhaps you can get engaged.'

'But if she goes to live in Italy, she'll probably run off with someone else.'

'If she did, then she wouldn't be worth waiting for, would she?'

'But if we get married now?'

'At twenty, darling?' she asked. 'What you've done, Larry – all that deceit in our own house – is not very nice, though I try to understand,' she sighed. 'I'm not angry with you. But your father is right. And I think you owe it to Sonia's mother not to hurt her. If she found out, it would break her heart. Later, if you want to get engaged, the past will be forgotten. You'll have made a clean new start.'

Alone in my room, still hearing the crunch of tyres on the gravel as she left in the Hisp., I opened Sonia's present, the one she had said didn't cost anything. It was a flat parcel. I tore open the flimsy white tissue paper, to reveal a Morocco-bound Italian diary, the sort with one whole page for every day.

And in it she had, throughout the weeks, filled every page for my first six months of 1932, ending on the previous day, my birthday; each page covered with her thoughts for me, the wonderful things we had done together, every happy day and night we had spent together, warmed by each other's love.

5

I would have been an abnormal twenty-year-old had I not for months displayed all the classic symptoms of a broken heart. I lost weight, I went for long walks alone, outwardly calm but secretly railing at the cruelty of life, at my parents, at my own stupidity at being caught, the greatest crime of all.

Two days after Sonia left I prepared to return to Paris, to work on the P.A. I had to. I also made a big decision not to live in the rue des St. Pères during the week. For I had guarded one secret the family *didn't* share – the existence of the tiny apartment in the rue de l'Université. Luckily I had signed the lease in my own name.

So, for what it was worth, I got a touch of revenge. The days at Douzy had passed in stony silence – not aggressive, more a silence because no one could find the right words to say to each other. But on the evening before I was due to leave Mama asked if we would all be having breakfast the following morning.

Breakfast at Douzy was a ritual, held in the large dining room, with its shining silver lining the back of the long sideboard. On it stood chafing dishes warming not only bacon and scrambled eggs but, from time to time, American hot cakes with maple syrup and even a mass of soggy, and delicious, corned beef hash with poached eggs.

Punctuality was never insisted on at breakfast. It really *was* a movable feast – until half past ten when the table was cleared. Otherwise people trooped in, some still rubbing their eyes, and took helpings of whatever was left, and filled their own cups of American-style coffee – Papa's only real addiction to an American habit: he could not stand the bitter chicory-flavoured liquid that passed for coffee in France.

We were all grouped round the polished table and Aubergine was handing some croissants or home-baked bread to Guy when I looked at my watch.

'Time to be off,' I said.

'Drive carefully.' Mama never changed her Monday-morning plea.

'I promise.' I smiled — though I felt miserable. I could see that *she* felt for me. Then I dropped my bombshell, enjoying briefly the casual words.

'And by the way,' I said, 'I shan't be staying at the rue des St. Pères any more.'

'What on earth do you mean?' asked Papa sharply.

'I need a change.' Adding almost defensively, 'I'm old enough to hold down a job. I'd rather be on my own.'

'But darling, *where*?' asked Mama gently. 'You can't just rush out and . . .' she looked hopelessly at my father.

'Yes, where?'

'You don't have to be scared, Mama. I've arranged to sublease an apartment from a friend, that's all. Just for a few months. It's handy for the office and the rent is peanuts.'

'But *where*?' insisted my father.

'On the Left Bank. I'll let you have all the details when I've got the place in order. I just don't want anybody to see it until then.'

At first there was a steady stream of letters, but Sonia was not a good correspondent, while I was always worried about pouring out my heart in case letters were opened by her parents, who had returned to Italy.

On the other hand, Sonia could have written to *me* without any danger of discovery, especially after I gave her details of 'a new apartment I've just moved into' — with the address of *her* place. She could have poured out her heart to me, yet she found herself incapable of translating the passion of the spoken word into the written language.

Both of us were frustrated, and in the thirties telephoning was virtually impossible. I tried from time to time, but France was cursed by a special brand of witches, usually female, who seemed to enjoy a fiendish glee every time they connected anyone to a wrong number after hours of delay. The Italian service was just as bad.

Still, though I missed Sonia, I loved her old apartment with its walls of red poppies. Despite the original fear that nostalgia would make me wallow in self pity, exactly the reverse happened. It reminded me of Sonia every day; I felt I was sharing it, but not sadly. I would have despaired much more had I stayed in the rue des St. Pères, knowing that someone else was living in our old apartment.

As I became more involved in my work as a newspaperman, my letter-writing energies began to dwindle. Apart from anything else, I had discovered that the newspaper world, which I had regarded as comparatively undemanding when writing only for the weekly *Paris American*, had become a tough, exciting, fascinating taskmaster.

'It's like having a new girlfriend,' said Oregon after I had done a major piece for the *Globe*. 'You just don't have time to go looking around for other girls.'

In a way it was true. Of course I still loved Sonia but, busier than ever, I didn't miss her on any particular day, that *very* day. Much more, I missed the memory of *all* the days of happiness we had shared.

And I discovered something else: the year of intense physical love-making before we parted, the physical expression of my love for Sonia, had been true, not just the randiness of a young bull. With Sonia's presence I had needed to make love all the time. Without her presence I didn't – apart, that is, from the occasional therapeutic night out with a pretty passing flirt.

But most important, the longer we were parted, the more exciting my work became. Each morning was a new adventure, a morning to which I awakened rarely knowing what it would have to follow.

If the weather was fine I walked to the office, making first for the river, with the tiny tugs straining as they hauled a line of barges along the Seine, or watching the first portable bookshops open under the huge elms or peeling plane trees, the first persevering fishermen reserving their places for the day. I crossed the Tuileries, walked up the avenue de l'Opéra, then bore right towards the Bourse until finally I reached the narrow, congested rue du Sentier.

The offices of the *Paris American* and the *Washington Globe* were at the top end, facing the boulevard Poissonnière. The narrow three-storey building looked as though it had been squashed between a textile warehouse and Madame Yvette's bistro where she served unlimited red wine, Pernod or *fine à l'eau* on credit to the small staff of four or five journalists and the handful of printers.

Each morning when I stepped into the narrow hall, its walls a 'post office' yellow, the air smelling of printer's ink, Charles, the porter, emerged from his *concierge*'s cage to greet me. Short, with rheumy eyes, he pulled open the latticed door of the ancient elevator where visitors were greeted with an uncompromising sign hanging on its surrounding metal cage: 'On no account must this elevator be used for downward journeys.'

The elevator shuddered to a stop on the second floor where the editorial staff worked, the squeaking machinery begging for oil as I tugged the latticed door open. The circulation department (consisting of one man) and the advertising department (more important, two men) were on the first floor.

Because Tommy Tomlinson, the Paris correspondent of the *Globe*, had rented rooms on the floor above me, he was giving me more and more work on a freelance basis, simply because if he wanted a rush job he only had to come down one flight of stairs to see me.

I found myself suggesting more and more exclusive stories for the *Globe*. The Astells *did* know many people in Paris, so that I often stumbled on fascinating titbits of news before anyone else. Also, Papa was a close friend of Bullitt, the American ambassador. A member of the Travellers' Club in the Champs-Élysées, he knew many politicians, he moved in the art world, and he often passed on to me casual information which might lead to a story.

Oregon helped even more. He was not only an experienced newspaperman who had deliberately opted out of the international scene to run the *Paris American*, he had become a living legend in Paris. He was, or had been, close friends with everyone from James Joyce to Hemingway, from Henry Miller to Gertrude Stein. They all loved Oregon, not only because he was wise, but because, with his private income from his share of the champagne estate, he was always willing to stake writers during difficult times.

Unlike my father who was tall and rather elegant in an aloof way, Oregon, his younger brother, was effusive, chubby, with a round face, alert eyes darting behind spectacles, eyes that were always alight with ideas. He talked with the same exuberance that made his articles twinkle – enthusiastic, always in such a rush to pour out his thoughts that often he had no time to finish his sentence. He chain-smoked Gauloises, lighting one with the stub of the last. A trail of ash always decorated his jacket lapels.

Since the day someone had dubbed him 'Oregon' years ago no one remembered his given name of Ronald, except on his passport and *carte d'identité*. He had long since discarded the name, like an old jacket which once fitted but which now sat oddly on his shoulders.

Often I drove him to Douzy, for I still spent the weekends there whenever I could. After the first anger, I had never really harboured a grudge against my parents; and anyway, if I missed Sonia, I also missed the gentle life of Douzy, its calm and peace, the warm hillsides clad in vineyards. At first the homesickness had been all for Sonia on those walks along paths we had known since we were children. But now, by the middle of the thirties, years had passed, and the homesickness was more for Douzy.

People came and went. Willi had become a regular visitor, for by now he was highly placed in Staffens, his engineering firm in Düsseldorf, and he travelled regularly to Paris. Anna adored him – much to Grandma's disapproval, for she still hated all Germans; even my father was worried, for the Fascists, then the Nazis, seemed to become more and more powerful and evil.

'It's not a question of whether or not there'll be a war next week,' said Oregon, one afternoon at Douzy. 'There won't be. But there *will* be a war before the end of the thirties. Impossible to stop it. Hitler's Nazis are winning everywhere. Mussolini is taking over any country he likes. The Spanish people are torn by civil war. There's no hope – not for Europe, anyway.'

'I see the French have agreed to extend the Maginot Line,' said my father.

'Useless!' shouted Oregon.

Willi had joined us, and, I'm not quite sure why, but

Oregon suddenly asked him, 'No offence, Willi, but do you ever feel you'd like to get out of Germany?'

'Leave my country!' Even his precise German accent betrayed his horror at such a step. 'You mean because of Hitler? Just wait till big business gets the wind up. They'll soon kick him out. And as for the German High Command — *they're* not going to take orders from a corporal!'

'I hope you're right,' said Oregon, 'but I think he's here to stay, and if the West doesn't do something to stop him — one day we'll have to pay the check.'

'*Nein, nein!*' cried Willi.

Olivia, who came almost every weekend to see Guy, said in a matter-of-fact voice, 'The Jews will come in for more beastly treatment, you watch. I'm Jewish, and when I listen to that sort of evil . . .' the words trailed off and her large brown eyes were sad.

Oddly enough it was Willi Frankel who gave me my first big break on the *Globe*. The paper had already printed dozens of my stories, but nothing could compare with this.

In July 1934 Willi had visited Paris on business, followed by the weekend at Douzy. And it was during a walk in the vineyards, beyond the orchard and the lake, that he told me the most extraordinary story.

We had read a brief account that Ernst Roehm, one of Hitler's oldest friends and head of the Brownshirts, had been executed. But that was all we knew. The details had been hushed up in Berlin.

'I heard a rumour that scores had been killed,' I said.

'Scores!' Willi looked at me with disbelief. 'Not scores, but hundreds, *thousands* even. Hitler himself is ordering the execution of thousands. Such a bloodbath it has been!'

'Then why are you a Party member?' I couldn't help asking Willi, as from the top of a rise we looked down on a magic carpet of blossom during the brief week of the flowering.

'This is a foolish question. You know that no one can get a big job in Germany unless he joins the Party. It is like being a member of a trade union in America. You are a member but it means nothing.'

'I'm sorry, I didn't mean it. But – know any more details?'

Ja, ja. One of the chief engineers at Staffens escapes by a hundred metres. Roehm is on vacation with friends at the Hotel Hanslbauer at Bad Wiessee near Munich for a jolly night or two. Roehm is homosexual, you know,' Willi continued. 'Most of his friends are. The men sleep together in the hotel. They don't like girls.'

'I'd heard rumours. You're sure?'

Ja. The Staffens engineer staying at Wiessee, he is very pretty, and several times the Brownshirts ask if he would like to meet Roehm.'

Slowly, as we walked, Willi filled in the background to the story. Roehm had started the Brownshirts – the *Sturm-abteilunger* or S.A. for short – and it had grown to four million strong, making Roehm more and more powerful, especially behind the scenes. Now, according to Willi, Hitler believed that Roehm had grown so strong that Hitler was worried. At the same time Hitler badly needed the backing of Germany's armed forces, which despised the one-time corporal.

'That is true,' said Willi. 'So it seems Hitler makes to get rid of Roehm.'

'But how, Willi? Hitler only came to real power early last year. You can't overthrow an army of four million men just like that.'

'Remember the German navy and army hates the rabble of the S.A.' Willi explained. 'So Hitler does a deal with them. Early in April – and this has never been told – Hitler left for a secret meeting on the pocket battleship *Deutschland*. They sail from Kiel. Admiral Raeder, the head of the navy, is there. So is General von Blomberg.'

'What happened then?'

'Hitler makes a secret pact. The German navy and army will agree that Hitler succeeds Hindenberg as head of the State if Hitler agrees to suppress the S.A. and kill Roehm.'

According to Willi's informant, Hitler and Himmler stage-managed a non-existent plot in which Roehm was supposed to be planning to kill Hitler. In fact Roehm and his cronies were at Wiessee, 'having fun and games', as Willi put it. To me the fascination of this inside story for the *Globe* was that though the bare details of Roehm's execution had been printed, lack of detail would whet the appetite for more. But how safe was Willi's source?

'As safe as — what is it you say? — as safe as my house,' Willi explained. 'My friend from Staffens is at Wiessee when Roehm is there — but he is lucky, his hotel is at the far end of the village. Finally Hitler drives to Wiessee — to confront Roehm. My friend sees him arrive. Hitler goes into the hotel himself. Roehm is arrested and taken to the Stadelheim prison in Munich.'

'It's sensational!' I exclaimed.

'Very much,' said Willi. 'This will become the — you might call it the turning point for Hitler.'

'But why didn't Hitler just order Roehm's execution?'

'Because he is an old chum of Hitler's — once they share a cell in jail — Hitler offers him a courtesy.' With a wry smile, Willi explained. 'He leaves Roehm a loaded gun in an empty room. Is a classic gesture, but Roehm refuses to be classic and ignores the gesture of honour. So he is executed by Himmler's S.S.'

According to Willi, thousands were shot in Munich, while in Berlin Goering supervised the deaths of hundreds more.

'I am telling you, Larry,' said Willi seriously, 'that this is very exact. Staffens are working on secret tank construction, there are many people close to Hitler. Even they are horrified. For twenty-four hours all Germany echoes to machine guns. The executioners, they must work in squads of eight, but only for an hour at a time.'

'But none of these details has been printed.'

'It couldn't be printed.' He shook his head. 'No German will dare to. And no American journalist in Berlin could get a cable through the censor.'

'Can I print it?'

Willi made only one stipulation. 'You must let me spend three days back home in Düsseldorf before you tell America. I would not like it to be associated with you here. And I am afraid of this man Himmler. He used to be a chicken farmer — did you know this? — but he has spies everywhere.'

I promised, of course. But five days later I had my very first lead story in the *Globe* — right across Page One, said the herogram, the name given to congratulatory cables from the *Globe*'s foreign editor.

Even Papa was impressed when the clip from Washington arrived by sea mail:

WHY HITLER EXECUTED ROEHM
THE FIRST FULL DETAILED STORY

and underneath, 'From Larry Astell, Exclusive'.

It was the first of many more scoops I landed during the next two or three years, when I often seemed to be working seven days a week – ninety per cent of the time for the *Globe*. The odd thing was that I had never met anyone on the Washington newspaper except Tommy Tomlinson, until the day early in 1937 when he phoned me in the P.A. office from his room above.

'Hi!' he greeted me. 'How's about keeping a day free for lunch?' Though this big, burly man had been correspondent in Paris for many years, he still couldn't speak more than a few words of fractured French.

'Could do,' I grinned. 'You paying?'

'Nope.'

'Then I'll have to think about it.'

'Please yourself. Only – I think I ought to tell you, Henry Vance, the owner of the *Globe*, is arriving on the *Berengaria* and has asked to lunch with me – and he wants to meet you too.'

I whistled.

'The big time.' Tommy had a sardonic attitude to newspaper owners.

'What gives?' I asked.

Tommy shrugged his shoulders. 'Far be it from me to unravel the insane workings of a newspaper baron's mind.'

'But seriously?'

Tommy harboured no jealousy because I wrote as a free-lance for the *Globe*. He was a tough old stager, quite content, now that he was in his early fifties, to stay in Paris until retirement age. 'He's obviously heard about your stories – or maybe' – with a wry smile – 'he actually reads his own paper. Most proprietors only look at the ads – the greenbacks. You

should get *your* old man to invite my boss and his wife down to
Douzy for lunch and dazzle him.'

I did just that. My father invited the Vances and Tommy for
the weekend, sending the Hisp. to Paris to drive them to
Douzy. And even Mr. Vance was entranced when he made the
usual first-time visit to drink a vintage Astell in the Douzy
pyramid.

'Never seen anything like it in the goddamned world.' He
peered up and down at the extraordinary white *cave*. 'What a
place to hide secrets. Yessir, thank you, I *will* have another
glass.'

Mrs. Vance was equally impressed, especially at the way the
servants looked after the guests — a tradition of Douzy.

'No one has ever looked after *me* like this before,' she said
after being cosseted by Aubergine, 'I just tell you, Henry
Vance, you'd better start improving the standard of house-
keeping back home, or I'll be pinching Aubergine, though
why she's called by that name I wouldn't know.'

We had to explain. And Mrs. Vance, when she left, gave
Aubergine the biggest tip she had ever seen.

Tommy's remarks about making friends with the boss were
absolutely correct. From that day, I was more than just a
cipher to old man Vance, even in faraway Washington. I was a
name; he could put a face to it; he had been to our home with its
strange white pyramid. I never looked back.

That afternoon, after the Vances had left for Paris, Mama
squeezed my arm and said to me, 'Be an angel, Larry, and help
me in the garden. It's a lovely day and, anyway, we never get a
chance to talk.' And when we were nicking off the crimped,
dead pansies round the border, she added, 'I'm so pleased
about your success with Mr. Vance, darling. I think he likes
you. You *are* clever.'

'Thanks largely to you,' I laughed.

'Not entirely. Your father says you're the sort of man who'll
always recognise a chance and seize it. It's wonderful.'

There wasn't really much to do in the garden. But I had the
feeling that Mama wanted to talk. Over the years, dealing
often with strangers from whom I was trying to extract
information, I had developed an instinct which told me when

the time was ripe for an imminent exchange of confidences.
Sure enough I was right.

'Do you ever miss Sonia after all these years?' Mama asked
me almost shyly.

'Not really – well, that's not true. It's a long time now –
three or four years – but of course I think of her often.'

'Any other girls in view?'

I shook my head. 'Nope,' I said firmly. 'Nary a one. A good
newspaperman must be a loner. Uncle Oregon told me that.'

'But you must have girlfriends?' Was Mama probing? Or
was this just normal parental interest?

'A few. Not very exciting, though. I like being alone during
the week, then coming to Douzy on Fridays – unless the *Globe*
asks me to do a Sunday stint.'

Mama sounded a little guarded, watchful when she asked
almost casually, 'Have you heard from Sonia *lately*?'

'Not for ages. Why? Any particular reason?'

'Only,' Mama hesitated, 'that I heard from Sonia's mother
the other day.'

'I didn't know you even wrote to each other.'

'Not often. But it seems there's a vague chance – nothing
more – that the Riccardis may be coming *en poste* to Paris.'

'You mean it – really! And? –' I left the question unfinished.

'I don't know, dear. I know nothing really.'

'But why Paris?' I blurted out. 'That's wonderful.'

'Why *not* Paris?' asked Mama with a laugh and explained the
details of the letter she had received. Apparently Riccardi had,
in the normal course of diplomatic duties, done a stint at the
Italian Foreign Office after leaving Paraguay and now, according to Sonia's mother, was senior enough to be given a fair
number of choices when the time came for him to take up a
new post.

'And he's expecting to be offered Paris,' she said.

'And Sonia?' I insisted.

'I don't know.' Mama laughed again. 'Really! Why Don't you
phone her and find out? I suppose she would come to Paris
– if this appointment goes through. Do you still love her? It's
been a long time since – but you say there's no one else.'

No, there wasn't. The thought – even the mere possibility
that Sonia might return to Paris after all these years – made me

realise how much I had missed her. How long was it now since I had seen her? Four years? No, more. Perhaps she or I or both would be different when next we met. Maybe the years apart would have robbed us of the innocence we had both at first enjoyed. I certainly didn't feel the white-hot surge which had always seized us in the past even when we brushed against each other. But you couldn't expect that sort of feeling to thrive on an absence of years. And during the years when I had moved ahead as a newspaperman I had become more preoccupied with living rather than loving. There was hardly time to *think* of love, let alone make it.

Of course, if I saw her again, God knows what my reaction would be. I don't think I could ever resist her – not only because of my feelings, but because she always made it so clear that she couldn't resist me. On the other hand, Riccardi might never come to Paris. And Sonia might be busy in Italy, or after all these years she might not want to re-open the past. She had hardly bubbled over with passionate letters in the intervening years.

'I'll believe it when I see her,' I laughed. 'In the meantime, I'm a loner.'

'You're right – it's probably only a rumour. All the same, Larry, I don't like to think of you so much alone in Paris. It doesn't seem natural.'

'Mama – I'm surrounded by friends – well, acquaintances. They're not so intense as' – I could afford to smile now at the memories – 'as Sonia was. Of course I'm lonely sometimes, but it doesn't worry me.'

As I shovelled up some dead flowers into a barrow, I had the sudden feeling that I wasn't the only one at Douzy who at times was lonely, and I felt a twinge of guilt at the casual way in which we accepted Mama, the dodges we got up to evade 'garden duty', forgetting that Mama didn't *need* to do any gardening. It had become to her a therapy more than a passion, something to do, something to keep her hands busy, her thoughts occupied, when she was bored.

'Yes, I am lonely sometimes,' she confessed, asking me for the secateurs. 'The trouble is – men change. At first when we were married, even if your father enjoyed his work it was only *part* of his life. But now he's become *too* successful.' With a laugh she added, 'All he had to do was watch people fill bottles of champagne and let nature do the rest. But now, my dear, he's the head of this and that, the vice-president of this, he works on the *Comité* and the *Appellation Controllé*. He's hardly time to say good morning to me. Yes, I am lonely at times,' she added thoughtfully, 'but thank God for Guy.'

'Let's hope he doesn't choose his new girlfriend Olivia instead of Douzy.'

'He won't!' she said almost ferociously.

'Mama! She's very pleasant. I admire Olivia. She's no Sonia, but she has a certain serenity. And she *is* a good painter.'

'I didn't mean it.' Mama straightened her back. 'I was only thinking. It's not my idea of fun living alone in this big house when you all leave home. You've gone already. And what's going to happen between Anna and that German boy? And after that' – suddenly she was sad – 'I'll be all alone except for Grandma and Mademoiselle Lisette. They're hardly scintillating companions. Soon there'll only be Guy left.'

'Don't you think,' I asked suddenly, 'that it's a bit of a bore having Mademoiselle Lisette around – I mean, an ex-nanny living in the house? After all, how many years is it since she *was* a nanny?'

Mama shrugged her shoulders. 'She's all right,' she said, curiously defensive. 'And there's plenty of room.'

'She's such a prune, it's bad for you to have her around. You need younger company. I think she should go.'

'No,' said Mama with sudden firmness. 'Let's forget the subject.'

'You're the boss,' I said cheerfully. 'But at least why don't you come to Paris more often? Even live there? Or visit America for a few months. How about that? Doesn't it tempt you?'

'Sometimes. At least shopping in Paris would make a change' – half humorously – 'from gardening.'

'Next time you come to Paris we'll go out for dinner. We'll find a boyfriend for you.'

'Maybe,' she said thoughtfully.

A few evenings later I mentioned to the family over dinner that I had been invited to meet Otto Abetz, the German minister in

Paris with special responsibilities. Grandma's immediate sniff of disapproval was distinctly audible.

'He should be shot!'

'But Grandma,' said Guy, 'you can't shoot everyone.'

'The Germans are the natural enemies of France.' She made statements like this with the air of finality that brooked no argument – and in fact we had long since found it easier to accept Grandma's dictums than to start discussions which we could never win. To her the French were God's chosen people, the Germans the devil's disciples.

'But,' wailed a pretending Anna, 'you can't want to shoot Willi – *please.*'

'You watch your step, young lady,' warned Grandma darkly, but without specifying any reasons.

My father helped himself to some more pink *gigot* – like most Frenchmen he preferred his lamb underdone – and some *mange tout.* 'I always thought,' he murmured, 'that in these dangerous times, with a lunatic like Hitler in command, we should all be trying to *avoid* war. *Really!* It seems to me that Mr. Abetz is at least *trying* to help – to promote understanding.'

'I still prefer dead Germans.' Grandma cut her slice of meat as savagely as the poor lamb's throat, then folded her hands across her lap, always a sign that the last word had been said.

'There, there, boys and girls, that's enough killing for one night,' said Mama tolerantly.

'We don't want to run out of coffins,' whispered Oregon.

Otto Abetz, it transpired, was paying one of his regular visits to Paris in his role of ambassador at large. Many French people were deeply suspicious of his motives. He was apparently very close to Hitler. The French anti-Fascist clique firmly believed that Abetz and his followers were building up a pro-Nazi fifth column strong enough to betray France in the event of war. Others, like my father, felt Abetz was striving to improve Franco–German relations. He *seemed* to be a Francophile with an impeccable pedigree. He had a charming French wife called Suzanne. He spoke the language perfectly. He was at home with French history and literature, and could keep his end up with any French intellectuals.

'He likes people to think,' said Oregon, drawing on his after-dinner cigar, 'that he's the one German above all others who's determined to prevent war with a country he loves. Personally I think it's a load of crap.'

'Well, the Europeans are behaving very strangely,' said my father.

'They sure are.' Oregon touched the plate with the end of his cigar so the ash would drop off gently. 'And not only with German-inspired riots in places like the Sudetenland, and Halifax in Britain crawling to appease Hitler. The Italians have joined the German–Japanese Anti-Comintern Pact – bloody strange bedfellows, I must say. And Franco is winning all along the line.'

'They should all be put behind bars,' said Grandma. 'And Abetz first – tomorrow. Better that than you, Larry, kow-towing to a German.'

'I still think it might be interesting to meet him.'

'Sure. But watch it. He'll be charming. My bet is that before the end of the party you'll be invited to a free junket in Germany.'

'And after the piece I wrote about Roehm? He must have seen it.'

'He'll have forgotten all about it. Anyway, he's big enough to take that sort of criticism in his stride.'

I met Abetz the following week in his house in the rue de Rennes. His French wife was at the door of the *salon* to greet guests and couldn't have been more charming. Almost in-stinctively I took in every detail of the room, the tall french windows, the pale green walls, the gold leaf that touched the mouldings of doors and ceilings – and of course an assortment of Louis XV furniture without which no political home was complete. It was a pretty room, particularly as a whisper of sunlight shafted through it.

Abetz obviously knew who I was for he came forward to greet me. I was surprised to find a handsome man, tall, with big shoulders, and a face that looked paler than it actually was because of his reddish blond hair. He had a big smile. It was his eyes, though, that fascinated me. They were blue, yet they didn't go with the smile. The smile and the eyes seemed to belong to two different people. The smile was wide and generous, the blue eyes above the smile like two chips of ice frozen with a bluish tinge.

'It is a pleasure to meet you, Mr. Astell.' He couldn't have been more charming. 'I have admired your work very much.'

The more I listened to him, the more intrigued I became. He seemed to make a great show of being an understanding friend of France; he exuded cordiality. He also made a great number of intelligent observations and yet, I couldn't tell why, I found him shifty.

There were about twenty at the party and we made small talk until another guest arrived with something of a flourish, as though the late timing had been carefully engineered for effect. It was the Countess de Portes, mistress of Paul Reynaud, the up-and-coming French politician, but she was not with her escort as Abetz stepped forward and kissed her hand while she cooed, 'So nice to see you again, dear Otto.'

I had met Hélène de Portes before, but only briefly in a crowd, and I had never studied her carefully. I found it hard to like her. She wasn't particularly good-looking. She had a somewhat angular face, a large mouth, and I noticed that her complexion was sallow. Still, she was dressed in the height of fashion, her dark curly hair swept upwards in the style of the day.

She had been Reynaud's mistress for nearly ten years, and behind her back her enemies called her '*la porte à côté*.' It was a double-edged nickname, for she *was* the side door through which anyone who wanted to see Reynaud had to pass; but *à côté* was also a snobbish term so that, to her detractors, she was 'a little *à côté*,' 'a little ordinary'.

'Perhaps, *chère madame*,' Abetz had joined us, 'you can help me to persuade Monsieur Astell to visit us in Germany. We have already invited several prominent writers, but not yet an American. All we ask of our visitors is that they write the truth and not propaganda lies.'

'You should go,' said Madame de Portes simply.

'May I introduce you to the writer Jean Luchaire?' said Abetz. 'He has already visited us in Germany.'

I knew Luchaire well by reputation. He had been Suzanne Abetz's boss before she married the German. Luchaire was blindly pro-Nazi.

'And his delightful daughter, Corinne,' murmured Abetz. Luchaire's daughter *was* delightful. Only seventeen, Corinne Luchaire had shot to stardom in a French film called *Prison Without Bars*.

'I congratulate you on your performance,' I said, adding sincerely, 'And – well, you *are* beautiful.'

Luchaire was accompanied by Paul Ferdonnet of the Agence Prima, another pro-German writer, and I knew that Abetz had arranged for several self-appointed intellectuals who were sympathetic to Fascism to have their unpublished books published in Germany – with Abetz footing the bill, and paying staggering advance royalties out of all proportion to possible sales. In short, bribery.

We had almost reached the end of the party, with guests beginning to drift away, when Abetz, seeing me in a corner talking to his wife, came up and said, with the studied air of someone skilfully planting a casual remark, 'By the way, I hear that an old friend of your family is coming to live in Paris.'

I was on my guard, for I could sense his interest by the way he watched my face.

'Oh yes?' I had an idea of what was coming, but looked suitably surprised.

'I mean Signor Riccardi. He's just been appointed to Paris.'

'Riccardi!' I echoed. 'How did you know he was a friend of the family?'

Abetz shrugged his shoulders as though explanation was superfluous. 'I can't remember offhand who told me. The countess, perhaps?' And with that charming smile of his, 'Did you mention it, Suzanne? No? Does it matter? The main thing is that old friends will be reunited. That *can't* be bad in these difficult days.'

I was puzzled. It was part of my job as a newspaperman to keep track of all the important changes at the Quai d'Orsay and on the Paris diplomatic list, and I would surely have known if Riccardi was about to replace the present ambassador.

'Oh no,' said Abetz. 'He's going to be an ambassador at large, so to speak. You may say that Signor Riccardi will have very much the same job as I have. In fact we will be working together – for peace and understanding, to encourage happy relations between our countries.'

I was still puzzled, suspicious. How could Abetz have possibly known that the Riccardis and the Astells were old family friends?

Then, even more casually, Abetz dropped his second bombshell.

'I hear that Signor Riccardi's daughter is positively beautiful,' he said. 'I'm looking forward very much to meeting her.'

'She is,' I said, and in my enthusiasm dropped my guard. 'A real stunner.'

'I'm only sorry,' murmured Abetz as he said goodbye 'that her fiancé, who works in the Foreign Office, won't be able to join her in Paris.'

6

I couldn't believe it! Sonia engaged! And without telling me! That angered me most. At first, filled with the indignation of a spurned lover, I was furious – forgetting that over the years I had hardly encouraged her to keep her love.

I slammed the M.G. into third and, taking the back way to the office, avoiding the Grands Boulevards, I roared up the rue du Quatre Septembre towards the rue du Sentier.

And there in the office, of course, was a letter from her. One glance at the postmark told me it had been delayed, as letters in Europe often were in those days. I was in no hurry to open it but for a few moments studied the Italian stamp, deciphering the smudged date, the blue envelope with its strong upward-sloping handwriting.

What excuse could there possibly be in the unopened letter lying on my desk, taunting me. Sadness? Apology? Reproach?

After a few moments, anger subsiding, I realised that she couldn't know how Abetz had deliberately told me in advance about her fiancé. Sitting at the old wooden desk where I had passed so many hours of my life, I was thinking of that sun-drenched day when I had driven her from Rolle and we had stopped the old M.G. in the cornfield and everything had happened, and the days which had followed and which could never be forgotten. I suppose that had been the happiest year of my life.

Sighing, I slit open the blue envelope with one edge of the pair of long scissors, without which no newspaperman's desk is properly furnished. I started to read.

'Darling Monsieur Coquelicot,' she began, 'I want you to be the first to know two things – that I am engaged to be married, and that I still hope you realise that I will always love you more than anyone else in the world.'

I straightened up, almost with a jerk, for this was no ordinary letter to a jilted lover.

'It looks awful, so stark, written like that,' she continued. 'But what I am trying to say, darling Larry, is that the love we have known for each other can never be replaced by any other man, and yet, though I have not written to you for a long time, there have been many reasons. Daddy has been in trouble – not yet resolved – and I have been able to help him, but in a way which has made it impossible for me to do what I really wanted to – run away to your arms and marry you, my love. One day I will explain.

'Italy is not America and the diplomatic service is not like producing champagne. I remember your papa once telling me that if he didn't approve of the harvest in any particular year he just wouldn't bottle any champagne. But you can't make decisions like that when you are a diplomat – or, alas, a diplomat's daughter. You have to carry on, and play a part if needed.'

I turned over to the back of the first sheet and read on. 'Francesco is a career diplomat who has had his problems too. We don't live in ordinary times now. *Il Duce* is in charge. Our problems are not terrible, but the life of a diplomat is not easy, and I think I have been of help. What I am trying to tell you is that in Italy – and certainly in the diplomatic service – it is sometimes more important for married couples to be good friends than passionate lovers like *we* have been. So, if we meet, you must understand that sometimes life is not easy for a dutiful daughter.'

There was a great deal more in the three blue pages, but I was wondering, what did she mean by 'having to play a part'? And that it was more important to be good friends than passionate lovers? It sounded like a recipe for a miserable marriage — not that she was married yet, only engaged. But was she whispering discreetly that love, as she had so often said to me, had nothing to do with marriage?

Mama received a letter from Signora Riccardi a few days later, and when I arrived at Douzy for the weekend and she told me, I professed only a mild interest. Mama and Papa exchanged noticeable glances of relief.

'Sonia's fiancé has a title,' said Mama. 'He is the Count de Feo . . . Francesco de Feo. But it seems they won't be having an early marriage. The Italian diplomatic corps likes a man to get settled before he saddles himself with a wife. Very sensible.'

Sensible! Who the hell wanted to be sensible with a hot-blooded girl like Sonia? What a terrible waste, I thought. But of course she must have changed. Now she must be twenty-three. Perhaps *she* was 'sensible' now.

Then, a few weeks later, Signora Riccardi wrote to Mama again, this time giving the date when Riccardi would be arriving in Paris, where they would live in a diplomatic house in the rue de Longchamps. Her husband would be ambassador without portfolio. And I knew that the appointment would cover many secrets. This had to be an important promotion, for it came after a previous promotion. Riccardi's stint at the Italian Foreign Office had been a direct reward for remarkable diplomatic help given by Riccardi — some said undercover help — in persuading the countries of Bolivia and Paraguay to end their bitter war in 1936. He was obviously a formidable man.

Sonia was engaged, of course, so that except innocently we would never see each other alone. But I couldn't prevent a tingle of anticipation at the prospect of meeting her.

The day after Mama had read the second letter she cornered me in the living room.

'I imagine we'll be seeing quite a lot of the Riccardis,' she began tentatively. 'After all, they're old friends – and you're bound to be thrown in contact with Sonia. But Larry,' she hesitated slightly, 'I trust you to – well, remember I *am* Sonia's godmother. It sounds so old-fashioned! But be *good*, darling, if you know what I mean. It would be very unfair to everyone.'

'I will,' I promised her, and I meant it.

Besides, I had other things on my mind: no time to moon over a schoolboy crush which had ended six years ago. I was now a professional newspaperman. I could say that. I had graduated. I was working so hard for the *Globe* that I had little or no time for the dear old *Paris American*, even though I still worked in its building. I wasn't a staff member of the *Globe*, but that was because I preferred it that way. As a 'stringer' – paid by the day or by the quality of a story – I was earning as much as a staffer simply because France and Europe dominated the news and Tommy Tomlinson couldn't cope single-handed. Yet the arrangement suited the *Globe* because as a non-staffer it wouldn't be saddled with long-term responsibilities if I vanished when war came. By now – 1937 – we all talked about 'when', not 'if'. I was equally satisfied with the arrangement because, though I was paid well, I retained my freedom. Naturally I consulted Tommy about everything, but I didn't have to send Washington a cable every time I took a day off.

'Once you're on the staff, they like to keep track,' said Tommy. 'You've got to send them a signal even if you fart.'

I worked hard. I was well paid. But the *Globe* didn't own me.

Yet apart from my work, and long before Sonia reappeared, all was not well, though I find it difficult, looking back, to pinpoint the moment when I realised how the calm and ordered life of the Astells was slowly beginning to show signs of strain. Nothing dramatic happened. No one ran away from home, Papa wasn't surprised in bed with another woman, we didn't lose our money. The *Paris American* actually put on circulation.

Perhaps it was an echo of the discontent, the masked fear that chilled all Europe each time Hitler tightened his grip on a dictator's world, each time the antics of Mussolini posed new threats. No one was *really* afraid – not day after day after day – but occasional stabs of fear came and went, like a tooth abscess that flares, quietens, then flares again.

I saw what was happening in the family mostly in episodic flashes when I returned to Douzy for weekends, or when members of the family visited our Paris apartment during the week. Perhaps I didn't realise what was happening at first because I was so busy with the *Globe*.

Then Sonia returned to Paris – and, despite all the promises, I was soon caught up in a web of deceit, smiling lies, broken promises, furtive meetings. Did that somehow help to sour the life of Douzy? Did the families suspect, did the ripples of what happened secretly turn into larger, eddying circles that touched others?

Because, of course, when Sonia finally arrived in Paris and drove with her father and mother to spend their first weekend with us at Douzy, we were lost. I was determined to keep my promise to Mama, and it never entered my head that an old lost love would be rekindled the moment our hands touched. It was electric, needing no words, the effect just of shaking hands, the feeling of desire, as though we had never parted.

She seemed hardly to have changed; the same perfect complexion on that heart-shaped face, the same wide, open blue eyes, as though she was always surprised at the joy of living, the eyes as bright as ever. I drew in a deep breath. Her tailored suit – even I knew that women liked their suits to be tailored by men – was in grey 'Prince de Galles' checks, a jacket and skirt that showed off her figure and long, straight legs, in their silk stockings. And when she took off her jacket I could see that she was as slim as ever, breasts pointing upwards under her silk blouse, just the right size, round and firm and angled gently, not aggressively.

The most extraordinary thing of all was that she knew she wanted me, without any words spoken, as desperately as I wanted her. And there was another extraordinary thing. It wasn't lust. I can't explain it – I was above that feeling; I just wanted to wrap her in my arms, smother her with kisses, and slide into her body.

I tried to think – what to do? I was bemused. At first I could only stand there, on the verge of panic. If I didn't control myself I would shout aloud, 'I need you! Now. *Now!*'

I remember that Anna had told me she was going into Reims to meet someone for ten minutes. She would drive over about five o'clock, then return in half an hour. It was my chance. Almost deliberately ignoring Sonia, who was talking to Tommy Tomlinson who had come for the weekend, I chatted first to Signor Riccardi for a few moments, glanced at my watch – half past four – then buttonholed Anna, showing her a book I had been handling, pretending to search for the illustration.

'Listen quickly,' I muttered as I turned the pages. 'Don't ask any damn fool questions, but for God's sake get Sonia to drive with you to Reims. Only drop her at the far end of the orchard. I'll leave first with Tommy, pretend I'm going for a walk. Sonia and Tommy can swap places, change back when you return home. I must see her alone. I *must.*'

I saw the quick glitter of conspiracy shine in her eyes. She had always known about Sonia and me since that first drive from Rolle in Switzerland. And now Anna had her own conspiracies with Willi.

'Okay,' she whispered. 'You go now. Take Tommy with you, and he can come to Reims with me for half an hour.'

It was as simple as that.

'How's about a walk through the vineyards?' I said to Tommy.

'Me? I'm no walker,' he began, fortunately out of earshot.

'Come on,' I muttered savagely and, to the others, 'Tommy and I have a problem to solve – our next assignment. We'll discuss it over a walk. 'Bye girls, see you soon.'

The far corner of the orchard backed on to the road leading through the vineyards, at the spot where each autumn village boys sneaked in to pinch apples. As we walked down the dell, I explained to a mystified Tommy what was expected of him.

'For a bureau chief you're very understanding,' I said.

'Anything to encourage romance,' he chuckled. 'Make a good story, wouldn't it?'

Five minutes after we had crossed the orchard, Anna's Citroën appeared round the narrow road, yellow as a lemon.

From this spot, the route led to the main Reims road.

My heart was banging against my ribs as though a hammer was striking them. The car always went slowly round the tricky bends of the drive and, when it stopped, Sonia jumped out without a word.

'Hop in, Tommy,' cried Anna, and as she started to move forward slowly, cried, 'Be ready to swap places in half an hour!' Then the back of the Citroën disappeared round the next bend.

Without a word we scrambled across the bank, stumbling through tall stalks of frothy hedge-parsley and poppies, on into the orchard. Then, and only then, we almost fell to the ground, hidden in the long grass, and kissed each other as though the world would end when we stopped.

Still without a word, lying on her back, she pulled up her skirt and there, after six years, was Sonia as I remembered her, the long, slim legs, the flat stomach creamy white against the black. It sounds incredible, but I had no time to think of her, I pulled down my trousers with one hand, stroking her with the other, feeling her damp with desire, and then, after barely one move inside her, it was over before I knew what happened.

Only then did she speak. Lying there next to me, stroking my hair, my face, she kissed me again and again and whispered, 'Don't worry, darling. I came before you – the second I saw you looking at me.' Kissing me again, she added almost wistfully, 'Almost at this very spot where I first let you look at me. Remember?'

I nodded.

'And here you are,' twisting my blond hair, 'the same Monsieur Coquelicot. Remember him?' She lay back smiling, shining black hair spread out in the long green grass. 'Do you forgive me?'

'Of course,' I said.

While we still lay back in each other's arms she whispered, 'Got a hanky – one you don't need again?'

I gave her the one from my breast pocket. She tucked it between her legs.

Watching her, filled with the electric clarity that always follows true love-making, I suddenly thought, 'I shouldn't be watching her – I shouldn't have done anything.' Aloud, I said,

'I am taking away another man's fiancée. I can't help having a feeling – well, you know . . .'

'Don't feel that way, my love,' she whispered. 'Remember the first time? It's me that should feel guilty. Do *you* forgive *me*?'

'Of course – if there's anything to forgive. Here – let me clean you up.' I was worried lest our parents would notice anything.

'It takes a lot to ruin a Caraceni of Rome,' she laughed. 'Brush my back, will you, darling?' With a kiss and a light laugh that showed she didn't care, she said, 'He's the only tailor in Italy who really specialises in Prince of Wales suits. Costs a fortune – fifteen hundred lire.'

'There! That's better.' I dusted a little dirt from her skirt.

'Thank you. And I'm so glad. I missed you so much. I find it difficult to write letters . . .'

'I know.' I laughed too. It was extraordinary how, in the space of a few minutes, we found it easy to joke, the tension eased after the urgent physical need.

'I know.' Echoing my words, she smiled back. 'You used the right words – a physical need – because the second we touched each other in the living room it was as though I could hardly stand up.'

'That's just how I felt. If I'd left the room, I wouldn't have been able to wait, even for you, even for this.'

We didn't make love any more that day. In a curious way there was no need. We had released the desire, and so, knowing that we did love each other, as we had done six years ago, the act of making love again wasn't necessary, for the moment anyway. Satisfaction was taking over from urgency, anxiety from desire. The moment of meeting had been the moment of falling in love again.

So it all started again. Only this time it was different from the earlier deception. It was better and worse. Then I had only kept a secret from my parents. Now I was involved in the betrayal of the man Sonia had promised to marry; though he was still in Rome, it would have appalled my father and mother, if discovered. To say nothing of Sonia's parents.

Yet there was no way in which we could stop meeting

during the months that followed. We tried. I wasn't an absolute fool; I knew I was behaving badly, and so was Sonia for that matter. Often I felt ashamed of what I was doing. Then at other times I caught myself thinking that it wasn't all my fault. Sonia was no quiet, unassuming fiancée. With her Russian blood, she had a temper that flared, she was impetuous, strong-willed, and though she might consider the wishes of her father, and thus never discuss the possibility of breaking her engagement — not at this stage — she was determined that we should not miss one moment of our love if it could be kept secret.

In an almost bizarre way, Sonia even advanced what she considered to be a perfectly rational attitude to our behaviour — one that made it clear (to her) that we had no need to be ashamed of what we were doing.

'After all,' she said, 'it's not as though one of us picked the other up and started an affair. We fell in love six years ago. The others stopped us. We're only' — she searched for the words — 'resuming where we left off.'

'It's not the kind of philosophical argument that would stand up in a debate!'

'I'm happy about it. It satisfies my conscience. After all, if we'd never been found out we might eventually have got married.'

'How extraordinary you should say that.' I was thinking back to a conversation at Douzy. 'Mama actually told me once that she was sorry we'd been discovered. What a pity, my darling Sonia. It would have saved me so much trouble.'

'It's too late now.' Her voice was suddenly abrupt. She seemed to hate discussing a more permanent relationship. But this time I stood firm.

'Look, we love each other,' I said, as though that solved every problem — which to my uncomplicated way of thinking it did. 'Breaking an engagement isn't the end of the world.'

'But it would be — for me.'

'But why? Is it your father? Or Francesco? After all, it *is* a bit odd, come to think of it: you become engaged to a man you obviously don't love — and as soon as we meet we fall into each other's arms!'

'One day I'll explain. I haven't done anything dreadful, if

that's what you're afraid of. But I need help and you can't help me. Kiss me – and don't look so worried. One day I'll tell you everything. But not now. Don't spoil everything.'

'But I want to know,' I said stubbornly. We were lunching at the Brasserie Lipp in the boulevard St. Germain. 'I have a *right* to know.'

The moment I used the word 'right' I knew I shouldn't have done.

Almost scornfully she looked at me – like a different woman. Her eyes seemed to narrow and she went almost white with anger. 'What *right* do you have?' she said furiously. 'How dare you lecture me about *right*? Isn't it enough that I give myself to you . . .'

'And take from me!' I said angrily.

'Oh!' Anger turned to sarcasm, 'Now I'm doing you a favour each time we make love.'

'I didn't mean that.'

'Then don't say it, you pompous idiot,' she flared up. 'Why the bloody hell can't you accept things as they are?'

At that moment the old waiter came in with our dish of *choucroute* and laid the tray on the table.

'You can throw that bloody stuff away,' she said to him, and without another word stormed out.

I tried to follow, to make peace – everything had blown up in a matter of seconds – but in my rush I upset the tray. The *choucroute* tipped over, much of it on my trousers, but some on the trousers of the waiter. The prim lady behind the cash desk screamed faintly, then beckoned to the head waiter, demanding payment before I left. 'He's drunk, he's a disgrace to a respectable place,' I heard her cry.

By the time I had paid, Sonia had vanished.

I too was boiling over with anger. That was the end of that! It served me right for getting mixed up with a woman about to marry another man. And what a bitch! No woman had ever walked out on me before.

On an impulse I walked across to the Deux Magots, bought a *jeton* from the waiter for the telephone call box and dialled Tomlinson's number. Only the day before he had asked me if I would like a quiet trip to Fontainebleau to write an undated piece for the Sunday supplement on 'the new Barbizon School' of painters – the inheritors of those who had worked mostly in the forest of Fontainebleau, people like Rousseau, Millet and Daubigny.

'Okay if I go today?' I asked him.

'You sound mad at someone. But sure.'

I spent three utterly miserable days at the Hôtel Fleuri et Floret at Barbizon, surrounded by the forest of Fontainebleau. The weather was warm and sunny but I felt cold and miserable; the food at the hotel was superb but I felt starved – for love. I drove round the area, searching out promising painters, making notes, yet all the time beset by a nagging whisper, 'Perhaps I should phone her?' I wanted to. And I swear it wasn't nastiness that stopped me. I didn't want to be nasty to *her*. It was a feeling I entertained, that even if I was miserable without her I must have a few days in which to breathe, to consider the future, the slippery slope down which I was sliding helplessly to what could only be a sticky end.

I didn't give in. I didn't phone and I never expected her to, for she also had a stubborn set to her jaw. Three days later I drove straight to the office, parked my car outside the rue du Sentier and, as I walked through the doors, Charles, the doorman, his watery eyes blinking as he opened the doors of the rickety elevator, said, '*Pardon, monsieur*, there's a lady to see you.'

'Now? It's only ten o'clock.'

'She's been here, sir,' he coughed discreetly, 'since last night.'

She was asleep on my leather sofa in front of my desk. By her side was a half-filled cup of cold coffee and the crumbs of a croissant. Charles must have brought her breakfast and she had fallen asleep again. But it wasn't that which first stunned me. The office was filled from floor to ceiling with poppies – hundreds and hundreds and hundreds of them. There must have been twenty or thirty vases standing on the desk, the floor, even the windowsill.

I leaned forward and kissed her gently on the eyelids and her cheeks and I could taste the salt.

Without rising, just emerging from sleep, she just put her arms round me and still with a trace of tears, murmured, 'Oh my darling Monsieur Coquelicot, never do that to me again, never, never. Promise? I'm sorry! I love you, I behaved abominably, you're the only real thing in all my miserable life. The rest is like acting out a horrible play.'

And when she had said that and made up her face and I'd opened a bottle of champagne from the office fridge – even though it was still only just after ten in the morning – she explained, though only in part, why she had agreed to the engagement.

'I didn't want to involve you and I still don't want to,' she said. 'But Daddy begged me to accept Francesco's proposal. He said his entire future – his very life – depended on the engagement.' But beyond that Sonia would not satisfy my curiosity.

So the quarrel was forgotten, and the secret months that followed were as wonderful as if we had never quarrelled or for that matter had ever been parted.

True, there were differences as the months slipped by. For one thing I still couldn't say that I enjoyed the thought of Sonia being engaged to another man, even though he was living far away in Rome – and didn't seem to love him. Yet there was a different reason why I was uneasy – her father's vaguely sinister work in France, something that seemed to arrest all discussion of our future.

I still thought it perfectly simple for Sonia to break off the engagement and marry me. But she was afraid to. She *wanted* to marry me, of that I am sure, but as she said time and again after that quarrel, she could do nothing that would upset the diplomatic relations between her father, Count Ciano – now Foreign Minister – and what was happening in France.

'And Francesco *does* come into those relations,' she sighed. 'Not with me – but with Ciano, and even Mussolini. I only pray that we can sort it out. You know I want to marry you one day. But be patient.'

There was nothing I could do – but carry on, work hard, and make love in secret.

First, I found a place where we could meet. I did once take Sonia back to the rue de l'Université, but it was more for old times' sake than as a refuge of safety, and both of us were nervous of being discovered, for both Papa and Mama had long since visited the apartment.

'We've got to find another place,' I said, and we did. I was an old friend of a tall American photographer called Alex Rhys, who often worked for the *Paris American*. He was a bachelor in his fifties and lived in the rue du Cherche Midi, across from the boulevard St. Germain. And when he suddenly announced that he was leaving for Asia on a year's assignment for a major American magazine I grabbed the chance.

It wasn't the rue de l'Université, though it was even smaller than that beautiful poppy-bedecked apartment. And it was on the fifth floor — without an elevator. But Alex had turned the one-room atelier into a charming apartment, every wall decorated with huge blow-ups of his photos. It had a shower and a bidet. The kitchen consisted of a glassed-in corner with a couple of burners and a fridge — enough for a bachelor, and enough for us. There were a couple of deep, comfortable armchairs, a table that would seat four at a pinch and, in one corner, a wide divan surrounded by bookshelves.

It was perfect, and within a month we had a second 'home', a beautiful and secret place of our own. There we could meet whenever we could snatch the time, and there both of us could live in a world of make-believe limited only by the time when Sonia had to go clattering down the rickety wooden steps.

7

Over the next few months I began to wonder more and more about the duties of Sonia's father. What exactly was the role being played by Riccardi? It must be very serious — and secret — for Sonia to insist that it would be impossible for her to break off an engagement to a man she didn't love.

I might have been unduly sensitive to Riccardi's behaviour, even his power to influence Sonia's fears, yet I had an instinctive feeling that he had not been appointed to Paris merely to initial new trade deals or discuss the plight of migrant Italian workers. His work smacked of intrigue, especially as he and

Otto Abetz met regularly. I knew that Abetz was trying to undermine French resolve in these critical years. It seemed incredible, but was Riccardi working with him?

'Daddy was supposed to retire even before he was posted here,' said Sonia. 'But when Mussolini appointed Count Ciano Foreign Minister, Daddy became one of Ciano's right-hand men. Mummy's delighted,' Sonia added with a laugh. 'The job rates a chauffeur and servants.'

Ciano was Mussolini's son-in-law, and I knew that when you marry the boss's daughter you often end up thinking and acting like the boss. And Mussolini, engaged in enlarging the Italian empire in Africa, was not my favourite character. He had poisoned the wells in North Africa, in effect murdering thousands of civilians. He had proclaimed King Vittorio Emanuele, Emperor of Ethiopia. He had already demanded – and *got* – part of France's East African possessions. He was finding it all so easy – easy enough to start demanding the 'return' to Italy of Nice, Corsica, Tunis. All over Italy the three words had become a battle cry.

'I shouldn't say this, but I have the feeling' – Sonia rarely sounded uneasy – 'that Mussolini is going to cause trouble in France. It's the hints my father drops.'

'Such as?'

'He told me to be careful because a number of Italians here are – well, spies, I suppose, though he didn't use that word. But they're reporting back to Rome on all Italians in France who are against Mussolini's régime.'

'I'm not surprised.'

'He was vague. Just said that sometimes countries don't see eye to eye. That it could happen with our two countries. And I don't like Otto Abetz. Father sees him all the time. He doesn't want me to be in the middle of any story.'

This particular conversation took place in bed – as usual in the early afternoon or lunchtime safely hidden in the one-roomed studio on the fifth floor of the rue du Cherche Midi.

'Sometimes I feel that we've never been separated,' Sonia said. 'As though this terrible interval has been just an awful dream.'

'It wasn't,' I said sadly. 'You *are* engaged to be married. And not to me. Why don't you –?'

She put a finger to my lips, and remembering that first day when we lunched together on the way back from Switzerland said, 'Here, let's share our food.'

'But I love you — more than ever,' I said. 'It can't be wrong to marry the man you love. Can it? *Can it?*'

'We've been through all that, darling. Don't spoil it. It *can* be bad. Daddy's walking a tightrope, and if he makes one false move — like breaking off my engagement to one of Ciano's most promising helpers — well, it's been made clear to me . . .' she sighed.

'Even so. If I spoke to your father? I could even turn you into an American citizen.'

From Sonia I had built up from casual remarks a picture of her life with Francesco in Italy as an engaged couple. The Count de Feo had great taste, a large estate, excellent manners. He was at his best chatting to any pretty woman sitting on his right or left at a grand dinner party — 'Rather different from this room,' I looked ruefully round Rhys's flat.

'You know how much more I prefer this one,' she replied.

I took some consolation from the fact that though Sonia must have been the most beautiful guest at any dinner, he seemed relatively immune. I couldn't understand how Francesco could resist her physically. 'How can any man keep his hands off a girl like you?' I asked, not exactly jealous but hoping she would say that he had never been to bed with her.

'He hasn't,' she said. 'It suits me perfectly. He doesn't like that sort of thing — not much. Anyway, I love no one else but you.'

But, I asked her, weren't there others, even if her fiancé was prepared to wait? Again I asked, how could a sexually stimulated girl like Sonia resist other men? Didn't she herself feel the urges of sex?

'You'd be surprised how it stops when you don't love someone,' was all she said.

'But your fiancé — how can *he* wait until you're married? Nobody does these days?'

'He does.' I began to understand in bits of conversation over the happy weeks, that Francesco wasn't what the Americans and British then called a nancy boy, but that even if he didn't like men he had never loved women. 'He loves to be sur-

rounded by them,' she laughed once, 'but not on *top* of them.'
He was, in a word, neutral.

'I think the term is "narcissus",' she said gravely.

'Then why the hell did he ask you to marry him?' I asked
almost savagely.

'Darling Larry,' she kissed me, 'don't talk any more, please.
We have an hour before I must go. Make love to me in our
special way. What did you call it once?' she laughed. 'The
nonchalant way! What descriptive powers!'

Lunchtime was the safest time to meet, and we usually ate
thickly buttered *baguettes* packed with pink, slightly moist
ham. We were already in bed, munching and occasionally
sipping cold beer, while Sonia snuggled closer to me as we
indulged ourselves in 'nonchalance'. It was exciting – and
typically Russian. Outwardly we were like a married couple,
tucked into bed, talking about the problems of life – the
office, my latest scoop, on this particular occasion the problems of Sonia's father. But that was only superficial. The
object of the game – which Sonia had invented of course –
was to see how long we could discuss mundane topics while
our hands were busy with each other underneath the bedclothes, sending delicious shivers of anticipation through our
loins. And yet – even by the time she could not stop moving
slightly when I touched her, and I was matching her excitement – we still pretended, even discussing the weather – until
finally neither of us could wait another second and without a
word I sank myself inside her, not on top, but both of us lying
fully stretched side by side so that not only our lips were
locked, but so were our feet, even our toes. This way,
smothered with kisses, I did not have to do a thing as she,
nearing her climax, moved faster and faster while I gritted my
teeth with the effort of waiting for her final shudder of
satisfaction.

For a few minutes afterwards I lay back, my breath coming
faster with the effort of making no effort. I reached across her
for a cigarette. Part of the game consisted of pretending
afterwards – until we got dressed – that nothing had happened, of carrying on the conversation where we had left off,
as though it had only been interrupted because the phone had

rung. Only this hadn't been a phone, and we each needed a few moments of relaxation, and during that time, almost like the schoolgirl I had first known, she lay back clutching my right hand in hers.

'As I was saying, there's one way out of your problem. All we have to do is get married,' I continued. 'Then you'll be an American. And whatever happens in Europe – even if there is a war – you'll be a neutral American. America will *never* get into a war in Europe, not after the Great War.'

She borrowed my cigarette, inhaled and said, 'Larry, darling, you're so *practical*. I love you, you know I do, but you know I can't.'

'But a broken engagement? That would soon be forgotten!'

'It wouldn't – not by Ciano,' she said.

'But if our love is so beautiful, why not get married, and to hell with everyone? Unite our families as well as ourselves.'

'You make it sound like a business merger. One day I'll tell you.' There was no irony in her voice as she jumped out of bed, beautiful when naked.

'I'm off to Douzy tomorrow,' I said. 'It's Friday.'

'Same time on Monday?'

I nodded.

'And darling Larry – never forget that I love you more than any man – and I always will. But don't worry – one day, who knows?'

One day? I had to wait many, many days before I learned why she and Francesco became engaged. Even then I never dreamed it would be Francesco, of all people, who would be the one to tell me.

Despite the late, watery sunshine, this autumn weekend had a sour note to it. The first thing I noticed when I arrived was that Guy and Anna weren't on speaking terms – and making it very obvious. Mlle Lisette, our ex-nanny, walked around the housing wearing a permanent sniff of disapproval. Mama was tight-lipped. Olivia, who had arrived at Douzy on the Thursday, looked embarrassed and almost anxious to leave. Only Papa seemed unperturbed. Normally Anna and Guy were as close as twins usually are, though their characters differed. But usually Anna took Guy's odd moods in her stride, never letting minor differences erupt into issues.

Mlle Lisette also usually kept herself to herself. It was a long time since she had bathed us all and looked after us, and now she had grown into a middle-aged spinster who had gradually taken on the duties of a general factotum, a kind of superior housekeeper who was regarded almost – but not quite – as a member of the family. The line of distinction had been subtly drawn. Mlle Lisette lunched but never dined with us. She didn't meddle in anyone's affairs, though she signified disapproval by the way she walked. To me she typified the frustrated middle-aged virgin.

'What the hell's up?' I cornered Anna. 'Anyone'd think the Eiffel Tower had fallen across our vineyards.'

At first she shook her head. 'Nothing.' She had Mama's habit of clamping her mouth closed with an air of finality.

'Come on, Anna, don't give me that crap.' I held her lightly by the shoulders. 'Not me!'

For a moment she hesitated, then she searched for her tiny white handkerchief and blew her nose – hard. I realised she was on the verge of tears.

'Trouble between you and Willi?' I knew he hadn't been to France for some time. I wondered for a moment if he had ditched her.

She shook her head. 'Willi's wonderful,' adding bitterly, 'when I get a chance to see him! He asked me if he could come to Douzy this weekend but Mama said it was "unsuitable".'

She drew another deep breath. 'Unsuitable! It's the last damn straw. Mama's allowed Olivia to come and live with us – yes, *live* at Douzy – all to make her precious Guy happy. She told Olivia yesterday.'

So *that* was behind the pursed lips. It seemed odd. I liked Olivia – she was quiet, a good painter. She had none of the arty-crafty mannerisms so popular in phoney art circles. Even so, a visit was one thing, but hell! *living* at Douzy was a very different matter.

'Did she ask to stay – or I suppose Guy asked?' I was still puzzled.

Anna sat down on a sofa. 'I'm so damn mad my hand is

shaking. Light a cigarette for me, will you, Larry? You're the only one I can talk to.'

I was horrified at the bitterness when she began to tell me the story. I already knew that Guy had several times hinted at leaving home to study art in Paris. He had cited me as an example, arguing that since I was following a chosen career, why shouldn't he? What was the difference between writing and painting? It sounded fair enough. To me he had said, 'Paris is the only place to study art.'

I had asked him then, half in fun, 'Would you be so keen to work in Paris if Olivia lived in Marseilles?'

Guy never did have a sense of humour. 'That's a bloody stupid remark,' he had said and then walked off in a huff.

I shouldn't have said that, I knew it. Poor Guy suffered from the curse of being a younger brother. And though I couldn't really see him as a young Picasso, I had the feeling that one day he would change. Mama had a streak of toughness in her. So had I. So had Anna. And I didn't doubt that eventually that toughness would break out in Guy.

Anna perhaps didn't see it that way. 'Of course it's Olivia,' she almost snorted. 'They've been lovers for ages. I've got eyes in my head. And so has Mama.'

'Well,' I said mildly, 'you can't blame Guy for that. You're not going to stand there and tell me that you and Willi haven't popped into bed together.'

'That's nothing to do with it. Of course we have – but *when*, dammit? Ten minutes in the orchard is about our limit. For Guy, sex is laid on. For me it's a crime!'

'You're a girl. Like it or not, it *is* different.'

'Okay, I'm a girl. So I try to be discreet and not upset Mama. But *Olivia*! She's not only come every damn weekend for the last year – even for Christmas – but now she's going to come and *live* here. Yet Willi can't come for dinner without special permission.'

I only heard later, from Anna, how the crisis had arisen. Anna was staggered when Guy first broke the news that he was planning to leave Douzy; for though I was in Paris, the family, according to Anna, was sitting down for dinner when Guy said, 'I've got something to tell you,' and drew a deep breath.

Everyone looked up.

'Mama,' he announced in a flat voice, 'I've decided to go and study art in Paris. I hope you don't mind, but I *have* to go. I need help in my studies.'

'I *say*,' said Papa. 'I might be able to get Raoul Dufy to find you a teacher. What about *that*?' He looked pleased at solving the problem.

Mama took a very different view.

'Oh no!' she wailed, as she had wailed every time Guy hinted at leaving.

'You'd want to stay in the apartment, I suppose?' asked Papa.

Guy shook his head. 'No, Papa. Larry's got his own apartment. I want to be on my own too. To work – and to learn.'

'You *can't* go. Please, Guy,' Mama begged. 'You're my youngest boy – the last one – all I've got now. Just wait a bit longer, darling, just a few months.'

'I've *got* to go,' said Guy desperately. 'I'm losing my grip. You're very kind letting Olivia come to teach me at weekends but I can't succeed alone.'

Turning to Guy, Mama added tearfully, 'Of course you have to leave home one day, darling – but not yet. *Please*. Just a little longer.'

All this I learned from Anna who, at this point, said, 'It was awful! I felt like throwing up. Larry, you can't imagine what the scene was like.' She hesitated, at a loss for a metaphor. 'I know I shouldn't say this about Mama, and you know I love her, but it was the way she *begged* – like an elderly girlfriend begging a young lover not to leave her. It was awful, Larry.'

'Poor Mama,' I said, 'it must be hell for her. She must love Guy very much. The youngest, I suppose . . .'

'Don't give me that garbage,' said Anna angrily. 'I happen to share that doubtful honour.'

'So what happened?'

'Can't you guess.' It was a statement more than a question. 'Mama knew perfectly well what she was going to do. Yesterday at lunch she told Papa that Guy *should* be encouraged to pursue his art studies, and then, turning to Guy, suggested that Olivia should come to live at Douzy. *Live!* I ask you. And, what's more, she could have the room next to Guy's. And that, as we all know, used to be a guest dressing room, with a communicating door. It's sick-making, Larry. It's perverted.'

'What did Papa say?'

'You know Papa. "Oh *really*,"' she mimicked his rising accent perfectly. 'He's sweet, he accepted anything. Thought it rather a good idea.'

'Well, it's kept Guy at home — for a bit,' I said.

'I've nothing against Olivia' — Anna's voice was a bit too harsh for truth — 'but Mama's actually encouraging Guy to sleep with a girl who's several years older than he is. And just in order to keep Guy at home.'

'I must say, it's a bit hard to take, but mother-love . . .'

'Oh shit, Larry,' said Anna inelegantly. 'It's unhealthy, especially as there's more to it than that.'

'What on earth do you mean?'

'Why do you think Mama's hanging on to Guy? It's not just because he's the last son at home. She's jealous because *she* hasn't got a man.'

'Honestly, Anna!'

'It's true. Mama *needs* a man.'

'You can't just talk like that about your mother . . .'

'"Honestly!"' she mimicked me this time. 'What's dishonest about saying so? Olivia needs a man. I need a man. What's so different about Mama — who's young and pretty and healthy?'

'But Papa?'

'Come off it, Larry. We all adore Papa, but as far as *that* sort of thing is concerned I'll bet he's as useless as a bottle of flat champagne.'

'Shut up!' I said.

'Sorry, Larry. But about the other thing — Guy and Olivia' — for the first time she laughed — 'you should have seen Mademoiselle Lisette's looks when she heard.'

'How did she hear?'

'No idea. But talk about virginal disapproval! If Mademoiselle Lisette's looks could have killed, Olivia would have been dead and buried before she had a chance to unpack.'

Anna was calmer now but, after she had started another cigarette, she added, 'I know that really it's no concern of mine. But what does make me mad is that when Willi rang up yesterday afternoon and told me he was coming to Paris unexpectedly on business, Mama said it was too late to make the arrangements for him to come to Douzy. It makes me sick. Anyway, I'm off this afternoon.'

'Off?'

'Sure. I'm off to Paris. In theory to spend the weekend with a girlfriend. But in reality – well, Willi's booked a suite at the Crillon and I'm going to spend most of the time in bed with him.'

I liked Willi, very much. He was decent, honest, good-looking in a Germanic way, and he was obviously brilliant, already well launched on a highly successful career at Staffens. All the same he *was* a German – a typical German in many ways. He walked in a determined, forceful way, so that sometimes I found myself thinking, there's a hidden goosestep in every stride. I wasn't being racialist; just realistic. After all, racialism and realism were often connected. One day – who could tell what might happen? The Germans were behaving like tyrants. The swastika was now Germany's official flag, and Hitler wielded supreme power. Conscription had been introduced. I knew that Germany was quietly building an air force, training its pilots of tomorrow secretly on gliders. Only a few days before Anna and I had our talk, Hitler had outlawed all Jews in Germany.

'So much for your Willi's Germany,' I said. 'I wonder how Olivia will react when she has to shake hands with Willi the next time he comes to Douzy.'

'That's politics,' sniffed Anna. 'Willi's not that sort of man.'

'Well, the Germans are on the warpath. I'm very fond of Willi, darling sister. But don't get too involved. One day Europe and America might even have to fight the Germans again.'

'Warmonger. What nonsense!' She was happier now, excited at the prospect of her secret weekend in Paris. 'Live for today!'

★   ★   ★

Anna had her own car by now, a Citroën, and I saw her off at the front door for one reason; I had grabbed my Malacca cane — 'Willi's present,' we always called it — because I had promised to meet Papa by the lake and go for a walk with him and I was just about to leave when I heard a voice ask gently, 'Larry — can you spare me a moment?'

It was Olivia, and at first I was irritated; she might be a good painter, she might be Guy's girlfriend, she might be very pleasant, but she *wasn't* an Astell, and as a family we had always abhorred discussing family affairs with outsiders. On the other hand no one could be irritated with Olivia for long, because her large, brown, pleading eyes disarmed all antagonism.

She was also very good-looking, with a long, intelligent face, the creamy white complexion accentuated by her hair drawn tightly at the back in what these days would be called a pony tail, showing off the back of her long, graceful neck.

'I feel terrible about Anna,' she said with a directness I liked, 'but I didn't *ask* to come here. When your mother told me, I was surprised as — well, as I suppose you were.'

'I was a bit surprised' — I thought she might like an equally direct reply. 'It was the adjoining bedrooms.'

'I suggested to your mother that perhaps I could live in one of the vineyard cottages, but she refused.'

'Did she now?' That did surprise me.

'It surprised me too, but I admire her for what she said.'

'What did she say?'

'That if Guy and I were in love with each other, she didn't want any hole-in-the-corner business. Sneaking in and out of each other's bedrooms. Those were her words. Then she added something I thought rather curious. She said there'd been enough of that in the house.'

'She said *that*!' For a moment a surge of anger towards Guy bit into me. God dammit, all those years ago I had had to leave the warm arms of Sonia in order to keep a secret — or so we thought — and now she was actually *helping* Guy to do what had been forbidden in my day, with only a communicating door to lend a spurious air of respectability to the proceedings. Did Mama know that Sonia and I had become lovers again, I wondered? Serve her right if she did! The stab of anger passed.

It wasn't Guy's fault; more his good luck. And anyway, thank God I was out of the house now, only a visitor at weekends. I loved Douzy, every stone of it, every square inch of our land, but in Paris I was free.

Olivia had spoken the words without any malice, and obviously hadn't the faintest idea what I was thinking about, for she said, 'So now I feel I ought to leave.'

'I wouldn't do that.' I chose my words carefully. 'I understand. But wait and see how things work out.'

'Thank you, Larry. And you know,' she said a little diffidently, 'I *can* help Guy. He does need me.'

'For art – or for . . .?' I left the sentence unfinished.

'One helps the other,' she said gravely, and without a trace of annoyance. 'Some people, Van Gogh was one, produce their finest work when they're miserable. They thrive on unhappiness. Others, like Monet, need to be surrounded by happiness. That's how Guy feels.'

'And you?'

'I haven't discovered yet.'

As she went back into the house I walked through the archway towards the dell, thinking of what Olivia had said – and without any thought of an extraordinary incident about to take place.

I was making my way to the lake, as it was always called, even though it only covered about two acres, with a man-made island in the middle just large enough for the wrought iron pergola which rose from its grassy slopes. The lake was ornamental really, part of the view, for even though it lay behind the orchard at the foot of the dell, its blue-grey sheen could be seen from the house, standing as it did on high ground.

My father had gone ahead to have a few words with Jacques Pagniez, the old vigneron who acted as general help; one of his duties was to clean up the lake from time to time, using a small rowboat from which he raked the dead leaves or algae.

At the bottom of the dell, with its long grassy slope, I was about to open the wicker gate leading to the orchard, which I would have to cross, when I heard voices. I stopped to listen, the action instinctive because in the autumn we were plagued by village kids pinching apples. It was easy for them to walk through the vineyards and, when they were certain no one was watching, wriggle through the high grass. I wanted to catch the youngsters red-handed, though I wasn't contemplating drastic action. I knew most villagers by sight, and the threat of telling their fathers – many of whom worked for us during the *vendange* – would scare them off for a month or two.

I crept behind one of the huge rhododendrons that served as a ten-foot hedge between the dell and the orchard. I could see no one, hear no more voices, and wondered if I had been mistaken – until I stiffened suddenly.

On the other side of the bush, only a few feet from where I was trying to hold my breath, a woman's urgent, angry voice cried, '*C'est dégoûtant!*' Then she continued in French, bitterly angry, 'You're all the same! No thought for other people. To bring that woman to live in the house!' She repeated her first phrase, 'It's disgusting! What you do in another house, or anywhere, is none of my business, but here – where,' the voice become a low hiss and I missed the words, until I heard, 'is living.'

I knew that voice, typical of so many nannies the world over. It belonged to Mlle Lisette. For a moment I thought she was angry with one of the man-servants – until the man replied.

'For Chrissake, Lisette!' said my brother Guy, equally urgently. 'You're not my nanny any more. You can't go around telling me what to do with my life.'

Lisette! Not *Mlle* Lisette! I had never heard anyone in Douzy use that name, yet Guy called her that. What was going on? By now, eavesdropping or not, I was curious – especially after Anna's disclosures. What had 'that woman' to do with Mlle Lisette, who in fact only lived at Douzy as an act of charity?

I heard no more.

'Damn!' I muttered as the voices faded and I heard feet walk through the long grass. What the hell had she meant? '*In another house*'?

I could hardly tell Papa what I had heard – especially as there might be an innocent enough explanation – but no, I thought, as I crossed the orchard, wading through the thick grass where

I had upended Sonia such a long time ago; no, there could be
nothing innocent about what I had heard.

When you are deep in thought following an experience that
leaves you puzzled it is a shock to be cheerfully hailed by
someone who hasn't the faintest notion of what happened to
you only moments ago. The fact that it *had* happened so
quickly made me feel that the other person must have known
too.

'*Ici*, Larry,' my father waved as I reached the gravel path that
ran round the lake. 'Been waiting for you. Look how Jacques
has tidied up the lake.'

The old vigneron gave me a '*Bonjour, m'sieu*'.

'*Really,*' said my father. 'Clean as a new pin. Splendid work,
Jacques, I *must* say.' And to me, 'Can you stand a walk to the
other side of Rilly? Take us about an hour. A bit chilly, but
we'll stop at the local bistro – they've just opened their 1933
Cramant – should be good and dry. Yes, *very* good, I *must*
say.'

He set off, long frame striding out, ashplant swinging
forward and then jabbing the ground with each step.

'Wonderful day for a walk,' he said exuberantly. And
indeed it was. The pale sun shining on the vines, and the
creamy yellow pathways gave everything a muted, gentle air.
The acres of stripped vines rolling away from us always
looked so *tidy*. They exuded an atmosphere of sobriety, of
thrift – very different from the exhilarating end-product. We
walked past a group of farm houses built of stone, solid, plain,
the rough plastered walls an austere grey, the narrow streets or
farmyards flanked by high stone walls concealing private lives,
with glimpses through heavy gates of an open courtyard with
a trough, a pump perhaps, a few dying hollyhocks straggling
near lines where lettuces and peas had grown and, at the back,
like a fence – as though the owner had planted something with
an eye to the distant future – a row of spindly poplars, their
bases and roots covered with straw as cosy, and as efficient, as
a coverlet protecting a child against cold nights. At that
moment a skein of geese flew overhead like a formation of
aircraft.

'It *is* wonderful,' I agreed. 'Like an aquatint.'

Papa's walks were rather special. He was, in his own words,

'a one-way walker'. Whenever he went for a walk, he never walked back, a habit which, looked at from his point of view, was eminently sensible. He would choose a target – one of the innumerable bistros, small hotels, even cafés, which dotted every village. He knew just how long it would take him to walk there. He then added half an hour for time to sample the local wine, at which time Gaston would arrive with the Hisp. and drive us home in time for lunch.

'May sound silly,' he confided to me once, 'but in fact if you look at it sensibly – yes, *sensibly* – it's a *good* idea. Walking never seems quite so attractive after a couple of drinks.'

We all felt guilty if we didn't occasionally walk with him – but he inevitably started long discussions on the champagne market, and the trouble was that none of us had any common ground for conversation with Papa, while he regarded a walk as a wonderful chance for talking about the vineyards.

He stopped to examine them for diseases, fungus, red fly. He passed the time of day with every neighbour and discussed prospects – either for frost, bloom, the *vendange*, according to the season.

As soon as we passed Douzy church and branched right along the track leading upwards to Rilly, he spotted one row of vines.

'Look at this!' he stopped and plucked off a leaf from a vine. 'Not one of ours, thank God. Not *ours*. *Very* bad management.'

The leaf was dented in the middle, as though someone had pressed its centre. The shoot of the vine had been flattened too.

'And that means *Court-Noué*.' I knew exactly what my father meant – a disease that normally attacked Chardonnay vines; no one had ever discovered what caused it. Some said it was due to a small fungus that flourished in the roots, others believed it was caused by poisoned soil.

'Thank God it's not infectious,' said my father. 'Half these vines will have to be uprooted. Who do they belong to?'

I had no idea and we walked on.

I don't know how the conversation started, but I suddenly found myself pleading the cause of Anna. It started innocently enough when I said, 'I'm sorry Mama wouldn't let Willi come for the weekend.'

'It's not a question of *not letting*. Really! Oregon is here for the weekend. Olivia is here.'

'I didn't mean it that way. But after all, if Guy can have his girlfriend here, it's a bit hard on Anna to leave Willi out. Instead, Anna's so upset she's gone to Paris to spend the weekend with a friend.'

'To Paris?' Startled, he jabbed his ashplant hard into the ground.

'Well, she's a grown-up woman,' I said. 'She doesn't have to account for everything she does. Any more than' – with a sly dig – 'Guy has to account for his taste in girlfriends.'

'Anna – well, it's different.' He jabbed his stick into the ground again.

'Because she's a girl?'

'Good Lord, no.' He looked positively astonished at my simple-minded attitude. 'No, *no*. Because Willi's a *German*.' And with a touch of asperity he added, 'And don't take me for a fool, Larry. If she's gone to Paris for the weekend, I don't imagine she'll be spending her time at the Louvre.'

'Sorry,' I laughed.

'It's Anna's future I'm thinking of, yes, her *future*,' said Papa. 'This fellow Hitler – to say nothing of Mussolini – neither of them can carry on for ever making an economic mess of their own countries. When they go too far down the slippery slope there's only one way out – blame neighbouring countries, and if necessary fight them.'

'Hitler doesn't *seem* to be making warlike noises,' I said.

'He's too smart,' said my father. 'I had dinner with Madame de Portes and Paul Reynaud the other day. He told me that Hitler doesn't *make* plans – he waits for other countries to make mistakes then takes advantage of them. And he watches while the morale of other countries crumble. Look at France. No resolve, no' – he searched for the word – 'no old-fashioned guts. Why don't the police do something about these anti-Jewish riots in Paris – the French Fascists, *Cagoulards*?'

'They're crackpots,' I said.

'I'm not so sure,' my father disagreed. Then, changing the subject, he asked, 'Do you think Anna is getting *really* serious about Willi?'

There was no point in hiding the obvious.

'Yes, I do,' I replied. 'I think he'll be knocking on your study door one day, clicking his heels, giving you a stiff German bow, and asking for permission to marry your daughter.'

'Oh! I *say*, not *really!*' Papa looked alarmed. 'I thought Germans only behaved like that in films.'

We had passed Rilly by now, ordered our drinks and he sat there, all six feet three of him, a man without an enemy in the world, but constantly surprised by the most elementary facts of life. '*Really!*' he said again, with his rising accent, 'I wouldn't know *what* to say.'

'I don't suppose it would make any difference.' I tried to sound philosophical. 'If Anna wants to marry Willi, she will. I think Willi would be worried if you said "no", for he feels he should ask you formally. But when the time comes, it'll not only be formally, it'll be a formality.'

My father called the waiter for another glass of the bistro's latest vintage. 'Really, *very* passable.' He held the glass by the stem to the light. 'Don't misunderstand me,' he said, 'I *like* Willi. A very intelligent young man. But just supposing . . .'

'You mean a war?'

'Exactly.'

Gaston arrived with the Hisp. and, as he drew up the car, Papa called out, 'There's a drink waiting for you, Gaston.'

'*Merci, m'sieu.*' Gaston pushed open the door of the bistro. He was well known in every village, for Gaston was not only their friend and neighbour, he was always offered a drink during Papa's walks. After all, Gaston was more than just a chauffeur; a handsome man, a worthy son of Jacques, the vigneron, he was an old friend.

Certainly he was a friend of mine, for I was a Walter Mitty racing driver and he was great at tuning the engine of my M.G. It was only natural that we had played together in the fields and the woods as kids. Everyone, including Gaston himself, had automatically elected to work with the family. And after he discovered a natural bent for tinkering with new-fangled motor cars everyone was delighted when he became the family driver, none more so than Jacques, who regarded Gaston's new job as a step up in the world. And life had also been made easier by a gesture of my grandfather's before he died: he had rewarded several old members of the estate with their own small plots of vineyards. They might not be extensive but, even so, everyone working in Douzy had a slice of independence, a few vines he could call his own, enough for each family to bottle its own wine or sell the grapes to the co-operative.

As Gaston returned to the Hisp., Papa asked him, as one villager to another, 'What do you think of this year's red, Gaston?'

'Not as good as Douzy, *m'sieu,*' said Gaston frankly.

'You're right,' agreed my father. 'Would you mind stopping for a few minutes at the *celliers*. I just want to see how the fermentation is going.'

We drew up at the entrance to the Home Farm, where the buildings at one end housed the machinery needed to produce champagne before it was taken to the *caves* below. The fermenting shed was at the far end, and it was like stepping into an oven; from the time of the harvest in late September, the wine juice had been kept in forty-four-gallon casks at a temperature of around sixty-five degrees; and in the thirties there was no air conditioning or modern tanks that could be heated.

'How's it going?' my father asked one of the *celliers*.

'Fine. We're in the fourth week,' he replied.

'We'll be able to let the fires die down in another two weeks. Then we'll open the windows and let in the cold air.' This sudden change of temperature was vital, because the cold caused a precipitation which threw off the impurities, allowing clear wine to be drawn off.

At this stage the casks would then contain only *vin nature*, but my father would be able to start judging, even from this rough wine, how to make it perfect by blending wine from our different vineyards to ensure that we maintained our special characteristics.

That evening Mama had invited several people to dine at the château, including the Misses Brewer and Barron.

'My spies tell me we're having *pintade* for dinner,' said Oregon, offering them champagne.

'I always feel so sorry for the poor guinea fowl,' Miss

Brewer said, nodding, 'being shot like that. It seems so cruel.'

'There, there dear,' Miss Barron consoled her. 'They probably suffer less than if they lived to be old, and then died
because they were too weak to find food.'

Did birds really become too old to find food, I thought idly
as the other guests arrived? Perhaps the Misses B and B were
right. The two old ladies fascinated me, for they, too, were
birdlike in appearance. What would happen to *them* if they had
to search for their food? If, say, a war came and their safety,
even their modest incomes, were endangered?

Looking at the two frail old ladies, Miss Brewer nodding
her head as she always did, Miss Barron eagerly agreeing with
everything anyone said — a legacy of her days as a companion — I had a sudden wild vision of German troops over-
running our beautiful countryside, shelling their pretty little
cottage, forcing their staid and uneventful lives to erupt into
violence and chaos. They would die of shock, poor dears,
though perhaps — like the *pintades* — they would suffer less
than by growing old and feeble. They would never be able to
cope.

Happily they were, like Grandma, convinced that war was
out of the question. I heard La Châtelaine say, 'I met Monsieur
Chautemps. He told me there would never be another war and
I believe him.' Miss Brewer nodded approvingly, and I wondered what she would say if I told her what I thought: that
Camille Chautemps was a weak, vacillating political leader
who might easily lead France into war. Of course I said
nothing, and luckily the silence was interrupted by two
sounds.

Just as we were passing into the dining room, Jean, in his
white jacket, came up to me and murmured, 'It's Mr. Tomlinson on the phone, sir. In Paris.'

'Excuse me, Mama,' I said, and went into the study where
there was an extension.

'Hi!' cried Tommy. 'Hope I haven't disturbed the family
dinner, but I've only got a couple of minutes. Gotta go to
Rome tonight. Train leaves at ten o'clock. Just received the
goddamn cable from Washington. I've got my interview with
Musso, and I've got to report to Ciano tomorrow lunch. It's
all been laid on at high level in Washington, but they only got

the okay today. Can you pinch-bit for me for a week? Usual dough.'

'Sure,' I replied. 'Need me tonight?'

'No – so long as you're on the end of a phone. I've told Washington where you are, and that you'll be in Paris tomorrow.'

That was that. No problem, especially as it was already the middle of the night in Washington. But after dinner the phone rang again. This time it was Willi Frankel. Thinking of Anna I felt a momentary apprehension, but Willi's voice reassured me.

'Sorry to intrude on you so late' – Willi was always very polite – 'but it is a big story I have for you. Yes, it is about Hitler and de Gaulle. *Ach*! It will be a scoop, *nein*?'

'Can I meet you Monday for lunch?'

'No, this is my problem. Before lunch I am to leave. Must be back in Düsseldorf. Any chance we have breakfast together?' I could hear the wry chuckle in his voice. 'Isn't that what Americans always do? The working breakfast?'

'You're sure it's worth it?' I asked.

'Is important, I assure you,' he said solemnly. '*Very* important.'

'Okay. I'll be there, eight-thirty for fresh orange juice and all the trimmings. Okay?'

After all, I was in charge of the bureau while Tommy was away in Italy. What a way to start the week if I could land another 'Willi' exclusive!

8

Willi was staying at the Crillon as he always did, and in a suite. He enjoyed the trappings of luxury that went with a good job.

I had been nervous that I might meet Anna when I parked my car in the Concorde at eight-thirty on the Monday morning. It was one thing for him to spend the weekend with my

sister, but I didn't want to see visible evidence of it in the form
of a bright and cheery couple sharing breakfast. I needn't have
worried. Willi was far too circumspect. Anna had already left.

Still, Willi did ask me as he helped me to coffee, 'It is at the
. . . the departure – Anna and me – well, we should get married. What would your father say to my – what is it? – my
troth?'

With a sigh I answered him, 'He wouldn't like it, Willi.
Nothing personal. He admires you very much. But she *is* his
only daughter, and he's afraid – of the future.'

'If there comes war, you mean?'

I nodded.

'If there comes a war,' Willi's tone suddenly became bitter,
almost savage, 'it will be the fault of France and Britain.'

'Hey!' I protested. 'You don't have to shove Hitler's propaganda down my throat, Willi – not at breakfast. Don't spoil a
good croissant.'

'Who is saying about Hitler? Europe it is who is *making*
Hitler. The French, they fight themselves, they are scared of
their own politicians, they do not like to think about Germany. France, she is very weak, so she gives Hitler more
courage – you understand? I hate Hitler. But French politicians are very pathetic. They are more scared of Communism
than Hitler.'

'You're exaggerating.' The waiter brought us more coffee.
But all the same I was wondering if Willi *was* exaggerating. He
had a new authority since he started climbing the ladder at the
Staffen Engineering Corporation – high enough to warrant
not only a suite at the Crillon each time he came to France but,
back home, so he said, a driver to take him to work. Success
had given him a new stature, even a slight touch of German
imperiousness. And he seemed to know what he was talking
about. Suddenly he said, 'Sorry for becoming angry. *Entschul-
digung!* – excuse me! Is only because I am frightened. But to
business – about one man in France I *do* admire, though. You
ever hear of a French officer called de Gaulle?'

I nodded. 'I've met him once or twice. Prickly sort of chap,
though he was polite enough to me.' I gave a short laugh.
'Perhaps because he was so surprised to find that *any* American
could speak French. I met him with Reynaud.'

'He writes a very good book,' said Willi. 'You are reading it?'

I shook my head. 'About tank warfare, wasn't it? You say it's good, but I read that it was an almighty flop. The military reviewers tore it to shreds.'

'I understand why. He calls the army leaders a lot of *Dummkopfs*. Is no way to help his military career.'

'I don't even remember what the book's called.'

'A good title: *Towards a Professional Army*.'

I wondered idly why Willi should be so interested in de Gaulle, or for that matter in military strategy, and with a touch of sarcasm asked, 'Don't tell me that Hitler is thinking of challenging the French army!'

'God forbid! Hitler is not being so foolish as to take on the finest army in the world.' He gave a sardonic grin. 'But I will tell you what *is* strange. Hitler gets hold of de Gaulle's book and he is going crazy about it.'

'I didn't know he could read.'

'He has ordered Otto Abetz in Paris to buy up all the copies he can get hold of – for his General Staff. They are being ordered to read it and send the Führer written reports.'

'Are you sure?' Willi had been right. It *was* a good story.

'Absolutely. My boss at Staffens is sent a copy, he is told to write a report. I see the letter myself.'

'I still don't get the idea.'

'I can understand. Our Führer believes he is a military leader in the Clausewitz tradition. And, ever since Germany occupied the Rhineland, he is dreaming of a new concept of war – self-supporting armoured divisions – using tanks as independent attacking units, not just to help the infantry. But all the top men – Keitel, Rundstedt and Guderian – are politely turning him down. They say to each other Hitler was only a corporal. But now all his theories are appearing in print – and by Germany's enemy.'

'So he's pinching de Gaulle's ideas?'

'Not exactly. They both have the same ideas but – please, never say this to anyone or it will be bad for me – the Führer is, well, not known for great thinking. He shouts a lot. But de Gaulle, he is a professional, and what he has done is give Hitler the practical explanation of how his dreams can come true.'

'It still has to be worked out.'

'It can be. After all, we make tanks, Larry – the men in our works are crazy about the book. It's not for any *aggression* – Hitler he says many times that he has no territorial ambitions – but he wants a strong Germany for world respect.' He looked at me almost defiantly. 'This is not unreasonable, is it? You admit, I hope, Germany has been very badly treated since the Treaty of Versailles.'

It was a hell of a good story for the *Globe*, though I realised I had to make sure Willi wouldn't be involved, just as I'd done on the Roehm massacre.

'I don't want you to be tortured,' I said half jokingly.

Willi laughed out loud – a real German belly laugh.

'So. Americans have amusing ideas about Germans. We are not eating babies for breakfast! The Gestapo? They are everywhere, but they are not *torturing* people. We are Germans – civilised people. Do not please confuse the Gestapo with Mussolini's bully boys who force people in their jails to drink castor oil by the pint as a punishment.'

I didn't need to clear the story with Colonel de Gaulle, because he hadn't given me the information, but I took care to describe de Gaulle as one of France's most exciting military brains, and to say that he had been attacked by the old fogies of the French High Command because they were jealous of him.

It worked. First I got a herogram from the *Globe* foreign editor saying, 'Your exclusive leads Page One', and when the paper arrived there it was under the headline:

HITLER STEALS BRILLIANT
FRENCH OFFICER'S IDEAS

And the strapline above looked good too: 'Exclusive from Larry Astell in Paris'.

I sent a clipping to de Gaulle, who wrote a pleasant 'thank you' letter, and the next time I met him at a reception he shook my hand.

'Well sir,' I said diplomatically, 'even if Hitler copies every idea in your book the Germans will never be a match for the French army.'

I'll always remember de Gaulle's reply, given in measured tones. 'The French soldier will fight to the last drop of his blood. Rest assured of that. But if German tanks – my tanks with German swastikas painted on them – turn the Maginot Line in the north and then sweep south, no one will be able to stop them.'

Willi had mentioned Otto Abetz, and the next time I met Sonia in the rue du Cherche Midi, she also mentioned him.

'Odd how that man's name keeps cropping up,' I said.

'I had lunch with him yesterday and dinner on Saturday.'

'Otto Abetz! You had two meals with him! Tommy Tomlinson calls him Hitler's hatchet man in France.'

'Horrible.' She screwed up her nose. 'He was lunching with Daddy and asked me along – deliberately, I think. Twice in a weekend.'

'What do you mean, "deliberately"?'

'He gave me the shivers. He meets Daddy all the time. It's spooky. We had lunch at Maxim's and he told me that he thought Mummy and I would be wise to leave France and return home to Florence.'

'But you've only been here a few months. Did he give any reason?'

'I wonder if Daddy put him up to it. His reasons were ridiculous. He said France wasn't safe. He said something about the *Cagoulards*, that they're going to increase their bombing campaign. Do you think Monsieur Abetz is behind them?'

'Abetz and – your father?'

'Oh no!' she looked genuinely horrified. 'Daddy's a diplomat. He'd never get mixed up in anything like that.'

That was probably true, but in addition to the Cagoulard evidence of Fascist activity there was the sinister, and unsolved, murder of two Italians in Paris. Both were violently anti-Fascist writers. One of them, Carlo Rossello, was shot dead; his brother Nello was stabbed to death in a wood near Bagnoles-de-l'Orne. The crimes had not only remained a mystery, but all news of them had vanished from the front pages of the newspapers. It smacked of a typical French cover-up.

'It's a bit sinister, all coming together,' I said.

'You don't think it was a political business, do you?' asked Sonia.

'I'm sure it was.'

Sonia was 'free' that evening, and we decided to risk detection and have dinner at Marcel's. Instead of walking directly along the rue de Seine we strolled along the *quais* towards the *Institut* before doubling back. It had been raining that afternoon, and it had given the *quais* a smell of freshness. The rain had washed not only the streets but the walls of the buildings and the trunks of the trees, so that the bare yellow patches of the plane trees shone golden in the lamp-lit evening and everything smelled good and clean.

Yet, as we sat down at Marcel's and looked at the blackboard to study the *plat du jour* – *daube de boeuf*, which we knew would have been *mijotée* on the stove for hours – I could sense that Sonia was unhappy.

'It's not your father who's worrying you?' I asked.

She sprinkled a little salt on her chunk of fresh *baguette*. 'No, not Daddy, but love – for you – and then, too, the fact that Abetz, a German, could warn me to leave – almost as though a German is giving orders to my father. That's what frightens me – the sense that my father is working with him, even for him, in such a mysterious way.'

'There's such an easy way out of everything,' I said again. 'Break your engagement. Marry me.' I reached out and took her hand, which was lying on the white tablecloth. 'Just marry me. After all, we love each other. It's only a question of going to the American Consul. You do love me?'

She was silent for some time, toying with her meal. 'I never realised until we met again how much I loved you. I *want* to marry you – but I'm afraid. It may sound over-dramatic, but I'm sure Abetz has some . . .' she searched for the right word '. . . some *hold* over Daddy. Or perhaps it's Ciano. As you know, he's Mussolini's Foreign Minister, and he certainly has the Duce's ear.'

'But it makes no difference, surely, if we break an engagement?'

'It does, I'm afraid. I daren't break it off. But I *have* done one thing. I've suggested to my fiancé that we should wait a bit longer – I'm playing for time.'

'That's something.' I tried to be cheerful. At least, I thought, it was a step in the right direction.

The next day in the office I cornered Oregon. 'I've got a question for you,' I said.

'What gives?'

'What's the latest news on Otto Abetz?'

'Just that he's still a diehard Fascist of the worst kind who poses as a friend of France. What's the drill?'

I explained what Sonia had told me – that Abetz might in some sinister way be 'using' her father.

'Sounds feasible.' Oregon lit another Gauloise and wiped the ash from his jacket. 'He's dangerous – got friends in high places – including Reynaud. Though Abetz isn't exactly Reynaud's friend, more his girlfriend's – the Countess de Portes.'

'I know. I met the Countess with Abetz. She's not my idea of feminine charm.'

'I don't suppose Herr Abetz is bothered with her charms,' said Oregon drily. 'It's her influence he's after.'

I found it difficult to imagine the rather dumpy Countess de Portes as a 'woman of influence'. Of course several French ministers had semi-official mistresses who seemed to run their political lives, but Reynaud hadn't struck me as a ladies' man, so perhaps he had to be content with what he could get. It never entered my head that it was the other way round, that it was she who had got him.

'Don't underestimate her, m'lad,' Oregon chuckled. 'Reynaud's intelligent and forceful, while she's consumed with ambition. That's a formidable combination. I wouldn't be surprised if she doesn't make Reynaud prime minister one of these days, then she'll be the power behind the throne. And if the political situation gets worse, it's always on the cards that Madame de Portes could hold the fate of France in her hands.'

'God forbid,' I said. 'She and Abetz!'

About a week later, Sonia and I dined 'officially' at Maxim's with Willi, who had unexpectedly returned to Paris and phoned Mama, asking if Anna and Sonia could make a four. It was all very respectable. Maxim's was off my beat – unless the

Globe was paying, or Papa was in Paris, for it was his favourite restaurant. But it gave us a chance to dance.

Anna was staying in the rue de Longchamps with Sonia, so I teased Willi while the girls were in the powder room. 'No hanky panky this trip?'

'*Nein*. Is time for truth, Larry. Anna and I want to marry. We need your help. Advice perhaps, but quickly.' In his excitement he lapsed into German, '*Ich fahre morgen ab.*'

'Leaving tomorrow?'

As we prepared to take the corner *banquette* on the left – Papa's usual table, given to us automatically by Albert, the imperious headwaiter with his fleshy, hanging jowls wobbling like liver about his tie – Willi whispered, 'Anywhere will do.'

'Anywhere will *not* do,' I explained. 'The top people in Paris always sit on the left as you come in. The right is reserved for tourists and riff-raff.'

A quivering Albert led us to Papa's table, facing the band. I had to admit that all the gilt and faded red plush did give one a feeling of opulence.

'Let's all have martinis for a change,' cried Willi.

'No champagne, Monsieur Astell?' Even Albert looked astounded when I shook my head. 'It's Mr. Frankel's party,' I said, 'so we'd better do as he says.'

Willi superintended the ordering. I think he rather fancied himself as a gourmet and he discussed the menu with authority, though I already knew I would settle for a *Sole Albert*. It was the best sole served outside Wiltons in London, where we always ate on our rare visits to England.

Finally the ordering was over, and then Willi said abruptly, 'Anna and I want to get married.'

'It's definite?' I looked at Anna.

'Definite.' Her eyes were sparkling with happiness and I thought (nothing to do with the subject under discussion) what a couple of corkers we had dining with us! I had already noticed a few pairs of tired middle-aged male eyes stray covetously in our direction. For Anna in her own way was every bit as attractive as Sonia – especially when she was happy. She had the same mischievous glint in her eyes, the same outgoing personality; only when she was in a bad mood or unhappy did her mouth become a straight line – rather like Grandma's.

How different she was now, here in Maxim's, with the band playing 'le fox trot'. Willi is good for her, I thought. She's a woman, she's in love, she's been having an affair with Willi for a long time: it's crazy to keep them apart, just because our parents think of her as someone who might be affected by international politics.

'Why don't you just *get* married?' asked Sonia.

Willi was really shocked. 'That is the last resort. Such a course of action is most improper. My parents would not like it, and I could never do such a thing behind Mr. Astell's back.'

'Then you'll have to go to Douzy and stand up to him.'

'I still can't see – why don't you just go off and get married?' said Sonia.

'You're a fine one to talk,' I said.

Looking back now, it might seem foolish of Willi to have been so nervous. Why shouldn't he and Anna just elope? But it wasn't as simple as that. The Astells were a warm, united, happy family, despite our problems. And in those days sons and daughters didn't *want* to upset their parents. They might hurt them if driven to take desperate measures, but not until every possible means of conciliation or persuasion had failed. We all wanted the best of all worlds. Anna wanted to marry Willi – and I sensed that, come what may, she would – but I am sure she would have been horrified if she had been told she could never return to Douzy, even for vacations. Life without Douzy was unthinkable. As a wife in a strange country, with no friends, living amidst a régime of which we heard awful rumours, she needed the *thought* that Douzy would always be there as a refuge.

We didn't solve anything that evening – but I don't think that was really the purpose of dining at Maxim's.

'What we really want is moral support,' Anna summed it up.

'When are you coming to Paris next?' I asked Willi.

'In three weeks.'

'Right. I'll start softening up the parents. I don't see how Mama can object to anything in view of the way she's behaved over Guy.'

'It's rather different.' Anna seemed doubtful. 'I'll have to go and live in Germany.'

'It's next door,' I said cheerfully.

We were soon to know how falsely founded was my optimism.

The next day, quite by chance, I again met Otto Abetz. The *Globe* had been so intrigued by my account of the way Hitler was studying de Gaulle's book that they asked me for a follow-up story. In the first article I had mentioned that Reynaud was a great admirer of de Gaulle's, and so Washington asked me to get a quote from Reynaud.

I telephoned Reynaud's secretary, explaining what I wanted. I pointed out that I had already met Reynaud socially and, no doubt, the name Astell meant something, for twenty-four hours later I got a reply. Reynaud was holding a small cocktail party at his bachelor apartment – as distinct from his main house, where Madame Reynaud presided. Of course many politicians, harassed by long nights of discussion at the Assemblée, kept small one-room flats near the parliament building, Reynaud included. His apartment was in the place du Palais Bourbon, very close to his work, but it could scarcely be called a 'bachelor' apartment since he had installed Madame de Portes in it.

Reynaud had a strong personality. Like many short men he was vain, with a tendency to aggression, as though to make up for his lack of inches. He was well aware of the power of the press – especially American newspapers, which was no doubt why I had been invited.

There were only a couple of dozen guests, including Madame de Portes – and Abetz. Reynaud immediately said that he had read my piece on de Gaulle, and had understood my request for some comments on it. 'And so, *mon cher*, I have already dictated some material for you.' He fished in his pocket for a neatly typed foolscap sheet, 'Efficient, *eh bien*? Now instead of talking business we can enjoy ourselves. *Voilà!* I will introduce you.'

Madame de Portes could not have been more charming. 'I too have seen your article on the colonel. Paul showed it to me.' She whispered almost as a conspirator. 'The colonel is a very intelligent man, but a bit hard to get on with, eh?' She laughed. 'You are as good a writer as your champagne is famous. Here we have Moët. I hope you are not insulted.'

'It makes a pleasant change from home, *madame*,' I said, and she thought that very funny. Madame de Portes took me up to Abetz, saying, 'You know each other of course, Herr Minister.'

I studied again the square shoulders, the cold blue eyes and the reddish blond hair. He seemed relaxed and cheerful.

'Of course, it is a pleasure,' he said, shaking hands with me.

I was about to make polite noises when Madame de Portes gushed, 'Herr Abetz is, as you know, one of France's greatest friends. He is the man who stamps out all the silly rumours about quarrels between our two countries.'

'A lot of nonsense is talked about Germany,' Abetz explained. 'It is my task to see that truth prevails. That is all.'

'Rather like a friend of mine from Italy,' I said, 'Signor Riccardi.'

For a moment, a split second, his mouth tightened. Then affably he said, 'Of course – I remember – we talked about Signor Riccardi the last time we met.'

'Yes. He's an old friend of the family. And so is his daughter. She was brought up with my family when her father was serving in South America.'

'A delightful girl.'

He lit a cigarette carefully, eyeing me. 'Very interesting, Monsieur Astell. I wish you well.' He gave me a half bow and strolled off to talk to other guests. I left soon afterwards – with an uneasy feeling gnawing inside me that, in front of this smooth and rather frightening man, I had behaved like a fool.

9

We were moving towards the winter of 1937 by now, and I was even more thankful that I still lived alone in the rue de l'Université – to say nothing of our secret hideout on the other side of the boulevard St. Germain. Paris was filled with people doing early Christmas shopping. Grandma visited the apartment regularly, as did Papa on business trips. So did Mama, who telephoned me without warning one day and said she was arriving to do some shopping.

'What about that lunch you promised me?' she laughed, sounding gay and happy.

'Wonderful. But dinner, not lunch. Remember your promise?'

'Darling, I'm in such a rush. Papa had to go to Bordeaux, he'll be back tomorrow night. And I've promised to dine this evening with the Sardis.' She mentioned a couple of old fogies I hardly knew.

'But Mama!' I protested. 'This is *Paris*! And the Sardis are exactly the kind of people we want to *avoid* in Paris.'

'Lunch, Larry, please. You'll just take me out like a young man escorting a lady.'

'You *sound* terrific,' I said. 'It's going to be quite a lunch. Where shall we go?'

'What about the Pré-Catalan? We can lunch indoors and look at the Bois.'

'Right. I'll pick you up at one.'

'I'll collect you,' she said. 'As Papa went by train to Bordeaux, I kept Gaston – he's got some relations in Paris – and then he can collect your father at the station when he returns to Paris, pick me up and we'll both drive home.'

'Suits me,' I said.

I must say, we had one of the happiest lunches I can remember. She seemed a different person. She was dressed in a Chanel suit which showed off her blonde hair perfectly. And the surrounding frame of green from the trees and the last of the flowers in their formal beds was the finishing touch.

'You look as though you've started a new life,' I said. 'Just watch that old man in the corner eyeing you! I'm sure he thinks you're my mistress.'

'Really, Larry.' But I could see she was pleased, as the *sommelier* filled her glass with Montrachet.

'It's very expensive.' She examined it. 'But never mind.'

'It beats me how you do it,' I said, 'how you look so young.'

She exuded a kind of suppressed sexuality, a hidden excitement that I had never seen in her before.

'Come on, Mama.' I offered her some more *quenelles de brochet*. 'Tell all. You been up to something?'

She almost giggled and shook her head. 'I just feel great, that's all.'

Even her departure had a touch of Astell style. This was still the era of great motor cars in France, the Delages and Delahayes, but nothing could equal the gleaming black and silver of the Hisp. when Gaston drew up in front of the gravel drive with its meticulously trimmed beds.

'Hiya, Gaston,' I greeted him.

'*Bonjour, monsieur.*' Gaston still had that rare knack of being able to translate a boyhood friendship into the different relationship of adults. There was nothing snobbish or servile in our friendship. Gaston was the first to crawl with me under the bonnet of the M.G. when it needed tuning, the first to shout, 'Pass me the number three spanner, Larry.' But with a true instinct he never used my name in front of others.

Mama had arranged to give me a lift to the office at the corner of the rue du Sentier and the boulevard Poissonnière, and it was the only time she mentioned Sonia. But what she *did* say left me dumbfounded:

'Do you miss her — do you still love her?'

'You shouldn't ask questions.' I avoided a direct answer with a laugh.

'Do you? I want you to be happy, Larry. And Sonia — you remember what I once said — what a pity that you were found out. Have you ever thought of — well, getting her to break off her engagement?'

'Yes,' I said flatly. 'I do love her, Mama. I always will.'

'Do you see her — I mean . . .?'

'How dare you!' I laughed again to cover the direct question.

'Well — I wouldn't blame you. Try again with her,' said Mama. 'Try, she's a wonderful girl. I blame myself a lot for — well, everything. And I want you to be happy. I want us *all* to be happy.'

★   ★   ★

It was strange how the smiling happiness of that lunch com-
municated itself to me. I had been very touched by Mama's
declaration, by her obvious happiness. But what I didn't
realise, until the next time we met, was that Sonia had changed
too.

We could still never meet regularly, of course. I had to wait
for her to telephone me, and sometimes we met in the
afternoon, sometimes in the evening.

'But this time, if you're free?' she began.

'I'm always free for you.'

'Well, darling – surprise! What about all night?'

'Explain before I burst a blood vessel.'

'Daddy and Mummy have left to open a new trade centre for
Italian goods in Lille. They've already gone.' She could hardly
contain her triumph. 'So if *monsieur* pleases . . .'

'*Monsieur does* please – see you in the Cherche Midi in an
hour. And, darling Sonia, let's dine again at Marcel's – to hell
with the risk. If anybody ever does see us we can always say
you phoned me because you couldn't find anyone else.'

'A likely story.'

I could sense the difference in her the moment she kissed me,
throwing her arms about me before we set off for Marcel's.
She was quiet in the warmth and cosiness of the restaurant. She
sat there after dinner, her coffee in front of her, just sat there
silently, eyes dreaming, looking at nothing, never noticing the
admiring eyes of the other diners, never realising her beauty.
Then, as I watched her, she put forward a hand, touched mine,
and her eyes told me she belonged to me again.

After our *café filtre*, walking back to the rue du Cherche
Midi, she was even quieter. Winter was creeping towards us; it
was a chilly night, so that, as she held me tightly and we
walked arm in arm, I thought that maybe she was keeping her
mouth closed against the bitter night air.

Once in our tiny apartment I poured out a *marc de Champagne*, the golden liquid made from discarded grapes, and
offered her a glass. She shook her head. I switched on the cheap
portable radio, and looked at her. At times – and this was
one – I would again catch her watching me quizzically, intently, with a faint ironic smile, as though summing me up.

'Why don't you turn off the radio, darling?' she said in her sleepy, dark voice, straight from the throat. As she spoke she slid out of the armchair and the next moment she was half-kneeling, half sitting on the floor in front of me.

For a few moments she said nothing, just leaned her head against my chest while I ran my fingers slowly through her silky black hair. Then she looked up. 'Have I been wrong all these years?'

'To love me? No.'

'No, not love. Wrong to think that this' – she waved to take in the room – 'is better than marriage?'

'You know what my thoughts are on the matter,' I said lightly.

'I think I *was* wrong.' Her voice had a slight catch to it.

I didn't say a word. I didn't dare. I just held her very close, stroked her hair and waited for her to speak again.

'Do you still want to marry a crazy girl like me?' She finally looked up.

'More than anything in the world. I've always loved you. I've always wanted you. But, darling Sonia, what about de Feo – the engagement? And your father?'

'I'm proposing to you, aren't I?' She laughed a little unsteadily.

'I can't believe it!' I held her away from me, looking at her from arm's length. How long was it since first we had fallen in love? How many happy, carefree years? That was the word – *carefree*. It was the carefree nature of our life and love that we had cherished, guarded so preciously.

'I'd almost given up hope,' I cried. 'Six years since that wonderful day when I brought you back from school. Come closer and let your fiancé – nice word that, I like it – let your fiancé kiss you . . .'

Later, I started to think about the future, thoughts racing through my head. What about this fellow de Feo? What about the so-called protocol of upsetting a diplomatic marriage which would probably infuriate Count Ciano? What about the 'hold' Riccardi had over Sonia or her fiancé? I was so excited, so happy, so tender with the excitement, that I found myself saying, 'Nothing matters really but us – all the other problems can be solved. But you'll have to tell your Mama and

Papa,' adding with a laugh, 'you can't have two fiancés at the same time.'

'Leave it to me,' she whispered. 'There'll be a hell of a row – but I can only say the truth. I can't live without you. I've known it all the time. I've tried to be a good dutiful daughter, but I can't – not any more. Even though it's going to hurt many people.'

'We could get married secretly?'

'We'll see, beloved. But just for tonight, let's forget all the problems and spend the night loving each other.'

I suddenly felt a wild desire to dash out into the street, maybe grab the M.G. and race round the block.

'I think I'll go and wake up Cartiers,' I cried, swinging her in my arms. 'Do you think they'd sell me a ring at this time of night?'

She kissed me, holding me tight.

'I'm overwhelmed,' I said.

'I meant you to be.'

'Well,' I laughed, 'you don't face any in-law problems. You're already a member of the family. Papa adores you – he'll be delighted. In fact I'm going to phone him. What time is it?'

'Don't do that, darling. Let's sleep on it. I was thinking it would probably be easier to get married quietly.'

'You really think so?'

'The thing is,' she said, 'that by marrying quietly, no one could do anything about it. People couldn't try to change our minds. And I *am* worried about Daddy. And that horrible man Abetz – and poor Francesco de Feo. If we got married secretly, nobody could do *anything* about it. Don't you agree?'

I had always dreamed in the past of Sonia and I getting married from the château and the village church in Douzy, surrounded not only by our champagne friends – hers as much as mine – but surrounded too by the vineyards and the villagers. I suppose the thought had first come to me when the Riccardis were thousands of miles away.

'Okay. Why not?' I agreed. 'I'll go to see the American consul first thing in the morning. Getting married is and should be our affair.'

Almost as an afterthought, I said, 'There's one point. As a good Catholic you'll have to have a church service later.'

'You're a Catholic too.'

'But not a good one. No, honestly, I'm thinking of our parents. Our mothers will be terribly upset if we don't have a church service.'

'We will. As soon as you like we'll have a benediction in church – but let's get the consulate over first.'

'Suits me. I just want to get married. I want to be your husband, not your lover.'

'Or both?'

'I hope so, darling. It's for ever, and the first thing I'm going to do tomorrow is to go out and buy you an engagement ring.'

'Oh no. Not yet.'

'Yes, I am. No discussion.'

'But Larry – this is still a secret, remember. And you're so crazy . . .' She was thinking back. 'Remember the day you bought me a hundred roses?'

'And you almost cried.'

'I did. It wasn't the money you spent on them – not even the fact that the flowers would have to die in a few days – it was *you*. You think of things. But a ring? Not yet.'

'I insist. What time is your father returning from Lille?'

'Tomorrow afternoon.'

'Right then. I'll be back before lunch. We'll have a sandwich here.'

'You shouldn't.'

'Please! You can pretend it's a junk ring, costume jewellery or whatever they call it. But let me buy it for you. And you can wear it on your other hand. A *secret* engagement.'

'Oh dear, you're already a bad influence. What can I say? Have you ever met a woman who doesn't love jewellery? But please, I'm coming with you to see you don't get swindled.'

'You're doing nothing of the sort. I know just what you want – and what I want.'

Finally she agreed. I went to Arnaud's, a small, beautiful jewellers in the faubourg St. Honoré, which Mama had patronised for years. I had been there often enough to be recognised by Monsieur Arnaud. Sonia would certainly approve, for I knew from the original presentation box that this was where she had bought my birthday cufflinks.

And at this moment in my life I came across perfection. There is no other word for it. Even I – with my total inexperience – recognised that I was looking at a ring more beautiful than any I had ever seen. It was a huge, pure, sky-blue star sapphire, its beauty caged in a brilliant circle of diamonds.

'Your mother admired this when she was shopping here the other day,' said Monsieur Arnaud, 'but she said it was too expensive. *Tout de même*, I thought you would like me to show it to you – it's one of the sad facts of life that beautiful things cost so much,' he sighed. 'Sky blue.'

'Is it very expensive?' I knew I had a sizeable sum of money left to me by my grandpa when he died, and I'd never touched a cent of it.

Politely – was he a shade condescending? – he mentioned a figure. Astronomical! Then he prepared to put the ring back into the safety of his counter case.

'Hey!' I cried. 'Is there any law stops me looking at it a little longer?'

'I'm sorry, sir.' Unobtrusively Monsieur Arnaud eyed his watch – Cartier, I noticed. He obviously felt he was wasting his time.

'Okay,' I said to his astonishment. 'Wrap it up.' Then as he gaped I added, 'Just one condition.'

I saw his eyes darting covetously, followed by doubt. Was I going to ask for long-term credit? Easy terms? It was a path strewn with hazards for any jeweller. You might start confidently buying something you couldn't afford but, when the crunch came, fathers and mothers had a habit of returning jewellery which their sons shouldn't have bought in the first place.

'No sweat,' I said. 'I'll give you a dollar check right away. The ring's perfect.'

'The condition, sir?' He seemed as puzzled as he was delighted.

'I want a certificate of insurance – for half what the ring's worth. Just in case the lady concerned needs to insure it. I don't want to embarrass her.'

He obviously thought I was dotty. So did I. I went whooping into the M.G. as though executing a war dance and, this time, when I reached the apartment just before lunch there were no tears. I patted a place for Sonia on my knees, then I let her open the velvet case.

She first gasped with sheer astonishment, then wonder, then gave a deeply drawn breath. And finally, when she had looked at it, she followed with a shriek of joy.

'You are mad,' she cried. 'You are crazy. I always knew you were, but this! Larry, my *pazzo* Larry, you shouldn't.' But, with a laugh, 'I'm a woman – so it's too late to take it back. It's *mine*. The most beautiful ring in the world. And it's mine for ever – like my idiot American fiancé who I will always love. I will keep this ring all my life – then one day, a long, long time ahead, it will belong to our daughter.'

Getting married – or rather making plans to get married – didn't seem to involve any serious problems. I rang up Jim Parks, one of the American vice-consuls with whom I played an occasional game of tennis at the Racing Club, and arranged to meet him that same day for a pre-lunch drink at Harry's Bar.

I was almost on my way out of the office, deciding to walk across the Opéra to the rue Danou, when a rewrite man on the *Paris–American* came in and asked, 'Got any more bumf for the "Comes and Goes"?'

This was our nickname for 'Arrivals and Departures'. As we were a local newspaper we printed a list of important Americans leaving or visiting Paris, and sometimes we didn't have enough material to fill the P.A. column because Oregon resolutely refused to dilute it by putting in trash.

I picked up a folder filled with leftovers for 'Comes and Goes' and was about to say, 'Take a couple from here if you need them', when my eye lit on a list of names. It is one of the odd factors of journalism that a practised newspaperman can look at a page even in a directory and pick out unerringly one significant name. Almost without looking I read in a list of departures dated some time back, 'Mr. and Mrs. Henri Sardi.'

Odd, I thought, trying to work out the date of my lunch with Mama. Well! Mama didn't dine at the stuffy old Sardis after all – for the very good reason that they weren't in Paris.

My first thought was that when I reached Douzy I would get Mama aside and tease her gently. But then I thought back to that happy lunch. Was the look in her eyes one of anticipation for the evening to come? Or had she in fact merely made a mistake in the date? No, that was impossible because the date had been arranged in a rush, with my father away. Conveniently away? It must be – well, I thought, I am not, repeat not, going to mention the Sardis to my darling mama. I don't know what the hell's happening, but she is my mama, and she deserves to be happy, and I'm not going to spoil it by putting my nose into some business that doesn't concern me.

At the Racing Club, Jim Parks gave me the necessary forms to sign, asked for the requisite photographs and birth certificates. That was about all.

'I'll process everything in about a week or ten days.' Parks assured me. 'Then I'll phone you, make a date and one of the consuls will marry you. After that it might take a while for Mrs. Astell's citizenship papers to come through, but if your pa has a quiet word with the ambassador I'm sure Mr. Bullitt will speak to Washington and there'll be no sweat.'

Sonia Astell!

10

That was Thursday.

Before I left for Douzy the following evening Sonia asked me, 'I know we must keep things secret, but you can tell Anna. We've been so close – she even fixed us up with our first date that time in Switzerland. I think you owe it to her.'

But I never had the chance to tell Anna. I drove down on the Friday evening. It was winter now, and it had turned bitterly cold. The roads were treacherous and, on some flat brown land, black skeletons of trees showed up against leaden skies.

Near La Ferté sous Jouarre I stopped for a swig of brandy

from my flask. People were skating on a small pond that came almost to the edge of the main road, men and women with woollen caps, brightly coloured, long scarves twisted round their necks and flying behind like pennants. One couple holding hands swirled to a stop by the grassy bank of the road which was stiff and white with rime. The man shouted, 'What time is it?' I told him it was nearly half past four. Then, waving to the skaters, I put my foot down hard and reached Douzy in fifty minutes, just as the sun was shrinking, burning away the last fiery particles behind the trees. And just in time to land right in the midst of the biggest family row I can remember.

As I closed the front doors to shut out the biting cold, I heard raised voices screaming at each other in the living room behind the formal salon. Suddenly one voice – Anna's for sure – screeched above the others.

'Goddamn hypocrites! That's what's wrong with this lousy family.'

'Anna darling, it's for your own good.' Mama's voice.

Throwing my thick coat and long scarf on the ormolu hall table, I strode into the living room, taking in the entire group at a glance – Mama, Anna, Guy, Olivia. Everyone seemed to be talking at once. They all looked up at the sound of the door opening. Anna was crying – but with anger, I thought. Mama was crying – but with sorrow, perhaps. Olivia – what the hell is *she* doing here in a family row? I thought savagely – had a stony, slightly aloof look. Guy was trying to touch Anna, to console his twin sister, but she turned on him shouting, 'Take your paws off me.'

'What the hell's the matter?' I asked.

'Oh Larry!' Anna wailed as she almost fell on to my shoulder.

'Here.' I pulled out my handkerchief and dabbed her eyes. 'Well?' I asked the others. 'What's the row about? And where's Papa?'

'Papa's gone out for a reception and dinner at the *Syndicat de Champagne*,' said Guy.

'You're the only man around the house – you tell me what's the trouble.'

'Better ask Mama.'

'Okay. Mama?'

Before my mother had a chance to speak Anna burst out, 'They've found out about Willi and me spending the weekend together at the Crillon.'

'Oh, *that*.' I tried to simulate a nonchalant approach. 'Is that all?'

'All!' cried Mama. 'The only daughter of the Astell family – in bed with . . .'

'Go on, Mama,' said Anna, her voice dangerously quiet, 'go on – say it . . .'

Mama hesitated, finally said, 'A man.'

'That wasn't what you were going to say, was it? You were going to say, "A German".'

'What the hell difference does it make?' I cried in exasperation. 'You can't make a row over the fact that a grown-up girl has been to bed with someone.' I was thinking, What about you, Mama? 'Come on, Anna, dry your eyes. Anybody'd think you'd murdered someone.'

Mama made no reply, but at least I gave everyone a breathing space.

'It isn't as though Anna is – well, *wild*, Mama,' I said. 'She's in love with Willi.'

Olivia hadn't said a word, and she shouldn't have spoken now, but she did.

'I think I should go to my room,' she said very quietly to Guy. All she meant, of course, was that this was a family row in which she had been caught by chance, and she was in fact withdrawing from a painful scene with tact and consideration. The pity is that she just didn't disappear without a word, for the enraged Anna seized upon those two words, 'My room'.

'Your room!' she shouted. 'Who the hell said it's *your* room?'

'Shut up,' cried Guy. 'It *is* her room. You mind your own goddamned business.'

Guy, I thought, is beginning to grow up. Perhaps it was Olivia who had made him tougher, taken him away from my 'elder brother shadow', given him a personality of his own. He had guts, and anger, and determination. His persistence in learning to paint was only a manifestation – one day to be forgotten, I was sure – of an inner toughness.

Anna was not so reasonable, for almost with a sneer she

asked, 'Is it? Well, I'd like to know how many hours of darkness she spends on her side of the communicating door.'

'Anna!' cried Mama sharply, the original cause of the row forgotten for the moment. 'Don't speak like that of Olivia.'

'I'll say what I like to who I like,' shouted Anna. 'That's what's so goddamn wicked about this house – yes, wicked. The hypocrisy. I'm a grown-up woman, I go off for a weekend of . . .' she looked at Mama almost with a sneer, 'fornication, I think that's the word. And you treat me like a kid. Yet, all the time you tell me I'm wicked, you, Mama, are letting my twin brother go to bed with . . .'

'That's the bloody end,' shouted Guy, and for a moment I thought he was going to hit Anna. Everything seemed to happen in one jumbled moment. I rushed over to try and quieten – protect? – Anna. Mama looked furious, yet strangely impotent.

Olivia said quietly, and I must say with great dignity, 'I didn't ask to come to Douzy. It wasn't my idea, and I'm sorry if I've embarrassed you. I'll pack my bags and leave as soon as I can.'

'Over my dead body,' cried Guy. Again I thought he was going to slap Anna's face but he thought better of it and said, 'If Olivia goes, I go. And for good.'

At that moment I tried to cool an explosive situation by asking Anna, with an assumed innocence, 'How was this terrible crime of yours discovered?'

'Mademoiselle Lisette saw us going into the Crillon when she was visiting Paris,' said Anna. 'Then she promptly came back to Douzy and told Mama. *Quelle vache!*'

It was not the first time our ex-nanny had told tales out of school – long after we had left school, so to speak, at least long after she had ceased to be our nanny. She didn't discover our innermost secrets perhaps, but she had a habit of telling Mama quietly that she didn't think we ought to go to a certain bistro, or that when Anna had said she was too busy to garden she had found her reading a sexy novel. It had been one thing to behave like that when we were under her charge, but what right did she have to interfere with our adult lives?

'Anna's right,' I said to Mama, still trying to divert attention from the main row. 'Mademoiselle Lisette *is* a troublemaker. I don't know why the hell we keep her.'

What I *didn't* know was that, typically, Mlle Lisette had been quietly listening to our shouting from the *salon* next door. When events didn't concern her directly she presumably stood there in the *salon*, drinking everything in. But suddenly *her* name was brought into the argument. She stormed into the living room. I had a sudden vision of a furious woman, wispy grey hair flat against her head, glasses with steel rims.

'Would you really like to know why I am still here?' she shouted.

'No, thanks,' I said quietly. 'Why don't you just go to your room, Mademoiselle Lisette?'

'Because I prefer to stay. Because I have every right to stay.' She spat out the words with fury, wielding a verbal dagger.

Olivia started to leave the room. Then Guy made to follow.

'Not you!' screamed Mlle Lisette. 'You stay. I know all about what happens in your room at night.'

'Everybody knows it,' I said airily.

'You should talk.' She turned on me. 'You're as bad as the rest of them. You think you can say anything you like. Do you really think I didn't know how Larry used to stand and watch me through the crack of the open door when I was getting undressed?'

I felt myself going cold. It was true. Mlle Lisette had been younger, prettier, when I was fourteen and discovered that she had the habit of leaving her door ajar when undressing at night. By peeping through the crack I could see everything, so I used to sneak up regularly to watch, confident she couldn't see me. I had thought it a great adventure in those days.

'That's enough,' I said thickly.

'No, it isn't! You're as bad as the rest. You thought I couldn't see you, but I could. I saw you all right, doing a dirty thing as you watched me. I used to stand there undressing until you'd finished.'

'Get out!' I shouted. 'Get out, you bitch.'

What I had done – and long since all but forgotten – was not very serious, even though in those days all boys were solemnly warned that if they played with themselves too frequently they would end up in an asylum. Still, it was not the kind of thing I wanted Mama to hear.

I saw Mama put a hand across her eyes as though to blot out some unpleasant picture, and I had a sudden premonition. Mlle Lisette's revelation about me was only a beginning. I sensed a fear in Mama, a real fear. It could have nothing to do with me.

'Are you all right, Mama?' I asked. 'Why don't you go upstairs and rest before dinner?'

Before Mama could get up out of the chair, Mlle Lisette started her ravings again.

'Come on, Guy,' I cried, 'kick that bitch out of here. Get her out before . . .'

But Guy stood silent. I looked at him. He was deathly white.

'Guy!' I cried more sharply, my mind flashing back to the incident near the orchard. This was not 'Mlle Lisette'. This was 'Lisette'.

'Guy,' I said, 'what's the trouble?'

'*She'll* tell you. She's been threatening to spill the beans for years. Go on you bitch – tell.'

'I will,' sneered Mlle Lisette. 'Pigs, all of you. Do you really know why your kind and supercilious mother keeps me on here – on full salary? Ask Guy!'

For a moment I thought Guy was going to keel over. I looked at his face – pasty, dirty, grey. Then I looked at Mama. Her face was creased with agony. I determined to kick the bloody woman out of the room, to use force. As I moved towards her, she shouted, 'Ask Guy! Ask your precious Guy!'

'Ask *what*?' shouted Anna as I struggled with the woman.

'Ask Guy,' Mlle Lisette shouted back at us. 'Ask Guy who's the father of my child.'

The bombshell was followed by an agonising silence, in which nobody seemed to have the courage to look at anyone else. Even the row over Anna was wiped off the slate – for a few moments, anyway.

As Guy stepped forward, Mlle Lisette, beside herself with fury, tried to grab Mama, shouting, 'Everyone was happy before that Jewish bitch came into the house.'

Guy tried to hit her. I somehow stopped him, almost pushed her out of the room as she shouted, 'Pigs! *Salauds!*'

Turning to Olivia, I said, 'I'm sorry you were dragged into this mess.'

She smiled. She had behaved with dignity, and now she turned to Mama, who was crying softly, and said, 'Please, Mrs. Astell, don't worry. It was a long time ago. I'm going to leave now.'

'No, don't,' Mama implored. 'Please stay.'

I stole a look at Mama, suddenly realising the one reason why she didn't want Guy to go. Was Lisette blackmailing her? How poor Mama had changed from that happy day of smiles at the Pré-Catalan! I caught myself thinking, it's bad enough about Guy, but what the hell? Who cares? It's Mama who counts, Mama who suffers, Mama who helps. And thank God Mlle Lisette had only been blackmailing Guy, and hadn't been snooping around Mama's private life. And thank God Mlle Lisette had only spotted Anna at the Crillon — and not Mama, dining with some unknown admirer at some secret rendez-vous. That *would* have played hell with the weekend.

'It could be worse, so don't worry, Mama.' I kissed her, but she looked agonised, almost as though she had painted on a new face suitable for a different occasion — or was it a new mask?

Of course you can't just ignore the sudden revelation that your brother has had an illegitimate child with the local nanny. A hundred questions danced before my thoughts. Where was it? Did Guy see it? Was it a boy or a girl? Yet, though I was flabbergasted at the news — Guy a father! — I had a curious sensation that Mama wasn't taking in the seriousness of the situation. Perhaps she had lived with the secret for longer than I realised. I had no idea when this wretched woman had gone to bed with Guy. Perhaps time, the situation itself, had dulled the effect for Mama.

But there was something else. Not for the first time during the quarrel, I wondered, was Mama more concerned about her own secret life than about Guy's and Anna's? She wasn't behaving as I would have expected in a traumatic row like this. Mama, after all, was self-possessed and quite capable of controlling a situation, especially in her own house. She might be lonely – she might be unhappy – but she could still with one sharp command have brought the rest of the family to silence, even that cow Mlle Lisette.

Maybe, only maybe, her mind was on other things, another man. And among all the family I was the only one to realise that Mama faced problems of her own. Did she guess that I knew? I couldn't tell, but I do know that, as we stood there, my heart went out to her, and fearful, fanciful impossibilities flashed through my mind in a second. She was about to run away and join her lover – for ever! That was why she hadn't controlled the family quarrel. Who gave a damn about Guy? No, she wasn't running away, she had been discovered, she was being blackmailed and suicide was the only way out. *That* would make Anna's problem unimportant. Crazy thoughts!

'Larry – you're the eldest son. Won't you help me – me and Willi?' cried Anna, breaking in on my thoughts.

'Leave this to me.' I patted her shoulder. 'This Guy business' – I nodded towards Guy, who was sunk in gloom in a chair – 'must have been a hell of a shock but' – I turned to Mama – 'let's deal with Anna. She's going to marry Willi. There's nothing you can do to stop it, Mama. And after all that's happened today, I think you should give Anna your blessing. I don't know where they'll be married, but if it's in Germany then I'm going there to give Anna away. She's had a raw deal – the toughest of any of us – and I for one am going to try to make up for it. I think you should, too, Mama.'

'You know I love you, Mama,' said Anna. 'I don't want to hurt you. But I *do* love Willi – terribly.'

'I understand – I try to – we all like Willi – we only want you to be happy.'

I felt like saying that our parents had chosen an odd way to prove their love for Anna, but instead I persisted, 'So it's agreed?'

Mama nodded and, after a long pause, she said, 'Of course, Anna. You can telephone Willi and tell him you both have our blessing.'

Not until after dinner did I drag the whole Mlle Lisette story out of my mother. Apart from curiosity at opening a cupboard containing such a fascinating skeleton, I was intrigued by one fact. If Mlle Lisette had had a baby, where was it?

'We had it adopted,' Mama told me when we were alone and she was more composed. 'It seems such a long time ago.'

Guy was only seventeen when it happened, while I was nineteen. Mama either didn't know or refused to discuss the details. However, the Astell children had long since ceased to need a nanny — so why had Mlle Lisette been kept on?

'You can only see one side of her,' Mama explained. 'You don't realise the way she brought you all up. She made you what you are today, darling.'

'For what it's worth,' I couldn't help saying, 'I'm not sure she did a good job.'

'It's human nature, I suppose,' Mama sighed.

'But what's that got to do with keeping Mademoiselle Lisette on after we'd gone away to school?'

'It's simple. She liked being with you all, especially Guy. So she's not only become part of the family, but nannies are getting harder to find, and I thought that one day — well, you'd all be getting married and she'd be able to look after my grandchildren. She's a queer stick, but I liked her — until Guy and she . . .' she shuddered.

'Didn't you fire her even then?'

'I wanted to.'

'But she did *stay*, Mama.'

'She went away to have the baby — four months before, so you and Anna wouldn't notice. The child was adopted. None of us, including Guy, ever saw it.'

'But then — she came back? After what happened with Guy. For God's sake, Mama, why?'

'She sort of — drifted back.'

'Deliberately?'

'I suppose so. Guy didn't seem to mind.'

'And since then? Look at me, Mama. You didn't *ask* her back, did you?'

Mama shook her head.

'She forced her way back. That's true, isn't it?' I asked. 'And since then she's been blackmailing you. Isn't that the truth? Come on, Mama.' I began to feel exasperated. 'I'm not a child. I'm twenty-six. Tell me everything.'

'Blackmail is such a nasty word – but' – rather patheti-
cally – 'I only paid her wages, Larry. Nothing more. And
she's been useful around the house.'

'And her keep – no wonder she can't stand the sight of
Olivia. Well, anyway, we've damn well kicked her out this
time.' A sudden thought struck me.

'Does Papa know? Know everything?'

'Oh yes. I couldn't keep a secret from him.'

Are you sure? I wondered, looking at her. I was sorely
tempted to tell her that Sonia and I were planning to marry in
less than two weeks, for she badly needed news to cheer her
up. And though I disliked the way Olivia had come into the
family, it was only now I realised that Mama hoped Olivia
might drive out Mlle Lisette. And, though much delayed, the
ploy had finally succeeded.

'Your troubles will soon be over!' I fetched her a *marc*. She
enjoyed one – but only one – small glass after dinner. 'The
main thing is, don't panic. Let poor Anna marry her Willi in
style. And don't worry so much, Mama. Anything could
happen. There probably won't be a war. Anna could leave
Willi if there is one. She'll keep her American passport. It's
such a crazy world there's no point in getting excited about
anything – because it may never happen. Promise me not to
worry.'

'You're very persuasive.'

'I'm not. I'm just practical. Since Anna's determined to
marry Willi, let's give her a good send-off. I'm going upstairs
to tell Anna to phone Willi again, and tell him they're going
to be married at Douzy. The first marriage here since
yours, Mama! We'll have a white wedding as soon as we can
fix it.'

'I suppose you're right. In fact Papa has already said that he
knows it was bound to happen sooner or later.'

And that, I thought – and hoped – was the end of a painful
day and night. I nipped off to bed as soon as I could after
dinner – partly because I didn't particularly want to have to
listen to Mama and Papa, or to have to intercede.

In the middle of the night, almost as though I was waking
from a nightmare, I sat up suddenly. One sound dominated

the blackness – the mournful tolling of a bell, driving all thoughts of the family quarrel away. It was the Douzy bell – and everyone knew what that meant in winter.

I heard my father's voice shout, 'Up everyone! There's not a moment to lose. Quick now!'

A stranger staying in the house might have thought it was a fire alarm, but it was nothing of the kind. That single sound of the bell told all of us who lived in the area that disaster was threatening the world of champagne.

I knew that from every house in every neighbouring village men and women would be scrambling out of beds, as I was, grabbing the warmest clothes they could fling on hurriedly, swilling faces to wake up – and then going into the cold night air in a race against time to save the vineyards from their greatest winter hazard – frost.

This was worse than fire; it was a malevolent nature's cruellest, craftiest enemy, for it struck simultaneously over an area. And so far no one had discovered a speedy way to outwit it, even though, when the temperature started to fall, 'sentries' were designated to make regular checks on the night time temperature.

Now it had fallen below zero.

I had felt the cold when driving from Paris, especially when I stopped near the skaters for a swig of brandy, but it was surprising how much milder it usually was in Champagne, especially in the protected folds of the vineyards planted on the sloping west-facing hilly areas. The vineyards are also planted between 400 and 500 feet above sea level, sheltering them to a certain extent from frosts, while the forest above them gives a soft moisture to the ground below which stabilises temperatures.

My father was running down the stairs, still crying, 'Every second counts!' For there was only way one to beat a sudden frost in those days – by employing an army of willing helpers bearing lighted torches, always kept in the outhouses of the Home Farm. As I ran down the lane, with Olivia and Anna just behind, I thought I was leading the way – until a wobbling figure flashed past the slight downwards slope. It was La Châtelaine cycling into the fray.

At the farm we picked up our torches – kerosene-soaked

rags tied to sticks – and made for the nearest vineyards. Old Pagniez and his daughter Aubergine joined us.

'Plenty of time,' grunted the vigneron. 'We'll have the smudge pots going full blast within the hour.'

Suddenly I saw another fleeing figure – right next to me.

'Oh no you don't.' I grabbed Mlle Lisette's arm roughly and spun her round. 'We can do nicely without any help from you.'

'Every helper counts.'

'Get off our ground. I'd rather lose everything. Clear out!'

Running on, I didn't see her again as I made for the first smudge pots, man's only invention against frost. They consisted of small rusted kerosene stoves, about two feet high, always left out in winter, containing fuel at the bottom with a chimney sprouting above. Hardly noticeable, half hidden in the vineyards, they stood at ten-yard intervals along every fifth or sixth row.

It was bitterly cold – it was now three in the morning – as the first men and women arrived, torches flickering, spreading out from the edge of a vineyard, slowly advancing, because every single kerosene can had to be touched with the torch to ignite it. And there were hundreds of them – yet this was the only way, in those days, to provide warmth. I often wondered what it would be like to fly in the dark over the vineyards and see below thousands of twinkling, slowly moving lights advancing in formation.

As we darted between the plants, more smudge pots belching black smoke, we started coughing and spluttering, for it was not the kerosene in the pots that warmed the vines against the frost, it was the dirty smoke – made worse by those who fuelled the fire with old tyres – that was effective. It settled like a blanket, loitering in every nook and cranny against the iron-hard soil, covering the vines with the warmth of the smoke, moving like an old quilt where it was most needed.

At 5 a.m. all helpers who weren't ready for bed trudged into the *salon* of Douzy château. It was a tradition, the equivalent of the British tot of rum after a naval battle. Only a few sneaked off home before gulping one, or two or three, glasses of *marc de Champagne*, fiery enough to melt an icicle.

Papa hadn't yet arrived. 'He's clearing up in the farm,' said

Mama, whose face was sooty, her hair bedraggled. She was laughing – just as Grandma dismounted and demanded her tot. She was wearing her 'emergency kit', consisting of a pair of old corduroy trousers tucked into fur boots, a long black cape with a fur collar, a woollen skiing hat and thick mittens.

'Bravo!' she toasted us. To the vignerons, this was high praise indeed, and there was a cheer as she downed her first glass of *marc* in one gulp as though it were water, then calmly asked for a second glass.

At least the night of crisis had one beneficial effect. It took Papa's mind off family affairs. At breakfast he was so full of the magnificent way the people had responded that he forgot the earlier problems.

'I'm very proud of everyone, *really*.' He helped himself to bacon and eggs. 'Such loyalty! *Really*.'

Only later did he remember Mlle Lisette, though Mama must have told him earlier of the terrible row. He only made one reference to our ex-nanny. It was a curious trait of Papa's, who had behaved in exactly the same way when he discovered me leaving Sonia's bedroom. He seemed to make up his mind, take a decision, announce it – and then, incredibly, forget it, or brush it from his mind as though it didn't exist.

'No doubt she egged Guy on, considering the difference in their ages,' he said. 'Yes, *probably*' – with his rising voice – 'but I can't allow a woman who has been wronged by our family to be thrown out and *forgotten*. Not after all the years she's spent here. *Really*, we've passed the days of throwing . . . er . . . immoral women out in the snow. Yes, the *snow*.'

'But she can't stay here, Papa.'

'Of course not. But we still have a few cottages in our Mont de Champagne vineyards, and it happens that one of them is empty. Madame Delamonde moved after her husband, who worked in the south vineyard, died a month ago. She's gone to live with her son. I will let Mademoiselle Lisette live there rent free and arrange for the *Crédit Lyonnais* to send her a modest monthly allowance. Yes, I think so, yes.'

'And Anna?'

'She will marry her Willi,' he said, adding with a touch of

wry humour, 'we don't want any more unexpected children in the Astell family.'

At that moment Anna came down for breakfast.

'Darling Papa,' she cried. 'I've spoken to Willi. He's so excited. Thank you for understanding.'

'Not actually *understanding*,' said Papa without any malice, 'so much as accepting. Your mother and I want you to be happy. Yes, *happy*. We may have had reservations, but never mind. It's your choice and we shall do everything we can to help.'

Later that morning, I told Anna, swearing her to secrecy, about Sonia and our marriage plans.

'What a pity we can't have a double wedding,' she said. 'I'm so happy for you, darling brother. Happy for everyone.'

Well, at least, I thought, we've had enough drama for one quiet weekend at Douzy.

Or so I thought.

I I

On the Sunday afternoon while we were having tea the phone rang. It was Paris: Sonia.

I had left her on the Friday, laughing and happy. Now on the phone she cried without preamble. 'Oh, Larry. It's Daddy. He's been expelled from Paris. Tonight. And I'm afraid for us.'

'What happened?'

'*Come to Paris!*' It was a cry of distress. 'Every second counts. The Quai d'Orsay has declared him *persona non grata*.'

'What on earth for?'

'I don't know, *I don't know*,' she cried, impatient with frustration. 'Just come, *please*. Mummy's still in the house packing up, but Daddy's taken a suite at the Ritz. Just come, for God's sake.'

'I'm on my way, darling. When does your father leave?'

'Midnight — in theory. But the Rome express leaves at ten. That just gives us time to tell him about us — because he said something I didn't understand — about me.'

'Don't worry, darling.' Without bothering to put on my coat I dashed round to the old stables on the far side of the courtyard and brought the car round to the front door, where I left her ticking over to warm up. When I went inside for my coat, Aubergine helped me into it and found me an extra scarf, for it was very cold by now, with a threat of snow in the leaden sky.

I had little time to explain to Mama what had happened to Sonia's father — and I deliberately didn't tell her about our wedding plans. Then I was off, twisting downhill past the dell towards the main road — and Paris.

I reached the place Vendôme at about seven and made my way straight to the Riccardis' apartment on the third floor.

Signor Riccardi opened the door of his suite the second I pressed the bell, almost as though he had been standing there to greet me before I saw Sonia. She gave me a wan smile. Riccardi's face looked more creased with worry than anger, but I could tell immediately that Sonia had told him about us.

'I'm sorry about the bad news.' I tried to commiserate, without having the faintest idea how much worse the news would be in a couple of minutes. 'It seems a bad time to talk about Sonia and . . .'

'A very bad time,' he said bitterly. 'To break up a future husband's life without so much as a warning . . .'

'It was my fault, Daddy. I couldn't go on with it.'

'This is no time for argument. I understand about people in love, I understand you two. But you play your cards badly. And you have no hope now.'

I didn't like the tone of *that* — though I didn't know why.

'May I say, sir, our families are old friends . . .'

'Don't be such a *cretino*,' he shouted suddenly. 'We're not playing *giro tondo*.' I remembered the Italian version of ring o' roses. 'You two couldn't marry now if you wanted to.'

'But I'm an American,' I blurted out.

'You can be Lord God Almighty,' he said. 'But what you

don't know is that Sonia has been expelled too.'

My mouth dropped open. 'Is this true?'

She nodded miserably.

'Tonight?'

'They've given me three days to leave,' Sonia whispered in a small, frightened voice. 'I can't believe it.'

'Three days! But that's eternity. I'm sure I can fix . . .'

'You can't!' said Riccardi harshly. 'Apart from her sacred promise to another man, you wouldn't have the time anyway.'

'I would,' I cried. 'Please understand, Signor Riccardi. We love each other – not only Sonia and me – but the families . . .'

As patiently as his Italian nature would permit, Riccardi explained that he understood everything I said. He had often thought in the past that Sonia and I would make a happy couple. But times had changed. Her fiancé was an important member of Foreign Minister Ciano's team. To start a scandal at this delicate moment – with her father kicked out of France – would be disastrous.

'There's something more you haven't told me,' I said. 'You can't stop us.'

'Diplomacy isn't just a question of giving orders any more,' he said bitterly. 'Why do you think I have been declared *persona non grata*? Intrigue – and not by the French. They are after Sonia too. I do not think you could marry each other if you tried.' With a wintry smile he added, 'Not even with your American influence.'

'But if I can?'

'I want to marry him so badly, Daddy. What does Mummy say?'

'I don't know. I don't know anything.' He wiped his forehead. 'She's still at the house packing personal things ready to be sent on. I don't know.'

'If I can?' I begged him.

He turned to Sonia, and stroked her blue-black hair.

'*Carissima,*' he said, 'I would like you to be happy. And I like Larry, I do. But you do not understand everything.' He was wavering.

I knew in my heart that I could pull the right strings. But

then Riccardi asked me, 'If there is no time to get married before Sonia is sent away, what then?'

'Then she'll go, and I'll wait a bit and say nothing – for the moment anyway – if that helps you,' I promised. 'I'm sure we *can* get married, but if there's a hitch I'll agree – if Sonia does – not to break her engagement to the other man until the timing is better.'

'I don't want that!' cried Sonia.

'We'll be married, don't worry,' I promised her. 'In a couple of days.'

'If not? It may sound silly to an American' – speaking softly Riccardi almost ignored Sonia – 'but to an Italian honour is very important. Especially in the Service. And I have problems. If Sonia stays here as your wife, it will be her honour that is dirtied. If she remains engaged and then breaks it off after a few months' honour will be satisfied all round.'

I didn't really like the sound of it – mainly because I was convinced Riccardi was lying, that he was using a feeble excuse about 'honour' to cover up a far more sinister reason why he hoped the engagement would continue. I knew Riccardi was in trouble, and perhaps needed Sonia, even de Feo. But what had he done? There were no clues, though the drawn face of Riccardi and the silence of Sonia told me it was serious. Yet I could not challenge Riccardi, could not call him a liar in front of Sonia.

'What do you think, Sonia?' She nodded – reluctantly.

'It is generous of you,' said Riccardi. 'I don't like what is happening, but we are in much deeper waters than you think, and there are people who will stop at nothing. Now I must prepare to leave. This suite will be kept on for Sonia until she goes.'

Inside me I was exulting. For I had made a deal which I was convinced would enable us to get married. And Riccardi had promised that if we got married before Sonia had to leave he would accept the situation – not that there was anything he could do about it, while Sonia was in Paris and he was in Rome. So the promise not to 'rock the boat' if she went to Italy would not apply.

'I do not have much time.' Riccardi looked at his watch. 'So perhaps I will say *au revoir* to you, as I am expecting guests before the car picks me up at half past eight to go to the gare de Lyon.'

He put his arm on Sonia's shoulder. They were standing by the window of the oak-panelled sitting room overlooking the private Ritz gardens, and he looked tired, though still hand-some – I could see where Sonia inherited her dark beauty. But I could also see a middle-aged man's dreams of his daughter making a good marriage to a titled diplomat crumbling about him. 'Yes,' he said sadly, 'all will suffer now, and we cannot fight them. They are stupid, these people, so stupid, they never listen to discussions. One man gets his orders – from whom? You may ask – and then everything goes on a belt of assembly and nothing can stop it.'

'But why?' asked Sonia desperately. 'They can't do this without giving both of us a reason.'

'They can. And do. I do not know why. The French at the Quai d'Orsay are very polite. However, they insist they have orders to cancel your residence permit.' He gesticulated as only Italians can. 'I argue with them, I tell them it is against all the code of diplomacy. They are very, very sorry, they say, but these are orders. Whose orders? I ask. They will not tell me. They don't even know why they do this; they cannot tell me.'

I had never seen Sonia so destroyed. Her face seemed to have fallen in with pain.

After I had said goodbye, I took the elevator to the ground floor and walked past one of the gilt and plush chairs opposite the concierge's desk – at the exact moment when Otto Abetz came marching through the front door. He had two men with him – bodyguards, I guessed.

He looked as he always did – tall, shoulders squared up as though for a fight, blue eyes seeing all, pale face contrasting with reddish-brown hair. And always carrying with him a sinister aura, like a cloak.

'Ah so!' he held out a hand which I unwillingly took. I hated myself for lacking the moral fibre to refuse it. 'When are you going to take up my offer of a trip to see our beautiful new Germany? The offer still holds, you know. We need good writers to see for themselves the wonderful things our Führer is doing.'

Abetz knew I would never go, knew I was violently anti-Fascist. So he wasn't *inviting* me. He was *goading* me, and the thought made me mad as hell. This man, I was convinced, knew why Riccardi and Sonia were being kicked out of France. He might even have engineered it to protect himself.

I saw it this way: obviously Riccardi's visits to Paris had held sinister motives; he might even have been involved in plans to liquidate the two Italian anti-Fascists murdered during the summer. If so, Riccardi would certainly have consulted Abetz as senior partner.

Above all, however, Abetz had to protect his own front as a lover of all things French, his rôle as confidant of Madame de Portes, his influence with the right-wing diehard French politicians, for this was his cover while he organised a fifth column in France. But what if Sonia's father had blundered somewhere, been indiscreet? If Abetz thought this had happened, he wouldn't hesitate to get Riccardi and his family out of the way before the French began to ask awkward questions, which might even implicate Abetz. This was speculation, I knew, but Abetz, I was sure, had used his influence among pro-Fascists at the Quai d'Orsay to declare the Riccardis undesirable aliens.

Abetz had one terrifying, snake-like trait in his character, one confirmed by many other newspapermen. It was an uncanny ability to read your mind. He could see the rage boiling inside me, and with his sharp intuition he immediately knew the cause of it. It must have been so for, standing there, slightly supercilious, he suddenly said the most extraordinary thing.

'So please come and see our Germany' – his voice was as smooth as silk – 'and I promise you, Monsieur Astell, an unending supply of our most beautiful *fräuleins*. We keep them handy' – his voice held a trace of a sneer – 'as a sort of therapy in case any of our guests are suffering from broken hearts.'

For once in my life I thought of the right answer before the other man had a chance to leave.

'I don't like making deals with men who fuck up my love

life,' I retorted, unable to control my fury. 'But I will make a deal with you. I'll come to Germany with *you* – the day the French come to their senses and kick shits like you back home where you belong.' Then I added one last home-made 'German' word which I had once invented as a joke to tease Willi. It had a very effective sound.

'*Gefundershite!*' I said and pushed my way through the swing doors into the clean cold air of the place Vendôme.

I was round at the U.S. Consulate almost before it opened, dancing with impatience until the girl led me to Jim Parks's door.

'Christ! You look mad,' he greeted me.

'Mad? I've never been so livid in all my life. Know what those sodding Frogs have done?'

As coherently as I could, I outlined the events of the previous evening. 'They can't *do* this sort of thing to innocent civilians,' I cried.

'It's life in *la belle France*,' Parks sighed. 'Might as well remember it.'

'I don't give a shit,' I cried. 'We've got three days. That gives us time to get married, doesn't it?'

Parks, jacket on its hanger, Arrow-type white shirt newly starched, fingered one of his embassy-issue yellow pencils with the standard rubber at the end, and said softly, 'I hate to say this, Larry, but no dice. You're out of luck.'

'But I'm *American*. Don't I have any rights?'

'In France, fuck all. And as for an Italian – she may be beautiful Larry, but when the French are looking for an Italian consider yourself lucky they haven't picked her up in the *panier à salade* and taken her to the local jail.'

'It's not possible that people can stand by and ruin other people's lives. I love that girl, Jim. If she needs guarantees, my father will vouch for her.'

'I wish I could help.' Parks shook his head, and he really meant what he said. 'But the only way you might have been able to pull rank was if you'd got the lady pregnant. And you've left it a bit late for that.'

After a few more moments of futile argument I stormed out of the embassy building, jumped into my M.G. and missed

almost every pedestrian unlucky enough to be on the avenue
Gabriel.

'I'll find some way,' I swore as I grated the gear into second.

But I didn't. I couldn't. When it became obvious that there
was no way of delaying the cancellation of her *permit de
séjour* – not even after I had been to the Préfecture – I had one
last thought: I would take her to America the following day,
and we'd get married there. But she didn't have a visa. And to
get one would take time. Finally I suggested that I travel with
her to Italy, and we could get married there. But she shook her
head. I had promised.

'Well, what about forgetting my promise and breaking off
your engagement?' I answered.

She looked at me. 'You heard what Daddy said. He's tied to
Ciano's apron strings.'

She held out her beautiful hand, displaying the sapphire on
the third finger. 'There's where it stays,' she promised. 'It's
our engagement ring – but it's an unofficial engagement, for
the time being. I don't want to tie you down. To tie *anyone*
down. Though Monsieur Coquelicot is mine for ever, whatever happens.'

And that, after a lot more discussion, was how we left it.
But when finally I realised that I must, for the moment
anyway, accept what had happened, I resolved on one thing. I
would never spoil the time we had spent together by a bitter
leavetaking. We would part as friends – can lovers ever really
be friends? Sonia had once asked me – until I came to marry
her.

I had Sonia's address near Florence, of course, so I decided
on impulse before she left to write to her so that a message
would await her when she arrived in Italy.

At the nearest souvenir shop on the rue de Rivoli arcade near
the statue of Joan of Arc, I asked the girl, 'Do you sell
postcards?'

'*Mais oui, monsieur.*'

'Give me fifty please,' I said with a deliberate nonchalance.
'As many different as you can.'

At the office I posted every one to Sonia.

★　　★　　★

I didn't go to the P.A. on the last day, for I was haunted by a feeling that we would never see each other again, certainly never as lovers. No doubt the Riccardis and the Astells – the young as well as the old – would meet again as old friends in years to come. But it could never be the same for us.

'It will, darling, it will,' Sonia promised as we sat down at Marcel's for our final dinner in the bistro we loved so much. Two or three of the elderly, solitary regulars bowed politely to us as they always did. I wondered what their reaction would have been had they known she had been thrown out of France.

I couldn't even begin to eat the *boeuf bourgignon*, which came to our small table piping hot, its sauce redolent of good wine. And matters were made worse when Marcel himself, in chef's hat and blue and white checked apron, looked horrified. *Nobody* refused Marcel's cooking (even though occasionally it was below standard) if only because most people who dined at his restaurant were so hungry and so poor they would eat anything.

'I'm just not hungry,' I apologised.

'Can I change it, *monsieur?*'

I shook my head. For a moment I had a wild impulse to blurt out, 'She's going!' But I resisted the temptation. There was nothing anyone could do about anything.

'I think he should have a cognac,' said Sonia gently to Marcel.

'On the house, please,' Marcel bustled over to the tiny zinc bar. Sonia took my hand. 'You should eat a bit, darling. Just a mouthful.'

'Plenty of time for that tomorrow.' I wallowed in self pity. Yet it wasn't only self pity that robbed me of my appetite, it was the fact that my misery was combined with a sense of foreboding which I could not dismiss from my mind.

Her leaving – and the sinister overtones that caused her departure – seemed symptomatic of the hatred, the beastliness, the downward trend of all life in Europe. It wasn't only our lives that were being torn apart, through no fault of our own. Europe itself was crumbling as it approached 1938.

'Let's go home, darling,' said Sonia when I had downed my cognac. 'Let's go to bed in each other's arms.'

We walked back down the rue de Seine, past the tiny

apartment where Gontchorova – who had painted my favourite sunflower picture – lived, then along the quai Malaquais until we crossed the boulevard to the rue du Cherche Midi.

Then we went to bed, but not to make love. I tried. Did I want to prove my love? I didn't know, but I couldn't. I lay there in her arms, wanting to. I tried again and again, waiting for the dawn, but I couldn't make love.

On the last day I took her to the gare de Lyon and saw her comfortably installed in her reserved first-class wagon-lit. After I had kissed her for the last time, she leaned out of the window and said, 'We'll meet again, my beloved Larry. I promise you.'

I wondered, as I drove back to Douzy, whether we ever would. When the car slid effortlessly round the bends towards the house, I felt that each rhythmic turn of the train's wheels rattling towards Italy was taking her further from me.

Reaching the courtyard, I had a sudden urge to turn round and race away. I resisted it, but I felt for the moment that I never wanted to see Douzy again. What had to us been a magic garden was, without Sonia, just another estate with its workaday chores.

I prayed we *would* meet again. Yet, somehow or other, I already had a premonition that the next time we did meet, she would be married. And not to me.

PART TWO

Spring 1938–October 1939

12

Anna was married at Douzy in the spring of 1938 'to her German', as Grandma said with a withering look which meant, 'Well, I did my best to stop them.'

Despite parental doubts, however, it was a beautiful white wedding. The couple were young and handsome and obviously very much in love, and if anyone had doubts about the wisdom of marrying into a German family in these troubled times, 'What the hell,' as Oregon said. 'Just think of Krug, Mumm, Heidsieck, and Bollinger – half the families of Champagne are descended from the Germans.'

Papa had decided on one thing: to give the guests the choice of wearing the traditional formal cutaway jacket with striped trousers or a dark, sober suit.

'That or a blue lounge suit I think, *yes*,' he said in his up-and-down voice. '*Really*, as this is a village wedding, a dark suit will be – well, quite *practical*, yes?'

'Blue suits! You mark my words,' Grandma snorted, 'this is the sort of thing that's turning France into a Communist country. Blue suits do *not* go with champagne.'

Oregon, the only one who dared to tease his mother (and still called her Grandma Jacqueline), said brightly, 'Let's serve beer instead.'

'It'd be more suitable,' muttered my grandmother, adding, when she was sure Willi wasn't in the room, 'It's the only thing the Germans drink anyway. They *swill* it down – by the bucket.'

'I do seem to remember wines like Niersteiner,' my father mentioned timidly.

Grandma glared at him. 'No one in France drinks *German* wine,' and, searching for a suitable simile, she sniffed and said, 'It's like serving mint sauce with a *gigot*. All right for foreigners.'

Most guests would wear cutaway morning suits – if only to do justice to what promised to be Anna's stunning wedding dress, for almost as soon as the date had been fixed Mama said firmly, 'It may only be a village wedding, but Anna is our only daughter, and she's going to wear the most beautiful dress in the world. Mainbocher promised me personally.'

This was the couturier who had designed the wedding dress for the Duchess of Windsor – a 48-year-old designer from Chicago. Originally called 'Main Rousseau Bocher', he had edited *French Vogue* in the twenties before telescoping his name and then setting up shop in the avenue Georges V.

'Main', as Mama called him, was a personal friend who took enormous trouble with clients he liked. He had arrived at Douzy with a selection of sketches and, when one had been chosen, sent a fitter to Douzy half a dozen times to make sure everything was perfect.

On the day, Anna looked exquisite. I had an impression of white lace that looked almost like a crinoline, hundreds of seed pearls, and Grandma's heirloom lace worked into the train.

'And no nonsense about etiquette,' Mainbocher had insisted. 'I know a train is only supposed to be three yards for a church wedding or six yards for a cathedral, but *you're* going to have a six-yard train.'

More than a hundred guests arrived from Paris. All the leaders of the champagne houses had been invited. Fifteen of Willi's friends came from Germany, including a charming couple called the Mollers, and Willi's mother and father who were quiet, very pleasant, but couldn't speak a word of English or French. A marquee, which could only be reached through the house, had been erected as an extension to the conservatory – deliberately, for though Papa hated class distinctions he knew that lines had to be drawn when the wedding guests included Bullitt, the American ambassador, and Paul Reynaud, who had each accepted.

'We couldn't . . . er . . . throw them in at the deep end with the vignerons,' Papa admitted. 'Both would be embarrassed.' He was right, for the villagers – friends to us, but unknown to guests from outside the area – arrived early, hungry, thirsty, and clutching all the sticky children in the village.

They made their way from every direction – up the dell, along the drive, through the orchard, past the cutting bed. Just behind the big yew trees and the courtyard arch, long trestle tables and three hundred folding chairs had been arranged. Everyone reaching the top of the dell was greeted by an unlimited supply of Astell non-vintage, with soda pop for the children. You could sit down where you liked; in front were mounds of food ranging from every kind of home-cured charcuterie or pâté to canapés of smoked salmon. Nearby, two huge pans hung over the embers of a large fire. One contained *boeuf bourgignon*, the other a *cassoulet*, in which even the geese had been fattened on the farm before going into the stewpot.

From time to time we left the marquee to visit the village celebrations at the top of the dell. The biggest cheer of all, however, was reserved for Reynaud when he made a brief appearance before the vignerons. After all, he was Minister of Justice; he apologised for the absence of his wife (and not, of course, mentioning his mistress) and then, a true son of France, insisted on toasting the bride and groom 'with all of those here who I know are her most trusted friends.'

A dozen arms held out champagne bottles from the tables. No one could find a clean glass, but that didn't worry Reynaud. He picked up the nearest cup, grabbed a bottle, poured in a little champagne, swilled it round to clean it, then refilled it and drank the toast.

The vignerons loved it – but soon the amount of champagne began to tell. I saw several sly boys and girls grab piles of smoked salmon canapés, stuffing them into their pockets or handbags. One little girl put some up the elastic of her knickers.

The young unmarried men and women began to disappear, making for the dark hidden corridors of the yew trees, from where I could hear sudden giggles, the rustling of hands in clothes, and the squeals of those who preferred necking – or anything else – to pâté and champagne.

The younger children played under the trestle tables, or rolled down the side of the dell littering it with paper, dirty plates, glasses and half-eaten *baguettes*.

'It's filthy,' I said to Mama as we looked out of the striped tent towards the dell. 'I'm not going out there again.'

'They'll be all right tomorrow; they'll clean up. You see, Larry, if one or two *do* get drunk, it's not because the champagne's free. It's because they *are* Papa's family. This is a great

day for them as well as for Anna. I only wish . . .' she stopped
short. I knew that just in time she stopped uttering the word,
'Sonia'.

'How do you think I feel?' I said bitterly. 'The only girl I've
ever really loved all my life – and Anna's best friend – yet
she's not even here. But perhaps it's as well she couldn't
come.' I muttered savagely, not saying it aloud. For despite
all the past, despite the uncertain future, I had – even to the
last second – hoped wildly, impossibly, that she might by
a miracle arrive at Douzy for this day and that I would suddenly see her, cool and beautiful, sipping champagne in the
marquee.

'I know, Larry darling.' Mama twiddled the stem of her
flute glass and smiled to someone. 'I only wish I could say
something. But, after all, she's living in Cairo now, it's a long
way away.'

Sonia had never been a prolific letter writer, but she had
dropped me a brief note – short and sweet – to say that her
father was being posted as ambassador without portfolio to
'handle affairs' along the North African coast. They would
live in Cairo – it was an obvious trouble spot. Italy was
demanding more and more territory in North Africa. The
French, on the other hand, were relying on their huge North
African empire to provide them with the cannon fodder for the
next war. They didn't put it quite so crudely, but that was
what they meant.

When I told Oregon of Riccardi's move to Cairo, where he
would have his headquarters, his first response was, 'Ciano
must think very highly of Sonia's father. She going with him?'

I nodded.

'North Africa could be a vital war theatre – if war comes,
that is,' said Oregon. 'Riccardi is probably laying the ground,
just as he did in Paris.'

'Maybe,' I agreed. 'And Sonia tells me he's got a new
assistant.'

Oregon cocked an enquiring eyebrow.

'Yes, her dashing young fiancé, the Count de Feo. It seems
he's gone to Cairo to be trained by Riccardi for a more
important job.'

'Espionage?' asked Oregon, not speaking sardonically as he so often did, but seriously.

'The Italians seem to specialise in it,' I sighed.

Feelings of depression were not confined only to thoughts of Sonia. As spring turned warmer, all Europe that summer of '38 was suffering from a kind of *malaise* as it was forced to face up to a question it had for so long tried to shirk: would Hitler fight?

Early that year, Hitler had assumed supreme power over all Germany. He had simply engulfed poor Austria. Against him in France Léon Blum had been no match, and had been replaced as prime minister by Edouard Daladier. In Vaucluse, where he had been born, the son of a local baker, Daladier was nicknamed 'The bull of the south', but though he had a tough exterior he was a hollow man inside. I was horrified at his appearance when I first met him. He looked dirty. A cigarette always hung out of the corner of his mouth. He stank of absinthe. He looked more sly than clever.

And because I knew Reynaud, I was fascinated by one other aspect of Daladier's character. Despite his dark-skinned complexion, his crude manners, despite the lock of greasy hair always hanging over his forehead (dreams of Napoleon perhaps?), Daladier, who was a widower, had managed to entice another titled lady into his bed as his acknowledged mistress. She was the Marquise de Crussol, and the Countess de Portes was her arch rival.

'The world's not big enough for both these women. One of them will have to go,' Oregon prophesied – a truth for which he didn't have to wait long.

Daladier was symptomatic of most French leaders – no guts. We all had *feelings* that none of them was strong enough to stand up to Hitler. And this indifference permeated through the entire European structure.

'It's hard for us, it really *is*,' said Papa one day, 'to realise that France is very *tired*. Yes, *exhausted*. You can't lose a million and a half men as France did in the Great War without having a feeling of "never again".'

'De Gaulle told me when I interviewed him recently,' I said, 'that France doesn't have enough tanks and planes to fight a war anyway. The French aero-industry is on strike. Tank production has been hit too. He says half the Renault work-force is communist. Arms production has declined every year – 1936, 1937 and now 1938.'

'That's all part of the "never again" malaise,' explained Papa. 'France doesn't *want* to fight. And really, I don't blame her. Especially on the pay they get. A few cents a day – it's appalling. Napoleon used to talk about an army marching on its stomach. They'd march better with full pockets.'

'And the fifth column doesn't help,' said Guy. Everyone nowadays was talking about the fifth column, the term which originated in the Spanish civil war when General Mola boasted that he had four columns outside Madrid – and a fifth one inside the Spanish capital.

'Led by Abetz?' I said.

'He should be shot,' interrupted Grandma, pausing at the door on her way to bed.

'But by whom?' asked Oregon slyly.

'Well, it won't be the army,' said my father.

The feeling of disquiet in those summer months was worse in Douzy than in Paris – because of the gap left once Anna had gone to live in Düsseldorf; the gap and the fear.

'It gives you an awful empty feeling without her around,' sighed Mama. 'I never realised how much you can miss someone you've always taken for granted.' With a worried look she added, 'I do hope she'll be all right. Things seem to be so gloomy in Germany – this talk about guns before butter. Do you think she's getting enough to eat?'

I could sense Mama's apprehension in the sudden, quiet evening moments at Douzy, the times when she looked at nothing, said nothing. I could almost hear her asking herself, Will Anna be safe? Can she ever be happy, an American living in a country like Germany? She had just been reading a report on the way children were being taught to inform against their parents and report them to Nazi bully boys.

'You mustn't brood on it,' I begged her on one of her 'down' days. 'You feel that way about Anna, but I feel that way about Sonia, living under Mussolini.'

'You know what I think,' said Papa, turning later that

evening to Mama. 'You should go for a week to Germany, and . . .'

'Hear, hear!' I interrupted. 'It's an easy journey and Anna wrote that her apartment is ready. Go on, Mama, phone Anna now.'

Well, Mama didn't phone that day – but I could see immediately that she was excited. And two days later in Paris I telephoned Anna from the office.

'Mama's thrilled at the idea of visiting you,' I explained. 'But why don't *you* phone *her* – without having phoned me, if you get my meaning?'

'And you can come another time,' said Anna. 'Split it up so I've got two visits! I miss you, Larry – and – well . . .'

'I will,' I cut her short before she started asking about Sonia. 'Now phone Mama right away.'

Originally Mama had planned to take the train to Düsseldorf, but somehow she gave us all an impression of worry, presumably because there had been several minor strikes on the French railways. She puzzled me, she wasn't the kind of woman to be nervous, yet a few days later she said to Papa, 'Wouldn't it be awful if there was another strike and I was stuck in Germany?'

'But they're not serious, Mama,' I protested. 'They're only one-day token stoppages – and there probably won't be any more anyway.'

'I don't like the idea of the train,' she said. 'Only . . .' The rest of the sentence trailed off.

I'm not quite sure how Mama's alternative suggestion was broached, though I do know that it came from Papa. But did he make his suggestion out of the blue? Or did Mama skilfully lead up to 'his' idea, plant the seeds in him? Or was the whole thing just an accident?

She did say, I remember, 'We'll go to see Anna another time. But,' – to Papa – 'it would be a good idea if I went the week you have to go to Switzerland on business.'

'Hardly business,' he said. 'More of a bore. It's the annual conference of the *Comité International des Vins* in Berne the week after next. Yes, really, a bore, I *must* say, but I'm the champagne chairman this season and I *must* go.'

'Of course you must,' agreed Mama. 'But' – I realise now that Mama knew perfectly well what she wanted, but was determined to let the suggestion come from Papa. And it did. As she said, 'But – I was wondering . . .' Papa said, 'Wait! I have an idea. Why not go by car?'

'By car?'

'Well, my dear, I'll be away for a week – going by train of course, the Swiss never go on strike! Why not take Guy with you? I'm sure he'd like to see Anna. Olivia's in Paris and he's simply moping about – especially after that scene with Mlle Lisette. And you, Larry?' he said, with a look in my direction. 'You'll be working, I suppose? Such a pity.'

'Yes, I will,' I nodded. 'But don't worry. I'm already planning a trip to Germany later for the *Globe*. I don't know how, but I'll make it soon.'

'Well, that's fixed then.' Papa seemed positively proud at solving such a 'difficult' problem, which had never been considered before simply because his thoughts were so concerned with champagne that he never thought of it – until somehow, skilfully, Mama jogged his brain in the right direction.

'And of course,' said Papa as an afterthought, 'you must go in the Hisp. No Citroën for you. Gaston can drive both you and Guy. After all, it's only a hundred and fifty miles.'

'You are clever!' Mama rarely displayed such open excitement. But then, it was her first trip to see Anna since the wedding.

That evening everything was arranged. Papa would be leaving on the Sunday to catch the train to Berne, so I would drive him to Paris the same day, and then collect him at the station on his return. No point in driving first to Paris in the Hisp. and then collecting Mama, as Reims was well on the way to Germany.

We telephoned Anna and started making final plans. The Frankels only had one spare bedroom but Willi arranged for Guy to sleep at the Borse hotel, just round the corner in a quiet street near the Kreugstrasse. In Paris we started filling in forms for the cumbersome bundles of paper required for an international trip by car – the *triptique*, the *carnet*, and international licence for Gaston, another one for Guy. Mama didn't bother.

She could drive – she held both American and French licences – but she hated doing so in traffic.

The visit started off without a hitch – well, almost. I telephoned both Mama and Guy in Düsseldorf to check. According to Guy, Mama found Düsseldorf pleasant, but with reservations. She thought the whole Ruhr area was pretty horrible, said Guy, 'and the noise was bloody. You know I can sleep, even if a hurricane hits Tampa, but the streetcars and buses start hooting at six o'clock. After the first night I swapped places with Mama.'

'How come?'

'Easy. I'm sleeping in the spare room, and I let Mama sleep in the Borse hotel. It's near the apartment and the street's quiet. So it suited everyone.'

'Guy is an angel,' said Mama on the phone the next day. 'I must tell you, Larry, it's a pretty horrible city. But the hotel is clean, and I come round every morning for breakfast before Willi goes to work. And Anna is wonderful.'

'It's a success?'

'It's more. It's a joy to see her again – and, if I'm really honest, the change for both Guy and me won't do either of us any harm.'

She certainly sounded happy.

13

Two events occurred the next morning. The first concerned Sonia and me only; the second had worldwide repercussions.

A letter from Sonia was waiting for me at the office. And, though her letters had always been tender and loving, this one held a note of despair.

'It's not a question of not loving you,' she wrote. 'You know I will always do that whatever happens, but there seems no hope now of planning to break off my engagement. It's always wait and see, wait and see.' She underlined the words savagely; I could visualise her anger when she wrote them down. 'I sometimes wonder if I dare run away, but if I did it would hurt and disgrace so many people. I'm so depressed because I can see no road leading from the present to the future. I am trapped here in Cairo by events which I can't control.'

What did the word 'disgrace' signify?

There was much more in the same vein so that I, too, became afraid. Worse still, anger and frustration were burning me up. It all seemed so pointless. She had only to *insist*. As she said – run away! I would do the rest. If she gave me the word, I would gallop in on the equivalent of my white charger and take her away for ever. And yet I knew in my heart that this was no solution, any more than it would have been easy for Anna to run off and marry Willi.

Sometimes I found myself wishing – oh! how I wished! – that I could find another girl who could wipe out forever the memories that haunted me. But I knew I never would.

The second event was very different, and tragic. That same morning a poor, half demented seventeen-year-old German or Polish Jew shot the third counsellor at the German Embassy in the rue de Lille in Paris, just round the corner from our apartment, and when the man died two days later all hell broke loose in Germany.

It was a tangled story. The youngster, called Herschel Grynsban, was living secretly in Paris with an uncle. Suddenly his German–Jewish parents of Polish extraction were among twelve thousand people deported from Germany to Poland. The trainload of refugees reached the frontier. The heartless Poles refused to accept it. The train set off on the return trip to Germany. It was not allowed in. For days the luckless men and women were shunted from one country to another. Four women on the train died. Herschel's father somehow got a letter to his son and, in a blind fury, the boy walked into the German Embassy and shot the diplomat, a man called Ernst Vom Rath, fatally wounding him.

It was the signal for an anti-Jewish pogrom surpassing in ferocity thus far anything ever witnessed, even in Germany. All Jewish newspapers were ordered to cease publication, cultural associations were dissolved. No Jews were allowed to attend university, all Jewish children were expelled from schools. Then bands of young Nazis, acting simultaneously all over Germany, set fire to synagogues, smashed Jewish shops, stoned Jews in the streets, forced many to crawl in public on their hands and knees. Men, women and children were dragged from their beds, the men taken to concentration camps.

Much of this fearful persecution took place near the area where Anna lived, for the Ruhr was ablaze with hate and vengeance. Papa was frantic; but we were helpless. As the pogrom gathered momentum all telephone communication with Germany was cut. We even thought of driving to Germany to rescue them, but the frontiers were sealed. Finally I asked Washington to try to contact Düsseldorf through the *Globe* bureau in Germany, while Papa begged Bill Bullitt to phone our embassy in Berlin. We did get a message through. No one had been harmed, the Frankel house had not been touched – and Mama would leave as soon as she could.

But that was days ahead, for the pogrom increased. On the radio Dr. Goebbels, the Nazi chief, screamed. 'The justified and understandable indignation of the German people at the cowardly Jewish assassination has been vented in a wide degree.'

In all, fifty thousand Jews were killed or wounded or lost their homes and the right to work. Inevitably the outraged Jewish communities outside Germany reacted violently – while all the time Mama was virtually trapped in Düsseldorf. As the pent-up hatred spilled across Europe we got a message from Bullitt. The U.S. Embassy in Berlin had secured permits for Mama and Guy to leave Germany. They had left that morning.

Almost at the same time, during the afternoon, Mama's voice came through loud and clear to my office.

'We managed to get to Copenhagen,' she said. 'Oh darling, it's been so terrible – and my heart breaks for Anna. I'll tell you everything when I see you.'

'Why Copenhagen?'

'It's the only border that was open – across Schleswig-Holstein – I hope that's how you pronounce it. We're staying at a hotel called the d'Angleterre, it's very beautiful and peaceful. We'll set off tomorrow for home. I've so much to tell you.'

As I was saying goodbye, Tomlinson rushed in crying, 'All hell's broken out on the Right Bank. Thousands of Jewish rioters. Let's go.'

Already on the previous day rioters in Brussels had gathered in the Grand Place, forcing their way into the beautiful fifteenth-century town hall, apparently searching for Germans supposed to be hiding there. A protest meeting in Trafalgar Square had been so jammed with Londoners that traffic was suspended round Nelson's column for four hours. Now, according to Tomlinson, a rampaging mob of thousands had assembled at the Châtelet, with the idea of marching to the French Chambre des Députés and handing in a written protest.

At first it was quiet and controlled, but by the time I raced along the Opéra and reached the area the mob had got out of hand. A few angry youths, a few officious policemen, started a minor scuffle. It spread with the speed of a bush fire. As the *flics* started swinging their murderous blue capes – the hems lined with lead – the first heads were cracked open. Within minutes infuriated men and women were tearing down railings, paving stones, upturning cars and setting them alight. The police brought in more reinforcements.

Clanging bells announced the arrival of the first ambulances – but they took away only injured policemen, leaving the Jewish protesters lying on the pavement, and ignoring frantic appeals for first aid.

It was then that I saw Olivia Jacobsen. The forward section had reached the quai du Louvre on its way to the Concorde, where the Jews planned to cross the bridge. But police arriving from the other end of the Right Bank started laying in to them, even though there was no fighting.

I had parked my car on the opposite bank, near the pont de Carousel – not far from the family apartment in the rue des St. Pères. By the time I saw Olivia police were chasing ahead, leaving the wounded to fend for themselves. Between twenty and thirty stunned and bleeding men and women lay stretched on the broad sidewalks bordering the Tuileries.

I had no time to think of the others. I picked up Olivia. She had what looked like a cut on the left of her forehead or cheek – the slanting, narrow split in the flesh that so often comes from a swipe with a policeman's loaded cape – but as I picked her up she actually smiled and said, 'Are you one of us?'

'You're too heavy,' I joked. 'Here! See if you can make the car, then I'll take you home.'

She was able to walk, dragging her feet, the strap of one shoe wrenched off – which made walking difficult – stockings torn, blood on her white blouse. But I felt that she looked worse than she felt, despite the cut.

When I got her upstairs I gave her a stiff *marc*, then went to the kitchen and returned with a basin of hot water and a cloth.

'This'll help.' I cradled her head on my shoulder and carefully dabbed the bloodied part of her face. Luckily her forehead was only scratched, but there was a nasty cut on the left cheek.

'I'm going to phone for Dr. Malherbe,' I decided. 'It's not a serious cut, but you might need a couple of stitches to make sure there's no scar on that beautiful face of yours.'

'I'll be all right,' she said. 'Sorry for all the bother I've caused you.' Then she almost laughed. 'Do you think I could have another *marc*?'

'And get plastered?'

'I won't, I promise you.'

Waiting for the doctor, I poured out another large measure, and took one for myself.

'But Olivia,' I said, 'you *are* a bit rash, dashing in like that. You could have been killed.'

'Somebody had to do something.'

'I understand. What's happened to those men and women in Germany is terrible. But you're not there, Olivia. A protest in France against the bully boys of Germany is like – swatting a fly.'

'It might stop people doing the same thing here.' She sounded bitter.

'They'll never behave like that in France. You know that. But I'm frightened for you – you're so fierce about it.'

'It has to be done.'

'But was it worth it?'

'My God – of course it was.'

179

'But that poor boy who shot the German – how many deaths has *he* caused?' I asked.

'It's terrible I know, but it's a kind of war.'

'I didn't even know you were in Paris,' I said.

'I came specially. I had to help.'

'But all the same, Olivia, you can't win the war in a day. You must be more – well, patient, even tolerant.'

'Tolerant?' she asked sadly. '*Tolerant* – isn't that just another word for indifference?'

The bell rang. Dr. Malherbe arrived and after a brief examination said firmly that he would give Olivia a local anaesthetic and put in two stitches. He finished quickly, packed his bag and said, 'She'll be all right after a good night's rest.'

'You'd better stay the night here,' I said after the doctor had gone. 'Does it hurt?'

She smiled – she had a very warm smile. 'Not a bit. But what would your mother say?'

'I think she would understand,' I smiled back.

'And,' she hesitated, 'Sonia, if she knew?'

'Ah, Sonia! She would be furious. She does get a bit jealous. Or did.'

'You really love her. I've always known it from the way you treated her when we were all at Douzy. I remember the first time I saw you.'

'You do?'

She nodded. 'Your sports shirt was open at the neck, as though the collar couldn't hold in your vitality, and your tie was knotted loosely, like a multi-coloured silk necklace. I thought' – eyes downcast – 'you were very beautiful. And in love with Sonia.'

'It's in the past tense now. She's engaged to an Italian diplomat with a title. My bet is she'll marry him, and we'll probably never see each other again. If there's another war we'd be enemies. Not like you and Guy.'

'My art teacher!' she murmured slyly. 'If you like to put it that way.'

'What other way is there?' I hesitated.

'It's difficult to explain.' She lay back on the bed. 'I have a kind of warmth for Guy but, you know, Larry, he doesn't

own me. And he's away – and you're away too – and Sonia
doesn't seem to own you either.'

'I love her – even though I had the real brush-off in her last
letter to me.'

'Well then,' she said gently. 'You and I are old friends
blooded in battle. And I read somewhere that violence makes
people passionate. And you can't take a vow of chastity just
because . . .'

'I never did take one.'

'And,' she hesitated and smiled again, 'my cheek doesn't
hurt any more.'

'We shouldn't, Olivia – and yet I do want to.'

'Do then,' she whispered.

'I don't want to hurt Guy.'

'He'll never know, I promise you,' adding almost gravely,
'just this once. To cement a friendship. Nothing more.'

After that there was no question of saying no. Apart from
the fact that I was on the rebound from Sonia, there *is* a curious
link that binds close friends who are the lovers of others.
Where did I read that most married men have an urge to make
love to their wife's sister? And, though I had never thought of
really loving anyone but Sonia, I wasn't a monk wallowing in
self-imposed continence. If I didn't do it as often as most other
men I knew, it was because I couldn't be bothered. But this
was different. It was an excitement adorned with the quality of
friendship. That, and the fact that Mama had telephoned after
leaving Copenhagen that she had reached Brussels, which
meant that she and Guy would be incommunicado until
morning. I know I should have harboured feelings of guilt
about Guy, but I didn't. And it wasn't as though I had made
the first move.

Quite apart from the beauty of Olivia, it was so long since I
had made love to a girl – any girl – that I had almost forgotten
the feeling of aching pleasure that comes when you are inside
the warm, soft, yielding flesh of a woman. For a few moments
I lay beside her in my own old bed, the one I used before I
moved out. My chest was squeezed against her warm full
breasts as if they were cushions, and our pubic hairs scratched
each other as she gently and expertly fondled me between my
legs. The whole of her body was the same creamy white as her

181

beautiful face, and when I started to speak she kissed me quietly.

'No need for words,' she whispered. 'It's as though we're two other people.'

'You mean it doesn't count.' I smiled as I looked at her body.

'It will count – in your memory,' she replied gravely, and stopped stroking me between the legs, fumbling until she found and gripped me.

'Do nothing,' she almost ordered me, but quietly, then rolled on top of me. She gave a secret smile and said, 'This is our way of making love.'

I didn't see how it could be that different, but she was exciting, and there was about this strange encounter an element of risk, of excitement, of once-and-for-all.

With her left arm holding herself away from me, she used her right hand to guide me, gently, just touching the entrance to her with the top of me until I was afraid it would all be over before I started. Then, still on top of me, half sitting, she pushed herself until I was inside her.

'I can't wait' – it was my turn to groan. 'I *can't*, Olivia, I'm sorry but . . .'

'You won't come.' She kissed me. 'Not yet. Can you feel anything?'

Suddenly, as she kissed me again, I felt the inside of her grip me, squeezing me inside her with such force that I could hardly move. Suddenly the grip relaxed. I was gasping – with the sheer pleasure of it, the excitement. It was a feeling I had never experienced.

As I lay there underneath her it came again. I was being gripped tightly, as though the velvet gloves of her soft inside had suddenly been replaced with the equivalent of an iron fist. She was so tight round me, I almost cried out with pleasure or pain. Then she relaxed, then used her muscles again. And again – and again. Starting me, stopping me, prolonging the sweet agony until finally, her lips wet with overkissing, she cried one word, 'Ready?'

I gasped out, 'Yes, yes!'

Almost frantically, she cried, 'Quick, quick!'

★ ★ ★

Later, as we lay in bed, each decorously wearing a dressing gown, each with a large Scotch and Perrier, I know that she shared with me the peculiar, if never to be repeated calm that is almost a sense of relief. It can only come to people who have made love yet who do not really own each other, but rather are long-standing friends like we were, enjoying themselves.

Raising my glass, I toasted her and said, 'Olivia, you are fabulous, truly.'

'I made you happy?'

'Christ! I've never known anything like it in my life. You're a witch – a sorceress. How do you do it? It's as though you've an extra hand inside you.' I laughed again, and said, 'You're out of this world as a lover. How, please?'

She hesitated, but smiling, and I knew she wasn't withholding any secrets. Perhaps, I thought, we just fit. Yet as I watched her, waiting for her to talk to me, I knew it was more than that.

'I know I've got a beautiful white skin,' she began tentatively, 'because everyone tells me so, but you might be surprised to know that though my father is Jewish and French, my Jewish mother – she's dead now – was half Egyptian. A small half by the look of me,' she smiled. 'I was born in Alexandria.'

'You can be a Hottentot for all I care.'

'But I'm explaining,' she laughed, and I felt a sudden quiver of pleasure as her dressing gown fell off one shoulder, uncovering one creamy, full breast.

'I'm sorry.' She saw where I was looking.

'No, don't please – leave it like that. You were explaining.' I poured two more Scotches.

'You'll make me drunk,' she laughed, and said, 'Egyptian Jewish girls are very special. And they have always had the reputation of making wonderful wives. They're' – a little more shyly now – 'supposed to be very beautiful as well.'

'They are – but . . .'

'Beauty is not enough,' she said modestly. 'Our mothers always told us that though women were treated as chattels by Egyptian men, a woman could always triumph over a man if she could keep him faithful. So we were taught.'

'But how? You can't be born like this.'

'We practised,' she said demurely. 'From the moment we started to menstruate.'

I couldn't believe it – or understand it. All I knew at that moment, looking again at that bared breast, was that she had somehow *gripped* me secretly and at will. I had never known a pleasure even remotely like this – a physical pleasure, not a love pleasure, but a pleasure to be enjoyed time and again, one that made me want to scream with the excitement of making it last for ever while at the same time wanting to reach a climax.

'It sounds awful putting it like this,' she explained, 'but girls are taught muscle control in order to please their husbands. Now you're making me feel embarrassed.'

'Go on – please.'

'Give me another drink.' She held out her glass. 'Then I won't be so embarrassed!'

She took a sip, then lay down, opened her dressing gown and stroked me. I began to feel stirrings again and as I touched her between the legs she too showed signs of excitement.

'We shouldn't,' she whispered, 'but this promise of only once does mean that "once" can last all night.' She shivered as I touched her again.

'Tell me, first, the secret,' I said. I wasn't ready yet, only fascinated.

'Put your finger in – go on, inside me,' she whispered.

I did – and immediately felt it gripped by her.

She laughed. 'It's an old method, practised by our mothers and their mothers for ever. I can't remember who told me, but everyone knew that girls were taught to control their muscles – inside. I used to be told how to sit with my legs as wide apart as I could, and exercise. It was hard at first, but in the end my muscles there were so strong I could control them. Now you know.'

And then we made love again. Afterwards, she whispered, 'Don't be angry with me.'

'Angry!' I echoed. 'How could I be?'

'And you don't have to feel' – she was searching for words – 'any sense of . . . obligation, that's the word.'

'I won't, I promise you – so long as you believe that I'm not a very good liar, and I don't want to lie to you, but I do want you to feel – forever – that what happened was a very natural coming together of two people who like each other. Do you understand what I'm trying to say?'

'Perfectly.' And almost sleepily, she said, 'I hope I pleased you, Larry.'

'You know you did. More than I can ever tell you.'

'That is *my* reward. Because you pleased me too. I know you'll always be in love with Sonia, but this doesn't count. I said that and I mean it. We're not in love with each other – I'm not even in love with Guy – but I think making love with an old friend you like is the most wonderful experience on earth. And I've just had that. I just wanted' – shyly again – 'to please you because you are a wonderful person. And in doing so, I pleased myself as well.'

The next morning I drove her to the station. As she jumped into the M.G. I examined the strip of plaster on her left cheek.

'Doesn't hurt too much?'

'I'd forgotten all about it,' she smiled, but even in the smile there was a special intimacy.

I would have driven her to Douzy, but I didn't dare to leave the office untended.

'I *do* work for a living,' I smiled. 'You know I'm not the sort who'd spend the night with you and then put you on the nearest bus to get home by yourself. But . . .'

'That night never happened,' she said gravely.

'But something did,' I said, 'and I think I ought to tell you. We *have* changed, Olivia. No, it's not love – I'm not going to make an idiot of myself. I just want you to know that from now on I shall always think of you not just as Olivia, but as a member of the Douzy family.'

'Thank you for that,' she said simply, 'and I promise you I'll always behave.'

'I know you will.'

'But' – with the faintest touch of a smile – 'it *was* fun, wasn't it?'

14

That was Wednesday morning. The next afternoon Mama and
Guy arrived back at Douzy. On Friday evening I drove home
from Paris, arriving too late for dinner.

'What about Anna?' It was the first question I asked after
Jean poured me a coffee.

'She's fine,' said Guy. 'A bit shaken . . .'

'She's *not* fine!' burst out Mama. 'Nothing happened to any
of us in Düsseldorf, but it was terrible and Anna was in an
awful state.'

'But if nothing happened . . .?'

'It was the knowledge that terrible things were happening
around us. That non-Jewish people' – with a look of apology
to Olivia – 'were unharmed, untouched. But even with censorship, people like Willi *knew* of the terrible things taking
place – literally round the corner. We all knew. One friend of
Willi's who worked with him at Staffens just vanished. Someone went round and found his apartment smashed up.'

'Were you hurt? Molested?'

'Not like Olivia here,' said Guy.

'You're all right now?' I asked her, carefully casual. 'Sorry I
didn't ask before.'

'Fine,' she smiled back, one stranger to another. 'I should be
thanking you for rescuing me and taking me to the train.'

I think all of us were anxious not to talk about Anna –
though that didn't mean we loved her the less, worried any less
about her, wouldn't have been glad had she come back to
Douzy. But casual conversation released the tensions. That
was probably why Mama said, 'Olivia must have been terrified. Knocked about like that.'

'You might have driven her back to Douzy instead of
dumping her at the station,' Guy said jokingly.

'You try working for a living, sonny,' I grinned. 'And
you'll find there isn't always time to drive a girl seventy miles
home.'

'Okay,' said Guy with mock resignation. 'I know I'm just a poor artist. They never work.'

'You're very conscientious,' Olivia defended him – and I felt the faintest twinge of jealousy.

'It's time you got a real job.' Grandma didn't realise that Guy was being sarcastic; she really believed that artists didn't work, just dashed off the occasional picture when inspired.

'When are you taking the stitches out?' I asked Olivia.

'Day after tomorrow.' We both spoke with studied normalcy, as though that eventful Tuesday evening had never taken place, that it was just a dream.

During the morning I took the M.G. to the small working garage behind the stables, for one of the mufflers on the exhaust pipe wasn't working properly and I needed help. 'It smells of burning,' I said to Gaston.

'I'll look underneath.'

'Sure you're not too exhausted after the trip?' I asked.

'Take more than that to tire me,' he grinned, and disappeared under the car, finally shouting, 'You need a complete new exhaust unit. The old one's cracked, burned through. I'll phone Paris to have one delivered to your office, then I'll fit it on your next visit home.'

Gaston had a knack of sliding out from under a car and, when he stood up, wiping his hands on a bit of rag, I said, 'Thanks. Hope you weren't too bored in Germany.'

'Not a bit,' he grinned, showing beautiful teeth. 'It was a change. I prefer our wine but . . .'

'I'm told the German girls are hot stuff!'

'Not for me. Too dumpy.'

'Anyway, thanks.' I walked back into the house, saying to Mama, 'I don't know how we'd manage without Gaston.'

'Why do you say that,' she asked.

I shrugged my shoulders. 'Nothing special – except that he's not only a good mechanic, he's so – well – even-tempered.' Then, changing the subject, I asked, 'What about Anna? We must do something about her.'

'She loves Willi – that's the real – well, I don't like to use the word "problem" about two people who are crazy about each other, but you know what I mean.'

. 'Then there's nothing to be done, *nothing*,' said Papa.

'And what does Willi think?'

'He says it's all madness. He was very upset, especially about the friend of his in the business, but he does believe it'll all pass over.'

'Did you ever suggest – yes, *suggest* but *delicately*, my dear, that Anna might – well – take a vacation in Douzy, perhaps stay here for . . .'

'I did, carefully,' Mama said to Papa. 'Anna was very angry – she said I was trying to break up their marriage. I said it wasn't true, and Willi said Anna was exaggerating. Willi is convinced that all this Hitler business will blow over.'

'Perhaps it will,' I said, lying.

'The trouble is,' Mama was trying to explain her attitude, 'that the *feeling* is so awful. We knew that not far away the Fascists were behaving like beasts, but we never *saw* anything. And when we got lost on the way to a museum, a policeman with a car actually told us to follow him and led us all the way.'

'All in the cause of art,' I laughed to Guy.

'I wasn't there. Probably the policeman took a fancy to Mama sitting behind Gaston in their flashy car.'

'You missing out on art!' I *was* surprised.

'Oh no, I wasn't,' said Guy. 'Anna took me to a staggering modern life class – there's no way you can get in without special permission – she fixed it. Mama wanted to go to the famous Museum of the Ages. It's Düsseldorf's greatest reason for existence.'

Later that evening when Mama and I chanced to be alone, I said teasingly, 'In fact, darling Mama, you seem to thrive on terrifying experiences. I know you must have been very worried about Anna . . .'

'I am.'

'But, well, you look as though the change – however brutal – has done you good.'

'I think it did. It took me out of myself.'

'You look so young – and – the word is "vibrant".'

'It did me good to see Anna. But vibrant? That sounds a wonderful thing to say.' She kissed me gently. 'Mmmm. Vibrant. Yes, I like that.'

'It's wonderful what mother-love can do,' I murmured.

'Would you look so happy if you were seeing me after a few weeks away?'

She *did* look attractive. There was a sparkle to her eyes, and she seemed to walk with a spring in her step.

'I haven't seen you looking so exciting for years,' I said. 'It's a good job you had Guy as a chaperone. We don't want another German in the family.' I was thinking of another day, another time, when she had also looked beautiful and happy beyond the normal.

'Of course,' I cried, 'I remember now. You remind me of that day when we had lunch together at the Pré-Catalan. You remember, I told you then – I'd never seen you look so beautiful, as though you were in love all over again.'

'Silly boy.' She kissed me on the cheek again. But not before I saw that those beautiful soft cheeks of hers were tinted with the faintest of blushes.

So the summer dragged on, a strange mixture of forced gaiety disguising apprehension.

'It's funny how much happier I feel about Germany now that I've actually seen Anna's apartment,' said Mama one evening. 'I can picture her whenever I want to. I'm not half as worried as I was.'

'You've no need to be, really,' said my father. 'I was lunching with Bill Bullitt yesterday and he's convinced that Hitler is bluffing.'

'There's no need to bluff if you're holding a straight flush.' Oregon still enjoyed the occasional game of poker.

'You mean he isn't bluffing?' asked Miss Barron, who had come in for drinks.

'Half and half, I *think* so, yes?' said Papa. 'All these threats about Czechoslovakia. It's a bluff in a way because he senses that France doesn't really want to get into a war. He trades on that – yes, *trades* on it.'

'I won't listen to a son of mine saying the French don't want to fight,' said Grandma angrily. 'They're the finest army in the world. We should thrash the Germans now – declare war immediately.'

'They'd need help,' ventured Jean-Pierre, who had also come in for drinks. 'Would England fight?'

'There's not going to be a war,' said Mama.

'No, Britain wouldn't fight – not at this time,' said Oregon.

'We don't need Britain,' Grandma snorted with finality, as though that problem had been solved, adding with a toss of her head, 'We're better off without them.'

Rashly I ventured, 'I'm not so sure about that,' but as Grandma started to bristle I caught sight of Mama, the trace of a sardonic smile lighting her face as she gave a tiny shake of her head. No use getting involved in an argument. I smiled my agreement back, though I was too late, for Grandma continued firmly, 'You should read more history, my boy – learn from it, learn the lessons of France's greatest leaders. Have you read the new biography on Napoleon?' And without waiting for an answer, continued, almost with relish, 'No! I thought not. Very silly of you. It's called *If Napoleon Lived Now*. That would put the Germans in their place.'

I dearly wanted to blurt out that Napoleon hadn't shown how to put the Russians in their place, so why should his ghost succeed against the German army of today? But I didn't like to disagree so angrily even though most reviews had panned the book.

Even so, I *was* worried about Hitler. I wasn't worried by actual threats – not any more than the average healthy young American could be worried. It was the unreal atmosphere in Paris that summer which left me disturbed, as if the city was determined to dance the night away until the dawn, knowing it would be bad.

There had never been a summer like it. There were an astonishing three million foreigners in Paris, many living there, others visiting. They included fourteen thousand Americans living there, plus all the visitors, bringing with them bulging wallets and insatiable appetites for a good time. To the dismay of French purists, pretty girls on the boulevards, using their own new slang, now said they had had a 'spiffy' evening – especially if their escorts looked 'snazzy'. Love letters from America started reaching France with the letters CYK on the envelope: 'Consider Yourself Kissed.'

The brooding image of Germany was so evident that I found myself hearing slang words borrowed directly from

Hitler. On the dance floor, a man complained, 'Hey there! I can't move. Give us a bit more *lebensraum*.' When I went shopping at the *marché* in the rue de Seine, one American who lived in the neighbourhood warned me, 'Don't like the flavour of those *saucissons* over there. They're a bit ersatz.'

The packed hotels, the rowdy night clubs in turn attracted top entertainers. Maurice Chevalier returned from Hollywood to sing at the Casino de Paris. The negro boxer, Panama Al Brown, won a fight in Paris and promptly doubled his fee by tap-dancing at the Cirque Medrano, the most famous circus in Europe. As if to provide an extra dollop of ice cream for the big spenders, the King and Queen arrived in Paris from London in mid-July. The Hôtel Crillon was decked out in cloth of gold. The fountains at the Rond Point des Champs-Élyseés managed to colour the water, giving the impression that the most beautiful fountains in Europe were spraying gold dust. The visit caused the biggest traffic jam ever known in the capital which went wild with excitement. 'The French love royalty,' said Oregon drily. 'They must be darned mad they cut off all those royal heads and did away with the system.'

It *was* exciting – but it was also make-believe. Until in September the warning bell in the office announced a 'flash' on the Associated Press teleprinter.

The French government had devalued the franc. And that – to politicians, let alone men like Oregon and Tomlinson – meant a political rather than a financial crisis, the one brought on by the other.

True, the Americans thought it great news. Until September 1938 you got twenty-nine francs for your dollar. With devaluation you got thirty-seven. The British now got 178 to the pound sterling instead of 147. It couldn't be bad – for those on holiday.

For the world outside, though, the fall in the franc – which had decreased by over fifty per cent in two years – was the signal everyone had been waiting for: that the mounting tension between Germany and Czechoslovakia had reached bursting point – one in which the French government was deeply involved. Within days France and Germany were poised on the abyss of war.

★   ★   ★

'But how does France come into this?' asked Miss Brewer, who had come with Miss Barron for a quiet supper at Douzy.

'It's simple really,' explained Oregon. 'Czechoslovakia is France's most powerful continental neighbour. The two countries have a mutual defence pact, binding each one to fight if the other's attacked. Now that Hitler is threatening to take over the Sudeten Czechs – and that will eventually mean the entire country – President Beneš of Czechoslovakia is demanding that France stands by its treaty obligations.'

'And the other countries?' asked Mama.

'They're not in it,' said Oregon. 'Britain, for example, doesn't have any defence treaty with the Czechs.'

That evening Tommy Tomlinson phoned that he had been ordered to Germany for a few days. Would I pinch-hit? I arrived on the Monday morning just as he was shoving some carbon paper into his typewriter case.

'I'll bet Daladier's scared,' he grinned, 'to say nothing of that arch creep Georges Bonnet. He might be Foreign Minister but he's the biggest appeaser in the business. And that's saying something.' To me he added, 'Mind the shop. I hear tell that Daladier's going to London to beg, steal or borrow some help, even if it's only words.'

'I don't see Britain offering to fight a war for France,' said Oregon. 'But France might try to get help of another sort. After all, Churchill said the other day that if France and Germany went to war, England would be drawn in.'

Fortunately for Mama's tattered nerves, telephoning to Germany had become normal again, in fact, comparatively easy. Unlike France and Italy, Germany was efficient; the operators rang the numbers you asked for. And Anna didn't seem in the slightest degree worried.

'It's all talk, Mama,' she said. 'The Germans don't want a war, and we're not going to have one. It's tub thumping, that's all. Did I tell you, we're just buying a new Mercedes? An office perk, but I'll be able to drive it.'

But the shouting didn't die down. Instead, the momentum of tension and fear increased, sweeping across all France. Daladier did fly to London, and as a result Chamberlain agreed to fly to Germany and try as an 'honest broker' to persuade

Hitler to moderate his demands. He spent several hours with Hitler at Berchtesgaden, the Führer's mountain retreat, but when the awkward, shambling figure of Chamberlain returned to Heston, then London's airport, it was clear that his mission had failed.

That was the moment when panic set in. Overnight the face of France seemed to change, as though the cheerful mask of those summer months had been ripped off by a mugger. It was not so much the nauseating sight of the rich fleeing Parisians in their expensive motor cars, but the immediate preparations for a war that everyone knew France could never win. It was as though Hitler had told the French via the British government that Germany would not hesitate to fight, knowing that the French *couldn't* fight, whereupon the French – who also knew that Hitler was more powerful – decided to bluff the Germans by preparing to fight.

Overnight almost every fit man in the country under sixty was mobilised – two and half a million of them.

Overnight there wasn't a mechanic, a plumber, a carpenter, to be found in Paris and other big cities. Yet there was no immediate threat of war. It was serious, yes, but the Germans were still talking. Chamberlain decided to make another attempt to save Europe, flying off within the week to see Hitler and try again, leaving a Paris shrouded in hooded street lamps, with piles of sand at every corner as the only defence against incendiary bombs.

The panic even spread to the Americans, for Jim Parks phoned me at Douzy that the State Department was planning to evacuate all fourteen thousand American residents in Paris.

'And if you take my tip,' he said, 'you'll get your folks away before the rush starts.'

'He's right,' said my father when I told him. And turning to Mama, he said with more firmness than he usually displayed, 'My dear, you must go – really, very quickly. For once I am determined, really *determined*.'

'You can be as determined as you like,' retorted Mama cheerfully. 'I'm not going anywhere – not while Anna is in Germany.'

'But you must . . .'

'I won't.' It was one of the few times I saw her eyes glint

with anger at my father. 'And anyway, even if there is a war, it won't be our problem.'

All the same, it sounded ominous. I was horrified the following day when I saw Jim Parks. 'You may be a hero,' he grinned. 'But the State Department doesn't rate your chances of survival in France very high. We've just anchored two American cruisers off Brest.'

'Two *cruisers.*'

'Sure. They're there to take off the U.S. citizens who're anxious to leave.'

The American Embassy, where I had gone to see Parks for a story, looked like the headquarters of a besieged city. Stocks of food, gasoline, with fleets of vehicles, had all been prepared so Americans could reach Brest.

'And then?'

'All U.S. nationals will be given temporary refuge in camps being prepared on the island of Madeira.'

'Always wanted to visit there,' I laughed.

'Now's your chance,' said Jim laconically.

Everyone had forgotten Chamberlain, who had returned from his second – and apparently abortive – visit to Germany. Many Frenchmen were anti-British anyway and derided him, for Chamberlain could hardly be described as *sympathique.* If not downright ugly, he didn't inspire confidence – any more for that matter than Daladier. The British fleet – the world's greatest – was mobilised 'as a precautionary measure' on 27 September, and another wave of fear gripped France, with everyone desperately trying to clutch at any straws.

The straws, however, were just out of reach – until two days later when, with an electric suddenness, a kind of excitement that really did hit you with the force of an electric shock, Daladier announced that he was flying to Munich to see Hitler. The conference had been arranged by the forgotten Chamberlain who would also fly to Germany. Mussolini was arriving by train.

'Well, that's that,' said Oregon to Mama. 'You can relax. Europe's okay – for the time being anyway. The big powers would never risk a full-blooded conference unless they'd fixed everything in advance. It's got the sweet smell of success.'

I didn't realise Oregon was being sarcastic until he added bitterly, 'and the sour stink of a sell-out. That's the end of the Czechs – they haven't been invited. They're being sold down the river.'

Oregon was right. When the conference ended, Chamberlain waved his piece of paper and cried, 'It is peace in our time.' Europe went mad with relief. I was at Le Bourget airport for Daladier's arrival. The long low terminal building, the apron behind, the parking spaces, even the main highway, were jammed solid with rejoicing people. Men wept with joy – or relief. Strangers rushed up and kissed each other – as though they had just won a war, instead of – well, avoiding one. All sense of shame evaporated. 'France has been saved,' someone next to me cried. Later, in the Deux Magots, it was drinks all round on the house. Within hours, President Roosevelt's photo – and a translation of his two messages of encouragement – were printed in tens of thousands, to be pasted on every shop window, every wall.

'I don't care,' cried Mama when she hugged me as I returned to Douzy at the weekend. 'I know I should feel ashamed and sorry for the Czechs, I know I *should*. But I don't feel any shame, darling. I only feel a sense of relief. And, when I think of those awful days in Düsseldorf, and poor Anna, I can't feel anything but gratitude to that Mr. Chamberlain for what he has achieved.'

Europe thought as Mama did. I showed her a copy of *Paris-Soir*. 'They've opened a special fund,' I told her before Papa arrived back from the pyramid.

'For what?' she asked.

'You guess. To help elderly cripples? Or cancer victims? Go on, you guess.'

'I never was any good at riddles.'

'It's a fund,' I spoke slowly, 'being raised by grateful readers of *Paris-Soir* to buy Neville Chamberlain a retirement villa with a trout stream somewhere in France.'

'I would like to send a contribution to the paper' – Mama was almost in tears – 'to say thank you – from Anna and me.'

A week later I received the first letter for weeks from Sonia. Before I tore it open, even while I was looking at the illustration of the pyramids on the Egyptian stamp, I knew the news would be bad.

It was. She had married, and her husband, the Count de Feo, had been posted to Paris as ambassador without portfolio.

15

I was determined on one thing: it was over between Sonia and me. She was married, and in a way I was thankful; it would save me from complications. I had been uncomfortable enough, lying and deceiving, as the lover of a woman engaged to be married to another. And though I knew that many married women had boyfriends, the deceit wasn't for me.

The feeling I had for Sonia was still confused. At bottom, everything was passion. A passion that over-ruled instincts which reason dictated should be kept in check; nothing to do really with marriage. She was not only Russian-wild but jejune on the subject of marriage. She'd never really been anxious to get married to me.

When I told Oregon – before anyone else, as Sonia's letters were always sent to the office – he had a theory of his own.

'Sonia's problem is very simple,' he explained. 'She's never grown up. She's got a childhood fixation, perhaps because her parents meant so little to her. She missed out on a childhood with them. So she's making up for it now.'

'Sounds a bit steep – a bit Freudian.'

'It's true,' he insisted. 'She's not really marrying this de Feo – at least she thinks she isn't. She's playing with her dolls. And all this nonsense you've told me about in the past – the blind obedience to her parents! I'm not denigrating Sonia – I adore her as much as you – but she regards them in the same way as a teenager. They're a symbol of authority – they have to be obeyed without question.'

Was that true? I wondered. She told me once that her ideal marriage would be to the kind of husband who wasn't too demanding. What an awful recipe for happiness! I remember thinking. Had Sonia tried to re-live the past, the happy days at Douzy when Monsieur Coquelicot slid under her blankets at night. Did she still feel like that? After all, I was thinking as I re-read her letter, sometimes first love *can* be best love. But this one had lasted long enough.

And, of course, people change. Does a girl change just because she becomes a wife? How, I wondered, had Sonia changed? After all, *I* had changed; I could view her marriage with some impartiality. Distance, a change of circumstances on her part, an increasing absorption with work on mine.

All the same, I couldn't help feeling sad at the finality of it all. Sonia had written that 'my husband and I' – and that did give me a nasty jolt, seeing it above her dashing, upward slanting signature – 'expect to reach Paris around April.'

She would, she wrote, be allotted the same home her parents had occupied in Paris, one which I had visited several times. It was in the rue de Longchamps, almost at the corner by the river, a long low house with a beautiful garden completely ringed by trees which effectively screened it from neighbours, making it a perfect setting for garden lunches or cocktail parties – and since the house was owned and staffed by the Italian Embassy, the food and drink were as good as any in Paris.

I couldn't help a wry smile and I told Oregon in the P.A. office where the new Contessa de Feo was going to live.

'Hope the food's as good,' I said.

'Under the same management, it should be. But you keep away,' he grunted.

'But if I get invited – in the cause of duty?'

Oregon hesitated, looked at me, his grey hair like a curly wig round his bald pate, his lapels covered as usual with a trail of ash, a man who had steered me steadfastly on the road to journalism.

'I hope not,' he said, deliberately pausing to light a second Gauloises with the butt of the first. 'No, no! Don't get mad. She's a great girl – and when I think of what you two have been up to for all these years, I'm jealous as hell of my wasted youth. Lucky dog! But you're no longer a carefree youth, you're moving forward, you're on the way to big things. And she's bad news for you.'

'I can take care of myself,' I said shortly, not sure whether to be annoyed.

'That's just the problem. Where Sonia's concerned, you can't – and even worse, *she* can't. You attract each other like iron filings in front of a magnet.'

'Well, this time it'll be different.'

'Hope so. Care to bet?'

'Ten bucks?'

'Make it fifty.' And more seriously, Oregon added, 'Watch it, Larry. And remember you'll be a neutral when – not "if" any more – when the war comes. And being American you'll have a head start as a neutral newspaperman in Europe, specially on the *Globe*. Don't spoil it. You're going right to the top of the heap.'

Mama gave me a similar comment when at the weekend she learned that Sonia and her husband were coming to Paris to live. It wasn't really a warning so much as a sigh of relief.

'I know you used to love her, Larry. Probably you still carry a torch for her.' She was arranging a mass of roses in her favourite blue and white Chinese bowl. 'So I'm glad for your sake that Sonia's married. So much more final.'

I almost laughed. 'It *is* final,' I promised her. 'Though not for that reason, but because I want it that way. Being married has nothing to do with still being in love, has it? Lots of married women have boyfriends. Why shouldn't Sonia?'

'You *are* a romantic. Pass me the secateurs, please.'

'So are you.' I handed them to her. 'And sometimes, Mama, I wonder about you. I've seen a sparkle in *your* eyes that makes me think twice.'

'At my age! Don't make me laugh. You ought to be ashamed of yourself.' But all the same I could see that the notion pleased her.

'For telling the truth?' I asked.

'For making up romantic nonsense.'

'Well,' I grew suddenly serious. 'Tell me, Mama – you and I, we've never had any secrets – dare I ask you?'

'No, you daren't.' She was suddenly sharp-tongued.

'Sorry,' I apologised.

'That's all right.' She put down the vase and abruptly left the room.

The early part of 1939, before Sonia's arrival, followed the same political pattern of the previous months – euphoria born of relief, all shame ignored, hidden like dirt brushed guiltily under the carpet.

There was even a new vacation idea to rival the normal skiing or winter sunshine holidays of winter. A French travel agent was advertising a regular five-day all-included '*Voyage de la Paix*' – from Paris to Germany, with stop-overs at Munich, Nuremberg, Bad Godesberg and Berchtesgaden. It was organised by the *Compagnie Française de Tourisme*, and it was a sell-out.

'Nice choice of words,' said Oregon drily when I told him.

But long before that, of course, the Germans had marched into the Sudetenland in a deal that spared the rest of Europe – but not poor Czechoslovakia – the agony of war.

I had no news from Sonia, and though we all wrote to her and her husband – polite letters of congratulation – I deliberately made no enquiries about the proposed date of her arrival. Apart from anything else, I was kept busier than ever before. There were political stories to be covered when Tommy was busy or away, as when he accompanied Daladier on a flag-waving visit to Algeria, Tunis and Corsica – a ploy to offset Mussolini's demands. When he returned, he asked me if I would like to visit the tattered remnants of five hundred Americans who had volunteered to fight in the Spanish civil war and who had suffered terribly during the closing stages.

The civil war was all but over, a towering defeat for those who had fought against Franco. Hundreds of thousands of refugees had fled across the frontier and were living in hastily erected camps near Perpignan. Conditions were appalling. Guarded by Senegalese, they were virtually without food. The lucky ones had a single blanket and slept on the ground. The vanquished who had fought against tyranny were dying every day, even as the foreign powers duly recognised the Franco régime.

My brief was to search out the remnants of the Fifteenth

International Brigade and write a story of the survivors. There weren't many left to interview. Out of about five hundred under the command of their American leader, Robert Hale Merriman, four hundred were either killed or missing. The picture of those bedraggled yet heroic men haunted me, and one night when I dreamed of the faces I had seen, I somehow mixed them up with Anna's.

Mama had been to Düsseldorf, for a second trip to see Anna, soon after the turn of the year. There had been no violence, no anti-Jewish pogroms on this occasion but, even so, when Mama returned home, she was very depressed. She had invited Willi and Anna to come to France for a holiday, but apparently everyone in Germany now faced difficulties in getting exit permits.

'I just have the awful feeling,' Mama told us, 'that they're prisoners – a jail without bars. After all, you should be free to go abroad if you want, but when the German government won't let you leave the country without signing dozens of forms, it's the same thing as prison.'

'But why? I really don't see the *reason*,' said Papa.

'The Germans say it's because they won't allow anyone any foreign exchange. The Deutschemark is in a terrible state.'

'But that's nonsense,' said my father. 'If we pay for their holiday it's no drain on the wretched Germans.'

'Exactly.' Mama sounded very weary. 'It's really because the Germans don't want their citizens – especially well-off ones – to see what a much better life they would have if they were allowed to go shopping in Paris or New York.'

I only hoped Anna would be allowed to, for Hitler was tightening his grip. The original sell-out at Munich had – by arrangement with the big powers – given autonomy to the Sudeteners, but in March Hitler flouted his earlier promises and marched straight into Czechoslovakia.

The French President and Mme Lebrun were on a state visit to London at the time. The glittering scenes, with Mme Lebrun dressed magnificently by Worth, the Paris couturier, and the Queen, in her tiara, were shown on newsreels in the French cinema – together with film of the German entry into Prague.

Probably the irony passed un-noticed, for to many French men and women Czechoslovakia was an unknown country, a hybrid one, and if anyone had ever heard of the Czechs it was as exporters of cheap gloves, boots and Czech glass. As for fighting for this unknown country – to the average Frenchman the idea seemed senseless.

All the same, Daladier was immediately granted wider powers in the Assembly to speed rearmament, and the man who had to find the necessary cash was Paul Reynaud who had been raised from his post in Justice to become Minister of Finance – a big step up the ladder.

'Not that *anything* makes any sense any more,' Papa sighed. 'No, *really*! Whatever happens, everyone is going to lose, yes, *lose*.'

'Specially here!' Oregon had come, as he often did, for the weekend, and I was spending the morning with them in the white and mysterious Douzy pyramid – still, even after all these years, invested for me with an eeriness when I looked up to the tiny hole far above, and imagined how, centuries ago, the Romans had started digging for chalk.

Spring was a critical time for Papa, for last year's 1938 champagne crop had been allowed to reach the high point of the first fermentation – for the first of the two fermentations that would eventually make champagne sparkle and pure. For at this time – spring – it was not a sparkling but a still wine. It had yet to be blended. Papa, with his flair for blending different wines, was quite at home with all the paraphernalia needed to mix different champagne wines from different localities. Even the grapes grown half a mile from the next vineyard had a different taste, and the skill of producing the best champagne in the world lay in mixing all the different wines together, through tasting and selection, to get a balance that suited Papa. He was the final arbiter.

'Taste this,' he said, 'and tell me what you think.'

Papa knew that my knowledge of champagne was negligible, but he liked to feel that this was a family concern, even though I was writing and Guy was painting.

'Actually, it *does* taste good.' I took a sip from another vineyard. 'We don't need to use any old wines from previous years, do we?'

Papa shook his head, delighted. If a crop from any particular year, like this one from 1938, hadn't been quite up to standard, Papa would have mixed in champagne from previous years, all stored deep down in the cellars; but once you added years to a new batch the champagne couldn't legally be classed as 'vintage'.

'But this one, I hope, *will* be vintage,' he said, beaming. 'We can mix enough of the '38 crop without adding any other years – and that will make a good wine.'

It wasn't champagne yet, of course. Papa had to add a small quantity of cane sugar and fermenting agents, then put it in bottles, resting in cool, deep cellars while the fermenting agents reacted slowly on the sugar, causing the 'head'. And even then, after months, the bottles had to be skilfully opened to get rid of the deposit – and closed before the bubbles escaped.

'But that's a helluva way off,' sighed Oregon. 'And I wonder if there'll be anyone to drink it by then – or come down to this pyramid. It's sad – a sort of second home to the Astells.'

'I wonder.' Papa washed his hands under the running cold tap. 'We've just started to get over the Russian Revolution and Prohibition and – and now? Just when the British market was starting to pick up too. It *really* is very discouraging.'

'Well, there's not going to be any champagne in England if war comes,' I said.

'You're sure right,' said Oregon. 'Seems a long time since that fat old womaniser Henry the Eighth used to keep a special envoy at Ay, barely ten miles up the road there, all year round, just to buy wines for him. Even though they didn't sparkle in those days.'

That spring the de Feos arrived to take up their post in Paris, and almost before they had settled in at the rue de Longchamps Sonia telephoned Mama. Mama, not me – as though Sonia, like me, was unwilling to reopen self-inflicted wounds.

I could also tell from Mama's replies, the excitement in her voice, what was happening.

'How wonderful for you, Sonia. Yes, I'm sure we'd love to come. Your *first* party as a diplomat's wife.' Pause. 'Sonia

darling, we didn't send a present, it was all so sudden.' Pause.
'It's just a party to meet your husband and his friends? Oh yes,
of course, your friends too.' Pause. 'Two weeks on Thursday?
Of course. If there is anything else, we'll cancel.' Laughs. 'And
your husband – it's terrible of me not to remember his name.'
Pause. 'Of course, Francesco, so beautiful. Yes, Larry is doing
very well – of course he'll want to come.' Pause. 'No, Sonia, I
can't say I'm really happy about poor Anna. I went to see her
just after Christmas. But the world's in such a state, who
knows *what's* going to happen.' Pause. 'Yes, they adore each
other but sometimes I get depressed about her future.' Pause.
'Yes, I've noted the date, all very informal, but as soon as you
can, you and your husband must come to Douzy for the
weekend.'

'That was Sonia.' Mama finally put down the phone.

'I rather gathered that,' I replied shortly, to mark my
disapproval – no, my irritation – that she hadn't even asked
to say hello to me. After all, she was my girl, not Mama's. Or,
I suppose, had been.

Mama looked at me a little oddly. She could always detect
any nuances in my voice. However, she decided to say nothing, except to add, a little too brightly, 'Sonia's giving an
informal party for her friends – and Francesco's. We're all
invited. I sometimes can't believe she's married, a countess,
the wife of an ambassador. And still only twenty-five.'

'At least she's not a mother yet,' I replied.

'You'll come, won't you?'

'I might,' I said airily. 'Depends on my engagements.' I
knew I would, of course, if only out of curiosity.

I had forgotten how beautiful the garden looked behind the rue
de Longchamps. It didn't depend on masses of blooms
arranged in symmetrical flower beds cut up into crescents or
circles. It had always been more of a wild garden, with a mass
of green trees forming a semicircular backdrop. Instead of
beds the flowers had been arranged in ochre pots, Italian
style – hundreds of them, some grouped round the trees,
others clustered round the steps leading from the terrace which
I had last visited to meet Sonia's parents when they lived there.
It seemed odd that though Riccardi had never owned this

embassy house his wife had been the mistress there, and now, Sonia was the mistress of the same house.

There was no protocol on this occasion, but there was a casual, cheerful 'line' so that as the guests arrived – some known to Sonia, others only to her husband – people queued up near the doors to the main *salon*, to shake hands or touch cheeks with perfunctory kisses, and offer their congratulations, before passing on to diplomatic flunkeys bearing salvers laden with drinks.

We entered as a group. Until she saw us she wore a slightly fixed smile of welcome, the sort duplicated in a thousand embassies the world over. But then Mama and Papa came just ahead of us, and Sonia's face broke into the old, warm, all-embracing smile and her entire face seemed to change.

'Mama! I can call you that?' She laughed and kissed them both. 'It's wonderful to see you,' and with a whispered aside, 'As soon as I've met the last of Francesco's friends, I'll come and look for you. I can't get used, really, to this formality.'

Then to her husband, 'Francesco, this is Mummy's great friend, Mrs. Astell my godmother, and her husband. They almost brought me up.'

He seemed a very pleasant man – tall, brown hair, good face, chiselled with a straight Italian nose, and he immediately grasped Mama's hand and said, 'I feel I've known you all my life. I've heard so much about all your family.'

'And this is Larry, and this is Guy Astell.' She looked at us both, kissed us on the cheeks and suddenly I found my heart pounding.

She looked more beautiful than I could ever remember her. Absence lending an added enchantment? No, it wasn't that. Her blue-black hair was done in a different way, more formal, not the sort of hair she used to shake out when she wanted to kiss me suddenly and it was falling over her eyes: the hair-do of a woman rather than a girl. That was it – she looked more grown up. Lips painted a different colour, nail varnish to match. Now, married to another, Sonia had reached the ultimate moment of peerless beauty. The schoolgirl who had fallen in love with Monsieur Coquelicot had been replaced by a person who exceeded even the promise of the past.

She looked at me, magically silent – yes, even though she

was talking, making introductions, small talk, she was still silent within herself. I knew she was occupied with thoughts of us, as though telling me in secret, 'Life has thrust us apart, but I was yours before anyone else possessed me, and I gave you everything I had to make you happy.'

For a moment I wondered if her husband could hear my thumping heart. I shook hands and Francesco muttered some polite greeting; and I wondered, too, whether Sonia's father had ever said anything to him about us. But of course no one was even remotely noticing my heartbeats and, as for Sonia's husband, he had the true trained diplomat's face. Not by the slightest gesture, hesitation or sudden emotion did he deviate from the automatic gestures of a warm greeting to old family friends of his wife's. 'You have to be trained to look like that,' I thought. A diplomat's disguise – it covers any emotion from jealousy to boredom.

As at most parties, Papa and Mama knew a fair sprinkling of the other guests, and so did I for that matter, but as soon as she could Sonia came across to us and hugged Mama again.

'Tell me first,' she said. 'How's Anna? You must miss her dreadfully.'

'I'm worried about her,' sighed Mama and, after Papa had made some non-committal remark and Guy had met an old friend who was also studying art, Sonia said, 'And you, Larry? I heard from someone that you're now the top man on the *Globe*.'

'Hardly. That must be Oregon talking – he always thinks in the future.'

'But work goes well? Still' – the slightest hesitation – 'still happy?'

I would have given the world to think up a brilliant retort off the cuff. But I could only say, 'Sure. And you?'

'As well as can be expected.'

A gushing middle-aged lady rushed up to her and kissed Sonia on both cheeks profusely, and wouldn't stop talking. As others moved around her, I realised how beautifully dressed she was. She had always been well dressed, but, I used to say in those days, she looked like a rich playgirl slumming on the Left Bank. She had dressed then with the simplicity of youth. Now she had an added sheen of beauty. She wore a pale blue silk crêpe outfit almost severe in its line, looking at first like a dress, but which was in fact a two-piece affair, with tiny self-buttons at her waist and wrists.

Mama, I realised suddenly, was watching me with an amused smile. 'That dress is a *marvel*,' she whispered to me. 'It'd make even a fat woman slim. But then it's a Mainbocher.'

'How can you tell, Mama?'

'To be frank, I'm surprised. I thought that as the wife of an Italian diplomat Sonia might *have* to wear clothes made in Italy. But it's by "Main" all right. I can tell his work anywhere. His flair sticks out, as though he's sewn his trademark all over the outside of the dress.'

The garden was soon crowded, and I was busy being civil to people I had never met before. It was so strange seeing Sonia again, so different yet the same, name different, status changed, an ex-schoolgirl now a diplomat's wife, married to an apparently agreeable husband.

Mama looked relieved that I had accepted the situation so cheerfully. I never quite knew what Mama felt – what son does? – but I had the feeling that the romantic streak in her imagined me starting a fight with Sonia's husband. Of course it was nonsense. Papa was much more down-to-earth. Probably he had long since forgotten our youthful indiscretion and presumed that I felt the same way. Only Oregon, with that conspiratorial twinkle behind the fringe of white hair, knew how I felt – or might feel.

It was strange for me though, because, despite the promises I had made to myself, the words of banality which she offered seemed unreal: 'Have another drink', 'Do try this caviar', 'I'd like you to meet Mr. and Mrs. Johnson', 'Yes, the trees are beautiful at this time of the year.'

I seemed to be aware of other drinks, other food, other people, trees, times, whatever she said to me. She didn't *do* anything. She laughed and joked and spoke the jargon of the day. She smiled politely to everyone – what she had once described to me as, 'Putting on my standard party smile'. She continued to introduce me to other guests but, though the movements of her eyes, her hands even, the way she spoke, smiled even, were totally normal, there was an almost imperceptible secret movement to every action. I knew that very first evening of the party that she was thinking as I thought: that though Europe might be poised on the brink of war, we faced an equally dangerous future: we were again poised on the brink of love.

When later, back home, I tossed and turned through a night when sleep eluded me, I tried to recall in my mind the series of secret signals she had emitted, yet which no other person in the garden could see, extra-sensory signals, like the unheard noises of some birds who can communicate with each other by sounds humans can't ever hear. We were like that.

I was thinking of the past, too, all gone, remembering for no reason half-forgotten moments which had made up our joint lives: the night I hurt my hand, the giggles and laughter when she tried to tie my bow for my dinner jacket. We had been going to someone else's diplomatic party that evening. Or the way we passed the later evenings, circumspectly, after she had become engaged to de Feo, planned excursions to our favourite hidden restaurant.

Lying there on my back, unable to sleep, the latest Steinbeck *The Grapes of Wrath* unread, turning over the imaginary pages of another book, my own life story, some of which I had re-read many times and yet, as I lay there, I was hesitating, almost afraid to turn the page over and start a new chapter.

Of course the thought that we could meet as 'friends' and cheerfully relegate all the memories of our past to semi-oblivion was doomed from the start. I fought against it, I even quarrelled in an attempt to prevent a return to the past. I really tried. I know Sonia did too, but she had more of a volatile temperament than I. She was apt to become 'Russian' at a moment's notice, as she did the time when we met during the Harvard Glee Club ball some weeks later.

Bill Bullitt had organised the ball to honour the visit of the Harvard Glee Club, and he had spared no expense. 'Everyone' was invited, including the Astell family *en masse*. There were two bands playing in turn in the main embassy ballroom, and in the immaculate gardens behind the avenue Gabriel two huge marquees had been erected, one as an intimate night club with Django Reinhardt, then the rage of Paris, the other as an outdoor-indoor running buffet where all the guests could help themselves whenever they felt hungry, with the promise that at 5 a.m. eggs and bacon would be served.

I can't say that as a rule I enjoyed this sort of shindig, but Mama did, and I danced the latest hit 'Begin the Beguine' with her and several other friends of the family, and it was almost by accident that I partnered Sonia. I hadn't gone out of my way to ignore her, we had just been at opposite ends of the rooms or even in different rooms until we met face to face.

'Come and dance,' I asked her, perhaps because she looked more breathtakingly beautiful than I had ever realised. She was dressed in pink, and even I could see that the chiffon skirt contained yards and yards of material, giving it a fairylike fullness. Her shoulders were bare except for two straps holding up the pink top encrusted in diamanté.

'You look ravishing,' I muttered.

I remember that I had some old-fashioned notion about married women; oddly enough, the prospect of going to bed with someone *else's* pretty wife just for the fun of it didn't really worry me – and there was plenty of temptation in the shape of bored wives during that last-fling summer of '39. Immoral it might have been, but that sort of adventure was to me unimportant compared with deliberately re-opening an affair with Sonia, recently married and closer in the past than she had ever been with her husband.

That was different. That, I felt in some silly way, was being dishonourable. I would never make any 'advances' to her. Nor was Sonia guilty of tempting me. For weeks we had met at parties, even a weekend or two at Douzy with her husband. Everything was very correct, though when we touched by chance, brushed against each other getting into a car or whatever the circumstances, I could sometimes feel her hand tremble, and I could tell by the way in which she touched the corners of her dry lips with the tip of her tongue that she was finding it difficult to control her emotions.

We danced round the room to the soft, lilting music of another new hit in Paris, 'South of the Border', until suddenly she held me slightly in front of her, away from me so that she could look at me straight in the eyes. Her face was almost desperate.

'I wish to God I'd never come back to Paris,' she said almost savagely. 'It's asking too much, here together like this . . .'

My voice was just as urgent as hers. 'I know, Sonia, I know – but come into the marquee. Only – never say you're sorry we've met again. Never say that.'

'Why not? What the hell good is it standing in front of each other like this? It's worse than being apart.'

We walked across the lawn and into the striped supper tent. Violins from Monseigneur, the Russian night club off the Champs-Élysées, had been engaged for the night, and they were playing a Russian folk song.

'Not that,' said Sonia again angrily.

It was a haunting, sad little Russian tune called 'Kalitka' – 'The Gate' in English, she had told me once – and the corny violins throbbed with love and temptation, and sadness.

'They *would* play bloody Russian music,' she went on. 'It makes me want to cry. Get me something to eat, will you?'

'What?' I began.

'Anything! Hell, I'm not going to *eat* anything. I only want to get my bearings.'

I walked over to the table along one side of the tent. It held a vast selection of cold meats. I put a little pressed duck and some foie gras on her plate; and some Waldorf salad, then the same for me. A butler brought some glasses and a bottle of champagne which he stood on a small table by our side.

'It's not even Astell,' she said curtly.

'Don't be cross, darling,' I said. 'We'll work something out. But you know – you *are* a married lady now. And we agreed . . .'

'I don't give a damn what anyone agreed, married or not. We've always loved each other. It's hypocrisy for you to sit here looking like a stuffed dummy.'

'Thanks,' I said.

'Well, dammit,' she cried, almost stamping her foot. 'If politicians can break agreements between countries, so can ordinary people like us. I hoped – I really did – that this would all be over when we got married. I hoped I'd never come back to Paris. But we're here. And I can't *help* myself. I *can't*, Larry.'

Only a few guests had started to eat, so for a few moments we talked without interruption.

'You talk like that,' I said. 'But what about Francesco? He's no fool. What about him?'

'Never mind him.'

'But you must – we must. Damnit, for all I know he's just outside the tent waiting for you. You're *married* to him now.'

'Marriage is one thing – and love – let's meet alone, soon.'

'That was fine when we were both much younger – but no longer. And after all' – I was beginning to get annoyed myself – 'you say it doesn't matter, but I *did* ask you to marry me. I even asked your father's permission. But *you* jilted *me*. And in my book that's a bloody good reason not to get entangled again – however much I love you.'

The violins were raking out the ashes of another sentimental love song, sweeping the haunting music past us like a warm wind. 'You've forgotten – I *wanted* marriage. Remember?' I asked.

Perhaps I shouldn't have added that last question, 'Remember?' It made her furious.

'Are you saying "no" to me? Are you?'

I shook my head miserably. 'No – but can't you see that I'll always love you, Sonia – always? And it's that which makes me hesitate. Love.'

'Are you?' Her voice was suddenly very quiet with anger. 'Are you saying "no" to me?'

'Let's see what happens, darling. Please! In good time, you know I will always love you – but, now?'

'I'm bloody well offering you myself – my body, my soul if I've got one,' she almost hissed. 'And you – you stuck up sanctimonious prig – yes, that's what you are. A prig. Perhaps this will cool you off.'

I didn't have time to deny the charge – or agree with it, for I realised she was right. I was a fool – and a prig. But at that moment, she whispered savagely, 'I don't want to make a scene so I won't throw the glass of champagne in your face. Instead' – and without another word she leaned across me, by the side of the small circular table, and poured the entire glass of bubbling liquid down the front of my trousers. With that, nobody noticing, she walked out of the marquee, head high, while I made my way to the washroom to explain a perfectly normal occurrence – that someone had bumped into me.

The Glee Club ball didn't end until 6 a.m. on the Friday morning and I think she must have left early, for I didn't see her again. I stayed on in spite of everything and didn't reach the office in the rue du Sentier until midday. I always had a weekly Friday conference with Oregon before he put the paper to bed.

What I liked about Oregon was that he could read my face like a book. 'Girl trouble?' he beamed knowingly, looking even pinker in the face than usual, almost cherubic – except that cherubs don't chain-smoke.

'Don't worry,' he lit up another Gauloises, 'where women are concerned, the motto is – masterly inaction. Always let *them* come round after a tiff. Never be the first to give in.'

'This one won't,' I muttered.

'Then I wonder why she asked for you on the phone about ten minutes ago?' he said drily.

Ten minutes later Sonia phoned again. 'Oh darling Monsieur Coquelicot' – it was years since she had used that word, the password that was supposed to heal all quarrels. 'No, no, darling Larry, I'm a beast, I hate myself, but you promised that whenever I needed help and called you that, you'd come to me. I need help now, Larry. I've only got a moment. I'm phoning from a call box.'

'Outside – not in your home?'

'No. All our phones in the house go through a central bit of machinery – oh, I don't know what you call it – a switchboard – but the Fascisti have their own men in the rue de Longchamps. Two live in my house. I just want to talk to you – to try to explain one or two things – and oh Larry, to tell you how much I love you. Can we have lunch in our old restaurant – on Monday perhaps, Marcel's in the rue Jacob?'

She must have sensed my hesitation because she added, 'I'll never ask you another favour, Larry. But *please* – if you want to make me happy, if you really love me.'

'All right,' I said. 'Anything you ever want – you know that.'

'I won't be able to phone back. And I don't think it would be very sensible for you to phone me at home.'

I agreed. 'One o'clock on Monday at Marcel's.'

★   ★   ★

On the Sunday morning I went for a long walk with Papa through the vineyards to the other side of the Rilly, past the neat little station with its old-fashioned instructions, and at the far end the yawning hole where the single-track line disappeared into the mouth of the tunnel.

The vineyards were looking at their most beautiful in July. They always did because of an added bonus. The flowering in the vineyards usually coincided with the flowering of the summer lilies that decorated hundreds of small gardens.

Papa examined some of the tiny vineyard flowers, and said in his sing-song accent, 'Well, I only hope we'll all be here for the *vendange*.'

By tradition the grapes were always picked a hundred days after the flowers, which lasted about a week, had died. There were exceptions, of course – sudden hailstorms or other acts of God or the devil – but we had stuck to that timetable in Champagne for longer than any of us could remember, and it usually seemed to work.

Rilly produced a very good still red wine – not as good as ours, we liked to believe, but still very drinkable and, after all, even though it wasn't sparkling and came in ordinary-looking bottles, it was still champagne.

'Yes, *very* drinkable.' Papa looked at his watch to time Gaston's arrival, allowing him time for a drink. 'Yes, *very*. I left the ball at the embassy early on Friday night – well, *really*, Saturday morning. What time did you leave?'

'Six a.m.' I grinned.

'Disgusting. How can you young people do it? Did – er – Sonia stay that long?'

A sudden sixth sense flashed out 'Warning, Warning, Warning;' as though a red light had signalled 'Take Care!' – that this was no innocent remark.

'No idea.' I was cheerfully able to tell the truth. 'I saw her in the supper tent about midnight, then I didn't run across her again.'

'I see.'

'Why? Anything the matter?'

'No, No. But I have a feeling, Larry – nothing to do with your past – er, escapades, yes I think *that's* the word – that we shouldn't see too much of the de Feos.'

'Why on earth not?' My mouth must have fallen open with astonishment.

'Well, it's not serious, but still . . .' he hesitated.

'But it *must* be serious – our oldest friends on a blacklist.'

'I say – *really*. That's a most unfortunate word to use. No, I don't like *that* word.'

'I didn't mean to use it. But what are you saying?'

'It's extraordinary, and probably it means nothing. But two things happened during the ball. Colonel Malcom, one of the military attachés at the embassy, told me that de Feo is very closely linked with Abetz, and is running an espionage network from de Feo's house.'

'I can't believe it,' I cried, but all the same, my mind racing, I was thinking of Sonia's warning, that her telephone was being monitored.

'I'm sure it's all exaggeration,' said Papa, 'but you know the Italians are becoming more bellicose in their demands against France. And there's something else. Reynaud told me that your old friend Abetz is being told to go.'

'Abetz!' I whistled with surprise. 'Leave for where?'

'Apparently the French have finally agreed to expel him from France for his pro-Nazi activities. I can't say I'm sorry.'

'That's the best news of the day.' I drained my glass as I saw the Hisp. coming round the corner from Rilly's main street.

'I thought you'd like it. But our embassy believes that any – er – abnormal tasks that used to be performed by Abetz will be taken over by de Feo.'

'But what tasks?'

'Well, someone will have to keep a secret radio transmitter open from France to Germany, and I'm told that it's going to be located in the rue de Longchamps.'

'And you think Sonia . . .'

'Of course not,' he retorted sharply, and with an irony he failed to perceive, 'Sonia's one of *us*.'

'Was,' I said.

'Better that way,' he agreed. 'Just for the sake of peace and quiet. I don't mean that we can't meet as a family whenever we want to. Of course we can – but – well. Don't start getting caught in any – I hate to use the word – but any compromising situations. Remember you are a newspaperman as well as an Astell.'

As Gaston drove us back to Douzy, I didn't think it was quite the moment to tell Papa that I was lunching with Sonia the following day.

That Sunday evening, at dinner, just as we had started the consommé, Jean leaned over my shoulder and whispered, '*Pardon, m'sieu*, there's a trunk call for you.'

Mama was used to my telephone interruptions by now. 'He's a newspaperman,' she would explain with a certain pride. 'He lives on the end of a phone.'

I hadn't the slightest idea who could be phoning me, especially as I knew that Tommy Tomlinson was in Paris. A disembowelled French voice said faintly, 'Please wait to receive a call from Lausanne.'

Switzerland? Who on earth could be phoning me from Lausanne?

'Who is it?' I asked.

'*C'est la gare à Lausanne, m'sieu. Attendez un instant, s'il vous plaît.*'

Impatiently I waited, racking my brains. It suddenly occurred to me that it might be Willi, perhaps on business and taking the opportunity to telephone freely from Switzerland – something that we had long since realised was impossible during the guarded telephone calls between Düsseldorf and Paris.

But it wasn't Willi.

'Larry! Can you hear me? It's me!'

'Me?'

'Anna, you ass.'

'In Lausanne?' I heard her laugh. She must have caught, even over the distance, the sense of improbability in my voice.

'Where's Willi? What on earth are you doing in Switzerland?'

'Willi's in Germany. Listen, Larry – I've only got a few minutes.'

'Fire away, I've got a pencil ready. What's the phone number of your hotel?' By now I always had a pencil, and I always asked for a phone number before anything else.

'I'm not at a hotel' – I *thought* I heard a catch in her voice – 'I'm calling from the station. I'm catching the night sleeper to Paris just before ten o'clock. I'll be in the gare de Lyon soon after noon tomorrow. Do you think you could meet me in Paris? Your darling sister – before – well, the others.'

'Of course. Anything wrong? You and Willi?'

'You *are* an ass. It's not Willi. He's the most wonderful husband in the world. But Germany – I'll tell you all about it.'

'Sounds great. *A bientôt!*'

'*A demain.*'

I went back to the dining room in a state of suppressed excitement.

'What is it?' asked Mama, suddenly worried. 'You look as though you've seen a ghost.'

'I have – in a way.' I hesitated; the news seemed too momentous to blurt out quickly. Then I drew a deep breath.

'Anna's coming back,' I said.

16

We seemed to stay up half the night talking about Anna's arrival, though I was careful to point out that Anna hadn't said she was returning to *live* in Douzy.

But the business of going to Switzerland, telephoning from a station, was intriguing. Anna would normally use an hotel phone even if she wasn't staying in the place. But a public call box in a railway station! It was quite out of character and, besides, the direct railway trip from Düsseldorf to Paris was much quicker.

The electric effect of the news was spiced by the unknown dangers of the future, for this was the summer of 1939 – early July, a time split by tension. Even the warmth of that last summer of peace could never dispel the chill winds of fear.

'I must admit,' said Mama, 'that I hope in my heart Anna

will stay a while. I'm sure she doesn't get enough to eat – you've all read about the guns and butter business?'

'They don't say guns before frankfurters,' said Oregon. 'The Germans won't starve. Not Aryans.' Then, with a look at Olivia, 'Sorry, m'dear.'

'Well, I'd like her to stay,' said Mama, 'for a long time if she wants to.'

'If she stays more than a few weeks,' said Oregon drily, 'she won't see Willi for years. Once the war breaks out, she'll be stranded – here.'

'Better here than there,' said Papa.

'Poor Anna,' said Olivia.

'Are you sure she will be better off in France than in Germany?' I asked. 'You're the one, Papa, who's always saying the Champagne area will be right in the path of a German advance.'

'If they ever reach that far,' said my father almost stonily. 'They haven't declared war, you know, and as for invading France – don't you think you're jumping the gun a bit?'

The first thing I had to do on reaching Paris was to let Sonia know I couldn't keep our lunch date. Yet I didn't dare phone her. The only alternative was to drive round to Marcel's and leave her a note, telling her I had been called away on urgent business, and that I would meet her in Marcel's several days later. I did so, though I couldn't tell Sonia that Anna was arriving, that this was the reason I couldn't meet her. I had been very shocked by Papa's remarks. And while I knew that Sonia would never have any direct dealings with the Germans – let alone an espionage network – I had felt for years that Riccardi had never been the innocent diplomat he pretended to be.

I caught sight of Anna as the conductor offered her a helping hand negotiating the steep steps of the brown and red *wagon-lit*. She saw me at the same instant, and for a moment I thought she was going to burst into tears – of relief. The porter in his belted blue blouse pointed out her two suitcases.

'This all you've got?' I asked.

Despite the relief, the hug of welcome, Anna looked tired, drawn.

'I didn't dare bring any more luggage.' She *was* on the point of tears, and her tone was bitter. 'I only got an exit permit for a week.'

As she moved towards the platform entrance, ready to offer her tickets, clutching her travel documents, I noticed that she was holding her American passport.

'You can still use it?' I asked.

'I did it deliberately,' she replied. Again the bitterness. 'You've got to learn how to keep ahead of the law in Germany. It's the only way to survive.'

'As bad as that?'

I didn't like to ask too many questions – not too soon anyway, especially when I suggested to Anna, 'Would you like to phone Willi from the apartment before I drive you to Douzy?'

'Phone Willi? From Paris? When I'm supposed to be in Switzerland!' She shook her head vigorously. 'My exit permit is made out for Switzerland only, and I can't afford to have any other immigration stamps on it. That's why I switched passports in Lausanne and used my old American passport. Perhaps later you could phone Willi? Discreetly. Don't mention my name, or anything like that.'

Anna and I set off for Douzy as soon as the porter had put the bags in the back of the car. I knew that Mama wanted to see her before anyone else. But the trip, less than two hours, gave both of us the chance to fill in some of the background to her life.

It was clear that Anna was deeply torn by three emotions – love, hate, fear. Love for Willi, hate for the Germans, fear of the future.

'Willi and I both share the fear,' she confessed, 'and that's really why I'm here. To have a breather. I hate Germany, it's so darned scary. And poor Willi tries to understand and be kind to me. But of course he's a German, so he can't see things my way.'

'In what way?'

'Two instances that are really extraordinary. The first is so ridiculous. Some bloody official came one afternoon, produced a card of authority – you know how the Germans like authority – and said he was from the Ministry of Child Welfare.'

'But we haven't any children,' she told the official.

'That's the problem, Frau Frankel,' said the man severely. 'Why not?'

'I told him that was our affair.' But, according to Anna, it was *their* affair. 'Germany is supposed to be surrounded by enemies and all that nonsense,' she said, 'and needs to produce more children!'

I couldn't help laughing. 'What did you do?'

'I tried the sob stuff. Couldn't have any children and so on. I'll tell you one thing, Larry, nothing would ever force me to have a baby at this time.'

'And the other problem?'

'More serious. It may sound melodramatic, but we're locked up in Germany now. No way to leave without official permission. I didn't *want* to go to Switzerland. I applied for an exit visa to visit France. Perfectly good reason – to see my family.'

'And what happened?'

'They turned my application down flat. Damn it, Larry, I'm an American – well, sort of.'

'Did they give a reason?'

'I gathered from Willi, who was furious, that some German bigwig is on the point of being expelled from France – there's already been a preliminary story about it in the newspapers – and so this is a kind of reprisal. No one is allowed to visit France.'

After some hesitation, I asked her, 'Do you ever wonder if you'll stay in France?'

'Willi wants me to,' she answered frankly. 'Even if it means being parted – for the time being. He's scared. But I love Willi, and we're so happy, despite the problems. And he can't go. He couldn't get a job anywhere abroad. And so we're trapped – because even if he wants me to go, I couldn't leave him. But at least, darling brother, I'm here breathing the good clear air of Champagne for a few days.'

'What fun we had,' I sighed, 'that night the four of us danced at Maxim's.'

'What a long time ago it seems,' she sighed too.

I told her the latest news about Sonia – omitting what Papa had said, but explaining that Sonia had specifically asked me not to phone her at her home. It would be different if Anna phoned later in the day, I suggested, with the perfectly inno-cent news that she had suddenly arrived in France.

She promised to do that, and by then it was time to sweep up the winding drive past the dell, through the arch to the courtyard, and as Mama came out and gathered Anna into her arms I could see that both of them were crying gently.

Even a couple of days of good clean Douzy air did wonders for Anna. The colour returned to her cheeks, but, more import-ant, she lost the tenseness I had noticed when we met. She was home – not at 'her' home really, I suppose, but still the home where she had been brought up.

'It'll always be home, always,' she said. 'I can't imagine life without Douzy. 'That's what tears me in two in Germany. I love Willi – but I love Douzy.'

We had set off for a long walk through the vineyards, and from the heart she said, 'We all seem to have made such a mess of our lives. Fancy *you* not being married to Sonia. It's unthinkable for you to marry anyone else.'

'I know.'

That morning, as I looked across the dell, opening the windows of the conservatory to invite the sweet smell of summer inside, I was thinking of the day of the thunderstorm when Sonia and I had raced from the orchard to escape the rain.

It was a day just like this, I thought, and looked down. By the far end of the drive a lane led to the Home Farm, lined with knotted hedges polished by the daily rubbing of the cows on their way to grateful milking. Wild flowers lined either side of the ochre lane – multi-coloured willow herbs tall as holly-hocks, the thick green stalks of hedge-parsley jutting out into spikes of creamy white blossom, and beyond the orchard and the lake the countryside spread out – the vineyards green and brown in rows, and beyond that the ripening corn, a glittering gold, while near the top of the rise beyond Douzy church was a carpet of more vivid yellow, a huge field of mustard, 'Champagne's other crop,' as Papa called it. Now that the flowering had ended, workers in the vineyards were trimming the ends of the vine stalks to make spraying easier and to give the sun more chance to ripen the grapes.

'It's the best time of the year,' Anna said as she walked along with pure pleasure. 'As though the whole world has been getting ready for me to come home.'

Slowly, almost hesitatingly, as though embarrassed by sharing secrets, Anna began to unwind. And in doing so, she told the family at Douzy some horrific stories.

'In Germany love isn't enough,' she said. 'I find it hard to explain. I know that in France everyone is scared there'll be a war. But that's a natural fear. In Germany, people are not only scared of war – but they're frightened of life.'

It was nothing one could lay a finger on, she told us; there was nothing tangible, but always there was a feeling of hidden terror. People were afraid to speak to each other, even to laugh openly. It sounded crazy, but people even disappeared – and with no trace, no warning, no clues.

Their neighbours the Mollers, who lived in the same apartment block, were such good friends of Willi's that they had even come to Douzy for the wedding.

'You remember, you liked them,' Anna said to Mama. 'And they were such fun. He worked in an architect's office, so in a way the two men had a kind of link, architects and engineers.' One day Mrs. Moller told Anna she'd be giving her some hard-to-get food she was getting from relations in the country – butter, pork products, all sorts of things.

Anna didn't have the cash ready when Mrs. Moller delivered the parcel, and Willi insisted that he would only accept the food on the understanding that it would be a 'business transaction'. Two days later Anna went up one flight to pay the bill and, she thought, have a coffee. But in those two days the Mollers had vanished. 'They'd gone,' cried Anna to Mama. 'Just vanished.' Another family had been allocated to the apartment, even taking over the furniture.

'But I must find out where they've gone,' Anna cried to the new neighbours. When she tried to get into the front door – half expecting to be invited in by the new arrival, a woman she had never seen – the stranger just stood there. But from the doorway Anna could see that one of the Mollers' own paintings was still hanging in the hall. And on a table she saw some old silver-framed family photographs that belonged to their friends. Pointing to them, she said to the new arrivals, 'So the Mollers are coming back? I see their photographs are still there.' Anna really thought they *were* going to return. But the new tenant, delighted to be allotted this apartment, said vaguely that arrangements were being made by the authorities to 'forward' all personal effects.

'It's the authorities this, the authorities that!' Anna exclaimed to me. 'It drives me mad. That – and the danger of asking too many questions. It's awful in Germany. The moment you ask a simple question, people begin to regard you with suspicion.'

Anna never did find out what happened to the Mollers – until Willi finally learned that Moller was part-Jewish and had been transferred to a different town.

'And I can guess what the word "transferred" means,' Olivia interrupted.

Anna nodded. Jews were being stripped of every penny then kicked out of Germany, often to Shanghai, where no passports or visas were required when landing at the International Settlement.

'Once they reach Shanghai, those who have some connections can sometimes get visas for America or Britain. But for every lucky one there are a thousand – ten thousand – who have nowhere to go. It's terrible. You know, Olivia, when I first arrived here at the beginning of the week, and I met you again, I felt a real sense of shame – of being German, of the way the Germans have treated the Jews.'

'You're not a German,' Olivia said gently. 'You never will be.'

I was concerned about one thing. 'What's going to happen if you don't return to Germany soon? You say you've only got an exit permit for a week – but the time's already up.'

Almost defensively, Anna said, 'They can't force me to go back to Germany right away if I want to pay a visit to my family.'

'But you switched passports.'

'Then when I return to Germany I'll switch passports again. I'll travel to Switzerland on my American passport, and go from there to Düsseldorf on my German passport, and just say I was taken ill.'

Almost without thinking I asked her, 'Where was your new American passport issued? In Germany.'

'What new passport?'

'Aren't you Mrs. Frankel now?'

'Oh, I see. I didn't bother to get a new one. This hasn't expired. I just hung on to my old passport – the one I had before I married. It doesn't seem to have stopped me travelling – so far.'

'All the same,' I said, 'I think you ought to get your marital status changed. You may find it very useful one day to have dual nationality. But if someone spots a technical error – like forgetting you're a married woman – well . . .'

'I'll get it done right away.'

'Don't leave it too long,' I warned. 'Jim Parks will fix it for you while you wait. It's only a question of writing your new name on the inside and stamping it.'

'I promise,' she said, but, knowing Anna, I doubted if she would remember.

Thank God I arrived first at Marcel's for the postponed 'reunion' lunch with Sonia. And that I had come by car – in my latest M.G., changed a year ago from the T model for a brand-new model WA, in 'racing' green, with wire wheels, four windows and running boards joining up to the rear wings. Altogether more luxurious.

Because Marcel's was closed. The standard sign read, 'Fermeture annuelle'. A smaller sign announced that the restaurant would re-open on Monday, 21 August.

Everyone – the butcher, the candlestick maker, to say nothing of restaurants and shops, closed each August. But it was not yet August, only the middle of July, and I had noticed that more and more places were closing down early. Oregon had had his own explanation. 'One hell of a lot of people are wondering when they'll get their next vacation,' he said.

Sonia arrived within five minutes. She was dressed in a blue linen two-piece suit, with a topaz clip on one breast, and a scarf casually knotted round her throat.

'Blue always did suit you.' I kissed her on the cheek, a brotherly kiss, smelling her faint perfume. 'And so does Arpège,' I remembered. 'But look,' I cried. 'Marcel's closed.'

'Oh no!' Her sudden exclamation of dismay, the way she put her hand to her mouth, was so genuine I felt a sudden urge to touch her on the arm. Years apart tend to make people forget the habits of others. Sonia had always felt a special bond towards people who had dealt with the two of us as lovers. She had a gift for sharing love, communicating it to others who could see how happy we were.

'That's terrible,' she said. 'Where shall we go?'

'Let's drive into the country,' I suggested. 'I know a lovely place at Marly.'

'You haven't been there with . . .'

'No girl, if that's what you mean.'

'I was so looking forward to meeting Marcel again. Oh! You've got a new car. How super. And it's bigger.'

'Yes, it's got a bit more room – and two-point-six litres of motor. It'll get us out to Marly before you know what's hit us. You're not afraid to be seen with me?'

'Maybe it would be better if you put the top up.'

Marly was only a dozen miles from Paris, a one-time royal hunting lodge surrounded by beautiful forests. A new road had been built bypassing Versailles, so that would be no problem.

'And the restaurant is pretty expensive,' I grinned, 'which means that it'll keep any tourists away. They'll be having their picnics. It's called the Auberge du Roi. Of course Charles the Fifth stayed there.'

We drove at speed along the flat straight road bisecting the beautiful forest, the thick green belts of trees on either side, with here and there sandy tracks or bridle paths, indicated by small green signposts.

Suddenly she said, almost breathlessly, 'Stop the car. Just for a second.'

I slammed on the brakes, slid off the road to the grass verge near the corner of a riding path and she said a little unsteadily,

'I know this is going to be a respectable lunch but, darling Larry, just one kiss before we reach the auberge.'

She leaned across – again the wisp of Arpège – and as I leaned across the low steering wheel towards her, she said in that husky voice of hers that always betrayed excitement, 'If you knew how long I've waited for this kiss, Larry. Oh, Monsieur Coquelicot, how I love you! And how I have missed you.'

I pushed one hand along her neck, underneath her thick blue-black hair; she kissed me, slowly at first, never to be rushed, until finally, when my breath had gone, I cried from the heart, all thoughts of behaving properly forgotten, 'Why did I let you go? Why, oh why? What a bloody fool I was!'

'No,' she said sadly. 'I let *you* go. I'm the fool, though I had no choice.'

We kissed again, and I could feel myself stirring, and I knew she felt the same, for she said, 'It can't be wrong to be in love. Not us. But where can we go?'

'Nowhere,' I said. 'You know that, darling – and perhaps it's for the best. This is just about the most public forest outside Paris. There's a peeping tom behind every tree.'

'But I must – I *must*.'

'I'll find a place after lunch,' I promised her, not knowing how – or even if I should. 'Take it easy.'

'Take it easy! You Americans! You must be mad. Can *you* take it easy? Let me feel you.' Almost savagely she undid my trouser buttons and pushed a hand inside my underpants. 'Oh darling, I want you – now. And you say take it easy!' She moved gently. 'We've got to do something. I don't give a damn if some tourists do see us. We must. Christ! We're as good as married – or we were. I don't care what you do – but I can't go into lunch like this – come on, darling, do it, do it and don't bother about anyone else.'

'I can't. Not in this bloody car.'

'Then let's do it to each other,' she urged me. 'Now, before lunch. Kiss each other in the car – and touch each other or ourselves. Nobody'll be able to see. Wait, I've got some paper hankies for you in my *baise-en-ville*.' She used the slang word for a large bag which girls sometimes carry when they know – or hope – to spend a night away from home, slang because *baiser* means to make love.

'Here' – she pushed the handkerchiefs inside my underpants – 'now nobody can see us, we can kiss and love each other.' She pulled up the blue linen skirt leaving herself bare, black and white, for there was nothing underneath.

It *was* all over in a few seconds. And when the kissing stopped, she said, 'That's better, isn't it, my love?'

She started to straighten her skirt, pull it down, then dabbed a little eau de cologne between the inside of her thighs – a typical Italian and French habit. Next she dipped into her capacious bag and took out a mirror and wiped away the lipstick. Catching sight of me through the mirror, she looked at me almost mischievously and asked, 'Now a glass of champagne will taste really perfect, *non*?'

We drove on – quite sedately, except that I was holding her hand most of the way.

'I suppose if our parents knew what we'd just done they'd be disgusted,' she wondered. 'But how sensible we are. We know everything there is to know about each other. And by a very simple process, we've' – she almost giggled – 'calmed ourselves down.'

'Mama would have a fit if she knew,' I laughed.

'Do you realise' – she still left her hand gently in mine – 'that this is the first time I've seen you laugh since I came back to Paris. Isn't it wonderful, playing with yourself and each other? And' – again mischievously – 'it's not only relaxed me, it's given me a huge appetite.'

The Auberge du Roi was suitably rustic, a reflection of the famous royal forest. A spattering of genuine antiques decorated the reception area. And behind the half-empty dining room lay a peaceful garden framed by an English-style herbaceous border with a lawn in the middle as green and smooth as a pool table. A large banknote discreetly pushed into a willing palm ensured that we had a quiet table in the corner of the open air veranda. And a bottle of champagne, which *did* taste good.

The menu looked enticing. 'And I'm just as ravenous as you are,' I laughed again. 'Just looking at you gives me an appetite.'

Drinking our champagne, we sat, silent in our thoughts,

looking over the garden with its bowers of roses and the bright green lawns.

'It's at times like this,' she sighed, 'that I wish we'd taken photographs of all our wonderful times together – pictures so that in the years to come, if things don't turn out well for us, we could for ever and ever turn to them and re-live our memories.'

'But I can remember everything. It's all there.' I touched my head. 'Everything. The beer in Pontarlier on that first day – you, dressed in pink. The cornfield, the gentle times we've had whenever other people would leave us alone. No, I don't need to be reminded by any fading photographs.'

We finished a whole bottle of champagne, leaning across the table, holding hands, the small vase of home-grown flowers pushed to the side until finally we heard a discreet cough and the waiter asked if we were ready to choose.

Before I could ask Sonia what she wanted, she turned to the old head waiter, gave him her most radiant smile, and said, 'Would you choose for us, please? We are very much in love, and . . .'

'I understand perfectly.' He was as gravely concerned as only the French can be when confronted with romance.

'Except *ris de veau*,' I said as an afterthought. I had never been able to stomach sweetbreads.

In the end he brought us some *feuilleté* of langoustines wrapped in puff pastry so light and flaky it almost dissolved as we ate it. And after that some breast of duck cooked in olives, and to top it off – 'You're still hungry?' I asked her and she smiled to the waiter – and ice cream over which the waiter poured a liberal portion of *framboise*; the lethal white distilled liqueur made from raspberries.

I had forgotten my cigarettes, and as I walked back across the lawn from the car I saw that Sonia was watching me intently.

'What are you looking at?' I asked.

'The way you walk. I love the way you walk – as though you want to dance. You'll always walk like that darling – not gangling, but an easy walk. *You* know. As though you haven't a care in the world – except me.'

'You always.'

'*Carissima*. I love the way you talk, walk, and . . .'

'Not now! Don't excite me again. It's not fair!'

It was over the second cup of coffee that I told her about Anna being in Douzy, and all about Anna's worries about Willi and living in Germany.

'How terrible for her, Larry! But naturally I'll be discreet. And I do hope not much time passes before I see her.'

And then Sonia had some news for me. 'I'm hoping to acquire – I think that's the right word – a small house in Switzerland.'

'What on earth for?' I was astonished. 'And what do you mean – "acquire"?'

'From Daddy. I know it sounds crazy, but if there's a war the Swiss at least might stay neutral – and it'd be a good investment.'

'Sounds wonderful. I still don't quite see why, though.'

'It'll be *mine*, don't you understand? And you will be able to come and see me there – a bolt hole.'

'I didn't think the Italians could export money.'

She looked embarrassed, just for a moment. 'Daddy's got a bit tucked away in Switzerland,' she admitted. 'I haven't got the house yet, but if I do – oh Larry, darling, just to have a place where we can go – a place of our own.'

'But you've forgotten you *do* have a husband. I feel guilty, even here with you.'

She hesitated, trying perhaps to arrange her thoughts.

'Don't,' she said finally and very gently. 'I'm not betraying anyone.'

'Your husband.'

'Least of all him. He's very understanding, very considerate. You see, everything was arranged – it had to be – and he knows about our past. All he asks is discretion.'

I didn't really understand. Her husband hadn't seemed homosexual.

'He's not,' she laughed. 'But don't *try* to understand,' adding gravely, 'After a wonderful day like this, just learn to accept.'

And so it all started again.

17

Midway through the summer, when the previous year's feeling of relief at the Munich sell-out had begun to evaporate, it suddenly dawned on France and Britain that Poland was now wide open to invasion, that the only hope of averting a European war with Germany was for Hitler's arch-enemy, Russia, to form a defence pact with France and Britain. None of the three powers was very strong, yet such a pact would surely mean that, in the event of war, Hitler would face enemies on both fronts. And even he could not be as mad, as suicidal, as to invite such a prospect.

By July the talks were proceeding slowly after a dismally ineffectual opening in June. Incredible Western bungling had virtually prevented any hope of success. Even the Poles – the only people to be threatened directly – flatly refused to allow Russian troops on their territory in the event of war.

'With the Germans we risk losing our liberty,' said Field-Marshal Smigly-Rydz, the Polish Commander. 'But with the Russians we lose our soul.'

The British led the Anglo–French delegation, with France very much the junior partner, and a British admiral was in charge.

'You'd have thought that since they're going to talk to the commies,' said Tommy Tomlinson, 'they'd have the brains to play down the English lah-di-dah lord stuff. But Jesus, they must be off their nut in Whitehall. Let me tell you the name of this guy – and imagine what the Russians are going to think. No' – as an afterthought – 'I haven't got enough breath to tell you his name. Here, read it yourself.'

And there, incredibly, was a copy of the London *News Chronicle*, announcing, 'The British delegation is headed by Admiral Sir Reginald Aylmer Ranfurly Plunkett-Ernle-Erle-Drax.'

'Can you beat it?' Tommy read it again. 'The Russians will die laughing.'

Before they started, the delegation ran into more trouble. To avoid crossing Germany by train the navy had chartered the *City of Exeter*, with the idea of meeting the Russians in Leningrad in four days. But only after boarding the *Exeter* at Tilbury, near the port of London, did the admiral discover that she made only thirteen knots, so couldn't possibly arrive in time.

'And I've heard a rumour from our Washington office,' said Tomlinson, 'that Ribbentrop has sent a team of his yes-men to Moscow to talk to the Soviet high-ups.'

Yet against all this background of mounting despair, Paris in the summer of 1939 seemed gilded by splendid receptions, dances, night-long festivities. The prospect of war was an ever-present ghost at every party, but even so people refused to acknowledge the reality behind the fears. Each new crisis was like a splinter of glass that scratched, might even draw a drop of blood, but was not savage enough to wound badly.

The madness in the air was a last-gasp attempt to enjoy ourselves while we could, a collective national need for illusion, by a patient with an incurable disease who knows that death will come at any moment.

Even the 1939 parade for the *Quatorze Juillet* on the Champs-Élysées, though splendid in its panoply, seemed out of place, an echo of past grandeur. The Foreign Legionnaires, the Zouaves, the polished glinting breastplates of the *cuirassiers*, even a platoon of British guardsmen in scarlet tunics and bearskins, seemed an empty gesture on this, my twenty-seventh birthday.

My duties for the *Globe* kept me from Douzy that birthday, for the first time in many years. But my photographer friend Alex Rhys had set off on another long trip, and I had been able to move from the rue de l'Université flat back to his fifth-floor bandbox of an apartment in the rue du Cherche Midi. And just because it *was* my birthday Sonia had somehow planned to spend most of the day with me at 'home'. Though cooking was hardly part of the daily duties of a diplomat's wife, Sonia, like many Italians, was a born cook and she produced an enormous dish of *spaghetti carbonara*. '*Al dente*,' she said, 'and

229

with real belly pork in it, not bacon, the way they do it in restaurants.'

I was sitting in the most comfortable chair, leaning back, legs outstretched, watching her.

'Cooking over a hot stove like any housewife,' I murmured.

'Just because I'm a diplomat's wife doesn't mean I can't cook,' she retorted. 'Specially *spaghetti carbonara.*'

But it wasn't cooking that intrigued me on this occasion. It was the way she had dressed – 'for comfort', as she put it. 'I hope you don't mind, but I decided to leave a nightie and dressing gown and one or two bits and pieces – just in case we can spend more time together.'

'These your cooking clothes?' I laughed, for she was wearing a beautiful white *crêpe de Chine* nightdress with a thin dressing gown over it.

'Mummy would have a fit if she knew,' she laughed. 'These clothes are part of my trousseau. All my lingerie came from Natalina Serni in Florence.'

'So long as they didn't come from . . .' I had a sudden stab of jealousy at the thought of him seeing her in that nightie.

'No, my beloved.' After biting off an end of spaghetti to check she came over and kissed me. 'He didn't buy them. I bought them – and I vowed, even then, that I would never wear them except for you. It was a present from me to you – bought by me, for the day when I knew we would meet again.'

With assumed nonchalance, I said, 'Very interesting. Lunch ready? I'm famished.'

'Horrible beast! I spend all my days cooking for you and . . .'

'Come over and kiss me again . . .'

'And then?'

'You choose. Lunch first or after.'

'And I've got another surprise for you,' said Sonia on the way home. 'I had lunch the other day with the Polish ambassador – I think he's got a crush on me. You've read about his ball in the embassy? Well, I've got invitations for the whole Astell family. You *must* get Anna to go, it will be good for her. It's going to be the greatest ball of the season. It's so sad to think,' she said, 'that this might be the last such ball for quite a while.'

'How did you fix it?'

'I asked him. He's met your family, and of course he admires both your papa and grandma for having stuck to their dual nationality – French as well as American. It's so easy to become American and forget the rest of the world.'

'Does Francesco know?'

She shook her head, but the very mention of Francesco's name jarred the beautiful sleepiness of the afternoon. I had been wondering about him, and what his specific duties were, because Abetz had by now been kicked out of France and replaced by another roving German diplomat, a fat lump of a man called Albrecht, who looked as prone to paranoia as his predecessor.

Albrecht was a frequent visitor to the Italian Embassy. I knew this from the *Globe*'s agency contacts, men whose job it was to cover the routine comings and goings of people at embassies, consulates, the Quai d'Orsay and so on. They obviously didn't report everything they saw or heard about, but somehow, over the months, pictures began to form which a trained political observer like Tommy could fit into some sort of overall shape.

It was these snippets of news that made Tomlinson say, without realising its significance to me, 'In the days when Abetz was top dog, first Riccardi then de Feo used to go and see him. They were ordered to go, I'd guess. But now it's changed. Albrecht goes to see de Feo. I wonder if Abetz blotted his copy book while de Feo is close to Ciano.'

Maybe, I thought, but close for – what? I had tried carefully over the years to prize clues from Sonia about her husband's secret work – and secret it was, I didn't doubt that. I had even told her once of a story in the Paris rumour factory that de Feo had only got his appointment because Count Ciano had been to bed with Sonia. But we both laughed at that.

Yet Sonia had always evaded any tactful questions with a sigh. Now I hinted again.

'Does your Francesco – and your father – have some secret – well, it sounds so melodramatic – but some kind of hold on you, darling? I don't mean anything wrong, but . . .'

'I know how puzzled you must be,' she said. 'We all have to protect our parents – and ourselves – from time to time. But don't worry. I've done nothing wrong. And now we are living today – don't let's force open any cupboards that might contain skeletons.'

There had never been a ball like the one at the Polish Embassy. The Astells went *en famille*; but despite my best efforts, Anna said she would prefer to stay at home. She was in a sad mood, wondering about Willi, from whom we had heard no word, but she did one very sweet thing. She gave her invitation to Olivia, and I was delighted – for Olivia's sake. She didn't go out much. Papa was in tails, I was in black tie, the girls looked wonderful, and the atmosphere of exhilaration – and a kind of gossamer make-believe – was so beautiful that at first sight even the most jaded guests gasped with phrases like, '*C'est merveilleux!*'

It *was* marvellous. In the beautiful gardens, the trunks of all the trees had been covered to a height of ten feet with garlands of fresh flowers. All the trees, lawns, had hidden lights so that the mood changed constantly, but never producing a glare, and with colour changes so gentle they ran into each other, like differently tinted clouds or sea. And it was more beautiful than ever because the scenes of unreality lent it a wistful note, a frenzied anxiety not to miss anything while it lasted. Julius Lukasiewicz, the ambassador, had spared no effort to make it a night no one would ever forget – especially by those who wondered if there would ever be another night like it. 'Luka', as he was known to his friends, knew perfectly well that the Russo–British deal had foundered and what that meant to Poland. I felt that he had decided the end was near and that he was determined to go out with a bang.

He had invited all the most beautiful women in Paris, and at three in the morning, under a warm sky, he made his final defiant gesture. He led his entire embassy staff, all of them barefoot – the ladies in crinolines – in a polonaise across the cropped embassy lawns, which were bordered with white marble statues. The effect was pure magic, for they and the beautiful girls were illuminated by large red Bengal lights; the pots of fire lit the lawns, the dancers, the white statues, with a macabre, moving red glow. Sonia was dancing with Francesco; I was dancing with Olivia, and, as she looked at me, smiling – Olivia was such a beautiful girl, I thought, remembering that one night together – her face was bathed in a soft reddish glow shining through her hair, and I shivered suddenly. The girls and those near her looked like corpses dripping with blood.

The moment passed, and the music changed into a fox trot, difficult to manipulate on grass. I suggested sitting down but Olivia begged me to continue, not possessively.

'I adore dancing,' she pleaded, 'and Guy – well, he's not much good at it. So give me one dance more, please, even though I have the strangest feeling, as though we're dancing ourselves into the war.'

'You look positively dazzling.' I tried to turn away any morbid thoughts. And she did look dazzling. Mama, who knew all the couturiers in Paris, had asked Edward Molyneux to lend Olivia a ball gown, a model dress. It was often done by good clients like Mama, who might ask a big house to lend a dress to a daughter for an important dance. It cost the dress house nothing, and providing the girl was pretty it was a good free advertisement. Olivia was wearing a long white dress that spread out from her waist almost like a crinoline – not really as full as that, but that was the only way I can describe it. 'Classical Molyneux,' said Mama.

'I suppose I ought to be grateful that Anna's not here,' said Olivia. 'I do hope you can help her to stay in France.'

'Germany *is* her home – well, her husband's.'

'I know. But if there's a war?' she said.

'What about here? And anyway, she'll decide. Anna knows what she wants.'

Mama came along and though I wouldn't have minded dancing again with Olivia I thought it more polite to dance with Mama – especially as I had already danced three times with Sonia. I was intrigued by Olivia, by the skill with which she wordlessly had made it quite clear that what had happened in that one night in the apartment was never to be repeated. She had never said anything – and I, being more in love with Sonia than ever by now, had never made any approaches. But Olivia did have extraordinary gifts.

'She's a helluva good girl,' I said to Mama. 'It seems a long time since we had that awful row.'

'I know. And now, with Anna away, she's become a kind of second daughter to me. Strange how it all works out.'

After another dance, I looked at my watch. Half past four. 'I'm pooped,' I told Mama. 'It's okay for you people to dance the night away, but I'm a working man. If the Hisp. is ready – and if poor Gaston isn't fast asleep – I think we ought to go.'

Mama nodded, and we started to collect the Astell brood.

As I waited in the hall for Guy to pick up Mama's wrap, a sixth sense made me turn round. I *knew* that someone was talking about me. And I moved so quickly that I actually caught Sonia's husband pointing me out – quite definitely. And the other man was Herr Albrecht. We had met previously, but now I saw the German nod to de Feo – almost as though he was obeying orders, being told by the Italian diplomat what to do. As soon as they caught my eye, they both waved.

We had all tended to shy away from the question of Anna's future plans – deliberately. All that any of us at Douzy could do was try to persuade her to stay but, understandably, too much persuasion irritated her, sometimes erupting in the kind of anger that makes people shout, 'Why don't you mind your own business?' or, 'Leave me alone, will you!'

She had to be handled carefully, poor Anna, her lovely young face now creased with worry bordering on bleak despair. She had to work out her future herself, while we could only hope she would stay. And she had stayed – so far. Her original permission to stay a week in Switzerland had long since expired. If she remained long enough, she might be too afraid to return. Wouldn't that be the best solution?

The chance scene at the Polish Embassy ball, when Sonia's husband and Albrecht had obviously been talking about me, had an intriguing sequel a few days later in early August, when Albrecht called me at the *Paris American* office.

Our meetings had usually been brief, often at the International Press Club functions, though, unlike Abetz, who had only toyed with writing, Albrecht was a professional journalist.

He tended to call all foreign correspondents by their Christian names, impervious to snubs by those who disliked him. Perhaps I was also prejudiced because his clothes seemed to hang on him, giving him a dirty, shifty look. His jackets had the tell-tale slanting pockets of the Germans, and no doubt they were expensive. If he looked a mess it was not the fault of his wardrobe, but of the shapeless mass of blubber struggling to burst out of it. On the other hand, he had been recruited by Germany's propaganda chief, Dr. Goebbels, and liked to be regarded as a 'fellow newspaperman'.

'How are you, Larry?' he began. 'Good. Listen. We've had an enquiry from a German national whose wife is missing. Enquiries have asked me if you can help.'

'Me?' I knew perfectly well what he was leading up to.

'Yes,' he explained. 'She's a Frau Frankel. It seems she's your sister. Is that right? I'm terribly sorry. Had no idea. But apparently her husband is worried.'

I said nothing, hoping he found the silence disconcerting.

'I'm sorry, Larry. Can you hear me?'

'Sure.'

'Well, then . . .?'

'But,' I said mildly, 'you didn't ask me any questions. You just made a statement. That's fine. Thanks for letting me know.'

'But your sister — we got a message — she went to Lausanne for a vacation.'

Again I said nothing.

'You are hearing me?' he sounded exasperated, as I hoped he would. Poor Albrecht was so used to making flat statements as a means of grilling people that he had lost the art of trying to frame polite questions.

'But she's left Switzerland,' he added.

'It's a free country and she's over twenty-one,' I said cheerfully. 'What do you want me to do?'

'Her husband is worried. He asked me to make some enquiries.'

That, I was convinced, was a lie. I had been trying for days to contact Willi. And high-ranking diplomats didn't waste their time making personal calls to newspaper colleagues just because someone had overstayed an exit permit.

'What do you think, Larry?' He finally asked a direct question. I answered with the first thought that came into my head.

'Do you think she's run off with another man?'

'Why you say that?' he asked.

'But you're sure she isn't in Lausanne? How can you tell? It can't be a problem for Germans – in Switzerland, surely?'

'We have discovered that she left suddenly. She gave no forwarding address. Perhaps she had come to see you?'

'If she's run off with another man? Hardly likely. Would *you* go to see your family if you bolted with a new girlfriend?'

'She might come to your château,' said Albrecht finally. 'You will let me know?'

'With her husband?'

'No. He is in Düsseldorf.'

'I've been trying to telephone him. I can't seem to get through. Could you help?'

'Perhaps his wife,' he persisted.

'From Lausanne?'

'She's not in Lausanne,' said Albrecht heavily, 'and I think you know this without me informing you.' With an attempt – equally heavy – at sarcasm, he added, 'Thanks for all your help.'

The more I thought about Albrecht's heavy-handed hints, the more I was convinced that de Feo was vaguely involved. I didn't flatter Anna by thinking that de Feo was moving heaven and earth to get one single German–American girl back to the Fatherland; but the Nazis and Fascists *were* dedicated zealots, and it was quite possible that Albrecht, knowing that de Feo's wife was Anna's lifelong friend, had mentioned her 'disappearance' at some routine joint meeting. And how astonished Albrecht must have been if de Feo announced that he had dined with Anna Frankel only the previous week – for Francesco and Sonia had been recent guests at Douzy.

That would have explained the talk between the two diplomats at the Polish ball. And the sequel. And it couldn't have come at a worse time, for finally Anna was beginning to crack.

On the Saturday – that would have been 19 August – she admitted to me that she had told Willi to phone me at the P. A. from an office outside his building for news, but no news had come through. She was sure Willi's phone was tapped.

Suddenly she burst into tears and cried, 'I'm going back to Germany. Something terrible's happened to Willi. I've got to go.'

'You can't,' I told her. 'You're in trouble yourself for overstaying your visit out of Germany. Knowing the Nazis, they could chuck you into jail.'

'I've got to go,' she muttered. 'I can't leave him without a word – oh! I hate the Germans. I hate them!'

'You're not going,' I said. 'Not yet.'

'You can't stop me!'

'I can.'

'How?'

'Because I'll go first and see what's happened,' I said – not suddenly, but after some thought. 'I can go on a trip as a newspaperman. No problem. I'll check out that Willi's okay, what he wants to do, then report back in a couple of days.'

She kissed me impulsively. 'You're an angel. You will? Right away?'

'Couple of days,' I said. 'Don't worry, Anna. I'll only be able to stay in Germany for a night or so, but I'll find out what's happened.'

I set off by train on Monday the 21st, and even I could feel the claustrophobia that gripped me as we passed the frontier and the guards examined our passports, with a couple of stony-faced men in Gestapo uniform watching in silence, unblinking, never missing a trick, spies not only on the innocents on the train but on the German officials checking our passports. It passed through my mind as the train restarted that the frontier epitomised all that was terrifying in Germany. I patted my Malacca swordstick with a sense of security – and irony that Willi should have given it to me. Not that I would ever use it – or need it – I thought.

I found a cab easily. No problem with the address, a prosperous-looking apartment block, Willi's name on a list by the front door, though when I rang his bell I half expected no reply. After all, every attempt to contact Willi had failed. Maybe he *was* having a secret affair with some local floosie. But no, Willi was highly intelligent. No man in his right senses would vanish without a word if he had a girlfriend. He would cover his tracks.

Then I heard movements inside the apartment – a vague shuffling from inside the room, behind the front door. A voice, which didn't sound like Willi's, mumbled something in German. I could just manage, in my limited German, to catch, '*Wie heissen Sie?*'

It *was* Willi! But a Willi who sounded disorientated.

'It's Larry!' I shouted. 'Open the door. It's Larry!'

'Thank God.' Willi's voice behind the door suddenly broke into a grateful sob. I waited impatiently to the sounds of bolts being drawn back – and then, with mounting horror, I managed to catch in my arms the broken, sagging figure grabbing a hall stand in a vain attempt to stand upright.

'Jesus Christ, Willi! What the hell's happened?'

'*Es ist ein Unfallpassiert.*' I could hardly recognise the bloody torn mess, as he repeated in English, 'an accident'.

His face was one blotch of purple and red bruises. Both eyes were blackened, barely visible. His lips were puffed or split, I couldn't tell which. The blood on his face was matted where the skin had split – obviously as a result of someone's fists.

'Come on, for Chrissake,' I cried urgently. 'Let me help you.'

I tried to take an arm. He gave an almost animal yelp of pain. 'Nothing fatal,' he gasped, 'but in the ribs there is much pain.'

Somehow I got Willi to the sofa in the living room. I had brought with me a bottle of Scotch and I poured a huge dose down his throat until he spluttered with the fire – and no doubt the stinging effect against his cut lips.

I took off his jacket carefully. His arms were all right, but his body was black and blue – and with the green and dirty yellow of bruises changing colour.

Willi's wounds were horrific – yet I didn't need a practised eye to realise that he had been beaten up scientifically: maximum pain but no broken bones. Lips split but no teeth knocked out. Puffy eyes almost closed, but no danger of losing his sight. Someone – and I could imagine who it was – had arranged for Willi to be taught a lesson – yet not a fatal one.

'When did this happen?' I asked harshly.

'Tuesday night,' he replied.

Tuesday! That was two days ago.

'Haven't you done anything? Seen a doctor?'

He shook his head. 'Too weak to leave the apartment. I sleep. No one comes in. I cannot eat. My phone is not working, and anyway, better not to involve friends.'

'But you could have died.'

He managed a feeble smile. 'Not likely. They could do this so easily, but they do not want to. Is good to see you, Larry, so good. And what news of my *liebchen*?'

'She's fine. She sends you a big kiss.'

He managed a twisted grin. 'No kissing for a few days.'

'Before anything else,' I said, 'you must get some medicine. And food. No, shut up, Willi.' I stopped his interruption. 'I'm going to put you to bed, then go out and find some cotton wool and bandages and iodine or whatever you need.'

He tried to stop me, but I managed to get the rest of his clothes off and put him between the sheets, though in truth he almost fainted with pain.

I managed to find a chemist who understood English and he gave me all the necessary supplies – as though beating up was a common occurrence. He showed me the salve to use for split lips, the iodine for cuts, the other medicines for bruises. On the way back I found some milk, a couple of loaves of dark bread and a pair of fat, long sausages. Willi would not be able to eat much until his mouth was better, but I could boil some milk for him to sip.

Almost the first question he asked me when I returned and put the food on the kitchen table was, 'And how is Douzy? Still as beautiful?'

I almost choked on the words. Douzy! Perhaps at this very moment Anna was wondering whether Willi and I had met yet. Perhaps she was having her pre-dinner drink, talking to Mama, getting moral support from Papa. But never – oh God! – never imagining such a horror as this: poor Willi broken and beaten. The contrast between Douzy and this apartment, reeking of blood and vomit, was almost more than I could bear.

'At least Anna is safe.' He managed a wan smile.

'She's fine,' I reassured him. 'We were worried about not hearing from you, so I came along to see for myself. Thank God I did.'

'I will be fine. And please, Larry, don't tell Anna about this I will be better soon. Don't worry her. What you see' – it hurt him to smile, but he still made an effort – 'what you see is fairly normal around the streets of Germany these days.'

'But why, Willi – *why*?'

'I'm not sure. They ask where is my wife.' He tried to sit up in a straighter position.

'Never mind the explanations now,' I said. 'The most important thing is – where can I get you a doctor?'

'No doctor. Better not. Maybe if you can get me into the hot bath, I soak in it.'

It did help, though only after a long struggle to get him into the big iron tub. His entire body was covered with bruises. I let him soak for a long time, topping up the water each time it began to cool. Finally I found a bath robe and half carried him back to the bedroom and poured some more Scotch into him before discovering what had happened.

Three Brownshirt thugs in uniform had rung his bell – and Willi remembered that for the first exciting moment of its sound he even thought that by some miracle Anna had arrived unexpectedly. Instead the three men marched in and closed the door behind them.

'One look and I knew why they were coming to see me,' Willi remembered. 'They didn't speak, they gave no reason, and for me there was no escape.'

'This is beyond all reason – they bloody well nearly murdered you.'

'Before I can argue, even ask why, they start to beat me up. Very methodical.' He winced with pain as he tried another smile. 'One man stick plaster over my mouth to stop screams, then they take the turns. Two men hold me from behind, while third man hit me. I can do nothing, not even move face. And they kick too. When one man is tired hitting me, another takes his turn. This way they go on hitting me for long, long time.'

'Poor bugger,' I breathed softly. 'You think it might be because of Anna?'

Willi was not sure. The punishment seemed to be too drastic for a husband whose wife had done nothing more terrible than overstay a holiday abroad. And it couldn't be anything to do with his work at Staffens. Willi was sure of that. He had recently been promoted; he was working on new and important contracts. He was, he said, a Party member in good standing. He had broken no rules, revealed no secrets. Yet suddenly his telephone had been disconnected, all attempts to call Douzy had been frustrated. He could only surmise that it was a warning – that Germans with foreign wives should keep them at home.

I found myself saying, 'I won't tell Anna the details, Willi, not if you don't want me to – but I hope you love her enough to stop her coming back to Germany for the time being. You've been warned, but what about her? I don't imagine they respect women any more than men.'

He shook his head. 'She must never come back,' he agreed, 'not till this madness is over.' He hesitated then added, 'I must write and tell her this, make her promise. Would you mind taking a short letter from me to Anna?'

'Of course not.'

Willi hesitated.

'I think you have to hide it,' he said. 'I want to beg Anna not to return to Germany. Is not enough if I ask you to tell her. I have to put it down in words. You understand?'

'Of course. Don't worry,' I said – but I was worrying.

When Willi finally handed me the letter it covered two closely written pages.

'No envelope?'

He shook his head. 'It must be carefully hidden.'

'But Willi,' I cried, 'surely they won't search *my* papers? I mean – I'm not German, I'm not Jewish, they've no reason . . .'

'They have. I know what happens when men like me get beaten up. They wait to see who your friends are – maybe they are hoping Anna is to return. Your presence here is probably reported – perhaps by the chemist where you buy the medicines. And someone will follow you to the station when you leave.'

'If what you say is true – it's terrifying.'

'It is terrifying, I tell you,' said Willi. 'Here! Flatten each page into a square, then put one inside each sock. Please!'

Though I took off my shoes and socks and put the pages against the soles of my feet, I had the feeling that everyone could 'see' them. I tried to forget my anxiety by preparing some food – Scotch was not enough sustenance for Willi. Rummaging in the kitchen, I broke up a couple of slices of bread, carefully taking off the crusts, then boiled some milk, dunked the bread in it until it was almost mushy, and produced that good old standby of nursery food – bread and milk. Willi managed to get some of it down, and afterwards he felt better.

'You know what they sometimes call bread and milk in America?' I joked. 'Graveyard stew!'

'The only thing that makes me happy is Anna – that she is safe,' he said. 'I didn't tell you until now, but as well as the beating one of the men demands my Party card and tears it up, and hands me official document that I am expelled from the Party. Why? I ask. They never tell. There can be no reason – jealousy, something I do not know about? I have been a good worker, I have helped very much. Now,' said Willi, 'this means I lose my job at Staffens. Is very secret work, only Party members can work in armaments division. For me there is only one thing – join the army.'

I hesitated. I was horrified at what had happened – at what I had seen, a generalised picture suddenly brought into the fine focus of a bleeding, torn mouth, black eyes, bruised ribs. This was Germany, I thought bitterly: 'The senseless brutes.'

'Yes,' sighed Willi, 'this is the master race that Hitler promises will rule the world for a thousand years.'

'I just can't leave you in the lurch,' I said. 'But I have to return to Paris. What are we going to do? Are you sure you don't want Anna to come back to Germany?'

'Nein, nein!' he tried to shout. 'It is over, life here in Germany. War comes very soon.'

'Sounds tough on you,' I said, 'but Willi, I agree. Anna may be married to a German, but she's still an American – and that means neutral. Looking at it from her point of view – and yours if you really love her – why should she suffer in a war that's no real concern of yours? But what are we going to do with you?'

'What can anyone do?'

'Can you get out? Leave?'

'Not possible, Larry. Germany is sealed tight. And even if I could go, where?'

'Do you mean to say there's nowhere you could go to?'

He shook his head. 'You do not realise how things are in Germany. I have no passport any more. How can I even get past a railway station? And if I escape, who will help a German? We are hated by everyone in Europe.'

Sealed tight. I had never before thought that people other than criminals could be denied the right to a passport, freedom to travel.

'I work all my life, very hard,' said Willi bitterly, 'I pass my exams, I am top class engineer – but maybe someone does not like the fact I have a foreign wife, or that my friend Moller's great-grandfather was half Jewish.'

I was thinking, trying to solve a puzzle which no one could solve. 'There's no chance,' I hesitated again, 'of – well, fixing you with a new passport? Or of escaping – is there no way out across a frontier?'

'Is impossible.'

'But if we knew in advance – if I could start the ball rolling – I'm sure that as the husband of an American citizen Papa could pull some diplomatic strings.'

'I tell you, Larry, war will come soon. I am lost in this kind of new Germany. The only way I will be able to find food to eat will be to join the *Wehrmacht*.'

I hated the idea of leaving Willi, and hated even more the prospect of telling Anna what had really happened. But I had to be back in Paris by the 23rd.

'Just tell her the half truth,' Willi begged me. 'That I lose my job, but not that I look such a mess. And one thing more; I would like a promise.'

'If I can.'

The war, he said, would be brutal and protracted. And France could never win against the might of Germany. 'This you must believe. We know from secret information that France will never be able to withstand Germany.' As for Britain, well, Willi felt that she would probably compromise. Hitler, however, would never dare to involve the might of America. 'So maybe I fight in France, who can tell? But maybe the Astells of Douzy remain neutral, *nein*? What I ask is – please to remember that when I join the army, I am like millions of Germans – I don't *want* to fight. But I have no choice. It is that or a camp. So please to remember this if we ever meet again. Remember I am not a free man – never until Hitler is dead and Germany is beaten.'

I left Willi in time to catch the early morning train to Paris-Nord on 23 August. On the way back to Düsseldorf station in the Bahnhofstrasse I decided that Willi was right. There was no point in telling Anna how badly Willi had been beaten up. Specially as he felt reasonably certain there would be no repetition.

Even in the comparative peace of the first-class compartment, the air of tension was suffocating. I sat down in a corner seat which bore my name on a ticket and put my briefcase and overnight bag on the rack above. A large fat woman sitting opposite opened a packet of sandwiches, looked at me suspiciously, and carefully held them so that I couldn't see what she was eating.

I stood up to take down the briefcase and get out the latest Eric Ambler, *The Mask of Dimitrios*, which had just been published in London. As I returned my briefcase to the rack the fat woman, still eating, looked down at my shoes. So did the other two people in the compartment – an insipid middle-aged couple. As though they had all heard Willi's letter crackling in my shoes because of my sudden movement, three pairs of eyes were suddenly fascinated by my shoes. The sweat broke out again on my forehead. Any of these people could be a Nazi agent. The fat lady pointed down without a word while the other couple looked on.

It took an enormous effort for me to look down, but I did. The thin leather bookmarker had slipped out of Ambler's thriller as I put it on the seat, that was all, but even so, I laughed nervously when I stooped to pick it up. I laughed, but it wasn't my laugh: the break in tension changed it into a high pitched nervous giggle.

At the frontier with France, we all had to get out, queue, have our passports stamped, check with the customs. I had been warned that any Jews would be stopped and searched physically in an effort to prevent them smuggling out valuables.

An officer in grey uniform, backed by a couple of armed soldiers standing nearby, looked hard at me, wrote down my name, then let me pass through to the customs, but only after he had whispered something to a nearby clerk.

In the next room where the customs search took place, I saw the clerk whisper to the officer, who asked me quite politely to open my bag. He must have known who I was – or at least that I was known to Willi – for he examined every single thing. He opened the screw top of my toothpaste, examined my toilet bag, felt inside the spare pair of shoes. After the bag, he searched every corner of my briefcase.

Even then the search was not over. As I prepared to return to the train a second officer stopped me and asked if I would turn out my pockets. They took out everything – from my *carte d'identité* to my fountain pen. But not until they actually started to frisk me did the sweat beads start again.

'Please to go!' he said and I saw him shake his head to someone. Thankfully I flopped down in my carriage seat. I felt as though I had been subjected to a third degree. But I had got Willi's message past the customs.

Two minutes later we moved across the frontier. As though a voice was crying 'Freedom' a Frenchman pulled open the sliding door of the compartment and cried cheerfully, '*Passeports s'il vous plaît!*' and '*Avez-vous rien à déclarer?*'

Hearing me reply in French, the fat woman leaned across and offered me a sandwich, saying, 'I was frightened to talk to you, I thought you were German.'

'I thought *you* were German.'

'*Mais non!* I come from Dieppe.'

Even so, I had to admit that as the train steamed away from Germany, I did wonder if I would ever see Willi again. It was a hope that had diminished to zero by the time I arrived in

Paris – just in time to read the sensational news that stupefied Paris and was now being announced in the biggest and blackest headlines ever seen in France.

While most of the country was on vacation, those two arch enemies Russia and Germany had brought off a coup that stunned the world. The headline in the evening papers told the story:

RUSSIANS AND NAZIS SIGN
NON-AGGRESSION PACT

At first I couldn't believe it. The German Foreign Minister, von Ribbentrop, had, it appeared, turned out to be a master diplomat. At one stroke of the pen, or rather two strokes, he and Stalin had removed the direst threat facing Germany – that of a war on two fronts, the danger which all Europe had hoped would prevent Hitler from his final act of folly.

Now there would be no danger of a second front, for Germany and Russia were 'friends'.

'And that,' declared Oregon when I reached the rue du Sentier, 'means certain war. It's a matter of days now, not weeks or months.'

18

The momentous news of the pact between Russia and Germany sent waves of apprehension through half-empty Paris which seemed almost visible – as though we had all caught a glimpse of the four grim horsemen of the Apocalypse riding by, licking their lips. So profound was the sense of shock that at first it seemed impossible that millions of people hadn't yet heard the news, didn't yet realise its significance – that the two ill-assorted bedfellows were preparing to carve up Poland between them, that Europe was doomed.

Why should they know? France was on vacation. In Douzy on that warm August Wednesday afternoon, with the sunshine rippling beyond the vineyards and over the yellow mustard fields, Papa was at the *cellier* and Mama never turned on the radio until Papa came back to the house. And so they still presumed that I would be returning late that Wednesday, as I had promised to tell Anna about Willi.

Of course I couldn't go – not immediately.

'On this date – the day the world has decided there's going to be a war!' exclaimed Tommy Tomlinson. 'Larry, I've had a telex from Washington,' he continued. 'You're working full-time on retainer as of now. I don't need you weekends – I'll mind the store Saturdays and Sundays. But even now Paris, like every other capital, is demanding reaction stories. I can deal with most of them, but you might ring up your chums in the army and politics – and Madame de Portes if you like.'

I couldn't say no to his offer. I didn't want to be on the staff for that would mean the end of my independence. There would be no way I could disobey an order – even if the paper sent me as bureau chief to any place from Singapore to Santiago. But being on a full-time retainer basis was subtly different because I could choose assignments they offered me, even take time off when I wanted – within reason.

I immediately telephoned Anna.

'Willi all right?' Her voice was harsh with worry.

'Of course. Super,' I lied.

'Why didn't he phone?'

'Phones don't work as well in Germany as they used to do. It's guns before phones now, not only butter.' I tried to keep my tone light, but with the first words she detected the half-truth in my voice.

'Something's wrong, isn't it?'

'Look, Anna. There are problems,' I admitted. 'But I can't talk on the phone.' I explained the news that had broken. 'This affects all of us – the whole damned world, including Willi as well as you.'

'Okay. What are you doing this evening?' Her voice sounded determined, edgy, bossy almost.

'Nothing. I'm on standby duty. Just in case . . .'

'Larry, bless you for phoning, but I can't wait till the weekend for news of my' – she hesitated – 'my husband. I'm driving into Paris right now. I'll spend the night at the apartment in the rue des St Pères. If I have to, I'll come to the office. Otherwise, can you spare time for a *casse-croûte* at home? I don't feel like going out to dinner. I'll cook for you.'

'Okay,' I agreed, 'seven o'clock.'

It seemed vaguely peculiar, the prospect of having a meal in the old apartment. So much had happened in those beautiful, spacious rooms, the grey panelled dining room, the tiny study with its sedate bookshelves, the bedroom Guy and I shared as kids when Papa and Mama took us to see the Cirque Medrano or the Eiffel Tower; all the beauty of youth, and often with Anna and Sonia there too. In those days it had been a real home; a second one, true, but we always *felt* at home there, as we scampered through its rooms. For long now, though, it had been relegated in my mind. The heart had gone out of the place, the excitement of youth had long been wiped off its walls. Now my Paris home consisted of my beloved *Coquelicot* rooms in the rue de l'Université. Going to the family apartment was like going visiting. Indeed, I felt like a stranger as I parked my car round the corner in the rue de Lille and passed through the courtyard before climbing the handsome, wide, circular staircase to the second floor. Anna had already arrived. She was sipping a Scotch and Perrier.

'And here's one ready for you.' She knew that I enjoyed an occasional whisky. As she poured out the Perrier in silence I looked at her, wondering what form the next few moments would take – and how much I could withhold. For she looked so miserable, I was afraid to tell all.

When she saw me watching her, she touched up her hair slightly, patting it into place.

'I'm afraid I look an awful sight,' she said.

It was not for a brother to admit this to a sister – even though it broke my heart to see her like this, so different from the beautiful bride on that spring day at Douzy, barely a few months ago. How she had changed! How was it possible that in a few weeks lines of worry or anxiety, or just plain fear, had furrowed her face, not only the forehead, the eyes, but two deeply etched creases leading from the corners of her nose to her mouth? And the hair of which she had always been so

proud, but which she now nervously patted again and again –
all the sheen and gloss gone. It looked dull and mousy, what
Oregon once described as 'old maid's hair'.

'I've got to begin with one bit of bad news,' I said heavily.
'Willi's lost his job.'

Anna didn't seem surprised. 'I somehow expected it,' she
said flatly.

I explained as best I could that Willi had been expelled from
the Party after some Nazi officials visited him at the Frankel
apartment.

'Did he say who?' She was asking questions almost like a
robot.

I hesitated.

'Come on – I'm not afraid,' she said harshly.

'Brownshirts.'

Suddenly she burst into uncontrolled sobs. 'Oh no, my
poor Willi,' she cried, and turned her tearstained face to mine,
'I knew them. Scum! Did they – hurt him?'

'No, no,' I lied again. 'According to Willi they roughed him
up a bit when he was slow answering questions. But' – and I
was on safer ground now because it was true – 'though there
was nothing for us to celebrate now he's lost his job, we did
manage to drink a bottle of Scotch between us.'

She tried to compose herself, but every now and then she
was racked with sobs.

'But Willi must have said *something*.'

'I think he was afraid his apartment was wired.' I told her
everything – everything except the naked savagery of Willi's
beating up – until she had quietened down.

'Sorry about this' – she searched in a blue bag for a wisp of
handkerchief and dabbed her eyes – 'but poor Willi – it's so
terrible for him – such a brilliant engineer, one of the best in
Germany. What will he do now? What *can* he do?' Her voice
trailed off.

Again I hesitated, but I had to tell her.

'He's talking about joining the German army,' I said finally.

'The army! Those bloody clod-hoppers!' she said savagely –
and I was glad: it was better to see her angry than weeping.
'What a *waste*, what a stupid waste.'

'I know, Anna.' I didn't really know what to say, but added,

'I think Willi felt that a few months of anonymity might be a good idea. I don't know what he's done . . .'

'Nothing!' she cried. 'That's what's so damnable.' She asked a hundred questions, wanting to know everything about him. Had Willi lost weight? Who was doing the cooking for him? And making his bed – 'Our bed,' she started to cry again, then said, 'It's the tank he was working on, at Staffens, that caused all the trouble.'

I didn't understand.

'It's highly secret,' she explained. 'Supposed to be the finest tank in the world when it's ready. And several times people came to question us – very politely. But in the end I realised that the friendly meetings were always directed at me. About my family. All of us at Douzy, and America. Everything. I'm the one who got Willi into trouble, I'm sure of it.'

'I think you're exaggerating.' It was all I could say.

'I know it. Willi was engaged on highly secret work – and he was married to an American. That bloody beast Hitler is paranoid about American spies.'

'Willi gave me a letter for you.' I handed the pages to her.

'Did he? Thank you, Larry. I thought everyone was searched. I'm surprised you dared carry it.'

'Willi warned me,' I said. 'Thank God he did. The Gestapo on the train had obviously been tipped off; I think I was trailed from Willi's flat to the station. They searched my overnight bag with a toothcomb. Even checked the contents of my pocket.'

'Where did you hide the letter?'

'One page in each of my socks.'

'Bless you, Larry. You've been wonderful.'

I hadn't read the letter, but of course I knew what was in it.

'And Willi told me to stress above everything else,' I said, 'that you mustn't return to Germany. He's a marked man, Anna – and technically, I suppose, you're a German citizen and you're marked too.'

She was reading the letter now, but it was so painful that she started crying again, and I took out my larger pocket handkerchief. 'Here, Anna.' I handed it to her. 'This is better.'

Later, after another Scotch, thinking that sorrows shared are sorrows halved, I said, 'If there *is* a war – and there's bound to be one – Italy will surely be dragged in as a partner of the Rome–Berlin Axis. And that means Sonia will be an enemy too.'

'I suppose so.' She stopped crying, perhaps grateful for a change in conversation. 'And you'll miss her. Do you see her often?'

'Whenever I can. I've never told you, Anna, but – well, we became lovers again soon after she married Francesco.'

'I wondered. And her husband?'

'He doesn't seem to care. And we're both very discreet.'

Anna sighed. 'Poor you. Poor us! I suppose if life had worked out differently it would have been better if I'd never married Willi and you had married Sonia.'

'Sonia wouldn't have me,' I said bitterly.

'She loved you. Still does, I can tell,' Anna insisted. 'I often wondered why she didn't marry you. I always felt there was some reason . . .'

'You feel that too?' I asked.

'Yes, I do. I remember Sonia telling me one day that you were the only man in the world for her – but there were problems. Those were her words – "problems".'

'One day we may find out,' I said. 'My own belief is that somewhere along the line Riccardi, who I have never really trusted, blotted his copybook – and the price of his future somehow involved Sonia not marrying me.'

'We'll never know. It is bloody, isn't it? You don't know why Sonia was afraid of some trouble – and I don't know why Willi's in trouble.' She thought for a while, then added, 'You know, Larry, this apartment makes me depressed. I'm not going to feel much better, but I don't feel like cooking – not even a *croque monsieur*.'

'Let's go round the corner,' I suggested. 'Better for both of us. I'll take you to Lipp's.'

So we walked along the rue des St. Pères, crossed the boulevard St. Germain and found a bench-type table in the famous Brasserie Lipp.

'*Choucroute garnie* for two,' I ordered. 'And two large glasses of ice-cold Slavia.'

'By the way,' said Anna during dinner, 'I forgot to tell you,

but while you were in Germany Sonia invited herself to Douzy
again for the weekend.'

I must have looked very pleased.

'Yes' – it was the first time I saw her laugh that evening.
'Her husband's been called to the Foreign Office in Rome. So
she rang up Mama. You mean to say she didn't tell you?'

'She can't,' I explained. 'It's awful, but the telephones in her
house are tapped. She daren't phone me except from a phone
box, and I can never phone her.'

'Still,' she said. 'You'll see her soon enough.'

Anna drove back to Douzy early on the Thursday morning,
and almost before I had reached the rue du Sentier, Sonia was
on the phone.

'From a call box – so early?' I asked.

'Francesco has already left for Rome.' She sounded breathless. 'Every foreign ministry in Europe is in a panic. I'm sorry
for *them*' – with her throaty laugh – 'but it's wonderful for us.
You've heard about the weekend? And our staff of spies are
now so overworked I think the Italian *Fascisti* have vanished.'

'For God's sake be careful   for your sake.'

'I'm not risking the phone – but I think the bloodhounds
have been called off – so any chance of lunch?'

'Can we go some place where I can kiss you?'

'That will be the most important part.' She still spoke in that
special voice of hers, almost as a signal, warning me she
couldn't wait long before we met.

'Think it's safe to go to Marcel's?'

'Is it open – in August?'

'Sure,' I replied. 'You remember it was closed last time – in
mid-July. And there was a notice, "reopening on 21 August".'

'Then Marcel's it is.'

Though times of crisis usually meant extra work for the
Globe, lunch was fairly safe, simply because, due to the time
difference, the editors in Washington were barely eating their
bacon and hot cakes as we ate lunch. But I did manage to sandwich in a reaction story before I made my way to the rue Jacob.
I went to see Reynaud to get it.

Reynaud had agreed to see me for ten minutes – in his
apartment behind the Chambre des Députés. And among his

remarks about 'grave danger for Europe' and the usual political guff there was one significant passage – though it didn't
come from Reynaud but from Madame de Portes who entered
Reynaud's private sitting-room without warning and said
briskly, *'Bonjour, cher* Larry. These are stirring times. But
exciting.' She caught sight of herself in an Empire-styled
gilded looking-glass, and automatically touched her bouffant
hair.

'But one thing, *cher* Larry,' she exclaimed. 'That man
Daladier will have to go if it comes to war. He's not the kind of
leader we need to rally France in times like this.'

'Then who do you think will succeed him?' It wasn't exactly
an innocent question on my part.

'Who do *you* think?' she asked almost archly, and her question was answer enough so that, when I wrote my story, I
started, 'Informed sources close to the Quai d'Orsay believe
that Monsieur Daladier may have to resign, and though no
one has yet suggested a successor many favour Monsieur
Reynaud.'

That, I knew, would please many people – especially one –
and make it difficult for Reynaud to refuse later requests for
interviews.

I arrived at Marcel's at ten to one and, five minutes later, while
I was waiting at the bar, Sonia opened the narrow door with its
frosted glass panes and stood for a moment framed in it,
almost like a model posing, dressed in a plain white and brown
dress with a narrow belt, a suede bag over her shoulder, and
wearing a tiny straw hat like one of Maurice Chevalier's. She
looked incredibly – well, saucy. She was wearing the sheerest
stockings that money could buy, and on her narrow feet a pair
of brown suede moccasins.

As I kissed her – no need for shyness at Marcel's; everyone
knew we were lovers even though we didn't go there often –
she looked up and asked, 'Do you approve?'

'I run out of words trying to describe you – and out of
breath. And that hat! Every time I see you, you look more
desirable.' I held her out at arm's length, studied her almost
clinically, then ordered a glass of champagne for her.

'Even three days away seems like an age,' she said huskily. 'I'm so glad to see you.'

'Me too.'

'Was it awful in Germany?'

I nodded. Anxious to change the conversation, I said, 'I love those shoes – they're new, aren't they?'

'You notice things!' Like any woman she was delighted.

'I just thought that moccasins show off your legs.'

'Made for me, that's why. By a man called Gucci who has opened a shop in the Via della Vignia-Nuova.'

'Never heard of him,' I said rather impolitely.

'Remember your twenty-first birthday party?' she asked as we sat down at our usual table. 'Such wonderful days – and nights.'

Nothing had changed – not there, not in Marcel's. Only we had changed. As the wife of a diplomat, Sonia was busy, much in demand, though always finding ways for us to meet. But I, too, had changed. Now I spent most of my time working on the *Globe* with stints helping out on the *Paris American*. I was earning good money, simply because there was so much news in Europe to be covered that Tommy Tomlinson couldn't cope unaided.

'It must be months since we were last here,' said Sonia. 'Hold my hand, darling. Across the table. Don't be shy.'

I wasn't shy, but she always pretended I was.

'You know, Larry, I don't think I've ever loved you so much. Perhaps it's because I'm afraid – no, that's not an insult. It's the truth. Francesco says it's only a question of days now. But darling, we'll always have a place to meet.'

I looked quizzical.

'My house in Switzerland.'

I had long since forgotten the cottage she had planned to buy.

'You mean you've got it?'

She nodded, the fear of war replaced by the excitement of a new toy. 'One we can share, neutral America, neutral Switzerland. Darling, it's for you and me. No one else will ever be allowed in.'

'Where is it?'

'You'll never guess. It's at Rolle, just behind the lake. Not

254

far from our old school. Remember St. Agnes? I don't know what's going to happen to Francesco and me, but if there's a war – well, I'm trying to think of the future. Switzerland will *always* be neutral – and as a diplomat's wife I hope I'll always be able to move around a bit.'

'And Francesco?'

'Papa's given *me* the cottage – it's *mine*. It's nothing to do with anyone else.'

'Has it got a name, in case I have to come and search for you?' I laughed.

'You remember the coffee shop? Well, almost opposite, by the fountain, a small lane leads off the main street. It's up there, first house after you pass under the railway bridge. It's got an odd name – "Three Circles Farm".'

'I wish we could escape now,' I said, suddenly thinking how awful it was soon going to be – both of us on our best behaviour for the coming weekend at Douzy.

'Why couldn't we?'

'Now, now,' I laughed. 'None of your mad ideas.'

'I love you, I love you, and we'll spend the weekend alone.'

'On Sunday Papa has called a family council of war – to discuss the future.'

'Well, Saturday – and Friday – with Douzy as a perfect alibi.'

'We couldn't. I wouldn't put it past your Italian blood-hounds to phone Douzy and speak to Mama – deliberately to check on you.'

She thought for a moment. Then, looking at me straight with those blue, blue eyes, she said, 'Why not tell your mama what we're planning?'

'But where would we go?'

'What about that place in the village near La Ferté sous Juarre? It's tucked away and half-way to Douzy. We could drive there on the Friday, and on Sunday just drive on and join the family for dinner. And your council of war.'

I wondered. Anyway, as I thought to myself, what the hell, I'm twenty-seven, I'm free and white, and if I can't tell my own mother my innermost secrets, who could I tell?

'You're right,' I admitted. What made it easier to agree was the fact that Mama was spending the Thursday evening in

Paris to attend some formal dinner. Gaston was driving her in, and surely there would be time for me to pop round to the apartment for a drink and sound her out before dinner. All the same, I was a little nervous. It was one thing for Mama to know about my affair with a married woman; something else to condone it.

That Thursday, sitting in the big *salon* in the rue des St. Pères, drinking my second Scotch, I summoned up my courage and said, 'Mama, darling, I want to talk to you. You can tell Papa later – if you want to. It's up to you.'

'You mean about you and Sonia?'

'You *did* know . . .?'

'I guessed. I'm not as old and decrepit as you seem to think.'

'But that wasn't what I wanted to talk to you about.'

'Oh!' she seemed surprised. 'I thought . . .'

'Now that Sonia's officially invited for the weekend – we wondered – well, her presence there with you could provide us with a super alibi. Could we sneak off for a couple of nights? It's so sad, always having . . .'

'To go home?' she asked and held out her arm. 'I know how sad it must be for you. Mornings are so beautiful, waking up, and . . .' she hesitated.

'Would you mind if I didn't stay at Douzy? On the Friday and Saturday anyway. Just so that we can be alone.'

Surprising me, she stroked my cheek, and said gently, 'Poor Larry, my love-child. You are doomed to love, that's the fate of the love-child. And we took Sonia away from you. I'll never be able to forgive myself for stopping you when you were young. I shouldn't say yes – I shouldn't. But' – almost mischievously – 'there's a world of difference between a snatched afternoon and an entire night.'

'Mama!'

'I understand – it's the least I can do, Larry. But come back Sunday afternoon – for the party at the pyramid. And I'll make apologies for you.'

'Mama, you are wonderful.'

'Where will you go?' she asked, suddenly conspiratorial. 'You two illegal lovebirds?'

I wrote down the name and number of the hotel.

'Have we time for another drink? To celebrate?'
'I'd love to, but I haven't time. I must dress for dinner.'
'Who with?'
'The committee of the American Hospital,' she laughed. 'So dreary. I'd much rather be with you.'

I had arranged to pick up Sonia soon after lunch, but before that I had to spend a morning at the office helping Tommy Tomlinson, and also Oregon, with the last lines of information for the *Paris American*. It was an uneasy morning, imbued with a sense of urgency, suppressed panic.

There could be no question of Chamberlain and Daladier trying to placate Hitler this time. Action was outstripping words, tomorrow's history being enacted as we gaped at the awful news, and I was horrified at the way in which we could only stand and watch preparations for the disintegration of the only world we knew.

Daladier, it appeared, was in a panic — almost more afraid of the French communists than of Germany. He banned *l'Humanité*, the official organ of the French communist party, and ordered the arrest of all its communist staff. Then he took an unprecedented step. He ordered the arrest of all communist members of parliament, though this was a direct violation of their parliamentary immunity. Known communists in the armed forces also were thrown into jail.

On the Friday morning — the day I was planning to leave with Sonia — Oregon and I went for a quick stroll along the Grands Boulevards to judge the temper of the crowds. The string of boulevards with their separate names joining one into the other, and called collectively 'Grands' were already pasted with mobilisation posters on every spare inch of wall.

'But Christ!' I pointed out the frightening headline *APPEL IMMÉDIAT* to Oregon. 'This is Friday — it's only a couple of days since the Russians and Germans got together.'

'Daladier's right. There's no time to lose,' said Oregon grimly. 'Look at that.' A convoy of trucks emerged from the corner of the boulevard Haussman into the boulevard des Italiens. They were packed with rows of helmeted troops, each man grasping a rifle by the barrel, the butt on the floorboards between his legs. 'They're on the way to the Maginot Line.'

Tommy Tomlinson had asked me if I could collect 'local interest' material for a piece that he would be writing later in the day. We often helped each other by pooling information.

'I'm going to take a quick look at the gare de l'Est.' I left Oregon and drove to the station – which I knew led to the Maginot Line area. The *gare* was jammed with the stark evidence of war, with troops everywhere. Some wore the khaki uniforms which had officially replaced the French blue uniforms of 1935. But many still wore the famous *bleu horizon*, not only out of pride, but because, as reservists, they had never been issued with replacements. Every man carried his manganese steel helmet with its unusual shape – still identical to the 1915 issue, stamped in one piece with an identifying badge.

Most of the men came from the infantry – it was easy to spot them with their blue uniforms, but even in khaki by the blue piping on the *képi*, or peaked cap, whereas other branches such as the artillery or infantry displayed different coloured piping. Here and there tank crewmen strutted past with their special pride in being part of the élite 'new army' which de Gaulle had envisaged. They had their own uniform, including their three-quarter-length leather coats and blue berets, and carried special helmets with neck guards and padded leather fronts.

There seemed to be hundreds of women crowding the station, some in tears, some kissing with the passion of a last farewell, sergeants shouting, officers swaggering in their neatly cut uniforms, and, above all, the long black columns of trains splaying out from each entrance to each platform, that and the steam above. It was a shambles of mixed patriotism and tears.

For every man there seemed to be two women, or perhaps it was an optical illusion, though there *were* two types of women: the younger ones – the sweethearts rather than the wives – locked in embraces, yet not crying, proud of their men, caught up in the infectious fervour of martial music calling the brave to arms, each girl convinced that her heroic man would return. It was the older women who had the drawn faces, the lines etched in by memories of another war, mothers weeping quietly when saying farewell to sons who had never known their fathers.

On the way back to the office I passed the Louvre. It was already closed, the trucks drawn outside, the first packing cases and crates taking away a national heritage to some secret destination. From the office I phoned the American Embassy for the latest news. Jim Parks told me that even the American Hospital at Neuilly was packing up, ready to be evacuated 'lock, stock and syringe', as he put it, to Étretat in Normandy.

The first early editions of the evening papers carried whole-page ads warning the people of Paris to leave the capital unless they were needed on essential work. 'Enemy bombs may be redoubtable,' cried one headline.

'But there's no war yet,' I said to Tommy as I typed out a few helping paragraphs. The ads, which were duplicated on posters on nearby walls, even across from the windows of the rue du Sentier office, urged people not to hoard food and staple necessities. But by the time I set off to pick up Sonia the first queues – for everything from sugar to gasoline – were form-ing. A sign *AVIS A LA POPULATION* gave instructions on how to shield car lights after dark and how to make impro-vised curtains for the home. The age of the blackout had arrived.

I had planned to meet Sonia in my M.G. outside the rue du Cherche Midi. She was always afraid of being seen, and as she jumped in and I kissed her gently, the sudden noise of a roll of drums startled her. An old-time village town crier – for Saint-Germain-des-Prés was a village in the heart of Paris – was beating a roll. A small crowd gathered as he announced in stentorian tones that under pain of severe punishment all members of the reserve must report to their units.

The decrees had already been promulgated, but the sight of this old man, crying to the 'villagers' as his forefathers had cried to our forefathers, before their past wars, before their past unnecessary deaths, made me shiver. It was a ghoulish illustration of the futility that gripped us all.

19

The Cheval Blanc, in a tiny village a few miles east of La Ferté, was the perfect place for our weekend.

I had stopped there several times for drinks on the way back to Reims and Douzy, and had fallen in love with its charm: a small hotel with eight rooms which had achieved gastronomic renown out of all proportion to its village location. Originally it had opened as a small bistro with a few simple rooms to accommodate visiting farmers or trade visitors – the sort of men who couldn't afford the better hotels. But then M. and Mme Roland, who owned it, began producing culinary delights far better than anything offered either in Reims or Épernay. Their food was superb. People started driving from Paris for weekends, even though six of the rooms only boasted a *cabinet de toilette*. And above all it was discreet. It had become not only a haunt for gourmets, but also an hotel where gentlemen could safely bring the wives of other gentlemen.

It stood in its own grounds – a courtyard lined with pots and tubs of annuals – of the type known to seed merchants as 'hardy' because they had to flower all summer through. There were tubs of orange calendula edged with lobelia, and the inevitable pots of petunias that grew, died and re-grew.

'It's so beautiful, isn't it?' Sonia squeezed my hand. Behind the restaurant was a large pond on which some ducks, no doubt kept for a specific purpose, quacked, almost the only sound to interrupt the magical silence.

The trees were coloured a dozen different shades of green. It all looked so peaceful that the impending beastliness of war seemed a million miles away. The Cheval Blanc cast a spell that made the short weekend as gentle and sweet as any I can remember. Perhaps it was also because we both knew there wouldn't be many more weekends together – that the same disruption in the lives of Anna and Willi would soon disrupt ours, make artificial enemies of each other. It was a weekend beautiful yet tinged with sadness.

We went for long walks. The countryside was different here. The fields of corn and barley were more sweeping, so that with each passing cloud a shadow rolled across the golden sea like a black wave. No one seemed to notice us, as if (though this was fanciful nonsense) all the world knew we were lovers on the verge of parting, and so tactfully left us alone. In truth the entire area seemed empty, as so many small villages are empty in France. This one didn't boast one single shop, not even a *tabac*. And the quiet village streets led across the fields which were different from those near Douzy. These were lazy fields, inviting, the fat black and white cows as much in place as the buttercups and other coloured wild flowers that dotted the green grass.

Hungry after our long walk on the Friday evening, we ate a huge dinner, in which almost everything was home-grown, home-made and home-cooked, from the *terrine de lapin*, the finest Charentais melons to start with, and the dish of succulent yellow *girolles*, the mushrooms which were sautéed, stalks and all, with a whiff of garlic so subtle it was as though Sonia had chewed a clove and breathed over the dish. Or for Sonia, as a vegetable, a dish of *haricots noirs*, the delicious skinny string beans that start out with blemishes of blackish spots which mysteriously vanish and turn green after cooking.

This weekend we made love in a peaceful, serene way, perhaps because of the war clouds rolling across our horizon, darkening the blue August skies. Perhaps also because for two mornings – the Saturday and the Sunday – we were untroubled when we woke; no anxiety, no need to dress quickly, no need to part hurriedly with backward glances. Instead we ordered our feathery croissants and coffee when we felt like it, not when we had to, before or after making love. Even the act of love-making was different here; it had a quality of gentle repose.

'It's like being married.' Sonia kissed me.

★   ★   ★

We arrived at Douzy during the late afternoon of Sunday, to find the family assembled for a champagne party that was about to start in the pyramid.

'I'm glad you both arrived in time.' My father eyed me warily. I was wary too; I wasn't sure whether or not he knew how I had spent the last two days.

'Why the party?' I asked.

'A sort of temporary farewell, yes, I think that describes it perfectly,' explained Papa, while I continued to look mystified.

'It's a mobilisation party,' explained Guy laconically. 'For those in the vineyards who've been ordered to report to the military authorities.'

A sudden rush of nausea hit me. It had been one thing earlier that week to watch the frenzied, excited crowds at the gare de l'Est on their way to the front – watching them as a reporter, as impersonally as if I were watching a newsreel.

But this! The men at Douzy were actually on the point of leaving for an unknown life. For where? For how long? For life or for death? Poor devils! It seemed only a few weeks since I watched the last remnants of the Spanish war victims – victims only because they had been on the losing side; several hundred idealistic young men who had volunteered to fight for a free Spain, many of them butchered by Germans with guns or planes. And now, all over again.

Oregon, who was spending the weekend at Douzy, must have seen my sudden silent anger, for he squeezed my arm gently. 'I know what you're mad at,' he seemed to read my thoughts, 'that a bunch of stupid political leaders are responsible for this – while we . . .'

'You're dead right,' I replied. 'Nobody wants a war.'

'I agree with you – but only partly.' He lit another cigarette in preparation for the short trip to the pyramid. 'There is one thing you can't really ignore. It's too easy to say that nobody wants a war, so therefore it must be the fault of the world leaders. But aren't we, the ordinary people, to blame too? It's not only the leaders who are tyrants – the masses can be tyrants as well.'

We walked down to the pyramid – all except Grandma who had been making her rounds of the vineyards, and whom we eventually saw approaching from a different direction – a stalwart old lady riding on her bicycle from one of the outlying vineyards where she had discovered some foliage which had not been trimmed well enough to let in the last weeks of the sun.

'Good afternoon, Grandma,' I said politely as she dismounted.

'And where have *you* been, young man?' she asked, though fortunately, perhaps with advancing age, she never bothered to wait for an answer. 'The number five field,' she said to one of the vignerons who was making for the pyramid, 'needs more trimming.'

He smiled assent. He knew that even if '*les sales Boches*' arrived at Douzy, La Châtelaine would make her rounds and give her orders – and expect them to be obeyed without question.

We trickled into the pyramid, more or less lining up at the tables, draped with white cloths, at the back of the observation platform, scanning the faces of those I knew would be going, feeling a twinge of guilt, even though it wasn't my war, that I wouldn't even be allowed to enlist had I wanted to. Which I didn't. If – that eternal if – it did come to war, I hoped that I would then be able to report it for the *Globe*.

Some of those who had received their mobilisation orders were sombre, some excited; looking at the white pyramid high above and all around us, I whispered to Sonia, almost shivering, 'It looks like a bloody shroud.'

One of Jacques Pagniez's family, a cousin of Aubergine's, came to shake hands. 'I'm leaving on Wednesday,' he volunteered the information. 'Ordered to the Maginot Line.'

'So he'll be safe, *monsieur*,' said Aubergine, with the touch of pride that signified an appointment to a 'safe' location.

'Yes, *monsieur*,' he said, 'I'm one of the lucky ones. One of the officers told me I'll probably never see a German. Do you know that some of our guns can fire twenty kilometres? Fancy shooting someone you've never seen!'

'Less uncomfortable for the soul,' said Oregon.

'Sir?' The young man looked startled at the mystic word 'soul'. Somehow the word didn't go with killing, and neither he nor Aubergine had the faintest idea what Oregon had meant.

The usual couple of formal butlers were serving champagne. Dressed in white tie and tails – a uniform to them – and wearing their badge of office, a silver tasting cup suspended round their neck by a multi-coloured ribbon, they dispensed champagne at every reception; they had never actually been vignerons – or full-time butlers – for when no one was giving a party both men worked in the accountancy department. Butlerage was a spare-time job which they performed with dignity and, by now, a professional touch.

'I'm afraid I'm leaving, sir,' said one of them, the middle-aged Pasteur. 'Called up with the reserves.'

'But who's going to . . .' I asked.

'We're not irreplaceable,' he smiled. 'Actually, *monsieur*, I'm really looking forward to it. I don't get on very well with *madame* – my wife I mean – and . . .' he shrugged his shoulders.

Papa turned to kiss Sonia on the cheek, 'We shall miss these boys. But I'm *very* glad to see you, my dear. And how's' – he stumbled over the forgotten name – 'your husband. Really! I've never got used to you as someone's wife.'

'Francesco's in Rome,' explained Sonia. 'Very busy, as you can imagine.'

'Yes, yes, of course. This must be a very busy time for him, very troublous, yes, that's the word, *troublous*.'

Anna was standing up by the rails, looking down into the white pit below, talking to Guy. Even though one was a man, the other a woman, at times the twins when seen in a certain light or at a certain angle were astonishingly alike – even though Guy looked quite masculine and Anna had a woman's face.

As Sonia walked over to talk to them, and I shifted away from Aubergine who had been introducing me to yet another relative, Mama came up to me and said, 'I think Anna feels much better – if that's the right word, but you know what I'm trying to say – now that the future is – well, resolved, I suppose you might say.'

'"Inevitable" would perhaps be a better word,' said Oregon.

'Whatever. But she's not torn by having to make decisions. She may be miserable, parted from Willi, but there's nothing she can do about it now.'

'One thing does worry me,' I said, talking directly to Papa. 'If the Germans do start a war won't Anna be in trouble? A German national, I mean – sort of an enemy alien in France?'

'She's American!' my father almost spluttered.

'Is she? She might be an American in America. But what would she be if the Germans occupied France and she was still here?'

'A disgusting thing to say!' La Châtelaine had overheard my remark. 'I would kill myself before I let the Germans take my home.' She gave an indignant rustle of her old-fashioned, rather long skirt. 'It's wicked even to suggest such a thing as occupation.'

'I'm sorry, Grandma.'

'I should think so. Occupied! By the Boches! Unthinkable!'

'Of course,' I agreed quickly. 'But I was thinking about Anna.' And then as Grandma, with a fine toss of her head, spoke to someone else, I elaborated to Papa. 'It's true that Anna has dual nationality, but even so you know how suspicious the French can get. It's not only the Germans – what about those French who whisper that she's married to a German, that her name is Frau Frankel, that she has a German passport? If war comes she would be an enemy alien, even if Germany didn't occupy France. She could be interned.'

'In prison!' cried Mama. 'Never. Not Anna.'

'You know what red tape is like in France,' I said.

Grandma was back, and snorted, 'The Boches will never beat the French. If this war comes it'll teach the Germans a lesson they'll never forget.'

'It won't be our problem, thank God,' said Oregon.

'Of course it will,' Grandma said angrily in reply. 'France is your country too, and don't you forget it, my boy.' The words 'my boy' made me realise how odd it was to listen to Grandma giving her son a dressing down. 'Never forget that even if America stays out of the war – and frankly it's none of our business, the French don't need them – we owe everything, our lives, our fortunes, to France. That's why both my sons have dual nationality. And that I am French. *Vive la France.*'

'*Vive la France!*' cried the others hearing her raise her voice, without having the faintest idea what she was talking about.

'Meanwhile, what about Anna?' I asked.

'We'll talk about it after dinner,' Papa suggested. 'Larry's right, of course. She should get out of France.' And to Mama he added, 'And so should you, my dear.'

'We've been through all that,' said Mama with a touch of asperity.

I was about to agree with Papa when – perhaps fortunately, as it broke the tension – Gaston came along. He was politely talking to Olivia, almost earnestly.

He approached my father and asked, 'I wonder, *monsieur*, if it would be all right to give Mademoiselle Olivia her final driving lesson tomorrow?'

'Driving lesson!' I looked at Gaston. 'What on earth do you mean? She's the best driver in Douzy,' adding with a laugh, 'after you and me.'

'I know, *monsieur*, but,' Gaston hesitated, '*monsieur* agreed that *mademoiselle* should spend a little time driving the Hisp. It *is* large for a lady driver, sir.'

'Ah yes, of course,' Papa agreed.

'But why?' I suppose I should have realised.

'Because on Wednesday afternoon,' said Mama quickly, 'we won't have a driver. Gaston's been mobilised.'

I couldn't believe it. Gaston and I had the bond that only two people who have grown up together *and* loved motor cars can share. The same age as me, a man of impeccable manners, a quiet charm, the son of an old friend of the family who had spent his life working for us, he was like another member of the family.

'But Gaston,' I suggested. 'Couldn't you qualify for a reserved occupation or whatever it's called?' I turned to Papa. 'Sure we could help.'

Gaston looked embarrassed. 'I don't want that,' he said. 'I'm only worried about letting you down.'

'And so,' explained Papa, 'we've got a new driver. A chauffeuse. Yes, chauffeuse, that's the word. What do you think of *that*?'

'And that's why I'm getting a few last minute tips,' Olivia laughed. 'I call the Hisp. the monster. I only hope I don't smash it up.'

'*Her*, please, not *it*.' I laughed too, but couldn't help asking, with a trace of sarcasm, 'Then what's going to happen to Guy's painting lessons?'

'Did I hear someone call my name?' Guy crossed the platform. 'Art? Oh that!' he said cheerfully. 'On the advice of my mentor and art master, I've decided to give up painting until the war's over. I'm going to work full-time for Papa in the vineyards or the *cellier*. Only until the war's over, mind you.'

'Hardly worth bothering about. If those Germans have the guts to fight, the war will be over in a couple of months,' said La Châtelaine fiercely – the look of fierceness accentuated by her eccentric clothes, the long tweed skirt and the thick leather belt with a huge buckle, and her hair in a bun.

I'm sure that Oregon loved his mother, but even so he couldn't stop the whisper, 'All she needs is a pair of cycling clips and she'd be a man!'

Turning to Gaston, I said, 'It's going to be tough without you, but let's hope Grandma is right – and that it'll all be over before it starts. Any idea where you'll be posted?'

'I'd hoped to go to North Africa in the transport corps or tanks. Thought I might as well get a free bit of travel on the government.'

'No luck?'

He shook his head. 'I've still got my application in,' he said, 'but now I've been told to report on Wednesday to Arras. I imagine my application has been pigeon-holed.'

'I think you're better off here,' said Mama. 'At least you'll be able to come and see us when you're on leave, and Madame Robert will be able to get you some extra food from the Home Farm. And you'll be with your family. Africa? It sounds horrible. Oh' – hesitating – 'if my husband can help . . .'

'I'm very grateful, madame.' I could see that Gaston really meant it, and was touched. 'And I'll continue with Madem-oiselle Olivia's final lesson?'

'Of course,' said my father as Gaston walked away. 'Salt of the earth, that lad, yes, the *salt*. Trust him with my life.'

The Misses B and B, together with Jean-Pierre, came for a quiet dinner that evening, and Miss Brewer in particular was a perfect foil for Grandma, nodding approval each time Grandma made a new and outrageous statement.

This was also a farewell dinner for Jean-Pierre, who had gained a commission as a second lieutenant and was being posted to the Maginot Line.

'On Thursday,' he said in answer to Papa's question.

'We shall miss Jean-Pierre very much,' sighed Miss Brewer. 'The cottage will be very empty.'

'Don't you think you should close it up and move to your small apartment in Paris?' asked Mama. 'If there is going to be any fighting, it's sure to be around the Champagne area, whereas the Germans will never reach Paris.'

'We did think about it,' Miss Brewer nodded more urgently than ever.

'But you see,' explained Miss Barron, 'it would suit us best to remain here. The cottage will be so much nearer for Jean-Pierre when he gets leave.'

To me it seemed incredible that though this nationwide mobilisation was urgent and for real, it was still invested with the unreal quality of an exercise. Nobody seemed aware that when the battle burst upon Europe leave wouldn't matter a damn – you could be shifted from one theatre to another without anyone being told – to say nothing of the fact that thousands would be killed or maimed. People like the Misses B and B seemed totally unaware of the disruption and bloodshed which war would inflict. Miss Barron had actually consulted the railway guide for information about trains between the front line and Reims. To her the front line was static, Jean-Pierre was safe, nothing would interfere with his routine leave or weekend passes. Did they really think war was still a game between 'gentlemen' who abided by a set of rules?

Of course, like everyone, I didn't think they would be killed, but when I said this to Oregon, he answered, 'No one would ever go to war again if they didn't feel certain it was the other guy who was going to get killed.'

'I'm quite looking forward to it,' said Jean-Pierre. 'Though I'm worried about what'll happen during the *vendange*.'

'We'll be short-handed too,' said Guy, 'so we'll have to help each other.'

In fact the *vendange*, though not due until the end of September, might well cause problems, for the speed with which the grapes were picked depended on employing casual labour from mining families in Lorraine who had over the years become regular visitors – and experts in harvesting.

'But as most are miners,' explained Papa, 'the government is certainly not going to let them have their annual vacations to pick grapes.'

After dinner Papa carefully broached the subject of Anna's departure. We were sitting in a corner of the conservatory having coffee.

'I don't really want to go anywhere,' confessed Anna miserably. 'If I can't stay with Willi, I want to stay at Douzy.'

'Very understandable,' agreed Papa. 'Yes, *very*. Nothing matters of course, if there *isn't* a war. But technically I suppose you are a German. And quite apart from red tape, people are getting, well, suspicious of their neighbours.'

'Suspicious of someone like me?' Anna almost laughed. 'But everyone round here knows me. Everyone!'

More gently than usual, Oregon explained, 'It's the fifth column, Anna. It's become a sort of cult. Everyone is looking at everyone else – looking for traitors, Nazi sympathisers.'

'It sounds awful,' said Anna. 'I don't want to go, but even if I did, where *could* I go?'

'America?' I asked.

'God forbid. At heart I'm a European, Larry, and you know it.'

'England?'

'They wouldn't let you in with a German passport, or stay with an American one,' said Oregon.

'Then I'll stay here,' decided Anna.

It was at this moment that Sonia drifted towards the conservatory, listening to the end of the conversation.

'I've got an idea.' She hesitated. 'What about my house in Rolle?'

'What's this about a house in Switzerland?' Both Papa and Mama looked mystified.

'Of course, I haven't told you.' Sonia explained how she had come by the house. 'It's not very comfortable yet,' she admitted, 'but Anna could stay there.' With a laugh at the happiness of the past, she said, 'At least it's got more comfortable beds than those we slept on at St. Agnes.'

I could see that Anna was tempted.

'It seems a *very* good idea,' said Papa. 'Just until this nonsense blows over.'

'I could come down with you to take a look-see and help put the place in order,' said Sonia. 'We could have such fun! It's probably in a terrible mess – but the Swiss are good at things. They'll fix it up in a week.' And squeezing Anna's hand impulsively, she implored, 'Come on, Anna! Just for the time being. Just the two of us.'

I realised for the first time that Anna was frightened. Not deeply. Perhaps 'apprehensive' would be a better word. But to her Switzerland represented a haven, while the prospect of living in America was too far from Willi – not to mention Douzy. Switzerland was different. It was small and cosy and next door to everything.

'Want a lift down?' I asked.

'Thanks – another time.' Even Anna was laughing again, and with a hidden meaning that only the three of us could understand, said darkly, 'We know what happens when you take girls out in your seduction cars.'

Before the end of the evening it was decided. There was no suggestion that Anna would stay in Switzerland for a long time. But even she had to agree that a German passport could be embarrassing.

'You two girls fix up the details between you,' I said. 'And I'll see you safely on the train.'

It was shortly after this that Mama came into the conversation, astonishing us with a rare outburst of anger.

The girls had gone off on their own – it always added to the warmth of my love for Sonia to see how close she and Anna had been, still were. Papa was explaining that Sonia had suggested taking Anna to Switzerland.

'A temporary refuge, yes, the word is *refuge*,' he said.

But this remark led to another. 'Of course I would have been happier, my dear, if Anna had gone to America – with you.' He turned to Mama. 'After all, you haven't seen your mother for years, and she's an old lady.' He added mildly, 'I see mine every day.'

'Too often,' grunted Oregon. 'No offence, but mothers should be seen and not heard. Why do you think I started the *Paris American*. So that I wouldn't be bullied in Douzy seven days a week.'

'Well, I'm not going anywhere.' Mama's voice was firm.

'I know how you feel,' said Papa. 'But it won't be much fun here, even for a neutral.'

This casual remark, directed originally at Anna more than at Mama, almost led to a row. I couldn't believe the intensity of Mama's feelings.

'We've been through all this before,' she said crossly. 'And once and for all, I'm not going to leave France.' As I looked up, surprised at the vehemence in her tone, she added, 'I don't know why you insist on carrying on about it.'

'The war could last a long time,' said my father drily.

'Or a very short time,' snorted Grandma as she entered the room. 'The Boches will never get past the Maginot Line.'

'There is one thing Anna would do well to consider,' Oregon was hastily changing the subject. 'She's going to find a German passport an – encumbrance. I don't know what she can do with it,' he hesitated, 'but if she can, well, conveniently forget she ever had it . . .' he left the suggestion in mid-air.

'You mean just use her American one?' I asked.

'Sure.' Oregon added, 'You told me the other day her American passport is still valid. Great. Only even though she does have dual nationality, she'll have to be careful . . .'

'About what?' asked Papa.

'About getting caught,' said Oregon. 'With the German one. By accident, I mean. Germans aren't exactly popular around Europe, and more and more travellers are being searched at the frontiers.'

I had had to work in Paris all that last week in August – and 'all that week' included trying to make head and tail of the abortive moves by Daladier and Chamberlain, both trying desperately to pacify the Germans.

'Daladier can't do a thing,' said Tommy Tomlinson in the office. 'He's too weak.'

First thing on Monday morning, I booked tickets for two sleepers to Switzerland for the Wednesday – 30 August. I had a hell of a job getting reservations, as everything was booked up, but with a little help from embassy friends I succeeded. The feeling of edginess in Paris was claustrophobic, yet I found, too, a ring of patriotism, as though everyone was echoing the cries of Grandma, 'The Boches will never stand a chance.'

On the Wednesday afternoon I took the girls to the gare de Lyon. Everyone seemed to be making for the southbound trains – or were the streets by the Hôtel de Ville always so jammed with traffic?

It was evening, and spattering with rain, as it so often was when the trains for the south departed. The rain added to the sense of foreboding. In normal times, trains are exciting, to watch, to board – but not now. The packed platforms were thronged with people, looking more bedraggled than ever in the blue wartime lighting, making the unending rows of platforms seem even longer under the huge arcs of the glass roof. People struggled at the narrow entrance gates, and at first a fussy ticket collector tried to stop me until Sonia explained her diplomatic status. We fought our way towards the train reserved for passengers to the south, hardly able to hear ourselves as the old-fashioned engine whistled away its steam.

It was deeply depressing. And yet I was delighted at our joint success in persuading Anna to leave, for what would in effect be the start of a new life.

The station was crowded, not so much with troops now – they would be making more for the gare du Nord or the gare de l'Est. No, the people jostling us now were mostly civilians in the process of running away. Like Anna, I suddenly thought.

Travellers going only to southern France – Lyons and the surrounding area – were able to board the train immediately they produced tickets, but passengers making for Switzerland, for which there were three special coaches at the rear of the train, had to go through immigration and a vague customs check. I knew that the customs operated at stations specifically to deal with occasional passengers about whom they had been tipped off, men or women carrying gold or perhaps drugs. In the same way passengers, especially those with foreign passports, were subjected only to a cursory examination. The police and immigration were more interested in looking for criminals.

I could see Anna and Sonia through the window of the immigration room off the station platform. The moment the officer looked at Sonia's diplomatic passport, he saluted smartly and even gave her a small bow. A moment later, Anna presented her American passport, and I saw the officer, apparently perplexed, motion to Sonia, asking whether they were friends and travelling together. Then I saw him consult a thick black loose-leaf reference book. I guessed it consisted of a list of names, and I saw, but could not hear, the beginnings of an argument. Barging through the door, I tapped Sonia on the shoulder.

'What gives?' I asked.

Anna had gone white. 'It's the passport!'

The French official was not only polite, he was plainly apologetic.

'Can I help, officer?' I asked. 'This is my sister.'

'It is unfortunate.' He displayed Anna's passport. 'And I can assure *m'sieu* that this is only a technicality. But the name of *madame* – and the passport.'

'Oh no,' I groaned. 'Oh Anna – you didn't get your passport stamped with your new name.'

Anna was in tears. 'There never seemed to be any time. . . .'

Sonia was whispering to the immigration officer, 'trying to pull rank', as she told me later. But there was no rank to be pulled. I saw the officer apologise profusely. Something about the man's manner, polite but acting under specific orders about a specific person, crystallised into a sudden suspicion that this was not an accidental problem at the station. Someone had warned the immigration authorities to watch out for a 'Miss Astell'. How otherwise could he have known that there was anything wrong with what appeared to be a perfectly valid American passport? How could he know enough to ask if Astell was her real name?

'I don't understand, officer,' my voice had an undercurrent

of anger. 'Why should you pick on my sister? She has dual
nationality. How did you even *know* she had a married name?'

'*Monsieur*, please, I beg you, this has nothing to do with me.
I am only presented daily with a list of names. As you know,
even if it is innocent, it is strictly illegal to travel under a name
that is not correct.'

I knew what had happened – knew inside my guts, even if I
could never prove it. I said to both girls, 'It's that sod Albrecht.
He knew you were in Paris, Anna, and he's tipped off the
neo-Fascists in the Quai d'Orsay.' Adding, 'My God! How
could you be so bloody stupid as to forget your passport
problem?'

As I led the girls back to the car I was thinking, How
powerful the Germans are – and the fifth column. And how
thoroughly ruthless, how deep-seated the determination to
beat the hell out of anyone who stood in their way. No wonder
that poor innocent men like Willi were watched, and beaten up
or exterminated.

I hoped, though I had my doubts, that the 'technicality', as
the immigration officer called it, could be resolved quickly.
And it had already occurred to me that if the Germans behind
the French were able to stop an American leaving Paris for
Switzerland, they might be equally capable of stopping a Frau
Frankel.

So it proved. It would take at least a week for the U.S.
Embassy to process the documents. New photos would be
required. They needed her marriage certificate, which meant
getting a duplicate from Douzy. The formalities were endless.

'We'll start the ball rolling,' I said. 'I only hope we get the
new passport through in time.'

I had to leave the girls after dropping them at the rue des St.
Pères. Sonia refused to travel to Rolle alone. Anna decided to
stay at the apartment until Friday evening when I could drive
her back to Douzy for the usual weekend break. But before
that – and right away – I had one phone call to make as soon
as the ancient elevator creaked and groaned on the second floor
of the rue du Sentier.

It was to Herr Albrecht.

Whatever he might have wondered, his first remarks on the

phone exuded his spurious air of camaraderie, that of the fellow journalist delighted to talk with a colleague.

'Cut out the hearts and flowers crap,' I almost shouted. 'I know bloody well you brought pressure to bear to get my sister stopped at the station.'

'That is outrageous, Larry.'

'You and Abetz. What a pair of shits.'

I could feel, even on the phone, his anger matching mine.

'I would remind you, Herr Astell,' – the 'Larry' had gone for the moment – 'that your sister insisted she was in Switzerland, *nein?*'

'Well, how do you know she isn't?'

'She shouldn't dine with an Italian diplomat, my friend. Women who are on the run should be more circumspect. After all, Italy is a member of the Rome–Berlin Axis.'

I felt sick. I had known that was the obvious link, but had thrust it out of my mind. Could it really be true that de Feo – the husband of Anna's oldest friend – had betrayed her?

At least Sonia could have nothing to do with it. So she must never know. If, that is, my guess was right. I prayed it wasn't, and said to Albrecht. 'Are you there, Herr Albrecht?'

'*Ja, ja.*'

'Then listen. Keep right out of my way. I warn you. I don't care if you're Hitler himself, but the next time I set eyes on you I'm going to beat the hell out of you, in the same way you beat up my brother-in-law. I'll start by crushing your balls together. Okay? Now just you remember – keep out of my sight.'

I felt better – a bit better, anyway – when I slammed down the phone.

After checking with Tommy Tomlinson, I left on the Friday for Douzy. I knew there was no hope of seeing Sonia that weekend and I had the feeling in my bones that the bubble of our lives was about to burst at any moment. So I set off in the M.G. arriving in the late afternoon.

The first person I saw was Gaston, polishing the Hisp.

'What on earth are you doing here? I thought you'd gone with the others, the day before yesterday.'

'I got some good news.' He seemed excited. 'They're drafting me to North Africa after all.'

'I knew you wanted to go. When?'

'On Sunday. Catching the train to Paris to report, then to Algiers.'

'Well – *bonne chance*. Algiers can't be that bad, though I don't suppose you'll ever see a German.'

The second person I saw was Papa, taking an early evening stroll in the courtyard.

'Just ten minutes for a breath of air before dinner,' he explained.

'Mama around?'

Papa shook his head. 'She's having a rest. She told Aubergine to wake her in time for a bath before dinner.'

'Nothing wrong?' Papa seemed tense.

'You obviously haven't heard the news.'

'Nothing – not since I left Paris.'

He sighed. 'It upset your mother. Germany has invaded Poland.'

'Oh my God!' I cried. Until the very last moment, despite the overwhelming news of sinister German troop movements, I had clung to the hope that it wouldn't, couldn't happen. 'So this is it,' I said dully. 'There's no way that France and Britain can keep out of the war now.'

'None,' said Papa.

'And Anna. How's she?' I picked up Willi's Malacca cane and found myself strolling out of the courtyard, in front of the yew trees towards the path at the top of the dell. In the early evening sun, the lake in the distance shimmered like a burnished tray catching the light.

'I'm very worried,' confessed Papa. 'Yes, really. This business at the station was *very* unpleasant. That sort of thing has never happened to the Astell family before.'

'The station business was deliberate,' I told him. 'A plant – set up by the Germans using French fascists in the government.'

'But what's going to happen to her?' My father looked anguished, nervously prodding his ashplant into the grass verge of the path. 'War is certain, yes. And then – do you realise Anna could even be interned?'

'She *is* American.'

Papa shook his head gloomily. 'She's not – not technically. She is American – but only in America.'

'If she holds an American passport?'

'I don't like it, Larry, I don't like it at all. If the worst comes to the worst and we can't get her out of France we may have to hide her.'

'You must be joking.' I could hardly believe my father's words, as though he was panicking.

'I am not joking,' he said crossly. 'Please realise that Anna is a German. And whatever Grandma may say about the French, we all know – you and I – that the Germans could cut through Champagne like a knife through butter. Yes, *butter*.'

'But we're neutral.'

'We may be neutral, but so is the lightning that strikes a neutral man dead in the middle of a field.'

'And Mama won't go to America? Definitely, not even now?'

'Absolutely not,' he sighed, jabbing again into the grass. 'Really, women can be very difficult. They don't understand that if they love a man in war-time all the husband wants is peace of mind.'

But astonishingly Mama confounded the family later that evening by calling us into the living room and announcing – without any arguments – that suddenly, inexplicably, she had changed her mind.

'Perhaps it's because my mother is getting old, and who knows if I'll ever see her again,' she said in explanation – or was it only part explanation? It sounded a little too pat for me. But then it occurred to me that perhaps she was doing it to try and get Anna away too.

'Is Anna coming with you?' I asked.

'That was my hope – still is,' said Mama, but Anna shook her head – firmly, as though she didn't want to discuss the matter. 'I wish,' began Mama, 'but I can understand about Willi.' And, changing the subject abruptly, she said, 'When do I have to leave?'

'Tomorrow, I'm afraid; it's the last chance,' said Papa, half happy for her, half sad.

Papa, it seemed, had made all the practical arrangements

long before. He had agreed with Bill Bullitt that she should leave on Saturday with a seat reserved on one of the many aircraft now flying between Paris and London. From there the embassy would look after her, meet her, transfer her to the boat train to Liverpool.

'I've never been on a plane,' Mama confessed. 'I'm a bit nervous.'

'No need to be,' said Papa cheerfully. 'People are flying all over the world these days. Why, there hasn't been a single crash since Pan Am started its first commercial flights between Europe and New York in May. I'd have sent you on one if you'd left earlier, but they've been suspended for the moment. However, it's okay between Paris and London.'

'And then there are those awful submarines.'

Patiently Papa explained, 'My dear. We're not at war, you know. We may never be. And you know, *really*, the Germans won't use their submarines when ships are going about their – what's the phrase – their lawful occasions on the high seas. *Yes.*' He seemed pleased to have discovered the exact description. '*Lawful occasions.*'

He paused for a moment, then added, 'And anyway there's no fear of being sunk even if Germany does start a war. No, certainly not. She's not only a fine ship, but she's carrying a couple of hundred children, nearly three hundred American citizens and around five hundred Canadians. Even the Germans wouldn't dare to sink a neutral passenger ship carrying over three hundred *Americans*.'

'When exactly does she sail,' asked Mama.

'Sunday evening – that's September the third,' said Papa.

'What's she called?'

'The *Athenia*.'

20

At 5 p.m. on Sunday, 3 September, France declared war on Germany. We sat waiting, ears glued to the radio at Douzy, though we all knew the actual declaration to be a formality, for Chamberlain had announced the grim news six hours earlier on the B.B.C., at 11 o'clock on that warm Sunday morning, and his quavering voice in London had been followed almost immediately by the dismal wail of air raid sirens as a signal for the people of Europe, friend and foe alike, to start the life of troglodytes.

It had been a false alarm as it happened, but now that war was a reality our first agonising thoughts were of Mama. Somehow I had always felt – or I suppose *hoped* – that in the end we would somehow settle for another 'Munich', that people couldn't be so mad as to go to war, that even if Mama did sail off to America she would be back once the hullabaloo had died down.

During the official announcement on the French radio, we were gathered in the living room – Anna, Guy and Olivia and, of course, Oregon. Jean had already prepared a silver tray with flute champagne glasses and a magnum of the prized '21.

'Shall I serve it, sir?' he asked, when Papa switched off the radio and rang for him.

'Please,' said Papa. 'And a glass for you too, Jean.'

The butler carefully eased open the cork of the large bottle, taking care to avert a bad-mannered pop. When our glasses were charged, Papa said simply, 'To Mama!' Adding hastily, with a quick look at Anna, 'To absent friends, all of them. Yes, *all*. And to victory. Yes, a *speedy* victory.' As we drank our champagne Papa looked at his watch and said, 'She should be sailing just about now. *Bon voyage.*'

Yet it was worry rather than fear. Though we had heard a great deal about the German submarines, even seen some photos of their ugly black silhouettes with the letter 'U' and a number painted on each conning tower, their presence was impersonal, it had nothing to do with us, they represented no danger to neutral passengers, to women and children.

There were others, too, who were worried that day. What about Anna? She was sitting on one of the deep oatmeal-coloured sofas near the big glass coffee table, twiddling the stem of her champagne glass, her thoughts miles away, eyes glazed with misery. She not only had Mama to worry about, but Willi too; an enemy now, an enemy of the France that he'd lived among so much.

And what of Olivia?

'*Santé!*' I toasted her. 'It's strange to think that here we are, in this beautiful home of ours, and you're the only French person among us.'

'Don't say that to Grandma,' Oregon chuckled. 'She may have an American passport, but that's the only American thing about her.'

'The *Athenia* is a good ship.' My father, miles away, was thinking aloud rather than talking, masking his worry.

'No point in upsetting yourself,' said Guy, trying to cheer him up. 'You'll only work yourself up into a state. Just put your mind forward a few days. In a week or so Mama will be hitting the high spots in New York.'

'I know you're right,' Papa admitted. 'Stupid of me, especially when I *am* so glad she took my advice.'

'But you can't help thoughts, can you?' asked Olivia gently. 'If only people could control their thoughts! Think only of happy things.'

'If only we could!' said Anna. 'If only Willi . . .'

Sensing the tautness in Anna's nerves, Oregon, trying to change the subject, asked, 'Where's Grandma?'

'Upstairs,' said Papa. 'She wants to stay in her room until dinner.'

'No doubt revelling in dreams of glory – how the French are going to thrash the Germans.' Oregon was chuckling.

'You mustn't tease her,' my father reproved his brother gently.

'I won't,' Oregon promised. 'But sometimes I think a bit of humour, even if it *is* forced, is the only way to keep sane. What about my problems?'

'What about them?' asked Guy.

'Never occurred to you, did it, that behind my cheerful exterior, I, too, could be in the dumps?' Striking an attitude of mock despair Oregon lit another Gauloise, looking round for an ashtray in which to put the stub of the one he had just finished. Then, peering through his glasses, cherubic in appearance, he added, 'I'll be out of a job soon. I'm going to have to close the *Paris American*.'

'But you can't!' It was Olivia, always sensitive to the unhappiness of others.

'You can't,' echoed Anna.

'*I can't,*' mimicked Oregon. 'But tell me – who's going to read it when the last Americans have gone? Oh yes, they'll go – the day after the first raid on Paris. And who's going to advertise in it?'

I said nothing, just felt sick at the thought of Oregon sitting there, not even noticing that the trail of ash from his cigarette was falling on Mama's precious thick white pile carpet, still trying to crack a joke, to take life as it came. The P.A. had been his baby – and in a way I was suffering too, for I had been weaned on it, learned my trade, helping to fill its columns; and, if it came to that, learning everything I had to learn through Oregon's selfless help.

Deliberately changing the subject Oregon turned to Olivia. 'And you? You're quite happy to carry on with your new work – Champagne's first lady chauffeuse?'

'If I'm good enough to keep the job,' she laughed. 'I've no desire to go back to the big city, apart from driving the Hisp. into Paris when I'm needed. But I love it here, especially since you've all been so kind.' I could sense that she was speaking under a certain strain. 'I never had a real family of my own until now. And I love the country. And I *hate*' – with a sudden rush of vehemence – 'big cities like Paris. You're never free in a big city.'

'Free?'

'From fear. You know what I mean, Larry. You're an understanding man.'

'You've never really got over that pogrom business, have you?' I asked.

She shook her head. 'I don't wake up at night with nightmares about it, if that's what you mean. After all, Guy and Anna and your mother had a far worse time than I did. They saw it in all its beastliness. I only saw the fringes. But it's not a question of being afraid *today*. It's the future that frightens me. If – well, you know, there is a powerful clique of right-wing Frenchmen who are as violently anti-Jewish as any Nazis. So you see, I feel safer here.'

'I don't think we've got anything to celebrate.' I tried to be cheerful. 'But I'm inviting anyone who wants to come to the Boulingrin.' It was months since we had dined at the brasserie in Reims.

'I'm just in the mood for a steak and *pommes frites*,' cried Guy. 'Specially if you pay. Remember! I'm no longer a struggling artist. Now I'm a struggling vigneron. The pay is even worse.'

In the end the four of us went. I think Papa and his brother Oregon were relieved to dine quietly at home with Grandma. For with my mother on the high seas, Papa was bound to be more miserable than we were – not because we were heartless, but because youth isn't as pessimistic as middle age. We were all certain that a cable from Mama in New York would arrive within days.

The Boulingrin was crowded, and Monsieur Leleu had great difficulty in finding us a table.

'How are you all?' To him we were friends first, customers second. 'Just have a drink at the bar, and I'll put you at the head of the queue for the next free table.'

A man drinking near us put his glass down on the zinc bar and slapped Guy on the back, crying, 'To victory! You see – it'll all be over in three months!'

He was half tight, but he insisted on opening a bottle of champagne – which none of us really wanted. Fortunately Leleu rushed up, a sheaf of red and white paper tablecloths in his hand, and whisked us away. The man promptly offered the champagne to someone else.

'What a sad day!' cried Leleu. 'But never mind, my old friends. There's no rationing of good red meat – not yet.'

Everyone was so busy eating and talking that it seemed almost embarrassing. This was a terrible day in the history of the world. Surely in British or German restaurants people would be eating quickly, imbued with a kind of decorum. But here? Crash! Bang! Wallop! as the American comics said. There were no inhibitions. We ordered our steaks, one *bleu*, one *bien cuit*, two *à point*.

'Here's to your mother,' said Olivia suddenly, gravely. And we all drank a toast to Mama in the first of four bottles of *vin ordinaire* which we knocked back between us before saying goodbye to Leleu, who doubtfully regarded my slightly raffish appearance and equally raffish M.G.

'Don't worry,' I laughed, 'I can drive this bloody thing blindfold.' I roared into first gear with a noise that could have wakened the dead, and soon rolled gratefully into bed.

At 2.30 a.m., I was sunk into a sleep so deep and concentrated that I didn't even hear the stutter of the special phone in my room, which usually jerked me into instant wakefulness as if it were a fire alarm.

For this phone was a kind of fire alarm. The normal phones at Douzy were used at normal times, day and evening, but some months previously, Tomlinson had arranged for a special phone, with its own number, to be installed in my bedroom to save the rest of the family being awakened if I was called in an emergency. It didn't happen often at weekends, but even so I could never ignore the fact that as far as the *Globe* was concerned it was only eight o'clock in the evening when it was one in the morning in France.

I knew it had to be Tommy on the other end.

'It's two in the morning,' he whispered instinctively. 'Sorry to wake you.'

'Two o'clock! You crazy?' I heard the noise of the office teleprinter. 'What the hell are you doing at the office?'

'Emergency. Called me out of bed from Washington via the embassy. I'm in my sodding pyjamas with a raincoat on top. It's bad news.'

Suddenly I shivered, a premonition of disaster.

'Bad news?' I repeated. I could smell it – seeping through the phone wires from Paris.

' 'Fraid so,' he said heavily. 'For you.'

'Well, tell me, for Christ's sake,' I almost shouted. 'I'm not a kid.'

'Easy, boy. There's no suggestion that anyone we know is dead or anything like that, but' – again the hesitation, the agony of having to impart bad news over the phone – 'Brace up, Larry, you've got to know.'

'It's Mama?'

'I hope not.'

'Then *what?*'

'The *Athenia* has gone down. Sunk by a German U-boat. The first casualty of the war. I had to tell you.'

'Of course.' I seemed to be discussing other people, almost as though I were writing an objective, unfeeling story about people caught in death, but people who didn't matter to me. A story.

'Go on,' I said after a pause. 'Any news of Mama?'

'No. The flashes are just coming through. There's every chance most people will be saved. She was torpedoed late yesterday evening, but all I know is that' – he hesitated again over the dreaded word of war – 'casualties are light. So your mother will probably be okay.'

'And other people's mothers?'

'Don't take on, Larry. There are lots of survivors, so keep your fingers crossed.'

'Mama?' I asked again.

'No news of individuals. And no news is good news. Sounds corny but it's true.'

'Poor Mama.' I suddenly felt the tears trying to push their way past my eyeballs. Oh God! What about the others? I would have to wake them up. For a few seconds, the prospect almost drove away thoughts of Mama herself.

'The *Athenia* – was she badly holed?'

'She's sinking. Those German pigs just opened fire without warning. They didn't care about the kids on board, let alone the women. No warning – the sodding captain just let her have a torpedo amidships.'

'God Almighty!' I was picturing Mama's body floating in the sea, and said, thinking aloud, 'How the hell can I tell Papa? And Anna?'

'Don't do anything now,' Tommy advised. 'I had to warn you about it, otherwise you'd have heard it on the radio first thing in the morning. But there's every chance that – hang on! I'm getting a new flash on the A.P. wire.'

In the background I could hear the stuttering wire machine, imagine the long snake of white paper tape trailing to the floor when the machine was unattended, the words spewing out letter by letter, as though some unseen hand was typing.

'Sounds much better. You there, Larry? A large yacht, the

Southern Cross, arrived on the scene almost immediately. Two British destroyers, the *Electra* and *Escort*, were right by. And a couple of Norwegian and Swedish vessels seem to have been around too. Here! Listen to this. Quote – several hundred survivors already picked up. Unquote.'

'Thank God for that. When did it happen, Tommy? Where?'

'Soon after dark, I guess, and a couple of hundred miles west of Ireland, place called the Rockall Bank, but it means nothing to me. Go to sleep now, Larry, but wake up early before anyone else listens to the radio. Give you a chance to break it gently. If I get any lists of survivors – if your mother' – again the awkward hesitation – 'I'll wake you.'

'Thanks, Tommy,' I said. 'But I won't get much sleep tonight.'

It was a long black night, and the morning that followed, after Papa had broken the news to everyone, was even blacker, despite the watery September sun. Everyone seemed to talk in whispers or, suddenly, loudly as though unable to control their voices. There was nothing any of us could do except listen to the radio.

Everyone was on edge, though the family was perhaps better equipped to hide fears or prepare for grief than the others. Jean served breakfast as though this would be the last meal ever to be prepared in the house. Aubergine sniffed so persistently that Papa, who rarely raised his voice, shouted in exasperation, 'For God's sake, stop that snivelling!'

The French radio, which we listened to in the living room, was spouting the nonsense which it always feels compelled to utter in times of crisis – declarations of the infallibility of French arms, the deterrent of the Maginot Line, the proud tradition of neighbouring Belgium, the German lack of aircraft. One announcer even proclaimed, 'The entire population of France is prepared to play its part, and *now*, for our latest information points to an imminent attack on Germany in order to neutralise the German air force before it has a chance to bomb our homeland.'

What nonsense! I thought. We *knew* this wasn't true and, at one time, when Papa was out of the room, Oregon sighed, 'The trouble with the French is that they despise everything that isn't French, so they can never bring themselves to believe the Germans are more efficient than they are.'

In normal times we would have switched the wireless off but no one dared to in case there was news of the *Athenia*. This, so far, was the only action of the war, and news bulletins about the U-boat attack constituted the only firm news amid a welter of theories, surmise and promises for the future. As a newspaperman I could hear the creaking hand of the censor in every official hand-out.

The sinking of the *Athenia* was not a 'French' story; the passengers were not French, neither was the vessel, but it attracted attention because of morbid discussions on whether the deaths would be an advantage in persuading neutral America to take stern reprisals against the Germans after the sinking of a neutral vessel, even perhaps help to draw America into the war. It gave us, the family waiting for news, an increased sense of the macabre as we listened to 'experts' discuss whether the loss of a few lives – perhaps Mama's – might not in the long run prove a cheap price to pay for extra American help.

'Not a hope,' declared Oregon. 'Someone will have to sink a few U.S. battleships before the Americans fight in Europe – or anywhere, for that matter.'

We didn't expect the French radio to announce any casualty lists. I don't suppose the radio newsroom even knew that the passenger list included one American wife whose home was in France. On the other hand, Tommy was keeping in touch through the wire services and had alerted the *Globe* in Washington. Papa had spoken to Bill Bullitt, so we had all avenues of news covered.

During the late afternoon Sonia managed to get through, but she asked for Anna, not me, as we were both convinced her phone was tapped. There was nothing she could do except hope. And then half-way through a dinner for which nobody had any appetite we heard. Mama was safe. It was about 8.30 when the phone rang and, as Papa was nearest the dining room door, he jumped out of his seat and almost ran into the next room. We sat on the edges of our seats for what seemed an eternity until he gave an almost wild shriek, to make sure we could hear: 'She's safe! She's all right!'

We had to sit in the dining room a few more minutes waiting for details, but when Papa returned his ashen face was touched by the first spot of colour I had seen during all that desperate day. Bill Bullitt had managed to get through from Paris. Mama, he told us, had been picked up by an American vessel, the *City of Flint*. Out of fourteen hundred passengers and crew, one hundred and twelve had been lost, including twenty-eight Americans.

After official confirmation we had to wait several days, for only then were passengers who had taken ten days to reach Canada able to send cables. Mama's read, 'All love but miss you terribly.' She had obviously been restricted to a short message. Five days later a second cable arrived from New York: 'Settled down none the worse for Atlantic ducking letter on way. Will miss you at the *vendange*.' I liked her reference to the *vendange*! But we still had to wait for our first letter . . .

I had almost forgotten this important autumn festival until Papa phoned me at the office a few days later.

'We're in trouble, yes, I think you could say trouble,' he began. 'We seem to be at peace with the world in Douzy, despite the war, but we can't get the usual labour for the *vendange*.'

By tradition the annual harvest in the vineyards took place a hundred days after the flowering – and we always relied on casual labour to help out.

'Guy is working like the devil;' I could sense a rare chuckle on the phone. 'Really, Larry, if he had painted as hard as he works now, he'd have filled the walls of the Louvre. Are you coming to help out – for a few days even?'

'It might be difficult. We're having a hell of a time. But I'll try, for a long weekend at least. Have you got the government's okay?'

'They agreed yesterday,' he replied. Even in wartime, government officials made regular tests throughout Champagne to ensure that the harvest contained a satisfactory quantity of sugar and the necessary acid content. Only after an affirmative nod would the strict controllers of the Champagne region allow the harvest to proceed.

'If I get a call from the *Globe* . . .'

'Of course,' replied Papa, 'I'll understand. But anyway, it'll be good to see you – and the family. And we need every man we can borrow, now that many of the regulars have let us down.'

'I suppose a lot of them are either mobilised or reserved as coalminers. But what about the women and children?' I asked.

'That's the trouble. They want to come, but transport is difficult.'

'Don't worry,' I promised. 'I'll be there if it's humanly possible, and I'm sure Oregon will be too. And since every spare body will be needed, have you ever thought of asking Sonia?'

'Would she come?' I could see that Papa was wondering what her husband would say.

'No harm in asking – providing the request comes from you, preferably to Francesco.'

'You'd like it?'

'You know I would. That's why I'm suggesting it.'

In fact Francesco agreed immediately that Sonia could stay at Douzy for a week and help out. I imagine he was so inundated with work that he was almost relieved, especially as this was an official invitation to work at a vital seasonal job Sonia had tackled many times in the past. Francesco even offered to come down to Douzy for a day and help, if he could spare the time.

So I had taken one major hurdle in my stride. Now I faced the next – how to get some time off. And that proved easy after I received an intriguing proposition from the *Globe*.

Back in Paris I warned Oregon that he would be expected to help for the *vendange*.

'Already!' he cried. 'The weeks fly by so quickly I seem to spend all my time reading the Sunday papers.'

Time did flit past – yet the war was less than three weeks old. Mama had barely had time to arrive safely in New York. No letters yet. And, most astonishing of all, hardly a shot had been fired in anger by either side.

I was talking to Oregon when Tomlinson phoned down to my office on the floor below and asked if I could spare him a couple of minutes. Something in his tone suggested an unusual request. There was a tinge of suppressed excitement in his voice.

'Larry, I've got news for you,' he started without preamble.

'Good or bad?'

'Depends on which way you look at it. Want the bad first?' I could tell from his banter he wasn't really serious.

Leaning back on his swivel armchair, feet up on his old-fashioned French desk, he said with mock sorrow, 'I've had a telex from Washington. Sorry about this – but they don't have any more use for you as a stringer. It seems they're about to appoint a staff man.'

It might have been said half humorously, but still, his casual drawl gave me an immediate reaction. I felt as though I had been pushed under an ice cold shower. 'Don't say that sort of thing. For a moment I thought you meant it.'

'I do. It's for real.'

'What the hell?'

'Temper, temper!' he grinned and explained the good news. The *Globe* wanted to employ me as a full-time bureau chief for France. They were offering me three times the amount I had been earning as a freelance, who is usually paid for material used or requested or alternatively by the day when sent out on an assignment. I had been happy with the arrangement, but I was beginning to realise that if I wanted to reach the top in journalism I should join the staff of a prestigious paper. And the *Globe was* the voice of Washington. To be appointed Bureau Chief in Paris, a senior member of the staff, was a big step up.

'And as far as money's concerned, you'll soon be matching me,' said Tommy. 'Not that champagne producers need any money.'

'But what about you?'

'Don't worry. I've got a new job too.'

He had indeed. Middle-aged but ever youthful, Tommy Tomlinson had been secretly nursing a dream which only Hitler could fulfil. He might not be ambitious for power at Head Office, but he had long wanted to be a war correspondent and had been furious when the *Globe* turned down his request to cover the civil war in Spain. When he threatened to resign, they had compromised by promising Tommy that he could be a war correspondent if ever there was a war in Europe – Vance being confident no war would interrupt Tomlinson's last years as one of the best Paris correspondents in the business.

'Vance sent me a humdinger of a cable when I reminded him of our arrangement,' Tommy chuckled. 'Practically said I'd fixed it with Hitler. I cabled back that I was being measured for my uniform.'

Now of course they couldn't find anyone but me to handle the political news. According to Tommy, Vance had had an eye on me as a possible successor in Paris since our first meeting but, excited though I was, two things worried me and I said so right away. It was one thing for me to write a 'set piece' – a 'situationer' as it was called in the trade – in which I had all the time in the world to research then write about something I hoped I knew about; it would be very different dashing off cables under pressure day after day as Bureau Chief.

'Don't worry,' said Tommy. 'I shouldn't be saying this, or you'll be asking for a raise, but you write like a dream, Larry. You're going to do the *Globe* proud, and I'll bask in reflected glory. And you won't be troubled by day-to-day chores. Routine filing is going to be too expensive, and all the routine business will be taken care of by the agencies. And your second gripe?'

'I don't want to leave France.' I knew it sounded impertinent for a beginner to start making terms after being offered a great chance, but I was operating from strength, not cussedness, because there was no way I *would* leave Douzy.

'No sweat,' Tommy agreed cheerfully. 'I knew you'd make that stipulation and told Vance as much. He agreed. He'll give you a contract for the duration, France only, and as a special feature writer.'

'Meaning exactly what?'

Tommy explained. Reporting a war was going to be very different from reporting in peacetime. What the *Globe* wanted were stories that no rival newspapers carried – stories in which the contacts I had cultivated so assiduously over the years would tip me off with fresh angles.

'If you can deliver one big French political story a month,' said Tommy, 'you'll have earned your pay. Now sign here.' Like a conjuror he produced a letter signed by Vance to be counter-signed by me. 'That will constitute a legal agreement.' He handed it over to me.

'What's the date to be?' he asked as I read it through.

Thinking suddenly of Papa's urgent request for help with the *vendange* – and that Sonia would be there – I said, 'Can we make it two weeks from now? Give me a bit of leave before I start.'

He nodded. As I signed, I said, 'You took a lot for granted.'

'I told your Uncle Oregon yesterday,' Tommy grinned an admission, 'and he told me he'd kick your ass to kingdom come if you turned the offer down.'

Later that week, I had new profile photos taken, for my press card and *carte d'identité* and for credit filing facilities. I had thought the old photos would serve, but the idiotic bureaucrats of the French civil service, puffed up by war, decreed otherwise: all official photos not only had to be in profile, but had to show the right ear clearly.

I soon received a couple of very agreeable cables. Tommy must have told Vance why I wanted leave, for he cabled, 'Welcome to the world of the *Globe*. And hope I may have a raincheck and visit you for the next peaceful *vendange*.' The *Globe*'s editor, Schill Scotter, whom I had never met, cabled more laconically, 'Welcome aboard stop any ideas proexclusives postvacation query.'

At the same time, I was introduced to the world of the censors and the Ministry of Information, a group of half-baked citizens who were already convinced they were the nation's guardians of truth, for even if there was no war to report that did not prevent the Ministry of Information from rapidly building up an enormous sluggish empire centred on the Hôtel Continental in the rue Castiglione. It was hardly the proper image for the pulsating heart of a grim operational war room. The wallpaper was pink and flowery. The uncomfortable gilt furniture was bogus Louis XV. The chief press officer dealing with the American and British reporters worked in an office so ridiculously large it could have been a banqueting hall.

Not even the remotest criticism was allowed to sneak past the censor. Every day Colonel Thomas, the Ministry of Information spokesman, held a conference for newspapermen. He was tall, thin, with closely cropped hair and a moustache. On the bridge of his long thin nose he affected old-fashioned pince-nez. He looked like a figure from a bygone age.

The weather was perfect as the time of the *vendange* approached. Yet it was extraordinary, that month of inaction by nations who in theory were willing to fight but who, in fact, were unwilling to commit themselves to large-scale losses. It was, as one newspaper put it, 'the war that never was'. Everyone had been preparing for a terrifying onslaught. The British cabinet had secretly estimated that the maimed and wounded in devastating air attacks would total a million casualties. Yet the French newspapers had to struggle to find stories of military fervour. The first British troops had arrived in France, at least giving the Paris press a few pictures of lads in kilts and girls draped over tanks.

Odd things, though, started to happen. While we were preparing for the *vendange*, as the nucleus of our temporary work force began to arrive, who should telephone from the Misses B and B cottage but Jean-Pierre. The war was less than three weeks old, he was an officer in one of the biggest forts in the Maginot Line, yet he was at home when I arrived to spend a Sunday at Douzy.

I went round to see him. 'How come you're back on leave so soon?'

'No place to sleep,' he laughed shamefacedly. 'I mean it. Sounds crazy but we're overmanned all along the Line. I had to sleep on the floor, so they sent me home for a week. Still' – proudly – 'I've already been in action.'

I looked surprised.

'Yes. I think our team was one of the first to fire the big guns. Though between you and me, the whole thing was a bit of an anti-climax.'

Jean-Pierre had been sent to the Hochwald Est fortress, and when he saw that I was interested, said, 'You won't breathe a word to anyone, will you? The press, I mean?'

I shook my head.

'Well, you know, three days after war was declared, we opened fire with a 75-millimetre gun. It jammed. Most of the shells were old and defective. We tried the bigger gun – the 135 – but two out of every three shells failed to explode. One of our guns at Hochwald Est fired shells over two thousand yards with one barrel, but less than nine hundred yards with the other. But the worst thing of all is the overmanning. It's crazy – even I can see that. Half the *poilus* should be sent back – to work in industry. At least I'll be here for the *vendange.*'

'And we've got air cover here,' I said. 'You didn't know? The British fighters have arrived to protect us.'

In fact a hundred and sixty Fairey Battle planes of the R.A.F. had arrived in the airfields of Champagne; and airfields in those days really meant fields, for there were no runways for the Battles, whose main duties were to protect French reconnaissance planes.

These first few weeks of war – as they affected me both in Paris and Douzy – left everyone bewildered by the almost uncanny lack of action, as though someone had forgotten to wind up several million toy soldiers. Nothing happened. War and violence were supposed to be synonymous, but there was no violence. In Paris the cafés were crowded each evening, and several times I could not find a table at the Deux Magots, even though I was a favoured old customer. The cinemas played to packed houses – especially *Ninotchka, Goodbye Mr. Chips* and *The Wizard of Oz.* Long queues formed to book for *Gone with the Wind*, which wasn't due to open until mid-December. Such was the faith of the average Parisian!

But though the threatened German attacks had never materialised – giving French newspapers the opportunity to jeer at German cowardice – I found the atmosphere chilling; the more so as no one in Paris made any adjustments to life as we imagined it should be in wartime. There was no point in hoarding, for there was enough of everything. Only the blackout was, in the words of one commentator, 'a ridiculous bore'. One newspaper headlined the front page satirically, 'Let there be light!' In a curious way the lack of heroic action made one feel almost ashamed. The only 'war' which we, as newspapermen, could discover was in the gilded halls of the Hôtel Continental where the censor waged an unremitting fight against all foreign correspondents. Their most positive action was to kit each of us out with a gas mask, to be slung around the neck in a cardboard box, and a tin helmet.

For the rest of it we soon became part and parcel of what was quickly labelled *le drôle de guerre*, and in England 'the phoney war'. I see it now in memory, those first weeks in flashbacks of war's oddities: the newspaper kiosks near the Métro stations all barred, and the days' papers, magazines, books, dumped unceremoniously on the sidewalks. The anger of thousands of crossword enthusiasts when their puzzles were suddenly banned from print in case the clues contained fifth column codes. The blackout with the street lamps painted blue or violet, giving an uncanny glow.

Unlike the famous Café Flore, which had closed down, the Deux Magots continued to open its doors, though outside the terrace, with its small circular tables squeezed as close to each other as loving couples, men were filling sandbags from a pile by the roadside while one solitary North African hawker did a good trade selling peanuts. When Oregon and I ordered drinks we could no longer, as we always had done, pile up the traditional saucers as a guide to our total bill. Now we had to pay cash with each separate order. Too many customers, it seemed, had conveniently bolted when the sirens emptied the streets.

From the inside of the terrace we looked up at the grey barrage balloons and – for the moment unthinking – I said to Oregon, 'This is the end of our world.'

'It isn't,' he growled. 'This is not the end of anything, it's the beginning of everything.'

We strolled after lunch on that sunny afternoon through the Luxembourg Gardens, I don't really know why. The first golden leaves were drifting down. A group of soldiers were digging trenches, but they had the air of men who didn't know why they were expending such energy, almost as though they suspected the work had been ordered only to keep them occupied. The lake in the gardens had been drained and we both had to hold our noses as we walked quickly past the stench. Not far away, three or four young women were arguing as they walked along, and I saw one soldier wave, another shout a garbled invitation, a third cry, 'They look as though they could do with a wash.'

It was a mild exaggeration, but it was a sign of the times: it was not done to be too chic any more. The French girls were already adopting a new fashion – not to use make-up or extravagant hair styles while there was a war on. Only there wasn't a war, not a real one.

21

On the day I drove back to Douzy for the *vendange* the first letter from Mama arrived. It had been opened by the French – there was no censorship in America, of course – but nothing seemed to have been deleted.

It was long, a little incoherent, and some of the earlier parts had been written on the *City of Flint* so it had become a kind of diary. Mama was not a very good descriptive writer, and it was hard to visualise what had happened. However, she was able to reassure us on several points which had worried us, for I had had visions of her struggling for hours in the water; in fact she had managed to clamber directly into one of the lifeboats, 'thanks to the wonderful crew members'.

There had been twenty-six lifeboats, Mama was told, and as the vessel took fifteen hours to sink most people got away. 'Most were killed near the number five hold, where the torpedo hit the *Athenia*. Someone gave me his lifebelt and then ran off before I could stop him. I was wearing a long evening dress when it happened. Do you know, I was still wearing it when the *City of Flint* reached Halifax in Nova Scotia on 13 September,' she wrote.

Describing the orderly scenes as she was lowered to the

lifeboat Mama added, 'I even had time to grab my leather attaché case containing my passport and other papers and money, and I hung on to it like grim death, but then when I was being transferred from the lifeboat to the *Flint* I dropped it and there was no time to retrieve it.'

I had also worried about the conditions on the *Flint*, but the Americans had apparently provided for possible Atlantic dangers and, though Mama had had to share a small four-berth cabin with no toilet facilities, 'they were very nice people who didn't snore too much, and we became great friends.'

Sonia had been driven down to Douzy by an Italian Embassy chauffeur, who had requested permission to remain at the château, offering to help in the harvest, while 'in the service of Madame l'Ambassadrice'. I had been warned about this via Papa, and in its way it was quite normal for a rich wife to ask for a room for her driver. The man – whom I regarded as a spy – would not sleep in the house, but in one of the farmer's rooms. I was beginning to feel sure that de Feo knew Sonia and I were lovers. But I also had the curious feeling that he wouldn't be unduly concerned providing we were *seen* to be behaving correctly.

Studiously I kept out of the way when Sonia's car crunched across the gravel courtyard and Aubergine emerged to help with the luggage. The next moment Anna arrived and the two girls hugged each other. From an upstairs window, I heard Anna cry, 'Oh! It's wonderful to see you. Just like the old days – the *happy* days.'

It was like that all the time of the *vendange*. Even though we missed Mama, and often thought of her with longing, the knowledge that she was safe had stifled all our worries about 'the war that never was'. And each evening, as we all sat down for supper and I touched Sonia's feet or leg, under the table, it was as though the intervening years had been a bad dream: even Oregon had overcome his initial depression at the closure of the *Paris American*.

There was something about the *vendange* that made you forget the miseries of the world. After all, the end of September, the vital ten days or so, represented the climax of a year's work and worry, so the harvest time always was a festive affair – not only for us, but evident in the holiday atmosphere of the pickers who not only earned good money but enjoyed magnificent food, served each evening on the long oak table in the kitchen of the Home Farm. Nothing seemed to have changed, not even the smell of freshly baked bread, not even the ceiling festooned with hanging food – the hams, the salamis, the sausages.

Due to the shortage of casual labour, there were some problems this year, though many of the regulars did turn up with their families, ready for a working holiday that would last until they all celebrated the end of the harvest with the *cochelet*, a traditional feast, washed down with unlimited champagne, with a local band engaged for dancing in one of the barns.

The day before work officially started we all went for a walk – the three girls, Guy and me – and it always gave me a peculiar feeling of continuity to come across old friends whose faces were familiar, even though we only saw them once a year.

Basically the activities would be divided into two sections: one, outside in the vineyards where La Châtelaine ruled; the other inside, where my father handled the problems of the pressing once the grapes had been gathered in. The division of labour worked without a hitch, but then as Oregon once explained to me slyly, 'Your father and his mother can't really have a row – because they never meet until it's time for dinner.'

'We're about a dozen people short,' said Grandma that evening. 'The wretched government doesn't seem to realise this is an emergency. Ridiculous! Not giving enough men permission to help the champagne industry.'

'Coal is important,' said Sonia meekly.

'What for?' snorted Grandma. 'We don't kill anyone, there's no fighting, we just let officers run around in big cars. Stop their silly war for a week, and we could have our harvest.'

We were having supper on the Friday evening after our arrival; the food was similar to a dinner but tradition dictated that supper, not dinner, was served at Douzy on the Friday before the harvest began.

At 7 the next morning, we all trooped out, meeting near the

barns in which the helpers had spent the night after supping at the big kitchen table. Grandma had been there for an hour. Every migrant helper who knew her reputation held her in awe. To them, she had as a widow inherited the vineyards and (with the help of a husband!) turned vines into liquid gold. Despite her eccentricity, especially in clothes, she was never reduced to a figure of fun. Not the indomitable, irreplaceable figure of La Châtelaine.

'I'm going to make a tour of the southern vineyards,' she announced to one of the vignerons. 'Keep these people on their toes.' A farmhand puffed out cold morning air as he pumped up her bicycle tyres. She was dressed in a green overcoat, rather long, and of the shade favoured by Austrians. It had large officer-like lapels with a double row of buttons which I felt should be brass instead of leather. A muffler had been thrown round her neck, for the early morning air had a keen September nip to it. On her head, hiding knotted hair worn in a bun, she sported a green felt Alpine-style hat – the same colour as her coat – with three or four brightly coloured feathers stuck in the band.

'She looks quite jaunty,' said Guy.

Four types of workers were involved in the harvest. First on the scene came the gatherers who worked in *hordons*, as they were called. Using secateurs they cut the bunches of grapes and stripped the leaves, putting them into small baskets.

By 10 a.m. I was at the south vineyard overseeing the *carriers* at work. They were loaders really, and their job was to empty the small baskets of grapes into wicker trays where the nearby pickers examined each bunch almost grape by grape. This was the *épluchage*, and it was vital to discard any grapes not up to standard. I saw a watchful Grandma, who had just arrived on her bicycle, pounce like a hawk as she noticed one picker sorting out bits of stalk and over-ripe or green grapes but not throwing them away.

'*Merde! Idiot!*' Grandma cried. She was merciless during the *épluchage*.

As the pickers filled their trays, the 'clean' grapes were placed carefully in 150-pound baskets called *mannequins*, then stacked with great care into carts, which took them to Papa's domain, the pressing room. Champagne, as he never forgot to tell us when we were young, was a blended wine, and the blender was the man who could make or mar the quality.

The shallow presses were designed so the fast-running juices would not have time to become stained red by the coloured skins of the *Pinot noir* grapes. And each press held exactly four tons of grapes from which Papa expected to extract thirteen casks of juice, each cask containing forty-four gallons; the ten first casks usually produced the *cuvée* – the best wine. In any event, the strict laws governing production imposed a limit of juice to each four tons of grapes. Once the quota of thirteen standard-sized casks had been filled, the remainder was sold off as still wine, either locally, or to mix in to *vin ordinaire*. It could never be called champagne.

As Papa ended the third day's pressing he said, with a satisfied aside to me, 'A very good harvest so far, yes, *good*. Of course, selling it might be a different matter, with all our markets closed. But we can always keep it.' And to one of the hands, he said, 'Well done, Georges. Take it to the boiling sheds after labelling.'

Each forty-four-gallon barrel was labelled to show not only the year but which vineyard it had come from – very important when it came to blending – and would be stored for several weeks in fermenting sheds for the 'boiling', as the first frothy fermentation was called. There the casks would remain for as long as necessary in a temperature, for once in their lives, well above that of the cellars of Douzy. When they were finally opened for a second fermentation, the contents of the casks would have no sparkle, of course, but at least the grape juice had become a still wine, ready for the long journey that would transform it into bubbling champagne.

Some of the casuals noticed differences at this *vendange*. For the first time that anyone could remember, two tall, white flagpoles had been erected. Atop one flew the flag of France; on the other the Stars and Stripes fluttered. In half a dozen places large wooden notice boards stuck on stout poles had been erected. They all read 'United States Property'.

One stood at the entrance to the drive where it branched from the road to Rilly, east of the main Reims-Épernay road.

Others boldly proclaimed America's neutrality on the main gates to the Home Farm, on several of the vineyards bordering local roads.

The most intriguing work, however, yielded no clues to the curious men and women who had arrived from Lorraine, for all questions about the construction work going on behind high wooden barricades were met with blank stares or vague shrugs.

In fact the construction work appeared to be an extension to the *cellier* at the far end of the Home Farm, near the building which housed the great press and the boiling room, and it was apparently taking place inside the farmyard, near the point where the steps led down to the cellar tunnels, lined with thousands of bottles, which continued all the way to the Douzy pyramid.

'It's just a precaution,' my father had explained mysteriously. 'Yes, I think that would *describe* it, but really, there's no need to advertise what we're doing. It's a private building, really.'

Behind the tall wooden screens Papa was constructing a sloping roadway about twenty-five feet long, running parallel to the cellar steps, and which, if you continued to dig, would lead into the old cellars themselves. However, the sloping roadway came to an abrupt end – blocked with newly laid bricks, the plaster still fresh.

'They're going to be dirtied, whitewashed, and then you'll never be able to realise that it's a new wall,' said my father. 'And behind that wall, completely bricked up, but with air vents, there are ten thousand bottles of the '33 vintage. Yes, I think you could say the finest vintage of the *decade*.'

'Papa! You cunning fox,' I cried. 'That's genius. At least if this war ever gets going we'll have something to celebrate peace with.'

'Absolutely. And a vintage that will shoot skyhigh in price if champagne production suffers.'

'But why the path?' I asked.

'You realise that originally, behind this hoarding, was the old wall of the warehouse. That will be replaced and then nobody will ever know that the wall was knocked down and rebuilt.'

'But still,' I said. 'What's the point of a road leading nowhere?'

'The Hisp.,' said Papa simply. 'I love the Hisp., and I'm not going to risk losing that if the war ever reached Champagne. Look.'

He had also built fireproof storage petrol tanks I had never seen before, housing thousands of gallons. They would be bricked up; a smaller store of petrol would be hidden in another cellar, so that if I needed any I could find it without knocking down the walls. He would, he explained, leave the hoardings up until the last minute if danger threatened. Then he would drive the Hisp. into its wartime cave, jack up the wheels and disconnect the battery. After that he would rebuild the wall: 'A few coats of whitewash on the bricks, and *really* nobody will be able to discover our secret.'

It was one thing to hide a car and a stock of champagne. It was a very different matter to hide something much more precious.

'What's going to happen to Anna?' I asked. 'Officially she's now a German citizen. The French have already announced that all German nationals in France are to be interned.'

'Not Anna,' said Papa. 'If the Germans ever come that *would* pose a problem. But for the present I've been to see the *préfet de police* and we have come to an understanding – yes, that's the word – to leave matters as they are for the time being. Yes, as they are,' he added in his up-and-down voice.

I didn't doubt that some consideration had been shown to the *préfet*, but to be on the safe side – in case the Germans did ever reach Champagne – my father had turned the old stables facing the main entrance on the other side of the courtyard into a self-contained little apartment stocked with the kind of provisions and articles like candles which many people had already stored in their air raid shelters. And in a business like ours, where loyal workers included odd-job men who could turn their hands to anything, it had been easy to erect a step-ladder at the back, down which anyone could climb and vanish into the woods behind.

'I only hope nobody talks – gives any of this away,' I said.

'You mean *spies?*' My father, who had a charming streak of

innocence, was horrified. 'What a terrible, yes, terrible thing to suggest. Why on earth should *anyone* do a thing like that? They're our friends, Larry. *Really!*'

'I'm sure you're right, Papa,' I reassured him. But all the same, I had my doubts. In this strange world of fifth columnists, anti-Jewish French fascists, men and women who believed the future of Europe lay in a strong Germany – why should *everyone* be a friend?

The week of the *vendange*, with Sonia so relaxed and happy, had been like a honeymoon. The need for brawn as a change from using brains, the outdoor exercise, the fun of everyone racing against time to gather in the grapes, the warmth of our love, the tenderness which sometimes springs from fear of the future, had all combined to make it a memorable week of – strange to use this word, but it was true – 'peace' in the midst of war.

Douzy was like an elixir of life. If you took it in regular doses no harm could befall you. And Douzy was an elixir of love too.

Now Sonia had to return to Paris, for a couple of days, before leaving to see her parents in Florence and then going to Rolle to visit her new house. She would be away for two weeks – and though she telephoned me once from a call box I was unable to meet her before she left.

Two weeks – it seemed an age. I felt the loneliness so acutely that, back in Paris, I went off by myself to the Apollo cinema near the boulevard des Italiens to watch the latest American hit movie called *Stagecoach*. It occupied me for a couple of hours.

Luckily I had a lot of work ahead of me, for as the new Paris Bureau Chief my first task was to land a major political article for the *Globe*. I faced an immediate problem of another kind, however. When Tomlinson had run the office, he had employed me as a stringer. Now I was Chief of Bureau and *I* needed a stringer.

Head Office agreed immediately to my request – and I already knew the man I wanted. He stood head and shoulders above everyone else and, as it happened, he had lost his job. He was, of course, the one and only Oregon. He knew more about France, politics, journalism, than I would ever know. What's more, the *Globe* was still operating from the offices in the rue du Sentier – paying rent to Oregon who owned it – so he even knew his way around 'the shop'. It would be an ideal 'duration' job for Oregon now the *Paris American* had ceased publication. The arrangement I planned was not without a touch of irony – the one-time pupil offering a job as assistant to the master who had taught him everything. But I entertained no worries that Oregon might suffer from hurt pride or wounded dignity. He was a pro – and proud of it.

When I tentatively suggested the idea to him, he positively twinkled behind his glasses.

'I've always said' – he lit another Gauloise – 'that I'll die the day I don't work for a newspaper. My boy! You've saved my life.'

I had been turning over an idea in my head since I found Jean-Pierre on leave so soon after the outbreak of war. After talking things over with Oregon and then meeting some high-ranking followers of de Gaulle, who favoured a streamlined army, I could visualise the headline in Washington before I wrote a word – 'French Army is Too Big'.

After a few days of research and interviews, I came up with an astounding set of facts and figures, proving that the French mobilisation machine was ponderous, bogged down with bureaucracy, over-ambitious. One man in eight was now mobilised in France – compared with one man in forty-eight in Britain. The French had called up so many men that industry was being crippled. Thousands of conscripts were already undergoing the laborious process of being demobilised. There was a tug of war between the army, which liked to control large bodies of men, even if there was no fighting, and the needs of industry. Then I discovered, after thinking about Jean-Pierre's faulty guns in the Line, that a huge proportion of French artillery was still in storage. By the third week in September, when mobilisation was complete, the French had in theory fifty-seven divisions – yet only seven were available for the western front.

'It's dynamite,' cried Oregon. 'Now let me dig out some facts about the effect on civilian morale. The fact that all the men have vanished, but there's no war, no work.' There was a bitterness among the civilians as well as among men at the front, a sense of anti-climax. The Germans hadn't rained destruction from the skies. Accidents in the blackout were more lethal than among the troops. There were restrictions on petrol – though anyone who knew the right friend could get as much as he liked.

'That's a fine piece.' Oregon read the finished draft through carefully, and that was high praise indeed. 'But you'll never get it past the censor.'

I had wondered.

'Not a hope in hell,' said Oregon. 'Your only hope is to file from Berne. No censorship in Switzerland. But even if you can get it there, you can't use your by-line, even on a Swiss dateline.'

'Well, then. What?'

There was only one way – and I knew it. Forget my by-line, make the ultimate sacrifice on my very first despatch as a staffer. But it had to be. If my name appeared on that story the French might well cancel my accreditation.

As Oregon added, 'Hell, Schill Scotter and Vance will know you did it, and they're the only ones who really count. The rest is just vanity.'

That was what happened. As a stringer – and as an American citizen – Oregon took the train to Berne one day, handed over the cable and some explanatory details to Tixerand, our man in Switzerland, and returned to Paris the next.

Three days later I received a cable from Scotter. It made no sense – except to me. It read, 'Unable contact Tixerand stop if you contact please onpass congratulations to Tixerand on gaining his majority.'

Scotter knew that in no way could I phone through to Switzerland. And as for Tixerand's 'majority', he was in the mid-fifties. It was Scotter's way of telling me, 'Good work, you've grown up now.'

22

Though I knew that Sonia was spending a few days in Switzerland, there was no way I could sneak off to meet her there. She did telephone the dates when she would be in Rolle, but I now had to realise that I was a member of the *Globe* staff; I couldn't just walk out of the Paris bureau for a couple of days to meet a beautiful girl.

It is curious how things work out in life. I didn't go to Switzerland for one simple reason – I couldn't. And on the very day when I would have been with Sonia in Rolle, had I been able to make the trip, I found myself instead dining alone with Sonia's husband.

I could hardly believe it when the Italian Embassy phoned.

'I'm the Count de Feo's personal secretary,' said the girl. 'His Excellency wonders if you would care to have dinner with him quietly on Thursday?' Before I could catch my breath, she added, 'His Excellency asks me to apologise for such short notice. He wondered if perhaps Maxim's would be agreeable to you.'

I gulped. Thursday! Yes, it was the very night I would have been in Rolle. And only two days before Sonia was due to return to Paris. Why the hell did he want to see me? He was the last man I wanted to meet alone over the dinner table. Though Francesco was, in fact, very agreeable and we had by now met often enough to use Christian names, no man can feel comfortable when dining alone with a husband whose wife is his lover. I wasn't thinking only of emotions like shame, embarrassment, guilt; I just didn't like the idea of sitting alone in a restaurant making polite conversation with a man of impeccable manners and breeding in such a situation.

I planned to arrive first, as a gesture to de Feo's status of ambassador, but he was five minutes early. Albert, the head waiter, fleshy jowls wobbling over tight collar, ushered me immediately to de Feo's table. 'I didn't order champagne' – de Feo always wore a slightly amused, almost ironic smile –

'because I feel you must drink so much of it at home. How are you? What'll you have?'

As I hesitated, he asked, 'May I suggest a new drink I've invented. Albert knows how it's mixed: Bitter Campari, vermouth, gin on what you call the rocks, with a splash of soda. Do try it. One day I'm going to think of a name for it.'

At that moment the negro boy who served coffee and was always dressed in fancy Oriental costume, came past and piped up, '*Bonsoir, votre Excellence.*'

'That's what I'll call my new drink,' exclaimed de Feo delightedly, 'A Negro! No – that would upset our African friends. I know – a compromise – a *Negroni*. Perfect!' He lit a cigarette in his long holder and, as I sipped the new drink, I found that it had a pleasant bitter taste.

I didn't often have the opportunity to size up Francesco; I had to admit that he was good-looking. He had what I can only call an 'open' face – something I didn't usually associate with diplomats. He had a good head of hair, slightly wavy – though not marcelled, thank God. He had the straightest of noses and he was no doubt generally regarded among the ladies as a dashing Italian Romeo. He had also become highly successful in his chosen profession while still in his early forties.

I continued to study him as we decided on the menu. His dark blue Italian-cut suit was exactly right. So was his bow tie – the *papillon*, as 'butterfly ties' were commonly known in France. The white and blue spotted tie matched a spotted silk handkerchief, and the initials under a coronet on his silk shirt were so discreet you could barely see them. He was, in short, very elegant, from his oval gold and enamel cufflinks to the distinctive gold watch with its 'D' strap which also whispered 'Cartier'.

We both ordered the same dinner – *foie gras* followed by roast beef. 'And some *raifort*, Albert,' adding to me, 'It's not so much the beef I like here, it's the horseradish sauce.'

Spreading the *foie gras* on a corner of wafer-thin warm toast cut in small triangles, de Feo said, 'I'm so pleased your father asked Sonia to Douzy for the *vendange*.

'The change did her good,' he continued, adding before I could say anything, 'One of the reasons I asked you to dine with me tonight was to talk to you about Sonia. I know that you're' – he coughed slightly – 'a very privileged friend, and I don't think she's very happy.'

I said nothing. This was one of those moments when, faced by a highly intelligent man, I needed to watch every single word – and let most of them be uttered by him.

'But first I have an apology and confession to make.' He paused while the *sommelier* poured out a little Pouilly Montrachet for him to taste.

'Thank you.' He nodded to the *sommelier*, then said to me, 'Larry, you have to believe me when I tell you that I had absolutely nothing to do with that terrible business in the railway station about Anna. I am as horrified as you. Apart from anything else, Anna is Sonia's best friend – I was shattered.'

'But you did give her away?' I asked.

'I had *nothing* to do with that,' he replied firmly. 'It was a mischance, and I'd better explain what happened right away.'

The 'mischance' – his own word – had, as I imagined, happened on the night of the Polish ball; he and Albrecht had been talking together while Guy was fetching Mama's wrap. How vividly I remembered the eerie sensation that I was being watched. What I didn't know until now was that Albrecht had been merely asking de Feo if he knew me, and Francesco had added innocently, 'My wife has known the family for years. And I know Larry Astell's sister. We dined with her last week.'

He motioned to the waiter to remove the small blue plates and replace them with warm toast wrapped in a stiff napkin.

'And that was enough,' said de Feo. 'I had no idea your sister was not supposed to be in France. Why should I? Sonia had told me that Anna was married to a German, but even so – why shouldn't she visit France? And I didn't know anything about Abetz running a vendetta against you.'

'A vendetta?' I echoed.

'Perhaps the word is a little dramatic. Do you mind if I smoke between courses? It's a deplorable habit.' He carefully pushed the end of his cigarette into its holder, and again moved his lips into that special, slow, slightly ironic smile. 'But I've known Abetz for years. Once he refused to drink Astell champagne at a party. When I asked why, he said you insulted him in public – before his colleagues. In the Ritz Hotel, I believe. What on earth did you say to him?'

'*Gefundenshite!*' I rolled the word round my tongue. 'I made the word up myself and it gave me one hell of a lot of satisfaction.'

'And caused you a great many problems,' murmured de Feo drily.

'How do you know about this?'

'I was posted to Germany as a junior in the Italian Foreign Service and worked with Otto Abetz. I was supposed to be his protégé. It was understood that if or when Otto wanted a key figure planted in Paris for the Italian Foreign Service, Hitler would ask Mussolini, politely, of course' – again that faint sardonic smile – 'to appoint me. Abetz wanted someone he could trust.'

'Does Sonia know all this?' I wondered.

'I don't suppose she does. We never discuss politics,' answered de·Feo after a pause. 'And that brings us to Sonia, doesn't it?'

What I have to tell now is the final unfolding of the tangled relationships between Riccardi, Sonia, de Feo and Abetz; how their fates were interlinked, and how, because of them, marriage had always eluded us. Each appeared in the drama, though only from time to time. Thus the problems appeared in episodic fashion, lacking continuity.

Now, however, at Maxim's, and later over brandies in the rue de Longchamps, I was able to piece together for the first time words and actions which had hitherto baffled me – especially as any suspicions had always been brushed aside by Sonia.

When it became obvious that de Feo was about to unburden his soul, my first puzzled question was: Why? Why tell me diplomatic secrets which had for so long been so carefully hidden? It never occurred to me that the reason was simple: Riccardi was dying of cancer and soon there would be no need for any more secrecy. This was why Sonia had gone to Florence. The second basic factor involved both Riccardi and de Feo. Both had skeletons in cupboards which they were anxious to keep locked. And the man who held the key to these cupboards was Otto Abetz.

Riccardi's troubles began in Paraguay, the landlocked country in South America which in 1932 went to war with its neighbour Bolivia; both countries laid claims to the vital Chaco River and the surrounding Chaco Plain, then – wrongly as it happened – believed to contain oil.

The Bolivian army was officered by Germans under General Hans von Kundt. Mussolini sent technical advisers to the people of Paraguay where Riccardi was ambassador in Asuncion, the capital. Riccardi became a kind of legend. With Italy's help Paraguay won the war at the end of 1935, and by 1936 their military'hero, Colonel Rafael Franco, a close friend of Riccardi, had been elected president in a coup. Immediately he formed a semi-Fascist régime modelled on Mussolini's Fascists. In it he appropriated four million acres of land from the rich, shared among peasants and soldiers – except for a 'present' of land worth $1 million which had quietly been promised to Riccardi as a reward.

There was one problem: it took years for Riccardi secretly to sell the land, which explains why he refused to leave Paraguay for better diplomatic posts. Nor could he easily siphon the cash to Europe. Mussolini had set up an Exchange Institution through which all foreign money transactions had to be routed. Riccardi *had* to work through secret channels. It was the only way. He finally managed to sell most of the land and transferred the cash to Switzerland.

While all this was happening – as I put de Feo's story into sequence – Francesco went as a junior diplomat to Germany. He had been picked to study infiltration and subversion under Otto Abetz.

Abetz, however, never trusted anyone unless he could control him, through fear or blackmail. Shortly after his arrival in Germany, de Feo was compromised. In the heady days when Hitler dreamed of an Aryan super race, with Francesco perhaps the most handsome man in their group, the cult of comradeship among men was strong. To be the friend of a man was far better than being the lover of a woman.

'That didn't mean that we all went to bed together,' observed de Feo wryly, 'but most of us did have friendships of the kind British boys at public schools go through. To be frank – Abetz trapped me one evening after we had all had a great deal to drink. It was pure schoolboy stuff. Nothing really sordid like sodomy.'

With a real sign of regret de Feo continued, 'I never wanted to get married. You have no idea how I used to *love* my bachelor life. It was perfect. I had marvellous servants, lots of women friends, who enjoyed a good dinner and were delighted not to be bored by amorous advances afterwards.'

To de Feo, who by now had returned to the Foreign Ministry in Rome, the Berlin episode had been forgotten. But then the ministry, guided by Abetz, called Francesco in and accused him of being homosexual. Though he denied the accusation, he was under a cloud. But Abetz had no intention of ruining de Feo's career; he just needed to control him. So, at a time when Mussolini was hysterically ordering every suspected homosexual in Italian government circles to be deported to Sardinia to work in the coal mines, Abetz moved to save de Feo, for he needed him. He suggested that Francesco could avoid the coal mines very easily – by getting married.

This was long after Sonia had been sent away from Douzy 'in disgrace', and Riccardi, working in the Italian Foreign Office, was behaving oddly, making sudden trips to Switzerland. Sonia was not stupid. She knew something was wrong.

But Abetz had heard the first whispers of Riccardi's 'secret treasure' – for a very good reason. Hitler had been furious at the way his general had been humbled by Italy in Paraguay – and Riccardi was the man responsible. The Germans kept files on Riccardi – and on left wing leaders in Paraguay. With the end of the Fascist government there, rumours about Riccardi multiplied.

As Hitler was deeply suspicious of all Italian motives, Abetz was ordered to have Riccardi watched. What better way to do this than through his one-time protégé, de Feo? And since Francesco was in trouble, what better way to use him than by forcing him to marry Riccardi's eligible daughter?

Riccardi was panic-stricken when he discovered from a German diplomat that Abetz knew that 'something intriguing had happened in Paraguay', and that a daughter married to de Feo would make Abetz ignore the conversation. No doubt the story was even more tortuous than the manner in which I have tried briefly to untangle it. But Riccardi *was* sitting on a million dollars – and liable to exposure. Sonia met de Feo, by arrangement. Francesco was presentable, with a title, and when he proposed Riccardi warned Sonia that, if she refused, he would commit suicide.

Soon Riccardi was posted to Paris. Sonia, by now engaged, returned there with him, relieved that she had not yet been forced into a quick marriage to de Feo. Once again the influence of Abetz prevailed. He was engaged in many devious plots while posing as an ardent friend of France, and he needed someone like Riccardi to do the undercover work for him in Paris, while Abetz posed as the Francophile.

In Paris, though, there was an unexpected development. Whispers of the 'Riccardi affair' had not only reached German Intelligence but also left-wing governments in South America trying to stage a coup in Paraguay. Left-wing anti-Fascist underground movements were beginning to work together, sharing information. Among the first to learn of the rumour were two Italian brothers, Carlo and Nello Rossello, who had fled from Italy and were plotting in Paris against Fascists. Finally, one of the brothers confronted Riccardi and threatened to denounce him unless he handed over the gold.

Riccardi realised that the two brothers must be eliminated, and arranged all the details through professional thugs. There is little doubt Abetz knew what was happening. From Riccardi's point of view it was a perfect murder. Mussolini even cabled him congratulations on the way in which the troublemakers had been removed.

Riccardi's stock actually soared – but not for long. Abetz never trusted *anyone* – especially someone who had instigated murder. He wanted to be sure that Riccardi was out of the way. So when he felt the time was ripe, he dropped hints to the French government about the murders. And Riccardi was kicked out of France. Of course Sonia had to leave too.

Now came the final silky twist in Abetz's devious plot. After Abetz was declared *persona non grata* in France, he asked Count Ciano to appoint de Feo roving ambassador in Paris, so that Francesco could keep an eye on Albrecht, his replacement. Moreover, Abetz insisted that de Feo and Sonia now marry. If

Francesco ever suffered an attack of conscience, his own wife would be involved in the crimes of her father. If Sonia refused to go through with the marriage, Abetz would leak the whole Riccardi story.

Our brandy glasses had long been empty, and finally I said simply, 'What now?'

'What indeed?' de Feo lit another cigarette. 'I am very fond of you, Larry. I would have been very happy if you two could have married. But' – he shrugged his shoulders – 'Abetz is still a powerful man – even stronger now, from a distance in Germany.'

'But you love Sonia, surely – in a way?' I hesitated. 'No one can *help* loving Sonia.'

'Of course I do. Sonia is wonderful, but believe me, when it was suggested that I marry her I was appalled.'

'It certainly took you a long time to get round to it.'

'Exactly. I know what you are thinking and the answer is a resounding "No". I am not – those vulgar words – a pansy, a queer, a pouff. But Sonia is my wife – and I have a name and family that is honoured in Italy, and I don't want it to be sullied.'

It was his turn to hesitate, searching for the right words. 'I know perfectly well that you love Sonia – and even worse, the poor dear loves you. I am very touched by it – this love of yours that seems to last for ever. I wish I knew your secret.'

He led me to the front door and opened it, the servants having long since gone to bed. 'But we must all take care. For if I'm watching Abetz's successor, you can be sure that he is watching us.'

'I will,' I promised.

He walked with me the few yards to my parked car at the bottom of the rue de Longchamps. 'I shouldn't be saying this, but make the most of this ridiculous *drôle de guerre*. Soon it will end – and when it does, when the Germans are ready, they will become the masters of all Europe.'

PART THREE

May 1940–December 1941

23

At half past six on the morning of Friday, 10 May, I was fast asleep at Douzy when the insistent ringing of the downstairs telephone stabbed my dreams. Had the noise come from my private bedroom telephone, I would have been instantly alert for only Oregon (and the *Globe* in Washington) had the number, but this was downstairs. And my father, who was a heavy sleeper, had long since disconnected the phone in his bedroom because it irritated him.

I switched on the landing light, cursing the prospect of answering a wrong number; but no, I thought, that wasn't likely; no one would insist on phoning for such a long time unless he was sure.

All the same, I almost barked into the receiver in the hall, 'Yes? Who is it?' as though saying wordlessly, 'And what the hell do you mean by phoning me at this time of night?'

Almost apologetically, the voice, which I recognised, astonished me. 'It's Francesco.'

I was suddenly wide awake, nerve ends tingling – with fear that something had happened to Sonia.

'Yes?' was all I could say.

But it had nothing to do with Sonia.

'I shouldn't be telling you this,' de Feo's voice sounded urgent, 'but it won't be a secret for long, and I thought you might be grateful if you could make an early start in Paris.'

'Francesco! You're talking in riddles. What's this all about? Nothing wrong with – your wife?' Hesitating over the last two words.

'Nothing – but the balloon's gone up!'

'How come?'

Speaking very deliberately, like a political spokesman reading the text of an official communiqué, Francesco said, 'At first light this morning, a hundred and thirty-five German divisions invaded Holland, Belgium and Luxembourg.

They're making straight for France, and the front extends from the North Sea to the Swiss frontier. My friend, *Dio ti protegga!*'

As I started to mutter a thanks for the warning, he added, 'I have to go. I'm speaking on my private line. *Arrivederci.*'

Without another word he hung up. As I stood there in my pyjamas, I suddenly shivered, thinking, Yes, we would all need God's protection now. And then another thought – how decent it had been of Francesco to call. He would realise that news of the German invasion could already have reached Washington from Berlin or neutral countries, and as it was now just before midnight yesterday in the *Globe* office there was nothing I could do in France. Even so, the sooner I reached Paris the better.

For this day, I knew, was the moment of destiny for France – and I was afraid. I was haunted by a few words which Hitler had said to his chiefs of staff the previous October and which I had read somewhere: 'I place a low value on the French army's will to fight. Every army is a mirror of its people.'

I only prayed that Hitler was wrong, but he had an uncanny instinct for hitting on the truth.

Rushing upstairs I grabbed my dressing gown then made my way to the kitchen to get some coffee. At first I thought no one else was up, but as I was heating the water Gaston poked his head round the kitchen door.

'Hello,' I cried. 'Heard the news?' I told him what I had learned.

Of course he knew nothing. Seeing him there, and with an oblique reference to Jean-Pierre's unexpected leave, I laughed, 'I thought you were in North Africa. Don't tell me you've got nowhere to sleep either.'

'Embarkation leave. Off tomorrow night.' And after a moment's hesitation he added, 'You're up early – not going to Paris by any chance? Could I beg a lift?'

'Sure. I'm leaving as soon as I get dressed. Have some coffee first.'

We sat across the kitchen table, the open door leading to the early sunshine at the rear of the house. Gaston explained that he had relatives in Paris and wanted to say goodbye to them. 'I'll get a lift back to Douzy or Reims somehow.'

I remembered that once before when Mama was being driven from Douzy to Paris, Gaston had stayed with friends there. 'Sorry I can't guarantee a ride back,' I said,' 'but God knows when I'll see Douzy again. Still – you never know,' thinking that maybe Oregon might want to go to Douzy while I remained in the office. 'Phone through to the office before you go back – just in case.'

Already, on the journey to Paris, there was an air of expectant secrecy, of pompous bustle. At half a dozen important junctions, officious military police demanded to see our papers.

'The news seems to have got around,' I whispered to Gaston. I dropped him at the Châtelet – what a long time ago it seemed since Olivia had been hurt during the riots there. 'This okay?' I asked.

'Fine, thanks. The Métro from here takes me straight through to Levallois-Perret where my aunt lives.'

Paris was beginning to awaken by the time I sandwiched my M.G. between two trucks loading cloth in the narrow rue du Sentier. Upstairs the tape machine rattled along in jerks, but there didn't seem to be any hard news beyond the original terse flash. We had reached the stage of reaction and background stories.

Oregon bustled in around nine o'clock, the prospect of action pumping adrenalin through him like a tonic. His eyes were alight with excitement, his voice had an undercurrent of exuberance that comes only to men and women – politicians, war leaders, and, yes, newspapermen – when they are destined to play a role in momentous events. And though it was true that journalists were only onlookers, we *were* privy to many secrets which readers of our newspapers were rarely permitted to see. Like Oregon I, too, felt a surge of excitement, even the macabre thought which I couldn't control, 'They might bomb Paris today!'

In fact at first there was nothing to report at all, though everyone knew the real war had started. When I passed Madame Yvonne's bistro, next door to the office, I heard a snatch of the radio announce that there was *'rien à signaler'*.

I could do nothing about the day-to-day reporting of the war – the agencies were faster and better equipped than I was; however, I could interpret, prophesy, seek exclusive interviews, while Tommy Tomlinson lived with the officers and men on the Maginot Line, sending eye-witness despatches.

The news on the whole was electrifying. But one thing never entered my head – that the German attack couldn't eventually be contained. The combined allied forces – French, British, Dutch, Belgian – were numerically superior to the Germans. We could muster one hundred and fifty-six divisions – twenty-one more than Germany. We had four thousand tanks – mostly French – and, though cumbersome, they should be more than a match for the Germans who had fewer than three thousand. Only in the air could Germany boast of superiority.

Even so, when I switched on the French radio, another solemn voice was crying, 'The nations of Europe are united as never before and we are ready to repel the invader and defend humanity against the hordes of Hitler.'

I switched off, irritated by this drivel, but then switched on again. It might be a good idea to listen in case there was a communiqué. Funnily enough I was more worried by Mama's reaction to American newspapers than I was by real fear. The Americans would splash the news, distort it, probably be drawing maps showing how the Germans hoped to break through Champagne – and we could do nothing to tell her that most of it was nonsense.

Among the papers on my desk was a message to ring Jim Parks at the U.S. Embassy.

'No, it's nothing to do with war – well, not directly,' and I could imagine his grin as he added, 'We leave that to you blood-sucking leeches.'

'Thanks a lot. So what?'

'An extraordinary thing has happened. Lots of unsorted cargo, parcels, even some luggage, was rescued from the sea when the *Athenia* went down. Don't forget she took fifteen hours to sink. Among the bits and pieces was an attaché case with your Mum's name on it. Not in mint condition; the clasps, locks are all rusted and so on. But it's got her passport and documents in it. Will you accept it on behalf of your father? He's next of kin, I guess?'

'Fantastic,' I cried. 'I'll call round as soon as I can. Keep it for me till then.'

As it happened I was summoned later in the day to the Hotel Continental by Colonel Thomas for a Ministry of Information briefing. I learned nothing – absolutely nothing – so after the meeting broke up I walked round from the gilded rooms in the rue Castiglione across the Concorde to the embassy. I was fascinated at the stroke of chance by which Mama's writing case had been saved, not least because it was well remembered. We three children had bought it at Hermès years previously for a joint Christmas present, and as I showed my pass and ran up the stairs to Parks's office, I could imagine the case bobbing in the water, remembering from Mama's letter how it had fallen into the sea just as she was being transferred from one vessel to another after the sinking. I could see in my mind's eye the anguish at that moment as it slipped from her grasp, as she tried in vain to clutch it, only to see it floating away. Probably it contained all her papers – not only her passport, address book, but even jewellery perhaps. According to Parks it had been sent first to Britain, then when the embassy in London discovered that it belonged to someone living in France it had been forwarded to the embassy here.

As I signed for it, Jim said, a trifle too casually I thought, 'It's not locked, of course. The clasps broke as soon as anyone touched 'em. But you'd better just open it for a look-see before you hand it over to your father. Never know, it might contain something that doesn't belong to you.'

What an odd remark! Back in my desk, I undid the string. The back of the writing case was almost coming apart, the clasps were rusted and useless, the beautiful leather with its distinctive Hermès stitching covered with circles of green mildew.

Almost without thinking I opened the case – and caught my breath – as though someone had thrown a bucket of cold water full in my face. I looked at the soggy mess on top. What I saw *couldn't* be true! It was a picture of an attractive, smiling woman embracing a handsome young man, an obvious keep-sake photo. And my mother had never looked more beautiful.

At that moment a knock sounded and as I hastily closed the top of the old writing case, Gaston popped his head round the door. I must have looked irritated – or maybe so stunned I hadn't yet recovered.

'Sorry,' he said, 'but I was almost next door and I thought I ought to tell you I've got a lift back tonight. Thanks for your help.'

'Okay,' I said almost absently. '*Bonne chance*, Gaston.'

As he closed the door behind him I opened the writing case again, almost savouring the moment of anticipation. There was my mother, and even through the once wet photo I could see the pure happiness shining out of her eyes and the adoration – yes, that is what it looked like, the real adoration for the younger man in the secret photo. And I knew the younger man too – in fact I almost ran to the door of my office to call him back.

Gaston of all people! *Gaston*. My age, Papa's driver.

I couldn't believe it. I closed the top of the case hurriedly as though someone had caught me peeping through the keyhole at a couple of lovers. A thousand thoughts flashed through my mind; the time when Papa was saying in his up-and-down voice, 'Salt of the earth, Gaston. Trust him with my life.' Life, yes. Wife? That was a different matter. How *could* she? I opened the case and looked again at the large photo. Of course he was handsome – even dashing. He had good manners, but in *bed* with my mother. Where? How? How had they done it?

I remembered the time Mama had lunched with me in Paris, refusing dinner because she had an engagement with some old fogey – and I had later discovered that the old fogey hadn't even been in Paris at the time. And then there was Germany. Of course! Mama had even managed skilfully to arrange to sleep in an hotel instead of with Willi and Anna. How excited she must have been when they couldn't get away, then the night in Copenhagen, another in Brussels.

My God, I thought. How long has this been going on? I had another sudden desire to rush down the circular stairs shouting 'Gaston! Come back!' I resisted the impulse. I would have been too late anyway. If Mama had still been at Douzy I might have done something – though I hadn't the faintest idea *what*. It wasn't *my* life, it wasn't *my* wife. Nothing to do with me. And I couldn't suddenly feel a surge of hate for Gaston because whatever had happened Mama must have been the one who instigated the *affaire*. Still, I could hardly look at him with the same eyes the next time we met. Thank God he was off to

Africa. And then I realised that this was the reason why Mama had at first refused to leave France, and then suddenly changed her mind. She had refused to leave Douzy, hoping that Gaston would remain in a reserved occupation, but perhaps Gaston had been torn by different loyalties; and once he decided to volunteer for service in North Africa, once he was booked to leave, Mama knew that she had lost him and decided to bolt.

Oddly enough, on this first afternoon, I didn't give much thought to poor Papa. After all, he didn't *know*; and indeed he hardly ever noticed anything. And I would take good care that he never would know.

A brief search showed that there was nothing else in the case that Papa shouldn't see. And I suddenly felt a wave of sadness for poor darling Mama, trying to pick an autumn crocus, thinking of the casual remarks she had made to me. 'Yes, it is a bit dull here in Douzy . . .' I was sure – hopeful? – that Gaston and Mama didn't really love each other, that it was the physical attraction which a beautiful middle-aged woman who sees life slipping by feels for a handsome young man, by a woman who asks for one more chance to remember her youth. 'Bless you, Mama,' I whispered to myself.

Before I could change my mind I decided to tear the photo to shreds – praying that Gaston hadn't kept one of his own to look at in North Africa. Well, we wouldn't meet – any of us – for months, even years, perhaps never. I felt almost guilty tearing up the photo, but I couldn't post it to America. Yet how she must have clung to it! How many times, I wondered, had she thought about destroying such damning evidence. She must on occasion have been terrified that it would be discovered by accident – an accident just like this. What torture it must have been for Mama, wondering, in love, or a kind of love, clutching to one photograph as the only tangible memory of those stolen nights in Düsseldorf, Paris or wherever. With real regret I tore the photo into hundreds of pieces, sprinkled the bits of paper with lighter fuel and then burned everything to the last morsel of ash.

Within a couple of days the first details of the German assault began to filter through, though all mention was rigorously suppressed in the press. It seemed that at daybreak on 10 May every available German aircraft took off. The *Luftwaffe*'s targets included Belgian and Dutch airfields, French airfields at Calais, Dunkirk, Metz, Bron and Châteauroux, and Valdahon camp. From the North Sea to the Rhône valley the sky was filled with a heavy drone. At the same time the Germans dropped almost the whole of their airborne strength over Holland.

At half past five that morning the bulk of the *Wehrmacht* attacked along the western front. The 135 divisions included ten armoured and eighty crack divisions, moving against Holland, Belgium and France.

Now the world as we had known it was really crumbling about our ears. Soon there were government changes. Reynaud, who had succeeded Daladier as premier, called in Marshal Pétain, the hero of Verdun, as vice-premier. General Maxime Weygand, who was seventy-three, replaced Gamelin as C-in-C. At Douzy, hordes of refugees from the Low Countries and Denmark poured across their frontiers into France, impelled by fear or an instinctive urge for security; long caravans of men and beasts, the Vikings with their blond hair and ruddy cheeks standing out against their dark-haired neighbours. Sometimes when I saw them approaching from afar on some distant hillside they looked for all the world like a covered wagon train awaiting attack by hostile Indians.

I was not often in Douzy during the early days, but according to Papa he managed to keep most of the nomads away from the precious vineyards. Some were aggressive, some violent – 'as though we owed them a living,' said Papa. They raided crops, became belligerent if we dared to protest.

'So what did you do?' I asked.

'I sent for Grandma.' He gave a wry smile. 'The first time she threatened them they thought she was a joke. But only once. I must say, only *once*. She laid about the largest man with her walking stick. In the end he bolted. Remarkable, *quite* remarkable, the way she followed it up with a tongue lashing.' At the memory of the moment, Papa chuckled, almost with relish, 'Yes, that's the perfect word – *tongue lashing*.'

'And then?'

'There must have been fifty in that group. Grandma chased some cows that were too near the vineyard, ordered the farmers to graze them in the orchard and shouted to the refugees, "Follow me!" They didn't dare to refuse, and followed her to the Home Farm where they were all given bread with ham or *saucisse* and as much wine or milk as they could drink.'

'And they behaved?'

Papa nodded. 'The word went round. Those who behaved as they moved on told the others they could depend on one free meal a day if they respected the house rules.'

This conversation took place a few days after the German invasion, on the first occasion when I was able to get to Douzy for a few hours to see how the family was faring. Five million men, women and children were on the march across Europe, all fleeing the spectre of German brutality, running anywhere, although they must have known in their hearts there was no real hope; the carpet of humanity was being trodden underfoot by the Germans with the indifference of men squashing ants.

'There's an old proverb,' said Oregon when we were discussing the refugees, 'which goes, "What's the use of running when you're not on the right road?" It's a German saying, by the way. Ironic, isn't it?'

The only information we could glean about these momentous events came through the Ministry of Information and, though any news of retreat was firmly withheld, I was able to fill in some of the broad outlines of the picture. Three Panzer corps were in the van of the German attack which had been launched that Friday morning. The Germans swarmed through the Ardennes in Southern Belgium and Luxembourg, obviously making for the river Meuse. Already by the end of the first day's fighting it was clear that the Belgians were retreating and there was no way the brave Dutch could hope to hold out. Though valiant, the Hollanders had only a quarter of a million men and fewer than 150 planes. They were doomed from the moment German airborne forces seized key airfields and bridges.

In fact, thinking back to those first days of the real war, the most extraordinary thing is that when the big push did come, even when almost immediately the Germans started pouring towards the Meuse, there was no sense of real panic. Sure,

France would receive a few hard knocks before the Krauts were beaten off, most people thought, but the issue could never be in real doubt because Europe was not only more powerful, but fortified with an even stronger weapon – right – on their side.

Of course the rich – as usual – took their precautions. A well known American hostess in Paris, Mrs. Laura Corrigan, promptly closed her Paris house and moved into the Ritz Hotel – it was said that she occupied the entire first floor. But, even so, that indicated a *lack* of panic. The Corrigans of this world could just as easily have flown off to Mexico or Rio, but all they wanted was to stay in Paris and be cosseted.

I could hardly get away from the office for several days, but on the Sunday – it happened to be Whit Sunday – Sonia telephoned me from the rue de Longchamps. Francesco had been ordered to Italy for a two-day conference with Ciano. We agreed to meet at the terrace of Fouquet's on the Champs-Élysées, so that if by chance she were followed our encounter would have all the appearance of a chance meeting.

Sipping a beer, I waited in the sunshine, glancing through *Le Monde* until she arrived. The Duke of Windsor had entertained King Zog of Albania at a charity gala in Paris. The Académie Française, busy composing its new dictionary, couldn't agree whether the wing of a chicken was a limb or a muscle.

She arrived along the avenue, gave a well-simulated smile of surprise and a wave as she greeted me, and I gravely invited her for a coffee, after which we strolled down towards the Rond Point. From some unseen window or café a gramophone or radio churned out the latest haunting hit tune, 'J'Attendrai'. Near the Palais de Glace gardeners were carefully planting early flowers.

'It's a perfect summer's day.' Sonia almost sighed with happiness, the long hard winter – the worst in the history of France – forgotten with the buds of the chestnuts opening out all along the Champs Elysées. It seemed impossible, feeling the sun on our faces as we strolled along, that during the winter, the Thames in London had frozen over and that Paris had been a city of burst pipes – with hardly a plumber in sight.

'Let's lunch at the Ritz,' I said suddenly, probably thinking of the unknown Mrs. Corrigan. 'It's a change and the food's good.'

'Anything you like, darling, even though, well' – with a low happy laugh – 'when you leave your beloved Left Bank for the Ritz it's rather like lunching in a foreign country.'

I just felt that the easy elegance of the Ritz matched the mood of the May sunshine and the phrase on everyone's lips, '*Chantons quand même!*' Why shouldn't we sing just because the bloody Germans wanted to stop us.

Georges, the barman in the small bar off the rue Cambon, always joked when I arrived, 'Sorry, *m'sieur*, but we've run out of Astell.'

'Don't worry,' I replied airily. 'I'll forgive you this once. Anyway, I have a sudden desire for a cocktail – a Sidecar.' It was years since I had tasted an old fashioned cocktail – and I couldn't even remember the ingredients, though I think it contained Cointreau and brandy. I just felt the need for a sharp, tangy flavour.

'Sorry, sir,' Georges looked at a sign over the bar. 'It's a dry day.' I had forgotten that on three days a week no hard liquor was served anywhere in France – excepting at home. But of course wine didn't count as 'liquor', so we settled for Astell after all. Georges also whispered a warning as I tasted the champagne. 'Only two courses allowed and there is no *pâtisserie* today. All cake shops close three days a week.'

'So we have to settle for a two-course lunch,' I cried in mock despair as I steered Sonia to a corner table in the quiet, panelled dining room – it was too early yet to lunch in the garden.

'Don't worry,' I added, 'we'll start with a *risotto con scampi* followed by *poulet de Bresse*.' I knew that at the Ritz they served the finest roast chicken in France.

Suddenly, half-way through lunch, without knowing why, I asked, 'I wonder what poor Willi is having for lunch today?'

'A tenth of what we are eating – if that,' said Sonia. 'It makes me feel embarrassed to think of it.'

'I was thinking how ridiculous it is that suddenly, Willi, a good friend, can so easily become an enemy.'

'Of the French, not of us.'

'You know what I mean. You might be the next enemy.

Francesco more or less said it was bound to happen in the end.'

'Not yet.' She laid a hand on mine.

'No, not yet,' I echoed. 'But one day for certain. What's going to happen to us then?'

'There'll be a way. There has to be.' She was suddenly silent, doubting perhaps, afraid, as the waiter poured out the black coffee and asked, 'Anything else, Monsieur Astell?'

I shook my head.

'I suppose,' Sonia was thinking aloud, 'that the real answer for me would be to live mostly in Switzerland. Francesco says all nations at war need one or two neutrals for convenience. And as you're a neutral American too – well, we could meet there.'

'And Francesco?'

'He'll have to understand – and I think he does. He told me about your talk.' She hesitated. 'You see, everything's changing. Poor Daddy is now in hospital. The end is very near. A priest is waiting to administer the last rites if necessary. I know I should be sad and weeping, but I can't really feel that way. He's in terrible pain in Florence, he cries to Mummy that he wants to die, and docs this sound brutal? – I want him to. And when that does happen, then the threat that hangs over him will die too – and I won't be needed again, not by anyone. Except you. Do I sound very – what's the American word? – tough?'

'Of course not. I understand. And for you as well as for me it's important that you say this and explain it to me. It's a terrible thing, talking about imminent death and suffering, but . . .' the words trailed off.

'What's so awful is that I can't see Daddy. I daren't go to Italy in case there's a war and the French wouldn't let me return. And if I have to choose I want to remain with you, the living, until the very last moment of our lives together. You don't think me heartless? And there's another thing – I'm really afraid of what most French people regard as the imposs-ible – a German victory. Do you think . . .?'

'I daren't *say* so,' with a smile that broke the tension. 'If Grandma heard me she'd flay me alive.'

Sonia smiled too, nodding as the waiter offered more coffee. 'Probably she's right, and I'm getting into a panic for nothing.

France *is* very strong?' She posed the last remark as a question, her voice betraying doubt, hoping for assurance.

'Not as strong as she pretends,' I had to admit.

'That's the real reason I don't want to leave you. It's because anything terrible could happen and I won't be away from you until we are dragged apart by events bigger than we are. If the war goes on with no result, why shouldn't I stay – at least until Italy declares war, if she ever does?'

'It's selfish, but that's all I want too. Every hour together with you is a bonus.'

We parted after lunch by different exits, for I knew by now that Francesco's main concern about us was the need for discretion. I walked back through the Ritz shopping arcade and out into the rue Cambon, turning right along the Grands Boulevards. Despite the war, despite the sandbags at strategic corners, despite the despondent groups whose rags and tatters and wide-eyed curiosity proclaimed them to be refugees, I felt the spring of love in my step as I strode towards the office. It had been a gentle, beautiful lunch filled with love. We had to stay together, we *had* to. I caught myself quietly humming 'J'Attendrai', for despite the refugees this seemed at a first glance like any other Sunday, with the crowds revelling in the Whitsuntide sunshine, even turning their faces upwards towards it as though to warm themselves after the cruelty of winter. Reality returned when I reached the office and opened the lift at the second floor to hear the jangling telephone.

It was Papa. I had been trying in vain since Friday to get through to Douzy, always to be told by the invisible vinegary spinsters who manned the French switchboards that the number was engaged. Papa had succeeded where I had failed – it was easier with local knowledge to pull a few strings – or telephone wires.

'It's bad news,' Papa said without preamble. 'We don't really know anything here at Douzy – except that the Germans are advancing everywhere. It's pretty awful, yes, *awful*. I went to Reims for a bite of dinner at the Boulingrin last night and it made my stomach turn – yes, really *turn*, to hear the army types swilling champagne and talking about their impregnable Maginot Line.' Then he came to the point. 'Any chance of you getting to Douzy – just for a night?' I could sense that my father needed me, if only for moral support. 'We must decide what to do about Anna. I don't like her staying here.'

'I'll try,' I promised him. 'I think I could get back for one night. How's everyone – Guy and Olivia?'

'I'm worried about her too of course.' Papa's voice rose up the scales. 'There was a nasty anti-Jewish demonstration near Reims the other day. But it's Anna who really worries me. She's German, Larry. She should go to Switzerland as soon as possible.'

'Could she?'

'Why not? Not by train, but is it too late to go by car?'

Papa seemed to ignore the fact that the Germans had at one point advanced almost to the borders of Switzerland.

'I'll try and get back home for a few hours some time this week,' I promised him. 'I want to see you too of course. Oregon can mind the shop.'

Papa was just explaining that he could provide me with a tank of petrol when the sirens sounded.

'It's a raid,' I shouted to him. 'I'll have to ring off but I'll be seeing you soon.'

The insistent wail of the air raid warning was, I thought, the most depressing of all sounds made by war. Gunfire was bad, and I had never heard the whistle of falling bombs or the terrible sound of the Stuka dive bombers, but the sirens had a depressing sound all their own; it was the noise of a world summoned to live underground, to revert to the life of the caveman. I could see through the windows the *flics* forcing people into makeshift shelters even though there was no sound of gunfire or planes overhead. I knew we should be grateful for their solicitude, but during the only time I had been caught in the street during a raid an officious policeman had insisted on bundling me down the steps into the nearest Métro station. It was jammed. The smell of sweating bodies, old women on the verge of panic, the claustrophobia, the feeling that if a bomb did fall and block up the entrance we would be trapped, was awful.

This time I was in the haven of the office, and I stayed there, listening to the concert of sounds, shouts, slamming doors, wardens' whistles.

There was no bombing and the 'flash' of the all-clear came up on the tape machine in the office almost as the sirens announced that the non-existent raid had ended.

The other news, however, was bad. By the Sunday, after little more than two days of fighting, the Germans had crossed the Albert Canal at Maastricht. A squadron of British 'Battle' planes based at the R.A.F. fields near Champagne had volunteered to fly suicide missions to attack bridges over the canal. All had been shot down. The only light relief came when a British correspondent arrived in Paris from London bringing with him the Sunday newspapers. The main headline in the *Sunday Chronicle* read 'Despair in Berlin!'

It was obvious that official communiqués were distorted but finally the foreign press corps cornered Colonel Thomas and literally demanded that they must be given regular off-the-record briefings, if only to combat German propaganda. It was not just a question of getting news, we all argued, but of being kept in the picture so that we didn't make fools of ourselves and thus unwittingly distort the truth through ignorance.

Colonel Thomas finally agreed and, adjusting his pince-nez on his aquiline nose, gave us a depressing but at least fairly accurate account. Not only had the Albert Canal been breached, but advance guards of the three Panzer corps had penetrated to the east bank of the river Meuse along an eighty-mile front between Dinant and Sedan. Within a few hours – 12–13 May – General Guderian's Panzers established bridgeheads on the Meuse by a sleepy old provincial town which meant much more to Hitler, and to France, than just another strong point to be stormed or defended.

Sitting astride the river, Sedan – as any of us who had studied European history knew – was one of those key points in war and peace whose fate had changed the destiny of Europe. Here, in the nineteenth century, it had been the scene of France's greatest humiliation when Napoleon surrendered unconditionally with a hundred thousand men to General Molkte of Prussia. Now Sedan was to be the scene of defeat again.

During the night German columns lining the Meuse positioned themselves for attack by seven armoured divisions supported by three air fleets. At Sedan the Meuse is a swift, narrow stream running between steep banks. The river line was an ideal barrier and the French were convinced they could hold it. They had reckoned without the superior air power of the Germans. For hour after hour, from early morning on 13 May, Stuka low-level bombers screamed over the Meuse, giving the defenders no rest. The covering guns were pounded into silence. The Germans crossed the river in boats and inflatable dinghies, setting up pontoon bridges, then establishing beachheads on the west bank. Within hours the advance guard of the German troops took Sedan without a fight, and as the news of the German victory rattled its letters along the office tape machine neither Oregon nor I needed to add the one significant factor which both of us knew: that Sedan was less than sixty miles from Reims – and Douzy.

'You'd better go and see your father,' said Oregon quietly. 'Only come back to Paris soon – all hell will be let loose before long.'

I drove down late on the Friday. With Whitsuntide behind us the weather had turned even warmer. The sun seemed to shine every day, and on the first evening Anna and I went for a long walk, up past the bleak outline of Douzy church, through the twisting streets of the village, stopping for a beer with Monsieur Roland, the *patron*, at the Café des Sports.

Even after only a short absence Douzy never failed to tug at the strings of nostalgia. Whenever I walked down past the dell to the orchard, or up to the village, I felt as though I could never bear to leave the place and sometimes would curse myself – muttering aloud – for choosing to live in a city.

'What *are* you chuntering on about?' Anna laughed. I hadn't realised I was talking aloud.

'I was thinking that there just can't be another place in the world as beautiful as Douzy,' I sighed. 'Listen.' We could both hear the growl of gunfire like a distant thunderstorm. 'And to think we're going to lose it all.'

'Nonsense!' Anna spoke quite sharply. 'Don't ever say that. It's defeatist – and oh!' with a catch in her voice, almost the kind of break that signals waiting tears, she added, 'If we don't look on the bright side — if we don't *hope* — what is there to live for?' She hesitated, and then added, 'I love Douzy more than life.'

We had finished our drink and Anna was walking by the side of the lane, framed to the waist in feathery cow parsley. 'If someone tried to take it away from us, I think I'd kill them,' she said.

'I feel that way too. And so in a way does Sonia. Never forget that. It's the only *true* home she's ever had. But Anna — don't you think you ought to get out of France? What if the Germans . . .'

She shook her head vigorously. 'Never! I still love Willi — I think of him more than you'll ever know — but I'm not going to be kicked out of Douzy by Nazis. And anyway I'm not going to leave Olivia. At least I do have a kind of American passport, but what chance is a Jewish girl like Olivia going to have if the Germans take France?'

'Not much,' I admitted.

'Nothing can happen to me,' she said.

'Don't tempt fate by saying things like that.'

'I said so and I mean it — I'll kill the first German who lifts a finger against me,' she said. 'I will, I swear it, Larry. I loathe the lot of them.'

'Not all. There must be millions of decent Germans like — well, like Willi.'

'Willi's only a German by accident,' she almost shouted. 'To me he's not German or American or French. He's my *husband*. My husband! Do you ever think of Sonia as an Italian?'

'I don't suppose I do — except perhaps when I worry about the future.'

'Well then.' She looked at her watch and suddenly changed the subject. 'Let's start for home, shall we?'

After dinner Papa also brought up the subject of 'the girls', as he called them.

'I must say we should do something,' he declared, but rather helplessly. 'Yes, I do, *really*. The Germans are less than fifty miles from Reims. You're cutting it rather fine, you and Olivia.'

Apparently, all attempts by Papa and Guy to organise some way of spiriting the girls to the South of France or Switzerland had been thwarted by one stumbling block: female intransigence.

'If it's dangerous to use the train couldn't we smuggle the girls across the frontier into Switzerland?' asked Guy.

'First, it's not so easy for an amateur to cross frontiers illegally,' said Anna. 'And second, we don't want to go.'

'Quite impossible, I agree.' Papa must have nursed some half-forgotten memories of an old war film, for he added, 'Girls scrambling over all that barbed wire. Out of the question. Yes, there must be a better way.'

'But what?' asked Guy.

'Please, Papa.' Anna was beginning to lose her patience. 'Don't worry. I'm a grown-up girl now – I'm married – and I can look after myself.'

I knew what she meant. But did Anna have the slightest idea of what the future might hold for her if the Germans over-ran the area? The trouble was that after the months of inactivity not a soul realised how subhuman the Nazis could be if anyone got in their way. I hated to think what they would do if they got their hands on Olivia in some anti-Jewish purge. 'Some of the stories of German savagery are unspeakable,' I said half aloud to Papa.

'I've heard about them.' But had he heard the real evil details? I wondered as he added, 'But still, I *must* say, this *is* American property. They'll have to respect it. They can't just . . .'

'Papa! Face up to the truth,' I cried, exasperated. 'And you've got to realise this, too, Guy. They can do *anything*. With the Germans, might really *is* right. Have you thought about the embassy? Couldn't the embassy help Anna? What about Bullitt?'

'Really, Larry!' Now Papa sounded annoyed. 'Do you think I'm a child? Of *course* I've been in to see Bill Bullitt. I think he could fix it. But there's one problem.'

Patiently Papa and Guy explained that Anna had become so close to Olivia that they had decided to stick together.

'They say they face the same problems,' said Guy. 'I don't really know how to explain it. Both losers, I guess. One without a husband, the other without a family, Jewish, on the run if the Germans arrive.'

'I can understand that,' I said. 'Each one is determined not to let the other down.'

'Really, it *does* complicate things.' Papa sounded frustrated, defeated by circumstances.

I felt a sudden pang of pity for him. We were all so busy with our own lives we forgot the quiet way in which he had carried on after Mama left for America.

'You must miss her.' I tried to console him. 'Have you heard from her?'

'No letters,' he shook his head. 'And as far as I can see not much hope of getting any for the time being. But I've had fairly regular short messages through the embassy. Mama's living in New York — and she's taken a flat at the corner of 55th and Lexington. A *very* convenient place for St. Patrick's.'

At that moment I heard the peal of the old-fashioned brass pull-bell outside the front entrance.

'Really, a bit late for callers, yes, it *is*.' Papa frowned and looked at his watch. He always considered it bad manners for anyone to arrive without warning after dinner and, as Aubergine came in to announce the visitors, he said almost testily, 'Do we know them?'

There was no need for an answer. The Misses B and B burst into the living room.

Miss Barron's face was drained of all colour. Miss Brewer's was streaked with tearstains.

'Jean-Pierre's dead,' said Miss Brewer dully. 'He's been killed in action.'

24

Daily the news grew heavier, though, as if deluding themselves — or being deluded by others? — only those in high places realised it. Even men returning from battle seemed under the impression that their personal experiences were those of an unfortunate unlucky episode. We knew — the foreign press corps particularly — for many of them came and went from one country to another and between them could piece together a more coherent picture of unmitigated disaster. To me it was as though the heart was being torn out of France. And I could sense something equally tragic – the sense of futility among men fighting under leaders with 1914–18 mentalities against a revolutionary war machine so fearsome that nobody believed it was possible.

One of Jean-Pierre's friends whom I had met when both were on leave had promised to call me when he reached Paris, where he lived, and tell me how Jean-Pierre had died. He had stayed with the Misses B and B the time when Jean-Pierre had been sent home because the Maginot Line was too crowded.

'That was the trouble.' He was a young man of twenty-two called Boisseau. 'As they had no room we were all sent up to the front line on the river Meuse. It was murder.'

We had met for a drink near the office, where he told me the horrific story. Jean-Pierre and Boisseau and their unit had been sent up the line to bolster the morale of raw recruits. Many had only been training for six weeks. The two thousand or so men had only eight hundred rifles between them. Only two hundred were modern *Mousqueton* French rifles, the rest were obsolescent, some rifles dating back to 1891. 'I had a long thin Remington weighing twenty pounds with a lock so worn the cartridges kept falling out,' said Boisseau. 'Others had rifles too rusty to load.'

When the unit set off for the front line they had no knapsacks and had to wrap their belongings in waxed cloth. They were issued with rations of eleven biscuits each, one tin of sardines and one of pressed meat. 'The tins were coated with blue paint and when I scraped the paint off my tin, I found I could read the date when the meat had been canned. It was 1917.'

Everyone could tell a similar story – but since none of them ever passed the censor, it was easy for the government to build up a false picture among civilians. By hiding bad news they gave the impression that though the French were suffering some setbacks nothing was out of control and soon the tide would turn. But we *knew*. The French government knew. It could pinpoint every disastrous defeat as the Germans thrust westwards and to the Channel ports, where more than a quarter of a million British troops had miraculously escaped after being trapped by the Germans at Dunkirk.

'Everyone knows how badly the war's going,' I said bitterly to Sonia during one of our quiet lunches. 'Everyone but the French. The Germans are taking France as easily as picking our grapes.'

We still met whenever possible at Marcel's, but even there it was hard sometimes to throw off the gloom. The sense of adventure which had made life so exciting had been drained out of both of us. Once or twice, when sitting at the square table, I caught her looking sad.

'A centime for your thoughts,' I smiled.

She smiled back. She looked so beautiful on that warm June day, no hat, black hair silky, lips slightly apart.

'I'm not *afraid* of war. It's only the dreariness of it all that terrifies me. We hardly ever laugh these days, it's as though we're already too old to enjoy life. A girl too old at twenty-five! Isn't it a terrible confession — not to have a sense of fun any more? That's what sometimes makes me depressed.'

She hesitated, still thinking, then asked, 'What do you think about?'

'I don't know.' The old waiter brought a small dish of charcuterie and some radishes, and we counted ourselves favoured clients. 'I just feel an awful weight of sadness, partly for a country that's going up in smoke around us, but — sounds selfish' — I tried a grin — 'but especially for us.' I was thinking, as though in the past tense, how we had shared such a beautiful, laughing love together, not just the physical side but the tenderness.

As if reading my thoughts Sonia sighed, 'I wish we were in Douzy now, this very minute.'

'The war can't go on for ever,' I protested. 'And then Douzy will still be there — to welcome us back.'

'But will it be the same? Will *we* be the same? You can't just brush away years apart and expect to remain unchanged.'

It was during this lunch at Marcel's that we finally agreed it would be stupid to ignore the fact that soon Italy would be an enemy. And that we would have to be parted.

'But where would you go?' I asked.

'The house in Rolle is ready,' she replied. 'I've got an official resident's permit. So it's my home — in theory. Our ambassa-

335

dor in Berne fixed it for me with the Swiss. But I should go there before Italy becomes involved, otherwise all of us at the embassy will leave together in a sealed train for Rome. It's the normal practice. And if that happens I might get trapped in Italy.'

It made sense – as long as Francesco accepted the situation.

'He will. He understands.'

'You'll have to go soon?'

'No, no, no,' she cried. 'Not until the very last second of the very last day.'

'I don't think it'll be long,' I sighed. 'The Italians are making threatening noises. And you know there are rumours that the French government is going to evacuate Paris. If that happens Mussolini will *have* to declare war – to be sure he gets a share of the spoils.'

My conviction that the government would leave Paris soon was reinforced after I met Jim Parks for a drink at the Tante Claire bistro not far from the embassy. Even Jim's image of the cool efficient young diplomat was getting a little frayed at the edges, as I noticed from the soiled cuffs of his shirt sleeves.

'Yeah, I know,' he said bitterly as he saw me notice them. 'Now I can't even get my goddamn laundry done.'

'Things must be bad,' I laughed.

'We're all set to run for it – contingency plans ready and tested.'

'For?'

'There's no secret about this. We reckon the government will have to make for Tours and set up some sort of government there and then we'll have to go with them.'

'And a temporary embassy?'

'We've already taken over the Château de Candé in the Loire valley, the place where the Windsors got married. It's been lent to us by its American owner. We've already got a skeleton staff there and we've prepared it down to the last bottle of vino.'

'Of course the government might not have to go,' I suggested.

'Nothing's certain in a crazy situation like this – with an enemy that sits on its arse doing sweet eff-all for nine months then bang! hits you in the crotch when you're not looking. But I don't see the French holding out for long. Take my tip, get some authority – a special pass or something to go south – just in case.'

He was right, and I decided to ignore all official requests for a pass. I would be bogged down in paperwork for the duration. Reynaud I could not approach, however considerate he was. With a country fighting for its life, I would never get within a mile of him. Madame de Portes, though, was different. It was worth a try. She was always accessible.

In fact she couldn't have been more helpful – though the scene when I met her was bizarre, even shocking, in the midst of a war.

Her secretary was arranging an appointment at six p.m. the following day when she must have grabbed the phone, for in that special voice of hers she interrupted, 'Come to the Ministry of Defence, *cher* Larry. Paul is up to his eyes in work and he's also got a cold, so I'm helping out.'

She was indeed.

I drove to the Ministry of Defence in the rue St. Dominique. Reynaud preferred to work there – where Napoleon had once had his offices – instead of at the Hôtel Matignon, the official residence of the Premier of France.

I arrived just before six. 'You're expected on the first floor, *monsieur*,' said the secretary.

As I reached the waiting-room the male secretary seemed embarrassed. So did the only other man waiting for an appointment – a man I knew, Pierre Lazareff, editor of *Paris-Soir*. He was gazing in astonishment through the open door leading to Reynaud's office – not at Reynaud, he wasn't there, but at Madame de Portes who was energetically presiding over a noisy conference of elderly statesmen.

'*C'est impossible!*' Lazareff nodded to me for I, too, could see that Reynaud wasn't in the room. How could you hold a war council, or whatever was going on, without the Prime Minister being there? And at the very moment when the government might have been discussing with anguish whether or not it should flee from Paris.

The countess caught sight of me, came out in a rush, crying, 'Please don't be impatient. We'll be finished soon,' then moved over to a third opening and, while Lazareff and I sat almost aghast, I heard her say through the door, 'Are you all right, Paul? Just relax. We're working.'

She bustled back to the conference room. Ten minutes later a group of dispirited cabinet ministers trooped out. Lazareff was waiting to see one minister. As they went downstairs together Hélène de Portes cried, 'Come in, *cher* Larry. It's good to see someone so young and healthy after talking to all these old fogies.'

'I hope the Prime Minister isn't too ill,' I said.

'No, no. Just a bad cold. But he has a great responsibility, you know, and I must make sure that he conserves all his energy. That is why I help if I can. Now tell me, Larry, what can I do for you?'

I explained – tactfully adding that I didn't for a moment suggest that the government would *need* to leave Paris, but that as the correspondent of an important Washington newspaper I must be prepared for all possible contingencies.

'You shall have it while you wait,' she said cheerfully.

I must say that, in direct contradiction to most French government offices, Madame de Portes did get things done. She worked like a dynamo.

'Sit down, Larry,' she said, and bounded into the outer office. I heard her dictate a letter of accreditation. When the secretary brought it in, she read it, then made Reynaud sign it in the adjoining room. The secretary stamped it with the official seal and almost with a flourish she smiled, '*Voilà!* These may be bad times, but even the Germans couldn't match that for efficiency.'

Back in the rue du Sentier I told Oregon what had happened.

'It's a madhouse,' he cried. 'With that bloody woman wielding all the power. What really frightens me is that if things go badly for France she'll make Reynaud sign the instrument of surrender as quickly as she signed your bit of paper.'

During the first week in June the phone in the rue du Sentier stuttered one lunch time, went dead when I picked it off the hook, then the bell shrilled again and a voice, croaking with exhaustion, but still with an unseen grin in it, cried, 'It's Tommy. Any chance of pinching a bath at Douzy? I'm at Reims, taking a couple of days off. Haven't washed for days.'

'Tommy! Wonderful to hear from you. Go there right away. Papa must be around but I can't phone, it's too hard to get through. I'm just filing a story, but I'll drive to Douzy when I've got my stuff through the censors. See you later this evening.'

I was so excited at the prospect of seeing Tommy Tomlinson again that I almost forgot to go to the Hôtel Continental for the afternoon briefing. I was on the point of leaving when the phone rang again. It was Sonia.

'Francesco's just left for Rome.' She sounded breathless. 'He says it's a question of days now. Ciano has sent for him. But Larry – it means that we're free for a couple of days,' adding with unconscious irony, 'Isn't it wonderful? I'll go straight to the rue du Cherche Midi and wait for you.'

'No, no!' I cried. 'I was just going to risk phoning you. Tomlinson's on his way to Douzy. He's driving over from Reims. I've got to go to the Ministry of Information for a briefing. Come to Douzy for a couple of nights, darling. I plan to leave as soon as I can get away. Can you get one of your embassy drivers to take you to the office? Wait for me and we'll drive off together.' I felt suddenly exhilarated.

I was kept at the Ministry of Information for nearly an hour for the afternoon briefing. Colonel Thomas was dressed in a beautifully cut uniform, specially tailored, severely masculine, the cloth pale khaki and the texture of tweed, with bound edges. He was being cross-examined (in effect) by another American correspondent who had just returned from the front line – part of France which Thomas had obviously never had the time to visit. He was forced to admit that, 'for the moment, only temporarily you understand, *monsieur*', the Germans had air superiority around the Meuse area. Yes, he agreed, civilian population masses were clogging the roads in many areas, 'but that, *monsieur*, is a situation that will soon cease and the requisite measures are in hand.'

'What measures?' asked H. R. Knickerbocker, one of America's most respected correspondents.

'That, *monsieur*, I am not permitted to divulge,' said Colonel

Thomas, picking up his briefcase and bowing as he strode across the splendid room with its gilded ceiling and ballroom chairs.

We reached Douzy just before dinner and it was extraordinary – especially when I thought back to our sad lunch at Marcel's – it was truly remarkable how the moment the car crunched on the gravel the air of depression lifted. The doors burst open before Aubergine could reach us and out rushed Anna, Olivia and Guy, together with a shambling figure balancing a champagne glass in one hand and with a huge cigar in the other.

'You old so-and-so!' I cried. 'That's my suit you're wearing, Tommy. And my silk shirt!'

'Everything is borrowed.' Tommy gave a lordly wave of his cigar. 'Even the cigar, one of Oregon's. I'll never be able to return *that*. My new friend Aubergine is washing my clothes, pressing my uniform and I feel like the king of the castle.'

From the very moment I hugged him, then kissed the girls and they in turn rushed to embrace Sonia who had appeared with me out of the blue, the few hours were like a birthday party. Everybody was suddenly on fire with happiness. We even started off with a joke after our first welcoming drink.

With mock gravity Anna announced, 'We're rather short of space now that Tommy's arrived unexpectedly but you won't mind sharing a room, will you, Larry?'

'Share a room – with Tommy! Never! He snores.'

'How do you know?'

'Not with Tommy,' said Anna sweetly. 'I thought Tommy deserves a long night's rest on his own. But if Larry and Sonia could be persuaded . . .'

We dissolved into laughter just as Papa, who had been working late, arrived home.

'You sound happy, *very* happy, yes, it sounds just like old days,' he beamed, and as he kissed Sonia he examined her more closely. 'You look more beautiful every time I see you,' he said as though it was a mystery and unexpected. 'Yes, more beautiful, very attractive.'

We didn't *do* anything to make that brief spell of freedom any happier than countless others. It just happened that way, perhaps aided by the presence of Tommy. An unexpected friend can often help to ease family tensions. Perhaps also it was because those hours were in a sense stolen, as though we were all on leave. Only Mama and Willi were missing to complete the family party.

At one stage, when Sonia and I sat together on the large sofa, my feet on the corner of the huge plate glass table, and the others talked or joked, I teased her, 'Another centime for your thoughts.'

'I was just thinking of the magic which this house holds for me. Douzy is our real home, isn't it? Where we first fell in love. Sometimes I imagine I'm married to you, not Francesco, and settled down here. It's so peaceful. So stable. It's the only home we've ever really had. If only we could stop the clock and stay here for ever.'

Later, as was inevitable, there were moments when the conversation grew more serious. Apart from anything else, I wanted to hear all Tommy's latest news. He was with the 35th Division in the French army where for three weeks he had been with soldiers holding a sector fourteen miles south of Sedan.

'After the big breakthrough?' I asked.

He nodded, explaining that after the Germans had crossed the river they had driven north and west, leaving German infantry to widen the gap and turn the Maginot Line. North and west the Germans were advancing up to fifty miles a day, by-passing strongpoints.

'You've never seen such a shambles,' said Tommy. 'The men in our sector were in some cases literally starving. The field kitchens were often ten miles behind the lines and the food was delivered once every twenty-four hours – each midnight – and stone cold. Sometimes the trucks couldn't get through and then there wouldn't be anything to eat – not a biscuit – for forty-eight hours.'

'Where does this leave us?' I asked. 'I mean Reims, Douzy, the family?'

'Not a hope. No use kidding ourselves. Reims will fall within a few days. Nothing can stop the rot; only the goddamn censor would never allow us to tell the truth.'

'Papa doesn't think so,' I said doubtfully.

'No offence meant,' Tommy hesitated, 'but there's a world of difference between your father and his brother. Oregon *loves* the French. Your father *admires* them. That's a helluva difference. And so you see your father can't realise that for a century – since Napoleon and then the great war that bled France white – France has been a second-class power flattering herself she was a great one. It's a pity, but it's led her into masquerading as an empire that's no match for the Germans.'

'Does it really matter if or when France gives in?' I asked Tommy. 'I'm not being cynical, but does it *really* matter? The British will have to sue for peace, won't they? After all, the French hate the British; they like the Germans more than they like the French. And anyway the British don't have a chance.'

'What about the Channel?' asked Tommy.

'Do you think the sea counts any more when the other side has mastery of the air?'

Perhaps the fact that Douzy was doomed – if only for the time being, we hoped – helped to sustain our feeling of exhilaration and to shrug off the doubts. It gave us an added impetus to enjoy those few hours to the full.

I had to leave with Sonia immediately after lunch, before Tommy, who had 'borrowed' an old Panhard, and planned to rejoin his unit a couple of days later. 'If I can find it,' he added drily.

The last lunch was subdued. It was as though the effort to be cheerful (even though it had been spontaneous) had sapped our reserves of emotion. In a matter of days Douzy would, even if neutral, be surrounded by German uniforms. This was surely the last time Sonia and I and the others would all meet in this beautiful home as one happy family, and the parting might be for a long, long time. Sonia would have to leave for Switzerland. Anna would become a fugitive in hiding. Olivia would live in fear if she ever dared to show her face. Already the process of disintegration in our family had begun now that Mama was in New York and Willi had vanished, swallowed up in the gigantic German military maw. Meanwhile I would probably leave for the south with the French government. Who could tell if I would ever be able to get north again to see Papa and Grandma? I even had to give up my M.G. – leaving it to be used at Douzy while I drove back to Paris after lunch in the less conspicuous Citroën, which I thought would be more suitable for the journey to Tours.

On the Saturday – that must have been 8 June – Sonia phoned me again when I was back in Paris. Her husband was not returning from Rome to Paris after all because the declaration of war was 'imminent'. That was the word she used.

'He told me not to worry,' she said. 'All embassy personnel would be given three days to pack up after the declaration, and of course the French would be given the same courtesies in Rome.'

'How will you go – I mean travel?'

'The officials here tell me we'll all be collected from the embassy in buses under French guard three days after war is declared and we'll be put in a special sealed diplomatic train. That's all I know.'

'But darling – war might come any day. And I might have to leave for Bordeaux or Tours at a moment's notice. Everything points to a sudden evacuation by the government. Time is running out. We must meet now – in case it's goodbye – until I can get to Switzerland.'

Then she dropped her bombshell.

'I'm going with you.'

'Hey! Wait a minute.'

'No, I won't wait. You listen, darling.' As calmly as she could – and she was never very calm – she outlined her plans. Italy would declare war within forty-eight hours, she was sure. She would be ordered to go first to Italy. 'But I want to go with you.'

'I know that, but it's impossible,' I cried. 'Apart from the fact that I don't know where I'm going to make for, if there is a war – and you're with me – you could be lynched if anyone found out you were Italian.'

'They won't. Don't be silly. Everyone at the embassy is getting a special pass with a time limit for the three days. Don't be so afraid.'

But I was afraid. Of course the prospect of travelling with her was wonderful. But there were fifth columnists everywhere, and if we travelled on crowded roads, where tempers could burst into angry confrontations, God knows what could happen. I explained as much.

'I'll take that chance,' she declared. 'I'll have three days of grace – of official protection, guaranteed by the French . . .'

'Sonia, please! The French can't even control their own troops, let alone civilians.'

'It's the only way. If we go south, then you can take me to Bordeaux. I'll get across the frontier into Spain, then go from one neutral country to another, Switzerland.'

'It's not on. Too dangerous.'

'Don't you understand *anything*, Larry?' Even at this moment of tension I almost smiled, imagining the way she was stamping her foot at the other end, as she often did when irritated by my imagined obtuseness.

'I'm throwing myself at you,' she cried. 'I want to marry you when we can. I'm leaving home to settle down with you. I don't know how or when, but this is our only chance. I'll tell Francesco. He'll eventually be able to get an annulment or whatever they do. But you are my man now, Larry. And despite this stupid bloody war' – she almost choked with anger – 'I'm coming with you.'

'Okay,' I said huskily. 'You're mad – crazy – but I love you, friend or foe, French or Italian or American. It makes no difference.'

'We'll do it, darling,' she cried. 'We will – and this time it's for ever.'

I never hesitated now the decision was made.

'Let's leave at dawn the day after tomorrow,' I said. 'I'm going to a press conference at the Hôtel Matignon this evening. The premier's official office, so it must be an upper-crust briefing. There's only one thing I must do – the only proviso I've got to make.'

'No conditions. We don't need any.'

'This one. If Madame de Portes is around – and she will be – I'd like to get an extra pass made out for you personally and get it stamped with Reynaud's official seal. She'll do it, I know.'

At least Sonia could hardly disagree with that useful information. 'It might not be necessary, but it's a good idea if you can pull it off.' Then she added, 'I'll see you this evening at the rue du Cherche Midi.'

'No, let's meet at the rue des St. Pères. I've got some petrol and food stashed away in the family flat. I couldn't face carry-ing the gasoline up five flights so I left it in our place. I'll pick you up at the rue de Longchamps after the press conference.'

That was how it worked out. Madame de Portes was there, and because I went to the Hôtel Matignon half an hour before the conference started she even invited me into her sitting-room for a drink and arranged a special pass without any problems.

We decided to leave at dawn or even earlier on the Tuesday, 11 June, and spent the last Monday pretending to be carefree lovers without an unhappy thought in the world, almost as though we were on honeymoon.

For in the hot sun of this Monday, Paris had the appearance of a stage set. The pavement cafés on the boulevards were as crowded as ever, a kaleidoscope of gaily flowered dresses, of men fighting for places at the minuscule tables, ordering a *vin rouge* or a *bière à la pression*; yet the roads were so empty they gave the city a nostalgic turn-of-the century character like an old sepia postcard unearthed from a dusty drawer. I almost expected to hear the clatter of a pony and trap. An occasional taxi driver sped along the Champs-Élysées with the verve of a racing driver who has no competition. And from time to time an ancient car – many of the rich had already left – would rumble up the avenue, always in the direction of the Étoile, to join the queue leaving the gates of the city for unknown destinations.

Even now, as we strolled along our favourite streets, the people of Paris seemed unable to believe that the worst could ever happen. I knew how their thoughts were running – that France possessed not only the Maginot Line but the finest army the world had ever known, the army that last time had stood for more than four years against German might, the army of glory that Lavisse once described as 'one of the most perfect instruments of war history has ever seen'. It was more than an army; it was the heart of the nation – it epitomised the very greatness of France. France might have changed, its politicians might be venal, but now more than ever people believed in the words of Anatole France that the French army 'is all that is left of our glorious past. It consoles for the present and gives us hope for the future'.

The heat shimmered and danced along the beautiful broad avenues, and although many shops were shuttered we saw few traces of war. Near the new Pont des Arts two formal gardens had just been planted on the embankment. In the symmetrical courtyards of the Louvre, men, brown and sweating though stripped to the waist, uprooted the early spring flowers and filled the bed with geraniums, from loaded trucks.

As we walked down the rue des St. Pères to the Left Bank the bookstalls were open and down by the *quai* – the dome of Les Invalides shining in the sun – a man in uniform calmly set up his easel and started painting. Below him a barge loaded with refugees sailed up the Seine. Not one in ten thousand realised that the Germans were on the point of taking Reims and had crossed the river Aisne and were attacking south of Soissons, while a Panzer division was moving on Rouen.

The last Sunday was beautiful – a tender make-believe day which gave us, as though handing out a farewell gift, a final picture to remember of the Paris we loved, unsullied by the dinginess of war.

'By the way,' I said as we prepared for bed. 'Got a visa to enter Spain?'

'Of course. And you?'

'Sure. The worst part of a foreign correspondent's job is keeping your visas up to date.'

We were both tired, but happily so. The last thing I did before switching off the lights was to turn on the radio for five minutes.

Italy had declared war.

25

The shrill of the alarm tore into the bedroom at 5 a.m. We had been fast asleep in each other's arms and, for a few seconds, as I leaned over to shut out the insistent ring, I hadn't the faintest idea where I was. Then, with a sick feeling, reality flooded in as I realised that our last hours together were running out for the third time in our lives.

We had two priorities: to get Sonia across the frontier into Spain; and at the same time do my job, find out what was happening among French politicians in Tours – if or when they arrived there – and file a story to Washington. This I hoped to do by sending a cable through Drexel Biddle, who was looking after the embassy task force in the absence of Bullitt who had elected, against the advice of Cordell Hull, Secretary of State, to stay in Paris. Biddle's headquarters in the Touraine was at the Château de Candé.

We set off in the Citroën at 6 a.m. after drinking some coffee and a couple of the previous day's croissants. I had managed to find some American tinned ham and loaves to make sandwiches. We put them in a separate carrier bag with two bottles of Vichy water and one of brandy. We each had an overnight bag with a few spare clothes, and in the rear boot I had locked a case of champagne – or what looked like champagne. I only hoped no one would try to drink it.

'For this,' I explained to Sonia, 'is vintage Astell petrol. I filled up a dozen magnums in case of emergency. Now let's go, darling. There's going to be a hell of a rush on the roads, though I'm not worried. We've made an early start. We should make Tours easily by tonight.'

How glib it sounded, how easy! Tours in a day! A mere hundred and fifty miles, even less. The trouble was that none of us had the remotest idea of the shocks in store. Around Douzy we had watched the long streams of refugees, but they had seemed to move along, however slowly. Why should our journey be so different?

The first few yards set the tone for that awful day. Not the traffic – not at first – but the atmosphere. Even in the early morning, as I drove across the Seine and up the Champs-Élysées, the city had a haunted, desperate air, so different at first light from yesterday's sunshine. It wasn't only the emptiness, the closed shops, the metal grilles, the drawn shutters, the naked newspaper kiosks on the pavements, the lack of movement. There was something more sinister: an air of dreaded expectancy.

Everyone 'knew' the French cabinet was pulling out of Paris, and this in itself was a signal for defeat. Everyone 'knew' the American ambassador had decided to remain in Paris to hand the capital over to Germany in some sort of neutral capacity. And that was a sign the French were being abandoned by the Americans. And so everyone 'knew' that it was only a question of time before the swastika would fly over the public buildings of an occupied city.

Only it hadn't happened yet. So we all watched, as though the patient was suffering from a terminal illness. It would have been almost easier to bear if death had mercifully ended the protracted suffering and put the patient – and his relations – out of their misery.

'At least the roads are quiet,' Sonia observed as she tucked herself into the right-hand seat of the Citroën. 'So there shouldn't be too many problems.'

It looked as though she was right. Half-way along the Champs-Élysées, at the Rond Point, an old flower seller was quietly preparing her stand of brightly coloured blooms as though this were a perfectly normal day. The few cars were mostly old, I noticed, probably dragged out of ancient garages at the last minute by people who had only just decided to abandon homes or offices and bolt.

We had decided to drive through the Bois, leave Paris by the porte St. Cloud, and make our way to Versailles, then Chartres and on to Tours. At first all seemed to go well, but it was an illusion. The roads were only empty at first because the exodus from Paris had started long before we had even woken up. Before we reached Versailles we had to slow down, though at first I assumed we had just been caught in a local traffic jam.

'We'll be through this in no time.' I patted Sonia's leg. 'Though we may find a few more bad spots like this.'

What we didn't know around seven o'clock that morning was that the traffic jam consisted of one solid block of vehicles stretching virtually without a break on any main road from Versailles to Chartres, more than fifty miles ahead. Nor did we have the faintest idea (until many years later) that we were living through one of the greatest mass flights of human misery in the history of Europe, with, in all, seven million people on the march across the face of France. They moved forward instinctively, as relentlessly as a colony of ants, some spurred by blind terror of the unknown, others impelled by a dogged determination to escape – struggling to reach a ghostly terminal that didn't exist.

I don't know the exact moment when instinct warned me that I had made a fearful error. I had chosen what I thought was the one main road and that was bad. I had to get on to the secondary roads.

'I've bloody well boobed!' I said as the traffic ground to a stop; an assorted collection of vehicles filled every inch of road ahead – everything from an expensive chauffeur-driven Delage with white walled tyres, in which a middle-aged woman sat in the back ignoring everyone around her, to a wizened old couple beside the car – old and panting, but insisting that they push their creaking overloaded handcart festooned with pots and pans that regularly clanked as they swung against the car.

Every few minutes the procession started up then stopped; as the old couple drew abreast of the Delage, the chauffeur became more and more enraged each time their pots and pans scraped against his immaculate maroon paintwork.

At one point he got out of his front seat and started to berate them. The old man doffed his blue beret to the lady in the car who didn't seem to notice him. Then, with an expressive use of the hands the old man made it as plain as if he had told her, '*Eh bien*! What can I do? It's all these people who keep pushing me.'

Every time the jumble of vehicles stopped the same thing happened, with the old man and his wife finding it impossible to steer the ancient handcart in such restricted space.

'I wonder if I can find a better way across country,' I said to Sonia. 'It might pay me, even if it's longer.'

The next time we stopped I jumped out and stood on the running board to see if there were any side roads or lanes I could take. Or even, I thought, I might turn round. I looked back.

'What is it?' asked Sonia.

'Come and see! We shan't be moving for a few moments.' She joined me on the running board, stretching on her toes for a better view. Now it was no longer just the road *ahead* that worried me. One look *behind* told me I would never be able to turn. Thousands of vehicles boxed us in – cars, horses and carts, a hearse, bicycles, and an old-fashioned three-wheeled tricycle with one wheel punctured. Every now and again a car wheezed to a stop, perhaps overheated or out of petrol, blocking the road. Those behind unceremoniously pushed the vehicle to the side of the road, the ditch or a village courtyard. I had the curious, ugly feeling that each time a car stalled everyone else experienced a moment of grim enjoyment. Each one that fell by the wayside diminished the number ahead.

In the open country linking the quiet villages many tried to bypass the traffic by driving across the fields. They vanished in the distance ahead, sometimes cheering at their victory. But sooner or later we caught up with them. Sometimes a field would end in a wall, a wood, even a ditch, and then there was nothing for it but for those who had taken a short cut to try to rejoin the main road. They never did. With an almost ruthless fury, those who had taken hours to cover their stretch of road blocked every attempt to let the clever ones back in the mainstream. With vehicles nudging each other nose to tail, this, too, gave those on the main roads a savage pleasure.

'We're trapped,' I said to Sonia. 'We couldn't turn round if we wanted to. We can only go ahead.'

Long columns of men, women, children, vehicles grunted under a hot sun. In front of us an elderly woman stumbled, too late for the helping hand offered by a father, brother or son. Someone behind pushed. The small group of walkers threatened to be engulfed, separated, to fall behind the others. I could see the old lady's arms, the wrists like knotted rope, then she started retching, the filth of the raddled old body pouring out of her mouth. Who would have thought that an empty shell of an old woman could vomit such a quantity of liquid?

Did anybody care in this torrent of frightened human beings? Yes, miraculously, love came in the form of the husband or son, or whoever he was. Gently he wiped the vomit from the old lady's face with the only piece of cloth to hand in the emergency: the tail of his shirt which he had somehow ripped away.

The old lady mumbled, but no real words came out. I glimpsed for a moment a look of terror in the sunken eyes and I knew what it was – the fear of being abandoned as those behind were forcing the press of people to move on. The father or son put a reassuring arm around her. All she wanted was to live! To suffer, to starve, to bring up a half-famished family with love and care, anything so long as she could live for another day, another hour, another minute.

There was hate too, hate and greed disguised with a smile.

'Look.' I pointed to some peasants leaning over the five-barred gate of their field. To the bedraggled tormented people, they cried out, almost cheerfully, as though offering sweets for sale:

'Come on, ladies and gentlemen! Out with your money! Ten sous a glass of water, two francs to fill your bottle.'

On the notice board outside one *hôtel de ville*, where the jam seemed never to end, I saw dozens of pitiful signs, advertisements for people trying to mend broken hearts:

Madame Lefarge, c/o Hôtel de Ville, asks for news of her daughters Marie-Louise and Hélène, 6 and 5 years old, lost near here on 9 June.

By noon we had covered perhaps twenty miles. The sun baked everyone; tempers frayed with heat as much as with the delay. The interminable changing of gears started to give me cramp in my right ankle as the muscles knotted up. I stopped for a moment to walk on it, to alleviate the pain. A cacophony of klaxons signalled their fury. More and more overheated cars began to stall. All were bundled on to the side of the road or a field, despite the screams of outrage from those who hoped (probably rightly) that the cars would start again after they had been cooled for an hour or two. With the heat and the stoppages, both of us were soon too tired even to talk.

Soon after midday, when we were well beyond Versailles, nothing moved for an hour. Nothing. It seemed as though all the vehicles in France had been welded into one solid mass, in the way old cars in America are crushed together into a block of solid steel.

'What the hell's happened?' I groaned, for always everyone was afraid to leave a car in case the road suddenly cleared. 'You can walk ahead a bit,' I suggested to Sonia. 'Stretch your legs and tell me what's happened.'

She returned a few minutes later.

'You'll never believe this.' She mopped her forehead. 'But

it's not a car that's causing the jam. It's a dustman in his cart.'

'A dustman!'

Others crowded around, besieging Sonia for news.

'What happened ahead?'

'Why can't we go on?'

'The dustman,' Sonia explained, 'has driven his cart from Versailles. It's filled with files and documents. But now it's stuck in a narrow street.'

Because it was hidden from our view, we never did discover how the dustcart was moved, nor did we ever pass it. Soon there was another hold-up when a charabanc stalled and was finally pushed off the road by a nearby tractor.

The coach was painted brightly, *'Paris de Nuit!'* It had been used for highly popular tourist traps, in which tourists paid a fixed sum for a tour of night clubs, with a glass of indifferent champagne at each stop, often ending at a *boîte* where girls were available. The coach bore the legend. 'We promise you the most beautiful girls in Paris'.

It was abandoned at the exact moment when I read the slogan, 'The most beautiful girls in Paris . . .' It was also the precise moment when the occupants of the coach descended – a couple of dozen decorous, fluttering nuns, all in stiff white coifs. They tumbled down the steps before deciding how to continue on their journey.

Not far from us – and the old couple pushing their hand-cart – the more healthy pushed their way through. A very old lady in a wheelbarrow was being carried by a young, stalwart *curé*, sweating in his long black soutane. He passed several cars and other vehicles by the simple expedient of keeping to the narrow edge of the road. The nuns fluttered round him and offered to help, but I heard him cry cheerfully, 'I'm only pushing my passenger to her sister in the next village.'

I looked at the *curé* and the old lady. She seemed very frail. Should I offer them a lift? More than once I had wondered whether I should make room for pedestrians, but several factors had prevented me. Above all others, I had not yet seen one instance of a *lonely* old man or woman, even a couple. Everyone had a handcart or a pram, and often seemed to move in families. There was another reason. Pedestrians made better time than we did. They could take short cuts across the fields.

All but the invalids could easily outstrip our car by walking.

'I do feel bad sometimes,' I confessed to Sonia, 'but I couldn't pack a large group in.'

And there was one more reason – selfish, but important. The crowd often turned ugly, and it was easy to forget that I was on an assignment for the *Globe*. However slow the progress, I had to reach Tours and file a story. I wasn't really part of the exodus; I was making my way to a specific place to do a job of work, and I didn't dare to let in strangers who might force me – even with violence – to change my route. I had already seen some nasty fights. Several toughs had tried to open the rear doors of the Citroën which I kept locked.

The *curé*, however, was different. When I heard him say that he was only going to the next village, I shouted, 'Why not jump in, Father – with your passenger?'

'That's very kind of you;' he seemed grateful. 'I'm fine myself, but my passenger is extremely old. Jolting around in a wheelbarrow can't be good for her.'

She looked very frail. Sonia got out of the front seat to help her get into the back. Then she sat down beside her and asked the *curé*, 'Why don't you sit in front, Father?'

'Thank you, my child. Perhaps you would be kind enough to hold this altar vase. My friend attaches great importance to it.'

'Of course.' Sonia looked at it casually. It was not particularly attractive, decorated with a frieze of religious figures.

'It was the only object I had time to take from the church,' explained the *curé*. 'This lady presented it to us many years ago, and we use it on the altar for flowers during the harvest festival or weddings. You understand – it's of no value really, but very precious to her.'

'I'll take care of it,' she promised him.

As we drove on a dozen men started fighting each other like savages – and all for the possession of the wheelbarrow which the *curé* had used.

'How can we expect to win a war when people behave like this?' I asked the *curé*. 'When half the people in France are greedy or corrupt? How can we *trust* the people of France?' As I spoke, one of the men lurched against the Citroën and started cursing, then peered inside and crossed himself. Another had already smashed up the wheelbarrow and hit the nearest man across the head with the barrow shaft.

The *curé* was young, with ruddy cheeks, and despite his bulky clothes there was the hint of a powerful country body beneath.

'You can trust them at first,' he replied cheerfully, 'because men at heart are simple creatures. They're easily dazzled. But then the shine rubs off, doubts replace trust. You're not French, are you? Your command of our language is to be complimented.' He spoke in the slightly old-fashioned way of someone who had spent years in a seminary.

'American,' I smiled. 'A newspaperman.'

'Ah! So you probably know about politicians. You sound as though you don't like them.'

'They make me angry.'

'Anger is a futile emotion,' he said gently. 'The man who is angry loses more energy than his victim. So if you are angry you put yourself at a disadvantage.'

'But I can't help it – not when I meet politicians who are . . .'

'Wayward?' he suggested the word. 'Does it really matter so long as men respect each other? All of us have to make the best of a bad job – which is what life is really all about.'

'It's sometimes easier,' I said, 'living in a village, in the country.'

'Yes, I am surrounded by peasants. I prefer them to city people.' Passing through the edge of a hamlet, he added, 'Look how the locals stand watching you.'

The farmers and their women, often leaning against their gates, silently studied the file of refugees as though watching a parade.

'When a war comes,' explained the *curé*, 'the only thing that matters to a peasant is its effect on his own personal life. War or peace are only extensions of storms or sun. Mobilisation or occupation are unimportant only when compared to sowing and harvesting.'

We dropped the *curé* at the next village – but it was not until we had driven through the straggling street that I realised the old lady had left the vase behind.

I peered ahead and around. Sonia opened the door as we

idled along, standing on the running board to see behind in case the *curé* called to us. There was no hope of stopping.

'I feel terrible,' I said. 'We promised. But it *was* such a scramble when they got out.'

'Don't worry,' said Sonia. 'We'll keep it in trust. One day we'll find him and return it.'

'Let's hope so.'

The *curé* had brought a breath of fresh air into our tiny, boxlike world. But did he really believe what he said about peasants, or were men of religion so isolated from reality that sometimes they were deluded?'

'I don't think he even realises the French are losing the war,' I said to Sonia. 'That what's happening is' – I searched for the word I wanted – 'cataclysmic.'

It was – to me anyway. This was not just a pitiful queue of craven men and women scrambling to illusory safety. In the sweat and the stench and the fighting, we were witness to the death of a nation, the last rites of France, of all Europe barring the master race. Each step forward on that hot dusty roadway was in reality a step backwards, another step on the road to defeat, another step on the road to victory for tyranny.

How wonderful the warm air might have been, with the sun shining, the fields of corn ripening! But the sun that baked us was also an illusion; the road of the exodus sloped downwards as man descended into the gloom of a night which would never see the sun.

'I'm sick of the French,' I continued. 'Not because a better army is beating them, chewing the so-called invincible French army into mincemeat. No, it goes deeper than that.'

What sickened me most was the all-pervading smell of corruption. The way people had been betrayed. This was the root cause of defeat, this far more than cowardice or ignorance. These people around us were running away because they were realists, aware that corrupt leaders were responsible for their plight.

There was a stop while a car ahead was pushed off the road. I took the opportunity to give Sonia a swig of water from the warm bottle of Vichy, then found a towel and wiped her face. Both of us were drenched in sweat, much of it brought on by our anger and impotence.

Most political leaders in France were rotten to the core, I thought. And everyone except country parsons knew it. Was it fair to blame some small-town clerk and his churchgoing family or some working man from a factory for the mess we were in, for not taking his cue in corruption from a political leader? After all, the French prided themselves on their logic. What could they say, how could they react at the spectacle of a middle-aged 'happily married' premier like Reynaud dyeing his hair in order to impress a mistress with whom he was infatuated? Who could blame the logical French for realising that as soon as the going got rough French leaders like Pierre Laval would sell out the French people to save their own skins.

In a way the ribbon of road ahead of us was like a river, the water dirty, yet composed of human beings. Tears, sweat, heat, the stink of selfishness and greed; the ever-present torment of fear surrounded us; the river of people and vehicles moved relentlessly forward like a tidal bore, slow but inexorable.

A commotion in a straggling hamlet halted the traffic yet again, this time barely a few paces ahead of us. A girl in her early twenties – long brown hair, a checked skirt, a pink blouse – screamed without warning and threw herself to the ground. Threw herself deliberately; she did not fall. She bent almost double, gave a bewildered look before she was seized by an epileptic fit, arching her body, writhing in contortions, the pretty mouth slipping into a slack, dribbling face as she twisted her body like a savage performing an indecent war dance. Two burly men pulled her screaming to the side of the road and the river of traffic poured on as though the sluice gates had been re-opened.

It was like that all day, a combination of all the worst elements in nature: heat and sweat, hunger and thirst, weariness and fear, cowardice and hysteria. Man was rapidly being reduced to the level of an animal. Men and women, cooped for hours in small square boxes that moved only in inches suddenly reached a moment – women in particular – when they had no choice but to squat next to the nearest man or woman to relieve themselves. For men it presented no real problem.

'You're lucky,' sighed Sonia. 'You're built in such a way that you can use the waterworks standing up.'

You could, standing against the side of your car. But the women had to rearrange clothes, pull up skirts, pull down panties, nervously realising that men could see everything, were almost brushing against them.

'I've been holding myself for hours,' confessed Sonia. 'I can't wait much longer.'

'You'll just have to squat next to the others.'

'I *couldn't*,' she said. 'I wish I could. I know that if I tried I'd seize up. All those men looking at me.' And then she added almost desperately, 'Haven't you got something I could use?'

A broken-down car ahead had caused yet another jam and I was able to lean over the seat.

'Only this.' I picked up the porcelain vase with the wide neck. 'We can't use that. It's the *curé*'s altar vase.'

'Give it to me.' At the sight of it Sonia gasped with the effort of controlling herself. 'Come on, for God's sake. I can't hold it another second. *Give it to me!*'

As always in summer, she never wore pants. With her skirt hiding her knees she perched on the edge of the front seat, holding the neck tight to the join of her legs. When she had finished, she edged the door of the car open a few inches and poured out the contents.

'I'll wash it when I get the chance,' she promised. 'I'm sure the *curé* would understand.'

'Don't worry,' I said. 'He would understand. Feel better?'

'A new girl. You know, this is the sort of problem you never see when the heroine faces a long and terrible journey in a romantic adventure movie.'

Yes, it was like that all day. Everywhere the once-beautiful countryside was littered with the signature of refugees – broken bottles, filthy paper, young people defecating, old people vomiting, torn umbrellas, punctured tyres, suitcases that had fallen off and burst open, straw mattresses split in two. Everything seemed to conspire to make the journey more frustrating.

Suddenly the dreary scene was enlivened by a breath of fresh air. Out of the blue, on a country road leading to Malmaison, we came across a truck drawn up by the side of the road. Grouped around it were some British tommies in their ill-fitting uniforms. Most were singing lustily, two were shaving, dipping their brushes in their tin drinking mugs. When I shouted a greeting in English, they crowded round our almost stationary Citroën.

'Blimey!' cried one. 'You English?'

'American.'

'Next best thing!'

'Got any fags, guvnor?'

'Know where the fucking 'ell we are? Begging your pardon, miss.'

'Don't let them offer you a cuppa tea,' another laughed. 'We've been shaving in it.'

It almost restored our sense of humour – the wolf whistles, the gratuitous advice.

'Keep the door of your car locked or someone'll nick your girl.'

With a wave we nudged forward, pushed there by the cars behind, klaxoning like mad; barely half an hour later we passed another bunch of soldiers. They were leaning out of the windows of a train that now ran parallel to our road.

But there were no songs, no jokes this time. These were *poilus*. Glum, silent human beings being shipped like cattle, ordered to some battlefield God knows where, probably by some idiots who would decide any moment that the war was in vain – apart from killing.

And there was something else.

'These poor devils are fighting in their own country,' said Sonia. 'Those British boys we saw – they looked as though they were *enjoying* the war. To them it was an adventure in a foreign land. But these French boys in the train – this is their own country they're fighting over. There's no spirit of adventure there.'

'It's not only the soldiers.' I ground in the gear to low, as some kids ran across our path. 'I never realised my different feelings about the refugees until now.' When we were at Douzy we had been surrounded by an endless stream escaping from Holland, Belgium, eastern France. Now, though, we were not watching the exodus of a nation. We were part of it. Every stumbling figure, every face torn with fatigue, had become a part of the patchwork of our lives.

Nowhere was the feeling of being part of the scene more evident than when we could see some distance ahead or behind. At the top of a small rise leading to Rambouillet, I looked back at the long, slow-moving procession, travelling along the white ribbon of road framed in poplars black against the sunlight, and on either side fields of corn. It reminded me of an old painting which La Châtelaine had always insisted on keeping in the *salon* – the flight of the Israelites, a long line of tired, broken people. It was a scene straight from one of those old-fashioned Bible illustrations. Only the trees behind me, the poplars, straight and dark, seemed suddenly to look like prison bars from which there would never be any escape for the innocents fleeing the enemy.

It took us nearly two hours to drive through Épernon, then finally I managed to leave the main road for one I knew would eventually by-pass Chartres.

'It goes through Maintenon.' I traced the route on Sonia's map. 'Better still, not far from Chartres, but in a tiny hamlet, there's a small gas station used mainly for tractors. I had a puncture there once. I know we've got spare gas, but we might as well top up if we've got the chance. Besides, with all this low gear work we'll need oil and water. She must be heating up like hell.'

Sonia put the question I hadn't dared to face.

'We'll never make Tours tonight, will we?' She flattened the map on her knees and traced the route.

''Fraid not. We'll be lucky if we get past Chartres. I'm going to try and make for a village called Blandy. It's near Châteaudun.'

'Not on the map.' Sonia was trying to find it.

'It's just a small village. But it's got a superb *maison de santé*, not really a clinic, but a plush kind of health farm for very rich people who want to relax and unwind. It's called the 'Bellevue' and it's run like a five-star hotel – with prices to match.'

'If we can get it?'

'We might be able to stay there for the night. I know the owner – I helped him with a piece in the *Paris American*, so he owes me one. Then we'll press on to Tours tomorrow.'

Once we left the N10 main road the route was much less

congested and we were making better speed when suddenly I heard the roar of engines, followed by a whine that turned into a terrifying screech, chilling the blood. Planes were diving out of a cloudless sky.

'Heads down!' I screamed, jamming on the brakes.

Only then, as the screech grew louder, did I realise that we were not the target. Out of the side window I saw four fighter planes attack the main road in the distance – the very road we had left. I couldn't see the target even when I opened the door, but I could see the planes and, even worse, hear them.

'There they are!' I pointed to the sky, instinctively clutching Sonia.

We could see the planes go into their dive. I knew where the main road was by the distant line of poplars on the horizon, marking the road along which we had expected to drive, perhaps the very spot where we might have been trapped. The planes wheeled like gulls, then in perfect formation roared into their dive. Until the very last moment they looked as though they would hit the ground and burst into flames.

'If only they would!' cried Sonia.

As I heard the distant rattle of machine gun fire, the four planes flattened out, then puffs of smoke covered the row of poplars. Out of the smoke, like genies out of a bottle, the planes zoomed up against the blue sky, sullied now with slowly enlarging clouds of grey, drifting smoke. Then they vanished high into the sky.

I hadn't realised that Sonia was crying softly.

'How can people do this?' she asked, leaning her head on my shoulder.

'I know, my precious, but this is what war's about.'

'But these are peaceful people.' She watched the smoke shrouding the main road. 'What have these planes got to do with them?'

'Just thank the Lord,' I said as I sat beside her, 'that we took this country lane. Otherwise . . .'

'Don't say anything,' she wiped away the tears, 'I just suddenly thought of one thing – it could have been us. I only pray that if anything does happen, both of us will be together at the same second.' She searched for my hand, squeezing it very tight. 'So that we'll never know.'

'Stop being so morbid.' But the same thought had flashed through my mind – 'Oh God! If it has to happen, let us die together.'

I remembered the small gas station, just a single hand-operated pump used mainly by locals filling up their tractors. It didn't have any forecourt or fancy buildings which, I felt, would make it less known. It was right at the end of the hamlet. I found the place behind a narrow street, deserted except for the occasional horse and cart returning from the fields at the end of the day's work. And there was the pump, with a solitary car just leaving, and a man standing by.

'Just what we need,' I said cheerfully, thinking that in a few minutes we should have passed Chartres. As I edged into the right position near the pump, I saw the man lock it up and pocket the key.

'No gas left?' I groaned.

'Doesn't look like it, does it?' He was surly.

'Not just a few litres? And I need oil and water.'

'We're closed!' shouted the man.

I swore softly and prepared to drive off. Then I caught sight of the automatic gauge with its figures on the side of the pump. Suddenly I realised that the pump *wasn't* dry.

'Hey!' I cried. 'You've got some gas.'

Though I knew I had spare petrol in the back of the car, I had, as always when working on a story, one thought – that nothing, certainly not some bad-tempered sonofabitch, was going to stop me taking every precaution to get to Tours, to save Sonia – and file my story. Every litre counted.

Without turning the man snarled, 'What if I have? I've been pulling that handle all day long. I'm tired. If you want some gas come back tomorrow.'

'But *m'sieu* . . .' I tried politeness.

The *garagiste* didn't speak English, of course, but again he snarled, and this time his words were the equivalent of 'Fuck off!'

'*Et ta soeur!*' I shouted the most pejorative insult I could think of and bounded out of the car.

'Come back,' shouted Sonia. 'Forget the bastard.'

'Just a minute.' I said.

'*Come back!*'

361

It was too late. I wasn't so angry about the lie he had told me, it was the pent-up frustration. I didn't give a damn *how* tired he was. Everyone in France was tired, an entire nation was tired. I offered to pull the handle of the pump myself, but he pretended not to hear, and instead said softly, 'What did you say about my family?'

He wasn't a big man, but he had the knotted, tight arms and shoulders of someone whose livelihood depended on his physical strength.

'What did you say?' he repeated menacingly.

'I need oil and petrol. I offered to do the work. I've got the money.'

'Fuck off!' he repeated.

'You shit,' I said in French. 'It's shits like you who are losing the war.'

He picked up a heavy-duty tyre lever.

'You'd better get out of here quick, sonny,' he said, 'before I bash your sodding brains in.'

'I won't budge,' I cried desperately. 'It's your duty. Here.' I fumbled for some money.

'I said get off my property.' His voice was soft, more menacing than when he shouted. 'I don't like little shits who insult my family.'

He moved nearer. I was frightened, praying desperately for some car to come along, to break the tension, to interrupt. Damn! All day we had been hemmed in by cars, now there wasn't one in sight. The pump was at the end of nowhere. I saw his knuckles show white as he gripped the tyre lever.

There was no turning back. I was out of the Citroën and that was that. I couldn't climb back in again and quietly drive off. I should have tried, I suppose. The old adage about discretion. But I *couldn't*. And anyway, I knew he wouldn't let me, I sensed that. All the same I realised that in a straight fight I would never stand a chance.

Sonia shouted desperately from inside the car, 'Please, darling – come back, forget this man.'

'Yeah – why don't you, sonny?' the man jeered.

The stubborn streak increased – determination born out of fear? Masculine pride in front of 'my' woman? I shouted back to Sonia, 'Stay in the car.'

In the seconds that seemed an hour I looked round for a weapon. The place was as empty as a padded cell. I might have grabbed the handle of the pump, attached to its rubber hose, but it was locked. The only object was an old watering can half filled. A sudden thought sent a fresh shiver of fear through me. Even if I dodged his raised arm, he could *throw* the lever at me. Even a glancing blow could break an arm or crack a skull. Again I looked round, ready now to shout for help if I had to.

At that moment I saw a second tube, longer, thinner, unlocked. It was near the main pump, but separate and with a much longer flex.

It was the pump used to force air into flat tyres under pressure. It took me half a second to remember how Gaston and I used to play a game with the tyre pump we always kept at Douzy, Gaston showing me how the force of compressed air could knock down quite large targets as easily as if he had been using a water hose. Air was as tough as water under pressure. Only you couldn't see it.

In one hand I grabbed the hose, in the other the watering can, hoping the man wouldn't realise the significance of the small nozzle. I knew now what to do – my only chance, ignoring one last wail of despair from Sonia.

It can't have been more than a minute since we first traded insults, but now I shouted, 'I'm going to smash the lock on your pump.'

Holding the half-filled watering can I swung it at the lock. I knew I could never actually break it, but I would take his mind off the nozzle in my right hand by giving a good imitation. I smashed the can at the pump again and again. He roared with anger, like a bull, arm upraised.

'Leave that alone,' he shouted. 'You bastard, you'll pay for this.'

In his anger I don't think the man realised that, as I kept on bashing the pump, splashing water all over it with each new effort, I still gripped the thin rubber tube in my right hand.

He charged towards me. I had to wait until the very last second, almost to the moment when he prepared to hit me with the lever. That was the toughest moment – waiting, controlling myself as he actually raised his arm for a blow that could split my skull, so close I could smell the garlic on his breath. He almost knocked the watering can, and then I pointed the nozzle – not twelve inches from his face. The jet of air came out of the nozzle with the force of a fire hose. It would never kill him but, for one second, two perhaps, I hit him full in the face with the blast, knocking him off balance. He screwed up his eyes, grunted 'Bastard'. I only needed those two seconds. I grabbed the tyre lever and hit him with it – straight across the nose.

I heard the crack as the bone broke. Then the blood poured out of nose and mouth as he keeled over, spitting broken teeth out of split lips. He wasn't unconscious – but he wasn't going to attack me because, apart from screams of pain, he was for a moment blinded with blood.

'Let's get out of here,' I gasped to Sonia and tore open the door.

I pressed the starter. Thank God it roared into life at the first touch of the button. I jammed in the gear – still shaking, though everything had happened in a couple of minutes. Then, through the rear mirror, I saw the man stumble to his feet.

'Quick, darling!' Sonia begged me.

'I'm off.' I inched the car towards the empty village lane that would lead me to the south.

Two seconds more and we would have been clear. But I didn't have those two seconds. Sonia, in the right-hand seat, was nearest the pumps. Even as we started to draw away, I heard the bellow of spluttering rage, the voice incoherent. With the instinctive reflex of a violent man the *garagiste* picked up the tyre lever and hurled it at me, at us, at the car.

It hit the right-hand corner of the windscreen, next to Sonia. And though we had safety glass, even in those days, it splintered. And Sonia was sitting in front. She must have seen the man hurl the lever, for I remember she instinctively ducked and shielded her face with her arm as I braked.

The bonded glass broke the force of impact and the lever fell to the ground outside. Jagged edges of glass tore through her silk blouse, ripping the right sleeve from shoulder to wrist in shreds. Without a second's delay – as though someone had thrown a tin of red paint at her – Sonia's right arm and shoulder were stained with blood.

She screamed. I held out an arm around her and steering with the left arm reversed towards the man. If Sonia hadn't screamed again I think I would have run over him. She couldn't possibly wipe away all that blood. Yet I could sense that the wounds were only superficial. Because it was safety glass the smashed window had fallen inwards. It hadn't sprayed.

'It isn't worth it,' she whispered. 'Please – I beg you – let's go and find a doctor.'

I raced around the corner, out of sight, stopped, tore off my jacket, then my shirt, ripped it into bits and tried to tie up her arm and wrists. The cuts weren't deep, though the forearm where she had held up her arm was bleeding badly. There were no deep gashes, but I realised that she must get the wounds cleaned in case they contained particles of glass dust.

The glass seemed everywhere – on her knees, the floor-boards, in the pocket on the dash. Every time I tried to wrap some cloth around her wounds I scratched myself with unseen glass.

'We'll be there soon,' I said with more assurance than I dared to hope for.

Just as I was turning off the back road to regain the road which I knew should lead me to Chartres, I saw an old weatherbeaten wooden signpost: *CHATEAUDUN, Route Inférieure.*

It might be inferior – it looked little more than a cart track – but it might be empty, off the beaten track, and the springs of the Citroën were tough enough to withstand any shock treatment.

'We'll try it,' I said. She looked pale, and I suddenly remembered the bottle of brandy. I had forgotten all about it until this moment.

'Here.' I held it up. 'Take a swig, darling – from the bottle.' She did and almost immediately a touch of colour brushed her cheeks. I could see that below the elbow blood had already started soaking through the makeshift bandage.

'It's all my fault,' I said. 'If I hadn't been such a bloody fool . . .'

'You're what we call *un tipo robusto!*' She tried to smile.

'Can you lie back a bit?' Seats in those days didn't recline, but I folded up my jacket to make a pillow, and as I drove on, bumping over semi-cart tracks, she lay back gratefully and closed her eyes.

Half an hour later the *route inférieure* suddenly blossomed into a proper, if narrow, road and before long we reached Blandy and I saw the white building of the Bellevue in the distance.

'We're there,' I said, and she opened her eyes.

'I'm not asleep,' she smiled. 'I'm fine. I'm only scared about these bits of glass.'

'We'll have you in bed in a few minutes,' I promised.

The Bellevue was on the edge of the place des Épars, the sprawling heart of the village with its market place, patch of green, rows of shops and the inevitable roofed washing trough of the local 'laundry'.

Because the Bellevue was a kind of hotel, hundreds of other people had made their way there, and the *place* was a jumble of cars, trucks, crowds, people sitting on piles of luggage round the edge of the square. Somehow I managed to double park the Citroën alongside the entrance.

'Hang on while I get the owner.' I didn't dare to imagine what would happen if he wasn't there. I remembered his name – luckily it was well known, Monsieur Lelong, the same as that of the couturier. I had once lunched Lelong when he visited Paris and I was trying to arrange for someone to keep us informed in the *Paris American* about Americans visiting the area.

'Hang on,' I said to Sonia again.

There was a moment of farce as I strode up to the ornate reception desk.

'No beggars or tramps here,' spluttered an irate clerk in striped trousers. 'Get out before I call the police.'

'My wife's been badly hurt . . .'

'No place for tramps. Get out.'

I had forgotten that I was bare to the waist. No wonder they thought I was a tramp. 'The name is Astell,' I said, knowing that everyone in the hotel business would recognise that name. 'Get me Monsieur Lelong.'

At that moment Lelong walked out of a *salon* leading to the main foyer.

'Hi!' I cried. 'Remember me? Larry Astell.'

'I didn't recognise you, *monsieur*, in those – er – sporting clothes. *Comment ça va?*' And more seriously, 'This is a sad time to be meeting.'

'Sadder than you think. A bloody maniac has attacked my – fiancée. She's bleeding. Can you help?' I explained briefly what had happened.

'Every regular room is occupied,' he apologised. 'The clinic is a shambles. But some of the *femmes de chambres* have bolted – and if you wish . . .? At least the beds are good.'

'You're too kind, *cher ami*. But first a doctor.'

'Don't worry. We have several resident doctors.'

Lelong snapped his fingers as though the milling crowds overflowing the foyer didn't exist. A hall porter materialised.

'I'll look after the lady,' I told him. 'Here's the keys, you take the car into the garage and bring in the luggage on the back seat – but leave the boot locked. Monsieur Lelong will tell you which room to go to.'

So we arrived at Blandy. It had taken us over twelve hours to drive there from Paris – a distance of around seventy miles as the crow flies.

Sonia was nearly done in. She must have lost more blood than I realised. I helped her into the foyer while Lelong prepared to take her upstairs when he had found the doctor. People on either side moved back in order to give her more space – or perhaps I thought, being French, to make sure bloodstains didn't ruin their clothes.

Once in the foyer I stood appalled. The Bellevue looked more like a transit camp than the elegant *maison de santé* I had known in the past. Everywhere was a shambles; ornate chairs were piled against the pink papered walls in a pathetic attempt to save their gilded value, mattresses were torn and bursting on the litter of the beautiful carpet. Every square inch of occupied territory was jealously guarded. I had managed to find a chair only because Lelong had brought it from the office. Anyone else searching for a place to rest was met with hostile stares. Luggage was piled in one corner, an uneven craggy leather hill. A vague smell permeated the room, a compound of tobacco, dead cigarette ends ground into the carpet or overflowing from ashtrays, or unwashed bodies, men and women past caring. It was the smell of war.

'What a bloody mess,' I said to Sonia.

She was obviously in pain, but even she was horrified at the spectacle of a beautiful hotel in chaos.

'We're *really* in the war here.' She smiled weakly. 'War is much more dangerous behind the front line than in it.'

She's right, I thought. Here in this beautiful lounge we were in the heart of war. War was no longer a set piece, the soldiers in scarlet dominated by unseen generals, in the days when war was a game of chess played by opposing military forces. Now it was *our* war.

The room under the eaves of the Bellevue was more comfortable than I had expected. Though small, ours had been used by two maids, so there were twin beds, and even a *cabinet de toilette*.

'But *hélàs, madame,*' Lelong apologised, 'there is no hot water.'

The doctor was professional and reassuring. He asked me to leave while he attended to Sonia, and by the time I had returned she looked a different person – still pale, still drawn, but the doctor had covered most of the wounds with plaster, though the forearm was bandaged where he had put in three stitches.

'Medically you didn't really need the stitches,' he explained, 'but it's a question of *esthétique*. This will prevent you from having a scar on your arm for the rest of your life.'

When he was on the point of leaving, I said, almost without thinking, 'We're off tomorrow to Tours.'

He looked at me in blank astonishment.

'You must be mad,' he exclaimed. '*Absolument fou*! You are proposing to take this lady who is suffering from shock to Tours – on roads jammed with traffic. Anything could happen. She needs her bed. Somewhere she can rest for at least twenty-four hours.'

'I thought if we had a good night's sleep . . .'

'My good sir, you are very young, and, if I may say so, very foolish. The after–effects of shock can be very bad. If she leaves the Bellevue tomorrow I accept no responsibility.'

At the door he returned to Sonia and said, 'I will come to

visit you tomorrow. And we may hope you may be able to travel the following day — if your husband insists.'

Outside our small room, while Sonia was washing, I explained to Lelong how urgent it was for me to reach Tours and contact the American Embassy. I did not, however, mention our plan to drive later to Bordeaux and then send Sonia across the frontier into Spain. Nor did I mention that she was Italian. Because of this Lelong made the obvious suggestion.

'Why don't you travel to Tours through the night? It'll be much quicker. I'll make sure *madame* is well looked after, properly fed, then you can drive back to Blandy tomorrow evening, sleep for a few hours, and return to Tours or wherever you go on the Thursday. Coming back to Blandy to collect *madame* shouldn't cause any problems. It's less than seventy miles from Tours. Travelling from Tours *towards* Blandy should be easy.'

It made sense. I was certain in my own mind that the French cabinet would eventually make for Bordeaux, and if I drove there with her after her day of rest I could easily drive on to the frontier later. The problem of filing urgently would have gone. Of course I felt torn on one point. I didn't want to leave Sonia, even for one night. But I *had* to contact the French cabinet at Tours. I should have been there already. And I was sure that cables from the *Globe* would be awaiting me at the Château de Candé, Drexel Biddle's American headquarters, which I would be using as a place to receive messages. And then, once I had got Sonia across the border, I could return to Bordeaux and await events, probably ahead of the competition. The *Globe* would, I hoped, put it down to my astute foresight. It was not for me to enlighten them that I was there partly because of Sonia.

I was worried about Sonia's reaction. I knew that she would be concerned about my job.

'I do hate being parted,' she admitted after I had helped her to drink a bowl of soup. 'But the doctor has given me one sleeping pill which I've already taken and another one for tomorrow morning.'

Lelong swore that she would be looked after night and day, and I believed him. It was just after 9 p.m. now, and he said, 'You must have a good meal. We have a small private dining room for the executives. Come. I will give you a steak.'

Long before I tiptoed out of the room Sonia was dozing. I ate my steak and chips and the Bellevue garage gassed up the Citroën and even replaced the smashed window from the spare Citroën parts which even the smallest hamlet always stocked.

Before leaving I said to Lelong, 'See you during tomorrow night. I'll just nip upstairs and say goodbye to Sonia.'

Half asleep she held my hand – hers was damp and feverish. She whispered, 'I know you have to go – but I hate the idea.' I sat on the edge of the bed and stroked her hair. 'I've got a sort of premonition,' she mumbled, fiddling with the cufflinks she had given me so long ago.

'Sssh. It's time you went to sleep, darling, and rested. And don't worry; I'll always be with you.'

'But if anything does go wrong . . .?'

'It won't – ever. We're going to be married somehow. Remember? Even after we've got you across the border, whatever happens to us, always remember – we love each other.'

She was already asleep when I kissed her gently on the lips. It was the sleep of a drugged patient, and I knew how badly she needed it.

'I'll be back tomorrow,' I whispered, though she couldn't hear me and didn't stir when I gently kissed her again.

It had to last us many months, that gentle kiss in the maids' room at the Bellevue.

26

I reached Tours around dawn, to find the city in a state of utter shock – disorientated, disorganised. On the verge of panic, every motorist moved towards the centre of this lazy old cathedral town, abusing each other as they fought for their right to put a few more inches between themselves and the Germans.

Above all I needed a shower and a change of underclothes and shirt which I had carried in my overnight bag. I managed to get a room at the Metropole in the rue Jean-Jaures where the Astells had stayed from time to time, and where I had a nodding acquaintance with the manager, the tall, elderly Monsieur Roland Audermard, possessor of a magnificent pair of moustaches which we had once photographed for the *Paris American*. He was also a fervent admirer of Astell champagne.

The hotel was packed, and even in the sedate reception area there was a great deal of squabbling amongst the indignant mistresses of government officials who felt that their status – or at least that of each political lover – deserved better accommodation.

'But the real problem,' confided Monsieur Audermard, 'is that when the government requisitions rooms from me, I am given a voucher in payment, a kind of promissory note. But I ask you, will it ever be honoured? I have to carry on paying the staff, but will I ever see my money?'

'Never,' I said firmly, producing a large wad of French francs and American dollar bills. 'If you can spare me a room – I only want it for a few hours.'

I planned to tour the government offices, see Reynaud, file my story, snatch a couple of hours' sleep in the evening, then drive back to Blandy by dawn the next day. There, all being well, I would pick up Sonia and return to Tours, then drive further south, even as far as the frontier if possible. Haunted by the memories of the exodus, however, I had as a precaution paid in advance for the second night at Tours.

Once I had showered the sleep from my eyes – only cold water, but that helped – shaved and put on a clean shirt, I made my way to the newly installed Ministry of Information, which was housed in a couple of buildings in the rue Gambetta, through streets crowded not only with cars and trucks but with the city's pretty blue street cars which would have been better left in the garage.

A colleague in the hotel told me the rue Gambetta led off a small square distinguished by a memorial to the dead of the Great War.

'You'll spot it easily,' he said. 'It consists of a statue of a nude lady wearing a helmet. She's sandwiched between a *pissotière* and a café. It's got food – some good coffee too,' he added as an afterthought.

The café was obviously a favourite haunt of newspapermen, no doubt because it was so close to the Ministry of Information. A. J. Liebling, the American writer, was there. He had spent the previous night trying to sleep in his car. Drue Tartière, who worked for the French *Radio Mondiale*, was luckier – she had borrowed a bed in the local brothel; while one junior British diplomat and his wife, who had arrived late, started the first night of their honeymoon dossing down on a bench in the nearby park. His name was Donald Maclean.

The ministry was a sorry comedown after the splendour of the Hôtel Continental in Paris with its rose-covered wallpaper and Louis XV furniture. One of the requisitioned buildings had been the *bourse de travail*, the other a dingy post office. Here the ministry had established a corps of censors.

Every newspaper despatch had to be passed by censor. For though I hoped to file through the embassy, they would never permit me to use their facilities unless I, too, had my copy stamped by the authorities. The press office was at the top of a flight of winding steps – a few dirty rooms furnished with ancient school desks – the kind with forms and desks in one piece. A British correspondent was listening to the German radio. The man was announcing in a throaty accent, and for a moment I imagined it was the voice of Willi speaking.

'The French government,' said the German voice, 'is now in Tours, the provisional – the *very* provisional – capital of France.' The tone was a sneer so pronounced that one French correspondent almost knocked the Englishman down as he switched off the portable radio.

'Hey, you!' shouted the Englishman. 'Leave my sodding radio alone. I'm making notes for filing.'

'You're a traitor, listening to that,' screamed the Frenchman.

'Nine out of ten Frogs are traitors, bud,' said an American, as the Englishman switched back to the German broadcast.

I bolted – just as one man punched the other and they started scrambling on the floor.

I had my own personal story to consider. I hoped to get an exclusive interview either with Reynaud or de Gaulle, or, if the worst came, with Madame de Portes. I wasn't in Tours to cover routine agency news; I wanted to cash in on my contacts among the politicians.

The greatest problem of all, however, was *finding* the government officials. The ministries had been dispersed to châteaux throughout Touraine – as a precaution against air attack, I was told; and at the same time, local newspapers had been forbidden to publish the address of government departments in case fifth columnists tipped off the *Luftwaffe*. In fact, the government, its cabinet leaders, the army, were totally cut off from the people of France, and even worse, from all reality.

I drove first to the Château de Candé – an American-owned fairy-tale pile of glamorous turrets and battlements, already famous as the place where the Duke of Windsor and Mrs. Simpson had married.

Now it had become the provisional embassy headquarters headed by Drexel Biddle. After crawling along dusty roads, it was as though I had stumbled on an oasis. The owner had installed a large pool – which, alas, I didn't have time to use – a badminton court, a golf course, archery butts, even artificial brooks to encourage ducks to breed.

More important, the generous owner of the Château de Candé had made his millions as an industrial efficiency expert; consequently, everything worked. A telephone had been installed in every one of its twenty rooms. It boasted its own internal switchboard. And when my car crunched to a stop on the gravelled driveway, I was even greeted by a real English butler in striped trousers; left behind, I heard later by the owner, in case Biddle needed personal attention.

'Whom would you wish to see, sir?' he asked gravely.

'Mr. Matthews, if he's available.' Freeman Matthews, known to everyone as 'Doc' Matthews, was a counsellor, always willing to help. He was a mine of information.

'Certainly, sir.' The butler ushered me inside with the urbanity of one greeting guests arriving for a weekend house party. 'And who may I say is calling, sir?'

'Mr. Astell of Reims.' I knew that any butler worth his salt would know *that* name. He did. 'Of course, sir, and if there's anything I can do to make your stay more comfortable, my name is James.'

He *was* able to help, for though Doc Matthews had driven off with Drexel Biddle to some other château, the inestimable James – I almost called him Jeeves – produced a list of personnel staying at the château to see if I could spot a friendly name.

'This one is fine,' I exclaimed as my finger stopped on the name of Jim Parks.

What's more, Jim had some cold American beer, and it was he who first outlined to me the state of panic already gripping the bewildered French government.

The British ambassador, Sir Ronald Campbell, was installed several miles away at the Château de Cleré. The French Foreign Minister was at Langeais, the Finance Minister at Chinon. Reynaud himself was installed with Madame de Portes at the Château de Chissay, above the river Cher, midway between Tours and Amboise.

'It's madness,' exploded Jim Parks. 'You'll never believe it, Larry, but when Reynaud arrived here he found three hundred coded telegrams waiting for him – and the fucking French refused to decode them because they said they were too tired.'

'I'm going to try and see Reynaud,' I said, 'but I'm worried about censorship. Even if I quote Reynaud's own words, the censors are liable to cut 'em out. They're a law unto themselves. Specially if you come across one who doesn't like the prime minister. I've got written permission to use the embassy line to Washington for cabling, but only if they're passed by censor. Anyway, can I get round it?'

Parks thought carefully. 'We don't expect the boss or Doc Matthews back until late' – he was weighing his words – 'but I guess that if you could get Reynaud to approve and sign every page – every one, mind you – and you got the cable to me before the others return, I'd just *have* to make the decision – and let it through. After all, if he is premier, he must be chief censor. Trouble is, Larry, you'll never get to see Reynaud.'

'I know him . . .' I began.

'Sure. I know you've got an in with lots of top brass. But how're you going to make contact? Set it up – make the date?'

'I'll phone Madame de Portes.'

'You'll never get through. Reynaud's got a hundred rooms in his château, but only one antiquated, hand-operated telephone. It's linked to the nearest village, where the goddamned lady in charge closes for two hours every lunchtime and switches off at six sharp each night.'

'Then there's only one thing to do.' I tried to disguise my misgivings with a laugh. 'And that's pop down the road to Reynaud's place and invite myself in for a drink.'

It was now 9 a.m. Candé must have been ten miles from Chissay – and Candé lay twenty-five miles east of Tours on the road to Orléans. But I still had a good road map (hidden, since all maps were now forbidden as a precaution against fifth columnists).

'I'll be back before six with my cable signed by Reynaud,' I promised cheerfully – though doubtfully.

Jim Parks looked worried – even more worried than I did. But at first I didn't realise why. At the last moment he hesitated, almost as I was on the point of leaving.

'I shouldn't say this.' He mumbled something like, 'Thank God this place isn't bugged,' then blurted out, 'Reynaud isn't at Chissay. Won't be there until late this afternoon.'

'Well, thanks,' I said sarcastically. 'You might have told me earlier.'

'I couldn't. I shouldn't even now. It's restricted.'

'But I'm on your side! Remember me? I'm supposed to be your buddy – and the voice of "Washington in print". What gives? Why the hell are you holding out on me?'

'I know, I know,' he said. 'But there are certain things I'm not supposed to talk about. Christ! you must know that, Larry.'

'Not with a guy who once tried his best to help me to get married,' I joked.

'For your eyes and ears only?' he asked. 'Promise?'

'On the flag if you say so. But what's cooking, for Chrissake. And where *is* Reynaud?'

He took a deep breath, hesitated, then finally said: 'Reynaud is with Winston Churchill.'

'*Jesus!* So Reynaud has flown to England?'

'No. Other way round. Churchill's here. Not far away; flew in yesterday.'

'In France! God Almighty! What a story.'

'You'll get me fired,' sighed Parks, 'shouting like that.'

'Where is he, then?'

'Place called Briare. It's the new French military headquarters. General Maxime Weygand, the C-in-C, met Churchill there last night.'

'Never mind Weygand. But Churchill in France!'

'He landed yesterday, in a foul temper I'm told. The car to meet him never turned up. It was a clapped-out old Citroën and broke down on the way. Churchill was furious – left standing on the tarmac fuming until they could find another vehicle.'

'Where's – what's the name of this place?'

'Briare. About thirty miles south-east of Orleans. Just follow the river until you smell an expensive cigar. But seriously, you've got a head start, because Candé is twenty or so miles along the main Tours–Orleans road.'

'Do you know who's going?'

'I don't know Churchill's gang, but I gather de Gaulle's there. And Pétain. And of course Weygand. Churchill's flying back to England this afternoon, but maybe you'll be able to pick over a few bones if you step on the gas and catch your chum Reynaud.'

I had no problem finding the headquarters of seventy-three-year-old General Weygand, the Commander-in-Chief, at the Château du Muguet – translated literally as 'Lily of the Valley Château'. It lay at the end of a narrow winding road past the village of Ouzouer, about eight miles from Briare itself, where there was a small airfield.

But there I was stopped. Two French soldiers stood guard in front of a pair of handsome wrought iron gates flanked by large stone pillars decorated on top with masses of petunias planted in two urn-shaped stone bowls. The soldiers had fixed bayonets.

'Restricted area,' the first growled, moving threateningly towards me. 'The grounds are private.'

It was hopeless even to think of asking for permission to pass those gates and eavesdrop on what could possibly be the most momentous war council in the history of France. And indeed, as I opened the door of my car, the sentry said something and waved me away from the gates with his rifle.

'Restricted area,' he shouted again.

'I'm a friend of the prime minister's,' I said. 'Here!' I produced Reynaud's letter of authority and he did allow me to step forward and examined it while the other sentry covered me with his rifle.

'Doesn't count,' he said. 'This is a war zone. Under military authority. General Weygand is the boss here,' adding with a laugh, 'Reynaud's got no power here – nor his girlfriend.'

I would never have a chance of entering a restricted military zone, I realised that immediately. But I also knew that so long as I remained in this country lane, minding my own business (and obviously not making a fool of myself by taking photographs), no one could really force me to leave. If on the other hand I behaved stupidly, threatened anyone, even the dumbest *poilu* wouldn't hesitate to shoot and ask questions after. My job was to play for time in the hope of picking up a few crumbs when the feast was over. In the meantime it was a waiting game.

I was half asleep in the front seat of the car. And I was hungry. But two hours of patience later I awoke as though shot. The sound of a hand-operated siren tore into the still air. Obviously it was a signal to the sentries at the front gate. I had long since turned the car around on orders from the sentry, and parked it on the grass verge well away from the gates. I jumped out – taking care to keep well away from the gates as the sentries spruced themselves up a bit.

In the distance I could see groups of men walking or waiting, gesticulating, strolling along the broad flagstoned terrace of the château with its classic façade behind, and its large French windows open to the warm day. Some seemed to be shaking hands, bidding each other farewell. I made out – vaguely but unmistakably – the tall figure of de Gaulle towering head and shoulders above the others.

I heard the spurting roar of motor cycle engines being kicked into life. Three cars came slowly round the back of the château which was hidden from me. Doors opened, bulky figures clambered in through the low French automobile doors. The motor cyclists opened the throttles of their noisy machines, the group which remained behind waved goodbye from the top of the terrace, the convoy slowly started to move across the long drive through open parkland dotted with drowsy cows, hidden only once for a couple of moments as it passed behind a clump of chestnuts.

Then the sentry was opening the gates. The four police motor cyclists roared past, helmets hiding faces. They hardly noticed me – their job was to make sure the V.I.P.s faced no traffic obstructions. Three Citroëns followed, slowing as they approached a ridge in the park drive just before the gates. As they passed the gates and accelerated I caught a glimpse through the nearest back window of a large man puffing away at a cigar. The car disappeared.

'Well,' said one of the sentries sardonically, 'now that you've interviewed your Monsieur Churchill, I suppose you've got enough material for your story.'

Actually I got the material, as the sentry put it, by luck less than half an hour later. Perseverance, too, though I say it myself. I had spent hours wasting time on a summer's afternoon, with droning bees and the sweet smell of the countryside making it difficult to stay awake. But some instinct told me I must hang on, because I knew that Reynaud would have to leave for Chissay before long, as he had a cabinet meeting and I did have his signed letter of accreditation. When he left, perhaps I could follow him, flashing passes, anything, to become part of his convoy until I could speak to him. For after all he knew me, trusted me, respected my father, needed help from the Americans. Everything was going in my favour – except contact. But when Reynaud passed through the gates I could stand near him, and he might recognise me – and give me a chance to ask if I could follow him to Chissay – 'officially'.

It happened almost that way – but then luck stepped in, when two motor-cycle policemen swept from the front door towards the main gates, followed by only one car. It *had* to be Reynaud's.

The gates were drawn open. The soldiers presented arms – sloppily, I noticed. I stood by the car respectfully – until, as I moved forward, the police officers waved me away with a shout. One just bumped me, throwing me off balance to the ground, forcing the car behind to jerk to a halt.

I jumped up, waved politely to Reynaud as he looked out to see if anyone had been hurt. Reynaud was seated in the back seat by the right hand window and he looked squashed and uncomfortable. He also looked astonished to see me there. I was even more astonished – at his cramped position. For five men and the driver were crammed into a car meant to hold four.

'What on earth are you doing here?' cried Reynaud through the open window.

I was so staggered by the mass of people inside that, almost without thinking, I cried: 'Excuse me, Prime Minister, can I drive any of you – help in any way?'

De Gaulle gave me a faintly ironic smile. He always seemed to find it hard to break into a real smile.

'What on earth are you doing here?' repeated Reynaud.

'I've been trying to get an interview with le Maréchal Pétain.'

'Waste of time!' snapped de Gaulle.

'Well, sir, I've got a car, and it's at your disposal.'

Their second car, it transpired, had also broken down and they were planning to drive to the airfield at Briare to pick up one of the extra cars used by Churchill's party.

'Well now,' mused Reynaud, 'we could save time if . . .'

I thought it better to say nothing – hoping, heart in mouth, as they looked at each other that I could drive them to Briare. At least it would give me a chance to ask for an interview later.

But then Reynaud made a suggestion that sent me into a newspaperman's seventh heaven.

'Let's bypass Briare,' he suggested to de Gaulle as I stood quietly by the open window. 'If we have to collect one of Churchill's cars at the airfield – and if by bad luck he's delayed – we'd have to remain with him, as a matter of courtesy. But since he's not expecting us to go to the airfield, we could possibly save hours of valuable time if we could ask Astell to drive one of the cars to Chissay.'

'I have to go to the American Embassy in the end,' I said politely, 'but if it suits you I could take you to Chissay first, Prime Minister.'

To de Gaulle, Reynaud said, 'You'll have to go there, won't you – for the meeting?'

He nodded.

'How did you know that Mr. Churchill was coming to France?' he asked.

'I didn't,' I lied. 'My whole idea was to ask for an interview with Marshal Pétain.'

'Done!' cried Reynaud. 'You will be enrolled – temporarily of course – as the only American chauffeur in the French civil service. You might get the *Légion d'honneur* for this.' To de Gaulle, he said, 'You sit in the back with me, *mon Général*. Astell will drive the two of us.' To the others he cried, 'You take the other car with the regular driver.'

Once inside the car, the policemen kicked their starters, the motor cycles roared, and we set off in style, sirens wailing on the two motor bikes clearing the traffic ahead, gesticulating, shouting, waving. Reynaud sat in the left-hand seat directly behind me. De Gaulle sat on the right, in a slewed position to allow him more room for his legs. I was astonished at the way in which even the most obdurate people ahead of us scattered when the police forced vehicles to the sidewalks. After the day of the exodus, it resembled a royal procession – which in a way I suppose it was. And though probably no one knew the identity of the tall, gloomy man with the big nose, the little cock-sparrow Reynaud was recognised instantly every time we slowed down.

He might be losing the war but everyone liked him, felt that he had guts, hardly realised yet that the war was being lost by others, more traitorous. As the Citroën edged slowly past a crowd, the men and women shouted, '*Bonne chance!*' or '*Bravo Reynaud!*' and often, '*Merde aux Boches!*'

At first the conversation between the two men was conducted in whispers, as though Reynaud and de Gaulle were discussing state secrets, or reviewing the vital meeting with Churchill. But during a lull, when Reynaud asked me where we were, and after hands pushed through his open window had tried to shake his hand, Reynaud spoke to me. In the rear view mirror, I could see that his eyes, below his slightly dyed hair, were lit with a trace of amusement rare in these harrowing times. Sardonic, perhaps?

'Tell me, Larry,' he asked me not unkindly, 'what do you propose to write about?'

My first problem was not writing, but bypassing the censor. With sudden inspiration I replied, forgetting all my earlier ideas, that I had come in the hope of seeing him for one reason only – to help France if I could.

'I know you must be overwhelmed with work, sir,' I said, 'but the *Globe* would be honoured if we could publish even a brief. . .' I just prevented myself from using the word 'appeal' and went on, 'a message of encouragement to the people of the United States who admire the wonderful stand you are making.'

'Are words enough?' Reynaud asked bitterly.

'We need guns and tanks and planes more than words,' said de Gaulle.

'I know, sir. But words *do* help. Roosevelt wants to do everything short of war to help France. A message might help. And sir, it could provoke the President into giving France a message of – of hope, sir. Hope that might persuade the French to send away their great navy, the planes that remain.'

'It sounds very fine in theory,' said Reynaud, 'but it is too late now to have any effect.'

'But sir,' I begged him. 'It's never too late. Not to hope. And anyway, sir' – it was very difficult trying to look disarming when Reynaud could only see the back of my head – 'it costs nothing to try. And if we could do this, sir, I'd arrange for the message to be made available coast to coast on the news agency networks.'

I knew the *Globe* would regard this as an astute move, a 'national interest' gesture, which would in no way nullify our exclusive, for the *Globe* was our local paper anyway, serving the nation's capital. It made no difference to our sales if we gave the story to anyone from the *Milwaukee Journal* to the *Los Angeles Times*.

De Gaulle was whispering. I kept silent, holding my breath. We were driving through a small town called Sully half-way between Briare and Orleans, a traffic cop's nightmare, for six roads met at the heart of the square. It took ten minutes for the police to force a passage and inevitably Reynaud became more and more irritated and the thread of our conversation snapped.

Somehow I had to bring him back to my suggestion, for apart from the value to the *Globe* of a major scoop I realised that if Reynaud *did* agree to back a nationwide appeal to Roosevelt, he would have to over-ride any censorship in the national interest of France.

'The problem is time.' At least ten minutes had passed since Reynaud last spoke to me. Now, out of the blue, he suddenly spoke as though I had made the suggestion only seconds before. 'But General de Gaulle agrees with me – a dramatic appeal to the United States could be of inestimable value to France.'

He was thinking, then he added, 'I have a cabinet meeting later this evening, but as soon as we reach Chissay I will ask you to help the countess to prepare a rough draft, then I'll go through it with you and make any suggestions.'

I stole a glance in the rear mirror at de Gaulle's face. It was expressionless, but I could sense, almost feel, his irony. There was no love lost between de Gaulle and Madame de Portes. On the other hand, from my point of view it would make writing the despatch easier and quicker. No one could say that Madame de Portes was hidebound or fussy. She was action-packed.

'I'll have to add a little background material, sir,' I suggested.

'Like how you were the only journalist to see Churchill.' Reynaud had a wry sense of humour and knew how to treat newspapermen – and the poetic licence they sometimes needed.

'Well, I did see him,' I laughed, adding more seriously, 'But of course, sir, Madame de Portes will show you every word we write so that you can cross out anything you wish.'

'With a carbon copy for Monsieur Reynaud,' added de Gaulle.

I decided deliberately not to mention the problem of censorship at this stage. I felt that if Madame de Portes became really enthusiastic she would deal with Reynaud as I had seen her handle a cabinet meeting in his absence. She could easily persuade the Prime Minister to exercise his right as chief censor. And that was all I wanted to satisfy Jim Parks at the American Embassy.

'I'm most grateful, sir.' I drove swiftly through the outskirts of Orleans. We were on the last lap now. 'And I hope I can be of real service to you.' Then, without thinking I added, 'it may even persuade the defeatists to delay going on to Bordeaux if necessary.'

'Bordeaux!' De Gaulle sat up so suddenly he almost hit his head against the low roof as he snapped, 'Who on earth said anything about going to Bordeaux?'

'I'm sorry, sir,' I stammered. 'I thought General Weygand . . .'

'Bordeaux is the road to defeat,' said de Gaulle loftily, 'the Prime Minister prefers the road to honour. We shall make our last stand in Brittany.'

I almost gasped, as he added, 'In Brittany large formations of troops will be able to hold out until British merchant vessels arrive to transport them to North Africa,' he explained, 'and Mr. Churchill agrees. We can embark half a million men from a Breton redoubt. I leave for Quimper this evening to make the necessary arrangements.'

Quimper, as I knew, meant the port of Brest – and the possibility of evacuating not only a fighting force but masses of equipment to North Africa.

I sped on towards Chissay, wondering how much of this latest startling development I would be allowed to print – if any. On the surface the plan for a Breton redoubt seemed brilliant. At least it would be able to halt the rout. I was equally fascinated by the irony of the choice, of the way various factions were 'using' Tours as they plotted for power. Everyone had made for Tours – but for different reasons. Weygand and Pierre Laval, whom I had never trusted, regarded it as a halt on the way to Bordeaux, whereas Reynaud and de Gaulle regarded it as a halt on the way to Brittany.

I would have a great deal to write about when I reached Chissay – if I was given permission: Churchill's visit (though I would never be able to mention Briare by name) and then the Breton redoubt and the emergence of de Gaulle as a more powerful figure in the struggle against those whom I was already beginning to label as defeatists – led by Laval and Marshal Pétain.

Yet all adrenalin flowing at the prospect of writing a major piece was dulled by one other thought. Sonia. For one thing was clear. The plan to establish a Breton redoubt meant the end of all our schemes to spirit Sonia away to Spain. It was now the 12th. By tomorrow at six o'clock (if she did not catch the diplomatic bus in Paris) she would be an enemy alien – subject probably to internment. It wouldn't have mattered had she been making for Spain. It was far from Paris, I had friends in high places in this region, I had always felt certain we could bluff our way through among the horde of refugees. But what could I do with Sonia if I had to go to Brittany – or even remain in Tours? I couldn't hide her for the duration of the war.

We reached Chissay in half an hour. The fifteenth-century castle, with its three round towers, lay in wooded parkland leading to an abrupt corner which in turn led to a courtyard. It was obviously a tricky curve to negotiate, especially if you met a car coming towards you. I was not surprised therefore that someone was needed to control the traffic.

But what *did* surprise me was the person in charge. It was none other than Madame de Portes, dressed in an outrageous bright red pyjama suit. She was busily directing the traffic like an expert.

Only when the police stopped with our car in front of the main entrance did she wave imperiously to someone else to take over her duties. She didn't seem unduly surprised to see me, greeting me merely with an 'Ah, Larry! *Bonjour.*' Before Reynaud started to explain everything de Gaulle gave her an almost perfunctory nod and, contrary to French habit, didn't shake hands.

'He's a cold one,' she muttered to me as de Gaulle moved through the door, '*Une grande asperge.*'

I grabbed my typewriter, found some carbon paper in an old study and composed the majority of Reynaud's speech for him, aided, I must say, by intelligent suggestions from Madame de Portes, who looked over my shoulder all the time.

As it was supposed to be written by Reynaud, I had to employ a few flowery phrases. I didn't want it to be too long because I also wanted to add a general story of the day's events – and some of this might have to be critical, for I couldn't possibly disguise the chaos, the disorder, the gloom, the horrendous defeats on the battlefields, though I *could* take care not to mention the incidents of cowardice, of French troops refusing to fight, the general feeling of betrayal from within. That would have to wait, and I knew that if any of this material reached Washington from agency sources the *Globe* would be able to work it in alongside my main story. Finally the 'Message from France' read:

> Friends of France! In this hour of greatest urgency, the fate of our land and our liberty rests in the balance as our valiant armies continue to fight against the forces of tyranny unleashed by Hitler. France and America have been staunch comrades in arms since we stood shoulder to shoulder against the selfsame enemy in 1914–18, and though I know you cannot join us at this time in the fight against evil I appeal to you now to give us all the help you can, even though it may be short of war, and declare America to be a non-belligerent ally.
>
> Such a gesture, though committing no one to armed conflict, would tell the free world that you are with us in spirit, and give hope to ourselves and Britain as the skies darken over Europe.
>
> I on my part promise our friends in America that, with the Germans almost at the gates of Paris, we shall fight in our fair country until if necessary the last soldier has been killed. If we cannot hold Paris, we shall fight in the provinces of France. If we cannot hold the provinces, we shall go to North Africa and fight from there. We shall never give in.
>
> *Vive la France! Vive Les États Unies!*

Madame de Portes read it quickly.

'*Formidable!*' she cried. 'It is wonderful. I will take it to Paul while you get on with the second part of your article.'

'It won't take long, *madame*,' I promised her, for I wanted to minimise the dangers of any high official interrupting Reynaud. If that happened I might not be able to see him for days. And anyway, I had already written some background material, particularly on Pétain, which had not been submitted to censorship, but which I could now tack on to the general story I tapped out.

I had been worried that Reynaud might cut out references to Churchill in France, and also the news about the Breton redoubt, but when finally he sent for me he immediately agreed with my point that Churchill's visit would be announced in a communiqué. Therefore mine would be an exclusive follow-up colour story – far, far better, for every agency would announce the communiqué but the *Globe* would be the only man present at the meeting.

Signing each page, Reynaud made no comments until I had almost reached the end and started to read the earlier material I proposed to.tack on. Some of it concerned Pétain.

'I can't pass this sort of thing,' he said testily. 'It's giving aid and comfort to the enemy.'

'Anything you say, Prime Minister.' I didn't hesitate, working on the principle that if I could get a quarter of my material past the censor I would be more than happy. 'What's the passage you don't like, sir?'

'It's where you describe Marshal Pétain.'

There was nothing wrong with the article, though I knew it might come as a shock to the less informed readers of the *Globe*. It simply stated a fact not often realised in America: that when World War One was about to erupt way back in 1914 – yes, World War One – Pétain was *at that time* already fifty-eight and looking for a villa where he could retire. And that was thirty years ago – yet now he was the spiritual leader to whom France looked. Wasn't that a bit old? I asked the readers in my article.

'It doesn't put him in a very good light, stressing his age – and for American readers,' protested Reynaud.

'It's true, sir, but it's been published before.'

'Yes, I know.' Reynaud was no fool. 'But by tagging it along on to the end of a message from me, it somehow reads as though I approve of what you say.'

'Please cross it out,' I said urgently. 'It's my mistake. You're absolutely right, sir.' I was suddenly sweating – one more stupidity and he might tear up the whole story. I breathed a little more easily when Reynaud finally signed the last page.

'Here's something you *can* put in,' added Reynaud suddenly. 'Much better than that absurd Pétain stuff. General de Gaulle told me we have absolute proof that the Italians have already started sending their Caproni bombers over south-east France and even as far north as the Loire valley. A great many casualties last night. They didn't waste much time.'

I scribbled out the addition on a spare sheet of paper and asked Reynaud to sign that page too. Then I returned to Madame de Portes.

'You are a fine journalist!' She herself made sure the pages were correctly numbered. 'Wait here. I will try and help you a little more.'

I stood in the study, idly looking at prints and old photographs on the wall, including an illuminated scroll bearing a French translation from Goethe. The first letter of each line was inscribed in flowery gold leaf and the text read:

Possessions lost, something lost;
Honour lost, much lost;
Courage lost, everything lost.

As I read it again, I felt a sudden shiver and had an almost irresistible urge to tear down the frame and its scroll and smash it against the table. Then Madame de Portes arrived. Leading me to the door, she indicated the two traffic cops sitting, legs astride, in front of my Citroën.

'To see you on your way,' she cried to me almost gaily, and to the policemen, '*En vitesse, s'il vous plaît!* This gentleman is carrying important despatches from the Premier of France to the American Embassy for transmission to the President of the United States.'

And that was how I returned to Candé to file my copy. Jim Parks could hardly believe his eyes when, out of the window, he saw the motor cycle *flics* tear up the drive and, as I emerged from my car, salute me briskly before roaring off.

'You sure travel in style,' said Jim.

'I told you I had contacts.'

'Anything to show for them?'

'Only this – duly signed for immediate despatch.'

'This' was my cable – with the note in Reynaud's own handwriting: 'This letter is my authority for M. Larry Astell to

file the attached cable, each page of which has been counter-
signed by myself.' And then following the legal phrase used
since time immemorial, he had added, '*Lu et approuvé, Paul
Reynaud.*'

Parks whistled as he read. 'Christ! You've hit the jackpot
this time. Oh, I almost forgot. There's a cable for you.'

It was from the *Globe*. It read: 'Paris declared open city stop
Tomlinson unable return exwar front stop Return Paris
soonest cover entry Germans stop'

Sonia darling, I'll be back in Tours and in your arms soon, I
was thinking, but I was also thinking: I'll have to take you back
to Paris and try to catch the diplomatic bus by tomorrow
evening. I can't disobey an order from the *Globe*. I might have
been tempted – but not now, not with you on the run and
nobody going to Bordeaux to help you. And, I was thinking
too, you *are* a diplomat, you *are* protected – but only if you
obey the rules. And if – no, damn it, when – the Germans
win the war, their Italian allies will be free to travel anywhere
in Europe. Even, as an Italian diplomat, to Switzerland, to
your bolthole in Rolle. I'll be there to see you, don't worry.

27

When I reached the outskirts of Blandy, making good time
against the mainstream of fleeing cars, I had no premonition of
the scene that would greet me as I turned the Citroën into the
place des Épars and saw the wisps of dying smoke, smelt the
sour aftermath of fire – burning wood doused with water.
Then I jammed on the brakes as I stepped into a movie scene
from an air raid. In the early moments of dawn, the sky was
streaked grey and pink. In front of me the imposing façade of
the Bellevue provided an ornate, smoking background. The
village square was filled with men, women and children lying
on the ground, crowded next to each other on pavements, in

shopfronts, snatches of grass, on benches, even on the side of the road, some huddled up close as protection against the twin chills of fear and night, some covered with newspapers, others with anything they had been able to forage – carpets, table-cloths, the lucky ones with blankets and pillows filched from the Bellevue. I heard cries for help, moans of people in pain. Ambulances, cars, even trucks arrived to carry people away as I watched. Others hobbled to hospital, if there was such a thing as a hospital in this small village. Mothers searched for children, everyone was coughing or spitting or vomiting because of the smoke.

It was the first I knew of a raid and I felt the actual stab of pain as fear clutched my heart. Where was Sonia? I had no clue to the events of the last few hours – only the obvious fact that the Bellevue behind the square had received a direct hit. And that I would never be able to drive my car, however slowly, across the mass of people. I started to reverse, remembering the side street leading to the Bellevue courtyard where the porter had first garaged my car.

Suddenly, despite the nip in the air, I began to sweat with fear – for Sonia – as a moving figure, a man in a daze, almost walked into my slowly moving Citroën.

'What the hell's happened,' I shouted.

'Air raid. Last night. Got a cigarette?'

I handed him a Gauloise, yelling, 'Was it bad?'

'Could have been worse. I hear that fifteen people have been killed. Everyone else had to be evacuated.'

'Where are the – the dead?'

'Don't know. Most of us grabbed our bedclothes and spent the rest of the night here in the square. A few people hurt – glass splinters mostly. I heard another bomb killed a lot of people in the suburbs of the nearest town. Could you spare me another cigarette?'

I scarcely heard him, mind racing with anxiety. *Sonia!* He must have thought I was scared – I was, but not for myself.

'Here, take the pack, I've got some more,' I shouted, and started to back the car until I was free of the square, heading for the rear of the clinic.

I *had* to find Sonia – there must be a first aid post some-where – but before anything else I had to make sure the car wasn't stolen when I went to search for her on foot. I must put it in the Bellevue courtyard which acted as a sort of open garage. The double wooden doors were locked. I jumped out and tried to force the lock. It was flimsy, the old doors rickety, but I just didn't have the tools to break the doors open. Finally I drove the car very slowly towards the doors, pushing the fenders against them, and nudging the car forward inch by inch. The doors began to groan and give – but I had to be careful not to overdo it, to smash the doors completely, for I had to leave myself a way to close them afterwards.

Slowly the doors cracked. Splinters of wood round the old-fashioned hinges broke off, and finally the square iron locks and bolts, screwed into the door, burst open. I jumped out and opened the doors completely. Once I had driven the car through, I closed the doors then backed my car hard up against them, forming a barricade heavy enough to stop intruders trying to enter the courtyard from the street.

The Bellevue foyer was a shambles of smashed furniture; debris everywhere, smoke, smell, crunching glass, the gilded reception area shrouded not only in dust and plaster but in uncanny silence. The elevators weren't working. The main staircase had been ripped apart but I knew the back staircase which we had used to go to the maids' room and this hadn't been damaged. I took the stairs two at a time, reaching the bedrooms under the eaves at the rear of the hotel, panting with the effort – and fear. The rear of the building seemed virtually undamaged. Yet as I reached the top of the stairs and turned the knob on the door of her room, a great fear held me back. Where was she? Why had I been such a fool as to leave her alone, unprotected, even for one night? And yet, I thought desperately, if she was searching for a place that seemed safe, this quiet backwater was the perfect one to choose.

Finally I burst open the door – half expecting the imposs-ible – Sonia still sleeping off the drug. The room was empty – but as neat as though a chambermaid had cleaned it up. Sonia's overnight bag was there, the room tidy, the bed pulled back, her pair of spare shoes under the edge of the coverlet. Nothing seemed to have been disturbed in the room while I had left her before driving to Tours – leaving her so drugged she probably never even remembered my goodnight kiss.

I could only hope and pray that she had left the hotel before the raid had started – perhaps for some simple reason, the need for a breath of air. I could imagine what happened then – panic, as only the French understand the word. But where was she? If she was unhurt why wasn't she standing in the place des Épars? Why wasn't she by the main gate, waiting for me since I couldn't know where she was?

There had to be a good reason – but what good reason? I must keep calm, I told myself, mind racing with possibilities. She might be in some makeshift hospital, evacuated perhaps, to the only available place in some nearby village – and then I would never have a chance of finding her.

I refused – by an enormous effort of will – to believe that Sonia had been killed. And yet, I thought in sudden panic, though our untouched bedroom indicated that she had left, it might not have been for that breath of air. She might have made her way to the main lounge, now a twisted, tangled pile of wreckage from which none could escape death or serious injury.

Shuddering, and suddenly cold, I realised there was only one way I could be sure whether or not Sonia was alive. I must go to the equivalent of the morgue. The village wouldn't boast such a place, but the police or air raid wardens must have designated some building in which the bodies would await identification and burial.

Angrily I stubbed out a Gauloise. I mustn't think of such an awful thing. I must think *positively*. I must think that this is Thursday and that in theory she had to be back in Paris and on that bus by the evening. She must be alive, and provided I found her soon we would still be able to reach Paris in time.

Outside in the square, struggling to move, I made my way past the front entrance, ignoring the shouts of the two police-men who wanted to know where I had come from. Half dazed with shock, I walked into the battlefield of the place des Épars. The 'bodies' were beginning to wake up, make more noises as the sun slanted over the village roofs. I trod as carefully as I could among whimpering, hungry children – the semi-sleeping figures stretched out, one or two with bandages on heads, arms or legs, though I could see that the most seriously injured must have already been taken away. Once or twice, coming across a huddled figure, I caught myself thinking, 'There she is!' but each time even before I spoke I spotted the telltale evidence that it wasn't Sonia – something as simple as a shoe peeping out from under a blanket, the kind Sonia would never have worn.

Two men came round the corner of the *place* wheeling a kind of trolley. On it stood a pail of coffee and some cheap cups and people began to form a queue. The children were the ones I was most sorry for, herded from one place to another as a farmer herds sheep, as bewildered as sheep, spindly legs moving wherever their parents told them to go.

I asked one of the men where the casualties had been taken. The dead had been laid out in the village church, he said. I knew I had to go there – and *now*. I had done this sort of thing before. Every trained newspaperman checks at the morgue before anywhere else when looking for a missing person. But I had never before done it when searching for someone I loved.

The fifteen bodies lying in the church were uncovered, as all the blankets had been needed in the village square. There was no sign of Sonia. So thankfully I was spared the agony of a long-drawn-out examination. The place smelt of death – and the all-pervading smell of wet, burned wood.

From the church I went round to the local *préfet*, asking if there were any reports of an accident to 'the Countess de Feo'. No one had heard of her. I made my way back to the Bellevue, in the hope that Monsieur Lelong had turned up and might have news. He had vanished. I wandered again through the crowds filling the place des Épars. One group had grown angry, demanded the right to return to the Bellevue now the danger was over. They didn't realise that the building could easily fall down if somebody interfered with the wreckage. The police were obdurate. Most sleepers had awakened, people were moving around as I searched among them – men looking for day-old *baguettes* to feed their kids. A bar in the corner of the square was doing a roaring trade in hardboiled eggs. I ate one before returning to the police station to see if there was any more news.

Where was she? What was happening? Beginning to feel more and more desperate, I even asked at several cottages in case she had been taken ill with shock. But nobody had heard of her. Fear that she was dead had been replaced by a kind of anger. Sonia was *there*. I felt it, I knew it, yet there was no way I could find her. She had to come to me, and if she couldn't there was no way I could meet her. Had I missed her through bad luck, stupidity? If I had reached the hotel an hour or two earlier, would I have found her then? If I had raced round the corners of villages when I almost fell asleep during the drive back to Blandy and had to slow down, would I have been in time to stop her vanishing? If I had skipped a mile and arrived just one hour earlier – even twenty minutes earlier – or if it had rained, or if it hadn't rained? The world of vanishing Sonia was a string of ifs . . .

With a sense of mounting despair I returned again to the place des Épars. She might have gone back, been looking for me while I was looking for her. Yet the search seemed hopeless. Apart from anything else, I didn't know where to start. The police seemed indifferent, they were busy, they either couldn't or wouldn't find time to help. I didn't know a soul in the village except Lelong, not even the name of the doctor who had treated Sonia.

It was at this precise moment that I did recognise a man and a woman. I didn't know them, I had never spoken to either of them, yet even the sight of someone I recognised gave me a surge of encouragement, a feeling of fear diminished when shared, even with a stranger.

The lady was sitting on a pink chair on the pavement in the square. She was the snooty woman in the maroon Delage who had driven near us almost all the way from Paris. Next to her stood her chauffeur in his matching uniform, though I noticed that he no longer wore his peaked cap or a tie.

Almost without thinking I rushed up to these 'old friends' and even though the woman didn't seem to recognise me – indeed she ignored me – I blurted out to the chauffeur, 'Do you remember me? We were driving just behind you from Paris – my fiancée and me. She's vanished. Have you seen her? And you, *madame*? Please forgive me.'

Very politely the chauffeur replied, 'I'm very sorry, *mon-*

sieur. I do remember the lady in your car. Next to the old couple who kept scratching *madame*'s car. But I haven't seen your fiancée since we arrived.'

It was extraordinary really, looking back to that strange tableau on the fringe of the large village square – the mass of people, sitting wherever they could snatch an inch of space, the crying children, the strident voices of parents disguising their fear, their hopelessness, their pessimism. The world seemed to have no existence beyond the crowded square that had become a casualty station in a battlefield, with a well-dressed, almost haughty woman ignoring everyone around her.

Then the woman spoke. She had a beautiful, gentle voice which was filled with compassion. It made a mockery of her attitude of imperious disdain.

'I recognised your American voice,' she said gently. 'You are enquiring about your Italian lady friend?'

As I gasped – had she actually met Sonia, confided in her? – the chauffeur interrupted, 'May I present Madame la Baronne de Lancourt.'

'Never mind, Jules,' said the baroness.

'But you've met her! Did she tell you she was Italian?'

'We didn't actually meet,' said the woman quietly.

'But we never speak Italian. How . . .?'

'I have a certain flair for accents,' she answered drily. 'Just as I could tell you were American immediately, even though you speak French perfectly.'

'But what's happened to her, *madame? Please?*'

'I cannot tell you much.' She smoothed the dress over her pink chair. 'I heard her talking to a policeman – just near here in the night just after the raid. I heard the policeman ask the lady for her papers.'

I waited impatiently, almost angrily, for she seemed determined not to hurry.

'There was a lot of noise, you understand,' she continued. 'A lot of crying children, some women screaming, and a great many words I couldn't hear. But this I *did* hear – and I can swear to it. I heard the policeman say, "I'm sorry, *madame*, but I must ask you to accompany me and prepare to return to Paris." I understood quite clearly that your friend was being

forced to go back to Paris for some reason I couldn't understand.'

'Back to Paris?' I echoed. Knowing more about Sonia's
plans than the mysterious baroness, I realised she was without
doubt telling the truth. Unless . . .

'You're sure, *madame*, it was my fiancée?'

She hesitated. Then, as though sensing that the chauffeur
was about to interrupt again, she said. 'Please, Jules,' and to
me with a touch of hesitation, 'I'm sure, even though I didn't
actually see the lady.'

'Good God! If you didn't *see* her − it could all be a mistake.'

'It isn't, I'm afraid. You see I . . .'

'But *madame*,' I said angrily, 'you didn't see.'

'It was an unfortunate choice of words, sir,' she said gently.
'I'm afraid I can't see. I'm blind.'

I could feel the rush of blood to my face as I stumbled for
words. Now, of course, everything that had happened on that
terrible day of the exodus fell into place − the lady's apparent
aloofness, the way she sat alone in her car, unconcerned at the
misery and suffering around her. What an agony it must have
been for her, seeking no special preferment. Not once had she
complained on that dreadful day.

An instinct warned me that she would not take kindly to a
stammered speech of commiseration. Much better to regard
her as a normal person, ignore her plight. She would take that
as a kind of compliment.

'You're right, *madame*,' I said instead. 'I can sense you know
you are right. I am very grateful.'

'Go and search for her,' she said softly. 'I feel that anyone
with such a musical voice as hers must be very beautiful. She
had a laugh in her voice even on that dreadful day.'

'Perhaps we will all meet after the war,' I said. 'I hope so.' I
took her hand. With a perfectly natural gesture she extended it
to be kissed in the manner of the French.

'*Bonne chance, monsieur, et vive les États Unies!*' she said, then
added a curious sentence, 'Do not worry, *monsieur*. All of us
have a life to get through. So we might as well get through it.'

After I had returned to the *préfecture*, I flashed my press card
and drew the officer's attention to the name Astell, which he
knew. Then he did remember the name and told me that Sonia

had been sent back to Paris for her own good.

'But officer,' I said, 'her letter was in perfect order.'

'That is true,' he admitted, 'but surely *monsieur* will realise that she has been told to present herself at the embassy by this evening.'

'I know.' It was hard not to show my exasperation. 'But you arrested her when I could have taken her back.'

'I didn't arrest her, *monsieur*. I did it also for *madame*'s safety. I could take no chances. If anyone in this area discovered she was Italian' – he shrugged his shoulders – 'she would have been torn apart.'

'But that's ridiculous.'

'No, it isn't, sir. You don't realise that it was an Italian bomber that killed all these people in the square.'

Of course the officer was right. And there was no way I could admit that by this very evening I had planned to get Sonia, an enemy alien, across the Spanish frontier if possible.

'I understand, officer,' I said – publicly, though inwardly I was thinking, 'Is the entire world crazy? All the way *back* to Paris? And when the French give in all the Italians in the world will be queuing up to take pleasure jaunts to Paris as well.'

It was mad.

Now I had to reach Paris as quickly as possible, not only in order to file my story when the Germans marched in, but to try and see Sonia at the Italian Embassy before the bus left.

I decided to spend a few minutes looking for a little food. I had hardly eaten for twenty-four hours, apart from that one boiled egg. I walked behind the hotel towards the serenity of the church, searching till I found a small shop where I managed to buy three tins of sardines and some pâté that looked none too fresh. Nearby was a bar, though the wrinkled old *patronne* was angry and impolite when I ordered a *bière à la pression*, and asked her if she could spare me a *baguette* to make a sandwich.

'I've been serving sandwiches half the night,' she shrieked as she wiped the froth off the *bière* with her wooden slat. 'Why can't you people stay where you belong?'

Everyone was in a foul temper. The solitary old waiter looked exhausted. When one man spilled a coffee he snarled,

'Why don't you get out of the way? I'd rather have the Germans here than you riff-raff.'

Not until I had flourished my considerable command of *argot* – accompanied by a note – did the old woman grudgingly give me a *baguette*. I grabbed the hunk of dry bread and bolted for the courtyard of the Bellevue to get my car. The sooner I set off for Paris the better.

I reached Paris at 4 p.m., driving against the stream of traffic still pouring out of the capital. It was madness, I kept on repeating to myself. Tonight my beloved Sonia would be forced to leave. Tomorrow her allies the Germans will be masters of Paris and (in theory anyway) she should be able to return whenever she feels like it.

I revved up the Citroën. She was beginning to make a few tired sounds after all the low-gear work, but she still responded as I drove across to the Left Bank and towards the Italian Embassy in the rue de Grenelle, quite close to our apartment. One look told me nothing on earth – no press cards, no plea of neutrality, no letter from Reynaud – would get me past the ring of police guards facing the gates of what was now enemy territory. I did try. I cajoled. Everything was in vain.

It suddenly occurred to me – as a forlorn hope – that maybe Sonia had been allowed to drive to her home first. After all, she was supposed to have three days of grace. But at the rue de Longchamps I drew a blank. There was no guard outside the beautiful low house, but there was no one in either. The shutters had been closed and when I rattled the doorknob the house sounded hollow and empty, as though all life as we had known it since the day of that first summer party had been whisked away for ever.

Half-way up the street I heard the sound of music coming from someone in a small bar. A group was drinking but not boisterous, and one played a guitar. I realised that two or three of them were American. I needed a drink badly – Scotch if it was still available – and I discovered that one of them also knew the words of the most popular song in Paris at the time. It was awful in a way, the contrast between the neutral Americans to whom war was an adventure, and some nearby sad-eyed Frenchmen waiting for the city to fall. It was a picture of haunting contrasts as one of the Americans strummed for a moment and then they all started singing:

> The last time I saw Paris
> Her heart was warm and gay,
> I heard the laughter in her heart
> In every street café.

I couldn't bear it any more. I gulped down my Scotch, left more than enough francs on the small round table, and drove back to the embassy to wait.

By evening, as though the news of the impending departure of the Italians had been spread around, a small, anti-Italian group gathered, shouting slogans, and when just after seven o'clock the wrought iron gates were opened by the police the crowd surged forward. The first of four buses appeared, armed guards on the step. It made its way slowly to the gates. I shoved and forced my way right to the front – haunted by a sudden fear that the bus might be attacked and that Sonia, as an ambassador's wife, might be given priority in the first bus.

Slowly the bus went past the gates. The small crowd – there can't have been more than a hundred men and women – shouted obscenities, there was a fusillade of rotten fruit – tomatoes and other things beloved by French crowds. And then, just for a second, as the bus swung right down the rue de Grenelle and headed towards the boulevard Raspail, I saw her.

It was nothing more than a glimpse, but through the unwashed windows of the bus, through the spattered remains of tomato pulp, I saw her and she saw me too. I didn't dare to make a special sign. I just put my fingers to my lips and smiled. She did too – a sad smile, but still a smile. Then as the bus drew away I felt as if it had taken a part of me with it for ever, that we would never again tread the paths of love, and that she was waving a farewell, not only to me, but a farewell to France.

28

On the last night before the Germans came I couldn't bear the thought of spending the evening alone in my apartment. In my mind's eye I could still see not only the Germans but the green bus with the obscene splash of squashed tomatoes and the face of Sonia behind the dirty windows, like a badly developed photograph.

'I need a couple of stiff drinks,' I said to Oregon when I reached the office. 'And I don't feel like drinking by myself.'

'Don't blame you. I've got some Old Grandad.'

'I've not sunk as low as *that!*' I screwed up my face. 'I think I've got a bottle of Scotch in my desk drawer.'

We drank almost in silence for a while, and then I couldn't even stand the office any longer. I wasn't only wallowing in self-pity because Sonia had gone. I was haunted by imaginary pictures of the awful spectacle that awaited us on the morrow.

'Let's go for a walk,' I suggested to Oregon. 'How about the embassy? Just to see what's happening?'

It was still light, of course, a balmy June evening of half empty streets which at first glance disguised the bungling, the wavering, the cowardice, the corruption in high places.

As we turned left out of the rue du Sentier along the Grands Boulevards, I sniffed the very special odour of the Métro when we passed the Richelieu-Drouot station. Without thinking I turned to Oregon and said, 'Something's missing.'

It wasn't the eerie quietness of the streets and the missing strident screeches of taxi tyres, it was something else and at first I couldn't place it. Then I realised – the rumble of the Métro beneath my feet was missing.

'Of course,' Oregon echoed my thoughts. 'We take it so much for granted. There's something else, the' – he hesitated to use the word – 'the *shame* of it. Paris is being given away. Compare that with the heroic stand of the Poles in Warsaw.'

'I know.' As we walked towards the Madeleine and turned

left, I asked Oregon, 'What do you think made Ambassador Bullitt stay on in Paris?'

'A sense of occasion,' replied Oregon promptly. 'The higher you rise in the pomposity stakes, the more you need to look for chances to show off your greatness – real or phoney,' he added hastily.

Even so, it was puzzling. Cordell Hull, as Secretary of State, was Bullitt's undisputed boss. Hull had insisted that Bullitt should accompany Reynaud to Tours. In other words, that the ambassador should follow the legal government – especially at a sensitive time like this. President Roosevelt, who had a special relationship with Bullitt and had often written to him without telling Hull, refused to give Bullitt an actual order, but *advised* him to leave Paris with the government. Bullitt grabbed the loophole and decided to ignore what was only advice.

'For Bullitt it's a perfect moment of destiny,' said Oregon. 'After all, Bullitt is rich – pampered, if you like. He's vain and flamboyant and he's captivated Roosevelt. Now, towards the end of his career, which has hardly been illustrious, he's been given the chance to preside at one of the greatest moments in the history of Europe. When the Germans march in they're going to go to see Bill Bullitt who is the only important foreign diplomat in Paris. And then he's going to hand over the keys of the city, so to speak.'

'It's like hiring a butler for the day to hand over the city, in the same way a servant would offer a drink on a silver salver.' I had never really liked Bullitt.

'That's all it is,' Oregon agreed. 'And mind you,' he was thinking out his next words, 'my guess is that when the history of this little episode comes to be written, Bullitt will go down as the one American above all others who let France down.'

We had almost reached the Hôtel Crillon when I heard a shout of 'Larry!'

It was André Guérin, a French journalist from *Paris-Soir*.

'They tell me the Germans are coming in tomorrow,' he said.

'That's what we've been told.' I shook hands.

'Britain has ratted on us,' said André. 'Refused to send in her last fighters to save France. And now America – well, I'm not bitter about America, *mon vieux*. But when I look across there . . .' he waved a hand towards the antiseptic-looking white building of the embassy, the Stars and Stripes, the marine guarding the entrance behind the railings.

'It seems incredible to think that when the Germans arrive tomorrow and start stripping Paris bare all you lot inside the embassy will be getting your normal clothes, Scotch, cigarettes – whatever you want – and all the food you can eat.'

There was nothing either of us could say, and anyway André liked us; his words weren't motivated by malice.

As he waved goodbye, I said to Oregon, 'It does give me a funny feeling – the thought that the embassy will be just about the only spot in Paris where war will never physically impinge on us, even if it's surrounded by starving French and overfed Germans.'

'It gives me a funny feeling too,' Oregon admitted. 'Those inside that building will be onlookers at everything that takes place in Paris – yet as safe from violence as the Romans were in their ringside seats at the Colosseum.'

Oregon left me soon afterwards and I strolled up the Champs-Élysées to Fouqets. Even though almost all the restaurants were closed, Fouqets offered me quite a reasonable snack, after which I decided to walk home, as though through a city of the dead.

When I crossed the Concorde to head for the Left Bank, I looked back at the yawning avenue, in its way the most handsome street in the world, now abandoned by everyone but myself and three stray dogs. Even the four huge flags at each corner of the square hung in lifeless despair on this last night before other hands would haul down the tricolours and replace them with the banners of the master race.

The first German troops planned to enter Paris before 8 a.m., and, according to an American Embassy official, General von Studnitz, the C-in-C German forces, would arrive at the Hôtel Crillon at 9.45 precisely. He had commandeered this building for himself, and arrangements had been made for him to set up his headquarters in the Prince of Wales suite on the first floor and to make a formal call on the American ambassador at ten o'clock the same morning.

Long before that, however, as Oregon and I walked the streets, the endless procession of German vehicles, with their troops looking like fresh, silent, blond robots, pounded through the empty streets of Paris on this, its blackest day. They entered the city north and east of Notre-Dame, their traffic regulated without a hitch by German military police using red discs attached to short handles.

Only a few people were on the streets. Most, I felt sure, were peeping from behind closed shutters, ashamed to be seen watching history in the making. Here and there, though, knots of people did stand and look glumly, most of them stupefied by the youth and discipline of the German soldiers, each one looking freshly scrubbed. No one really knew what was happening, even how to behave. Paris, by deciding to become an open city, had fallen without a shot being fired in anger. But that was all they did know. Had France lost the war, or had they only lost a battle? Their confusion was increased by the thousands of French policemen in neatly pressed uniforms, lining the streets with their white batons at the ready. They almost looked as though they had made a special effort to smarten up for the occasion – as though royalty was going to visit Paris.

'They look as though they're enjoying it.' I instinctively lowered my voice.

'I don't think so,' Oregon said. 'It's their way of holding up their heads, as though telling the Germans that, though they're beaten, they're French and proud of it. Poor devils. They must be suffering.'

Perhaps surprisingly, I didn't feel much emotion. Significant occasions, I had already discovered, tend to freeze one's feelings, especially if you are occupied storing up facts and impressions for an article to be written later in the day. I was too busy to feel – except for the passing thought that only a few days ago I had been strolling down the Champs-Élysées in the sun with Sonia, and now she was God knows where, locked up in some bloody train heading for Italy – and not neutral Switzerland.

And so in a way the day passed by in a series of snapshots. I certainly wasn't going to miss the German commander's visit to Bullitt and, for this ceremony – if that's the proper word for it – Oregon and I and several other American correspondents were able to flash our press cards and stand inside the embassy courtyard. What happened had all the trappings of farce – if it hadn't been so pitiful.

The Hôtel Crillon was, of course, separated from the American Embassy by only one narrow street, the rue Boissy d'Anglas. Yet, though von Studnitz could have walked in three minutes to his nearest neighbour, so to speak, he was apparently determined to observe strict attention to protocol for the visit to the American ambassador. He was also determined to extract the last ounce of drama from this historic moment. From the American Embassy courtyard I could see the German commander climb into a large black Mercedes, flying the swastika. In this the German commander set off for the hundred-yard journey, preceded by an escort of motorcyclists, black leather contrasting with gleaming machines. At the front entrance to the Crillon they revved up their motors, then the cavalcade covered the distance in under two minutes, halting with shouted commands in the embassy courtyard.

Von Studnitz stepped out. I caught a glimpse of a short, dapper man wearing a monocle and a small moustache, reminding me of a *démodé* cavalry officer. Spurs clinking, his chest a spectrum of medals, his monocle firmly screwed into his right eye, he walked into the embassy – and out again ten minutes later.

I wondered what Bullitt must have been thinking.

'He's too goddamn vain to realise that by staying in Paris instead of following the government it was as though he's slapped every Frenchman in the face and told them they're finished,' said Oregon.

The day was not entirely devoid of humour. After the ceremony of handing over the city, Oregon was talking to a group of correspondents and embassy officials in the avenue Gabriel, outside the embassy gates, when a German lieutenant stopped, saluted politely, and asked, 'You're Americans?'

There was a chorus of affirmatives, after which the German asked, 'Can you tell us where we can find a decent hotel?'

'You must be joking!' We could not help laughing. 'The

city's yours, there are hundreds of empty hotels all over Paris. All you have to do is take your pick.'

So the miserable day continued. Following hard on the heels of the stormtroopers came experts ready to take over every section of Paris life. Their efficiency was incredible. One group of uniformed engineers drove to the main telephone exchange in the rue de Louvre while trained announcers and operators, also in uniform, seized the main radio station in the rue de Grenelle. Before midday Radio Paris was broadcasting programmes in German and music by Wagner. Before midday, too, four blood-red German flags dominated the Concorde – two over the Ministry of Marine, the other two over the Hôtel Crillon. Others floated over the Chamber of Deputies, the Senate, even over the Arc de Triomphe, with the tomb of the unknown warrior and the eternal flame beneath.

I walked towards the Eiffel Tower to see what was happening. The first flag the Germans tried to fly there was too large. It had taken some effort, for the lift had been sabotaged and the Germans had to walk all the way up – nearly seventeen hundred steps. I could see the flag flapping like a sail and then hear the sudden noise of ripping as the wind tore it. Half an hour later more German soldiers climbed the tower again to replace it with a smaller flag.

All this we took in our stride, eyes on watches to make sure we gave ourselves enough time to meet deadlines.

'This has to be a humdinger of a piece,' said Oregon. 'For once in the war you won't have to face a censor.'

It was true. The Germans planned to open a censor's office the following day, but for twenty-four hours Americans – and a few other neutral correspondents – were being permitted to file anything they wished to write. There was an obvious reason for this. There was nothing they could say that could irritate the Germans and there were no military secrets involved. I had arranged to file through the embassy, so I had plenty of time to return to the office and type my piece. Then I made my way back to the embassy to file. I wasn't particularly looking forward to the night that lay ahead – for I knew that as soon as I had handed in my story to the skeleton staff at the embassy I would have to set off and drive through the night to Tours. Only by leaving around midnight could I hope to beat the jams that would surely build up and choke the roads later in the day.

As I walked out of the embassy doors after filing, I had to stand on the steps for a moment to wait as a low gleaming Mercedes swept through the double doors of the courtyard and drew to a stop with a flourish. Everything about that moment infuriated me – the soldier in his jackboots clicking his heels as he opened the rear door, the exaggerated salute, the polished car, and above all the flag, the swastika, on a pennant near the offside fender. Without knowing why, I suddenly thought of poor, shy Jean-Pierre lying alone – dying before he had even begun to live.

The military driver held out a hand to help the unseen passenger as he leaned forward from the deep back seat. I watched – vaguely irritated but still intrigued, wondering who in the German hierarchy could possibly be visiting the American Embassy so late at night.

Since he was arriving in a chauffeur-driven German limousine, it never entered my head that the mysterious visitor wouldn't be a German.

But it wasn't a German. It was an American. Unsmilingly, the tall thin man declined the offer of the helping hand, stepped out, peered through the dim light as he climbed the steps and then, seeing me, exclaimed in his special up-and-down voice, 'Well *really*, Larry! A one-man reception committee? How did you know I was coming to see you?'

I stood there, almost gasping with horror, staring at my father as though unable to believe what I saw. Then I looked at the sinister long black car, the Nazi flag, the Nazi military chauffeur, and I suddenly realised that it *was* Papa – and that he wasn't being facetious, he wasn't trying to disguise anything, he wasn't even attempting an apology or to show some sense of shame. What he was doing seemed to him perfectly natural.

'But Papa!' I exploded. 'What the hell are you doing – being driven around by a German soldier? With a Nazi flag in a German military car?'

'Eh?' He seemed genuinely surprised. 'Oh, that's easily explained. Quite *easy*.'

'I can't see any easy explanation from where I'm standing.'

'Really, Larry – why *do* you jump to conclusions?' He started to climb the embassy steps.

'I can see the conclusions,' I cried bitterly.

'I *must* say, Larry' – he was suddenly testy – 'you are a very stupid man. There is a perfectly logical reason,' and with a short laugh, 'I'm not a – collaborator. I'm a perfectly good American citizen, even if I do have more than a dash of French blood in me.' Holding my arm, he guided me up the steps and inside the reception area where he said more gently, 'I have a few minutes before I see Bullitt.'

For a moment I was so stunned that I almost rushed down the steps without another word. But reason told me there must be some explanation – however misguided. There had to be. Whatever he might do, he wouldn't make a fool of himself like this. And he would never treat with the Germans, even though America was neutral and the Germans were not therefore our enemies. Not technically – but Papa was half French, he had dual nationality, while Grandma was a hundred-and-fifty-per-cent French. And so anti-German she would, I thought, even shoot her son on the spot if she had seen what I had seen that night.

'Come inside,' he said quietly.

My father whispered to the clerk behind the desk, presumably asking him to wait before announcing his arrival to Bullitt. Then he sat down on one of the blue *banquettes* facing the desk, back to the tall elegant windows.

'Young people get so excited, yes, *very* excited,' he exclaimed. 'Anybody'd think . . .'

'I did think,' I said, but more slowly now, more quietly.

'It's so very simple,' he sighed, as though tired with the effort of having to deal with idiots like me. 'When General Guderian occupied Reims the first thing he did was to appoint a German civilian to control the entire organisation of the champagne market. He's called' – even Papa couldn't help but chuckle at the absurdity of the title – 'The Führer of Champagne'.

'But what's that got to do with you in a German car?'

'Please Larry, *really*! "The Champagne Führer", whose name is Herr Gaertner, interviewed the head of several champagne houses to discuss the future. Very bleak, yes *very*,' he shook his head. 'But Gaertner is an expert on wine. He has vineyards just across the border from Alsace and he's a very sympathetic man. All the same the Germans have ordained that champagne sales to civilians are to be banned. Production will continue – but most of the output will go to the Germans. This was what I was told,' added my father. 'I didn't meet Herr Gaertner at the earlier meetings.'

'And then?' I was beginning to get more intrigued.

Slowly the story unfolded. It seemed that Herr Gaertner had discussed with all the champagne growers the prospect of electing one man to liaise with all the members of the Bureau de Champagne, the affiliation which since the turn of the century has always protected the interests of champagne.

'Well,' said Papa, and I could feel that he was pleased with himself, 'all the champagne houses unanimously asked me to become the delegate to deal with the Germans.'

'But is that such an honour?' I couldn't quite eliminate the edge of sarcasm in my voice, though Papa didn't notice it.

'Not an *honour*, good gracious no. But my colleagues feel that even though I am half French, the fact that I am a neutral American might help the – well, the common cause, yes, the *cause* – perhaps getting certain conditions eased.'

'What does your Herr Gaertner think of that?'

'In fact,' said my father, 'he's – well, a gentleman. Intelligent, educated at Harvard, and owns some very large vineyards.'

'And the car – why the German car?'

'Really, you *are* cross-examining me! It's no mystery, goodness me, no. I agreed to serve as chairman of the committee, but on one condition – that I went to see Bullitt and placed my problem on record at the embassy. I don't see that there's anything wrong in what I'm doing, but I wanted it clearly understood that I wouldn't take the job if the embassy didn't approve.'

As I sat there he added drily, 'Anyway, there was no other way I could drive to see Bullitt, thanks to you, I *must* say.'

'Me!'

'Well, you did take my Citroën and I'm too old to tear around the countryside in the dead of night in an M.G. Besides, an official German car makes it much easier to pass through road blocks.'

'I hope you won't regret it,' I said. 'Treating with the Germans . . .'

'I'm not treating,' he was suddenly angry. 'What a stupid thing to say. Yes, *really* stupid!'

'I'm sorry . . .'

'You should be. I've taken this job not to make life easy for the Germans but to make it easy for the *French*. To increase production and to make a profit and to provide jobs for the French. Really, you make me *very* cross, Larry. Now goodbye. I must talk to Bill Bullitt. Will I see you?'

'I'm off to Tours but . . .'

'I hope to see you in Douzy soon. Meanwhile I will look after the family, my friends – and if I can help them by borrowing the occasional German car for official business with the Germans, I shall not expect you to stop me.'

With that he turned to the desk without looking at me again. I had rarely seen him so furious. Or was it something else than anger, I wondered, as I walked solemnly across the courtyard to find my car? Was it a simulated anger disguising hidden doubt? Did my father secretly feel a sense of shame at being driven in style by a Nazi chauffeur – and on the very day that a fellow American had handed over this beautiful, tragic capital? Perhaps in a curious way Papa didn't realise the shame of it until he saw me and saw the look of horror on my face when he stepped out of the German car.

29

Long before I set off for Tours after the encounter with Papa the French government, unknown to most people in Paris, had been evacuated again – from Tours to Bordeaux. The idea of a Breton redoubt had, I learned later, been abandoned, largely because Madame de Portes and Weygand disliked what she called 'a stupid gamble'. Anyway, she didn't like de Gaulle. So I bypassed Tours, though I did not cross the

Gironde and struggle into the great seaport of Bordeaux until the Saturday afternoon – and by then even I could smell the air of defeat in the endless trail of haggard failures. Twice before, Bordeaux had been the provisional capital of France – in 1871 when the Germans occupied Paris, and for a brief spell when the capital was threatened in 1914.

The city was overflowing with refugees. There was hardly a hotel bedroom to spare, but I managed to park my car in the place de Quinconces which stretched in front of the striped awnings of the Hôtel Splendide terrace. The *place* was not a paved square in the usual sense of the word, but an open space normally reserved for fairs or exhibitions. It was bordered on the far side by the river. The authorities had obviously been preparing for a new fair for there were several abandoned pavilions advertising 'Les Vins de France'.

I had already spent one night in the Citroën on the way down, and was reconciled to spending another. The American Consulate in Bordeaux was in the rue Esprit-des-Lois where Jim Parks told me it had been elevated to the status of temporary embassy, adding sourly, 'I've got to share a twin-bedded room with nine people.'

At least Jim was able to put me in the picture. 'It's all over bar the shouting,' he admitted. 'But the boys tell me that de Gaulle is the man to watch. There's a vague rumour going round that if France gives in he's going to bolt for it – and try to fight on.'

Reynaud had set up his headquarters in the Quartier-Général, the headquarters of the Eighth Military Region in the rue Vital-Carles, a short street leading off Bordeaux's main shopping centre quaintly named the 'cours de l'Intendance'.

'I'd better go and see if I can contact him,' I said.

'Your best bet would be to check with the British,' Parks advised. 'They've taken over the Hôtel Montré – five minutes away from Reynaud's house – and if anyone does bolt for England you can bet your bottom dollar the British will be around to help.'

'I'll go there right away.'

'Go to one other place,' Jim said suddenly. 'The Portuguese Embassy. I gather it's just about the only place still issuing visas and it's hell there – even fighting in the queues. Shouldn't that make a good story, if nothing else?'

I'd already seen that the visa section of the American Embassy stretched in a queue half a mile long on the pavements outside. 'And it's as bad at the British Embassy,' said Parks.

Fear born of ignorance had struck terror into the hearts of a population swollen by hundreds of thousands of refugees. Only the brave or the foolish still dared to hope for a miracle. For the rest, nothing could throw off the stupor that blanketed the city. I could see the ugly mood among men and women of many nations who had been funnelled by circumstances into this one city, and who could no longer disguise from themselves that they had reached the end of their tether.

Outside the Portuguese Consulate, which was near the place des Quinconces, men fought like savages as they vainly queued for a visa to freedom. Jews, Czechs, Poles, German and Austrian refugees – all knowing they were marked for the concentration camps – tried to storm the consulate building. The Portuguese officials phoned the police, who did not even bother to answer the distress call.

Knowing the nature of their fate if the Germans caught them, these people did not realise that the Portuguese were issuing transit visas only, and these only to people whose passports were already franked with a visa for the country of ultimate destination. And for ninety-nine out of a hundred there was only one chance of getting this – unless they happened to know that the Republic of Haiti was prepared to stamp any passport with a resident's visa for a hundred and fifty francs.

The Portuguese Consulate was near the Splendide, and as I walked past the crowded terrace of the hotel I could even hear the welcome sound of ice tinkling in glasses.

During these fateful hours no one had any real news of the actual fighting. And there was no way of finding out. Anyway, what did it matter? I tried the British as well as the Americans. The British were probably better informed because after all it was their war as well as the war of France. But *no one* knew. At the embassy, though, I did meet an old British colleague, Harold King, who worked for Reuters news agency; he was one of the best informed English correspondents in France. He had driven down to Bordeaux and had a cubbyhole of a room at the Splendide with a sofa which he offered me in place of a bed. Better still, it had a bathroom, and after a shower King took me for dinner in what was recognised as the finest restaurant in all Bordeaux. It happened to be next to the Hôtel Montré, the 'temporary' British Embassy, and they had booked a large 'embassy table' at the Chapon Fin for every lunch and dinner. The food was impeccably cooked – everything from lobsters to soufflés. In the far corner of the room I spotted the swarthy features of Pierre Laval.

But then there were two worlds in Bordeaux during those last hours before the Germans snapped the handcuffs on France. If refugees without rooms filled the park benches, shopkeepers filled the shelves of their windows. In the cours de l'Intendance almost every imaginable article was on sale. Provocative dummies flaunted the latest fashions in dresses and hats for women. I replaced my wardrobe with a couple of the latest style shirts, a pair of slacks, socks, shoes.

It was the same even in every food shop. Though penniless thousands were unable to get a square meal, confectioners crammed their windows with mouth-watering displays of chocolate, the perfumiers with scent, the grocers with cheeses, rows of hams, mounds of pâtés, bottles of wine – at a price.

As far as the *Globe* was concerned I had plenty of colour stories, but I gave up trying to compete with spot news. I tried again and again to contact men close to Reynaud, but as the panic spread nobody had the time even to be polite. On the other hand, I didn't have to worry. It was by now becoming increasingly obvious that Pétain and Weygand (with Laval in the background, I was sure) were winning the battle to capitulate against the frenzied efforts of Reynaud and de Gaulle to continue the fight. And Jim Parks told me one other sobering fact: that Reynaud's mistress now believed it would be better to give in and was trying to influence Reynaud. The poor French premier was on the rack – and now his mistress was going to give the screw an extra turn. How long ago it seemed – and yet it was only a matter of hours – since Reynaud and de Gaulle shared a dream to continue the fight in

North Africa with its great fleet, and so keep the symbol of a living France in front of the world.

The dream seemed to have been shattered, but the one thing that never entered my head was the possibility of an alternative dream – one which, though in a different way, could still be the symbol of a living France. It came about late on the Sunday night when finally Reynaud had resigned and Pétain had succeeded him, and though he had not yet formed a cabinet it was obvious that he would immediately sue for armistice terms with Germany. To all intents and purposes the French had given up the fight.

I heard the news first from someone in the British-occupied Hôtel Montré which I visited every day. I walked the five minutes across the cours de l'Intendance to Reynaud's office in the hope of seeing him – or perhaps Madame de Portes – to pay my respects to the premier who had fought so magnificently, if in vain.

Reynaud's house and office in the Quartier-Général had a small courtyard facing the rue Vital-Carles, and behind the large front entrance an imposing hall. There were no longer any sentries at the door. It seemed impossible to realise yet that Reynaud held no more rank, but was just a private citizen of a country that had lost the war. As I reached the door another man approached. It was Major-General Sir Edward Spears, Churchill's liaison officer with the French, and a close friend of de Gaulle's. I had met him at the British Embassy and I nodded to him, and said, 'It's darned dark in here.'

It was. The spacious hall, which boasted several stone pillars, had a wide staircase at the rear. The only lighting came from one miserable bulb. The entrance hall was empty except for us. I realised that if I wanted to see Reynaud I must climb the wide stone stairs. As I stood there undecided, both of us heard in the eerie semi-darkness an urgent whisper, 'General Spears! I must speak to you!'

The man was French – and Spears spoke French as well as I did. To my astonishment, I saw a tall figure flattened against one of the columns, shrouded in its shadow.

It was de Gaulle. I couldn't believe it – this haughty, almost disdainful leader hiding like a criminal in an entrance smelling of dust. Urgently he whispered again, 'It's extremely necessary that I talk to you.' He caught sight of me. 'Oh! It's only you, Astell.' It was not a phrase expressing arrogance, more relief.

Spears whispered, 'I can't speak now. The British ambassador is going to take me to see Monsieur Reynaud.'

'You must,' insisted de Gaulle, still whispering and carrying on speaking. 'I have very good reason to believe that Weygand is planning to arrest me.'

Spears whispered to de Gaulle, warning him to stay just where he was, virtually hidden. He would, he promised, be back soon. I had at first been astonished to see de Gaulle at all, for I knew that on the previous day he had flown to London to see Churchill.

'I arrived back this afternoon,' he explained to me. 'In a British plane. Churchill gave orders for it to return to Britain tomorrow morning. And the crew knows that if I want to go to London they have orders to take me – but they must leave at nine o'clock in the morning.'

'If there's anything I can do . . .' I began, still whispering.

'Perhaps,' said de Gaulle gloomily. 'Weygand *is* going to try and arrest me. I insist that in some way France must continue the fight. He says that it's treason for anyone to continue fighting after an official armistice. I have great faith in the British – though we don't always see eye to eye. But I'm going to fight on.'

'Do you mind if I stay?' I asked. 'Or do you want me to leave?'

'Stay if you wish,' said de Gaulle. 'But no *reportage* until I am safely on British soil.'

Of course I promised. But I did need de Gaulle's permission, for Spears was known as a prickly British general who would be quite liable to kick me out of the place without a word. 'Perhaps you'd tell General Spears that I'm to be trusted,' and hesitating, for I didn't want to sound banal, added, 'and your friend.'

'I'll do that,' he muttered. 'Where the devil is Spears?'

A few minutes later the British general returned to the cavernous hall. I heard his footsteps on the empty stone floor. De Gaulle was so well hidden that at first Spears didn't see us, with de Gaulle standing bolt upright, his back to a column so that he couldn't possibly be seen by anyone entering through the front doors.

Moving to the rear wall where we were even more hidden, we held an impromptu conference. The gist of it, in whispered conversation, was that de Gaulle had decided to accept Churchill's offer of a seat on the British plane which was waiting at Merignac, the military airfield for Bordeaux. But he had to make his way in secret early on the following morning, for which he needed a car. He also needed a place to hide for the night.

Spears had his car but didn't advise de Gaulle to take it over. No doubt he thought, as I did, that de Gaulle's presence in an official car would probably be reported back to Pétain or Weygand in a matter of moments.

'As to hiding, well, there must be some spare place in the Hôtel Montré,' said Spears. 'And that is only five minutes away.'

'We will take a chance and walk there together,' said de Gaulle to me. 'Astell can show me the way.'

'And I do have my car if you need it tomorrow,' I offered.

Spears drove ahead. De Gaulle and I followed, and as soon as I had slid his tall frame past the glass entrance door to the hotel we looked around for a place to sleep. To the right of the hall was the old-fashioned salon, reached by steps lined by statues of semi-naked ladies. We sat down on the red plush Empire-style chairs while de Gaulle explained more fully to Spears why he felt he must go to London immediately. He not only wanted to continue the fight – and that would be impossible in France – but he wanted above all to broadcast to Frenchmen, to appeal for continued resistance before the defeatists broadcast *their* message. De Gaulle's only chance was to reach Merignac airfield which could soon be in Weygand's hands, and fly to Britain in Churchill's aircraft.

Finally, after de Gaulle prepared to doss down in a small *salon*, on the largest sofa he could find to accommodate his lanky legs, it was agreed that we would all prepare to leave the Hôtel Montré at 7 a.m. the following morning.

Sleep was out of the question for hours. The excitement of being an eyewitness to history kept my mind so alert I could think of nothing except the prospect of the following day. If I did manage to help de Gaulle to escape, how the hell would I ever be able to get the story out? And could de Gaulle escape? I hoped so. I admired him greatly, though whether he could do anything from Britain, already girding itself for possible invasion by the Germans, was a different matter. Thoughts kept crowding in, until at last I fell into a troubled sleep. I awoke early to go and fetch the morning edition of *Le Journal* which had continued publication in Bordeaux. I took it to de Gaulle, with a roll and some coffee, and let him see the headlines himself:

PÉTAIN A LA TÊTE DU GOUVERNEMENT
PAUL REYNAUD A DÉMISSIONÉ

'He tried his best,' was all de Gaulle said, then added with his usual irony, 'He might have succeeded but for that woman.'

Within a few minutes, with me driving, Spears next to me, de Gaulle half crouching, sitting sideways in the back seat, we set off. We did not take the direct route to the airfield. Still convinced that Weygand planned to arrest him, de Gaulle was determined to disguise his flight in case any officials saw him and reported back. He seemed afraid that the French commandant at the airfield might already have received orders to prevent him flying to Britain.

We stopped first at the Ministry of War where de Gaulle, without leaving his seat, made a great play of arranging a number of appointments for the rest of the day. While he made plans, I kept the motor running just in case we had to make a dash for it.

We enacted a similar drama at another building housing some war ministry personnel. Only then did de Gaulle agree to make for the airfield, which we reached just before 9 a.m. As the car turned onto the bomb-pitted apron in front of the control room we all looked round in disgust. It was not a scene of pillage or destruction that made us angry; the airfield was filled with hundreds of aircraft packed wing to wing – and none of them was apparently preparing to take off for North Africa.

Now we had to find the solitary British plane, and our task was made more difficult because we could hardly manipulate the car through the tightly packed lines of aircraft. Yet we needed the car because de Gaulle had piled in a lot of luggage. At last I found it. There was an agonising delay while the luggage was stowed. All seemed ready, but then the pilot insisted that de Gaulle's heavy trunk, filled with papers, should be lashed in case they ran into bumpy weather. This was more easily said than done, for there was nothing with which to tie it up. One of the aircrew ran off to find some rope; it all took another precious ten minutes.

Still worried that he might be stopped if anyone saw him get in first, de Gaulle insisted on playing one last scene. When the luggage was stowed and the propellers turning, Spears jumped into the aircraft. I followed him while de Gaulle, pretending to wave farewell, stood by the plane. At the last second, at the very moment when the chocks were pulled from under the wheels, de Gaulle leaned forward as though for a final handshake. Then as we jumped out he clambered aboard. The pilot revved up the engines and roared along the runway. Within a few minutes the tiny plane was over the sea and heading for Britain.

For me, that was the end of the fight for France. What follows was anti-climax, including the armistice terms and the eventual partition of the country to give Pétain a government in Vichy. In the here-and-now – a matter of hours – I had to make an urgent decision. I was sitting on one of the hottest stories any newspaperman had ever had – I had helped de Gaulle to *escape*. But de Gaulle had told me that Churchill not only approved of the French setting up some sort of Free French movement, but that he wanted to broadcast to France the day after he arrived in England. And that – however important to history – would kill my story stone dead unless I could print the details of his flight beforehand. I had to file this day.

I could almost feel the sharp intake of excitement, the electricity of achievement at the prospect of the challenge, the hunger of my own ego. This was an exclusive account of a major historical event, one in which – did I even dare to say this? – I had played a minor role by helping de Gaulle on his way. It might well rank as one of the supreme moments of my life as a journalist — and a signpost to my future.

But how would I achieve this? With the new government thirsting for de Gaulle's blood I knew that no cable office in France would ever transmit my story without higher authority. The makeshift American Embassy couldn't help, simply because they had given an undertaking to cable only messages passed by the censor. And though Reynaud had helped me once, he could not help me now.

It was 10 a.m. Spears got a lift back to Bordeaux in the car which had brought the aircrew to Merignac. I stayed — for the moment — all manner of wild ideas crossing my mind. Could I rent a speedboat at the mouth of the Gironde and make for the Spanish coast by sea? If only I could charter an aircraft! Impossible, of course. I discarded them — although discard is perhaps too strong a word. It suggests a choice, and in fact I had none.

Except one. With the time difference between Washington and France, I did not need to file a story before midnight. That gave me twelve hours, even longer. Why not drive to Spain and phone my story directly from there? It was barely a hundred miles, and I had the last of my petrol in the champagne bottles. I had also a fair supply of dollars as well as plenty of French currency. And I had a Spanish visa.

It was the only way. And since there was no hope of filing from France I would be no worse off if I failed to reach Spain.

I crossed the bridge at Hendaye at 7 p.m., my eyes tired from peering through the dirty, fly-specked windscreen. The motor was burning hot from hours of stopping and starting. On the whole, though, the trip had been much easier than the earlier one down to Tours, simply because half-way along the crowded roads the French police turned everyone back who didn't have the necessary visa. I had to queue before we reached the police, but after that I had a straight run into the checkpoint at the frontier and then I was only thirty miles or so from San Sebastian, the nearest large town in Spain.

I made my way to the biggest hotel, the Reina Cristina, booked a room, then walked up to the *concierge*. In nine cases out of ten the *concierge* is the man who can achieve the impossible — especially if you flash a few dollar bills around.

417

But when I told him I wanted to call Washington – and for around twenty minutes without being disturbed – even he looked dumbfounded.

'Look,' I said desperately. 'I know it can be done if someone like you really tries. I know the connections are always difficult, but can't you have a word with the girl who operates the switchboard? I'll pay in dollars and I'll tell you what, *concierge* – if you can get me through to Washington I'll give you a couple of hundred bucks and you can tell your girl behind the switchboard that I'll give her an extra hundred for herself. Is that fair?'

Dollars still talked – especially in miserably impoverished Spain. I booked a person-to-person call to Schill Scotter, the editor, and when I finally got through, two hours later, he gave almost a yelp of surprise.

'Where the hell are you?'

'San Sebastian, Spain. This morning I helped de Gaulle to escape. Absolutely exclusive.'

'Jesus! I'll get you through to dictation.'

'I'm frightened of getting cut off. And anyway I haven't written the story yet I haven't had time.'

'Don't worry.' Schill acted swiftly. I'd never met the editor but I could tell that he was a man of action. 'My secretary's right here. I'm listening in on the extension. Just start telling her the story in your own words and we'll lick it into shape when you've finished.'

I spoke for fifteen minutes. 'You'll have to polish it,' I said, voice croaking with the effort of talking.

'Terrific!' he cried. 'We'll have a brand new slant on the whole war. Jesus! Is this going to make your name for ever.'

It sounds crazy – even indecent weighed against the tragedy of France – but I was a newspaperman, and I couldn't help feeling an excited glow which only someone in the newspaper business can understand; not only *managing* a scoop – but the even more difficult business of getting the news out when everyone else wanted to hide it. The greatest story in the world has no real value to a newspaperman if you can't get it to your editor.

The *concierge* had entered into the spirit of the adventure and was delighted that I had succeeded. I paid him and his assistant off – and by the time I had settled for the phone call I had only a few dollars left in my pocket, though I had plenty of French currency, which the hotel would have to accept.

However, the enthusiasm of the *concierge* made me want to try another 'adventure'. I was in a neutral country. Why couldn't I try to phone Sonia at her father's home in Rome?

'Why not?' said the *concierge*, still excited by what we had done – but also making it clear that he would expect further remuneration for any new service he could render me.

'I'm running short of dollars,' I said. 'Are francs possible?'

'I regret, sir.' He spread out his hands in apology.

'But I have no more dollars.'

He hesitated, thinking. 'This is not a matter for the Spanish authorities,' he said. 'For them I can exchange French francs and put the call to Italy on your bill, sir, but – well, I am not supposed to do this, sir, you must understand. I'll risk my neck. The new régime in Spain' – he didn't need to elaborate. He wanted a bribe – and he didn't favour French francs which might be worthless in twenty-four hours.

Finally he explained, 'You see, sir, we are all so poor – especially here in the north – many dead – and although I look as though I have a good job we can only make both ends meet – if *monsieur* has perhaps a *very* small piece of jewellery I could sell for him, or a gold coin perhaps?'

'I don't wear jewellery;' I forgot the irony of my reply. 'No rings. And in this weather – but wait . . .' I had a sudden thought.

I hadn't even been to my room yet; the overnight bag was still in the front hall. And I remembered that I *did* have some jewellery. When Sonia and I set off from Paris I was wearing the shirt with her cufflinks in it.

Her cufflinks. Solid gold with four small emeralds, one in the centre of each link. The ones Sonia had given me for my birthday, and which I had promised her I would never lose.

I had promised. But now, what were the true values we faced in the blue carpeted entrance of the Hôtel Reina Cristina? What was more important – a pair of cufflinks she or I could replace when peace came, or five minutes of spoken words at a moment in our lives when both of us were beset with anxiety about our immediate future? If a pair of cufflinks – wrapped in a promise – could give us the opportunity to tell each of us that we were safe at this climax to the war, surely the price was cheap. And the cufflinks could be replaced. If I kept them, those words of love and encouragement would never be spoken.

There was no choice. Minutes later I was giving him the number of Sonia's parents' house in Rome. 'Person to person,' I said, 'to the Countess de Feo. And no connection, no pay.'

'I will make the connection.' He eyed the cufflinks greedily. 'There may be a delay, so may I suggest that you take the call in your room.'

The call came through at two o'clock in the morning. Her words, her voice, her love distorted by distance, the seas separating us, the neutrals from enemies, but still, it was her voice.

'My darling,' she cried. 'Where are you?'

'In Spain!'

I told her I was returning to France the following morning, and in the faint voice that somehow seemed washed by the waves that separated us she told me that she was leaving soon for Rolle. Everything had been fixed up and if I could go there she would be waiting for me.

'I'll try,' I promised.

'Give me a couple of weeks and I'll be in Switzerland.'

'Still love me?' It was a stupid question, but suddenly after all the talking to Washington I couldn't think of anything new to say.

'Never so much as now. Oh darling, thank you for phoning. I've been so worried – and now, just hearing you, I feel safe and secure. And darling – I've seen Francesco and he's told me . . .' At that moment the phone clicked and we were cut off. I rattled the ancient instrument. God! How infuriating. Told me what? Yes or no? Yes to a new life? Together? I banged the instrument in desperation. But I never got the call reconnected.

30

In the months following the armistice it was as though I lived in two countries, the difference was so marked between country life in Douzy and city life in Paris, the hub of occupied France. Several factors enabled me to spend so much time away from Paris. First, there was a dearth of news from Paris. Britain, with the possibility of an invasion, then the Blitz, soon replaced France as a news centre. Then I was able to travel fairly regularly between Paris and Douzy because the Germans, with typical thoroughness, had improved the telephone system so that not only Oregon could phone me but at times even Washington was able to reach me on my direct line. Finally, now the war was over, Tommy Tomlinson had put his uniform in mothballs and was in Paris waiting for transport back to America, where he had been appointed Foreign Editor of the *Globe*. So he was at a loose end – and this could provide me with an extra insurance against being caught away from Paris if a major news story developed.

So I got into the habit of visiting Douzy almost weekly, not only because I felt less lonely there without Sonia but because I had this feeling that I could give the troubled family – Papa, Grandma, Anna, Guy and Olivia – a kind of moral support.

Though outwardly unchanged, nothing could disguise the difference in spirit. Our neutral enclave had been invested with sinister overtones of a prison without bars. There might be no barbed wire, no probing searchlights on squat watchtowers, but once outside our own land the Germans were everywhere. It had been like this ever since the armistice was signed, when the town crier stood on the village square at Douzy and gave a roll on the drum to summon the villagers.

'*Avis!*' he had cried, the signal for doors to fly open, shutters to be thrown back, windows to be pushed open.

'Today, 26 June,' announced the town crier sonorously, 'is a day of national mourning. At 11 everyone will gather at the war memorial. A one-minute silence will unite the nation's homage to the glorious dead of 1914–1918 and those no less glorious of 1939–40.'

The people dispersed; they had fifteen minutes to change into black which, as most of them were peasants, meant their Sunday-best clothes.

The next day the swastika flew over the ugly square tower of Douzy church. Signs appeared everywhere. Each empty house bore the warning, 'Anyone found in an abandoned habitation will be considered a looter and will be liable to capital punishment.'

Every night German soldiers policed the winding narrow streets of Douzy to enforce the blackout. When a chink of light showed in the Café des Sports the first that Monsieur Roland heard was the blast of a whistle. Roland had no idea he was in trouble, until three minutes later – the official time allowed – when a German shot all the glass out of his windows.

'It wasn't the shots that frightened me,' Roland moaned later, 'but the fact that it took three months to get the panes of glass to mend the window.'

Not far from Douzy, in a large field where the corn had been reduced to stubble, fifteen thousand French soldiers spent a miserable three weeks behind barbed wire, with no real shelter and very little food. On my next visit to Douzy they had vanished; I could only hope that with peace they had been sent home, but I never found out what happened to them.

Germans from country areas even tried to help fellow peasants as the time for the *vendange* approached. Douzy certainly needed help for the harvesting of the grapes, for there was no way we could expect the usual transit harvesters to travel from the coal mines of Lorraine to Douzy and other champagne vineyards as they had done in the past. And these men and women were experienced by tradition.

'It looks as though we'll have to rely on inexperienced volunteers,' said Papa. '*Very* disturbing.'

Then one day a German sergeant arrived on a dusty grey motor cycle. His name was Sergeant Bischwihr – a typical Alsace name. According to Papa the man said, 'Yes, sir, I come from across the border beyond Colmar.' He was with a unit, he explained, which included many men who worked in the vineyards.

'We are about twenty,' he said in passable French, 'and if you wish, sir, we would like to help out with the harvest. We are bored here — there is nothing to do. Our commandant has given his approval.'

At first Papa thought it was a great idea. 'He was all for it,' said Guy when recounting what had happened. 'And, to be frank, so was I. I was getting more involved with the vineyard and the leader seemed a decent enough chap, a vigneron like us. It wasn't *his* fault he'd been dragged into a war, any more than poor old Willi's.'

'And I have to admit — yes, I *do*,' said Papa, 'that the soil — er — brings all people *together*.'

During this brief moment when the German was politely standing twiddling his field cap, fully expecting to be thanked for his offer of help, Olivia walked in. With an almost rueful grin, rather like a boy caught doing something he knows he shouldn't, Guy told me, 'she went as white as a sheet, and as soon as she heard the German discussing the prospect of work, she stormed out of the room. I dashed after her, she shouted — yes, shouted, I never heard anything like it — that if just one German worked in the vineyards, she was leaving Douzy for ever and would never come back. Phew, Larry! She was tough. And outraged. But that was nothing to what happened next.'

Grandma, it transpired, had come into the hall during the brief shouting match in the salon next to the living room. When she opened the door, Olivia burst into tears and cried, 'The Germans are in the next room!'

I could imagine the set of Grandma's jaw. And the look of astonishment on the face of the quiet German as she walked in wearing her cycling uniform of slacks, green jacket, broad belt and felt hat — the uniform which was the trademark of La Châtelaine. Guy followed her in, watched, listened as, in her haughtiest voice, Grandma cried to my father, 'Who is this creature?'

'A German soldier who . . .'

'I can see he is a German. But what is he doing soiling this Aubusson carpet?'

The German began to flush, first pink, then slowly turning to puce. 'My boots are clean, *frau* — and I'd thank you to mind your manners.'

'He only wanted to help with the *vendange*,' Papa tried to explain.

'Don't worry, old woman,' the German replied. 'If that's all the thanks I get for helping people in a country that's rotten to the core . . .'

'You may leave my house,' said Grandma without losing her dignity. 'I would rather lose the entire harvest than let one Boche touch one grape on our vines.'

'I've heard of you,' sneered the German, and how astonishing, said Guy, it was to see the way quiet people can be transformed by anger, aroused by circumstances. 'They call you La Châtelaine. As far as I'm concerned you're *une vieille chatte*.'

I said to Guy laughingly of the confrontation, 'She's sure got a temper! Olivia, I mean.'

'Doesn't show often,' Guy laughed too. 'Normally she's very quiet, almost placid.'

I wondered, thinking back to the night in the apartment. Did a woman become placid – or unplacid, if that was the word? – because of the influence of her partner? Olivia hadn't been placid when rioting near the Châtelet or in bed afterwards. But Guy had settled down to a quiet, easygoing life – after the one moment when he gained his demand – and perhaps, like a good wife or lover, Olivia had accommodated her life to Guy's. She couldn't always have been placid by nature. Nor for that matter could Guy. After all, he had gone to bed with Mlle Lisette, with disastrous results, and yet, didn't he ever want to know what had happened to the child? His child. It seemed as though to Guy it had never existed. And Guy didn't invite confidences. He was never affable when asked leading questions; he just smiled vaguely and made no reply. I tried him now with one.

'She's a great girl,' I said. 'Do you and Olivia ever plan to – well, get married? You've been together for a helluva long time.'

'Never given the matter any thought,' he replied. 'I suppose if Olivia got angry and started demanding her "rights" – or whatever you call them – I'd have to start thinking. Don't know what I'd do. But I have a feeling that Olivia might not want to marry me.'

Anna came in just as Guy, still in the same vein, asked me, 'And what about you and Sonia?'

'Never mind us − you have bigger problems.' I turned to Anna. 'What are *your* plans?'

'I don't care,' she said. 'I've decided to stay − and in a way I'm much more worried about Papa. He's working himself into the grave trying to help the French to produce champagne − all for the bloody Germans to swill down.'

'But what exactly is he doing?' I asked.

Guy shrugged his shoulders. 'I dunno. But the commander of the German garrison in Reims and the German Champagne Führer seem to agree with everything that Papa wants. I suppose it's because Papa keeps production up − and keeps all unrest quiet.'

Though I didn't really understand what Papa was doing I couldn't keep from asking, 'Is it right for an American − or a Frenchman − to encourage the French to work harder?'

Some weeks after this I was again visiting Douzy, and this time I was actually there when a German officer arrived and asked to speak to Papa. Though he looked presentable and polite, with none of the swagger which films of Nazi parades had led us to believe was normal, I still found it hard to be civil.

'I'm the son of the house,' I said. 'My father has just gone out for a walk.' I felt a sudden anger at his presence − nothing to do with the poor German, but because I knew that the moment Aubergine had seen the Nazi flag on the car at the bottom of the drive she must have rushed to warn Anna to stay in the stables. It was so bloody demeaning − for Anna to have to hide in our own house.

'May I wait, Herr Astell?' he asked politely.

I couldn't say no, but left him in the uncomfortable salon until Papa arrived a quarter of an hour later. He, too, always panicked on the rare occasions when we were visited by Germans. 'There's always the feeling at the back of my mind,' he confessed once, 'that they've found out about Anna and have come to fetch her away.'

This time, however, the visit had nothing to do with Anna. The officer, a Captain Deschuer, had come on a very different matter.

'I have been asked by Major Kissling, the commander in Reims, to request' – he hesitated, politely trying to make an order sound more like a request – 'that the pyramid at Douzy be closed forthwith and placed under a German guard.'

My father jumped up. I'd never seen him so suddenly angry.

'Close Douzy pyramid! What on earth for? This is American property, I would remind you!'

'I'm sorry, sir, please do not be alarmed.' The officer looked more terrified than a symbol of German might. 'There is a very good reason.'

'It is American property. There can be no good reason, and I refuse to listen to one. I shall telephone to Major Kissling immediately.'

'Perhaps, Papa,' I tried to soothe him, 'we should find out.'

'Why, Captain?'

'I have the papers here, Herr Astell. Four men were arrested two nights ago in the cellars of Douzy pyramid. They were Frenchmen who were discovered manufacturing explosives. I regret, Herr Astell, but there is no doubt about it.'

'Who are they?'

'I do not know. They are now in jail. The pyramid is too difficult to guard, Herr Astell. If it is locked up you will be saved much inconvenience.'

'And my stocks of champagne! Really, Captain, my *champagne*.'

'It will be sealed and remain untouched,' the officer promised. 'The commander has told me he's given you his word.'

In fact the idea of closing off the potential hide-out for the few Frenchmen did make sense. Many men were beginning to form a resistance in country areas. Anyone could get lost in those tunnels of Douzy and make all the explosives they wanted without being discovered. But it was a sudden twist to the conversation that made me open my eyes.

'I was planning to use our pyramid to increase production,' my father protested – to my astonishment. 'It has been arranged with Major Kissling.'

'The major regrets,' said the captain, 'and suggests you might like to do the extra work in the pyramid at Rilly.'

'What's all this about?' I asked.

'It's nothing, nothing really. Our pyramid seemed a good

place to store champagne when production increases. Really – the Germans are' – my father hesitated to use the word 'stupid'.

'Like any army we are bogged down in red tape, Herr Astell. I apologise. But please do understand that the cellars in the pyramid at Rilly are smaller, safer, and next to the village, so that the danger of' – he coughed again – 'unauthorised entry is minimal.'

He was right. Douzy was a huge pyramid in comparison with Rilly – and who wanted a deep cavern like that just to make champagne for the Germans? It was a showplace rather than a going concern.

The Douzy pyramid lay between our house and the main railway line linking Reims and Épernay, close to the point at Rilly station where it entered the tunnel under the Montagne de Champagne. Rilly pyramid lay on the other side of the railway. Each pyramid was so close to the tunnel that they even had underground passages, formed many years ago, leading to platforms on either side of the tunnel in the days when the champagne was pushed from the cellar to the railway and loaded up by the end of the tunnel fifty yards distant. But they had been closed for years.

Some weeks later two curious events happened in quick succession. First, the Germans blocked the southern end of the Rilly tunnel. Not at Rilly village, but at the southern end, where it emerged in the sunlight before travelling on the last lap from Reims to Épernay. The entire south face of the exit – exit, that is, if you were travelling southwards – was blown up and left a mass of debris. It seemed to be the height of folly. Trains would now have to take a slow circuitous route between the two most important towns in the area. And anyway, if the Germans had blown up the southern end of the tunnel, why not the north end as well?

Two weeks later, on a bright moonlit night, a small force of R.A.F. planes flew straight to a pinpoint they had obviously marked exactly on their charts. There they unloaded every bomb in their planes – all of them on the sleepy little village of Rilly. It seemed crazy, even more so when they returned three times to bomb the village again.

'I did have faith in the R.A.F.' Guy summed up bitterly what everyone thought, 'But they must be stark staring mad to bomb an unimportant village like Rilly.'

Not for a long time did it occur to me that the Germans had deliberately left the north end of the tunnel open, and that the R.A.F. had been trying unsuccessfully to close the tunnel by bombing it – obviously to seal it off, but for what? The pyramids? The tunnel itself? It didn't seem to make sense.

Then the German army picked up Olivia.

I was virtually alone in the house when it happened. Anna was upstairs, Papa in the Rilly cellars, Grandma out in the vineyards, while Guy and Olivia had cycled across the valley road to take some eggs from the Home Farm to the Misses B and B, who still lived in their small cottage on part of our land.

I had seen Guy and Olivia set off on their bikes – Olivia, as one might expect, sitting upright and steady, Guy wobbling a bit and laughing as he hit a rut and nearly knocking into her. I was thinking, 'How ironic that Grandma's insistence on cycling everywhere for all these years should now be copied by all of us.' We cycled all over the vineyards, conserving our petrol for longer journeys, even though we had our secret stocks.

Anna almost never went out – which was why she was upstairs; she was intelligent enough to realise that it was dangerous to go into the village of Douzy even, especially as the end of the war had been followed by dozens of sinister promulgations. It was now an offence punishable by the death penalty to harbour a German refugee – and Anna *was* being harboured. I don't think the Germans would have dared to arrest the other members of the family, all of them neutral Americans, for hiding a German relative – but they would certainly arrest Anna. She knew that.

I also had twinges of apprehension whenever Olivia went out. She didn't go far, and never into Reims, but she made regular trips in the countryside. Apart from anything else, some of the vineyards were quite a distance from our home. In theory there was no real danger because we had our own I.D. cards (and for the family, American passports). She was 'accredited' to the neutral Astells, and though the countryside was at times crawling with Germans from a large camp in the hills behind the B and B cottage, where they had a firing range, they didn't seem to interfere. On the other hand, by now – the autumn of 1940 – both the German and French attitude to Jews in France was hardening. Many shops displayed signs: 'Out of Bounds to Jews'. Anyone asking for a job now had to swear on oath that he or she wasn't a Jew or a Freemason. Olivia, who didn't look particularly Jewish, had never registered as a Jew. Papa had declared firmly, 'She's a member of our family. That's the end of it. Her race has nothing to do with anybody, *really*.'

He was right, but we all prayed that it would never come to a showdown.

It did – half an hour or so after she and Guy had left on their bikes. I was in the courtyard when Aubergine fluttered out crying, 'Please, sir, Monsieur Guy is on the telephone. He says it's very urgent.'

I had no sense of premonition – just the niggling fear that was always present those days at the mention of the word 'urgent'. Grabbing the phone, I said, 'What's the problem?'

'It's Guy here. Where the hell have you been?'

'I am allowed to go for a walk,' I said.

'Cut out the crap, Larry.' Guy's voice warned me that he was on the edge of panic.

'Sorry. What's the trouble?'

'Olivia's gone.'

'What do you mean – gone? Where are you?'

'Near the Grand Champagne.' He mentioned the name of the large hotel half-way up the hillside. 'They've taken Olivia away.'

'Taken her?'

'For God's sake, do something . . .'

'But who took her?'

'The fucking Germans, who do you think? They just walked in, grabbed her and took her away.'

'But they can't . . .'

'There's a bloody war on, Larry – and she's Jewish. They even knew her name – who she was.'

'That's impossible.'

'It's happened.'

429

'Stay put. I'll come over. It'll only take me a few minutes. Any Germans around?'

'Not too many. That's what makes the whole thing so goddamn mysterious.'

'But what exactly happened?'

'We decided after we'd dropped the eggs to go and have a drink at the Grand Champagne. A German officer came in – he was expecting us. Or it seemed like that. He was very polite – saluted, heels clicking and all that crap. He didn't even look at my passport closely. All he said was, "I advise you, Herr Astell, to stay indoors for the moment."'

'He knew your name?' According to Guy, the German officer turned to Olivia and said not quite so politely, 'Are you Fräulein Jacobsen?'

Then he told her she was wanted for questioning. He clapped his hands, soldiers approached. Some of the hotel staff were peering from behind half-open doors like rabbits, mesmerised. Olivia, it seemed, was suddenly grabbed by two of the German soldiers. She tore her arms free and stood there. Guy, as he told me later, rushed up to put an arm round her shoulder. The German soldiers looked at the officer, who nodded.

'You would be wise to observe your American neutrality, Herr Astell,' said the officer.

'Tell your bloody goons to take their hands off this girl,' shouted Guy. 'Then we'll talk.' The 'goons' hesitated.

'The girl is not under arrest,' said the officer, obviously trying to prevent a fight with a neutral. 'She is only being detained for routine questioning.'

'Well, you can detain her another time,' shouted Guy. 'She's under my protection now – and I know my rights. I'm an American citizen.'

The officer, Guy remembers, gave another almost imperceptible nod. Three soldiers grabbed Guy from the back, pinning his arms back from the shoulders until he could feel the pain that almost dislocated his joints. He kicked and struggled to free himself, screaming to Olivia to run for it – an instinctive scream, for he knew in his heart there was no way of escape.

Held by the vicelike grip of three burly German soldiers,

oblivious to Guy's kicks as he struggled to twist himself free, he watched as the two other soldiers grabbed Olivia and marched her outside the hotel. Guy could see her being bundled into a large grey truck with flapping canvas roof and sides. A group of soldiers was already sitting in the back and started laughing and shouting as she all but fell inside.

'As soon as she had gone,' said Guy, 'the soldiers freed my arms, but by then the truck had disappeared.'

I wasted no time on further questions.

'Stay where you are at the Grand Champagne,' I suggested. 'I'll be round in ten minutes in the Citroën.' I set off on the winding road up the hill under which the Rilly tunnel stood. There was something sinister about the whole affair, dozens of unanswered questions. How had the Germans picked Olivia out? There must be dozens of Jewish girls in the Champagne region, but they had even known her *name*. Why should the mighty *Wehrmacht* send an officer to one specific hotel to meet one neutral American whom he greeted by name, then take away his Jewish girlfriend? And what worried me too was the thought that if they could do this to Olivia – know all about her – might not Anna be the next in line?

The road was virtually free – by which I mean I was only stopped at one checkpoint where a polite officer saluted me when I showed my pass and waved me on. Then, as the Citroën climbed the hairpin bends leading to the hotel, I had a sudden thought. I would telephone Papa and tell him what had happened – but not from the hotel; there might still be a German sentry around, and I didn't want to look for trouble. Much better to stop first at the cottage where the Misses B and B lived, though Papa had tried to persuade them that they must leave Champagne and return to their apartment in Paris.

I stopped the car outside their trim white cottage, which the Misses B and B had furnished as though they had gone to painstaking trouble to provide a place which exactly reflected their characters. The cottage itself was small and old, and the gate creaked as I pushed it open and strode down the small crazy-paving path with its carefully tended flowers on either side – geraniums with borders of bright blue lobelia, and behind that windows framed in rambler roses. The interior was hidden by white curtains. I was convinced that the living room would have an old-fashioned barometer and – yes! – there was a rocking chair, which I had also expected. It was very clean, and there was the unmistakable odour which goes with sachets of lavender in every drawer.

'I just wanted to use your phone,' I asked Miss Brewer. 'Do you mind?'

'Of course, Larry. You know where it is.'

Local calls were much easier now and I got through to Papa in the new headquarters of the German-run Champagne Bureau at Rilly. Without preamble I told him what had happened to Olivia, adding, 'I'm on my way to the Grand Champagne now. As far as I can see, Guy's very lucky he didn't get beaten up.'

'There *must* be a mistake,' Papa was horrified. 'Must be, *yes*. I will go and see Gaertner right away – and the German officer, Major Kissling. I have met him several times. He will help if he can. Yes, he *must*.'

As I begged Papa to hurry, he cried, 'I'm going right now to see Major Kissling at the *Hôtel de Ville*. And as you're at the cottage, don't you think you should warn the – er – ladies to return to Paris? Yes, *really* it's very silly for them to live alone in that small cottage.'

Before leaving I said to the Misses B and B, 'There's been trouble. Olivia has been arrested by the police.'

'Oh dear,' said one of them, 'she and Guy didn't seem to be in any trouble just a short time ago.'

'Well, she is – and *you* might be in trouble one day. I don't want to frighten you, but I really think you should prepare to go to Paris.'

'Oh, we couldn't do that, we couldn't leave the garden,' said Miss Brewer, nodding. 'Not until we've decided to go for good. But' – with a smile – 'we do keep a couple of suitcases packed ready.'

'You may need them.' I was anxious to get away, to see Guy, but there was no way you could ever shorten conversations with either of the Misses B and B.

'The only trouble,' said Miss Barron, 'is that I can't close my suitcase.'

'Let me help you,' I said desperately. 'Then I *must* go.'

'It's in here,' she said.

Closing Miss Barron's suitcase wasn't difficult. She had left some clothes hanging out. I helped to tuck them in. On top of the dresser was an open American passport with a school-boyish face staring out. It was poor Jean-Pierre.

'Poor boy,' Miss Barron sighed. 'Such a short life, and he was so much in love with Anna.'

'He never had much chance there.' Miss Brewer picked up the passport, eyes bright with unshed tears, as she kissed the photo.

At the gate I paused, remembering the comment that hadn't properly registered. 'You say you *saw* Guy and Olivia.'

They nodded. 'They said they were going to the hotel for a drink.'

The thought that anyone had warned the Germans about Olivia was preposterous, so it was almost idly that I asked, as I jumped into my car, 'Did you have any other visitors?'

'Only Mademoiselle Lisette,' Miss Barron said. 'She often drops in to see us, you know. Her cottage is only a quarter of a mile from us, on your father's property.'

I suddenly went ice cold, almost trembling.

'She just missed Guy and Olivia,' said Miss Brewer bright-ly, nodding in emphasis. 'They were just leaving, but I know mademoiselle saw them because she asked where they were going.'

Pressing the starter ready to make for the Grand Cham-pagne, I suddenly realised that my forehead was covered in sweat. I could feel a twitch in the corner of my left eye, a trembling like a tiny tic, as awful, impossible thoughts came tracking through my mind. It was too wicked for words – and yet, suddenly on the hillside, looking down on the valley in the sun, I *knew*. I had the deep-rooted conviction that Mlle Lisette had informed on Olivia.

Was it possible, I asked myself, that our ex-nanny har-boured such an intense hatred for our family that she had denounced Olivia to the Germans? It seemed inconceivable, but we weren't in our world any longer, we were in Hitler's world, where it was considered honourable for a son to betray his father, for a daughter to inform on her loving mother. And there were plenty of French who hated Jews.

I decided it was better not to voice my suspicions to

Guy – not at this moment anyway, for when I reached the hotel I found him in a terrible state of anger, nerves, a tinge of fear, I couldn't be sure what.

'There's probably a perfectly logical reason for it,' I tried to reassure him, lying.

I explained that I had arranged for Papa to phone me at the Grand Champagne when he had news.

'But in the meantime,' I knew I was being idiotic to advise him, 'just relax.'

'Relax? God! These sodding Germans actually grabbed me – that's virtually an arrest. I'm going to the embassy to complain.'

'Let's see what Papa says first.'

'Papa! Come off it, Larry. Papa can't do a thing. He couldn't even let us keep the Douzy pyramid open when it was closed for no reason. He's too busy looking after champagne. There's nothing he could do for us – or for Olivia.'

But Guy was wrong, completely wrong. Fifteen minutes later Papa was on the phone to me at the hotel and almost with an air of disbelief I heard him say, 'It was a mistake. I've been on to Major Kissling and Herr Gaertner. Olivia is waiting at the Hotel de Ville. You must go and see the Major personally and sign for her release. I am very angry at what has happened. Yes, *very*.'

'But that's fantastic, Papa!'

After a moment's hesitation he said, 'You'd better not take Guy. He can be very hot-tempered, and after what he's been through . . .'

So Guy cycled home and when I reached the town hall Olivia was waiting on the steps for me and I drove straight back to Douzy. She was remarkably calm and poised. She told me that she had not been ill-treated in any way, but that she had just been taken in for questioning.

'Thanks to your father I'm all right,' she said calmly, but then, almost fatalistically, she added the chilling thought, 'I might not be so lucky the next time. Or Anna.'

'Why Anna?' I asked.

'One of the things they asked me,' said Olivia, 'was a long string of questions about Anna. They got nothing out of me but they asked about her all the time.'

What puzzled me above everything else was the power that Papa wielded. For there was no doubt that he had intervened and secured Olivia's release. To get a Jewish girl who had been arrested out of the hands of the Germans! It was unheard of. And I also began to wonder, not for the first time, why it had been so comparatively easy to keep Anna in Douzy. Surely if the Germans were anxious to trace a missing national who they believed was in the area they could have over-ruled our neutral objections? The occasional German visits of enquiry seemed almost too casual; put on for show. It all seemed curious.

Papa was vague in his answers. Only once was he really firm.

'Watch your step, all of you,' he said. 'Do nothing to provoke the Germans. I've managed to insist on our neutral rights so far, but one false move — one act of provocation — and you could let the Gestapo in. And once *they're* in, then none of us can do anything.'

Papa never talked much about his work, but by chance I met someone in the champagne business who had to sit next to me in the Boulingrin because it was so crowded.

'Remember that your father is the president of the syndicate dealing with the Germans,' he said. 'And the Germans respect him.'

'They must do,' I said drily. 'But do the French respect him too?'

'The French! Your father's a hero to the French. He's saving hundreds of lives by producing work that *he* has persuaded the Germans to undertake — to construct a series of new cellars linked to each other around the Rilly pyramid.'

'But if the Germans are going to use these cellars, surely my father shouldn't be helping them?' I asked. 'Isn't it aiding the enemy?'

'They'll never use them,' said my colleague. 'There are hundreds of miles of cellars in Champagne. Who wants any more? I tell you, your father is playing it brilliantly. He's got the Germans eating out of his hand — and employing Frenchmen who'd otherwise be sent to labour camps.'

It was certainly true, I thought, that Papa's influence had saved Olivia. But now there was Anna — and this worried me even more. I didn't like the way the Germans had questioned Olivia about my sister. Whatever else I did I must stop the Germans arresting her – or even finding out where she was living.

I suppose it was on this day that I decided there was only one way of trying to get Anna to safety. I must ask Sonia to help. I couldn't phone, I couldn't telegraph, but surely if I went to see her in Switzerland, explained everything, she would be able to pull diplomatic strings.

I decided to return to Paris the next day, then take the first available train to Lausanne. I knew there was a massive delay in railway travel, but I had to get to Switzerland as soon as possible.

31

Quite apart from helping Anna, the prospect of seeing Sonia, of putting my arms around her, of kissing her, of taking her to bed, filled me with an intense longing and excitement. At times over the past months I would think of her with a physical desire I could hardly control; at other moments, a mental longing would engulf me, the subtle joy of good times remembered, incidents returning like snapshots – Sonia laughing, Sonia angry, Sonia wistful.

Now, though, it was different. There was war, separation, the absurd twist that made us into enemies while still remaining lovers – and friends. Separation was a way of life to millions of people who like us had been torn apart by war. Yet none of this mattered because the growing pains of youth, with their jealousies and torment, had ended; I knew now with a certainty that I would love her for ever and, equally important, I knew that she loved me and would for ever too. It was strange, thinking back, to realise how we had altered. I had in a modest way succeeded in my chosen profession and that had changed me; but she, twisting this way and that to free herself from the unwelcome parental chains – she had *suffered*, men-

436

tally if not physically; now, though, it was only a question of waiting, and after the years apart I could face the future.

On the Tuesday Guy rang through to say that a German officer had made yet another routine call to enquire if there was any news of 'the missing Frau Frankel'.

The shiver of apprehension, as Guy told me this on the phone, emphasised the urgent need to contact Sonia, and gave me a spasm of guilt for thinking of us rather than what she could do to help my own sister.

Were the Germans baiting Anna? Did they *know* that Anna was at Douzy, hidden in the stables as soon as anyone saw a German car approach? I couldn't believe it – and yet, why would the Germans bother about one unimportant missing German national – unless the apparently innocent requests masked hidden threats?

I had to get her out of the country because, without realising it, she needed our help to escape from her own devils. And Sonia presented the only chance. After all, Italy and Germany were allies. Sonia moved in diplomatic circles. Couldn't she persuade someone in Rome to plead her cause to the Germans? Wasn't she – or Francesco – very close to Ciano? Surely one of them could pull strings in high places.

'*Maybe*, Sonia,' said Oregon. 'But don't you think it's asking quite a lot for her husband to help? After all, you are in love with his wife.'

'Well, Sonia then,' I said defensively. Everyone knew about Sonia and me, but when someone put it into words it always embarrassed me.

I couldn't, of course, warn Sonia. What a hell it was having no international telephones, no cables, no way of contacting each other quickly. But I could see how matters might be arranged. I felt sure that she would be in Rolle now. I would try to take a day off in Switzerland. I could see no dangers in leaving the office. Not only was Oregon there to file on my behalf, but Tommy Tomlinson was still in Paris, hanging around, still waiting for transport back to America. He might have to stay in Paris for weeks before leaving for Portugal where he hoped to book passage on a neutral ship.

*　　*　　*

Apart from the danger facing Anna – and the overwhelming desire to see Sonia – I needed a change anyway, for I was heartily sick of Paris. Douzy, with its German troops everywhere, was bad enough, but Paris with its hypocrisy was rotten.

In the months following the armistice and the creation of the Vichy government in unoccupied France a profound change had gripped the city. It was the metamorphosis from apprehension to acceptance.

'It's not a *willing* acceptance of defeat,' said Oregon, 'but before the war Paris was a nervous, anxious and downright scared city. Like someone waiting to have all his teeth pulled out. Well, now they've got their dentures and it's turned out not to be so bad.'

It was true. The city was more tranquil now than it had been for years.

'Nine out of ten people still hate the Germans,' one French friend confided, 'but we've got to make the best of a bad job because there's damn all we can do about them.'

In a way I could sympathise. Even André Gide said after the fall of France, 'To come to terms with yesterday's enemy is not cowardice, but wisdom.'

Certainly life, though tougher physically, was more relaxed. The Germans had been ordered to maintain a polite presence and cause no problems. There were obviously many hardships, often because everything had to be paid for in occupation marks which could only be changed at the official rate of twenty francs to the mark. Just before the war, however, the rate had hovered around four francs to the mark. It soon became clear that with this artificial rate of exchange France was being stripped of sugar, tobacco, coal, clothing, all paid for in occupation marks – and that meant a polite form of looting.

'I like the French description of Germans who pay in occupation marks,' chuckled Oregon. 'They call them *doryphores*.'

It was one of those catchwords which immediately became used by everyone, for the doryphore is a potato beetle which strips the leaves from the fields, leaving the plants dying and the farmers with no crops.

The discomfort was accentuated in other ways. Most of the

cars had disappeared. Hundreds had been commandeered by the Germans, though as a neutral my Citroën was safe – even if at times it was difficult to get petrol until I could refill my tank at Douzy. Taxis had virtually vanished. Some ran on gas cylinders, others on contraptions filled with charcoal. But the most popular 'taxi' was a western imitation of an eastern rickshaw – a kind of bath chair pulled by a tandem bicycle. At the stations – still crowded with refugees – men had developed a new enterprise: carrying luggage. For forty francs they would carry your trunk. For eighty they would take a cabin trunk, hauling it in an ancient soapbox fitted with two old pram wheels.

Food was very scarce. The rations were soon reduced to the barest minimum – twelve ounces of bread a day for people who normally nibbled their *baguettes* even on the way home from the baker's. There was only about twelve ounces of meat a week. Most Parisians were reduced to smoking tobacco concocted from Jerusalem artichokes, nettle leaves, or even lime flowers.

Many of the food shops I had patronised for years – the little shops with stalls in the rue Jacob, the rue de l'Université and so on – had closed. I noticed that when I did find a shop open I was one of the very few men patronising it. Paris had become a woman's city, and time after time I heard the same whispered question, 'Heard any news of him?' and almost always it was answered with a shake of the head.

Yet despite the deprivations the capital was filled with dozens of oases of plenty – and I found this sickening. You could still find all the caviar you wanted at Petrossian's, all the food you could eat at Maxim's, which was by now being run by Herr Horcher, a renowned Berlin restaurateur. The flabby-jowled Albert, however, was still headwaiter, but bowing and scraping now to Goering instead of to the Astells. All the great couture houses quickly reopened – Lelong, Dior, Balenciaga, Coco Chanel (who made doubly sure of her comforts by becoming the mistress of a high-ranking German officer). Writers and painters carried on as usual – Paul Valéry continued to lecture, Simenon continued to write, Cocteau even advised writers in an article that autumn, 'Seize your chance, it's here!'

Famous painters, like Braque, Vlaminck and Picasso, continued to paint, famous singers like Yves Montand and Maurice Chevalier continued to sing. Even the most exclusive brothel in Paris, the 'One Two Two' – which theoretically did not permit German clients – was booming, according to Fabienne Jamet, its *madame*, who admitted cheerfully, 'I have never been so happy.'

On the other hand, for me there was little work, for there was little news likely to interest American readers. As one French friend said to me, 'Killing time is more difficult than killing Germans.'

After all, correspondents did need a change of scene, something new to write about, and though there weren't many neutral countries left there were always stories to be picked up in Switzerland, Spain, Portugal, even Sweden – if you could get there. A new dateline meant a change of pace as well as a welcome break; and our press card allowed us to go to neutral countries and then re-enter France without formality. I could hardly wait to get away.

Then the blow fell. It came in a circular, from Otto Abetz, now back in Paris as German ambassador. The warning was blunt: no foreign correspondents leaving France would have the automatic right to re-enter the country. 'This is not a threat to muzzle the press,' explained Abetz in his signed letter, 'but rather a precaution to prevent correspondents making a quick trip to a neutral country in order to file material that has not been censored by the Germans.'

It was an old trick and I could see the reasoning behind the edict. Especially when the circular added, 'The Ministry of Information has no wish to be hard or obstructive. Anyone who is in good standing has nothing to be afraid of from the Third Reich.' For most correspondents it would still be possible to get re-entry permits, even before leaving France for a trip abroad.

I had to apply, of course – and with Abetz behind this new move I wondered whether I would be considered 'a correspondent in good standing'. I soon discovered the truth when I made a routine application to the Ministry of Information for an exit permit to visit Switzerland for a week's vacation, with the understanding that I could return to my job in Paris as soon as the trip was over.

'There's nothing to stop you leaving France,' said the official, 'but permission to return to France if you leave the country is not granted. If you leave the country your press card is annulled.'

'But why?'

'We are not required to give reasons,' said the official, throwing my card back on the desk.

'But it's unfair — I haven't done anything wrong. What's the *reason?*'

'No reasons need to be given,' he repeated, closing his book with a bang. 'If you wish you can apply to the ambassador's office.'

I knew there could be no successful appeal — not from Abetz, of all people. If I once crossed the frontier to see Sonia it would be as though a portcullis had clanged down behind me.

'We should take it up at the highest level in Washington,' said Oregon. 'It's monstrous.' Then he thought, 'But why *not* try a direct appeal to Abetz first? I know he hates you, but it's just possible that he doesn't know about what's happening.'

I didn't believe this for a moment. At the same time, though, knowing the grudge which Abetz bore against me, I had the feeling that if I applied for an interview he would get a curious satisfaction in watching my reaction. That's exactly what happened.

Sitting at a large desk, on which was a picture of Hitler, Abetz was in no mood for small talk. Gone were the pleasantries about trips to the Fatherland which he had promised me years previously.

'I'm very busy, Astell.' He fiddled with a paper knife and had deliberately dropped the 'Herr'.

'I just wanted to know, Mr. Ambassador' — I tried to be polite — 'why I can't have a re-entry permit?'

'Shall we say that this is a privilege reserved for friends of the Third Reich.'

'But that's grossly unfair. I am a friend — I am neutral.'

'All who are not involved in war are neutral, but' — his voice was silky – 'some men are less neutral than others. You come into that category.'

'That's your final word?'

'It is. Except for one more thing.' He put down the paper knife and stared at me with those unblinking flinty blue eyes which – so long ago it seemed – had scared the hell out of me.

'You asked to go to Switzerland. Alas, perhaps you didn't know but for the moment your – well, "mistress", I suppose is the right word – is in Rome.'

I must have looked startled. 'Ah! So you didn't know? Of course not, how could you. We in Germany are better informed than you Americans. I hear that the beautiful contessa is neglecting her husband . . .'

My nerves grated at the cold, supercilious sneer, the insult, compounded by his almost feline gestures, but I kept silent, raging inwardly.

'No, my dear Astell, not for you. Distance, a cynic once told me, makes the heart grow fonder – of someone else. The contessa's regular escort these days is Count Ciano.'

And as I choked back the words that I fought not to shout, he added contemptuously, 'Quite a step up from a newspaperman.'

I knew he was lying, of course, but still, I could feel the prick of tears brought on by my anger. Memory plucked at my last encounter with Abetz. I wanted to smash his face in – but the price would have been too tough – for all of us, the family, Sonia, never mind me. I would have gone straight to jail.

'I know how you feel,' Abetz almost chuckled as I reached the door. 'You'd love to throw the chair at me, wouldn't you? I don't advise it.'

With my hand on the knob, I shouted, 'Thanks for the help. Remember my last word to you? I'll refresh your memory – *Gefundenshite!*'

'And the same to you,' Abetz said softly. 'I'll remember that stupid word of yours when we run down your sister – as we surely will do one day. I'm waiting for the moment.'

Now I began to panic. If I left for Switzerland I could hardly expect the *Globe* to let me stay on as their correspondent, just because my married girlfriend lived there. Quite apart from that, the prospect of leaving the family was unthinkable.

I tried to thrash out the problem with Tommy Tomlinson, leaving nothing out. I emphasised the danger to which Anna and Olivia could be subjected. I had, I told him, finally persuaded them that they must be prepared to part. Olivia herself had told Anna that she would be mad not to leave France.

'Since you can't get out,' said Tommy finally, 'I'll go as your messenger. It makes no difference to me whether I stay on here until there's a ship available to get back to the States. I could go to Switzerland — and wait there until I get the call to go to the port from which I'm sailing.'

My heart leapt. I had, almost without realising it, hoped for just this to happen.

'She might not be there yet — but she will be soon. Would you really do this? Don't you agree with me that it's time we got Anna out?'

'I do. I know that in a way Anna's still American, but this shit Abetz is gunning for her — or perhaps for you. The sooner she's out of France and then Stateside, the better. The obvious thing is for me to fill Sonia in on all the details, and then she can travel to France. That shouldn't present any problems. She's got a diplomatic passport.'

'I'll never forget this, Tommy.'

'Anna should have bolted months ago. As I see it, when Sonia gets to Douzy she'll be able to sort things out, make plans, then go back to Rome and start the ball rolling.'

I heard no direct news of Tommy for two weeks, though I did get a signal from Washington that he had arrived. Then at eleven one morning the phone rang in the rue du Sentier and a voice I didn't recognise asked, 'Signor Astell, *per favore?*'

'That's me. Who is it speaking?'

'The Italian Embassy has just been re-opened a week ago. I have a message for you, sir. I am to let you know that the Countess de Feo will be visiting Paris the day after tomorrow.'

'You know the time? Where she will stay?'

'I am sorry, sir. That is all I have been told in the message. *Buon giorno, signor.*'

*　　*　　*

Sonia arrived the following Tuesday and was met by a diplomatic car which took her straight to the rue du Sentier. I was
in my office, sitting on the edge of the desk talking to Oregon,
when she rushed past the door, gave him a dazzling smile, and
without a word threw her arms round me, hugging me,
kissing me, opening her mouth slightly, crying *'Baciami!
Stringimi!'* and only after I had kissed and hugged her did she
gasp, 'Sorry, Uncle Oregon. Oh darling, I've waited so long
for this moment!'

She had never looked more radiant. I caught a glimpse of
grey and pink – her favourite autumn clothes, a Prince of
Wales check jacket and skirt, with the ruffles of a pink blouse
peeping out, framing her neck. I held her away from me to see
her better, the black crocodile shoes, the matching bag, the
long slim legs in sheer silk stockings – increasingly hard to
find.

When I had caught my breath, and Oregon had thoughtfully made an exit, I asked her, 'Where are you staying?'

'Nowhere. I mean, I haven't got a room. I thought – how
about the family flat?'

I shook my head. I was still holding her, running one hand
through her silky black hair, and when I pressed her close to
me I could feel the giving in her breasts and asked laughingly,
'Still no bra?' She never had worn one.

She shook her head. Her eyes were bright with tears, but
they were signals of happiness renewed.

'Where then?'

'The rue de l'Université. The family flat has been commandeered by the Germans.'

'*Our* apartment! I couldn't ask for more.'

'It's a bit cold at night,' I warned her.

'We'll spend all the time in bed keeping warm, making
petites chaises.' I had almost forgotten the old French phrase,
used so many times so long ago when we cuddled each other,
the front of one circled round the back of the other.

'I know we've got to get to Douzy right away,' said Sonia,
'and I've already started planning to help Anna – but, Monsieur Coquelicot, can't we just have this one night alone – in
the old flat – and is Marcel's still running?'

'Of course.' My voice was husky. 'We'll go home now.

We'll do anything you want, anything you say, *anything* to make you happy. And tomorrow we'll go to Douzy.'

I held her hand, lacing her long, beautiful fingers in mine. On one finger blazed the engagement ring I had given her when we first hoped to get married.

'Come on, darling,' I said. 'Let's go home!'

I had wondered if distance, war, the last sight of her leaving in the bus, would make any difference to our love-making. We had changed, both of us, we must have done. And yet I need not have worried.

On the way to the flat she told me that Francesco had agreed to an annulment. He had, she said almost shyly, even wished us well, and I wondered if the shyness would persist as we entered our tiny flat again. I wondered whether yesterday's impulsive love, with an ending which we had never been able to foresee, a live-for-today love, would change now that we were, so to speak, engaged, settled down, secure at least in the knowledge that, however long we might have to wait in order to be free, we would one day marry.

I needn't have worried about any shyness, any modesty. She slid off her grey skirt, then her stockings, standing only in her slip – beautiful blue satin, covered with the finest lace.

'Scratch my back!' she whispered as I slid off her slip, and as she stood there naked I scratched her gently between the shoulder blades, my hand slowly moving downwards.

'Don't catch cold,' I whispered. 'Come into bed.' Her feet *were* cold, and as we lay facing each other, kissing, I warmed her feet with mine, pressing them together until, still cold, she bent her legs and cuddled up to me, putting her feet between my legs, rubbing against the insides of my thighs until the cold had vanished. And at the same time kissing, stroking gently, while I aroused her.

'Don't touch *me*,' I entreated her. 'Or it'll be all over before we start.'

'Never mind.' She twisted round, facing me, and kissed the edge of my ear, then closed her lips on mine and she was kissing me, biting me, and I was doing the same with a kind of wild frenzy and disregard for anything else in the world. In that moment nothing mattered, not even the actual joy of making love, for we never had time – not that time – to make love properly. We were kissing, fingers and arms grabbing for each other, legs entwined with lost love regained. I gasped, 'I can't wait, I just can't,' and she cried, 'Me too. Do it now!' But I couldn't find her, she was moving with an ecstasy which she couldn't stop, she just couldn't lie still. I tried, but I couldn't. With every movement the rhythm accelerated, her mouth searching for mine, until before I could enter her she gave a gasping cry of, 'Oh Larry!' A cry of pain or pleasure – I couldn't tell which – and one last movement was all I needed so that, before we could actually make real love, both of us suddenly went lax and drained.

'It'll never happen again as long as we live and as long as we love each other.' She lay back in bed. 'Do you realise that we didn't even make love!'

'Well – we did – in a way.'

'We *thought* of each other, but without actually doing anything. It was just all the love locked inside us.'

She lit a cigarette, lying back in bed, her head, as she used to do in the old days, on my right shoulder, one breast crushed against my chest.

'I know I'll never feel anything like it again. It was like' – she searched for words – 'like an explosion because I didn't want it to happen, I wanted you inside me, but there was no power on earth that could have stopped me moving. It was overwhelming, *piercing* – I wanted to scream. I knew I was coming, that I was robbing you, but I couldn't stop, darling, it was beyond me. And then, oh God, as I stopped, feeling as though my insides were pulling out of me, I felt the sudden heat of you pouring over me, I knew it was all right.'

There was still about an hour before dinner so we opened a bottle of Astell while Sonia outlined how she would try to help Anna. Everything had of course been explained by Tommy – and Sonia felt sure she could help. But she did need to collect all the documentation, the details of Anna's life, as soon as we reached Douzy – things like birth certificate, marriage certificate, American passport numbers and so on.

'Once I've got something to go on,' she said, 'I'll get her out

before the Germans get her, even if I have to go and see
Mussolini personally.'

'Or Ciano?'

'Maybe.'

'But since you know him' – I wasn't really jealous – 'I hear
that he's become a regular dinner date of yours.'

'Who on earth told you that?'

'Our friend Abetz.'

'Darling Larry, you don't have to be jealous. Galeazzo –
yes, that's Ciano's name – is a compulsive womaniser. I *do*
have dinner with him occasionally – but no more than that.
He's repulsive.'

The real problem, as she explained, was that under new
decrees Italians were forbidden to export money out of Italy
without express permission for each separate journey. This
was the sort of thing that applied to almost every country at
war. 'And I have to get permission from the *Valuta Estera* –
that's the foreign exchange control – because I don't want the
Italians to know I've got money already in Switzerland.
Otherwise the Fascists might seize it. Of course I do use my
Swiss money, but I have to make a pretence by obeying the
Italian rules and keeping up appearances. And it's virtually
impossible to get an export licence from the *Valuta Estera*
unless someone pulls strings.'

'Like Ciano?'

'Exactly. Not personally, but he orders someone to deal
with it for me. But there's another reason, darling. By being
friendly to Ciano – no, no, not *too* friendly,' she kissed me, 'I
may bè able to make use of him after I've learned more about
Anna. He's a short cut to power – he's Mussolini's son-in-
law – and he could get Anna out like *that*,' she snapped her
fingers, 'if someone could persuade him.'

I wasn't jealous, I told her, but I caught myself wondering
what price a man like Ciano would demand for the safety of
my sister. It wouldn't be cheap, that was for sure.

We decided to have a scratch dinner in the flat. Sonia and
Tommy between them had bought a suitcase half filled with
food from neutral Switzerland – huge steaks, even some
morilles, the most wonderful mushrooms in the world, butter,

cooking oil, slabs of chocolate, even a two-pound chunk of *grana*, the name by which Parmesan is known when it is still so fresh it would be a crime to grate it. When we opened the second bottle of champagne, after she had cooked dinner, we toasted first each other and then, 'To Anna and a safe journey.' After that we went to bed.

It must have been nearly midnight when there was a banging at the door outside, just below my window.

'It can't be the Germans?' Sonia woke up terrified.

'Hope not. Wait a second – I'll peep out of the window.'

No, it was not a German – nor the police. I opened one of the windows to try to get a closer look.

'Good God!' I cried, 'It's Oregon! What the hell does he want?' thinking it must be a major story that had suddenly broken, and that Oregon wanted me to go to the office.

'I couldn't get you on the phone,' he shouted. 'I've been trying to get through for a couple of hours.'

I rang the bell which opened the outside front door and then opened the tiny door to our poppy-coloured little flat.

As Oregon walked into the tiny hall I thought I was looking at a ghost. I was horrified. The normally dancing eyes were dulled, hardly seeing me, the ruddy complexion as grey as ashes, even the fringe of white hair below his bald head looking an off white or grey.

'What the hell is it?' I whispered. 'What's happened?'

'What *is* it, Uncle Oregon?' Sonia had slipped one of my overcoats over her thin nightie.

'Oh! Both of you!' he cried in terrible anguish. 'I have to tell you, and yet I daren't. Douzy got through to me at the office when they couldn't get through to you at home.'

At the word Douzy I felt suddenly ice cold, knowing instinctively that everything we had feared had come to pass.

'The Germans?' I could feel anger – and fear – swamp the room.

He nodded. 'Worse, Larry. It took six hours for your father to get through on the phone to the office.'

'*Worse?*'

'The Gestapo. They've arrested Anna and Olivia – both of them.'

32

Painfully I pieced together a picture of what had happened, drawing on the experiences of all who were there, then trying to sort out in my mind the relevant facts, putting them in a coherent, composite form.

Papa was working in the Rilly pyramid when Guy, looking out from the window of the observatory, saw Germans at the bottom of the two-mile drive, beyond the tip of the dell. It was mid-afternoon. All previous visits by the Germans had been limited to a car or even a grey motor cycle coming up the drive on some obviously unimportant mission. This time there were three cars, all black Citroëns with yellow wheels, making their way slowly towards the château. And everyone knew by now what those yellow wheels signified – the Gestapo.

Before anything else Guy shouted, 'Anna! The Germans are here! A bloody convoy!' Then he ran upstairs to get a better view.

Aubergine was in the living room and Guy told her to run to fetch Anna, and tell Olivia to remain upstairs. They all knew what to do. No one was really afraid; the family felt that Papa had sufficient influence whereby the Astells would not be harassed providing they behaved and observed their strict neutrality. Even so, at the first sign of any German, Anna always made her way to the 'suite', as she called it, the rooms arranged over the one-time stables on the opposite side of the courtyard, facing the large double front doors of the château.

The German convoy crunched into the courtyard, two of the cars slightly ahead of the third. Doors opened, slammed. And Guy, who had crossed the landing and was overlooking the courtyard, saw several men looking like army privates. They wore field grey uniforms and carried rifles, though they weren't wearing helmets. But then one of the soldiers sprang to attention and saluted briskly as the third car stopped. From each side of the back seat a man climbed out. One look warned Guy that there would be trouble. The one nearest to the house was wearing a peaked cap, jackboots and breeches, a black leather overcoat with the swastika armband, black gloves and – even though the sun was not shining – that most sinister of all trademarks of the Gestapo, dark glasses.

Out of the other door a man in grey uniform emerged – the official uniform, with its insignia of the *Waffen* S.S., the dreaded élite detachments of the *Schutzstaffel* – the S.S. – the army's corps dealing mostly with special police duties. Sometimes the S.S. and the Gestapo worked together, sometimes they were deadly rivals.

Guy peered down from behind the curtains. At the bottom of the stairs he could hear Aubergine panting with fear – though she couldn't have been more frightened than Guy was. Jean, the butler, appeared at the front door even before anyone pulled the old-fashioned bell. The open window made it easy to hear as Jean nervously stuttered a few remarks. Then in a loud voice the S.S. man said, 'I am Sturmbannführer Rascher of the *Waffen* S.S. I wish to speak to your master or mistress.'

'They are both out,' stammered Jean, terrified out of his wits. '*Monsieur* is in the cellars and La Châtelaine' – he instinctively used Grandma's nickname – 'is out in the vineyards.'

The S.S. man – his rank was the equivalent of a major – looked at the Gestapo man, who slowly pulled off both his black gloves, studied his fingernails, and said only three words in a tone that sent a shiver of fear through Guy's veins.

'Where's the Jewess?'

Stumbling for words, Jean replied, 'I don't know. I know . . .'

Without a split second warning the Gestapo man, with one swift movement, slapped his black gloves across Jean's face. The old butler almost fell, but with a cry Aubergine ran out to the door and caught him. With a handkerchief pulled out of a sleeve, she wiped away a small trickle of blood.

At that moment, a voice roared from the far end of the courtyard. It was Grandma, who had entered by the small gate leading from the back to the vineyard and the Home Farm. Looking every inch La Châtelaine, she stalked up to the Gestapo officer, a formidable, even frightening figure in her long green cloak, and raised her stick as though about to hit him over the head. Two German soldiers rushed in and seized the stick. Grandma looked the black-coated man up and down scornfully and then, quite unafraid, said to him, 'You German pig! How dare you hit an old man?'

'If you were not an American, I would hit you,' the man replied silkily. 'On the other hand, why should I bother with an old cow like you, dressed up to look like a lampshade.'

Grandma looked as though she would explode. The soldiers stood alert – not threatening, but ready to act if Grandma provoked the Germans. Villagers, attracted as always when bad news travels fast, gathered by the back gate – including old Pagniez, the father of both Aubergine and Gaston, Madame Robert from the Home Farm and half a dozen others.

The S.S. major clicked his heels and said almost politely, 'We have orders to detain Fraülein Jacobsen. She is liable to punishment for not registering as a Jewess. I must ask you to send for her – or my man will fetch her.'

Scorning to reply at first, Grandma took out her own handkerchief and said to Jean, 'Go inside and clean up your face.'

All this happened in a few seconds, long before Guy had even had time to think of running downstairs. Guy's own fear was that Anna would boil over with anger and run down the stable steps into the courtyard. Before anything could happen, Grandma walked with dignity to the front entrance, stood on the steps, and said firmly, 'This is American property and you are not going in – unless you kill me.' And to the Gestapo man, she added, 'Not even you, you – *petite crotte! Merde.*'

The S.S. man whispered to the Gestapo man, who said in an almost cheerful voice, yet in the tones of a man suggesting that he was enjoying a sinister joke, 'If the laws of neutrality don't permit us to enter, we must try other methods.'

As this was happening, Olivia had run across the second floor of the house and joined Guy, whispering, 'I'd better go. There'll be trouble if I don't.'

'Don't be a fool,' Guy whispered. 'Not while Grandma is here. They're bluffing. They *can't* come into this house. If you go it'll all be over. Grandma might be able to beat them.'

No one, however, realised what the Gestapo would do next. The man snapped his fingers. A soldier brought a loudhailer. The Gestapo man said casually, 'Fraülein Jacobsen

is wanted for questioning. This is her last chance to come out
of the house where she has no right to be. I would remind you
that the house might be neutral but the *land* of France is now
under total German authority.'

As Olivia started to run down, Guy grabbed her and
clamped a hand over her mouth to stifle a cry. 'Hold it!' he
hissed. 'Hold it – and hope.'

The Gestapo man waited a minute – certainly no longer –
then walked across to the wicker gate leading to the fields at
the rear of the courtyard. He pointed.

'You!' he cried. 'Who are you?'

'Pagniez, sir,' Gaston's father fumbled with his old cap,
terrified out of the normal stolid reaction of old age to a
lifetime of security.

'Come here!' commanded the Gestapo man. A terrified
Pagniez slowly advanced, each step a sinister crunch. From
upstairs, Guy prepared to run down and, as he told Olivia, 'I
must do *something* – though God knows what I can do.'

As everyone watched fascinated, Guy almost tumbled
down the stairs. Unceremoniously he pulled Grandma off the
front steps and inside the house. 'Get inside, Grandma,' he
shouted. 'This is no place for you.'

She was so astounded at being ordered around that she
obeyed. The Gestapo man turned to Guy.

'Who are you?' he asked insolently.

'Guy Astell.'

'What do you want?'

Pagniez made to move away to the knot of onlookers which
had grown. The Gestapo man shouted, 'Stay where you are
until I give you permission to move.'

'You ask who I am,' said Guy, adding with a courage which
he admitted he didn't feel, 'but who are you? What gives you
the right to come barging into a private home and to hit an old
man?'

'We are German. That is enough. My name is Hoess.' He
held out a hand – almost as though to taunt Guy.

'No thanks,' muttered Guy.

'As you please.'

'Then get out of here. This is our house. What do you want
anyway?' Guy, knowing perfectly well that the Gestapo were

after Olivia, could only try to stall, hoping that Papa might suddenly return – a forlorn hope. Guy knew that Papa never returned early from the office.

'There's a cold breeze,' said Hoess. 'May I step inside to discuss this matter?'

'*Non, jamais!*' screamed Grandma from inside the door.

'What do you want?' asked Guy.

'The Jewish girl.'

'She's under my father's protection as a worker. Major Kissling has agreed.'

'Mr. Astell,' said Hoess, still smoothly. 'I am in authority here. The Jewish girl should have registered by now. She hasn't. She has broken the law. Therefore I am taking her in for questioning – whether you like it or not.'

'You're not stepping inside this house. You have no right,' said Guy.

'Germany respects the law. And we have no wish to antagonise Americans who are not our enemies. But the girl has *broken* the law – she is Jewish. And Germany has won the war. Therefore she will come in for questioning. I will demonstrate how. But first – and for the last time – send the Jewess out of the house.'

Guy stubbornly shook his head.

'It's your fault,' said Hoess almost regretfully and suddenly barked out some orders. As Guy tried to intercept, two guards stood in front of him. It was madness, he remembers thinking; this was a scene out of Dante's *Inferno*, a scene etched in his memory – the silky, sinister figure in shining black leather, the black Citroën, poor old Pagniez wringing his hands, looking to Guy for protection and help, Aubergine sniffling, Grandma inside the door bursting to come out and hit someone, while above and still hidden Olivia must have been standing behind the window, and opposite, in the stables, the hidden figure of Anna, watching. And all this set against the white archway leading to the park, the dell, the orchard, the vineyards, every stick and stone of it a haven of peace and love and gentleness into which this black-coated monster had suddenly intruded. During the few seconds when Hoess was talking, Guy took a look at him – tall, a wisp of nondescript mouse-coloured hair behind his cap with its shiny peak, cold grey eyes, an aquiline nose, not hooked, but narrow, with flared nostrils above thin supercilious lips.

'We'll use this old man to teach the Jews a lesson,' said Hoess.

As two soldiers all but gripped Guy, two more grabbed old Pagniez. What happened then was so fast it was all over before anyone could prevent it. Pagniez had no chance to struggle, and at first Guy was convinced the old man was going to be shot.

'Don't worry,' said Hoess. 'He's not worth shooting – not for a Jewish bitch. This'll flush her out.'

The two soldiers dragged Pagniez across the gravel towards the stable door, above which Anna was hiding. While Hoess stood barely a couple of yards away, Grandma was stationed behind the double front doors of the château. Still nobody realised what was going to happen. There was no suggestion of shooting – even the crossed rifles held against Guy were being used mainly as a 'fence' to prevent him charging forward. The two Gestapo men who held Pagniez forced the old man against the stable door which opened inwards. Hoess almost languidly uttered one sentence: 'The right hand.'

Even then nobody realised how the Gestapo men were going to 'set an example'. A guard gripped Pagniez's right hand by the wrist, another moved forward to help. They told him to spread out his hand, fingers together, almost as though they were going to fingerprint him.

The third man opened the wooden door – inwards, as usual. Wide open. Pagniez, two men gripping his right wrist and hand, was pulled round the edge of the door. Then, with a quick movement, they forced his fingers into the opening made between the gap of the wall and the hinge formed by the door. Before anyone could see what was happening, a third man inside the ground floor of the stables opened the door to its widest then with all his force slammed it closed. There was a terrible scream, and Guy caught a glimpse of the mangled bloody fingertips opposite as Pagniez slumped to the ground. So, with a scream, did Aubergine. All caution forgotten, Guy ran forward, pushing the sentries aside and, wresting one of their rifles, tried to hit Hoess. He almost missed, but somehow Guy tripped. As he did so he at least managed to hit Hoess full on the thin bony nose. Another soldier hit Guy over the head. He remembered a glimpse of Olivia walking scornfully out of the front door into the courtyard. But what horrified Guy in the split second before he passed out was the terrible cry of anger and despair from Anna, running from the stable door and shouting, beating the Gestapo man's chest with her fists and shouting like a madman, 'Let her go! Let her go!'

She was flailing her arms wildly. A soldier grabbed her and then Guy passed out. Luckily for him, though he didn't realise it at the moment, he fell forward on the steps of the house, half way through the door where Jean and Grandma pulled him inside. That probably saved Guy from arrest, for he was on neutral ground once he was inside the house.

The others by the back gate could all see, even hear, what happened next. Olivia was handcuffed without ceremony and pushed into the back of a car. Pagniez was left on the ground screaming with pain, tended ineffectually by Aubergine until Madame Robert dashed across the courtyard to help.

It was Madame Robert, the farmer's wife at the Home Farm, who, being more composed than the others, saw a soldier grab Anna from behind and pinion her arms behind her. Somehow Anna managed to lean backward and spit full in the face of the Gestapo man.

For one second Hoess, the blood pouring from his nose, was so astonished he did nothing. Then, with Anna helpless, he hit her across the face with his right hand.

'You will pay for this for as long as you live,' he said softly, and then, with Anna still held tight, he used all his force to tear open the front of her clothes, her blouse, her bra, leaving her breasts naked. He touched them and then shouted, 'Let's see the rest.'

Anna tried to kick. She never had a chance. Other men gripped her by the ankles. Hoess tore the band round her skirt till it broke, then ripped open the front, leaving her clad only in panties. He ripped them off too, almost with a grin, then rifled one hand through her blonde pubic hairs.

'This is an unexpected bonus,' he said. 'Herr Abetz has been looking for you.'

Almost crying with anger, and oblivious to the weal across her face, or the fact that she was standing naked, Anna screamed, 'I am an American citizen. Take your dirty hands off me.'

'Silence!' said Hoess. 'You know perfectly well, Frau Frankel, that the Reich never – but never – acknowledges the right of a German to change her nationality just to suit herself. You became a German when you married. You stay one until you die. And before long you will be *hoping* to die.'

That was the moment Guy came round – just in time to see his sister naked except for her torn silk stockings and shoes. As he screamed and tried to rush out of the door, Hoess said brutally to him, 'Better stay where you are, sonny boy, safe in your house. Because if I ever catch you outside this building, God help you. Meanwhile I'm going to enjoy your sister. Yes, I'm going to – what do you Americans call it? – I'm going to lay her. And I think I might try the Jewess as well.'

Between them, distraught vignerons and women like Madame Robert managed to get La Châtelaine to bed. Even her immense powers of resistance had – for the moment – been shattered by what she had seen. That, and the awful agony of wondering what would happen to the girls now. Two hefty men carried her upstairs. She was conscious, but her brain was not working properly. There was a skim of froth on her lips, and she was muttering French, but the words were unintelligible. Someone gave her a brandy. Guy decided that before anything else he must phone a doctor – even before phoning Papa. Pagniez's right hand was crushed, the bones little more than fragments in a bloody, fleshy pulp. Grandma needed medical help too. Everyone was suffering from shock.

Above everything else Guy dreaded phoning our father. Trying later to rationalise what he had done, he realised he had phoned the doctor, then Oregon in Paris, and only then did he have the courage to know that he could no longer evade telling Papa. And he knew, too, that he had to go to Rilly himself and break the news to him man to man.

'It was the worst moment of all my life,' Guy confessed when finally Sonia and I arrived at Douzy. 'Papa went deathly pale, then he kind of crumpled up. He actually seemed to shrink, to bow under some awful weight. It's a moment I never want to see again as long as I live.'

Douzy was like a haunted house by the time we arrived. We had been unable to leave before dawn because of the curfew and we didn't reach Douzy until just before lunch. In a selfish way I was grateful for our delay in arriving because it spared us the initial agonising shock of that terrible afternoon. By the next day everyone had calmed down, and despair, though never absent, had in part given way to a positive feeling, a desire for action, however ineffective any action could possibly be.

First Papa telephoned Bullitt in Paris, who promised to help – though warning him that it would take time. Papa went to see Major Kissling, the commandant in Reims. But though he was sympathetic and said he would try to find out what had happened it was, as he admitted, almost impossible to find out the secrets of the Gestapo.

'Had it been an army problem I could have helped,' he explained. 'But the Gestapo makes its own laws.'

The fundamental problem which faced us was simply that Anna and Olivia had vanished completely. On that afternoon they had been there in the château. From the moment they had been forced into the black Citroën they might as well have ceased to exist – a terrible prospect which I refused to consider, but which I couldn't altogether banish from my own haunted thoughts.

We tried everything. Major Kissling gave Papa the address of the Gestapo headquarters in Reims, a dingy building in the rue de Venise, near the old so-called port which served the canal – and in whose waters, it was already rumoured, many corpses had been thrown. I went there, thinking that as I hadn't been involved in the scene, and as I had a press card, I might be able to see them; but I couldn't even get past the sentry at the door.

Poor Papa was heartbroken. Over and over he repeated the same sentence, 'I told you not to rock the boat!' Sometimes he added a curious remark, 'I have no power with the Gestapo,' as though to affirm that he *did* have power with the *Wehrmacht*. Guy, too, was at his wits' end – and he had not only lost a sister and a girlfriend: he was now a marked man.

For four days, while we explored every possibility, Guy wandered round the house like a tormented soul. He didn't shave and hardly ate, though he knocked down more than his share of whisky. Without knowing what course of action to take, Guy had assumed that, for the time being, anyway, he would be safe if he remained in the château. I felt uneasy. This arrangement was too simple for someone like Hoess. That kind of man didn't accept a public humiliation and do nothing about it.

Sure enough, on the fourth day Papa returned home from Rilly early, and highly agitated. 'Major Kissling has told me unofficially that the Gestapo have persuaded the French to take out a warrant for Guy's arrest. When the paperwork is done, they'll probably arrest him. It could be tomorrow.'

'You've got to get out fast,' I warned Guy. 'You can't come back to Douzy until the war's over.'

'But Papa?' Guy was tormented. 'I can't leave him on his own. And I might be able to help to find the girls.'

'Don't be a fool,' said Grandma almost harshly. 'I refuse to believe that Anna is dead.' And to Papa she said in a tone more kindly than I had ever heard her use, 'Don't worry, *mon fils*. I know you feel bad, but you must have patience. Patience and planning. You and I and Larry are neutral, so we can plan. But Guy is a wanted man – and if he's going to help us, he must be free. Out of France if necessary. Perhaps – who knows? – to make contact with Sonia.'

Sonia was also a tower of strength.

'It may take months to find Anna.' She wasn't forgetting Olivia; it was only that Anna had been brought up with her, was her oldest friend. 'I don't know how to go about it – but I will. I swear it. And don't look so sad, my beloved' – she stroked my cheeks gently – 'I know the agony you're going through. But I, too, am sure she's alive.'

'And Olivia?' asked Guy harshly.

'I'm sure we can find her as well,' said Sonia. 'But it's a different problem. Anna is a German or an American citizen. Olivia is French – and Jewish. It must be dealt with by different departments. But you know I'll do all I can, Guy.'

In many ways Sonia emerged as the most authoritative voice in the agonising days that followed – partly of course because she was the only one who might be able to exercise power to secure the girls' release. Grandma could give moral support, but her help was limited to making threatening noises. Sonia was *practical*, but she did say to me, alone in our old bedroom, 'I think I ought to get out of Douzy quickly.'

I must have looked baffled.

'Darling, I *am* – in theory – an ally of the Germans who took away the girls. If I'm found here – collaborating, so to speak, with the other side – oh darling Larry, it's so awful, but if the Gestapo did find me it would spoil all my chances of getting help in the future.'

'But why should they care?' I said, adding bitterly, 'They've got what they wanted, the girls.'

'No, they haven't got all they wanted,' replied Sonia. 'They want Guy. Remember what happened – a high-ranking Gestapo officer has been publicly insulted in front of other Germans. The Gestapo will never stand for that. Never.'

'But Douzy is neutral. You can't get away from that.'

'You can. He could be arrested by the ordinary police on an assault charge, and then handed over to the Gestapo. Guy must escape quickly. If he once gets into the hands of the Gestapo – after what he's done to them – Larry, I would rather he was dead. I mean it.'

Guy came into the room just in time to catch the last part of the sentence and asked, 'What's this about me escaping quickly?'

'Sonia's right,' I said. 'They're out to get you – and being defiant isn't enough. They're in the box seat.'

'I give the Germans twenty-four hours to do the paperwork – and then get official permission to have you arrested by the French,' said Sonia.

'But I'm an American!'

'That's precisely the reason for the paperwork. Normally the Gestapo or S.S. just bash a door down and grab you. But you're neutral. So they're going to make a formal charge through the French.'

'When I tell the court . . .'

'*Please,* Guy. Don't be so naïve. You've seen what they've done to the girls – taken them by force. God knows where. You talk about a court! You'll never have a trial. You'd just vanish.'

'But if I run away, what about Anna and Olivia? I can't just leave them.'

'It's your only chance,' I insisted. 'If you can get out, escape to Switzerland or wherever, at least you can keep on fighting somehow, getting some action from the government, perhaps. But if you're in some stinking prison . . .'

'Maybe you're right.'

'Of course he's right.' Grandma had walked into the room. 'I'm not going to have a grandson of mine ordered around by those – those *scum*. Understand?'

'There are army patrols by the gates at the bottom of the drive,' said Sonia. 'You can't just walk out.'

'I've got it!' I cried suddenly. 'If we act quickly you can get out now – it's your only chance, your last chance before they come to arrest you.'

'How?' He seemed doubtful.

'The Misses B and B are leaving for Paris today. It's all been laid on with Papa. They'll take you along.'

'Holy cow! You must be mad,' cried Guy. 'Those two twittering old maids – are you *trying* to land me in jail?'

'Trust me.' Even Sonia looked doubtful.

'But if we're stopped,' Guy objected, 'if there was a confrontation, they'd just go into a dead faint.'

'They're tougher than you think. And you won't be stopped. Listen. I'll explain!'

33

The idea had come to me because I had insisted that the Misses B and B must get away from their lonely cottage in the vineyard. They had finally agreed, and the date had been fixed in advance for one particular reason: understandably, the old ladies were frightened of driving all the way through German-held territory to Paris in their ancient Renault.

Papa had therefore asked Major Kissling to issue them with specially franked passes, dated for the day they had chosen. These were, after all, two elderly American ladies, and they were neutral, so there was nothing unusual in a request for them to have a safe conduct. Their route had been mapped out, command posts had been alerted to expect them and to look after them; Kissling had apparently done this willingly, at a time when the German High Command was doing everything it could to create an atmosphere of goodwill between America and Germany.

Indeed, vast sums had been spent on propaganda to make the Americans believe that Hitler's quarrel was only with Europe. Oregon himself had once told me, as we puzzled over the way Papa treated the Germans, that a desire to create goodwill towards America was a major factor contributing to Papa's success: that, and the fact that the Germans were delighted with the increased production of champagne.

'That's why the Krauts are treating the Misses B and B as minor V.I.P.s,' I explained. 'It's a propaganda exercise. I'll bet the Germans even arrange to take their photos and distribute them to the press. And some'll probably find their way into the *Chicago Tribune*.'

'But hell,' cried Guy impatiently, 'how do I come into the act? Them and their clapped-out jalopy?' I could see that Guy was rattled, the shock of what had happened to the girls overtaken now by a very real fear. Guy knew now that if he didn't escape from Hoess he would never see either of the girls again.

The plan was simple and depended entirely on the Misses B and B's Renault, an old model which had not been produced for years. It was an odd machine, considered very snappy in its day, but I was convinced that, as it was so outmoded, no German stopping a couple of sedate elderly American ladies would realise that every Renault made in 1931 contained a secret compartment.

There was the normal small boot opening from the rear – and unless anyone stripped the car down this appeared to be all the luggage space there was. But the Renault of that vintage had a second luggage compartment behind the back seat. If you pulled the back of the bench seat away, it revealed a narrow space in which the spare wheel was housed, together with the jack and other tools. It was narrow, a tight fit, but it might be possible to hide a man in it, provided no one sat on the back seat.

I had told the Misses B and B earlier when discussing the route and the passes not to call at the château, really because I thought it more sensible for them not to while Anna was there. But their route down the Mont de Champagne came past the Home Farm before it joined the main road to Paris. I had told the ladies to stop at the farm and pick up a supply of food – eggs, butter, fresh bread and *saucisse* – which Madame Robert would prepare for them.

'I can't see any problems,' I told Guy. 'The most important thing is for you to stay alive – to help all of us, wherever you escape to. Alive you may be able to do *something*. Dead or in prison you don't have a chance.'

Getting Guy to the Home Farm presented no problem. The ochre lanes bisecting the vineyards, leading from the rear of the château, were hidden from any but the most vigilant German soldiers who might be patrolling the main entrance to the drive.

'I'll come down as far as the Home Farm,' I suggested, 'then return to Douzy and pick up Sonia. Then, after the Renault has gone ahead, Sonia and I will drive to Paris in my Citroën. No problems there. We'll drive slowly, follow you in case of trouble. I don't see what I could do if there is any trouble, but' – with an attempt at a smile – 'we'll give you moral support.'

'Do you think they'll take me – the Misses B and B?' asked Guy. 'Christ! I'm bloody scared myself, but what about those two old maids?'

'They'll go along,' I promised him. 'Remember poor Jean-Pierre. Those two old girls aren't the only ones who have a debt to settle with the Germans.'

Not for the first time I felt that behind the twitterings of two old maids there was a longing to be loved by us all, perhaps born of a fear that one of them must die before the other. Even as I was talking to Guy, I was thinking of the dinner at Douzy when one of the old ladies had talked about guinea fowls, and the awful prospect that faced birds and beasts when dying alone. One of us had thought then of them as guinea fowls, doomed to die in loneliness.

But behind every man and woman is a second character – one which isn't needed perhaps except in dire peril, just as a frail old lady can sometimes draw on a greater store of hidden strength than some stronger woman in the ultimate crisis of a loved one's death.

Now, for the first time perhaps, the death of Jean-Pierre might have stiffened characters that hadn't needed stiffening beforehand. I was sure that at the prospect of action they would change, as though they would suddenly produce a surprise present, kept hidden all these years.

We both reached the Home Farm unseen and settled down to wait until we heard the warning sound of their old rattle-trap. It arrived around three o'clock and of course the ladies were totally unaware of what we hoped they would do. As quickly as I could I outlined the dangers and the plan.

'Guy is a wanted man,' I felt I had to warn them. 'If you're caught hiding him, you could both go to jail.'

It was almost comical really – or would have been had it not been so tragic. The two ladies looked at each other, nodded, and then Miss Barron said almost briskly, 'Well, the sooner we start the better. I don't like driving after dark. My eyes, you know.'

'I could drive,' Miss Brewer offered, nodding hopefully.

'Now Millie, you know you can't tell left from right,' said Miss Barron, adding by way of explanation, 'She has a small wart on her left arm. That's the only way she can tell the difference.'

In a corner of the farmyard we pulled out the back seat and removed all the tools and the spare wheel.

'We'll have to risk a puncture,' I said, and rolled the tyre out into the yard.

At first I didn't think we could squeeze Guy into the hidden compartment. It was such a tight fit that he had to take off his shoes. By saving that extra inch or two he could just manage to lie on his back, head on a cushion, knees bent, bracing his stockinged feet against the offside of the car. It was going to be a rough ride, and if any official – French or German – by chance pulled away the back cushion of the rear seat, he would arrest Guy on sight. With four days of stubble on his chin, Guy looked every inch a man on the run.

'But if there's any real trouble,' I said before the Misses B and B set off, 'I'll be driving behind you, and Sonia will create a diversion. I don't know how or if' – I shrugged my shoulders – 'but after all she *is* a friendly ally of the Germans – and the wife of a diplomat. The Germans love kow-towing to authority, titles and all that.'

I wanted to give the Renault a good start because Miss Barron drove slowly and I thought I would look conspicuous, suspect even, if I dawdled on the main road leading to Paris; but I planned to catch them up before we reached Château-Thierry. It wasn't big as big towns go, but a German garrison was stationed nearby at Condé-en-Brie, and what little traffic passed through Château-Thierry would automatically be stopped for identification.

By the time we reached the checkpoint I was perhaps a hundred yards behind the old ladies and there were no cars in between us – in fact there was virtually no traffic other than German cars and trucks. As we reached the town by the rue l'Hermitte, large signs blocked off the through road and forced us to drive along the rue de Fère next to the château in its beautiful old grounds. A German military policeman held up a red disc on a short stick – how long it seemed since I had first seen those discs when the Germans marched into Paris! – and I drew up a few yards behind the Renault, heart quaking, as one German officer saluted and asked the old ladies to show their papers.

Gripping Sonia's hand I had a sudden irreverent thought: what would happen if Guy suddenly sneezed! A soldier opened the boot in the back, gave the suitcases a cursory look, nodded; the officer saluted, still politely, and within a couple of minutes the two innocent elderly ladies received a signal to drive on.

We were equally quick. A one-way detour took us slightly out of our way; but soon we were driving along the north bank of the river Marne, then forking right to join the road which I knew led to La Ferté, and straight on to Paris, only fifty or sixty miles away.

All went well for the next twenty miles or so. Both cars

passed two smaller checkpoints without problems. We must have been about half-way to Paris when we passed through Meaux. The checkpoint was on the far side of town, giving us the opportunity to drive slowly behind the Renault. This time there was a barrier across the road. It consisted of a striped pole, weighted at one end, so that it could swing up and down, like those one sometimes sees at frontier posts.

A few yards behind the Renault I watched as a German officer saluted, and then with a gesture of the hand ordered the two women out. At the same time a man in German soldier's fatigue overalls — not unlike those of a mechanic — started examining the wheels, opened up the uniquely shaped bonnet to examine the engine. A third man took a look at the interior, even taking out and examining the rubber mat beneath the foot pedals, before taking a look at the contents of the glove compartment.

I began to feel the sweat on the palms of my hands. Sonia clutched my right arm more tightly than before.

'Wait a minute longer,' she whispered.

At that moment the officer examined the documents signed by Major Kissling and with an arrogant gesture which seemed to indicate that it was of no value as he was in charge, threw the piece of paper back on to the front seat of the car.

'I don't like him,' I whispered.

In front of us the officer barked an order to a soldier. The soldier opened the back of the boot. Only a thin slip of plywood separated the suitcases from the doubled-up figure of Guy squeezed behind the cushions. You could have heard a man breathing behind it. For a moment the soldier poked round the interior of the small compartment, then he took out the hamper. With a gesture of triumph he opened it, eyes wide with greed at the display of food.

'Look here, Herr Hauptmann!' he cried. 'A real storehouse. The *marché noir*.'

The captain bustled over and barked to the Misses B and B, 'Where did you get this food?'

The Misses B and B fumbled for words. They looked terrified. They exchanged glances, desperately searching for a way out. The bullying German shouted again and Miss Barron nearly jumped out of her skin. Miss Brewer looked imploringly in my direction, then dabbed her eyes.

I, too, was terrified, especially when the captain shouted, 'If there's all this in the back, there must be more hidden. Strip the car. Take out the seats.'

'No, please.' Miss Brewer gave an anguished cry. 'We are Americans. Please leave us alone.'

Again the captain asked, 'Where did you get this food? I demand to know! You may be neutral Americans, but when you deal in the French black market you are robbing German soldiers of their rightful rations.'

'It's from a friend,' said Miss Barron faintly, looking desperately at us in the car, for I had told her that we had planned a diversion. But we had to wait until the very last second.

It came when Sonia stepped out of the car. I had always admired the way she could act the part of a diplomat's wife, and she now turned in a performance that could not have been bettered.

'Herr Hauptmann!' she called imperiously to the officer. 'A word with you, please!'

He looked the apoplectic type, the fussy, arrogant kind of man who wore his officer status like a uniform that didn't fit very well. I could see, even by his gestures, how much he enjoyed exercising power over people who couldn't answer back.

For a moment he looked as though he would splutter with rage, but then – perhaps with an eye on the vision of beauty which suddenly appeared before him – he softened visibly, but still growled, 'Can't you see I'm busy, *Frau?*'

'Herr Hauptmann, why am I being delayed?'

Without waiting for a reply, Sonia added, 'Here is my diplomatic permit to travel. I am the wife of the Count de Feo, one of the chief assistants on the staff of *Il Duce.*'

His eyes popped out at the mention of Mussolini's title and, with a pathetic attempt to air his spurious Italian, he cried, '*Signora Contessa! Mille scuse!*'

'An American is giving me a lift to Paris,' she said, less imperiously.

'Please – you can pass, *signora.* It is my pleasure.'

'And the car in front?' asked Sonia.

'Black-market goods,' he said pompously. 'I am going to confiscate the lot after I have searched the car.'

I could hear every word, even sense the hidden menace. I licked my lips – there was no saliva there for my parched throat. I was scared stiff – for the Misses B and B and for Guy as much as for myself.

'I don't think so, Herr Captain,' said Sonia. 'Mr. Astell – you know his champagne by repute of course – gave the ladies in the car ahead of us some produce from his farm. They are rather . . .' she whispered something and he smiled conspiratorily.

'Ah! I understand, *signora*. Perhaps we must be understanding to older ladies. One moment, *signora*.'

The captain barked an order. I didn't understand it, but then, with a show of ingratiating gallantry that made my sweat turn to bile, he said, 'Of course, *signora*. If it has been legally acquired I will allow the women to proceed.'

He shouted another order.

'*Zu befehl, Herr Hauptmann,*' a soldier shouted back. The officer stiffened into a salute and one of the soldiers put the basket of food back into the car. The captain aired his Italian once more – with a final, '*Buon viaggio, signora.*'

We drove straight into Paris without further incident. By prior agreement, we had agreed to part as soon as we reached the city proper. The Misses B and B – and Guy – made for the apartment they shared in a modern building in the rue Balny d'Avricourt round the corner from the Arc de Triomphe. I dropped Sonia at the embassy, knowing that she must leave for Rome as soon as possible.

'But not before tomorrow,' I pleaded at the gates. 'I know every minute counts, but please, one more night.'

'I'll try,' she promised. 'It does depend on the trains – when I can get a seat.'

'And I must go back to the office.' I looked at my watch. 'Give me a ring later – and I'll fit in with anything you can fix.'

'*Stringimi!*' she cried, 'Give the embassy staff a treat!'

I did hug her, not caring for anyone else in the world. The Italian word itself excited me, pronounced with the soft 'g', as if she had murmured 'strinjimi'.

467

'See you later, beloved.'

As usual there was little news at the office – except the personal news about the girls which I recounted in detail to Oregon.

'It's terrible,' he sighed. 'And it's the lack of information that's worst of all. It seems incredible that people – Americans, dammit – can just disappear, vanish without a trace.' Then he chuckled. 'I'd have given a year's pay to see Grandma trying to hit the Gestapo shit with her walking stick.'

I couldn't help smiling. 'Or the moment he said that she looked like a lampshade!'

'Poor Grandma.' Oregon never called her Mother. 'She never did have much of a dress sense. Odd! I thought all Frenchwomen knew about clothes instinctively.'

It was a tiny effort to make each other smile, but neither of us could dispel the emptiness of not knowing. Where had those monsters taken Anna? Where was Olivia? My mind kept dwelling on the terrible stories I had already heard of men and women deported to labour camps. I'd already heard rumours of vast concentration camps – one at a place called Dachau – where Jews were being killed by the thousand – some said they were gassed, others that they were kept as slaves until they could no longer work. Anna, as a German–American, would surely merit better treatment, but Olivia was different. For all we knew she was at this very moment being tortured by sadists like Hoess and others.

Not for the first time I thought too of Mlle Lisette. I *knew* that she had betrayed Olivia – and I thanked God that I hadn't told Guy of my suspicions. But by betraying Olivia she had indirectly betrayed my own sister, the baby which Mlle Lisette had brought up, handled in her cot, cuddled in the nursery, helped with her first steps as a toddler. True, she had not deliberately betrayed her, but she would have to bear the responsibility for the rest of her life.

'Where are they?' I asked for the fiftieth time.

'Sounds damned stupid advice,' said Oregon, 'but our only hope of finding her depends on Sonia – one of our enemies.'

My thoughts were so depressed, so deep, that the jangle of the phone made me jump in my seat. For half a second I nursed the wild hope that the girls might have been freed. Instead, a cold impersonal voice, with a strong Teutonic accent, asked, 'Herr Astell?'

'Who is it?'

My dashed hopes turned to ice as he replied, 'The S.S. You are the brother of Herr Guy Astell?'

'I am.'

'The French police have issued a warrant for your brother's arrest, but the Gestapo in Reims inform me that he is not there.'

'Well,' I said shortly, masking my fear with bluster, 'what the hell am I supposed to do? Don't you know this is a newspaper office? It's our deadline time. I'm busy.'

'I advise you not to be angry — or attempt to terminate this conversation.' The voice sounded as silkily offensive as that of Hoess. 'Your brother has escaped.'

'Bully for him!' I shouted into the receiver.

'Fortunately for you, you do not appear to have been implicated. We have checked at the roadblocks you passed.'

Then at the next words the fear leapt inside me. 'But I notice that your old friend Madamoiselle Barron and her companion have also left today. Do you know where they are?'

'Of course I don't,' I lied.

'No matter,' he said. 'We have the address of their apartment near the Étoile.'

I told Oregon what had happened.

'We must warn the Misses B and B,' I concluded. 'There's no place to hide a mouse in their tiny apartment. But maybe Guy can do something — run for it — Christ! If they catch Guy too we might as well all give ourselves up.'

'I'll phone from Yvette's.' Oregon made for the lift. 'I'm sure your phone is tapped.'

He was back in five minutes. 'Got through right away. They're fantastic, those two. They just told me not to worry, they'd arrange everything.'

What's more, they did. But as the Misses B and B recounted the story to me later, it must have been touch and go.

Outside their apartment in the rue Balny d'Avricourt they had waited until the street was empty after they had parted from the Citroën. Then the two women went in first to make sure the elevator was on the ground floor. Guy followed, and Miss Barron pressed the sixth floor button. The lift took long enough to reach the top of the Empire State Building before finally it stopped at the sixth floor. The three hurried inside and Miss Barron threw herself against the door, pushed the safety bolt in a state approaching panic, then tottered towards a chair and sat down.

The other lady seemed to have stronger nerves. She actually remembers that she laughed happily and said, 'Who would believe us if we told the Germans that we had smuggled a wanted man past hundreds of guards into Paris and into our apartment?'

It was shortly after this that Oregon managed to telephone them a warning – and only just in time.

The Misses B and B and Guy were still sitting in the living room with its large leatherbacked divan and gay warm colours when the doorbell rang.

Miss Barron bundled Guy into her bedroom, and whispered, 'Quick! Take off your clothes and jump into bed. Pretend you are ill. Leave the talking to me.'

Guy was in bed in seconds. Miss Barron tied a towel round his head just as she heard Miss Brewer call out, 'Where are you, dear? This gentleman wants to see your room.' As Miss Barron walked out into the living room, it seemed to her that the piercing glance of the Gestapo agent bored right through her. Two plainclothes men stood in the doorway. Miss Barron opened the bedroom door for the Gestapo man, saying, 'You'll have to excuse the mess. We have a patient who is quite ill with intestinal flu. I hope you won't have to disturb him too much.'

As the German walked into the big bedroom, she said in what she hoped was a soothing voice, 'It's all right, Jean-Pierre, don't try to talk.' And turning to the agent added, 'This is Jean-Pierre.'

'His papers, please,' the German asked.

She had kept all Jean-Pierre's papers in a red wallet which I remembered seeing when she had helped me to close her emergency suitcase. Now she took out his American passport which she had left on top of the other clothes. The Gestapo man flicked through the papers casually while Miss Barron thanked God for Guy's unshaven face and also for the fact that the passport, issued some years' back, carried a picture taken when Guy was nearer Jean-Pierre's age.

It seemed to satisfy the German, for he walked back into the living room, asked Miss Barron a few noncommittal questions and left. Within seconds the two women heard the peal of the next doorbell and then the pale-faced, unshaven face of Guy appeared – in his underclothes, a towel tied round his head.

'Where is Guy now?' I asked when she told me the story the next time we met.

'I don't know. But not in France. He has his own friends and he planned to leave for the unoccupied zone or for Spain. But I don't know how or where – we thought it better not to know, in case the awful Gestapo men took us to prison and tried to make us talk to them.' Miss Barron smiled while Miss Brewer nodded. 'But we do know that he escaped.'

'You do? How?'

'Guy had promised he would let me know. One day the phone rang and a French voice just said, "*C'est bon.*" Then the unknown voice rang off. It was a code we had arranged.'

'You're very brave, both of you.' I kissed them gently, thinking back once again to the twittering concern of the two old ladies for the guinea fowls.

34

For months we had had no news of either Olivia or Anna. Sonia tried everything – but she was powerless because she had no starting point from which she could work. Had she known the destination to which one or both of the girls had been sent – a prison, a work camp – she might have achieved something. But the girls had vanished. Every attempt to see Hoess was brusquely refused. The S.S. had also refused to

meet me. There were no records – none available, anyway –
for us to study, to give us a reference point. They might by
now both be dead; in fact I was more and more beginning to
believe they had been murdered.

And then in the spring of 1941 I learned that Anna was
alive – from one of the men I hated and despised most in the
world, Otto Abetz.

I had finally approached his office for an appointment; for as
ambassador to France he could surely request details from the
Gestapo. I also realised that blustering demands would get me
nowhere with a man so close to Hitler, and that my only hope
of success lay in being polite, even servile.

It was a difficult confrontation, for me certainly. As I was
ushered into the imposing embassy building in the rue de
Grenelle, still with the photo of Hitler on the big polished desk
in his study, Abetz looked at me coldly, the periwinkle blue
eyes staring with hostility. But at least he motioned me to sit
down in the leather armchair facing him on the opposite side of
the desk.

'Well?' he asked.

I swallowed, and said, with as much politeness as I could
muster, 'Mr. Ambassador, I know that we don't particularly
like each other, but that's no reason for bad manners. And I've
come to apologise. I'm sorry, Herr Abetz. You are an ambassador and I am a neutral, and I should at least – well, respect
your rank and be polite.'

His entire face changed, breaking into a smile. It was
astounding. It was not a smile of victory, but (or so it seemed)
a smile generous to a defeated opponent, an all-is-forgiven
grin – though I knew that for me the work was yet to come; I
had to beg abjectly for news of my sister.

'My dear Astell,' he said. 'Forget it. I hate to see two
intelligent men fighting over nothing.'

Thwarting my marriage to Sonia was hardly nothing.
Neither was the murder of the two Italians years ago; but I let
the remark pass.

He rang the bell and gave an order to a man in livery.

'Let's drink a glass of champagne,' he said as the man
appeared with tray, glasses, ice and a bottle which he proceeded to open.

'I'm afraid it's not Astell,' Abetz apologised. 'But as you know, my boss, Herr von Ribbentrop, the Foreign Minister, used to be a champagne salesman for Pommery, and he won't let us have any other brand in any of our embassies. He is loyal to his old life, *hein?*'

I looked at him. Young – still in his thirties – his fresh complexioned cheeks looked even healthier than I remembered, and after a drink I was less hesitant about approaching the subject of Anna. With a swallow, I said, 'I wonder if I could ask you a favour, Herr Ambassador?'

'Ask away!' he said magnanimously.

'It's about my sister.'

'Your sister? You mean Frau Frankel?'

I nodded. 'She was taken away by the Gestapo some time ago. We haven't heard a word from her. Since she's done nothing . . .'

He hesitated, and I was aware of the tiniest touch of cunning as he said, 'I had no idea she was missing.'

It was a lie, I could feel it in my bones, the split second of hesitation neatly covered up.

'I knew,' he added, 'that she had been told to return to Germany, but – missing! It's hard to believe.'

'Well – we haven't heard a word,' I said bitterly. 'Not a word. Even the American Embassy can't help. The Gestapo picked her up, and for all I know she's dead.'

'No, no, I'm sure she's not,' he assured me, and this time I did believe him. It was queer, one moment scenting a lie, the next moment the truth. With mounting excitement I suddenly realised that perhaps Abetz actually knew where Anna was, what had happened to her. The way he had emphasised 'I'm *sure* she's not.' He *was* sure. I couldn't explain my feelings but I was convinced that this time Abetz was telling the truth.

'Leave it to me.' He rose out of his chair, a polite signal that my time was up. 'I'll make enquiries, I promise you. Right away. And I'll let you know. Please don't worry. I'm sure your sister is alive.'

As I got up, heart tingling with hope, lightened as though I had thrown away a millstone, he came round the edge of the desk and held out a hand.

It was the second time I had shaken hands with him and I

remembered how on the first occasion in the Hôtel Ritz I had been ashamed of myself for lacking the moral fibre to refuse such a handshake. This time, though, it was different. I still hated him, but I needed him too – and politeness had paid off.

Sure enough, within a week I received a summons to the embassy.

'Good news!' Abetz cried almost jovially. 'I'm afraid I can't give away information that might be of military importance, but I am glad to assure you that your sister is well.'

'Where is she?' I asked.

'She's working – serving the Third Reich. And for that reason I can't say where she is.'

'But why not?'

'Please be reasonable, Astell. You must realise that I've gone to a great deal of trouble on your behalf – not the kind of work, either, that an ambassador . . .' he left the rest of the sentence unsaid.

'I'm grateful, very grateful, sir. Don't think I'm not. It's only that . . .'

'I know, I know. You must be very worried. I understand your anxiety – and your father's.'

'She's not in jail?'

'Of course not.' He almost laughed. 'You have my word on it. I told you she's working – with some German officers, and in a very worthwhile job. But military secrets are – well – you understand.'

'She's happy?'

'She has realised where her duty lies. She's performing a very useful service.'

'What's she doing – her actual work, I mean?'

'That I can't say.'

'Can I write to her?' I asked. 'Or can my father?'

'I don't see why not. But not directly. On the other hand, if you let me have letters for her I can see no reason why I shouldn't arrange for them to be delivered.'

'And letters from her?'

'That's a military problem, I'm afraid. I'll try, but Germans aren't really allowed to write abroad, as you know, except to a military post office.'

I did know that. But Anna was alive! Where, remained a

mystery. But at least Abetz, in return for a grovelling apology, had tried his best, and I was convinced that his information continued to be genuine. For the first time since we had met I felt a little more kindly disposed to him as I rushed to telephone Papa with the news.

That piece of good news helped to make a new man of my father. But in the same Spring of 1941 he had yet another welcome surprise. One day, unannounced, Gaston just walked into Douzy and reported for work.

'Well, *really*, this is *most* unusual,' exclaimed a delighted Papa. 'I thought you were in North Africa.'

It transpired that, with the armistice, soldiers who had sick or dependent relatives had the opportunity from time to time to return to civilian life. Gaston, by ill chance, came into that category because his father, old Pagniez, had been so brutally tortured by Hoess of the Gestapo that he was too crippled to work. Gaston, therefore, was able to argue that he was needed to help his family on the land. It took months for the papers to be processed, but finally he returned home. He looked leaner, even tougher than I had remembered him when he was our family chauffeur. His fair hair had been cut short, he was tanned, while his face had more resolution to it than in the past. From my father's point of view his arrival was a blessing. We were shorthanded, and of course Gaston had been born and bred in the vineyards. It was not long before he took the place of Guy.

Grandma was also delighted to see him, though she issued a stern warning when first they met. She was still as ramrod straight as ever, still looked 'like a scarecrow', as someone once said, but she ran the vineyards as professionally as ever.

'And I'm also a professional hater of Germans,' she declared when Gaston reported for duty. 'But don't let what happened to your father make you so bitter that your anger will run away with you. Don't do anything that could get you into trouble. Wait – and the moment for retribution will come.'

'I am proud to be working again for La Châtelaine,' said Gaston a trifle theatrically. 'And one day I am going to kill Hoess. But I am not going to hang for it, *madame*. I shall wait.'

Later on as we talked he said to me with a smile, 'She's pure *sauce tartare*, La Châtelaine. And it does one good to see someone hate the Germans as much as she does.'

'I was sorry about your father,' I said awkwardly – partly because I was sorry, but also because I could never be sure whether Gaston knew that I knew about Mama.

It was strange how, after months of inactivity, when nothing seemed to have happened, everything was bustle and movement. Soon after Gaston arrived two unexpected letters reached us from America, one for me, the other for Papa. Both had been sent to Paris in the diplomatic pouch. It was the first news for months, even though in theory letters could be posted in America and delivered in France. The only thing was – they never arrived. We knew that Mama had written many times, but somewhere along the line letters just disappeared.

I didn't read all of Mama's letter to Papa, only the bits he wanted me to read. But it was enough to confirm that she had written regularly and that it was Tommy Tomlinson who had arranged for them to be sent via the bag. She asked after us, and was desperate for news of Anna, but what did astonish me was the information that Guy had actually met her in New York.

Guy in America! I had been there years previously, so that I not only felt a surge of relief but a shaft of envy. Life was so depressing in France. Sonia was so far away, Douzy was so empty and sad, that I found myself imagining Guy strolling along Fifth Avenue in the special crisp spring weather which is one of New York's most nostalgic trademarks. In her letter Mama simply wrote, 'Guy visited New York for a few days and came to see me, but said he was just passing through and wasn't sure where he was going. How very odd!'

I was astounded. We had been able to let Mama know all the latest family news through Sonia, who wrote regularly from Switzerland – from one neutral country to another – but the relief that Guy was safe after months when we hadn't heard a word from him was tinged also with speculation. What was he up to? Where was he going?

I got my first hint from Tommy Tomlinson, for my second letter from the States came from him. As a journalist he was not only accustomed to writing factual letters, but he didn't like leaving loose ends. So he wrote (without mentioning Guy's name) that 'our friend has already left for Spain and then intends to look up old friends with whom he's lost touch' − the inference being that those 'old friends' could only be Anna and Olivia − which in turn meant that Guy must be planning to return to France, where there was a warrant out for his arrest. He must be crazy!

There was also a long typed screed from Tommy giving me the latest news from Sonia, who could, of course, write openly. Again, just in case the diplomatic bag was mislaid, Tommy had called her Poppy − not a bad *nom de guerre* bearing in mind the infamous M. Coquelicot.

She had, she confessed, got nowhere. She had met the leaders in the Fascist party − 'I have even been out for dinner several times with Count Ciano,' she wrote to Tommy and said that he had personally promised to do anything he could, but that she must have a starting point. Once she knew what had happened to the girls, where they were, then the rest, as she put it, would only be a matter of asking Ciano to help. And then, as she wrote to Tommy, 'I'll do everything I can.'

Tommy had also visited Mama in her new apartment on his first visit to New York, and he wrote, 'Your mother has never looked more beautiful − or younger. Seems incredible, but despite the problems you all face she's taken on a new lease of life. Don't misunderstand me. About the rest of the family she's doing everything she can to help − pulling strings wherever she can − but it's not what she *does*, it's the bevy of men I met who surrounded her on the two visits I made to New York! Without making an effort she attracts men like flies round a honeypot. Honey's the word! She's a real beauty. America sure agrees with her.'

Re-reading the letter I had a sudden picture of Mama − and of course the photo of her and Gaston. How infuriating that a picture which had nothing to do with me, had never been part of my business, had caused nobody any harm, should refuse to be forgotten. Each time I saw Mama, I saw him. And now − a 'bevy of young men' surrounding Mama. Did that mean a new young man in her life? Papa forgotten? Or at best ignored, Mama still searching for youth, if at one remove? I would have laughed off any such suspicions but for the fact that Tommy was not a man who used words lightly. I had the feeling that he had penned the lines thoughtfully, paying as much attention to what was written between them as to the lines themselves.

All in all, the letter that I had opened with such anticipated excitement left a sour taste. Guy behaving like an idiot by planning to return to France – as though we didn't face enough troubles. Mama enjoying herself! The insensitivity of it seemed somehow to be in bad taste, unworthy of her, though of course she could not spend the rest of the war knitting socks in New York.

And then there was Sonia. I trusted her, and at long last I had the sure feeling that one day we would be married. She would never do anything to harm our love; yet the nagging thought persisted: Sonia loved us – Anna as well as me. Given the opportunity to save Anna, what price would she be prepared to pay?

At least with spring on the way Papa had less time to dwell on the fate of Anna, for though Grandma's work in the vineyard was less arduous at that time of the year this was the moment when Papa came into his own – during the process of the *cuvée*.

It gave a curious sense of permanence to realise that though Champagne was now ruled by different masters, nothing had really changed since Dom Perignon found out how to put the bubbles into white wine. The Germans queued as avidly as the French had done to hear and see the mysteries of the *cuvée* explained, only now, of course, the audiences were hand-picked. They included officers and men from the region opposite Alsace who were experts at producing white wine, and there was therefore no rancour on these occasions. The processes leading up to the *cuvée* were magical, depending on the whims, taste, knowledge of one man, in the case of Astell champagne of Papa. It was an individual achievement as personal as painting a picture, for he could literally change the taste of the grapes he had grown.

I visited Douzy as often as I could that spring, for Papa needed all the help – moral and physical – that I could offer him. Gaston was invaluable. I never realised how much the family depended on him — a wry situation, I reflected, thinking of the photo of Gaston and Mama looking so happy, long torn up. Gaston wasn't an expert in the *celliers*, but he had been born and bred in the vineyards and his general knowledge and aptitude was considerable. And my father, who had always liked him, soon began to use him as a replacement for Guy.

One day a score of officers had assembled in the *cellier*, the large area of outhouses, including the big winepress, above ground, at the far end of the Home Farm, and from which there were passages leading to underground cellars, even all the way to the most famous cellar of all, the Douzy pyramid, now blocked off by the Germans.

Papa had several stock speeches which he used to explain highly technical terms, and though he tried his best now, the enjoyment of similar past occasions in the days before Anna disappeared was sadly lacking. He tried. He introduced his *chef de cave* and other experienced men, and as I looked at the German officers, for all the world like a group of interested businessmen, I found myself thinking, 'Is it possible these men could treat Anna as they have done?'

But of course they weren't to blame. It was almost unfair to think ill of them, to compare the polite Major Kissling, whom I was watching, with someone like Hoess.

'This is the moment, yes, the real *moment*,' said Papa indulgently, 'when we can watch the profit emerge out of thin air by adding the bubbles which come for free.'

There was a polite titter from the captive audience. 'Since the *vendange*, the grape juice has been stored in forty-four-gallon casks over there' — he pointed to an adjacent building — 'and considering that we like to store our champagne in cellars at a steady temperature of ten degrees all year round, it may seem odd that we have just finished boiling the juice.'

'Boiling' was the technical term used during the winter, when the casks were stored above ground — in the *celliers* as apart from the *caves* — and maintained at a constant temperature of nearly twenty degrees centigrade, causing the first fermentation, usually ending in the spring.

'After the turn of the year the *cellier* windows are opened,' explained Papa. 'The heat is turned off and the cold causes a precipitation which throws off the impurities, so that we have been able to draw off the clear wine. Now we come to the preparation for the *cuvée.*'

It was a complicated business, but simplified it meant what Papa called 'composing' a champagne to his taste. As always each cask which the Germans watched had been labelled with the name of its special vineyard. The twenty or so wines from different vineyards were now 'married' to produce a balanced individual wine, as near as possible similar to that of previous years.

'People like champagne to taste the same every Christmas,' explained Papa, 'and how we achieve that – our own formula – is our most seriously guarded secret.'

'You haven't mixed in any black grapes?' asked one knowledgeable German.

Papa shook his head. 'We will for some blends, but here we're blending our speciality – we're very proud of our *blanc de blancs*, and for that we use only white grapes, even if they come from different vineyards. And now I have to add the bubbles.'

The remark was always greeted with another ripple of polite laughter, though in fact the only additives consisted of a small quantity of cane sugar and fermenting agents.

'Now we bottle it,' explained Papa, 'and put it to rest in deep cellars – but of course it's not ready to drink for at least a year, even many years if we decide to keep it.'

During this period, he explained, the fermenting agents would react slowly on the sugar, causing a second fermentation. The sugar was transferred into alcohol and carbonic gas which was imprisoned in each bottle. 'And that's why' – he picked up an empty champagne bottle and put his hand into the hollow at its base – 'champagne bottles are never flat at the bottom. They have to be strengthened like this or the fermenting bubbles would blow the bottom off every bottle.'

I always had the feeling on these conducted tours – and God! how many thousands I had been to as a kid – that many of the people thought the champagne would not be ready to drink. But the incredible fact is that every bottle, after it was aged, would have to be opened once more. Before this the bottles had been stored, neck tilted downwards, during which the second fermentation had formed a deposit which had to be cleared from the neck of the bottle.

'This is called *dégorgement*,' explained Papa. 'It's a highly skilled operation. A man has to remove the sediment by withdrawing the cork, wasting as little of the froth and wine as possible, then topping the bottle up with a few drops of liqueur composed of reserve wine and sugar. I'm told that someone is inventing a process in which the sediment in the neck can be instantly frozen and automatically taken out in seconds before the bottle is recorked and held in place with a wire cage. That'll be a wonderful improvement – if it ever comes.'

After the morning lecture Major Kissling – who, I had to admit, was very polite and very helpful – asked if he could take a look at the Rilly pyramid. Papa was delighted.

'Come along too, Larry,' he urged me, and I felt that he really wanted me to come, needed me.

'Sure,' I agreed. 'I won't guarantee that I'll like it after our pyramid, but . . .'

'I'm sorry about that,' said Major Kissling to me. 'But you know, Mr. Astell, the trouble is that if the' – he hesitated – 'the wrong authorities arrest people suspected of anti-German activities, then often we can't even discover what has happened to them. By closing Douzy, I have tried to protect your father from trouble. If, for instance, any resistance elements use Douzy, it would embarrass your father.' That was very true – and thoughtful.

We walked towards Rilly pyramid. To get there we had to pass through Rilly – once a picturesque village with its trim station under the lee of the Mont de Champagne where the tunnel started, but now disfigured by different mountains – grey, dusty hillocks of rubble, pockmarked with the skeletal outlines of once beautiful houses, sticking out like rotten teeth.

'All this,' I said bitterly, picking my way through the debris, 'is the result of *British* bombing by the R.A.F.'

'They are crazy,' Major Kissling agreed. 'The war is over. We are at peace.'

I wasn't so sure of *that*, but even so, each time I visited Rilly I became more and more angry at the futility of the R.A.F. bombing raids on a small unimportant village which could not possibly have any strategic value.

The Rilly pyramid was considerably smaller than ours, but of much the same structure; a tall narrow white underground pyramid, with steps and small terraces or balconies hewn into the white chalk. Chains and pulleys hoisted up wine from the ground floor to the cellar passages above, some of them visible on the sides, like black holes because of the lack of light. 'Too much light is bad for storing champagne,' my father was always fond of explaining.

The place seemed busy. Some men were trundling cases, the contents of which I could not see. Rilly produced an excellent local wine, but not in any quantity, and of nothing like the same standard as ours, and I had always assumed that the pyramid was never really used for practical purposes as it was in Douzy. But everything seemed very busy. Yet, what was everyone *doing*? I watched from a balcony as Papa pointed out to Major Kissling one large hole, darker and bigger than the rest, perhaps fifty feet from the apex of the pyramid, where the small rectangular light shone from the sky above. Steps led up to the hole in the wall. Papa was explaining, 'That's an old passage which leads directly to the railway line, almost at the beginning of the tunnel.'

'But it's not used?' asked the major.

Papa shook his head. 'Not for years and years – and the same thing applies to the Douzy pyramid. Someone had an idea years ago that they might be able to take advantage – yes, *advantage* is the word, I think – of the proximity of the railway to both pyramids, and load champagne straight on to goods trains from this tunnel and the one like it at Douzy.'

'But nothing came of it?' asked Kissling.

Papa shook his head again. 'Not worth it. We had by then installed trucks, rather like small streetcars, running on rails directly to our headquarters. Both tunnels were blocked up near the railway – except for small emergency exit doors.'

On one side of the Rilly pyramid gangs of men were actually hewing new passages to link up with other cellars, some perhaps half a mile away. It seemed crazy. There were around fifty pyramids on the outskirts of Reims alone, to say nothing of hundreds of miles of cellars. And with the biggest champagne drinkers in the world cut off from supplies, there seemed no point in digging out new corridors, new cellars. I almost blurted out as much, but then Major Kissling, watching the workers, said enthusiastically, 'Excellent, Herr Astell! Thank you for the tour.' He clicked his heels and smiled to me politely, but didn't offer a hand to be shaken, realising perhaps that he didn't want to risk rebuff.

'But *why*, Papa?' I asked when he had gone. 'It seems ridiculous.'

'Don't worry,' Papa said testily. 'You don't understand. My job is to look after the French — and keep the Germans quiet.'

I didn't like to argue. I wasn't sure that efforts to keep the French happy should be made if the price was making the Germans happier. Wasn't it more honest to make the Germans *less* happy? Gaston, for instance, was already talking — still in a vague way — of starting up a resistance movement. Preliminary plans had been formed. He talked vaguely about blowing up bridges and derailing trains later on.

'One day the people of France will rise up and fight against the Germans,' he insisted. 'De Gaulle has given us the lead. And in the south — where the Maquis is already operating — the French have formed teams to rescue British fliers, get them home via Spain. And at the same time, to make life hell for the German occupation forces.'

'And you plan to do the same?' We were walking round the lake. It was a cold day, the grass stiff with rime, but the sky a blue canopy above.

'One day — but not yet. We're not strong enough. And anyway, your father is doing his bit to help the French.'

'But not by blowing up buildings?' I laughed.

'You don't realise, but by using the Germans he's got the same objectives as we have. The week before last your father actually saved three men whose deportation orders had been signed and processed. They were due to leave the next day for some terrible camp. Instead they're now working in the Rilly pyramid. Your father arranged it. He's a hero.'

That *was* good news — and yet, unfair thoughts niggled me. Papa was no collaborationist, of course, yet would any German in authority — even an apparently agreeable man like Kissling — let a Franco–American champagne shipper cancel deportation orders, dig unnecessary tunnels, without asking for something in return? The Germans didn't operate that way. They were too tough.

'I can see your point of view,' said Gaston, 'but it's got one flaw. The Germans are *not* asking for anything in return, except more champagne for the Germans to guzzle.'

It was some time after this when, for no reason I can explain, I suddenly revealed for the first time to anyone my feelings about Mlle Lisette. Thinking it over, I *do* know why I spoke about her. I had cycled up to the cottage once used by the Misses B and B (now settled in Paris) on a routine check to see that the building had not been vandalised or occupied by the Germans, who were always threatening to seize empty houses. From the hills above, I could hear the sound of firing from the hidden range where Germans practised pistol shooting.

Cycling down the hill towards the hotel where Olivia had first been arrested, I saw Mlle Lisette in the garden of her neighbouring cottage. I hadn't set eyes on her since that day and for a moment I thought of marching into her garden and confronting her, with violence, if necessary, to extract a confession, but stopped myself in time. That would do no good. Indeed, if she had admitted anything and I had beaten her up, I would be the next Astell in trouble, and that was the last thing I wanted, especially as I couldn't be *sure* she had informed against Olivia.

Perhaps this was why I told Gaston, to unburden my soul of suspicion.

'It was all too pat, the way the Germans seized Olivia that day,' I explained. 'I can never prove that Lisette did it – but how else could the Germans have found out about her – and been there just at the very moment when Olivia was there?'

'Thank God you didn't do anything – it's much more important to keep suspicious people around as possible contacts in the future. You understand? I don't say you will ever need Mademoiselle Lisette, but if she was out of circulation she could *never* help. If she's around, she might be able to. There's one sure thing – you can't get a confession from a dead man.'

'You make it sound very – well, technical.'

Gaston hesitated. 'In a way, you being neutral, I shouldn't tell you, but I don't see why I should hold anything back from you. I came back from Africa with a lot of troops who were specially trained just outside Switzerland in sabotage and so on. The day will come when we will form a real French resistance. Not in this sleepy village, perhaps, but somewhere. It's too early yet – just as it would be too early to confront Mademoiselle Lisette. But some of us are laying the foundations for the future. And keeping tabs on the Lisettes of this world will help.'

'Be careful,' I warned him. 'And, of course, I haven't heard a word you've said.'

'I'll make a few enquiries, though, all the same,' Gaston promised me. 'Not me personally – others.' And then, as I was about to go, he asked me an odd question:

'Does La Châtelaine have any suspicions about Lisette?'

Grandma! I was astounded – also in a way at the use of her nickname again. 'Good Lord, no. What on earth made you think she'd possibly know?'

'Just a question. La Châtelaine gets around much more than you think.'

Around the end of April I was sitting in the conservatory with its commanding view of the dell stretching to the entrance gates in the distance, when I saw a car draw up. Someone leaned out and spoke to the sentry. I saw the sentry salute, then the car drove towards the house.

It was a black Citroën.

'It must be the Gestapo,' I cried to Grandma who was sitting with me, cutting up pieces of old material to stitch into a patchwork quilt, just as Mama used to do before she left for America.

Grandma got up angrily.

'Are you sure? Don't let him in, whoever he is. No German has any right to come into our house. Be firm, Larry.'

'I will, I promise.' She had no need to persuade me.

'They're vultures, the lot of them. Where's your father?'

'At Rilly.'

'Be firm. I'm going upstairs – I just can't even bear to set eyes on any of them.'

Half-way up the drive I saw the tell-tale yellow wheels of the Citroën. I only hoped – for the sake of all of us – that it wasn't Hoess, because I don't think I could have kept my hands from his throat. And violence could only lead to arrest – and one more Astell out of circulation. On the other hand, they couldn't arrest me for words spoken in my own home; for refusing them admittance. And I didn't need La Châtelaine to urge me on.

I called for Jean. It was pitiful to see how the war had aged him. He was years younger than Grandma, but it wasn't rheumaticky legs or rheumy eyes that painted him with age, it was the spirit. He had had the stuffing knocked out of him – perhaps for him encapsulated in that terrible few minutes when Hoess had tortured Pagniez and 'Mlle Anna' had been arrested.

'Whatever you do, Jean,' I ordered him, 'don't allow any of the Gestapo into this house.'

'But sir, if they use force . . .' he began.

'That's different. I don't expect you to knock him down.' Jean joined me in an attempt at a smile. 'But if anyone asks to speak to me, tell them to wait outside while you come to see me. And close the door. You know, there's not much I can do to help people like you, but at least we'll show who's the boss in our own home.'

I could hear the car rumbling along the drive, past Grandma's cutting bed until it finally came to a stop on the gravel terrace. By then I couldn't see if it was Hoess. I heard voices, an indistinct blur, then Jean came in. Despite his clean white jacket, the small silver salver he carried almost as a badge of office, he looked more agitated than I had ever seen him.

'Good God, you look as though you've seen a ghost.' I was vaguely irritated because he didn't look afraid, more astounded. 'Is it the Gestapo?'

He nodded.

'You kept them out?'

'There's only one man, sir – alone.'

'Keep the bastard waiting. I'll see him outside.'

'But sir . . .' At first Jean couldn't force the words out, when he blurted, 'It's no ordinary Gestapo man, sir. It's – you'll never believe this, sir – it's Monsieur Willi, Miss Anna's husband.'

486

I too must have looked as though I had seen a ghost, for Jean said tentatively, 'Are you all right, *monsieur*. Shall I . . .?

Willi! Of all people! The man I had last seen with his face smashed in, telling me he was going to join the German army. The *army* — yes, that was one way out of the mess he had been in. But the Gestapo, the scum of Germany?

'By Christ!' I said savagely to myself as I strode to the door, 'You've got a bloody nerve — you've got a hell of a lot to answer for. The *Gestapo*.'

I wrenched open the door with almost a shout of anger. 'You! How dare you show your face in that uniform?'

Willi looked terrified, quite different from the sophisticated German engineer ordering meals at Maxim's in Paris. At the sight of my glowering face his own was stamped with apprehension.

'How dare you come here?' I asked again. 'Have you heard about Anna? Your wife? Vanished! My God, Papa was right to warn Anna against marrying a German.' I looked at him with loathing. 'If you've got business,' I said, 'let's get it over with. Otherwise get the hell off our property.'

'It's not what you think . . .' he began.

'You want to see your wife?'

He nodded eagerly.

'Well, you can't — because she's been taken by the Gestapo — your lot. And since then not a trace of her any-where.'

For a moment he stood there, almost rocking with the suddenness of knowledge.

'I know you had to be a soldier,' I said bitterly, 'but *this* — this hideous uniform.'

'But will you listen . . .'

'No, I won't. I've got nothing to say to you.'

'Let me *explain*!'

'Just answer me one question. Are you — or are you not — in the Gestapo?'

After a long pause, Willi answered with one word: 'Yes.'

'Then get off my ground.'

'Listen!' he shouted. 'God dammit, you listen to me for once.'

His voice was so angry – and, if that's the word, *sincere* with anger – that I stopped shouting.

'You remember the promise you made when I was beaten up in Düsseldorf? You promised then to believe me when I told you that I was not a free agent and that anything I did you had to believe in me. You *promised*. I believed you, I came all the way to see you, and instead I find you a liar. You're the one to be ashamed.'

Suddenly, embarrassingly, Willi stood there just outside the front door and burst into tears. Huge sobs racked his body as he stuttered, 'I'm sorry.'

'Better come in,' I said gruffly. I couldn't ignore that hideous uniform, but somewhere at the back of my mind was the thought that maybe – only maybe – I'd jumped to the wrong conclusion. Though how could I? He had *admitted* being in the Gestapo.

'Sorry about this;' he wiped his face as he walked into the living room.

I got him a drink. He downed it at one gulp. I had a drink too; I felt I needed it.

'I had hoped that Anna would be in America by now,' he said when he was able to speak a little more quietly. 'I've lost everything in the world worth living for but I risked everything to come here because – it was foolish of me, I see that now – I thought I could count on *one* friend.'

I felt awful – yet what else could I say?

'But Christ, Willi! Your lot have tortured one poor devil in Douzy, you've abducted Anna and Olivia – you can hardly expect me to welcome you with open arms.'

He shook his head. 'I'll go,' he said slowly.

'Then why are you here?'

'To help.'

'You, help!' I cried. 'How can the Gestapo help, for Christ's sake?'

A sudden voice stilled my anger.

'Let Willi explain before you condemn him.' Grandma had walked into the room. She must have been listening.

'But Grandma, he's a German!' I said, as though that explained everything.

'I know. But I think Willi has suffered a lot and – well, tell me what happened, Willi, then we'll see.'

At first I was puzzled by her ready acceptance of *any* German. But when I looked at her enquiringly she just said briefly, as though in an aside that explained everything, 'We need all the help we can get – even from the enemy.'

Willi's story was quickly told. He had at first joined the army, as he said he would, but his only thoughts were to find Anna. Or at least to get news of her. The army offered no such opportunity, and he was on the point of being sent to the eastern front in Russia when he learned that the S.S. was asking for volunteers with specialised knowledge of languages and geography in France.

'They were recruiting experts for occupied France in various regions, to enforce civil government,' he explained. 'I was the perfect choice for this area. We've been stationed in several places, but now I'm at Châlons-sur-Marne, less than twenty miles away from Douzy. I didn't dare to drive over before, but today I was able to get a car. I wanted to find out – and Larry, believe me, to help – to do *anything*. Half Germany is disillusioned with Hitler, the war, now the Russians. We *know* it's a hopeless cause, now the invasion of England has failed.'

'I'm sorry, Willi,' I apologised.

'It was understandable. The German people don't have a very good image these days. Tell me – do you know the man who arrested Anna and Olivia?'

'His name is Hoess. He's stationed at Reims.'

'I'll kill him!' burst out Willi. 'I know all about him. He's a sadist.'

'Don't be a fool,' I said. 'He knows the name Frankel. He'd realise who you were right away.'

'I'm still going to kill him.'

'You're going to do nothing of the sort,' said La Châtelaine in her own special voice of authority. 'Are you with us – or neutral?'

'With you?' Willi looked from me to Grandma.

'Yes – will you help us?' She sounded almost impatient. 'I don't expect you to start killing Germans, but all information is useful, and if you have any . . .'

'I'll do what I can,' Willi promised. 'It won't be much. I

can't get involved. It might ruin everything – there are spies spying on other spies in the Gestapo.'

'All the more reason to stop telling us how willing you are to kill Hoess,' said La Châtelaine acidly. 'If you actually did kill him you might destroy the one man who could tell us where Anna has got to. Get your priorities right, young man. The time for killing Germans will come later.'

35

For some weeks I had been undecided what tactics to employ about a major piece I was anxious to write for the *Globe*, but which I knew I could not file from France, not even under my own name. I wanted to write the truth about the hypocrisy among many Frenchmen, living comfortably in occupied Paris. I'd been thinking about women like Coco Chanel and her German lover, and many other French men and women who seemed – well, at least not to suffer under the occupation.

Stories like the one I had in mind don't boil up overnight, but gradually in the mind, and mine, I think, was born partly because of the difference between city and rural life – the different standards between Paris and Douzy.

Country life in Douzy might be uneventful, even gloomy, with only Grandma and Papa as companions most of the time, but at least the air smelt clean, and I *felt* clean, whereas Paris depressed me – I always had the feeling that, whatever you were doing, you had to watch yourself because someone else was watching you.

One day I saw a man in a shabby suit sit down at the Flore and order, '*Café crème, s'il vous plaît.*'

There was nothing to mark him out from his fellows. He was nondescript, the kind of man turned out by the thousand, seemingly mass-produced for large cities, enduring lonely, friendless lives, living each day as they lived yesterday and tomorrow. Yet at his request the waiter looked at him suspiciously, and within seconds two plainclothes Germans who had heard him give the order demanded to see his papers. Eventually they took him away — and roughly. I never discovered what happened to an apparently innocent man, but the waiter explained *why*. 'Those men were Gestapo in civilian clothes,' he spat in disgust, 'and the minute they heard him ask for a *café crème* they were suspicious that he might be a spy. There hasn't been a drop of milk in a café for months. Everyone knows that *café crème* is unobtainable.'

This is what I wanted to write about, the way in which every move was dictated by fear, while collaborators thrived on the miseries of others.

Even if they weren't arresting people, the Germans became more ill-mannered. The early veneer of politeness had been rubbed away. In the Métro German soldiers often entered by the exit stairs, pushing civilians aside. Places in trains were desperately hard to find, yet dozens were reserved for the army, the half empty compartments bearing stickers on the windows, '*Nur für Wehrmacht*'.

In contrast to the spit and polish of the Germans, most Parisians looked dowdy. The hat had given way to the bandeau. Stockings had vanished. Girls painted their legs, even down to the black line of the non-existent seam at the back. The first wooden soles were appearing. Bottles of liquid saccharin had replaced sugar in ersatz coffee. Bread was now a dirty grey — and you were lucky to get any. In place of the renowned French *confiture* you could now only buy what was derisively called 'approximate jam'.

And always it was the Jews above everyone else who lived in fear, especially since the anti-Jewish police — known as the *police des questions juives* — was established to enforce new legislation under which thousands of Jewish refugees who had acquired French citizenship were liable to have it rescinded.

Many Jews had been hidden by friends just as we had hidden Olivia; I knew of at least one who had been hidden by Sylvia Beach at her bookshop 'Shakespeare and Company'. I hadn't seen her for several weeks so I decided to pick her brains and ask for specific instances about life in Paris which I would then incorporate in my article, to be written under a false name, of

491

course. I had gone on the spur of the moment, but I walked into a real life drama.

An arrogant Prussian-type officer was having an argument with her. He obviously wanted to buy one particular book from Sylvia, who equally firmly was refusing to let him have it. Sylvia was an even-tempered woman, but now she had dug her heels in and said, 'I'm sorry, this is my last copy and I don't want to sell it.'

The book was James Joyce's *Finnegan's Wake*.

'I demand to buy it. That's what a bookshop is for, isn't it? You sell books?' asked the German angrily.

To ease the tension I cried cheerfully, 'Hello, Sylvia. All going well?'

The German looked me up and down with the kind of insolence that only Germans can put into a stare – especially when they are victorious.'

'I warn you, *fraülein*,' he ignored me, 'that you will sell that book.'

'I won't!' she shook her head.

'Very well,' he shouted angrily. 'We'll see. I'll be back tomorrow with a squad of soldiers and I'll have your bookshop closed down.' He stamped out.

Sylvia looked at me. 'He means it,' she whispered.

'He does,' I agreed. 'The Germans have the power to close any foreign bookstore. Any excuse will serve.'

'He's not getting *Finnegan's Wake*,' she cried. 'In fact I'm fed up with even having to serve these bastards. I'm going to close down for myself. I've turned fifty and I've had enough. Come on! Let's go to work, Larry.'

We did. We had several hours' start – and my car. And friends. Before nightfall we had removed all the books, taken them into hiding, and knocked down all the shelving. We couldn't carry the wood away, but the crowd which gathered round the shop, intrigued by our activity, was delighted to take away shelving, no doubt hoarding it for the winter's fires. Sylvia gave away all the furniture. Finally, early the following morning, I tracked down Fernandez, the Spaniard who had papered the poppies all over the walls of the rue de l'Université, and he painted out the name 'Shakespeare and Company'. By the time the officer arrived the next day, together with four armed soldiers, the most famous foreign bookshop in Paris had simply ceased to exist.

These were the thoughts I wanted to write about, but obviously such a story could never be written from Paris. It would not only be censored, but I would probably be kicked out of Paris. My best plan was to file the story under another name from neutral Switzerland – which would have the added bonus of allowing me to see Sonia.

Once I had decided to go, the question was, how? I couldn't leave France legally, for I would get no re-entry permit. So the simplest way would be for me to smuggle my way across the border into Switzerland and then file from there. I decided to tell Oregon what I had in mind.

Wise old bird, he spotted at once the factor I hadn't mentioned and with apparent innocence said to me, 'Great idea. But dangerous. If you really want to safeguard your name for the *Globe* much better let me go. I'm only a messenger. Unless, of course,' with a twinkle in his eye, 'you're thinking of popping into Rolle to see a certain young lady.'

'Okay,' I sighed. 'I can't fool you, Uncle Oregon. I should have known better.'

'Actually,' he said, 'I would have gone as a messenger because I think you do run a serious danger of being discovered. But honestly, I'm too old to climb mountains and hide in woods.'

'I do want to see her,' I admitted. 'I've also got a great story to tell, and I'm even willing to sacrifice my by-line. I can't do more than that.'

'You can't write it and then carry it back with you,' he said.

I shook my head. 'That would be too dangerous, I agree. But I can remember everything – and I'll write it in Switzerland and send the copy through our Berne office.'

'But what if you're caught? I mean, if you're an American correspondent you have every right to travel about France, but you can't leave the country and get back.'

'It's absolutely essential there's no suspicion that I've left the country. The way I plan to go is to get a new identity card with a French name on it and smuggle my way into Switzerland. After all, if I cross the frontier at, say, Divonne, overlooking the lake, I'll only have to cover five miles or so to get to Rolle and I'll lie up there, get our man in Berne to come and meet me, and hand him the copy. Then, after I've said goodbye to Sonia, I'll go back – as a Frenchman.'

'But getting a French identity card might be difficult.'

I shook my head. 'It's easy. I know a chap who turns them out by the dozen. Very smart. I'm not in a rush to go to Switzerland but I want to be prepared and I'm going to start the ball rolling right away.'

In fact my plan, though ingenious, took a little time. Through a friend I spent a morning at the faculty of the Sorbonne and started leafing through the register of enrolments. When I found one of about my age, I wrote down his name – Henri Vasson – and the department in the Seine-et-Oise where he had been born. This happened to be at Pontoise. Then I wrote under the name Vasson to the local records office at Pontoise, giving details of my birthday, the clinic where my birth had been registered, and so on, asking for a copy of my lost birth certificate, saying I needed it because I had mislaid my identity card.

The copy of the certificate was duly delivered in a matter of days, then all I needed was a couple of friendly witnesses after which the nearest police station issued me with a genuine duplicate identity card, though this one was decorated with my own photograph and even my own fingerprints, and of course, the name 'Henri Vasson'.

'Here you are.' I showed it to Oregon when it finally arrived. 'It's a funny feeling – like being given a present of a new life.'

'For God's sake hide it until you need to use it,' said Oregon, quite sharply for him.

'I will,' I promised, never realising how valuable that card would become, that a journey planned almost as an escapade to land a story with a derring-do dateline to thumb my nose at the French would result in a desperate bid to help in the rescue of Anna.

I had no idea when I returned to Douzy on my next visit that I would hear the first rumours of Anna's fate. They were only rumours, there was no confirmation, and I didn't hear about them at first. But they came eventually from Gaston.

Gaston had now assumed the role of Grandma's right-hand man in the vineyard. She was as active as ever herself, cycling indefatigably from one vineyard to another, a straight-backed figure recognisable from a distance. Grandma liked Gaston, I could tell that, and not only by the way she spoke about him whenever we were at home. I found a touch of cynical amusement in the way first my mother and now my grandmother had taken to him.

'He's dependable, that's what it is,' said Grandma.

'I quite agree, yes, I *do*,' said Papa. 'Without doubt he's learned very quickly and he's an admirable – yes, *admirable* – replacement for . . .' Poor Papa, he couldn't bring himself to utter any of our names, not even the word 'Guy', though he at least we believed to be safe. Absence really had made Papa's heart grow fonder. Perhaps it had this effect on everyone? I remembered the rows when Olivia had moved in – and, not without a touch of bitterness, the row when Sonia moved out. One law for Guy, another law for me. Still, as I looked at Papa, older, worn by sadness, drinking his soup up carefully, sometimes finding it difficult to bring spoon to mouth without spilling a few drops, I knew that my thoughts were unfair. What had outraged Papa years ago was that I had betrayed the trust which he had placed on Sonia. With Olivia there was nothing to betray. Guy had demanded, she had moved in. After a few weeks she had become part of the family.

'I'm so glad *you* like him,' I said to Grandma.

'Of course I like him,' she all but snorted. 'He hates the Germans as well as being a vigneron.' Grandma's priorities were intriguing. Hatred before skill!

I noticed something else about Grandma. She accepted Papa's work as necessary and useful in helping the French, but I had the feeling that as far as she herself was concerned she would be happier in a more active role, more anti-German.

'If I was younger,' she said at dinner one night, 'I'd go south like a shot and join the Maquis.' Still hatred before skill! She had just finished saying this when, almost without a second's pause, she turned to the butler and said, 'Jean, this chicken is vile. Tastes like old string warmed up.'

Jean muttered apologies. I heard a whispered 'I'll tell Madame Robert, but there's no feeding stuff left.' Poor Jean! It wasn't his fault, he wasn't the cook; and no one could produce first-class feeding stuff for the animals when the Germans grabbed everything. We were darned lucky that we could kill a pig or wring the neck of a chicken or turkey or duck whenever we felt like it.

'You're a little bit hard on Jean,' said Papa when the butler had left the room.

'Fiddlesticks! Keeps everyone on their toes. A bit of complaining doesn't do any harm. Doesn't make any difference who you complain to, the message always filters through.' Then, returning to the subject before the interruption, she said, 'Yes, I would like to have joined the Maquis. Maybe later – perhaps if we start up here – who knows?'

'You are a *neutral*,' said Papa almost severely. 'You mustn't *entertain* such thoughts, really!'

'I'm no more neutral than a . . .' Grandma started witheringly but couldn't think of the right word, so rose from the table, glowering.

'She's very headstrong,' Papa sighed. 'I hope she doesn't do anything foolish.'

'Headstrong! Papa, that's the last word you could use to describe Grandma!'

'She's *La Patronne*. She likes the title and feels the need to live up to it. She's a *leader* in the area, yes, more than I ever was, and she could do something rash – I'm sure if she'd had a gun in her hand she'd have shot that Gestapo man on that terrible day.'

'Who wouldn't? But thank God she didn't.'

'Me too,' said my father. 'I hear rumours about Frenchmen starting to form groups to fight the Germans – a sort of Resistance. If your Grandma gets involved in that sort of thing our last hopes of ever finding the girls . . .' he left the sentence unfinished.

I mentioned Grandma's rashness to Gaston next time we met, saying I hoped she wouldn't become involved.

'No danger of that – not yet,' he said. 'There's nothing to

get involved about. But she's a wonderful old lady − and, who knows, one day America might be in the war.'

'Think so?'

'It's not inconceivable. Though less likely now that Britain has won the Blitz and the German invasion of England has failed. Pretty good stuff. I wish I'd been able to get to Britain and fight with the Free French.'

'You might do more valuable work here.' Gaston had already confided to me that he and his friends were completing a dossier of all German activity − and rumours of fifth columnists.

'The Germans can't control Europe for ever,' he said. 'But it will be a terrible struggle to get them out, even though they have now invaded Russia. The only way the French people can help is to collect every scrap of information about the Germans. One day it will all be of value.'

'But events − conditions − they could change.'

'Well, we'll have to keep our information up-to-date. We can't do anything now, but one day'− he was speaking almost dreamily − 'we'll use the British and the Free French and send in saboteurs: parachute them down into the dozens of hidden valleys in Champagne. The Germans can never patrol them all.'

It was about two weeks later that Gaston came up to me, looked round, and said, 'I've got something extremely important to tell you. Can you meet me in the orchard − say five o'clock?'

'Sure. But remember that as a neutral I can do more for you than if you drag me in . . .'

'Don't worry. Promise.'

I had hesitated at first, making the excuse about neutrality, because a horrible thought had passed through my mind. If Gaston wanted to see me so urgently − and alone − what could he possibly want to see me about − except perhaps Mama? Had he heard from her? No, that was impossible. Or had Papa found out? No, that was also impossible. But what else could it be? Anyway, I decided to go and have a word with him.

Instead of making my way directly down the dell to the

orchard, I walked along the back paths leading to and past the Home Farm. The country always gave me a sense of permanence. The house, with its walls of hand-shaped stones three to four feet thick, had stood for centuries, and war or no war, the open sheds in the yards were still being used to dry corncobs for the pigs and cows. One of the farm lads was walking a horse to the nearest blacksmith near Rilly. The nine cows were ready to be milked; despite the scarcity of food by our normal standards we were almost self-sufficient.

'I've wrapped up some *saucisse* and ham for you to take back to Paris,' said Madame Robert, adding the question everyone asked, 'Any news yet?'

I turned up to say hello to old Pagniez, who hailed me with a greeting, and I thought then that even with his crippled right hand he had come to terms with life much better than if he had been a town-dweller. He was an old man, stooped after a life bent over the vines, but he never complained. I shook his left hand, and crossed the bottom of the dell towards the rhododendron bushes where I had first overheard Guy and Lisette quarrelling, and then through the wicker gate into the orchard. I was suddenly stabbed by the painful memory of the day I up-ended Sonia in the tall hayseed grass, and the intriguing look she gave me when, without warning, as I held her up by the ankles, she let her skirt fall down almost over her face. It wasn't a painful memory, of course; more a beautiful one. But I actually felt a short stab of pain in the chest thinking of the past. Then Gaston appeared and the vision flew away.

I had never seen him so ill at ease, metaphorically shuffling his feet as we stood in the long grass. The secrecy of the meeting made me wonder again if he wanted to talk about Mama. Well, I wasn't going to stand for *that*.

'You didn't suggest this talk because you want to go for a walk?' I said lightly, swiping at some weeds with Willi's Malacca stick.

'No, no. But it's very hard to tell you, very hard indeed. But I have to. I didn't like to talk to you about this until I was ninety-per-cent sure.'

'Well, for Christ's sake, come on! What's it all about?'

Finally he asked, 'Did you know that in the rue Christina, just off the boulevard de Pommery – about half-way between the cathedral and the town hall − the Germans have established a brothel for German troops and officers?'

I had heard rumours − terrible ones. The Germans had not only rounded up every known street walker, they had imported some from Paris and also forced dozens of local girls, many of them Jewish, presenting them with an alternative: either work in the brothel or face a firing squad or deportation. The desire to cling to human life was so strong that though some girls were shot many had entered the bordello. Even so, as Gaston stood there, the truth never entered my head.

'The brothel is in two sections,' explained Gaston. 'One for officers. One for other ranks.'

'What are you trying to tell me?'

For a moment Gaston hesitated, obviously scared to tell me; and then I knew what he was trying to say.

'We don't know who she is,' he said. 'We can't even be certain our information isn't just a rumour. But we've had seven different reports from contacts who have never even met each other, and they all confirm that there's a blonde American girl being forced to work in the' − he didn't like to use the word bordello − 'in the *maison de plaisir*. The one reserved for officers only.'

At first I couldn't assimilate the shock, perhaps because Gaston had attempted to soften the blow by saying 'It's not certain, of course,' rather like a doctor who tells a relative, 'She's very, very ill,' when in fact the patient is already dead. But when the full impact hit me I couldn't even say a word to Gaston. I left him there, stumbling back to the dell, hardly seeing the grass, eyes brimming with tears. For in a way death would have been easier to bear. It can help blot out the past. Death is final; you know where you are. But now, as I stumbled up towards the house, I suddenly thought, 'What's she doing? What's she doing at this very minute while I'm alive and free?' Try as I might I couldn't eradicate a picture from my mind. Anna on her back, legs spreadeagled and a man − a German − grunting on top of her. Oh my darling Anna! I can do nothing − nothing to help you. Poor Anna, how many times did she have to do this? How many men queued up every day to take her? For a moment I couldn't go on. I'm not the one suffering, I thought, and yet my legs felt like jelly. I retched, and all my guts seemed to spew out of my mouth. Some of the sick caught where the nose and throat meet, so that as I blew my nose out came the last remnants of vomit.

I knew it was true. For a moment I tried to believe the whole thing was an exaggeration – a case of mistaken identity. But suddenly a picture from the immediate past flashed before my eyes, telling me it was true, that Anna was being subjected to a systematic, degrading torture as brutal in its way as the pain meted out to other victims shackled in the cells.

I was thinking of the friendliness of Otto Abetz when he assured me that Anna was alive, his smile as he said, 'She is serving the Third Reich.'

The words had been deliberately chosen, of that I was certain. And one day, I vowed, I would revenge myself on him.

The most awful emotion was the loneliness of my knowledge. I couldn't share it. I couldn't tell Papa – unless I believed he could help to free her. He would go berserk, kill somebody, or curl up and die, if not in fact, then in spirit. I couldn't just burst in and tell Grandma, saying, 'Your granddaughter is working in a brothel.'

She could have borne the blow better than my father – better than me, for that matter – but what good would it do to worry an old lady in her seventies?

But there was another reason why I didn't tell the family. We didn't know for sure. Instinct told me it was true, but I still had to make certain. Instinct wasn't enough on its own. The unknown blonde in the bordello might have been brought in from anywhere – if, that is, there *was* a blonde American girl in the *maison de plaisir*. So far we only had unconfirmed reports. Even so, dozens of wild thoughts raced through my mind. I had a map of the underground passage linking our cellars with others. I knew the address, and could pinpoint almost the exact spot directly underneath the buildings in the rue Christina. But the chalk passage would be, perhaps, fifty feet under street level, and there was no way I could dynamite my way up. I didn't want to blow up Anna when trying to rescue her.

In my heart I was already aware of two facts: I had to be sure it *was* Anna in the brothel; and then I would have to get to see Sonia as quickly as possible and beg her to help. Over and over again she had promised that if she could only find out where Anna was she could pull the necessary strings and obtain her release. I believed her. But I didn't want to bring Sonia into this until we were absolutely certain, if only because Sonia might not be able to exert her influence a second time if we made a mistake at the first attempt.

I determined to tell Oregon as soon as I reached Paris, but first I went to see the outside of the bordello. It wasn't just morbid curiosity – far from it. I wanted to be sure of the geography, I wanted to *feel* the agony of propinquity, however nauseating.

The brothel consisted of a group of several large houses each distinctively painted with yellow doors. They lay almost under the shadow of the cathedral, each door for different soldiers who were lined up outside. Their sex life was organised according to rank. Officers stood in line outside a two-storey house on the right side of the street. That would be the place where Anna was. The next house was besieged by sergeant majors, recognisable by the narrow silver stripes on their collars. The drill sergeants, with stars on their epaulettes, stood at the foot of the stairs leading to an old, half-dilapidated house. Privates and corporals waited outside the other houses.

As I watched them, like cattle waiting to be fed, an old military saying kept running through my thoughts: 'A soldier's pay, a soldier's risks'.

From the ground level room I could hear the sound of music blaring. Now and then one of the closed windows on the first or second floor opened and a girl would lean out and scream. Gaston told me later that sex could be bought for between twenty and fifty occupation marks.

Large signs along the street read, 'Members of the German Armed Forces are permitted to enter this street only between 6 a.m. and 10 p.m.'

I don't quite know when I first realised that there was only one way to find out about Anna. Since the bordello was reserved for officers only, I would never be allowed to patronise it. But I *did* know of one German officer – and so the macabre, ghoulish thought persisted. Willi had promised to keep in touch – he was as desperate as I for news – and on his next visit to Douzy I would have to put it to him: Willi was the only man who could find out if the girl in the bordello was Anna. I hadn't worked out the details, but the scheme – if Willi would agree – was so crazy that we could get away with it. And once we knew that it was Anna then I could use my false identity card to rush to Switzerland and Sonia could move into action.

Willi didn't visit Douzy very often; it was too risky. Though to the enemy the Gestapo exuded an aura of being all-powerful, it had its own rigid code of discipline, including geographical areas of operation. Nobody trespassed on another officer's preserves without risking embarrassing questions. It was almost as though even poaching for torture victims was frowned upon. So, as Willi was stationed at Châlons-sur-Marne, each journey to Douzy posed a hazard. He was always accompanied by a Gestapo driver – and, as Willi had pointed out to us, every member of the Gestapo was as eager to spy on his colleagues as on the enemy. Consequently Willi's visits to Douzy had to appear important with, whenever possible, a different driver each time. He tried to visit us about once every five or six weeks, but this time when he arrived – two weeks after Gaston's news – he didn't have the faintest idea of what to expect.

'Any news from your end?' I asked, pouring out a drink for him.

He shook his head. 'And your side?' For a split second I hesitated. It was a terrible moment to tell him what I suspected had happened, but he pounced on that split second with the speed of a panther – and also, I thought wryly, with the expert training of a professional interrogator. He jumped up and grabbed my shoulders.

'*Wass ist?*' he shouted almost hoarsely. 'What do you know?'

'Take your hands off me, Willi.' Angrily I thrust his shoulders away. 'I'm not being bashed around by your lot.'

'I am sorry. I feel . . .'

'I'm sorry too, Willi. But don't shout. You don't want the driver outside to hear.'

'But what?' he demanded. '*Mein Gott*! I can tell you have news. Why are you torturing me?'

Torture! Willi's unconscious irony was lost in the rush of thoughts.

'Sit down,' I said. 'For Chrissake. At least do as I ask you in *my* house.'

He sat down, almost glowering. He took off his jacket, tie, collar. 'You are trying to inform me she is dead.'

I shook my head. 'This is only a rumour, Willi.' I didn't know how to begin. 'So don't count on it. Don't get all het up. It's possible that Anna is here – in Reims.'

'But where?' he shouted. 'You speak in a riddle, in a roundabout way.'

'It's a roundabout story,' I said shortly, and then as calmly as I could I told him everything.

His face seemed to crumple into a thousand creases, then without warning he burst into a spasm of terrible sobbing – just as he had done the last time, only now in great animal cries, so loud that Jean came in alarmed.

'It's all right,' I told him. 'I'll give Monsieur Frankel another brandy.'

'My *liebchen*, my *liebchen*,' he cried, holding his face in his arms, rocking backwards and forwards and groaning. 'My beautiful innocent lovely *liebchen*. My Anna – why did they do this to you? Why did they make you a *mädchen für alles*.' I knew the German phrase: a girl for all purposes.

'They did it to your wife – the Germans,' I said, because I thought it would bring him down to earth. 'But don't forget that the Gestapo also did it to my sister.'

He looked at me, incongruous in his shirt, without jacket or tie, as though trying to disguise the uniform. Now, confronted with the terrible news of how the Gestapo had treated his own wife, Willi looked at the jacket, crumpled, lying on the floor, with loathing – the symbol of the brute, of the degradation inflicted by one human being on another – and often for no other reason than to satisfy a sadist's whim.

'Does anyone know?' Instinctively Willi lowered his voice as though to hide the shame.

I shook my head.

'Not even your father?'

'No, no. I said nothing to him. After all it may not even be true.'

'You know it's true. Yes?'

I hesitated again, then repeated, 'All I can say is that several independent reports confirm that there *is* a blonde girl with an American accent working there.'

'Where is it?' he asked in a flat, dull voice.

I told him – explaining where the rue Christina was, how to recognise the group of houses with yellow doors. Though I couldn't keep the bitterness out of my voice when I added, 'It's easy to find – there's always a queue outside.'

Willi held his head in his hands again as though trying in vain to blot out the picture of life behind those doors.

'I cannot even *begin* to imagine it,' he groaned. He was begging me for comfort. Again I couldn't help thinking – however swiftly – how ironic it was to find a member of the mighty Gestapo begging a neutral civilian for help, for advice, for – and I knew this as I looked at Willi – for forgiveness, not for what *he* had done, but as a measure of the contrition he felt on behalf of his countrymen.

Of course, I thought as I watched him, it wasn't all Willi's fault. One fault lay in the happy-go-lucky way we had all blithely swayed our parents away from their own doubts, had persuaded them to let Willi marry Anna. We were to blame. Yet who could have known?

'What are we going to do?' In his white shirt without its collar, the brass stud sticking out of the old-fashioned neck-band, the face sagging with despair, he could in peacetime have passed for some scruffy down-and-out asking for a job.

The master race! How much simpler brutality was when you were dealing with cyphers, not friends. I stole another look at Willi. Yes, he was broken. Yet it was the fate of his wife that must have been a factor in persuading a 'good' German to become an enemy of the Third Reich. But what had he been like before that? Had Willi ever tortured a victim with the same indifference that Hoess had tortured Jacques Pagniez? Had Willi ever torn off a woman's fingernails just because she was a Jewess? Or inserted electric bulbs in a girl's vagina as part of a routine way of getting more information?

Of course it was unfair of me to think like that. Willi

couldn't have behaved in such a way. The German forces were full of men who never wielded any weapon more lethal than a typewriter.

'Do you think if I went to see the Gestapo in Reims,' asked Willi, 'they might release her in my custody?' It was a forlorn hope.

I shook my head. 'If they trace you back to her,' I warned him, 'you'll be for the high jump. And, besides, we don't *know*. Above everything else we must *know*, we must be certain we're not making a mistake.'

'Then what?' he asked helplessly.

'I have a plan,' I said slowly. 'It'll work – but only if you keep cool.' Jean brought in another bottle of cold Perrier. 'Better have another brandy and soda,' I urged him. 'The plan is based on several factors. But Willi – remember this is *my sister* just as much as she's your wife. And if you think that as a German you can get her out of this bloody place you've got another think coming.'

'I'll do anything I can,' he promised.

'I'm sure you will. Because, Willi – better get this straight – you do *exactly* what I say because if anything goes wrong I wouldn't hesitate to kill a German – even one particular German – to get Anna free.'

'I know, I know. But remember I too hate the Nazis.'

'I hope so. But I recall the day at Douzy, sitting in this very room, when you said the Nazis didn't count. Your lot brought the Nazis into power, Willi, so cut out the crap. Anyway, I believe I've found a way I might be able to get Anna out.'

'I'll do anything,' he begged me again. I saw him look nervously at his watch. Rightly, he was afraid of staying too long at a place where, as he had told the driver, he was making a cursory inspection – presumably on some non-existent orders.

'You'll have to go?'

'Five minutes. Can you tell me – now, quickly. I cannot get her out, *nein*? Not possible. Nor you, Larry. So who?'

I hesitated, almost for effect.

'Sonia,' I said softly.

'Sonia!'

'Who better? She's an ally of the Germans. She's the wife of a high-ranking Italian diplomat. I understand that Mussolini himself admires her – when his mistress isn't around.'

I explained as quickly as I could how Sonia might be able to help – once we were all sure that Anna was in the rue Christina.

'For there's one other problem,' I said. 'We can't send Sonia out on a wild goose chase. We can't set a complicated plan in motion unless we're a hundred-per-cent sure the girl behind the yellow door *is* Anna. And that's where you come in,' I added as Willi started to put on his collar and tie and shake the creases out of his uniform. 'That's the moment when you're going to have to keep cool. If you don't, you lose your head.'

Willi was so numb with despair, shock and anguish that he looked at me, mouth open, as though he hadn't the faintest idea what I was talking about.

'If I can help,' he mumbled finally.

'Willi,' I said gently, 'we must have a positive identification of Anna before we drag Sonia into this. I can't help. You're the only one who can make sure if she's there.'

'But how?' he asked almost stupidly.

'You've got to go to the bordello in the rue Christina, pay your money, queue up with the other officers, and insist on having the blonde,' I said almost brutally.

For a moment I thought he was going to throw up. His face went a sickly colour, he leaned forward, he started to retch again. In a panic I looked round for a vase or a *cachepot*, but as the wave of nausea passed he shouted, 'I couldn't do it.'

'You will,' I said, adding with deliberate brutality, 'Don't be such a fucking coward. It's the only way, and you owe it to us.'

'I couldn't, I couldn't!'

'You will. This is my sister. And at the rate Anna is being used, she probably won't last much longer. If you want to see her alive . . .'

'*Mein Gott,*' he groaned. 'If only I was dead, how easy.'

'How easy it would be for you. To let her spend the rest of her life in a whorehouse. Yes, bloody easy – for you.'

'I'm sorry. But even if I do this thing will she ever be the same again? How can she be?'

'I don't give a shit about that. That's a problem for the

future. First things first. Identification – then I'll contact Sonia
in Rolle. Sonia will have no problems travelling to France. But
you come first. And remember' – my voice hardened again –
'quite apart from what *you* want I want my sister back. If you
love Anna then you'll go through with this. You'll just have to
go to the brothel and confront her. It's the only chance you'll
ever have of saving her.'

So it was arranged. We couldn't fix on a definite date for
Willi to visit the house with the yellow door; he couldn't just
walk out of Gestapo headquarters in Châlons without making
arrangements. But he did promise to go as soon as possible and
then let me know if it was Anna.

'You'll be on your own,' I said, 'and the most critical
moment of all will be when you go into her room. She
probably won't have the faintest idea it's you – or that you
know her. That's bad enough for any woman – going whor-
ing and then finding it's her own husband.'

'I could hold my hand over my face?'

'I don't give a damn what you do. Because even this isn't the
most important moment. If I know Anna, the moment she's
going to scream – to lose all her control, irrespective of what
might happen to her – will be the moment of *double* shock.
First when she recognises you, second when she sees the
Gestapo uniform. It's enough to make any woman go mad.'

Willi looked at me helplessly.

'Somehow you've got to stop that first scream, Willi – but
it must be with your first words. *Your very first words.* Even if
you have to grab her mouth for a few seconds, tell her before
anything else, "I've come from Larry. Help is on the way."
Once you get that message across, even if she doesn't believe it
at first, even if she's about to vomit, *you've got to stop that first
scream.*'

36

It was three weeks before Willi was able to manufacture an adequate excuse to get away from Châlons and spend the day at Reims. He had taken care to have a different driver, and only called in at Douzy for five minutes.

'I go this afternoon to the rue Christina,' he said dully, his precise Germanic English failing to mask his obvious distress.

'You'll call in on the way back?'

'Of course,' he nodded. What would happen, I wondered, at the moment of meeting – if they met, that is. How could *anyone* suppress a shriek of despair at the sight of him? There he was, hateful black uniform, the sharply angled peaked cap, the death's head emblem, the exaggerated cut of his tightly fitting breeches, even the equally exaggerated shine on the polished jackboots. He looked every inch a figure of fear.

'It is the uniform,' he apologised, seeing me look at him. 'If I want to make certain of demanding the blonde girl, then I must *look* like the Gestapo officer – you know, I am used to being obeyed. I must give this impression. We go now. Do not think this will be easy for me.'

'I know that, Willi. But it's the only way.'

For the benefit of the driver, Willi marched out of the front door, all but shouting, 'These papers must be found, you understand! I am going to Reims on business, I will come back. You may be neutral, but everything must be ready, understand?'

'But I'm not sure . . .' I said, playing my part.

'No excuses!' cried Willi as the driver jumped round to open the back door, and I heard him mutter, '*Dummkopf!*' That was at 11.30 a.m. I settled down to wait.

Willi did not return to Douzy until nearly four that afternoon. As the driver rushed round the car to open the door for him, he stumbled out and I thought he was going to die on the spot – or at least faint. But somehow, dragging out the last reserves of his strength, he shouted, 'The papers? *Ich habe es eilig.*'

I realised what Willi was saying, for the benefit of the driver, that he was in a hurry. He told the driver to wait, muttering, '*Bitte warten Sie hier ein Paar Minuten.*' As he stumbled to the front door, Willi whispered, 'It's her, *mein leibchen*. For God's sake, get me a drink.'

I had to help him to the sofa. I poured out a stiff brandy – which he downed at once, and held out the glass for a refill. I could see the flush slowly spreading across his face, which had the deadly pallor of a man who has seen a ghost. He undid his collar in a fight to ease his breathing, and now that I knew it was Anna I didn't rush him. He had another drink, and I waited with a patience I certainly didn't feel, thinking of the time we had met in Düsseldorf, when I had opened the front door to look upon the bleeding pulp of Willi's smashed-in face. I knew that this was far worse for him, for now he had been beaten mentally, and at first it was impossible to force a word out of him. He was half sobbing, his face at times buried in his hands. Finally he became composed enough to give me a coherent account of what had happened.

He had, he said, informed his driver where he was going, and why, telling him to report for duty in three hours at the officers' car pool near the cathedral. Then he walked to the rue Christina, panicking at the prospect of seeing Anna, though it never entered his head that there would be much delay. He was astounded to find the rue Christina crammed with Germans – laughing soldiers queueing in front of one house, N.C.Os at another, a couple of dozen officers at a third, the one sporting a yellow door. From the man in front of him, a regular officer, Willi learned that each man was allowed thirty minutes with a girl. It cost fifty occupation francs, payable at the desk.

Forcing himself into a pretence of conviviality, Willi asked, 'Can you pick and choose?'

'Of course. There is a sitting-room and, once you are inside, then if you want a special girl you can't be kept waiting more than half an hour, can you? I have a favourite. Many do. We have a nice waiting-room, some champagne – it is very civilised.'

Civilised! Willi almost retched at the thought, but somehow he managed to keep up the appearance that he was enjoying the outing. 'They tell me there's a blonde American in there?' he jerked his head to the yellow door.

'I hear there is. Can't say I've ever seen her. Too frustrated, the Americans. Don't know a thing about the art of pleasing a man. Now a French whore . . .'

They queued for an hour before the officer ahead and Willi were allowed in. Behind them the queue in the street had grown – there must have been fifty officers alone standing in line for sex.

'There are only twelve girls, all hand-picked,' confided the young officer. 'I'm going to wait for Olga. I've been with her several times. I always bring her a bar of chocolate or something as a present.'

The house, Willi learned, had once been a small residential hotel before the *Wehrmacht* took it over and the reception room looked unchanged. A lady in black wearing glasses sat behind a desk. As Willi approached her she looked up and asked, 'Any particular girl?'

'The blonde, please – the American blonde.'

'She's busy – half an hour, if you don't mind waiting. A bottle of champagne?'

Offering champagne was obviously one of the ways *madame* increased her income, and a girl assistant led the way to a sitting-room where half a dozen officers, awaiting their particular choices, sat talking and drinking. It was like the front parlour of a middle-class home, and Willi found it almost impossible to imagine what lay upstairs, behind the secret doors. Everything bore the stamp of mediocre respectability – the antimacassar, the potted green shrubs, the brown at the tips, the round table in the centre covered with a crochet lace cloth on which stood several empty bottles. Leather chairs were grouped round the wall so that men could stretch their legs. On second thoughts, Willi reflected, it didn't look like the front parlour of a home; more like the waiting-room of a provincial dentist.

Most of all, Willi was dreading the moment when *madame*'s assistant would beckon him. He was terrified, because he knew that at the first sight of the uniform Anna – or whoever she might be – would stiffen with revulsion. Even while Willi was waiting, as the only Gestapo man in the room, he noticed that the banter among fellow officers waiting their turn did not include him. Virtually all German regular army officers – many brought up with a strict code of tradition – looked upon the Gestapo officers as pariahs.

Worse, Willi did not have the faintest idea what to expect. Ordinarily a man visiting a brothel wasn't unduly concerned, and just took everything as it came, but to Willi the unknown drama assumed an importance bordering on panic. Would she be on the bed? Would she greet him? Would she be fully clothed or lying there naked? Above everything else, would she scream? He decided that he must try at first to hide his face, to turn in sideways, shield himself somehow to stop her crying out. But how?

Two or three officers left the room, each one summoned by the *madame*'s assistant, who told them which numbered door was theirs at the top of the stairs. A few minutes later the girl approached Willi and tapped his shoulder.

'Number nine, *m'sieu*.' She pointed the way, and Willi felt his skin crawl, though his forehead was suddenly bathed in sweat. He climbed the stairs and opened the door marked '9' at the far end of the corridor. He caught a glimpse of a bidet and wash basin, a brass bedstead with a pink woollen coverlet and two pillows, and the back view of a woman in a pink dressing gown. Though he had planned to clap a hand over her mouth, the woman was too far away. Hiding his face as best he could with his cap, he coughed, then said his first words, very quietly, knowing that if it wasn't Anna what he said would mean nothing.

'Larry has sent me.'

She spun round, hand to mouth in her shock, suppressing her own scream. 'Larry!'

At first she didn't seem to realise who it was for she cried, 'Oh my God! My God,' and then she saw him and whispered, 'You! What are you doing here? The Gestapo?'

Willi had to rush his words, not give her time to think.

'Larry sent me to help.'

'But the Gestapo?'

'No, no. Forget this uniform. It's a disguise,' Willi urged

her, the words tumbling out. 'Larry found out where you are. He sent me to let you know. Sonia is going to help you.'

'Is it really you? Willi? In this hateful uniform?'

'I had to put it on to get in here,' he lied. 'You will be free soon. Sonia has promised.'

Terrified, she looked at the door, then fell into his arms, sobbing, 'Get me out, for God's sake get me out of this terrible place. You're not one of them, are you?'

'No,' he lied again. 'I will get you out, *liebchen*. I promise.' He led her to the bed, sitting down beside her.

'Don't look at me,' she whispered. And when Willi did, she covered her face with her hands. 'No, please! I feel so old – and tired – so dirty. Oh Willi, I'm so tired. I just want to die, to end it all, I'm so miserable.'

'Listen, *liebchen*,' he said. 'It's hard to tell you this, to think of what is happening to you – but *please*, one woman at Gestapo headquarters had her nails pulled out, one each day. Another had electric light bulbs pushed inside her. Be brave, Anna. Yours is a filthy torture of a different kind, but it will be over soon. Larry has made the promise. And we will get you away, to Switzerland to live.'

She looked at him, almost with wonder. 'Is it really you? Am I *really* going to be saved? Are you sure? How can you tell?' The questions tumbled out as though she couldn't believe what she was seeing or hearing.

Willi nodded. 'It's taken all this time to find out where you were,' he explained. 'I'll tell you about it all later. Meanwhile this nightmare is nearly over.'

Willi looked at her face; the bloom of youth had gone, to be replaced by ugly lines etched on a grey skin, a map of despair.

'Never mind my face!' she cried suddenly. 'Look at this.' With a sudden angry gesture she tore away her dressing gown so that Willi could see her stomach, thighs and blonde pubic hair. And surrounding it the mottled yellow and purple bruises.

'They don't even know when they're hurting me.' With a sudden defensive gesture she closed her dressing gown. 'They're often in such a rush they force their way inside me. Yes' – in a melancholy voice loaded with tears – 'up to twenty times a day. With three days off once a month when I have the curse.'

'I can't tell you any more,' Willi finally said to me. 'I can't *remember* any more. I was in a daze all through the time I was there.'

'But she realises − well, that there's hope?'

'I'm sure she does. I'm only hoping that she understands. She's very, very tired.'

'Poor Anna. How she must be suffering.' My first fury had been followed by utter dejection, a sense of shared degradation for a sister I had once seen laughing and gay.

'I'm going to leave for Switzerland tonight,' I told Willi suddenly. 'Right away. I'm going now. You see, it's still going to take time. There's no way I can explain this on the phone to Sonia − even if I could get through to her, which I can't. And if I did the phone might be tapped. The most important thing of all, Willi − for God's sake, not a word. One leak and we're done.'

'How do you mean?'

'There's one good reason for not phoning. If Hoess ever gets a hint that we're on the track of Anna, she'll be whisked out of the rue Christina before we can do anything. And then − even if they put her in a house in the next town − in the next street, even − she'd be lost again. So, Willi, do me a favour. However you feel, don't go back to the rue Christina. Don't fall into the trap of trying to see Anna again, just to cheer her up. Wait till I come back − I'll be back in less than a week − then come to see me first and I'll tell you all my plans − Sonia's plans. *Then* you can go to see her and tell her what to expect. But until then − you promise?'

At first he looked horrified. I think he had planned to try to see Anna regularly − maybe twice a week, I don't know. 'But you can't,' I urged him, '*anything* can arouse suspicion − you yourself said that the Gestapo spies on its own members. It must be dangerous going off from one headquarters to visit another where you're not supposed to be. It was okay when we had to do it − but don't give anyone the slightest chance to find out. You of all people know how the Gestapo works.'

'You're right,' he admitted. 'When do you expect to be back? You said in a week.'

'Maybe four or five days. I'll stay one night to tell Sonia and then I'll return as soon as I can.'

'I'll come to Douzy in a week or ten days.'

'Do that,' I said, and as an afterthought, for everything else had been driven out of my mind, I asked, 'Did you hear any news about Olivia?'

He nodded. 'She was also in the rue Christina, but then an extraordinary thing happened. Hoess sent for her. Apparently he decided to keep her as his – well, for himself. So now she lives in his house. Anna told me that much, but she wasn't sure of the details.'

'He's next on the list,' I said savagely. 'If we can find a way to get Anna out, then we'll find a way to deal with Hoess.'

The journey across France to within a few miles of the Swiss border presented no serious problems, because I planned to hide my false French identity card and travel legally as a neutral American journalist. But I didn't dare to cross the border legally, on my American passport, in case I was caught, or even if a check was made with Head Office in Paris. If that happened I would be prohibited from returning. So I decided to swap identities as I approached Divonne, the nearest town to the frontier, because if I was caught then, as a Frenchman, I might be able to bluff my way out of an argument with the French.

I decided to drive north from Reims through Châlons then cut across to Troyes and on to Dijon, after which the main road branched left and led to Dôle, instead of missing Switzerland if I had gone straight on to the south coast of France. I decided on the route for two reasons: I knew it well, and at a time when the Germans had removed virtually all signposts and it was impossible to buy maps this was a major factor. Also, if I had taken the northern route through Vesoul, crossing the frontier near Belfort, I would have had to spend at least two days crossing Switzerland itself – an added hazard, as I had no papers permitting me to stay there.

On the other hand, Divonne was almost within sight of Nyon on Lake Geneva in Switzerland, and Nyon was barely seven miles from Rolle. In fact, by not going into Nyon I could reduce the distance considerably by taking the short cut along the mountain roads.

I also had a contact in Divonne, thanks to Gaston, to whom I explained my plan.

'Divonne can be tricky,' he advised me. 'But about two miles out of the town – and that means away from the border post, but nearer the lake – there's an old inn called the Bois Joli. I stayed there after leaving North Africa. You remember our training? Well, it included two days in Switzerland getting kitted out. I had a wonderful holiday there too. As for Madame Gavroche, who's the boss of the inn, she'll help if she can. There's a regular traffic across the border. But be careful – it's pretty rough going, through wooded country.'

'You think she won't be suspicious if I ask for her?'

'You'll have switched nationalities by then,' Gaston reminded me. 'She's very pro-French. You'll like her.'

'And I can mention you by name?'

He nodded.

'She might have forgotten you,' I laughed.

'She won't,' he said.

It turned out to be almost as simple as that. I was stopped several times at German checkpoints, and I'm quite sure that each time details of my passport, identity card, car registration papers and so on were noted and sent back via local headquarters to some vague central authority. But I was doing no wrong, so I didn't care. As long as I had petrol, and that was stored in the magnum champagne bottles, and as long as I stayed in France on legitimate business, no one really had any right to stop me except in a military area. Even the champagne bottles filled with petrol had a legitimate look to them, for the labels bore my name. And I did keep a dozen bottles of non-vintage to offer occasionally when I wanted to smooth the ruffled feelings of any official in a bad temper. The difference in the size of the bottles made doubly sure that nobody would get a dose of petrol by mistake.

Now and again I had to stop to find a bite to eat, and I retraced my steps to two places where I had once spent such happy hours. I passed one night in the old mill near Dijon where, greatly daring, I had checked in with Sonia when she was seventeen; and when I reached the frontier town of Pontarlier on the second day I stopped for a beer at the same Western-style bar in the main street, before passing through the ancient gates of the city walls and plunging into the dark caverns of the thickly wooded, twisting roads of the Jura mountains.

I found the hotel which Gaston had told me about without any trouble after hiding my American passport and becoming a Frenchman. But once there I got quite a surprise.

I don't know what I had expected – I suppose my mental pictures hovered between two extremes: on the one hand a buxom, motherly type who would make me welcome, on the other the vinegary spinster type all dressed in black with rimless glasses tied to a cord, and a sharp eye on the cash register. Madame Gavroche was neither. The building was unpretentious, and could have done with a lick of paint, but it was attractive in a village sort of way, and I made my way to the small entrance hall with its inevitable polished reception counter and row of a dozen keys on hooks behind an extremely pretty woman who stood waiting at the desk. Tentatively I asked her, 'Can I please speak with Madame Gavroche?'

She smiled, showing beautiful teeth. A touch of hidden amusement made her eyes twinkle.

'*C'est moi-même, monsieur.*'

'You, *madame*! *Pardon*!' Confused, I added, 'I expected someone – well – a little older.'

'Everyone does,' she laughed. 'I'll have to try and grow older more quickly.' And then in a more businesslike tone she asked, 'What can I do for you, sir?'

'I wondered if you had a room for the night. And a garage for my car, perhaps.'

She shook her head. 'I'm sorry, sir, we're full up.'

I looked at the row of keys dangling on the wooden plaque, as though to say, 'You don't *look* full up.'

'No rooms available,' she said more firmly. 'I'm sorry, sir.'

'So am I,' I said slowly. 'Because I have a message from a friend of yours.'

'Who is that?' For the first time she looked interested.

'Gaston. He said you would remember him.'

'Gaston!' She almost blushed, and at once her attitude changed. 'How is he? Is he well? He's not being foolish – on dangerous missions? Oh Gaston! Come inside, *monsieur*. I think I can offer you a cup of *real* coffee – not this ersatz. We get supplies sometimes from across the frontier. Please do come in!'

She showed me into what I supposed would be called the parlour. Once we were both seated she cried, 'Tell me more – about Gaston – and your name, if I may ask?'

'Henri Vasson.'

'Monsieur Vasson. Ah! Gaston. *Quel homme*! He didn't stay long training in the mountains – two weeks maybe, then' – a little shyly – 'he took me for two days to Switzerland, to Geneva. In the middle of the war, it was a very pleasing interlude.'

I had no doubt it was. A pleasant change from Mama! Younger, too. I suppose I must have looked puzzled at her youth, for she explained gently, 'My husband was killed in the first two weeks of June, a year ago. I can hardly believe it. We had been married for six years and we bought this place with his savings. Since then I've helped anyone I can – anyone who hates the Boches.'

'I do,' I said. 'The Gestapo have taken my sister.'

'If I can help?'

'I have a very good friend – I hope to marry her one day – and she lives in Rolle. I want to go and see her. That's all.'

'Of course. I understand.' I caught a look – regret? – and thought that for a moment she eyed me rather wistfully, thinking perhaps of a substitute for Gaston; but I am sure I was flattering myself.

'And the room?'

'Of course. I always say no at first – because we have to fill in *fiches* for the police, and I am afraid unless I trust someone.'

Later she took me up to the loft under the roof, steeply sloping to guard against the winter snow. From there I had a perfect view of Lake Geneva, shining like a grey slate on which you could have drawn with a pencil. She pointed out Nyon in the distance. It looked ridiculously close. 'Rolle is over there;'

she pointed to the left. 'You see, you don't have to go to Nyon at all. You can bear left, walking across the side of the hills, then eventually you'll see the town hall of Rolle below you. It's the next town after Nyon.'

In some detail she explained the topography. The town of Divonne, with its customs post, was away to the right, out of sight. Below us were thick woods which lay spread out like a carpet in front of me. The belt of trees, she told me, was two miles deep and I had to get through them, but they were only a few hundred yards wide. Even so, I must on no account try to make my way across open ground.

'And be careful,' she warned me again. 'The vineyards you see *before* the bottom of the trees, on either side of the belt of woods, they are in France. And though the actual border is only a barbed wire fence at the bottom of the woods, if you stray outside that woodland in order to try to get across quicker the area is still busy with police. This is still occupied France, remember: we're just inside the demarcation line. Many of the police work directly under German supervision. That's why I didn't want to tell at first – in case the French tip off the enemy. Be very, very careful. Sometimes Germans come on patrol with the French police. And if you try to cross the vineyards or open ground and you are spotted – and the countryside is pretty bare at this time of year – you only get one warning. Then they shoot. It's not fair to blame the French entirely' – she shrugged her shoulders – '*They* would be shot if they didn't uphold the German orders.'

It was very clear. She arranged for me to leave the car locked in a shed attached to the house; I removed the ignition keys and gave them to her for safe keeping, then went upstairs to rest, coming down around five o'clock to get something to eat. Half a dozen people had by now gravitated to the pub's bar, the zinc top being wiped clean by another girl whom I hadn't seen before. I fell into conversation with some of the men – well, I didn't *fall* into conversation, they seemed so anxious to talk to a new face that they pushed me into the talking. But it was all very harmless and helped pass the time. It also allayed suspicion, and since I had to wait until ten o'clock at night when the moon was up before setting off for the woods I played a few hands of piquet with three of the men. One man, called André, left early, but two of the others, Louis and Valéry, stayed on and we drank our share of rough red wine, though I was careful not to overdo it, and at nine-thirty I announced that I was going to bed.

I went upstairs, took a flashlamp and my Malacca cane-cum-swordstick, not so much as a weapon of protection – I would have been terrified had I been forced to use it – but because I thought I might need it to feel my way in a dark wood, in much the same way as a blind man tests the way ahead when walking. The thick foliage would probably be impenetrable even though there was a moon.

Madame Gavroche's last words as she handed me a packet of sandwiches were, 'Be on the look-out for the police. We've had a couple looking around, but I think they've gone. But *do* be careful, I beseech you.'

Then I set off. Following her instructions, I walked about a couple of hundred yards along the roadside and then entered the wood, plunging from the moonlight into thick darkness. Thank God for the shape of the forest! If it had been square I don't think I could have ever found my way out of it, but because it was long and narrow I knew that if I strayed too far to the left or right I would see the lightness of the sky through thinning trees. It gave me an added sense of security – and I needed it, for it had never entered my head that the under-growth would be so dense, at times almost impassable. Thank God too for my malacca! By waving it in a semicircle ahead of me I could make slow progress. And every now and again I switched on my torch, literally for a second.

What really held me back was the *nature* of the under-growth. It seemed to consist entirely of thorn bushes, gorse perhaps, holly maybe, and from time to time the sounds of the forest would be broken by another sound – that of tearing, ripping cloth as I stumbled against a bush tougher and higher than the others. There was only a glimmer of light from the moon shining directly down, and my eyes gradually became accustomed to the darkness; but it was tough going all the same.

The only trouble – apart from my torn clothes – was that without warning I suddenly sank over my ankles into some sludge – a shallow pond. My feet were covered. Worse, in the effort of getting out I fell, covering the bottom half of my trousers with filth and losing one shoe altogether. That I *had* to find – for even if I reached the frontier, there was no way I could walk seven or eight miles to Rolle with only one shoe.

Cautiously I switched on my torch and managed to retrieve the filthy thing. I had to pour the mud and water out before I could put it on, squelching ooze out as I walked. Then I pushed ahead.

To this day I can never be sure of the exact moment when I realised I was being followed. The thickness of the forest at first muffled the sound, or perhaps I didn't want to hear it, was afraid to. But then I heard a twig snap. It was definite, no doubt about it. Then an eerie silence, though *not* a silence, a semi-silence broken by the sound of panting, of heavy breathing, the sound a dog makes when it has been running. Only this was no dog, or else it would have smelt me, approached me, friend or foe.

I reckoned I had to be fairly near the frontier by this time as I had been forging ahead slowly for over two hours. Now I had to get out quick. Once I was over the frontier the French police would be powerless, and only the Swiss could touch me – if, that is, they were there, which was unlikely. I was confident I could find Rolle, for there would be signposts again to help me. Even the name of the house on a wooden board, 'Three Circles Farm'.

But that was ahead.

Behind me the breathing grew nearer – and I suddenly realised there was more than one man. I had to run for it. But I couldn't. No man could run in this tangle. I was young and fit – and I did manage to increase my pace, reckoning that if the *flics* gave chase in the dark I would be less encumbered, could probably outpace them. But why didn't they shout? Order me to halt? I had no time to think. On my credit side was the fact that they didn't know exactly where I was, or where I was making for. Against me was the fact that they must be familiar with the terrain.

So I crashed on ahead, an unknown in a wilderness, all sound confined by the darkness, making no attempt at silence.

Flashlamps stabbed the night, went out. Then I heard French curses: '*Halt!*' '*Merde!*' '*A gauche!*'

And then in French, 'Don't kill him.'

The last gave me a mite of consolation − at least they weren't going to shoot me. And thank God they didn't have any tracker dogs.

Cursing, I almost fell into a gorse bush, the prickly needles tearing at my clothes again. The backlash of taller branches whipped savage scratches across my face and forehead. I could taste blood − my blood. Panting, I scrambled headlong, oblivious to the tears in my clothes, the ripping of cloth I could feel. Once or twice resolution almost gave out. But always a picture of Anna was there to goad me on as, gasping for breath, I tried to cover the last few yards of the forest.

What worried me most of all was that I might be running off my track. I knew the wood was narrow, but still, I was afraid I might turn full circle, back into the same gorse bush.

It was panic, of course. Reason told me that I was in the right place, but even so I was almost exhausted when two circles of light blazed at me and a voice shouted again, 'Halt or I fire.' They couldn't have been more than twenty feet away. I kept still, hoping the undergrowth, the bushes, the thick leaves of the evergreens would hide me. Then the man spoke again, but this time in a hoarse whisper to his colleague.

'*Il est là, Louis. J'en suis sure!*'

At the sound of the name the penny dropped. Louis! Christ! All this time I had assumed that the police were searching for me; the alternative had never entered my head. But Louis! Suddenly I realised that this was no police matter. I was up against a couple of thugs whom I had met in the bar and who had laid in wait for me, presumably to rob me.

Fury − at my own stupidity as much as at the two men − pumped in the adrenalin. I wasn't going to let a couple of thugs beat me! How many others, perhaps even more helpless, had been robbed by them as they were on the point of gaining freedom?

Well, I had one weapon they didn't expect. And it could be frightening. I realised now that I mustn't run any more. I must wait for them. I hadn't dared to wait and provoke the police; for an attack on an officer of the law would be flashed across the frontier in no time. But a couple of amateur Al Capones was a different matter. I was scared, yes; but they would never be in a position to press charges if I hurt them.

I waited. They switched on their searchlights, on and off, searching, only the nearness of the breathing telling me they were getting close to the tree behind which I was crouching. I had never used my swordstick, and my heart was pumping with fear, but I did know the cardinal advantage of the weapon: you didn't *unsheathe* it if defending yourself. You used it first as a stick, which a couple of assailants could grasp, imagining they would wrest it from you – especially two to one.

That is what happened now. I couldn't see either of them, but I knew one at least – probably both – had reached the other side of the tree.

At that moment, praying it was the right second, I shouted out, screaming an unearthly sound – merely for effect – then switched on my flashlight with my left hand. As it showed up Louis, I slashed his face with all my might – *but with my stick.* It must have been a terrifying blow. A scream of rage erupted and at the same moment Valéry, the other man, plunged towards me – to save Louis, to attack me. Louis almost fell with the force of the blow, and I prepared to strike again.

'Oh no you don't,' you bastard,' growled Valéry and, warding off the second blow, he seized the stick with both hands.

That was his mistake. He thought that with his powerful arms he could wrench the stick from me, and then I would be helpless. He did wrench it from me – but with a difference.

With all his might he pulled, cursing, ready to kill me – and then fell over as the sheath of the sword came away in his hands. Meanwhile Louis was screaming with pain, but I didn't have to worry about him – not for the moment. Instead I charged over to Valéry and, standing on top of him, one foot digging into his crotch, said viciously, 'Now, you sonofabitch, it's my turn!' With that, and without waiting for one second, I thrust the swordstick as deep as I could into his right shoulder.

I felt it go in – oddly enough, for a first time swordsman, it gave me a curious immediate sensation. 'That's like a rubber ball that's sealed itself up,' I remember thinking.

As I pulled out the blade, I looked for the stick, and found it. Valéry screamed, not only with pain but with fury. 'You could have killed me!'

'I still can,' I said. 'And if you try to follow me any more I will. *Salauds!*'

The other man was bleeding more badly. I hadn't used the sword on him, but the force of the slash had split open his right cheek – there was a wide, bloody gash that would leave a scar for life, stretching from forehead to chin.

'You'd better go and see a doctor,' I said, 'you and your mate.'

I found the edge of the wood ten minutes later, almost out on my feet, not only with fatigue but with reaction. I was trembling all over. But it seemed a different world when I emerged from the trees, so thick they had blotted out the moonlight. It was like being presented with a new pair of eyes.

The actual frontier-post was a couple of miles away at Divonne, but here I was faced with only a barbed-wire fence near the edge of the woods. For one moment I was scared that it might be electrified, but I had to take a chance and clamber over it, ripping my sports jacket once more. I knew – apart from the map – that it was now downhill all the way until I reached the lake. From the point where I had emerged from the woods I had to travel left. At least after the horrors of the wood I felt at home in vineyards – more like my usual friendly territory. All I had to do was walk and be sure nobody saw me.

It was by now one in the morning. I had to cover the seven or eight miles to Rolle before daylight – earlier even than that, before the first farmworkers were astir. If anyone saw me in my present state he would call the police before touching me, for I looked like a scarecrow. My clothes hung in ribbons, my shoes were filthy, my face was torn and bleeding.

The lake below, shimmering in the moonlight, offered the perfect guide. All I had to do was walk parallel to it, leaving Nyon behind. I was very tired, but Madame Gavroche had given me sandwiches and an apple which I chewed as I trudged along.

It was nearly half-past four when I saw the outline of Rolle – the nearest town after Nyon – picked out in the moonlight of the lake. I had to skirt several small villages – all of them signposted, of course, but with street lamps blazing so that I gave them a wide berth. I also had to be very careful of dogs, who I knew would start barking as soon as I approached within range of any houses. I started climbing downwards, and eventually made out a signpost for Rolle, barely half a mile distant.

I found the little road at a quarter to five. There was only one house on the left, as I peered ahead at the outline of the railway bridge; so I knew exactly where I was. Almost trembling with fatigue of a kind I had never believed possible, I pushed open the five-barred gate and found myself in the courtyard where I knew there would be the sound of running water from an old horse trough fed by a spring. There was.

I just managed to reach the front door and started to pull the bell and bang on it. I heard a voice, angry at being awakened – Sonia's voice? – then lights, then a man's voice, another woman shouting, then a figure coming out in the cold on to the first-floor balcony. This time it was definitely Sonia who shouted, 'Who are you? What do you want?'

I just managed to croak, 'Sonia! It's me!'

I heard a shriek – 'Larry!' But I had passed out before she had time to open the door.

37

The scramble through the forest must have taken more out of me than I realised for when I woke up – feeling new pyjamas, clean sheets, feeling *clean* – in a four-poster bed draped in white at the corners, I held out my arms to Sonia and before uttering any other words could only demand hoarsely, 'I heard a man's voice – whose is it? Does he live here? Was it he who carried me upstairs?'

'Yes, he did – and that's a fine way to greet me!' She must

have realised the strain under which I was still suffering, but she still added, 'I do believe you're jealous.'

'I am!' I blurted out. 'Who is he?'

'I'll ask him to come in. But first – let me kiss you with your poor, torn face. Be careful, my darling. But your lips are all right. There! My beloved Larry, here in *our* home.' Then she opened the door, and with a touch of laughter in her voice called, 'You can come in for two minutes to say good morning to the invalid.'

There was a vague clatter of footsteps on the staircase – I had a sudden half-conscious recollection of a sweeping circular stone staircase – and then a man appeared in the doorway. He had fair hair, but most of his face was hidden in a bushy, reddish-blond beard. I screwed up my eyes to see him better, but I couldn't focus properly. Then he spoke, and voices are sometimes easier to recognise than faces.

'What the hell have you been up to?' he asked cheerfully.

'Guy!'

'None other! See you for breakfast if you're up to it. Meanwhile I'll leave you two lovebirds together.'

'What's he doing here?' I asked weakly when we were alone.

'It's a long story. But, in a few words, he's in and out of France using false French papers, organising a Resistance group – and then when he needs to he comes back to Switzerland as an honest American neutral. In fact he's attached to the Red Cross in Berne. But don't worry about that now, darling; I'll explain later. Much more important first – you haven't even told me you love me.'

'I'll prove it after breakfast.' I put my arms round her and as she put her hands on my chest I added, teasingly, 'You wait – Monsieur Coquelicot is still waiting for you.'

'Always, I hope.' She was suddenly serious as she kissed me again. 'I haven't had the chance to tell you yet but, though it's going to take time, the annulment is on its way. Francesco has done wonderfully. I don't know how long it'll take, but things are on the move. We're cutting through the red tape.'

After breakfast, sitting round the old square table in the dining room-cum-entrance hall, I outlined everything that had happened. I told them about Mlle Lisette. Sonia and Guy listened, horrified, for I spared them nothing – nothing about

Olivia, nothing about Anna. It was too terrible even to imagine, to realise that it was actually happening, this very day, this very minute. Sonia was not crying audibly, but her face was streaked with tears. For there was no way anyone could soften a blow like this, no way to minimise it or skirt round the truth; the wicked things that other men were doing to those we loved were there, were happening *now*.

Sonia proposed to take immediate action. 'If you're going to return to France,' she said firmly, 'I'll go straight to Rome. Tomorrow Ciano has promised me he'll do everything he can.'

As she explained, she had already broached the subject to Ciano. 'He's not my favourite character,' she confessed, 'but he does have the power to ask favours – after all, he *is* Mussolini's son-in-law, and now that I have the precise details of where Anna is . . . considering he's the Number Two, he won't be asking for a great deal.'

'I only hope the price that he demands isn't going to be too much,' I said, half-jokingly.

'No price is too high to get Anna.' Sonia was serious. 'But I think I can manage him. He's a smarmy brute – a great one for ogling and pawing you – but I think I can handle all that.'

I knew that Sonia, who really and truly loved Anna like a sister, almost more than a sister perhaps because of us, was thinking how every day counted. She said to me, 'If I can get her out of that hell one day earlier then I'll save her . . .' She didn't have to end the sentence; she was thinking, 'If I can save a day – that's twenty times less she'll have to do it.'

We didn't have to talk openly of that, but it was always in our thoughts – the number, the pictures that came to us and couldn't be stamped out, that refused to be wiped off the slate of our imagination.

And there was Olivia too. We tended to forget that she, too, had spent several weeks in the bordello before being transferred to Hoess's house – and what happened there? I tried not to think. Guy and I went for a walk immediately after our breakfast conference, while Sonia drove the few miles to Lausanne to make sure of her train ticket and reservation for a sleeper to Rome. She was also, she said, going to send a message to Ciano that she would be arriving, while at the same time the *Globe* man in Berne was setting off for Rolle to meet us that evening so that I could hand him the story for Washington.

'Before we decide on what we can do to help Olivia,' I said to Guy, 'it might be a good idea to tell me what you're doing already. What's this about your French nationality?'

As we walked round the small garden, he told me. In brief, he had become an unpaid assistant to the Red Cross who were always looking for volunteers. Apart from providing them with invaluable information, it gave him a kind of cover to use Switzerland as a base while in fact helping to organise Resistance groups inside France. He was ideal for the job, for like all of us Guy was more at home speaking French than English, and he had acquired French papers, a new nationality – everything.

He also told me how he had come to grow a beard. 'Apart from the fact that it's a good disguise,' he said almost with a grin, 'I actually started it when I escaped in the car with the Misses B and B – and then like Topsy it just grew and grew!'

'But what do you do, exactly?'

Guy's activities were very different from the kind of work which men like Gaston undertook, for Gaston was basically planning for the future in that part of France directly under German rule. Guy, on the other hand, worked in unoccupied France, passing the frontier near the south-west tip of Lake Geneva. He was helping to organise escape routes and active resistance circuits inside the demarcation line. He mentioned a series of code names, none of which meant anything to me, of course – the 'Autogiro' circuit near Dôle and the 'Spruce' and 'Pimento' circuits near Lyons. What he did in actual fact he also never told me until years later, but it was obvious that he was crossing into Switzerland in order to return and pass on vital information to the Red Cross.

'Now,' he said, 'I'm going to switch plans because of Olivia. I don't know how yet, but we've got to get her out. I can't do anything more for Anna: that's up to Sonia. But we might be able to use Willi to help us again. What do you think?'

'Perhaps, but one thing at a time,' I cautioned him. 'Let's be certain we get Anna out of France first. God knows how Sonia's going to pull that one off.'

'That sonofabitch Ciano will do it for her,' Guy said savagely. 'God! He's a double-dyed shit. He rings her up regularly – oh yes, he's mad about her – and she has to go to Italy now and again anyway to get her permit or whatever it is renewed. He insists on it.'

'I don't like it,' I said. 'The thought . . .'

'Forget it.' Guy had grown more aggressive; perhaps the nature of his work was making him tougher, more abrasive.

'You can't *forget* like that,' I protested. 'Any more than I can forget what Lisette's done.'

'You have to,' he said roughly. 'I hope Sonia will be able to handle Ciano, but if you want Anna back – well, let's hope she can feed him on promises.'

'I'll drink to that.'

'So will I,' he said soberly. 'One thing I've learned from a lot of very brave women I've met since I joined the Resistance is the women pay, they really do. But you must never ask them questions. That way you'll never know what price they *have* to pay in order to save you.'

'But if you can rescue Olivia? Won't you want to know?'

'I would never ask her, never, ever,' said Guy. 'That way at least I will give Olivia a little present – her private self-respect.'

'And what are your plans for Olivia?'

Guy had obviously been thinking it over a great deal. 'One thing is certain – I've got to get back to Reims.'

'There's a price on your head there – and don't forget that Hoess has a long memory.'

'They'll never recognise me behind all this fuzz,' he laughed and stroked his beard. 'In fact I might travel back with you.'

'Not a hope!' I said flatly. 'And you know it. As soon as I get over the border I'm an American – and I'm not giving a lift to anyone.'

'I suppose you're right. It was okay when I went with the Misses B and B. God! That seems a long time ago. I'll never forget that moment when the Gestapo men came into the room and I pretended to be Jean-Pierre. They were tough, those two. B and B – are they still all right?'

I nodded. 'Still living in Paris – and firmly determined to stick to their neutral status.'

'They might not be neutral that long,' said Guy.

'Roosevelt would never get us into a war.'

'I wasn't thinking of that,' said Guy. 'There's a helluva lot of funny business going on in the Far East. Even in Paris you must have read about it. Japan is getting uppity. We've cut off her oil and the Japs are making threatening noises.'

'They may threaten, but they can't fight America – the very thought is ridiculous.'

'I guess so. But they're a lot of doubled-dyed bastards. And they seem to have a passion for committing suicide. You know – *hara-kiri*. Maybe they'd like to do it on a nationwide scale – Tom, Dick and Harry Kiri.'

We both laughed.

'By the way,' I asked almost as an afterthought. 'You saw Mama in New York. How was she?'

'Don't ask me,' Guy almost groaned. 'Honestly, she never moves without a retinue of men.'

'Well, it's not her fault she's so attractive,' I said lightly.

'In a way it *is* her fault. She can't help her attitude towards men.'

'Nothing serious?' I was thinking of poor Papa all alone and so sad in Douzy.

'If you mean marriage – no.'

'But . . .?' I left the question unasked.

'Jig-a-jig – sure.' Guy nodded vigorously. 'Making up for lost time, I'd say. The big city life after the country blues.'

I was almost tempted to tell Guy about Gaston, but thought better of it.

'Mind you, she's discreet – at least the bed part of it,' said Guy. 'She's just having a whale of a time. As I say, making up for lost time. I have the feeling' – he was obviously thinking of Douzy – 'that Papa was never a greater performer in bed. Takes after me. Whereas Mama takes after you, you old ram.'

How odd it was to hear Guy say that about himself – an echo of a remark made years ago by Olivia.

'I hope she'll be happy,' I said, 'and come back when this bloody war's over.'

'She'll be back,' said Guy cheerfully. 'She'll probably be so fed up with men, it'll be anything for a quiet life.'

Sonia arrived back at the farm before lunch and we walked round the small grounds, so quiet, so gentle – God! What a wonderful feeling not to have a German at your back.

Three Circles Farm was beautiful. It was long and low and white, set back from the house so that no one using the lane could overlook it. The stone horse trough which I had seen in shadow during the night matched the house perfectly; the water gurgled and spilled into it from the pipe, and above it like a gigantic umbrella were the bare branches of an enormous plane tree. Behind it the courtyard, with its circle of tubs, empty now of flowers, shielded a dozen or so fruit trees set in knee-high grass. Bordering them, but without a fence, was a large wheatfield. It was secluded rather than isolated, with the nearest house about four hundred yards away, only hidden by clumps of big trees.

'What I really like about it,' I said to Sonia, 'is that it's not a chalet, it's not a house, it's an old *farmhouse*. Only, why did you call it Three Circles Farm?'

'I didn't.' Holding my hand she walked to the gate and looked out across the vineyards sweeping up the hillside. 'I inherited the name. All I know is that it used to belong to a journalist and he christened it. Why, I've no idea. But since *you're* a journalist I thought we should stick to the name. Anyway, in Switzerland it's very complicated changing a name.'

She gave me a squeeze, and we turned round and looked again at the long low house. 'I have a dream sometimes that you'll come and live here,' she whispered. 'That this will be *our* home when we're married. It's so peaceful. Even the fact that the Swiss are pretty dull and that life is boring doesn't matter – it's so regulated, so safe, so secure. You feel you don't have to lock your doors at night.'

'But you did lock yours last night,' I teased her.

'Habit,' she confessed. 'Just old habits left over from France and Italy.' Sonia had booked to leave the following night on the express for Rome, while Guy, around the same time, would drive me through to Nyon to the point where I would cross the frontier.

'But you will be careful, Sonia, won't you? Don't think I

don't realise what you're doing – and that our only hope for Anna is you.'

'I will be careful, I promise you. I can handle all this.'

She had planned exactly how things would go. She would go to see Ciano – 'I'm having dinner with him the night I arrive in Rome.' Then, once the request to the Foreign Ministry for Anna's release as a favour was official, Ciano would contact the Italian Embassy in Paris and they would relay messages to me. 'It's far easier than us trying to get in touch on the telephone, which as you well know is virtually impossible,' she said.

'How it's going to work, I don't know,' I said.

'I've told Ciano that Anna was born American, made a disastrous marriage, and now her husband has vanished, and I want her to come to Switzerland. Then, if she wishes, she can go off to America. Just keep your fingers crossed, darling.'

'And you keep your legs crossed,' I said with a touch of vulgarity I immediately regretted.

'That wasn't necessary,' she said quietly. 'You forget something. I've been yours since that first day near Dijon. I'm going to be yours for ever. When we marry and our children arrive, I'll still be yours – so don't worry, whatever happens.'

That afternoon I typed out my story – after all, that was the original reason for my visit to Rolle – and the *Globe* man in Berne duly passed by the farm to collect it and then spent the night in Lausanne. Meeting him, I found it almost impossible to adjust to the tempo of *peace*. The casual way in which, when I had handed over my copy and we had sipped a glass or two of *fendant* Swiss wine, he picked up the telephone and calmly ordered a taxi to take him to Lausanne. *Ordered* a taxi! And it *came*! I hadn't seen a proper taxi in Paris for two years. And I had forgotten the shabbiness of life in France. Old clothes were worn almost as a badge of courage to begin with, and by now a lack of new clothes was so commonplace that no one noticed the shabbiness any more. But now, as I watched Sonia's housekeeper, a middle-aged lady, very pleasant, very quiet, no doubt not that rich, but still wearing good clothes and new leather shoes, even new stockings, I saw the difference. Everything about her looked so new; everything in France looked so old.

38

In mid-November the Italian Embassy official phoned me at the rue du Sentier. It was the same man who once before had relayed information.

'Signor Astell,' he said. 'I have a message for you. La Contessa de Feo says she will be arriving on Thursday and that everything has been arranged to pick up the parcel.'

Thursday! Two days away. *The parcel*. That could only mean Anna. My heart started thumping with excitement, though I knew – indeed Sonia had warned me – that I must be most careful to play only a passive role. I could do nothing but await events – await Sonia's orders, in fact, for only she knew what had been planned. And too, during the brief stay in Rolle, she had impressed one other thing on me: the need for secrecy.

'A few days this way or that may make all the difference to Anna,' she had said then. 'But the others – your father, Uncle Oregon, Grandma – an extra day of waiting won't make any difference because they're not expecting any news at the moment. If they were to get excited beforehand, I'd be scared they might give something away. And the stakes are so high we can't afford to take even the slightest risk.'

This was the advice she had given me in Rolle, and I was glad of it now because on the Wednesday a heavily bearded 'Frenchman' who gave the name of 'Guy Marchand' turned up at the office and asked for me.

It was Guy, of course. He had arrived after a series of hair-raising adventures, travelling through unoccupied France and then into Paris, breathing fire. He wanted to make straight for Douzy and then – at least this is what he said – quickly strangle Mlle Lisette.

'And ruin everything?' I asked. 'We keep Lisette on ice for just as long as we need her. You know that better than I do – after all, you're a professional. And then,' I shrugged my shoulders. 'She's all yours.'

'What's happened to Sonia?' he asked. 'And plans for getting Anna out?'

'Nothing really dramatic.' That was both a lie and the truth. 'We're in Sonia's hands.'

'And that bastard Ciano.'

'You don't have to remind me,' I said coldly.

'Sorry.'

'Well, do me a favour. Don't go to Douzy right now. You're safer in a big city. Let me sound out plans with Gaston – for your approval, of course. And I think you're right – Willi could help us. After all, if we get Anna out Willi owes us one more favour. And he'll make it. In fact he's told me he'd like to defect, cross the border into Spain or Switzerland and give himself up.'

'He'd be interned, wouldn't he?'

'Yes. But at least he'd stay alive. I've got a plan formulating. It includes Willi. And if he'll help you to get Olivia out then we could help him to get across the frontier. But wait, Guy, till I give you the word. And for Chrissake remember – for the moment most of the Astell family have kept their lives neutrally clean. Except you. You're on the list. So don't get caught or you'll be no damn good to anyone.'

'Okay,' he promised. 'I've got my own contacts here. I'll tell you what – I'll be back in four days. How's that? You outline a plan and then we'll crack this goddamn thing wide open.'

'Four days.' I was relieved – above all that he obviously didn't have the faintest suspicion that Sonia was about to arrive in Paris. It seemed a bit mean not to tell my own brother good news about our own sister, but Sonia was right – a couple days more of ignorance couldn't make any difference.

I didn't really feel guilty about withholding the truth from Guy. But I *did* feel guilty about not telling Oregon, for we had a mutual trust which, oddly enough, was shared by none of the rest of the family, not to the same extent. I think it was because we shared the common denominator of being newspapermen. It was a link in which every secret had always been shared. All except this one.

Sonia arrived around 10 a.m., the time I knew the train from Switzerland was normally due, and I reached the office early because I had the feeling that she would follow the same routine as she had done the last time, being met by an embassy car and driven straight to my office.

She did exactly that. I was peering out of my office window on the second floor when I saw the car draw up, with a green, red and white flag on the bonnet. My heart missed a beat as I saw her step out, slim and desirable. Even the way she climbed out of the car had an elegance about it, the way somehow both feet seemed to land on the pavement at the same time without showing a lot of leg; the way she shook out her black hair, the glance at her watch, her orders to the embassy chauffeur, all given with a warm smile. I heard the shuddering elevator groan its way towards the second floor and I waited to open the trellised iron gate as it seemed to hesitate before stopping with a jerk. Then she was in my arms, on the landing, before gently pushing me away, again shaking out her shiny blue-black hair, and saying, 'Let me get my breath back! Oh Larry, it's wonderful to see you again. But . . .'

'But nothing!' I led the way into my office. 'I must look at you.'

'Larry – we don't have much time!'

'Not even for looking?' I said jokingly. I could sense the tautness in her voice, almost as though she had made an effort to embrace me. Though that, of course, was nonsense. She must be tired after a night in the train.

'Sorry,' I said, for after all there was one reason above all others for her being in Paris – Anna. Even my presence was incidental to that.

'It's all arranged;' she sat down on my office sofa, then said in that same rather strained voice, 'But there are several conditions. The first that I'll become entirely responsible for Anna while she's on French soil – in other words till we get her to Switzerland.'

'But that's all right. We can spend a night or two at Douzy – poor Anna, after what's . . .'

'Poor Anna!' She was almost mocking. 'You make it sound as though she's getting over a dose of flu. Really!'

'But what do you mean? Are you trying to tell me something?'

'Of course not. How could I know? But my God, Larry, you don't expect her to be the same girl who was arrested in Douzy, do you? She could be – well – ill.'

I had considered that. I was not quite as stupid as Sonia thought, but I had always tried to pretend – except in my innermost thoughts – that this kind of problem didn't exist, and I had thought that way for one reason only: the less we dwelt on the terrors of the future, the more we pretended to act normally, the less danger of all of us becoming morbid. That was one reason why I hadn't told Papa where Anna was.

'I'm not quite a fool,' I muttered shortly, all thoughts of a romantic meeting dashed under the cold shower of reason.

'I know, but' – with a sigh – 'it's been a great strain for me too.'

I looked at her. She did look tired – beaten, in a way, just as she had looked once before when her father had said we couldn't marry. Yet people of our age didn't get tired just because of a few missed hours of sleep on a train. Had the 'great strain' really been brought about by one night's jolting train journey? Or anxiety, while waiting for the news to come through? Or had it something to do with Ciano? Almost harshly I said, 'We're all under a strain. But yours – was it . . .?' I was on the point of asking her when I remembered Guy's remark – 'Never ask a woman what price she has paid.'

Instead I said, swallowing hard, 'I know, but we're going to save Anna – thanks to you. What are the plans?'

She hesitated before saying flatly, all the emotion drained out of her, 'You and I are going to fetch her – now. In half an hour and then . . . we take her to Switzerland tonight.'

'Tonight!'

'There's nothing any of us can do about it,' she said wearily. 'And please, Larry, don't shout. I've got a blinding headache. The authority to release her has come through, but it's a condition that she leaves with me tonight. Don't blame me for things like this. The train reservations have been booked by other people. I've even arranged to have a special set of papers issued for her.'

'But tonight! It's criminal! She needs rest. Dammit, she *is* my sister – and what about Papa? Doesn't he want to see his own daughter? Shouldn't he?'

'He shouldn't – not right away, and you know it. It would be too painful. You've done your share. So has Willi. Nobody could have rescued Anna unless you had found out where she was. But after that, there's nothing you can do. Once you had located her, you needed me to help. Well, I've done it – but,' she added bitterly, 'I've had to fight – remember the Germans are the bosses now; the Italians play second fiddle. A lot of Italian pressure had to be brought to get Anna out. And getting her out is the only thing that matters. We could never demand conditions. Good God, Larry! What do *conditions* matter?'

'So what's the drill?' I asked dully.

'Anna is to be handed over to me at the *hôtel de ville* in Reims between three and four this afternoon. I'll have to sign for her as a sort of legal guardian while she's on French soil.'

'And what about the others?'

'You come with me.'

'Why me especially? Why not Papa?'

She passed a hand across her forehead wearily and explained, trying to be patient, 'Because I had to make all the decisions on the spot without consulting any of you. I had no choices. I'm taking responsibility, but the German authorities demanded the presence of one member of the family to sign a declaration that she *is* Anna Frankel, or Anna Astell.'

'I see. And then?'

'Nothing, Larry dear. Try to understand. In a way it's not me you're talking to; I'm just a messenger from the Italian government. There's no time – not even any desire – to kiss each other and swear undying love. This isn't the time or place. We're sure about our love anyway – or I wouldn't be here, would I?'

'No, I do understand. But . . .'

'First I need a wash;' she interrupted me almost deliberately as though to prevent me arguing. 'Can I use your "gentleman's" place, please?'

I nodded. She had used it before, the time she waited to greet me with a room full of poppies; and there was no one around on the second floor at this time of day. 'I'll stand guard,' I laughed. She went in. There was a toilet, a wash basin and it was always clean and always with fresh towels.

'I'll put on a new face,' she said, 'and have as good a wash as I can.'

During the quarter of an hour I stood guard outside I was thinking – jumbled thoughts tumbling one over the other; above all of Anna. Soon she would be free. But what would she be like? She would be changed – but how? In a way I was almost afraid of the meeting that lay ahead. She couldn't be normal, couldn't expect to be after the horrors she had passed through. For a moment I almost wondered whether it wouldn't be better to let Sonia take Anna back alone. But no, that would be a coward's way out. Even if no one else in the family could see her for the moment, at least I should, to show her that we were all together in this.

Sonia agreed when she returned to the office and Charles had brought up some ersatz coffee from Madame Yvette's bistro downstairs. 'You're her favourite brother. She'll look to you for – well – moral support, I suppose you'd call it.'

'And Papa?'

'You forget one thing,' Sonia reminded me. '*You* may have problems crossing frontiers but that's only because you choose to be a newspaperman who's unpopular with the Germans. But your father is a true neutral. He's respected by all sides. He can travel to Switzerland to see Anna whenever he wants – next week, if you like. And stay at Rolle.'

'But why not today? At Douzy? On the way home?'

'No risks, Larry – not until we get her out of the country. I never trust men like Abetz. God knows' – she still sounded bitter – 'we realise how wicked he is – and don't forget, this is an *official* diplomatic visit by me, as an emissary of the Italian government. The orders for release, the details, everything I have in my handbag' – she held it up – 'are here – but there are copies in the embassy. This is *official*. Even a visit to your office has been noted here. And the itinerary is in the embassy hands as well as in mine. I have to drive back from Reims after

537

Anna is handed over and stay inside the embassy until it's time for the train to leave.'

'But that means . . .'

'There's no other way. You can imagine that the driver of the embassy car has been specially chosen.'

'But to come all this way, darling – and never even to see you alone.'

'I came for Anna,' she said simply. 'Nothing else matters. These few moments are the only ones we'll have alone – this time.'

'Well, dammit,' I said almost savagely, 'I'll come back the same way as I did the other time – through the woods.'

'I hope you will. I hope so with all my heart when all this is over,' she said, suddenly gentler, her lips trembling, eyes bright with tears. 'But on the next trip don't scratch your face, like you did before.'

For a moment I clung to her, neither of us kissing but holding each other in our arms. Then she said, 'We must go. And be careful in the car. What we talk about, I mean. And no holding hands.'

The journey to Reims was utterly miserable. We sat like a couple of strangers in the back seat, talking inanities, while I let my mind wander around phrases she had used: 'when all this is over,' and the reference to Ciano. I thought, too, of the innuendos which Abetz had made, which even Guy had hinted at. Yes, a journey to rescue my sister, a journey that should have been an occasion for joy, for the pealing of bells, proceeded with the glum silence of a funeral procession.

We didn't even stop for lunch. However, Sonia had packed a picnic meal, which she had put in the car at the station, and now proceeded to open.

'Some for us,' she said as she unwrapped the square parcels of tissue and greaseproof paper, 'and some for Anna if she wants it.'

There was an assortment of Swiss food easy to eat in the car – even though it was a raw November day; some salami and other *charcuterie* and a *tarte de blette*, a kind of quiche made of Swiss chard with cheese and eggs. There was a huge chunk of Emmental, the best Swiss cheese. 'With the best holes in it,'

Sonia said, laughingly for once. And there was some late fruit from the Rhône Valley, together with two bottles of good Swiss wine, a *fendant* which fizzes very gently because, as Papa had once told me, it was bottled without being separated from its yeasty sediment.

I did drink my share of wine − I loved it for a change − but I could hardly eat a bite. Neither could Sonia. The tension was too oppressive, not only the anxiety but in a curious way an apprehension of the confrontation to come.

When the moment did arrive it proved to be almost an anti-climax. I helped to direct the chauffeur, telling him where to turn left off the Paris road when we reached the boulevard Louis Roederer, leading to the place de la République. From there it was only a few yards along the right fork of the rue de Mars, named after the famous Roman gate.

As we stopped outside the steps of the *hôtel de ville* where Sonia had been told that Anna would be ready she whispered − instinctively − 'You'd better come inside too.' I followed her up the steps. A French policeman stood to the left of the door, but a German soldier stood at the other side, as though sharing responsibility for law and order. Seeing the chauffeur and the Italian flag on the right bumper, to say nothing of the C.D. plate at the rear, the German soldier stepped forward, saluted smartly, and said, 'You are expected, *madame*.'

Once inside the main entrance, he beckoned us to an ante-room, looking as if it hadn't been dusted for a year. A man like a clerk was introduced to Sonia. 'This is Herr Weiss. He is dealing with your problem.'

Herr Weiss didn't seem very enthused. Ignoring me completely, he motioned Sonia to a hard chair opposite the cheap desk, asked her to show him her papers, read them, then finally turned to me and asked, 'Are you the relative?'

'I am,' I said.

'The lady is outside. Will you please identify her?' I must have looked puzzled.

'Through the window behind you,' said Weiss in a tired voice. I walked to the end of the room, which overlooked the main entrance lobby through which she had come. And there she was, Anna − sitting straight up on a hard chair. I didn't take time to study her face – perhaps I was frightened to look too closely – but returned quickly and said, 'That's my sister.'

'Sign here, please.' He might have been asking me to put my signature on a new driving licence. 'This is your sworn declaration in front of me that this is your sister. You understand? It is a formality, but for our records. And' – turning to Sonia, he offered her some papers – 'here is the safe conduct from Reims to Lausanne, countersigned by the S.S. That will be all.'

And that was all. Even Sonia had turned pale with the anticipation of the moment. The clerk-like Weiss left through a different door after a curt 'Good afternoon'. I held Sonia's arm – more for support than a gesture of love – and we walked out into the large entrance hall.

Anna still sat on the chair, as though rooted to it – or was she afraid to move without permission? Sonia ran across the room, arms outstretched, and only then did Anna get up. She said nothing – nothing I could hear – as Sonia put her arms round her and then Anna was looking at me, full in the eyes, and I kissed the cheek of her grey, lined face below its stringy hair and said nothing. She let her arms fall on my shoulder, smiled at me, a tired smile, and kissed me back.

'Let Sonia help you to the car,' I said gently. There wasn't much to say, really. The girls sat in the back seat. I got in front, next to the driver. Half-way there Anna began to ask one or two questions. 'How is Papa?' I told her Papa was well, and when she asked, 'Does he know where I am – was?' I replied, 'No, Anna, I didn't tell him. He doesn't know yet that you're free.'

'And Guy?'

'He's fine,' and with an attempt at humour, 'he's grown a huge beard.'

I turned my head to look at her in the rear seat – an uncomfortable way to talk to anyone for a long time; but perhaps it was just as well. I didn't want to give her the impression I was examining her. But at the mention of Guy's beard she did manage a wan smile. 'I'm so glad,' she said, though I didn't quite know what she meant by that remark. But then she didn't say much. It was an awful journey back to Paris, both Sonia and I silent in the face of Anna's total resignation, mental exhaustion, acceptance. Looking back, I find it hard to analyse what Anna was feeling, not that I could have expected to know what her emotions were, except that I could *see* them in her grey, tired face. I caught myself thinking, half-way along that interminable, cold November drive, I hope to God I never have to make a trip like this again as long as I live.

The thought was immediately followed by one of guilt – how shameful to be thinking like this, how wicked of me to be so selfish. But the trouble is that you can't harness thoughts, you can't make them do what you want. And of course there was one other reason I felt the way I did. I shouldn't really have been in the car, I realise that now. Brother I might be, but I was unwanted at this reunion, and understandably so. A man was the last repository for a girl's confidence, confessions, at a moment like this. I realised that I would actually have helped Anna to overcome the initial shock of freedom had I greeted her in Reims and then let the two girls drive back alone to Paris, with promises that I would come down to see them. Instead I was here, inhibiting any chance that they might want to talk to each other, of giving way to their emotions. Well, we would be back in Paris by six o'clock and they would have all the evening together in the embassy; and then all the night in the train to talk to each other.

Once or twice Anna did speak, especially as we reached the outskirts of Paris. I hadn't been thinking of the route, but as we reached the porte de Pantin I suddenly realised that I wasn't being invited to the embassy anyway. Normally when we drove to our flat on the Left Bank – and the Italian Embassy was also on the Left Bank – we came in by the porte de Vincennes, and then passed the place de la Nation, along the boulevard Diderot, past the gare d'Austerlitz. I could drive it almost blindfold.

But now, after entering by the porte de Pantin, we drove along the avenue Jean-Jaures and the rue Lafayette, where Anna, suddenly sparked by memories, cried 'Oh! There's the Galeries Lafayette.' We made our way along the rue Hauss-mann, then to the Opéra – and then, with hardly a moment to say goodbye, Sonia had ordered the car to stop along the Grands Boulevards at the corner of the rue du Sentier.

'It's better this way.' Her voice wasn't meant for argument. 'And for everyone. You'll come to see us as soon as you can, won't you?'

'I promise.'

'Give my love to Papa,' said Anna. 'And please come soon.'

Sonia stepped out of the car to have a word with me in private.

'No kissing,' she whispered. 'Except on the cheek. The driver's looking. And don't be angry, darling. Anna's in a state of absolute shock. Believe me, this is the best way. It's our only hope of bringing Anna back to normal. And don't tell anyone until the embassy phones you tomorrow confirming that we're on Swiss soil.'

There was nothing left for me to say. I waved to Anna, she waved back, and as Sonia prepared to get back into the car, she whispered, 'And remember – all this business has upset me too, you know – but it hasn't stopped me from loving you. Please don't *you* stop loving *me*.'

The telephone message arrived two days later. It was simple. After identifying myself verbally, the same man from the Italian Embassy announced on the phone in the same deadpan voice, 'Monsieur le Comte de Feo has asked me to pass on a message, sir. *Madame* and her friend have arrived in Switzerland.'

I had known it would be all right. The arrangements, backed by officialdom, were too watertight to admit of error, but even so, I startled Oregon in the next room by shouting, 'Whoopee!' And as he came in, looking almost Pickwickian with his fringe of white hair, he was even more startled.

I had committed the sin, usually indulged in by victorious racing drivers, of uncorking a bottle of Astell, and thumb in neck, was shaking it until, just as Oregon opened the door, I pulled out my thumb and a fountain of froth and bubbles shot out into a shower, spraying the entire room.

'What the hell?' cried Oregon. 'Your father would be furious' – for it was considered very ill-mannered even to make a 'pop' when uncorking champagne. 'What's happened? You've been appointed editor of the *Globe*, or what?'

I shook my head.

'Well – we haven't won the war – not yet.'

'We *have* won our greatest victory of the war – Anna's safe. I've just heard that she's in Switzerland – with Sonia.'

'*Anna!* I can't believe it. But how? When?' Almost fervently Oregon lit one Gauloise from the stub of the last, brushing the ash off his jacket lapels. 'Sit down!' and laughing with happiness he almost shouted, 'You may be the boss around here, but remember – I taught you all you know!'

'Oh Oregon!' I did sit down and poured out a glass of the remaining champagne. 'I'm so happy. Poor Anna. I was sworn to secrecy until she was actually safe in Switzerland – safe from that bastard Abetz. And no one can touch her now. So I couldn't even hint. But now I must takę a day off and go and tell Papa. He'll be overjoyed.'

I knew I merited a day or two of leave because by now the piece I had written on life in France, and filed from Switzerland, had been published, causing one hell of a row in France. The *Globe* had been officially proscribed by Vichy France – not that it ever arrived there. It was not so much the Germans who were angry; more the French. The French police, who couldn't take any serious action without consulting the Germans, came to see me, studied my papers, asked me where I had been around the time the article was printed. I had a perfect alibi, inasmuch as I had never left France – not officially. But the article was not only a major scoop about conditions under the Germans in France, it bore the stamp of my writing, which by now had, I realised, its own character, as clear to an expert analyst as my signature. Only this story had appeared under the name of our Berne correspondent. And so long as I kept out of trouble, and the identity of Henri Vasson was never discovered, the French and Germans in Paris could think what the hell they liked. All I had to do was say, 'Of course I never wrote it. It's unthinkable.' My only regret was that I could never see the copy of the newspaper. I did get news of it from Jim Parks, the consul, who had remained in Paris as part of the skeleton staff now that Admiral Leahy had been appointed U.S. Ambassador to the Vichy government. Parks didn't get copies of American newspapers, but the office did get a daily Roneoed digest of what the American press was saying. And the Berne story figured prominently.

On the Sunday I drove to Douzy – just for one night, arriving very late. After breakfast I told Papa and Grandma. To spare their feelings I had never revealed the truth about Anna, only that we couldn't trace the prison where she was being held. But by substituting 'prison' for 'brothel' I didn't have to get involved in too many lies, and I stuck to the story that she had been arrested and put in jail. I didn't want Papa in particular ever to learn the truth: it would haunt him for the rest of his life. So all I said was that Anna had been held in detention without trial and that we had discovered where she was. Apart from that, everything I said was true – that Sonia had arranged for Anna's release, how she had done it, the conditions which had been imposed, even the need for secrecy.

After the first shock had passed, the near tears, Papa said, 'I think we should go to Mass, yes, yes, even *you*, Larry.' And as an afterthought he added, 'This is a moment of great *rejoicing*, yes, that's the word, *rejoicing*, so let us ask the congregation to join us in a glass after lunch.'

It sounded a little complicated to me – for how could you ask all the people at church? You couldn't expect the good priest to announce it from the pulpit. But I needn't have worried. I was so out of touch it never occurred to me that Douzy's congregation would have shrunk to a handful of people. Apart from anything else, the cold of this November – without any heating of any sort in this old stone church – kept them away. Papa warned me of that, yet the idea of a 'welcome home' party for the absent Anna *was* a good idea, for everyone knew she had vanished, and this was the simplest way of telling them that she was alive and well and safe.

'Go to the Café des Sports before the service,' suggested Grandma when Papa had gone to his study. 'Monsieur Roland will pass the word along. Thank God this nightmare is over.' And then, with a secret look at me, she asked, 'Did her husband help? Willi?'

'Yes, Grandma, he did. But he doesn't know yet that Anna is safe. He told me that he wants to try to escape to Switzerland – to "defect", is that the word?'

'Best thing in the world,' she grunted. 'One less German to fight. Good or bad, one less. Come on, let's walk to church.'

She set off at a brisk pace, still upright, tall and angular. For church she wore a hat which helped to hide her thinning grey hair, only allowing a few wisps to peep out. She walked as she cycled, always with determination, with purpose; just as she walked now, straight backed with long strides, as though to save shoe leather.

It was wonderful to sense the happiness that suffused the faces of all our villagers after church. Almost all were connected in one way or another with our family. Papa asked for silence, and announced, with his standard introduction to any speech, 'I don't propose to make a long speech.' Only this time he didn't. 'I just want all our friends here, all of us suffering under a cruel war, to share in our happiness – yes, our *happiness* – at what has happened.'

He didn't of course announce that Anna was free; the word had spread through the village in a matter of minutes. But it was touching to see men and women like old Pagniez and Madame Robert hold up their glasses and cry, '*Bonne chance, Mademoiselle Anna!*' and 'Bravo, Miss Anna.' I didn't hear one person toast 'Madame Frankel', but it wasn't done deliberately. If Anna had married a dozen times the people of Douzy would always call her 'Miss Anna'.

39

As the drinks party was about to end, Gaston, who had been there, whispered to me, 'Did you know that M'sieu Guy, the so-called Guy Marchand, is here?'

'Already?' I nearly spilt my drink. 'He did say he was coming in four days – I suppose that was four days ago.'

'He's come to discuss plans to rescue Olivia. Now that your sister – it was wonderful what you all did.'

'But Olivia?'

'Well, I agree with Guy Marchand. Apart from the fact that a friend of your family is involved – Miss Jacobsen, I mean – I think it's time some of us in the Resistance showed the stuff we're made of. Marchand has been telling me what he's being doing near Lyons. We're just beginners here.'

'How do you propose to set about it, Gaston? I mean, you can't just raid Gestapo headquarters, abduct Hoess and whisk Olivia away.'

'Not quite;' he gave a wry smile. 'But we might do the next best thing. We might lure Hoess away from Gestapo head-quarters and *then* abduct him.'

'Be careful,' I warned. 'I'm all for anything we can do, but my brother – he's a very brave man but he's a daredevil.'

'We need a daredevil. Guy's all right,' said Gaston.

Guy! So they were on first name terms. But then they *were* members of the same army. Half humorously I asked, 'Isn't it a bit unwise calling him Guy?'

'Not Guy as in "Guy Fawkes". Guy as in "Gee". And it's Guy Marchand. No, it's not dangerous.'

'No more dangerous than calling . . .'

'Calling you Larry? No;' he shook his head. 'In a way, after what you've done, you're one of us whether you like it or not. We have no ranks, only Christian names in our groups.'

And that is how, without any fuss, I was accepted by the Resistance – if only as a passive member. And now, equally without any fuss, he started quite naturally to call me Larry. His next remark, however, shook me.

'We've been having preliminary thoughts on how to go about it. I'd like your advice. It's about Willi Frankel of the Gestapo?'

I gasped – not at the idea – and asked angrily, 'What the hell do you know about Willi Frankel?'

He had the grace to look a little uncomfortable, and finally, dragging the words out, he said, 'You'd better ask La Châtelaine.'

'La Châtelaine! I bloody well will.'

At first I was furious – and I remembered feeling the same anger years previously when Olivia first came into our lives; it was 'the family' – and the Astells didn't like 'outsiders' discus-sing the family. But when I confronted Grandma with Gaston's statement she became almost angry with me for being angry with him.

'Be more intelligent!' she snorted. 'There's a war on, remember?'

'Not ours.'

'Nonsense. You think it's important to write your articles
for the *Globe*. Maybe it is. But my boy, life has changed since
you and Oregon started playing with words. It's *changed*, do
you hear?' she asked almost fiercely. 'We've reached a stage in
history when the sword is now mightier than the pen – and
the sooner people help with the sword the better.'

'But Grandma, I think you've been unfair. And as
Americans – we *are* neutral.'

'Fiddlesticks! To pretend as much is stupidity. And I can't
abide stupid people. As for Willi, without his help we would
never have freed Anna – and you know it. He proved that he
was capable of keeping calm in a crisis.'

A dozen questions leapt to my mind. Why should Grandma
decide so firmly? Had she and Willi met? I asked.

'Yes, we have. Twice,' she replied, adding a trifle ironically,
'After all, you don't live here, Larry. We do have visitors when
you're busy in Paris.'

Of course I could hardly expect Willi to send me a cable
telling me when he was going to pay a visit to Douzy, but
somehow I was irritated.

'So I arranged for him and Gaston to meet,' said Grandma.

'Was that wise?'

'Of course it was' – with the return of her old fire – 'otherwise I wouldn't have done it. And perhaps now you realise we
have a German agent working for us in the Resistance.'

Again I looked at her, this time aghast. Grandma was over
seventy. 'What on earth do you mean – "Us in the Resistance"?' I asked.

Almost with a grin, she replied, 'Let's just say that I'm an
ex-officio member. If I can help, I mean to. Till the last
German is kicked out of France.'

Thinking it over on the drive back to Paris, I wondered if all
this plotting and secrecy were worthwhile – or whether
Grandma, Gaston, Guy, all the others whom I didn't know,
were of any real importance in the business of war – leaving
out Anna, that is, and of course Olivia. Take the plans to blow
up railway lines. Were they really of any value, or were they an

extension of irresponsibility, like the stuff we used to read about in schoolboy magazines? I didn't see how a handful of Resistance men and women, however brave, could take on the might of Germany – could ever be of any account. What did it matter, blowing up a bridge or a tunnel? After all, the R.A.F. had tried to blow up the Rilly tunnel and had only killed some innocent civilians instead. And if the Resistance did blow up a train, then what about the reprisals? We had already heard terrible stories from central France where whole families had been executed – children as well as grandmothers – after a couple of German soldiers had been killed. Could such an act of violence ever influence the war sufficiently to justify the deaths of innocent children?

As I continued on my way towards Paris – this time taking the road through La Ferté that would lead to the Left Bank – I realised I hated the idea of being thought a cynic. I *wanted* to believe in heroes. After all, having obtained the release of Anna, I was inwardly excited at the prospect of helping Olivia to escape.

'Well,' said Gaston the next time I met him, which was during the last week in November, 'we're going to – what's the word they use in American movies? – we're going to "spring" Olivia next week. But remember, there's only one way we can do it. It will involve tortures, and then coldblooded killing. So there will be reprisals when the Gestapo discovers what we've done – and who we've killed.'

'Hoess?'

'Absolutely. Apart from Olivia, who to be frank I only know as a member of your family, I haven't forgotten what Hoess did to my father.'

'I understand. But if you hardly know Olivia, it seems a little extreme.'

'It's not my idea. It's Guy's. He wants her freed. And he's an experienced senior member of the Resistance. I know he operates mainly in Vichy France and I don't come under his orders, but he is experienced. He knows what he's doing, and he can help.'

'Where is Guy now?'

'He's still at Douzy, staying in a safe house.'

'Where?' I persisted.

'He's not far away. As I say, in a safe place.'

'But where?'

Reluctantly Gaston finally admitted, 'He's been staying with my father. But now we've arranged a local place to meet secretly if we have to pass on messages or hide.'

'But where?' I repeated. 'Or would you rather not tell me?'

'Well, yes, I think I can. You'd have to go there sooner or later as we will need your help. It's in Douzy church. Up near the belfry there's a tiny room, which we've turned into a place where you can sleep – only a straw mattress, but it's safe so long as we can get food in.'

I had to admire Guy. Of course he couldn't have gone to stay at Douzy, for he would be on the wanted list as long as there were Germans in France. Still, it was one thing to do what he had previously done – slip over the border, however dangerous, and then return to the comfort and safety of Switzerland. But this – living like a hunted animal – it must take a lot of guts. Either he loved Olivia very much or he had seized on her release as a focal point, a challenge he had to meet.

'I hope Grandma won't be dragged into any of this?'

Gaston was truly horrified. 'You must think I'm a wicked bastard,' he said. 'All she does is relay messages – verbal messages – to and from Willi Frankel whenever they meet. Of course La Châtelaine will never become involved – any more than she did when, as she told me at a meeting, she was the only one who saw the value of Frankel, of how he could be useful.'

'A meeting?' My amazement never stopped. 'You mean to say La Châtelaine is not involved, yet you're having secret meetings – about a man in the Gestapo?'

'It wasn't a meeting, really. She sent for me. I had no option.'

'But a *meeting*?'

'It was in the vineyards.' With a shrug, he added, 'La Châtelaine does – well, tend to give orders. And as you know, there's an enormous amount of work to be done in the vineyards in November and December – turning over the earth, covering the stocks, protecting them against frost, banking up the soil, fertilising, replacing worked-out soil. It's a heavy programme, and our talks started when La Châtelaine came and worked alongside me.' Gaston looked at me almost pleadingly. 'I couldn't do *anything* – you must know that. La Châtelaine is – unique. She decides, everyone else obeys.'

I couldn't help but grin. 'You're right there,' I said. 'She really laid into me the other day – more or less told me I was wasting my time writing. So, I would like to say hello to Guy. And to help if I can. After all, I do have a good neutral cover.'

'I'll tell Guy, and of course he'll want to see you. But as for helping,' Gaston sounded doubtful, 'all the plans are laid now, everything's prepared.'

However, I did meet Guy, though not in Douzy. When I returned Paris he left a message for me at the rue du Sentier, asking me if I would meet him at the Deux Magots.

'I didn't know you were back in Paris,' I said when we met. 'You could have phoned me at the office.'

'I didn't dare. The phone might be tapped.'

'I'm sure it is,' I agreed. 'What are you doing here? I thought . . .'

'I came to reassure you. *Garçon*! Two beers please.' When they arrived he sipped his with distaste. 'Tastes like weasel pee,' he said disgustedly. 'Ah! For a pint of good Swiss *Feltschlossen*.'

Finally he came to the plan. 'Grandma knows nothing about what we're going to do,' he said, anxious to reassure me. 'And I hope that we'll be able to go it alone; but we need someone as a back-up, in case things don't go as smoothly as we hope they will.'

'And what are those plans? Am I allowed to know?'

'You shouldn't.' Guy almost grinned, and then without stopping said in a loud voice, 'God! It's late. I must be going.' As we both fumbled with money to pay, he whispered, 'Don't look round, but we're being watched. See you at the Boule Blanche this time tomorrow and then' – with a touch of irony he added in a whisper – 'I'll tell all.'

The Boule Blanche was round the corner, just off the rue Jacob, and the next day at four o'clock Guy was waiting for me.

'Sorry I had to rush off yesterday,' he explained. 'I could smell the Gestapo a mile away. And they always get suspicious if they see two men talking earnestly at the same table for too long.'

The first thing that Guy and Gaston had learned was that Mlle Lisette had not just betrayed one woman, Olivia. She was a regular traitor, working with the Gestapo for money.

'My first thought was to kill her right out,' Guy admitted. 'But that's a stupid thing to do. Never kill anyone you might need to use.'

Where had I heard that advice before?

'But how do you *know*?' I asked. 'You can't be sure, I mean you can't know what goes on in Gestapo headquarters.'

'No, but Lisette is too scared – and too useful – to risk visiting the Gestapo. So they come to see her. Even Hoess pays her regular visits, presumably to collect information. And Gaston has virtual proof of five people who have mysteriously disappeared – and who were known to Lisette. She's one of dozens of French bastards who believe Germany has won and are backing the right horse – or what they think is the right horse.'

'Still – how can you trap her? And get Olivia out? After all, Olivia is the main object of the exercise.'

This in brief was the plan. It was almost the end of November by now, and on the following Friday – that would be 5 December – Guy and Gaston planned to make the bid for Olivia's freedom. Willi apparently was due to visit Douzy on the Thursday evening – the Thursday before the plan went into operation.

'Yes, we've had to make this one a firm date for Willi,' said Guy.

'But how do you know he can keep the date?' I asked.

'Don't worry, Willi will keep it,' said Guy. 'We know he will because this is going to be his last trip. After that he's going to try to get to Switzerland and give himself up.'

According to the arrangements Willi would drop off his driver at Reims on the Thursday evening, giving him a three-day pass to Paris – it was a rare privilege to be allowed to stay overnight in Paris – and then Willi would make for Douzy.

'Why on Thursday evening?' I asked.

'We need two cars and to rearrange Willi's Gestapo car a bit,' said Guy. 'I hope you don't mind, but we plan to take off the number plates from your old M.G. and use them. That should get us through.'

I gulped. I didn't expect to use the M.G. for a long time, but she was my pride and joy, even though she was in the garage. But Gaston promised to get a replacement set of number plates. Once Willi reached Douzy on the Thursday, Gaston would take away his Gestapo car, change the number plates and paint out the yellow wheels; the car could then be used to escape to Switzerland.

'That's fine in theory. But you've skipped one important part of the story,' I objected.

'You mean – how we're going to get Olivia out?' Guy smiled.

I nodded.

'Let me outline our plans,' he said. Someone in the Resistance would make sure on the Friday that Hoess was in Gestapo headquarters. Then Gaston and Guy would drive an old tractor up to Lisette's old cottage at the end of the same lane as the cottage once used by the Misses B and B. Gaston on a tractor would excite no comment.

'But wouldn't she recognise you?'

'Doesn't matter,' said Guy. 'She won't know it, but she'll be for the high jump before the day's out.'

Once in the house, a quarter of a mile from the B and B house, Lisette would be forced to write to Hoess. 'We'll have to persuade her to write that letter,' said Guy unemotionally. 'But we know how to do it.'

'And then?'

Lisette would tell Hoess she had important news that couldn't wait. 'She's done that before,' said Guy bitterly, 'and if it's hot news Hoess always comes. After all, she can't be seen at Gestapo H.Q. and it's only a couple of miles' drive up the hill for him.'

Guy realised that Hoess would never come alone to such a lonely spot. But Gaston's Resistance fighters would have half a dozen picked men hiding in the woods round the cottage. They had arms stolen from the Germans.

'It sounds damned dangerous,' I said.

'It is. But you've got to understand one thing, Larry. The fact that I want Olivia freed is of course important, but the others want something bigger – to prove themselves, to stage a major coup, to kill a Gestapo man who is hated all over the area. Why, even Willi Frankel says he's a swine.'

'Where does Willi come in?' I asked.

That was the second stage. Once Hoess had been trapped into visiting Lisette's cottage, he too would be subjected to what Guy called 'persuasion'. He would be forced to write a letter to the house where he lived in the rue St. Julien, where Olivia also lived as a prisoner.

Hoess in theory would say in the letter that he wanted Olivia sent to see him under Gestapo guard. Willi, in his own Gestapo uniform, would then drive in his own car to the rue St. Julien. It would look perfectly normal – one Gestapo officer bearing a letter from another, ordering a prisoner to be sent to him.

'But Hoess will never agree. Never. And what about noise? The soldiers outside.'

'Hoess *will* agree. You wait. And there'll be no noise.'

'You might be able to force Lisette to give in, but Hoess isn't the sort to crack early, quickly, is he?'

'Not easily. But we'll have to make him crack. And we know how to do it.'

'And then?'

'Once we get Olivia out, she'll be driven back to Lisette's cottage. But she'll stay in the car at the bottom of the lane. Willi will run up to the cottage to tell us she's free, and also to help if needed – disposing of the bodies, or whatever. Yes, of course we'll have to kill them both.'

His matter of fact statement not only sent a shiver down my spine, it made me realise how Guy had changed, what an extraordinary life he had been living – proving that his particular sword was far mightier than my own particular pen. He was *saving* men and women, he was *killing* enemies. Once the couple had been killed, Willi would go out to tell any waiting S.S. men that they could return to barracks. He would be in Gestapo uniform of course, and it would seem quite natural for him to tell their sergeant that he was driving Hoess back home. Once the S.S. had gone, everyone would make for the belfry at Douzy church, where peasant clothes for Willi would be waiting, together with food and anything else needed for the journey to Switzerland. Guy and Willi planned to leave with Olivia for Switzerland immediately.

'Only one thing is missing,' I said with a touch of irony. 'Where do I come in?'

'Not very heroic,' admitted Guy. 'But we don't want your identity known to the Gestapo – to those who start panicking when they find out that Hoess has been murdered. There'll be hell to play. But there's one thing you can do. While we're changing in the church, you can drive Willi's car to our secret petrol pump in Douzy and fill her up. We need all the gas we can get.'

'And Gaston?' I asked.

'He doesn't want to go to Switzerland. I can understand. After all, he works in *this* sector,' said Guy.

'But won't there be a danger that he'll be traced – seen?'

'I don't see why.' Guy shook his head. 'All witnesses will be dead – they won't be able to tell any tales. It's important that Gaston tries to keep out of this – tries not to be discovered. And of course the same thing applies to you, Larry. It's just as important that you keep out of this, as a neutral, as a newspaperman. That applies to Papa too.'

That was all – and to be frank I didn't like it. It all seemed too pat, too easy. But it was their plan, and they were the professionals.

40

Guy planned to reach the cottage around nine o'clock on the Friday morning. If all went well, Olivia would be freed in a few hours, leaving several hours of daylight to drive as near to the Swiss frontier as possible. If anyone in the party ran into trouble they would take the road or the railway. Somehow they would move southwards. It all seemed very hit-and-miss to me, but then I supposed this sort of operation always would be.

The first real snag came on the Thursday. Aubergine asked me very politely if I could go to see Gaston who was working in the vineyard. It was perfectly normal for him to be there when he had nothing else to do. To any outsider my presence in the vineyard seemed perfectly innocent, reinforced in the eyes of anybody who might be suspicious by the presence of Grandma, bossing everyone, walking with long strides along the lanes of bare stalks, shouting an order here, giving an instruction there, eyes missing nothing. All in all it was a perfect picture of a law-abiding neutral vineyard at work − and a perfect cover for meeting, passing plans, arranging secret rendezvous.

'We've hit a snag.' Gaston bent over and from a container replaced some sour soil with fresh while I helped, squatting down.

'What's the trouble?'

'I've just been tipped off that Lisette's cottage is fitted with an alarm. The Gestapo calls it *notknopf* − a panic button.'

Gaston explained in detail that about fifty French informers whom the Germans thought worth protecting had been linked up with Gestapo headquarters by an alarm system; doubly dangerous, according to Gaston's informant, because it wasn't a shrill alarm inside a house − the kind of alarm that would scare off people − but a silent alarm which, without the knowledge of the intruder, would alert Gestapo headquarters, so that anyone suspicious could be caught red-handed.

'We had planned to send Guy in first. He might be suspect, but at least he could argue with Lisette, saying anything he wanted as − well, as an old friend. Even if she was suspicious, there'd be nothing she could do about it once Guy got past the front door.'

'But now?'

'I understand these panic buttons, as the Gestapo calls them, are always hidden near the point of entry − obviously they would be, so that if anyone does panic he or she can press the button without the visitor knowing. That would *have* to be the reaction of Lisette if she suddenly saw Guy, whom she must

know is wanted by the Gestapo on charges of assaulting
Hoess. Their last words were filled with hate – or so he told
me. She's a woman who must live in fear – all informers do.
So she'd take no chances.'

'Will *you* go?'

'I could, I suppose,' said Gaston, 'but I'm the only one who
can manage the tractor. It's got to be turned round, prepared,
ready for the escape before there's any alarm.'

'What about Willi?'

'He won't be there – not to begin with.'

'So . . . what?'

Gaston lifted his head from the chalky soil which he had
been patting round the roots of the vines, and his eyes stared
straight into mine.

'You'd be perfect,' he said, almost with a twitch of humour.

'Me! But you said my value rested on being really
neutral . . .'

'I know, I know, and we still don't want to involve you.
But this is our only chance to get Olivia out. Willi has burned
his boats. He'll never be able to operate again. Guy's waiting
for you in my father's cottage. He's gone there for some
food. Go and see if you can find a better way of solving the
problem.'

In fact Guy could offer no other solution. Old Pagniez had
gone off to the Home Farm and we sat in the tiny kitchen of his
thick stone cottage, trying to keep warm with a fire made of
bits of wood hauled down from the hillside. I wasn't that
worried about getting involved, of taking a chance, except to
protect Papa's reputation and the work he was doing for the
French. And if Lisette was going to be killed anyway I
wouldn't be taking that much of a chance. After the fight in the
woods I didn't feel as squeamish as I had done before – or
thought I didn't. Even so, I didn't relish the prospect of
actually killing a woman – even someone like Lisette – in cold
blood.

'You don't have to do it,' urged Guy. 'The way I see it,
you're the only Astell, except for Grandma and Papa, who
isn't connected in any way with the Germans. You don't have
to creep up to the cottage. You don't have to hide. You can
drive up openly in our Citroën, give a toot so as not to frighten

Lisette, and when she peers through the window she won't have the faintest idea what you have in mind.'

'And what will I have in mind?'

'Not killing, that's for sure; we want her alive. But you are the only one who can talk to her at the front door, tell her any story you like – why not say Grandma is ill and could Lisette help? I'm sure she'll say no, but you can *beg* her to come. Then ask if you can talk it over, invite yourself inside, worm your way in – *get past the panic button* – then grab her. We'll follow. After that you can go home and leave us to clean up the mess.'

Though I drove up the Mont de Champagne outwardly calm, I was quaking inside – not with fear; I had nothing really to be frightened about – except letting down the others. I was nervous because I knew that everything depended on my ability to get past the intriguing but invisible panic button.

I wanted to make some noise, draw attention to the fact that I was not making a secretive excursion; so I called in first at the old house to which the Misses B and B had never returned since they left with Guy hidden behind the back seat. All pretty gardens look at their worst in winter, but the B and B garden looked worst than most, for it had lost its neat and tidy trade mark. The grass in the small patch of lawn had not been mown since the previous summer. The trim flower beds were overgrown with weeds, the hanging basket over the door, once filled with geraniums and lobelia, looked as though it should be thrown away.

The B and B house – like Lisette's – belonged to the Astell estate, and had been built originally by Grandma's father for house workers; but over the years they had tended to congregate near Douzy, forming a village. We had, however, a perfect right to check our houses on our land, and as I drove slowly on towards Lisette's home at the end of the lane I heard the steady clop-clop of a farm horse with a young ploughman called Fresnay sitting sideways on its broad back, legs dangling over the side.

I stopped the car. The knowledgeable old carthorse stopped instinctively, and I was delighted, for I knew I was in earshot of Lisette's house.

'Haven't seen you for a long time,' I shouted – deliberately loud.

'No. Whoa! I suppose with your work in Paris, Monsieur Larry, you're too busy.'

'Well,' I laughed. 'There's not much good news to write about these days.' I kept young Fresnay talking as long as I could – in the hope that Lisette would be curious enough to see what was going on. Sure enough, she did eventually open the front door to her house at the bottom of the lane. I left the car where it was and walked towards her.

'Good morning, Mademoiselle Lisette.' I instinctively used her nursery title as I added, 'I was on my way to see you to ask for some help.'

'I don't see what you can possibly want with me,' she replied coldly, no doubt remembering the terrible scene when we had kicked her out of the house after learning what had happened between her and Guy. She didn't sound *too* aggressive, and I smothered a temptation to say, 'Well, you are living free in one of the Astell houses! You might try to be polite.'

Instead I produced a hypocritical smile and said, 'I know we've all had our problems but did you know that Grandma is very ill?'

'La Châtelaine?'

I nodded. 'She needs someone to help her.'

Standing by the front door – with the panic button just behind that door? – she said abruptly, 'I'm sorry. I'm busy. And anyway . . .'

'Anyway what, *mademoiselle*?'

'How do I know your grandmother would *want* me?'

Was she weakening? I didn't believe it. She was stalling. Perhaps she didn't want to set foot in our house. Or . . .? Perhaps I was wrong. I decided to test her.

'I think you're wrong.' I forced a smile. 'Perhaps. I certainly hope you'll come – and after all' – with a laugh – 'Papa is the one who counts. He's the one who pays the bills. And he's asked you to come.'

The inference was clear, I hoped, though without a scrap of truth in it – a veiled suggestion that if she didn't help a family friend in a desperate hour of need Papa was quite capable of cutting off the modest allowance he paid regularly as 'conscience money' to the Crédit Lyonnais. I knew that Papa would never be a party to blackmail – not unless he knew the truth about Anna. What I was trying to do was persuade Lisette to ask me in; not for me to say, 'Can I come in?' I wanted to make sure she was completely off her guard, for her to take the initiative, for her to feel that perhaps she ought to help; anything so that I could get her into the middle of the house, away from any hidden alarms.

'I *am* busy, teaching part-time at school. I expect you know. But maybe I could – I don't know – manage once or twice a week – what's the matter with La Châtelaine?'

I looked suitably sad and lied through my teeth. 'We're afraid it's cancer,' I said, crossing my fingers for poor Grandma who had never looked fitter.

'Oh dear.' Lisette's face fell. 'I *am* sorry. I never had any quarrel with La Châtelaine.'

'And there's no one to help,' I said desperately. 'Not a soul except Madame Robert.'

'That one! She can't do anything except bake bread.' And then, so suddenly it took me by surprise, 'Come in. Let me look at my book and see what times I have free.'

I walked in – thinking as I did so how life can twist you round. Here was this plain middle-aged woman, hair like grey string, the classical nanny and, for that matter, the classical virgin. Yet once, long ago, she and Guy had tumbled into bed; then hate had warped her mind and she had turned into the most degrading kind of human being, the informer, the traitor, sending people to their deaths – or worse.

'That's very kind of you,' I said, once inside. 'It's a very pretty room you have here.'

'Thank you.' She leaned over her kneehole escritoire, halfway into the living room, along an inside wall. 'My papers are always in such a mess. Ah, here!'

As she bent forward, presumably to find her diary, I realised that this was my chance, perhaps my only one. It was safe now, she was well past the front door. As I sprang forward from behind and grabbed her throat, my thumbs on the back of her neck, my fingers squeezing into her windpipe, she cried out once, then scrabbled with her hands for the bureau, pushing the chair out of the way as she struggled. She had sunk down to her knees, so that I all but lost my grip. I had to keep her quiet, to stop the screams by pressing on her windpipe, and in those first seconds it seemed to me that she was not only trying to pull herself away from me but, gasping and panting, was trying to do something else. After the first instinctive wrench with her hands on my wrists, those hands of hers were outstretched towards the desk . . .

Grabbing a defenceless woman by the throat isn't as easy as it sounds, as I had expected it to be. She was grunting, foaming at the mouth, and all the time kicking, arms flailing, so that I had my work cut out to hold on. She managed to grab the side of the kneehole desk, in order, I thought (if I thought at all), to get leverage to push me off; but it wasn't that. Even as her breathing turned to more ugly gasps, as her face turned almost puce, she still instinctively fought, fingers outstretched, only not to loosen my grip so much, not to fight me. Her fingers were searching for a different solution, moving around, as though anxious to grab something, to press up against it.

'Christ Almighty!' I yelled, suddenly realising as I pulled her away from the desk that she was searching for her panic button – it must be there, not at the door. I let go of her throat. She gasped, but she wasn't finished yet, and began to crawl like an animal towards the kneehole.

'No you don't, you bitch!' I cried, and as she almost reached the desk, fingers outstretched, I picked up the nearest chair and hit her across the head. She dropped like a sack.

Trembling all over with the sudden surge of relief, I pulled down the curtains to tie her up. But where the bloody hell were the scissors, where was the handy piece of rope or whatever which always seemed so convenient in the movies? I threw the curtains aside. She would be out for another minute or two, I guessed, so I dashed into the kitchen and grabbed two tea towels and a carving knife. Ripping one cloth in two, I managed, however roughly, to tie her wrists behind her back – hard and tight. With the other half of the cloth I tied her arms above the elbow as a double protection. I ripped the other cloth and tied up her legs, again tightly. Then, using the carving knife, I managed to cut up some of the thick curtain material and tied it round her mouth, making her bite into the corners, to form a gag. Just in time. She was beginning to move, to gurgle and gasp.

Then and only then I spared a few seconds to leave the writhing figure and examine the desk. There was the button, almost invisible; it was on the inside of the kneehole, so unobtrusive that if she had needed help she could even summon the alarm by sitting at her desk and operating it with her right knee. And no one would know except at Gestapo headquarters.

The others would be here at any moment, but as I waited I was amazed to discover what a lot of damage Mlle Lisette had done to me, merely in defending herself. My legs and arms were bruised where she had slammed her pointed heels into my shins. One trouser leg was torn, buttons had been ripped off my sports jacket, even off my shirt.

Four or five minutes later I heard the growl of the tractor arriving. I opened the door – to show there was no danger – as I saw Guy at the foot of the lane. He jumped off as planned, while Gaston started to turn round the cumbersome old machine.

'You've got her?'

I nodded. 'Yeah. She's tied up.'

'Great. Where's the button – by the door?'

'No – under the kneehole of the desk.'

As Guy followed me into the room, Mlle Lisette had somehow managed to slide off the sofa where I had left her tied up and was wriggling like a worm along the floor – in the direction of the desk.

'Stop her!' I cried. 'She might be able to press the button by lifting both her feet.'

I would have hesitated, I suppose. Guy raced across the tiny living room and without hesitation hit Mlle Lisette with a clenched fist on the side of the face. The force of the blow turned her over. For a second I was appalled. I knew I had fought to control her, but to hit a defenceless woman in the face – and so savagely! I'd never seen anything like it.

'Don't be so fucking squeamish.' Guy pulled Lisette by the feet into the middle of the floor as she moaned, her blood soaking into the gag in her mouth. 'Every time you are, just think how many times Anna was raped – because of her.'

'I know. It was the shock.' I was thinking how curious it was, the almost grim pleasure I had got from beating the two hoodlums in the forest not so long ago. And they were only robbers. Lisette was a million times more wicked. A woman beyond redemption. Yet I had been shocked. For the moment, anyway.

'I know what your instincts are,' said Guy gruffly, 'but believe me, that business about the female of the species – they may not be *more* deadly than the male, but in war they're equal. And you've got to treat them as equals. The enemy, I mean.' He added kindly, 'You'd better go now, Larry. You've done your job better than anyone else could have done it. You've got the first stage over with by capturing Lisette. But what you've seen so far is kid's stuff to what's going to follow.'

'No. I'll stay.' I had my own sudden thoughts of Anna and Olivia.

'Please yourself – only one thing. You may be the boss of the family, the eldest son sort of thing, but I've been doing this – extorting confessions – for over a year. It's not pretty work, especially with women, but honestly, I reckon our teams in Vichy France, where Laval *encourages* traitors to betray France – I reckon we've saved hundreds of lives. So what I do, I'm doing to save those that are going to *live*. Kill the ones who are trying to kill them – you get my meaning?'

He leaned over and turned Lisette round with his shoe. As she opened her eyes he hauled her up to a sitting position and looked at her frightened, almost glassy eyes and said, 'Remember me? Guy – behind this beard. Yes, it's me. Now you can co-operate with us or be hurt. The choice is yours.' Then, leaning closer, he said, 'I'll take this gag out of your mouth if you promise not to scream. If you *do* scream, you'll be kicked in the face again. And you'd better realise that I mean it. If you promise not to cry out, nod.'

She nodded her head furiously.

'We'll try you – but watch your step. Untie it, Larry, will you? No, just loosen it, so that it hangs round her neck. That way we can pull it back if we have to.'

She nodded more furiously. I loosened the gag, caught sight

of the bleeding where the corners of her lips had been cut. She seemed to choke, drawing in huge gasps of breath, panting like an animal, until finally she gasped, 'You'll pay for this. You'll never get away with it. Stop it at once, I tell you.'

It was extraordinary how instinctively, with the return of her breath, she had become our nanny again, almost telling us how to behave.

'We want you to write a letter,' said Guy, ignoring her words.

I could see for a moment her eyes light up – or at least a glimmer of excitement over the film of pain from which she was suffering. She obviously thought that she would have to go to the desk.

'No, not the desk,' said Guy. 'Larry found out where the panic button is, so you can forget that.'

She seemed to sag with despair. 'What letter?' she asked, frightened by the hate in Guy's voice. 'I can't write anything unless you untie my wrists. You're hurting me, Larry. Undo them.'

It was a command – an order from the nursery!

'What letter?' she asked again.

'Telling Standartenführer Hoess of the Gestapo to come and pay you a visit.'

'I don't know who you're talking about. Get me a handkerchief to wipe my face, please.'

'Yes, you do know. Hoess comes here regularly – to collect information.'

'I'll write no letters to anyone.'

At that moment Gaston appeared.

'You'll be sorry about this, Gaston,' she cried when she saw him. '*Very* sorry. I'll have you reported for this.'

Gaston looked straight at Guy and said, 'There's something wrong with the tractor. It goes in fits and starts so I've managed to get it to the bottom of the hill. That's why I've been so long. When I saw that Larry's car was still here I thought that maybe we could use it – that or Willi's, when he arrives – instead of the tractor.'

'Good,' said Guy briskly. 'Good. Now, Mademoiselle Lisette, you will write a letter to the *Standartenführer*' – Guy had carefully used the proper rank for the Gestapo equivalent

563

of a colonel – 'telling him you've got some vital information and you want to see him urgently.'

'You're crazy!' she gasped. 'Even if I wanted to, you'd never get away with it.'

'Why not?'

'You *are* a fool. Even if I wrote your ridiculous letter, who would believe it?'

'The Gestapo. Don't you worry.'

She was gasping for breath, and I could see that her neck was hurting.

'We've very little time,' said Guy. 'And I don't want to hurt you, but . . .'

She seemed to sag again, yet she still had a curl of hatred and disbelief on her cut lips, perhaps knowing that the manners she had instilled into the Astell boys from birth would prohibit Guy from hitting her again.

'We've all changed – since you betrayed Olivia and Anna.'

'I did nothing! It wasn't me,' she cried, not with defiance now but in a kind of whimper. 'It was all an accident.'

'And do you know what happened to Anna?' Guy didn't wait for an answer. He told her – brutally, no details spared. 'You were responsible for that. *You*, and now it's our turn. Will you write the letter?'

She shook her head. 'I can't. I don't know what . . .'

'What if she doesn't write it?' I began to think the whole plan might not work.

'She will. I've seen this sort a dozen times. Cowards at heart,' said Guy.

'What are you going to do?' I asked.

'Watch – or rather don't watch if you'd rather not. It won't take long.'

He took a copy of the *Écho Reimois*, rolled it up, and then with the carving knife that I had used to tear the curtains, he ripped open her skirt.

'Stop it!' she cried. 'Stop being so disgusting. You wouldn't dare.'

'No, I'm not going to do *that*;' he tore off her skirt, her slip, panting with exertion, leaving her in a pair of pink panties. 'I'm going to light a fire between your legs.'

As he put a match to the rolled up paper and barely touched

her thighs, she screamed. Guy shouted to Gaston, 'Put the gag over her mouth.' Then to me, 'Larry! Take your car and hide it behind the end of the lane. We don't want anyone to see it. Willi should arrive any moment in his car.'

Mlle Lisette didn't hold out for long – thank God I didn't see what happened. What fascinated me about my single involvement of someone being tortured was the belief that if they talked their life would be spared. If Mlle Lisette wasn't killed she would eventually denounce us – so how could she escape death? Surely she must realise that death was inevitable, not so much to mete out justice as to safeguard ourselves. Yet each time she passed out, each time Guy dashed a pail of water in her face and she revived, moaning with pain, she had, as he told me, *believed* what he had promised her – despite the brutality, the pain. Each time he leaned over and said, 'You see we mean business. All you have to do is write the letter – it's Hoess we want, not you. Once we've got Hoess we'll leave you alone if you give us your word to forget all this.' And she believed it!

'They all do,' said Guy almost sadly when she had finally written the note. 'The only thing that matters to all of them is the instinct with which everyone is born – the desire to cling to life. They want to believe they're going to live, so they're confident that they will.'

'It beats me.' I looked at the pitiful bundle of the woman who had brought up the young Astell family.

'And when I started out on this lark – after I decided to join the Resistance, and the Red Cross, some of us went to a lecture by a psychiatrist. He explained another fundamental truth – the way pain distorts your thoughts. It makes you believe what you otherwise couldn't believe.'

I didn't understand.

'Well, Mademoiselle Lisette is an example. If she was behaving rationally she'd know that she was the primary cause of what happened to the girls. But through what this man called the three Ps – pain, persuasion and promises – it's been quite easy to make Mademoiselle Lisette believe that Hoess is the guilty man, that the girls would have been arrested anyway, that her betrayal was incidental – or even accidental.

Therefore she feels she has a right to be allowed to live. At least in her mind. Whereas we know that exactly the opposite happened – Mademoiselle Lisette is the real guilty party. Hoess is just an agent – a sadist, no doubt, but an agent.'

I had earlier heard the sound of Gaston driving off in my car. Now I heard another car arrive.

'That'll be Willi.'

It was. It was the first time I had seen him since he learned that Anna was safe. He thanked me effusively, until Guy cut him short – kindly but firmly.

'If we're going to make a getaway by lunch every minute counts.' He took an approving look at Willi's neatly pressed Gestapo uniform. 'Now, here's the letter from Mademoiselle Lisette. You drive directly to Gestapo headquarters. When the S.S. man salutes, hand in the letter and rev up the Citroën before he has a chance to ask who you are.'

Willi read out the letter: 'Dear Standartenführer Hoess, This is a very urgent request. I must see you. Guy Astell is back in Reims and I think I know where he is but I'm told he is leaving tomorrow.' She signed, as she said she always did, 'L'.

'That should fetch him,' said Guy. 'Stroke of genius on my part to name myself. I know he hates my guts.'

Looking round uneasily before he left, Willi asked, 'Where's the woman?'

I explained that she was bound and gagged in the kitchen, and that now we had to persuade Hoess to write a letter for Willi to take to his house in the rue St. Julien asking to deliver up Olivia.

I heard the sound of Willi setting off down the hill. Soon Gaston arrived back on foot.

'With luck Hoess will be here in an hour.' Guy looked at his watch. 'But being the Gestapo he's bound to suspect a trap.'

Gaston nodded. It intrigued me, the way in which I, as an amateur, was watching the professionals at work. Gaston was not a real mature professional killer of Germans yet, but still, he was dedicated and he shared with Guy an almost clinical approach to the whole business of outwitting the Germans. It was curious. Nobody, for instance, could have hated the Germans more than Grandma, nobody could have called more loudly for the last German on French soil to be killed, but she inveighed against them with the fervour of an elderly Joan of Arc, or a member of the Crusades ridding the country of the infidel. Gaston and Guy were more cold-blooded, as though they were soldiers and not permitted to give way to their emotions. They, too, wanted to kill the last German in France, but as executioners, not as religious maniacs. The change in Guy's character was enormous. Nothing illustrated it more than his remark when Gaston returned from the kitchen, where he had been checking on Mlle Lisette's bindings, and warned Guy that he would be surprised if the woman wasn't on the point of dying.

'Save us a lot of trouble if she does,' Guy shrugged. Then he asked Gaston, 'All the men in position?'

Gaston nodded. 'Seven men, all armed, in the surrounding woods.'

'Good. So long as your men don't panic and kill Hoess. And don't shoot too soon, or we'll never get Olivia out. Odd, isn't it,' he asked no one in particular with an almost philosophical detachment, 'how much easier it is to kill people than to capture them alive?'

Willi arrived back, having left his Citroën behind the turn of the lane, away from the direction that would be taken by the Gestapo cars, so that unless they backtracked there was no reason why they should find it.

'All okay?' asked Guy.

'I do everything I was able to do,' said Willi in his rather stilted English. 'I give in the letter, then say my mission is very urgent and leave quickly. I am ready for the next letter when she comes.'

That, as Guy had said, would be a tougher proposition, and now we all had to wait. I carried no arms – I could have asked for a gun, I suppose, but I honestly didn't know how to handle one in a crisis. Both Guy and Gaston carried guns, however, Guy a Luger P. 08, stolen from the S.S., and Gaston a Walther P.P.K., a brute of a German pistol, also stolen.

'We won't have to use them, I hope,' Guy reassured me. 'But it gives you a feeling of confidence – and without sounding morbid I like to keep one up the spout for myself, in case. I've seen the torturers at work. I've no desire to be one of the victims, whose only prayer is for a merciful death – which the Germans never permit.'

'Do I know the men outside?' I asked Gaston.

'Perhaps. Every one I'd trust with my life. They're armed with whatever they can get – shotguns, one with a .22 rifle, one with a Luger taken from a German corpse. But they have the great advantage of surprise. If the worst comes to the worst, they could, from the cover of the trees, pick off the bodyguard one by one without any trouble.'

'I'm not worried,' said Guy, and he explained what he meant. First of all there was a special camp about a mile above the hill where new German arrivals trained for occupation duties. 'It's a very different kind of war for them,' he said. 'Fighting battles is one thing, being an occupying power is rather different. They undergo an intensive course up there.' With a nod in the general direction of the camp, which no civilians had ever seen, Guy added, 'They train them in the use of pistols instead of guns. They are also training for ambushes rather than straightforward attack. And I've often heard shooting on a rifle range. Anyway, it won't come to shooting.'

But it did. For all of us had made one major miscalculation.

41

An hour and a quarter after Willi had left to deliver the message to Hoess, we heard the sound of a car coming up the hill. No, it sounded like two cars.

'They're Citroëns,' whispered Gaston. 'I can read the sound of motors just like a book.'

With four or five men to a car, the thought of the two Citroëns coming up towards the cottage meant a force of possibly ten men. That didn't worry Guy as we prepared for their arrival. Gaston was in the kitchen in case anybody started checking round the back, while Guy and I waited at first from behind the curtains of the upstairs front bedroom where we could see what was happening.

From there I had a bird's-eye view as the two black Citroëns arrived. The driver from the leading car jumped out, saluted like a robot as one man alighted and whispered an order. The S.S. man saluted again, barking out, '*Jawohl, Standartenführer.*'

'That's Hoess,' whispered Guy as he ran downstairs to hide behind the front door. I saw the other Germans tumble out of both cars, eight men in all. All were armed, each one almost caressing his ugly-looking weapon which I knew was deadly: a Schmeisser machine pistol. One man, a sergeant in the S.S., walked up the pathway covering Hoess as he advanced.

I had assumed – we had all assumed – that Hoess would knock to let Mlle Lisette know that he was there and then perhaps slip inside, thinking she hadn't heard him. It would be a natural reaction. She lived alone, there was no phone in an isolated cottage. After all, he was well guarded; he had no real need to fear a trap. But he didn't knock. Instead he called out, a low voice, 'Mademoiselle Lisette. *Her ist Hoess.* Where are you? *Ich habe es eilig.*' Meaning that he was in a hurry. When there was no reply he shouted again for Mlle Lisette.

Still silence. Hoess drew his Luger. From the upstairs room I could see that he was really suspicious. He barked out orders, and in the cold-carrying air I could hear the sinister sound of magazine clips being snapped into automatic weapons. Slowly, machine pistols at the hip, the German troops advanced. They were now in a tight ring almost surrounding the cottage. Hoess stood his ground. But it was obvious he wasn't going to enter the house.

I couldn't see, of course, what was happening inside the house, but I *did* realise that if the French Resistance were going to pick off the Germans they would have to act quickly. Yet they had to avoid killing Hoess.

At that moment there was a diversion. Because I could hear everything, I could easily imagine what was happening. In a desperate attempt to break the deadlock, Willi, despite the drawn gun of Hoess, opened the front door and shouted, 'Standartenführer Hoess? *Heil* Hitler!'

Hoess, still gripping his Luger, let his arm fall downwards and, presumably seeing the junior status of a man he didn't know, shouted angrily, 'What the hell are you doing here? Who are you?'

'I am Obersturmführer Brandt, sir.' Willi gave the S.S. equivalent of a first lieutenant's rank, adding urgently, 'Fraülein Lisette has been taken ill. I am a friend.'

'A friend!' shouted Hoess scornfully. 'Since when does the Gestapo become friends with traitors? There's something funny going on. Explain yourself, *Obersturmführer. Was ist los?*'

I knew that Willi was playing for time – and time was fast running out.

'*Est hat einen Unfall gegeben!*' he cried.

'I can see there's been an accident, you *dummkopf*,' roared Hoess. 'Right! Turn round. I'll find out later what the hell you are doing in my territory. Now' – he stabbed his gun into Willi's back – 'I'll follow you. You take me to Mademoiselle Lisette. And if there's any monkey business – you won't know what's hit you!'

Even I could appreciate that two things were vital: if Hoess saw the bound and gagged body of Mlle Lisette, now on the kitchen floor, he would take no chances, but would shoot Willi on the spot. And without Willi as a messenger there was no way to approach Hoess's house and save Olivia. Secondly, if we saved Willi by killing Hoess we would also fail – for there would be no one to write a letter of authority demanding Olivia's release. So we needed *both* men alive. But how?

As Hoess passed through the door, gun stuck into Willi's back, the S.S. sergeant who had been guarding him fell behind him, following; Guy made a decision.

In the split second before the inevitable discovery, Guy, from behind the door, shouted to divert Hoess's attention. The Gestapo man wheeled round, drawing up his firing arm, but Guy got in the first shot, hitting him on the right side and smashing the gun out of his hand. As Hoess screamed with rage Willi turned and grabbed hold of his legs making Hoess fall over so that Guy could hit him.

He did – over the head, with the butt of his gun. Then, as the N.C.O. behind Hoess dashed in to save his master, both men seemed to fire at each other simultaneously. Only one man screamed, though. And luckily it was Guy who cried out, 'They've got me!' I say 'luckily' because the other man couldn't scream, couldn't do anything. Guy had shot him through the head, whereas the N.C.O. had only winged Guy, a nasty flesh wound just below the thigh, though we didn't realise how bad it was at that moment.

Now all hell seemed to erupt as the house – every single corner of it – was sprayed with automatic fire. Glass smashed, and there was the sound of air as bullets rushed past, as the Germans prepared to assault the cottage. But the Resistance men, shielded by the trees, were able to pick them off in seconds, for though the S.S. had surrounded the *house*, the Resistance had surrounded the *S.S.* – and by the very nature of the operation the S.S. had their backs to their attackers. Not one of them had the time to turn round and return the Resistance fire or enter the house. They were too busy to look both ways at once. I was safe upstairs. Willi was safe. The only other casualty was Gaston, hit in one arm, but not badly. And Mlle Lisette. A stray bullet through the kitchen window had perhaps mercifully robbed one of us from assuming the role of executioner.

As Guy shouted to me, I clambered downstairs, and Willi and I tied Hoess to a dining room chair, each arm to one chair arm, each leg to a chair leg. Guy was in severe pain, I could see that, and losing blood, but we managed to find a first aid kit from the back of the Citroën. 'That needs stitching,' I said.

'Not a hope,' grunted Guy. 'Not until I get to Switzerland.'

'You'll never be able to drive.'

Outside it was like a battlefield. But with an extraordinary methodical discipline, the Resistance fighters were stripping the German bodies outside of everything they might need – not only precious machine pistols and ammunition, but even uniforms in case they needed them for disguise. Then they dragged the bodies in their underclothes into the forest.

'Now,' said Guy savagely as he faced Hoess, 'we'll deal with you.'

The German's face was drained of colour. His right arm was covered in blood. Even so he sneered at Guy. 'You amateur bungler. Do you think an overgrown schoolboy like you can take on a member of the Gestapo? What do you want?'

'The girl in your house. Olivia Jacobsen.'

'The Jewess! Ah! I see.'

571

'No, you don't,' shouted Guy and slapped him across the face.

'That's the second time you've hit me,' said Hoess. 'I didn't recognise you behind that stupid beard. You'll pay for that. Do you think you can intimidate me, as you have presumably intimidated that wretched woman who betrayed your family?'

'You will write a letter to your home, asking for someone in authority to hand over Miss Jacobsen to the *Obersturmführer* here, and then . . .'

'And then you'll kill me?' He actually laughed. 'Do you really think I'm such a fool as to let this,' with a withering look at Willi, 'this despicable traitor to the Führer take a letter that I *write*? And sign my death warrant? You must be mad! And do you think I'm afraid that you might engage in a little torture? Try it, my friend. Just try it. You need quick results, eh? Otherwise someone's going to realise that something's wrong. And then you'll have to kill me!'

'I wasn't thinking of killing you,' said Guy, almost with an air of apology.

'Very considerate. So. You are not going to kill me, eh? You fool!' It was extraordinary really, the *hauteur*, the disdain with which he, as our prisoner, regarded the rest of us.

'Willi,' cried Guy. 'I think as a German you had better leave the room.' Willi went obediently through to the kitchen – I think he had a feeling of guilt at the sight of Hoess. He wanted to help us, but he also had a loyalty to the German people, and anyway he was obviously mixed up, so it was much better for him not to be present. Gaston came in. I listened to the threats made by Guy – and looked at my watch.

'You, Hoess,' said Guy, 'are the lowest of the low. Our sister . . .'

'She betrayed Germany!'

'No betrayal deserves that kind of revenge. Nor did she ever truly betray you. Yet you tortured her in a way that will affect her mind for the rest of her life.'

'Well – kill me,' said Hoess. 'I'm not afraid to die. And as for torture – try it. You fool. I am a *German*.'

'No torture is bestial enough to avenge our family,' said Guy.

'You think' – Hoess wriggled in his bonds to make himself

more comfortable – 'you really think that a German officer – *Heil* Hitler – is afraid? What do you plan? To pull out a few fingernails?'

'No. That's one of your favourite methods, no doubt.'

'It works with the weak, but not with the strong. And I am strong.'

'You may change your mind. I'm not a sadist like you are, Hoess, but I know two things. I have a picture of my beautiful sister before you wrecked her life. And of Olivia. And second, I know that you're not as feeble as Mademoiselle Lisette, who is dead of course. We're aware that you can resist torture – you've been trained to it. And I don't think you are afraid of death.'

'Your assessment is correct.' Hoess didn't even seem to be aware of his bleeding arm, the blood now dried. He still managed to convey a touch of irony, even sarcasm.

'And we know that in hundreds of German camps tortured prisoners are begging only for one thing – for death, for release,' continued Guy remorselessly. 'And you won't give it them, will you?'

'Go on. You don't have much time left before the alarm goes off.'

'Plenty of time yet, Hoess. Despite what you have done to my sister and Miss Jacobsen I'm prepared to be merciful. I'm prepared to give you my word of honour that if you ask me to I will shoot you.'

He looked at Guy as though he were an idiot. 'Schoolboys!' he spluttered. 'Are you mad? Germans don't ask to die. They don't ask anything, except to serve the Führer.'

'You will.'

For the first time a flicker of unease passed across Hoess's face. I was as puzzled as he was, for I hadn't the faintest idea what was coming next.

'You will write a letter to the *Obersturmführer* and he will take it to the rue St. Julien and ask Miss Jacobsen to come and join you here. Once we know she's free, you have my word I'll shoot you.'

'And otherwise?'

For a moment – but only for a moment – Guy hesitated, then in a dead level voice he said, 'We shall blind you.'

The words were like a cold douche, as though draining the room of every sound except one lonesome bird outside.

'Yes,' said Guy quietly. 'With this.' He picked up a paper knife from the desk. 'Remember what you did to my sister and Miss Jacobsen?' he added softly.

'You wouldn't dare.'

'I have a debt to repay – and a girl to be freed. Why shouldn't I dare? I don't want to do any of this. But I have had to find a way of making sure that I can give you the ultimate gift – *you* begging *me* to kill you. When you're blind, if you don't crack by then, we'll break both your elbows. Then we'll make sure you're rescued by the Gestapo. You'll be a shell – valueless – but they'll look after you, try to help you – or what's left of you.'

'You'd never dare,' Hoess repeated. 'Anyway, Americans don't behave like that.'

'American sisters don't get treated like whores. It's true we don't behave like this. But you've got Olivia Jacobsen, and I'm going to get her back – or you're going to live, a blind man with crippled arms for the rest of your life. If Olivia wasn't a prisoner I would be merciful and shoot you. But she *is* a prisoner and so I'm going to make sure you don't die – until she's free. Then I'll be merciful.'

Guy turned to me. 'Larry! Go and wait in your car. Tell Willi to wait in his and as soon as we finish off our – well, our business – I'll give Willi a shout to pick up the letter and set off.'

It was Guy's way of getting rid of me, and I was glad to obey, for I knew it had to be done – even though I was beset with confusing thoughts. Was it *ever* right to stoop to the level of a man you despised? Wasn't a man demeaning himself by so doing? And yet there was poor Olivia being demeaned by this warped monster who could, it seemed, only obtain sexual gratification from the excesses of cruelty. And could we so easily forget Anna? None of us had seen her since the escape, but we were all haunted by the possibility that she would never *really* recover. And it would have been simple for Hoess to send her to an ordinary jail; instead, and no doubt to crush the Astells, he had consigned her to a bordello.

I was thinking thus when a scream pierced the still winter

air. A terrifying wail of anguish. I had never heard a sound like it in my life. A moment or two later another scream tore into the silence but this time a blubbery muffled scream of someone on the edge of fainting. Gaston rushed to the front door and shouted, 'Willi! Come here.'

Instinctively – morbid curiosity – I ran to the door, almost bumping into Willi.

'He's agreed,' panted Guy, and that was all he said before *he* fainted. I just managed to keep on my feet. All this had taken perhaps ten or fifteen minutes while we were outside in the car waiting. On the chair, moaning, was the wreck of the once proud Hoess. I had never seen a blind man before, the black, bloody holes out of which presumably the eyes had been torn. Blood was seeping slowly down both cheeks, but Hoess was coming round and shouting, 'You promised to kill me, you promised! Your word as a gentleman!'

I tried to bring Guy back to consciousness, pouring some water over him. Even Gaston looked as grey as the wood ash in the grate, his face incredibly older – for the moment, anyway.

'You tell him what to write,' Gaston said to Willi. 'In German. Not at the desk – it's still got the panic button. In the dining room – where he can sit at the table and you can guide his writing.'

The fight had gone out of Hoess. I don't think he could ever have believed that normal 'simple' Americans would behave like this. I couldn't have done it, I admit it frankly. But Hoess hadn't realised that Guy was not only motivated by a desire to get Olivia free, but had been working with the Resistance for a year, had known from first hand experience the terrible tortures that the Germans and the Vichy French inflicted. Guy had known that no 'normal' torture would break Hoess. But Guy, having seen the victims who had been forced to stay alive, denied the promise of death after repeated tortures, sometimes for months – Guy knew that the only way to beat Hoess was to promise him an end to the living death we *could* inflict on him.

The letter took some time to write. Willi had to make four attempts, and Hoess was by no means in control of himself – he couldn't see, he couldn't find the edge of the paper. He was blubbering, whimpering with pain, but even Gaston, who looked as though he would pass out any moment, whispered to me, 'God! The man has got guts.'

'You will shoot him?' I asked.

Gaston nodded. 'I hate what we've done. But when I think what they did to your sister – it's nothing compared to that, is it?' He was almost apologising, trying to excuse the brutality of it all, to erase it from his mind. 'Isn't it ironic,' he continued as we waited for the letter, 'that the world only begs to stay alive – yet here we have a man who is begging to die.'

Guy was better now, lying back on the sofa, panting a bit. A lot of blood was seeping through the bandage we had taken from the first aid kit in the German car. Gaston was much better. The bullet had just sliced the flesh on the left arm, and he wasn't in any pain.

Willi came through with the letter. 'The writing is not good for a German, is very shaky,' he admitted. 'But the signature, she is firm. Please look.'

We all examined the letter. It was just good enough. 'Right,' said Guy. 'Off you go. Call back here with Olivia and then . . .'

As Willi put on his ugly, shiny peaked cap and ran out of the house to drive to Reims, he cried, '*Bis bald*,' and I echoed, 'See you soon.' At that moment I heard something move in the next room. It was Hoess. By God, he was like a worm you cut in half but which still goes on moving. Do the Germans never give up hope? Blind, he was feeling his way along the side of the wall, trying to find the desk.

'The panic button!' I screamed, throwing myself across the room and into the blind man just as he had reached the side of the wall. Even as he fell, screaming with pain and fury, he was scrabbling with his left hand, trying to find the button as I pushed him away and tied up what was left of him.

The rescue of Olivia took place without a hitch, according to both Willi and Olivia. Smart and trim in the uniform of a Gestapo officer, there was no reason for the servant or soldier – presumably a batman – to doubt the authenticity of a letter asking for Olivia to report to the *Standartenführer*. It was the sort of thing that could happen to a prisoner at any time.

When I ran out at the sound of the Citroën, leaving Guy waiting on the sofa, I could see that Olivia was still afraid. All the honeyed words in the world couldn't hide the evil uniform of the man who was driving her.

But then I cried, 'Olivia!' and she jumped out of the car and ran towards me, half crying, trying to smile through tears.

'We got you out!' I cried. 'Let me look at you.'

'No, no. Please don't look. And thank you, Larry. I didn't recognise Willi at first and then I thought . . .'

'Guy's waiting for you − here in the cottage,' I said gently.

'He's here?'

'Yes, he's lying down. He's been hit − but not badly.'

As we walked towards the house, I stole a look at her. She was wan, tired, still suffering mentally from what had happened to her, but even so − and taking everything into account − she didn't look as bad, as grey, as taut, as I would have expected. It did occur to me, a fleeting thought, that however terrible her life had been she had perhaps not suffered as much as Anna had, who had had to serve every customer she was offered. Olivia had been forced to live with Hoess but, in a sense, living in his home, she was in the position of a married woman who is forced to copulate with a man she loathes and despises. But only one − and there is a limit to the endurance of even the vilest pig of a man.

As we reached the door a shot sounded inside the house. That would be Hoess.

'Wait here,' I said to Olivia and ran forward, almost forgetting her.

'That was Gaston,' said Guy. 'I kept my word. We'll throw both the bodies in the cellars underneath the trapdoor of the kitchen floor. With luck they may not be discovered for months.'

At that moment another shot rang out − this time outside.

For a moment I thought we had been ambushed − I had visions of being surrounded by the Germans who had come to the rescue of Hoess. Instinctively we all ducked − until Guy cried, 'God almighty! It's Willi.'

Olivia ran to the door and helped him back into the room: Guy could barely walk. I raced to the back of the garden; Willi was sprawled out along the shrubs, his gun in his hand, not quite dead, eyes glazed but fluttering.

'Willi, you idiot,' I cried, not realising how little time he had left.

'Is best,' he gasped. 'I do what I can for the Astells, yes?'

'Don't talk like that, Willi.' I felt the tears stinging my eyes. 'Oh Willi! We were going to get you away.'

'Can never be same with Anna;' he tried to smile. 'No future for me − a good past, yes?' Gathering his breath as though for a huge effort, he gave a genuine smile, and cried out, just before he died, 'We had good times dancing at Maxim's, Larry, yes? Remember? Give my love to Anna.'

42

Everything was changed now. We had no time to waste − ironically, no time to think even of Olivia. Poor Willi was dead, but had to be left unmourned.

First things first: we had to get rid of Willi's body. It seemed unceremonious, but he had to be lowered into the cellar below the kitchen trapdoor together with the other bodies.

After that Gaston, despite his wounded arm, had to make for Pagniez's house − his father's house, of course. He drove Willi's car, taking with him Guy, who had to be helped into the seat next to him. But now what? Guy had planned to drive Olivia and Willi to Switzerland. With no Willi Guy couldn't possibly drive, certainly not until he had received proper attention and been strapped up. And he might not be in a fit state to drive even then.

I didn't want to go to Switzerland. I had driven to Douzy to help, to do everything I could to free Olivia, but I had a job to do, the *Globe* to serve, and after I had done all that was expected of me I wanted to return to Paris as fast as possible. Not a soul knew of my involvement with Hoess or the rest of the dead men. I had taken care not to contact Papa on this trip – no one knew – but within a very short time the Germans would be looking for the missing men, trying to find out what had happened. I wanted my alibi established – Paris.

I drove Olivia to Pagniez's cottage. 'But I'm only staying a second,' I said abruptly. 'I don't want my Citroën to be seen.' We had originally planned to hide Olivia in the belfry at Douzy church until Guy was ready to leave, but of course there was no way Guy could climb the belfry steps unless at least two of us helped him.

'I've got to get back too,' declared Guy. 'I've a job to do in Vichy France. But I can't drive you, Olivia. I just can't. Can you, Gaston?'

'If I have to.' Gaston hesitated. 'I'll do anything I can to help, but I don't want to spoil *my* cover. I'm regarded in the Douzy area as an honest vigneron, working for La Châtelaine. It's a vital role I play. If I'm caught driving a car a hundred miles from Douzy, me, an ordinary worker in the fields, how can I be expected to answer any questions at a roadblock? I may never be able to return to Douzy: then I lose half my value.'

'You're right,' Guy acknowledged. 'I'll have to stay for the time being. Hide up – perhaps here. I think I could make the steps to the belfry.' He thought for a moment. 'You'll want to stay here in your father's cottage, won't you?'

Gaston nodded. 'If I can.'

'I'll make it easier,' said Olivia, sitting down, hands cupped round a big bowl of hot, ersatz coffee. She looked up and said slowly, 'I want to stay in Douzy.'

'That's crazy!' I said.

'Is Guy crazy, helping like he does? After all, he's neutral. Are you crazy, fighting for me?'

'Come on.' I tried chaffing her. I knew from the past how determined Olivia could be. 'That's different. We all love you – and we're going to look after you.'

'Thank you all for everything you have done,' she said looking round. 'I feel new, cleansed – and grateful in a way you'll never be able to understand. But I'm not going.'

'Well, you could repay us by getting to Switzerland,' said Guy gruffly, twisting his leg round in a search for comfort.

'No.' She sipped her coffee then put down the bowl. 'No. I want to repay what you've done – but at the same time get my revenge for what the Germans have done to my people. I want to fight – here.'

'We need trained men and women,' said Gaston shortly.

'Then train me!' retorted Olivia.

We might have argued for hours, and I wanted to leave because it really did mean a great deal to me to preserve my job, to get back to Paris. And yet – I couldn't leave Guy here. Apart from anything else, he would eventually need medical attention. And there was bound to be one hell of a fuss soon. Gestapo men couldn't suddenly vanish without an intensive manhunt. Guy had to leave.

'Well,' I said, though I couldn't hide my reluctance, 'I'd better take you to Switzerland. But I think we'll go in my car. It's safer. I've got my set of French papers anyway.'

'I can't let you do that,' said Olivia. 'I want to stay, but I'll drive Guy down to Switzerland if you like. Remember, I was the chauffeur of the Hisp. Then I'll drive the car back to Douzy.'

'A Jewish girl, on her own in France? You'll be asking for trouble at the first checkpoint.'

'I'll go,' said Gason.

In the end, the matter was settled by the development which nobody envisaged. Looking through the front window, Gaston saw the figure of a man cycling, shoulders hunched forward, pedalling hard, up the incline to his cottage. 'That's Pinot,' said Gaston. 'I wonder what he wants. He's one of us, but he'd never come here unless the matter was urgent.'

The man, whom I recognised vaguely as a farmer's son, almost tumbled off his bike as he arrived. He took one look at me and gasped, 'Monsieur Larry! Go quick! The Gestapo are after you.'

'Me? They don't even know I'm here.'

'They do. You must go. Only don't go to Douzy.'

'What on earth are you talking about?' asked Gaston.

'Look.' The man pulled the bottom of his jacket up over his shoulders. I realised that despite the cold he wore no shirt or vest. His back was red-raw.

'They picked up half a dozen of us. I don't know what happened, or why, but I heard that a lot of Gestapo men had been killed. They beat me, but I couldn't say anything because

I didn't *know* anything. In the end they threw me out. But one of us, Fresnay, did talk after they had torn out two of his nails.'

'Fresnay? Who's he?' I asked.

'He mentioned you, Monsieur Larry. Said you'd been talking to him this morning near Lisette's cottage. It didn't seem harmful but the second one of them heard your name . . .'

Of course! I had forgotten Fresnay, the farmer's boy on horseback. Probably he hadn't the faintest idea that he had done me any harm.

'That changes everything,' said Gaston. 'I'll be able to repaint the Gestapo car – don't worry about that. But you, Larry – bolt for it. Now. Not in ten minutes, not in five minutes, get off, now – for Switzerland, I suppose. We'll get a doctor up to Guy.'

'I can't. The *Globe* . . .'

'Damn the *Globe*,' cried Guy. 'I'll have to stay now. I'll get to the church belfry, don't worry about me. It's too risky you coming with me. This is a completely new ball game. Your neutral image has been split wide open. You'd better get the hell out of here – out of France – before the Gestapo grab you. I can imagine that nothing would give Abetz more pleasure than taking you inside. And there are plenty more men where Hoess came from.'

Almost in a daze, I agreed. It's hard to explain how, in the midst of a near panic, after a morning in which I had actually seen a man who had been deliberately blinded, how Willi had said goodbye with his last breath – how all this tumult had raged in a few hours, and yet all I could think of was the *Globe*. 'You're a stupid bastard to care so much,' I said to myself.

Ten minutes later I was on my way south.

As I set off, making for the secondary roads round Dijon and then Dôle, I wasn't sure which of my identities I should use. If, as seemed certain, I had even been seen in the vicinity of the gun battle, I would certainly be wanted for questioning. For one moment, before I set off, I wondered whether running away was wise: it would certainly be taken as an admission of guilt. Yet I knew I had to run for it. Once they found the bodies, then discovered that Olivia had been freed – and after that the other bodies in the woods, the two empty Gestapo motor cars – no, it was too big a risk to be ignored. I would be implicated, and I didn't relish the likely Gestapo method of extracting what my explanation might be.

I decided to go 'French'. With my papers as Henri Vasson and my profession as a champagne salesman, it did not seem likely that anyone would have the number of the car – the most common make in France. I didn't even know whether it would be possible for the German authorities to flash messages giving my name and American passport details by radio all over France. After all, Reims was only a local Gestapo office. But I couldn't take that chance, for Guy was right – Abetz might take a hand, seeking a personal revenge. I hadn't seen him since Anna was freed, but he couldn't have relished our victory.

I wondered when I would see Oregon again – to say nothing of Papa and Grandma. Gaston had promised to explain carefully that I had left Paris, and to pass on the news to Papa. It would soon be around Reims anyway. Talking to myself as I drove along, I found myself saying, 'I know I won't see the family again until the war is over, and that looks like dragging on for ever.'

I knew that if I made for the Bois Jolie and sought help from Madame Gavroche I would have to go through the woods again – though I imagined that the two toughs I had beaten up wouldn't yet be fit enough to plot revenge! But there I was. In for yet another surprise.

It was like coming home to reach the warm country atmosphere of the Bois Joli with the lake in front of me in the moonlight, and to find a warm log fire in the sitting-room, for the night was cold and miserable, a typical early December wet day, a touch of snow on the Juras, otherwise rain.

Madame Gavroche welcomed me with open arms – and some rough bread, much better than the bread of the north, and with a bowl of home-made soup, filled with chunks of parsnips. I realised I had hardly eaten since dawn.

'Going over again?' That was her way of saying, 'Are you crossing the frontier?'

I nodded, busy dunking bread into the thick hot soup.

'Well, you won't have any trouble this time – with, you know, the two men. The police moved them out of the area. The *gendarmerie* were furious. There are a great number of policemen here who try to help – if they can.' She poured out more wine from a *pichet*.

'Thank God. Even so, I'm dreading the trip through the woods.'

'You have to go that way? Through the woods, I mean?' She asked the question guardedly, as if trying to encourage me to ask *her* questions, for then she added slyly, 'It's a pity you're not an American.'

'Would that be easy?'

'Straightforward.'

'You guessed?'

'I thought from the way you behaved. English perhaps, but the English are fighting, so they have to hide more. Such brave boys! But you didn't have to hide. So why can't you cross the frontier normally?'

'Well, Gaston and I – we had a bit of a fight this morning. Killed a lot of men.'

'Gaston is safe?'

'Yes. But I was identified after someone had been tortured.'

'*Salauds!*'

'So I daren't go by the normal frontier, in case I'm on a wanted list.'

She poured herself out another glass of wine and one for me. '*Santé.*' She touched the rim of her glass with mine. 'Let me find out if they are looking for you.'

'From the Germans?'

'No, no, not them. Quite often they leave the frontier post to be checked by the French, and every day they issue what they call the "prohibited list". People on it are stopped, but not if the right police can help us. It only applies to foreigners, of course. There's no way a Frenchman can cross the frontier legally.'

'Even so, it seems risky to me,' I said doubtfully.

'Safe as houses – at the right time. And also, if you're going to stay some time in Switzerland, surely it's much better to enter legally? The last time you went you only stayed for a night or two, but if you plan to stay longer, and they pick you up without the proper stamp at the frontier, that could mean trouble for you.'

I had thought of that, but had decided to take the risk of being picked up, and if my papers were not in order I would bluff it out with my press card, American passport, and if necessary a diplomatic push from Sonia.

'The Swiss are getting tougher. But what time is it?' She looked at her watch. 'Seven o'clock. The frontier closes at nine. And le Capitaine Dumont of the Immigration Service will be in charge of the frontier tonight. He's an old friend of ours. How you say – very close?' She smiled engagingly, really a very pretty, lonely widow. 'When he's on duty he always comes here for supper at seven thirty. Then at eight o'clock he goes back and the German officer slips into town for a bite of food. The captain says the food is better here. And as he has an eye on me, and . . .' she paused, 'when I tell him you're an American he will let me see the "prohibited" list. If you're not on it, I'll introduce you, and you can both go to the frontier together. Or perhaps follow just afterwards to give the German officer time to go for his supper.'

Captain Dumont turned out to be a genial, vaguely anti-German middle-aged man who obviously had a soft spot for Madame Gavroche and would do anything to help.

'The French are the masters of the blind eye;' he exercised his rather cryptic English. 'No see, no action.'

I didn't like to be too pushy, and I was still a little afraid that it was all too easy, but the immigration officer and Madame Gavroche studied official lists together, and though she now knew that I was an American, and my American name, she hadn't told the officer, so she went through the string of names carefully.

'*Eh bien,*' she said finally. '*Pas de problème.*'

And there wasn't. Before driving to Divonne I unloaded Madame Gavroche a few bottles, to be hidden for safe keeping if I was refused permission to leave, but as a present for her if she didn't hear from me by midnight. It consisted of four magnums of precious petrol, and my remaining five bottles of Astell.

'I don't want to be caught by the Swiss trying to smuggle in my own champagne,' I laughed.

Then, after letting Captain Dumont cycle ahead in the rain and dark, I followed him, arriving at quarter to nine.

There was no German officer at the post, though two German soldiers had been left on guard. Dumont behaved as though he had never seen me before, an obviously intelligent ploy in front of witnesses, and rather grandly asked for my passport, examined and then stamped it, adding a perfunctory, 'We also look after the Customs to save money. Have you anything to declare?'

I shook my head. 'Nothing, *monsieur.*'

On the other side of the road, barely fifty yards away, I could see the grey and green uniforms of the Swiss; I was glad I had got rid of the champagne and petrol, for they searched the car thoroughly, even checking on the chassis number on the engine in case it had been stolen. But my *carnet* and *triptique* were in order, and I had nothing to hide. I had even left my false French papers at the Bois Joli.

This time I arrived at Three Circles Farm in style, tooting as I opened the five-barred white gate and drove in. Two minutes later I was inside the house, my arms wrapped round Sonia.

43

It was the peace, the feeling of relief, of safety, that was so wonderful after all the events of that terrible day. As soon as I had washed, cleaned up a bit and swilled my eyes with cold water, I had to tell Sonia everything that had happened. We sat down in the living room, and I recounted how Olivia had been freed, Guy wounded, and how I had become involved – and identified by the Germans. I left out most of the details of the torture.

'Does that mean you can't go back to France?' Sonia asked eagerly. 'That you'll be staying?'

'For some time, I suppose. I'll have to phone the *Globe* after I've got my breath back – and after we've spent a little time together. God! How I've missed you. But' – with a sudden thought – 'where's Anna? I must see her.'

'She's not here.'

'I don't understand.'

'Don't panic, but she's in a superior sort of clinic just outside Lausanne.'

'Clinic!' I knew the French used the word clinic more than we do to denote a more elegant kind of hospital, but the way she said it, slowly, started a rush of terrible anxiety into my head. 'You don't mean' – I could only think of the French words – '*Un asile d'aliénés.*'

'An asylum! Darling, of course not.' Her genuine laugh was like throwing a great fear out of the house. 'No, my dear. She's exhausted – and she's *not* normal. She won't be for weeks. But you'll go and see her tomorrow; we'll go together. And now let me look at you.'

She held me away from her in the way she often did, hands on my shoulders, looking at me critically before she said, 'You look grey with fatigue!' She riffled her hands through my thick blond hair. 'But at least you haven't started going bald.'

'I'm surprised,' I laughed. 'After all I've been through.'

'Poor Larry. And you *have* lost a lot of weight.'

'A bit,' I nodded.

'And those patches of red on your cheeks,' she touched the two spots.

'Fatigue – and fear,' I laughed again. 'The two Fs – they'll disappear right away.'

The housekeeper, who I remembered as being so well dressed – her good quality shoes somehow stuck in my memory – came in to ask if there was anything *monsieur* needed.

'I've had some supper, thanks,' I said. 'But I could drink some really good coffee.'

I'd almost forgotten what the taste of genuine coffee was like, for though we received a small ration from the U.S. Embassy in Paris it was of a new kind, already prepared. Here, that moment in Switzerland, I could smell the coffee before it arrived – and hear the old lady grinding the beans in the kitchen. What luxury! What peace! and soon there would be crisp sheets and the warm naked loving body of Sonia next to mine.

During the night I had a terrible nightmare. I dreamed that I had to shovel the bodies of Hoess and Lisette down the trapdoor hole of Lisette's cottage into the cellar below, and as I did so I turned over the dead man's body and the corpse was that of Guy with two sightless, bloody holes where the eyes should have been. And the body of the girl had a creamy white complexion and the eyes were filled with fear – in the face of Olivia.

I must have screamed, for Sonia turned me over, then put on the bedside light. I was drenched in sweat; pillows, pyjamas, even the sheets were wet through. She got up, rubbed me down, and then I left off my pyjamas and wrapped myself in the bathrobe of thin towelling, and moved to her side of the bed, which was still dry.

I overslept, physically exhausted. When in the morning I peeped out at the courtyard with the horse trough and the huge umbrella of a plane tree, and the stumps of the vineyards beyond, the world was covered with snow. I must have fallen asleep again, and when next I woke it was to see Sonia standing there in her dressing gown, holding a tray.

'Breakfast, *monsieur*,' she cried, then put the tray down carefully and leaned across the quilt, whispering, 'My *monsieur* – for all time, for ever now.'

I ate every scrap of breakfast, the grapefruit, the bacon and eggs, the croissant and black cherry jam, and, perhaps, best of all, three cups of *real* coffee. Then I said, with a pretence of sternness, 'If I *am* your *monsieur*, you are my *madame*, and I order you to enter my bed.'

She laughed, face lighting with pure happiness and relief. I don't remember Sonia ever looking more beautiful, eyes shining with the joy that comes from knowledge that whatever the price we had paid we had succeeded. She put the tray down on the floor, turned the key in the doorlock, took off her dressing gown and then, by the side of the bed, pulled her blue nightie over the top of her head and slid under the covers.

Long after – or so it seemed – she kissed me gently and whispered, 'I've got to go shopping in Lausanne, and then we'll go and see Anna. Is that all right with you?'

We drove to Lausanne quietly, the lake on our right, the vineyards hugging every inch of hillside on our left.

'I'll park the car here in the place St. François,' Sonia said. 'Then we'll walk down the hill and buy provisions for the weekend.'

The 'hill' consisted of the narrow, winding chéneau de Bourg, and it really was narrow, for 'chéneau', literally translated, means 'gutter'.

After two years of war I gazed in wonder at the shops on either side of the narrow street. Habit had made me forget the variety of cooked meats, the mounds of pâté, the pink ham, the darker tongues, the even darker *viande de Grisons*. A dozen different salamis lined one counter, together with the larger white and pink Italian *mortadella*. Next door a butcher displayed joints of beef, decked out to look attractive enough to pop straight into the oven, together with chops and fat chickens. It was the hunting season, so there were saddles of venison ready for the kitchen.

I wasn't being greedy, looking at these shops with wide open eyes, smelling the nearby bakery with a dozen different kinds of bread. It was my instinctive reaction to the plight – not mine, I was luckier – of millions of Frenchmen who for months had been grateful for a few turnips or fish-heads as a staple diet.

Of course there was more to it than that. Plenty was a sign of peace, but it could also be a sign of conquest – or, for that matter, of an undeclared war between poverty and wealth. But here in Lausanne it was the breath of freedom, the lack of an instinctive need to look over a shoulder. I would have to make up my mind what to do soon, I thought; but until I did I was at peace, with no wish to re-enter the nightmare world from which I had just escaped.

Shopping over, Sonia drove me in her little Fiat, with Swiss number plates, to the Cecilia Clinic on a hillside above Morges, a lakeside town, little more than a village really, midway between Lausanne and Rolle.

I had, without realising it, been prolonging the shopping expedition partly because I was dreading the meeting with Anna. I wanted to see her – of course I did – yet I was nervous, afraid perhaps that I would be shocked by what I saw, that Sonia had been hiding the real truth from me.

After all, I knew Anna had suffered, but a 'clinic' did smack of something worse than shock, a period of rehabilitation. The word held a vaguely sinister note, and my first impressions did little to allay my apprehension – the smell of antiseptic, even the floor polish, the bustling, efficient nurses, so busy with patients that they seemed to have no time for a patient's visitors.

A sister nodded to Sonia at her office on the second floor; she obviously knew her, and preceded us towards a room, peeped through a small window and said, 'That's all right, countess. She's presentable. A bit sleepy, but . . .' she smiled and shrugged.

The sleep, I learned later, was drug-induced, as the doctors had kept her sedated during a period of nightmares often violent and resulting in screams that would have awakened the hospital if the room hadn't been sound-proofed.

We walked in on tiptoe, but almost as soon as I leaned over the bed Anna opened her eyes. They met mine and, though hardly awake, she recognised me, smiled and held out her fingers. I couldn't make out what she said – something on the lines of 'Wonderful to be home' – and then she faded away into sleep again, her hand still clutching mine, locked to it.

I remained with her for an hour or so and once or twice the semi-consciousness was interrupted by open eyes, recognition, smiles of joy, mumbled words.

'It's all over now,' I whispered. 'We're here to protect you. For ever and ever. The nightmare's finished.'

She smiled and closed her eyes in sleep.

'She's much better,' said the sister, when she decided we had stayed long enough, 'but we mustn't tire her.' Later that day Sonia told me, in outline, the problems which the doctors had faced, the reason for helping Anna to sleep as much as possible. It was not only the nightmares, but the fears when she was awake. At first the sight of even the most inoffensive doctor in his white coat sent her screaming with rage, the violence spilling out when she jumped up from bed and tried to attack any man. And she was very strong. One male hospital orderly was severely bitten when Anna dug her teeth into his arm as she was being lifted. Two received heavy bruises.

'The only way was to keep poor Anna quiet,' confessed Sonia. 'The specialist – you'll meet him – has given me his word that there's nothing really wrong with Anna. No real mental disturbance, though she's not' – she hesitated – 'not quite normal yet. You can't expect her to be.'

'Poor Anna,' I said as we walked along the corridor to the stairs and the outside world. 'If only I could do something.'

She pressed my arm, linking hers with mine. 'You may not realise it, Larry, but Anna's taken a gigantic step forward today.'

I must have looked astonished.

'You are the first man to see her alone in her room. We'd planned it in advance with the doctor. But he was so frightened of violence that he agreed only if he was outside, with two male nurses to overpower her if she attacked you.'

'And she didn't.'

'No, she didn't,' Sonia smiled happily. 'She took one look at you and I could see the Astell affection darting between the two of you. And when she woke up again too.'

'Was it as bad as that?'

'It was never bad.' She walked towards the parking space and offered to let me drive but I shook my head. 'Never bad. I was impressed by this doctor from the moment I met him. It was never hopeless. But lengthy.' Sonia started up the Fiat and crunched in the gears professionally before backing out. 'Anyway, it's all different now. She obviously believed when she first came to Switzerland that every man was trying to rape her. I think you've speeded up the improvement by months just because she trusts you. She'll be all right, you see. Go and visit her every day until she associates you with love – and not hate.'

'I will,' I promised.

That Saturday we went for a walk – and that in itself was a symbol of our freedom. We drove for dinner to a small inn at a village called St. Saphorin, where the owner bottled his own white wine and we had the most famous of all Geneva dishes, *filets de perches*, small fish caught that morning in the lake and sautéed in butter with *pommes frites* such as I had never tasted since oil became virtually unobtainable in France. We washed it down with local wine followed by Espresso and a glass each of Kirsch.

On the Sunday, after I had visited the clinic again, I had the feeling before dinner that Sonia wanted to talk to me – and seriously. The living room was warm, white walled, with sofas on either side of the large fireplace; its logs sometimes crackled, sometimes hissed, as tongues of blue flame settled down to a more normal colour.

I was drinking a Scotch and cold water. We were not great whisky drinkers at home, but we did enjoy it from time to time and Oregon had always drunk his favourite, 'Old Rarity', which in the old days was delivered to Douzy by the case. It came in grey and green stone jars, and looked as good as it tasted. I had found a couple of bottles in Lausanne and was sipping it gratefully, my left arm around Sonia's shoulders, her head resting on my shoulder.

'Bliss,' she said, 'that's the only word to describe it. Bliss. Does it ever have to end?'

'Meaning?'

'Well, I mean . . .' She sat up, turning slightly to look me in the face. 'For a country that isn't at war, you've not done badly. You've written nasty things about Hitler, you've nearly been killed, you saved two innocent girls from . . .' she shuddered. 'I'm very proud of you, darling, but isn't enough enough?'

'I must contact the *Globe*. I've phoned our man in Berne, passing them your phone number so that Washington can phone me here.'

'But what can they, or you, *do*?'

'I don't know,' I said, adding laughingly, 'I wonder what would happen if they sent me to Rome.'

'Oh no! Then I'd have to leave Rolle.'

'Well, if I don't stay in Europe we'd be worse off. I might be sent to, say, Argentina or China. Then we'd *never* meet.'

'Why go anywhere?' She hesitated. 'Why not stay here? You have money in America, and I have all the money we need

here – from, well, Paraguay if you want the truth. You've
done your share. It isn't your war. Let the other people fight
it.'

'What about people like Guy?'

'Guy chooses his way of life. In a way he enjoys it. At least, I
think he does. In a way – it's nasty to say this, but you know
what I mean – he's trying to compensate with action what
you've achieved by thinking. Now you're the opposite.'

'Hey!' I protested. 'What about my fight in the woods on
my last trip here? No action!'

'I still say you're not an action man. Have you ever thought
why you got involved in fighting – and killing now? Not to
win the war, Larry. For you the pen *is* mightier than the
sword. No, you only get involved in fighting to save your
women! Me, Anna, and then you felt you had to help Guy get
Olivia out. And look where it's landed you.'

I knew what she was driving at. And yet I had a niggling
feeling that even a neutral couldn't just walk out on a tortured
world because it wasn't his problem. It would be like walking
past, pretending not to notice some bully beating up a
woman.

And I was thinking not only of myself, but of Sonia as well.
How could both of us spend years hiding from the truth,
shirking it? Wouldn't it be impossible to live that way, after all
that had happened, all that would happen in the days to come?
With each year – and each new experience of work or war – I
felt the need to go on. Looking at her, silent for the moment, I
wondered. I *had* changed. In the past I had been happy with
each day we had loved together, and all I had asked of life then
was that the next day be as happy. But now – I needed more,
with Sonia of course, but *more*.

'I don't want to be a hero,' I protested, 'but I can't just sit
around enjoying the view of Lake Geneva for the rest of the
war.'

I knew that in a sense Sonia was fighting for us both, for our
future together, especially when she said, 'Couldn't you write
a book? Surely after what you've seen and done and with your
name splashed all over American newspapers – well, nobody
has written a good book yet on how France lost the war. Or
what life is like in France under the Germans. The material you

sent from Switzerland the last time you were here was terrific.'

That was an idea that *did* tempt me. Like almost all news-papermen I had toyed with the idea of writing at length – we all wanted to write 'our book' – and I had wonderful raw material. But I faced one snag: there was no way I could complete any extra research I might need without talking to French friends. Though, sitting there in the living room sipping Scotch before dinner, it did occur to me that as a neutral in search of a book I might be able to visit England and talk to de Gaulle. It was a thought, anyway.

'I don't know,' I sighed.

'Don't worry now.' She took a sip of wine. 'We'll work something out.' Almost ruefully she added, 'Life has a habit of working things out for you, whatever you decide yourself. Specially in these days.'

It was a casually uttered prophecy uncanny in its accuracy – and the speed with which it was fulfilled. We were sitting drinking coffee after dinner on that Sunday evening when I switched on to the B.B.C. to listen to the latest reports on the siege of Leningrad, now in its third month. I listened with only part of my mind – until I exclaimed, 'Jesus Christ!' I sprang up suddenly, switched the radio to full blast, spilling my coffee over my only suit. For the impersonal B.B.C. announcer, after warning listeners to stand by for important news, announced in a calm voice, 'This morning units of the Japanese navy and air force attacked Pearl Harbour without warning.'

'Jesus Christ!' I cried again.

'It's not possible,' said Sonia. I waved her to silence, listen-ing intently as the announcer filled in the details. The attack had taken place in Honolulu that morning – the evening of the same day here in Switzerland – by more than three hundred and fifty torpedo bombers and Zero fighters from six Japanese carriers. The *Arizona* had exploded after a direct hit, four other battleships were sunk, half a dozen more damaged, and nearly two hundred American aircraft destroyed.

'They must be mad!' I switched off at the end of the bulletin. 'They must be absolutely crazy. They may have sunk half the American navy, but the Japs just can't take on the United States. It's a preposterous thought.'

'It's terrible,' she cried.

'It's war – now it really *is* a world war. Everyone's in it. All of us.'

'Us?' she echoed. 'What's it going to mean to us?' she asked in a very small, sad voice.

I hesitated. 'I don't know. But it looks as though you're right. Events *have* had a hand in shaping our destinies.' I sighed, because I knew from the moment of the broadcast what I would have to do, though I did not tell Sonia until much later in the evening. Then, very quietly, I said, 'I'll have to go back to America and join up.'

'You can't,' she said dully. 'I know how you feel, but . . .'

'There aren't any buts. The fact that I could get out of the fighting – by being, say, a war correspondent in the Pacific – well, that only makes it more important that I *do* join up of my own free will.'

'But my own Larry,' she was almost crying, 'this will make us – enemies.'

'I know. But only our countries.'

'It's so wicked, Larry. So unfair. At least until now we weren't enemies.'

'We're not, darling. Not really. The bloody Japanese! Now they're in, we'll have to fight – Europe as well as Asia. And that includes me.'

'But why? Why try to become a hero? If they order you to, that's one thing. But you don't have to volunteer – to fight me, and that's what it means.'

'Sonia, don't be angry if I say something that's going to hurt you. You know I love you. But, like it or not, the Fascists in Italy are in their way as bad as the Nazis in Germany. Not as powerful, but as bad. You know this in your heart. And if the Germans can torture Anna because some sonofabitch squealed on her, the Fascists can do exactly the same to you. Without warning. That's what I'm fighting for, darling. You.'

I said it that night, and a month later when I got the chance to fly to Portugal where a boatload of Americans was being evacuated for the States I said it again, lying in bed, kissing her.

'*That* is what I am fighting for, Sonia,' I said on that last night. 'You're the love of my life – and I'm going to fight to free you, so that you can marry and have children in a land of peace. When I join the U.S. army I won't be fighting to win the war. I'll be fighting to win you.'

PART FOUR

December 1942–August 1944

44

Perhaps it wasn't surprising really, the change I found in Mama when I arrived in America. Vague remarks by Tommy Tomlinson had prepared me. Early in the spring of 1942 I arrived on a Swedish freighter at Pier 86 in New York City, without having been able to warn anyone of my arrival.

All the shipping schedules, passenger manifests and so on were secret in case of U-boat attack. So I checked in at the St. Regis in East 55th Street and the first thing I did was to wallow in a hot bath, then have an Old Fashioned in the Old King Cole bar before dinner in the Oak Room. I knew I had arrived in America when I heard the waiter, laden with a tray of food, hold out one plate and bellow to the diners at a nearby table, 'And who gets the frogs' legs?'

Mama lived only a block or two away, across Madison and Park at the corner of 55th Street and Lexington. I phoned her in advance at her apartment and by mid morning the following day I had reached the fourteenth floor where she had a corner flat overlooking 55th and back towards 3rd Avenue. She was waiting at the door at the end of the corridor with open arms.

'I was listening for the elevator to stop.' She hugged and kissed me. 'Larry, you look *thin*.'

'And you look stunning.' I laughed.

She did. Still under fifty, with good legs, she was beautifully dressed. Her hair was still a natural blonde which had never been rinsed in bleach. Her nails were long and painted pink, her teeth small and white, and after another look I summed her up with another laugh, 'What a dishy blonde.'

She obviously liked the compliment. But what I didn't say, but felt, was that she glowed with a kind of inner satisfaction. She wore the same look of happiness blended with contentment which used to suffuse Sonia when we were able to translate our love into physical terms. I knew that look of Sonia's well, and it gave me an odd sensation, seeing it reflected in my own mother's face.

She was bursting to learn all the family news, especially about Anna, and I told her everything – everything, that is, except what had really happened to Anna and Olivia. As far as Mama was concerned, they had just been 'wrongfully imprisoned'.

As we talked, I looked around the apartment. It was very attractive, the front door opening directly onto an L-shaped room, the far end furnished with a glass-topped table leading directly to a kitchen.

'It's just what I need,' Mama said as she showed me round. 'Handy for the 5th Avenue shops. I didn't really need two bedrooms and bathrooms, but it was the only one I could get. And I did hope that at one stage Anna might come and join me.'

'I know,' I admitted. 'But in a way I think she's better off with Sonia. They always have been close and . . .'

'And how is Sonia?' asked my mother gently. 'Still in love?'

I nodded. 'Francesco's trying to get their marriage annulled; it's a long, dreary business, but apparently he has a lot of influence and it'll come through eventually.'

'And then – at long last?'

'Yes. We'll get married. I've always wanted to. But this bloody war – I can't see it ending for years.'

'With America so strong?'

'I know. But the physical problem of actually invading huge countries like France – to say nothing of Japan. There aren't enough men in the world to kill all those Germans and Japs. We will never be able to knock them out.'

'And what are you going to do?'

'I'm going to join up. There's no nonsense about being heroic. I just feel that I might be useful if I can get into some sort of – oh! some sort of undercover job or something like that.'

She didn't really want to talk about the war; naturally all the conversation revolved around the family, the latest news, what had happened to Papa – and to everyone at Douzy.

'It seems like a different world.' She pulled open a bureau, revealing a selection of bottles and glasses. 'I've already got the ice prepared,' she said. 'Are you going to take me for lunch? Shall I mix a drink? A martini? Or something else American?'

I don't know why, but I had the impression that Mama was making small talk. She never mixed drinks at home. She never asked what we wanted. She was nervous.

'Here, let me do it.' I started to stir the gin with its few drops of Noilly Prat. 'And what about the "21" for lunch?'

She prattled on for the hour or so before lunch, bombarding me with questions, but all the time I had the feeling that, though she certainly wanted to know everything there was to know about the family, she was carefully avoiding another subject. Surely after all that had happened, the life so different, it couldn't still be Gaston?

It wasn't – because I asked her. Not brutally, but firmly; not to upset her, but more to put her mind at rest. It came out naturally when I asked, 'Shall we have a quiet dinner tonight before I leave for Washington tomorrow to see the *Globe* people and then see about volunteering for active service?'

'Oh darling!' She seemed genuinely sorry. 'I know you couldn't let me have advance warning that you were coming, I realise that, but I do have another date for dinner. Such dreary old people. But . . .'

'Like the – what was their name?' I asked slyly.

'Who?'

'Don't you remember? When you were in Paris and I asked you out for dinner, you said you were dining with these people, but later I discovered quite by chance that they weren't even in France at the time.'

She looked at me and murmured, 'I must have got mixed up. I don't remember.'

'Mama! I adore you,' I laughed. 'But you've turned quite pink. You don't fib very well. If it's any consolation, I know who you had dinner with that night.'

'Now, Larry!' She tried her 'mothering' tone.

'It's past history And' – airily – 'I opened the attaché case that was saved from the *Athenia* before anyone else – and I threw away the incriminating evidence.'

'Oh Larry! You did?' She was bright red now.

'I did,' I said. 'Did you know that Gaston is back in France? He's Number Two to La Châtelaine.'

Impetuously my mother took another sip of her martini and laid her hand on mine. 'It was just a . . .'

'I know, of course,' I said. 'And I never let on to Gaston that I knew.'

'It's strange you should know,' she said finally after I had poured her out another drink, 'but Gaston helped me – yes, a lot. I was so depressed, so lonely, so *bored.*'

'With Papa?' I hope I didn't sound reproving, but I did feel slightly embarrassed.

'Not *with* Papa! What an awful thing to say, Larry. But with life and . . .' She was talking frankly but a little sadly, though I realised that she was aching to talk to me. 'I suppose that does include Papa in a way. I don't mean that nastily. I didn't realise until Gaston – and that happened all by accident, you know – I never intended – but until then, I never realised what I had been missing. I shouldn't talk to you like this. Your own mother! But I can't help it. Your father gets so involved, he's no time for me – or didn't have. For any woman. I'm not being nasty. He's a man's man. But I – well, you must understand – after you and Sonia – I used to be so envious, so jealous of your happiness.'

'And are you happy now?'

She hesitated. 'You can never be entirely happy in a situation like mine – the family split up – by war, I mean,' she added hastily.

'But still?' I persisted.

'I've achieved a kind of happiness,' she admitted guardedly.

'Which means you have a boyfriend?' I wasn't sure whether she would be irritated or treat my remark as a joke.

She made no reply. She didn't have to. No mask could have disguised her face – that of a woman in the midst of a love affair.

I went to Washington the next day to tell the *Globe* that I wanted to volunteer for the army, and they understood, but when I asked Tommy Tomlinson, now firmly established as our foreign editor in Washington, whom I should approach to find out if there was any outfit that worked with the underground or clandestine forces – so that I could put my knowledge of French to good use – nobody seemed to know. In fact of all people it was Mama who put me in touch with just the right man after I had returned to New York.

I had already firmly established in my mind that I wanted to do something different from the ordinary run of things – partly due to something that Guy had said in a casual conversation months previously, when I had tried to pump him about his work. 'Sure, my job is clandestine,' he said, and this was *before* Pearl Harbour. 'But who do you think's paying for it all?'

'The Red Cross?'

'You must be crazy! The Red Cross is neutral. The Americans – they're the chaps who are paying. We may not be at war, but we know where our sympathies lie. I'm working underground for an American military outfit.'

It transpired that almost as soon as Roosevelt appointed his old friend Admiral William Leahy as ambassador to Vichy, F.D.R. made it clear that he expected Leahy to gather secret information which could be passed on to the British. In turn, Colonel Robert Schow became military attaché to Leahy. His job, said Guy, was to keep in close touch with the Resistance. Though I did not learn this until much later, Guy passed his information direct to Schow.

Even before the war Roosevelt had set up an agency to organise propaganda and espionage under the umbrella of the C.O.I. – Co-ordinator of Information.

I didn't know much about it, but these were the people I wanted to join. I hated the idea of a stick-in-the-mud job where my knowledge of French would probably lead me into a dead-end desk role as a translator of leaflets to be scattered over France.

Yet that's what I might have been had it not been for Mama.

'Come to the apartment next Tuesday,' she said. 'Some friends of mine are coming in for drinks. One of them you must know by repute: Bill Donovan. Bob Sherwood, the playwright, is coming too.'

I didn't know either of them – though I did know that Donovan was a legend from the last war, a millionaire Wall Street lawyer known to his cronies as Colonel 'Wild Bill' Donovan. Nor had I ever met Robert Sherwood, but as it happened we had corresponded. Years previously I had seen a movie of Sherwood's play *The Petrified Forest*, and as I was unable to get the book of the play in France I had written to

Sherwood. He immediately sent me a copy in which he had written on the flyleaf some very complimentary things about my writing.

Bob Sherwood, who was the boss of the C.O.I., arrived first and couldn't have been more agreeable. He was tall, loose-limbed, handsome, and reminded me in a way of Jimmy Stewart the actor. He spent most of his time these days in Washington. He read the *Globe*, and he remembered our correspondence. Before long Donovan arrived, a stocky, grey-haired man who exuded power and imagination. If Sherwood was the titular head of the C.O.I. Donovan worked for that section of the organisation devoted specifically to intelligence and underground activities.

I was intrigued at the way they – and the other guests – adored my mother. I thought back to the way she had entertained Vance, the owner of the *Globe*, and his wife on their first trip to France so long ago, and the easy way she had made everyone feel at home and wanted. Here, reflecting again as I watched the others relax, I realised what a flair she had for being an ideal hostess, full of fun, easy, unfussy.

'You're very lucky to meet both Bob and Bill,' said an amused Mama when we were all talking. 'I'm sure they can fix you up with any kind of uniform you want.'

I was not quite sure at first that I would be interested. They gave me the impression of being planners – and I didn't want to be an assistant to a planner. In the end, incredibly, each of them offered me a job! Not, I am sure, because of nepotism, but more because of the timing; for what I didn't know then was that I had entered the scene – enacted really in Mama's flat – just at the very moment when Sherwood and Donovan were deciding to divide up their 'empire'.

'The President has decided that shortly – in July – I'll run a new department called the O.W.I.,' explained Sherwood. 'The Office of War Information. We'll be handling propaganda. I plan to set up our own radio station called the Voice of America, to serve all Europe. You're exactly the kind of man we're looking for. Knowledge of the countries, fluent in French – you're a cinch for us. Consider yourself booked for the duration.'

I felt almost embarrassed by this flattery. I might be a

bilingual newspaperman, but still I was not trained in propaganda. However, my reaction was nothing to the blush I could
feel on my cheeks when Bill Donovan said, with a glint of
amusement in those piercing eyes of his, 'Just a minute, Bob.
You've got no right to go taking my boy just like that.'

It was said in fun, but then Donovan explained – and I
began to tingle with excitement. For Sherwood's O.W.I. was
one thing, but Donovan was setting up something very
different – an entirely separate organisation, the O.S.S. – the
Office of Strategic Services.

'And I'll be the boss of the dirty tricks department,' said
Donovan. 'On the ground, in the ditches, the front or wherever. Volunteers only. And they'll be trained by the British
S.O.E. the Special Operations Executive. It's concerned with
intelligence organisation for the Resistance and sabotage in
occupied countries. It's headed by a Britisher who used to be
the boss of Fords in France.'

I was very impressed with the prospect of working for the
O.S.S. – if I could wait until it was established. But Donovan
made it clear that the O.S.S. wasn't even formed yet, and that
very few Americans were allowed to work with the S.O.E. in
England.

'There's no problem if you're right at the top,' said Donovan. 'The S.O.E. is the most professional bunch of men I've
ever met in my life. And you've got to be professional to stay
alive in their kind of business.'

Donovan knew what he was talking about. As far back as
March 1941 he had, he told me, been taken round some of the
S.O.E. training establishments in England from where the
first intelligence agents had already been sent by parachute into
France.

That settled it. Because the O.S.S. was not even formed, it
took several months before I gained my commission. I was
posted to G2, Military Intelligence, underwent preliminary
training at Fort Benning and half a dozen military bases in
America, and was then posted to London on attachment to the
British – 'for special duties'. I sailed from New York in a
blacked-out *Queen Mary*, one of sixteen thousand troops on
the world's most prestigious liner, now converted into a
troopship in which the same beds or berths were used for

eight-hour shifts, leading to the boast, 'Our beds never get cold.'

It had never entered my head that any training of human beings could be so exhausting. I naturally heard of the rigorous preparation that goes into the making of an American Marine, but this was different. A 'civilian' job – in a way that was what I was being trained for. And somehow I had rather expected to receive a course concerned mainly with formal problems: identities, methods of transmission, code names, perhaps elementary training in the use of weapons. I had not envisaged a commando-type physical training programme that left me exhausted physically and mentally.

At first I was utterly miserable. There were no other Americans training with me. There was no way I could write a letter to anyone in France. And of course from the moment America entered the war even Mama in New York had no way of contacting my father or Grandma. The only guarded letters Mama could write were to Sonia in neutral Switzerland. England, being much deeper into the war, and struggling at this stage to stay alive after heroic resistance, could offer no sort of fun for anyone. The only way I could write after I landed in England was through the Army Post Office. And this would be forwarded eventually to Mama in New York. Other than that I had virtually ceased to exist.

From Liverpool I was first sent to be interviewed in London, my acceptance approved for F section of the S.O.E. – F for France – then I was told that I would have the rank of major which had been my rank in America, though it would not be gazetted. And there was one simple order in addition to this:

'We would like you to grow a beard, starting this morning.' Seeing my look of surprise the spokesman added, 'It's quite understandable, really. We expect to be sending you over to France. You might as well have a little elementary disguise in case someone you know runs into you. It's not likely, but it's a sensible precaution – and it's about the only thing in this war that costs nothing.'

Then I took a slow, cold train in streaming rain to Guildford from where a bumpy truck transported me to an old English country house called Wanborough Manor. Inquisitive locals had been told that it was a commando training course – and it might just as well have been, for the P.T., as the British called physical training, was designed to toughen me up.

We started with square bashing, carrying twenty-pound. packs. We were bombed with flour sacks from nearby roof-tops, and if we were hit we were ordered by tough British army sergeants to clean up our uniforms and be on parade in twenty minutes looking spotless. The hotter the weather, the heavier the clothes we were forced to wear. From time to time exhausted men keeled over, fainting; I almost did myself half a dozen times. Anyone who fell had a bucket of cold water dashed over him by a soldier who was screaming, 'Defend yourself! Otherwise you're dead!'

It was a rigorous kill-or-cure-régime, and just as I thought I had got over the worst I was sent on a paramilitary training course in another country house near Arisaig on the wild west coast of Inverness-shire. Security was tight. There were few roads, and because the Admiralty had some nearby naval bases the entire area was restricted anyway. It was the perfect place to train for a new life in a world I had never dreamed of entering – a very different world from that of the ordinary soldier, whose instilled discipline taught him to obey every single order without question. I was taught to think, act, kill on my own initiative, once the original order had been given.

There I was taught everything that I might have to know – how to kill silently, with a knife or by strangling, or by pistol, using British, French and German weapons in case we cap-tured any. On one occasion two of us were sent off for four days without a penny in our pockets or a scrap of food and told to reach a point eighty miles away in those four days. We had to beg or steal food, if necessary robbing lonely cottages, and all without being discovered. I thought I had done very well considering all the problems, and was rather pleased with myself as I flopped down on my bunk. Two hours later, after the shortest sleep ever, when my vision was blurred with tiredness, I was called out by a screaming sergeant-major for pistol target practice at mansized moving targets ranged be-hind the wall of the house. The fact that it was pelting with rain didn't make sighting the targets any easier, but as the instructor put it, 'None of you'll ever be a shot until you can shoot straight by instinct out of your pocket or lying on your back in bed.'

We used a fearsome but exciting murder weapon, a silencer pistol with a long thick barrel full of baffles. It even had luminous sights when we set off for night firing practice.

The only language spoken throughout the course was French – even in the unarmed combat which we practised daily, even during demolitions when we blew up old buildings using P.E. – plastic explosives – because P.E. was considered safer than anything else. It would not detonate even if hit by a bullet. A detonator embedded in it was essential. It was so soft that one night a trainee ate some, mistaking it for chocolate – and lived.

When I was considered expert enough small parties were told to report back to London, to S.O.E.'s F section in a small house in Harley Street. It was one of those typical long, narrow (to American eyes, anyway) streets lined with dignified Georgian houses, most of them bearing the highly polished brass plates of doctors or dentists. There I was received by a British lady in the Women's Auxiliary Air Force, the W.A.A.F. A neatly-uniformed flight lieutenant, Joyce Brock, seemed to handle all the details, and informed me that I had passed all my examinations and would be told when to report for duty.

My first three trips to occupied France were brief, dangerous and yet in a curious way uneventful. I was dropped twice by parachute on northern France, helped local Resistance groups to be reformed, took them canisters of arms, and returned across the Channel by fishing boat. The third time I was sent both ways by fishing boat, landing at Le Touquet, and making my way inland to report to a local Resistance group.

I loved the work. I hope that doesn't sound pompous. I was never in any real danger, though there were moments of disquiet. But every mission I undertook was, I knew, preparing me for what I hoped would be the 'big one' on home territory. For I had more and more been receiving hints that 'something big was brewing' in the Champagne area – and that I might be sent there. I hadn't the faintest idea what was exercising people's minds in Champagne, but if there was trouble it would seem natural for me to be sent. Apart from anything else, S.O.E. was a professional outfit, and I would obviously have a head start if I knew the geography of the area. And I was fretting for action, like a runner who has been trained for the one race of his life and has now reached his peak of training. I was ready – now, this minute.

My instinctive belief that I would be sent to an area I knew was increased when I was asked specific questions about my family: was my sister still in Switzerland? Where was my brother? Did my grandmother still live in the château at Douzy? And my father? I answered as best I could, and certainly the heads of F section seemed to know all the good work that Papa was doing.

Early in 1944 I was ordered to visit Harley Street to report in the first instance to W.A.A.F. officer Brock.

'You're to meet Major Turbeville,' she said briskly, 'for a preliminary discussion. Then you'll receive a detailed briefing. After that, if all goes well, we'll give you your orders and then – I imagine you're anxious to be off.'

'I can hardly wait,' I admitted.

'I know,' she sympathised. 'You get all steamed up and then – nothing happens. There's always a good reason for it.'

'But any action?' I started.

A phone rang. She listened, said, 'Certainly, sir.' Then she turned to me. 'The major will see you. You can go into his office now; Room Eleven.'

Major Turbeville seemed a pleasant, middle-aged man – he might have been a commercial traveller or the owner of a small prosperous factory. It was hard to say. And it was equally hard to determine whether he was French or English, since he greeted me in impeccable English, after which every word was spoken in French. The name seemed vaguely French, but I had long since learned never to ask questions of anyone in S.O.E.

'I expect you've been wondering about your next assignment,' began Turbeville, 'and hoping it will be in a part of France where you can capitalise on your local knowledge. Well, I'll put you out of your misery – we *do* plan to send you to the Reims area. But not for three months. And because we need your specialised knowledge of the area, we don't want to send you on any other missions of – well, risk.'

'Champagne is wonderful!' I cried. 'But three months! Why do I have to wait that long? If you've got a job earmarked for me, why not now?'

Turbeville sighed, "'Fraid not, but don't blame me. It's a question of waiting for the exact moment. When we're ready to launch the second front. Yes, of course we know it's coming, but the job waiting for you is so big that it must be timed almost to the hour. Don't worry, we're keeping it for you; but it's supremely important not to act too quickly. Could ruin everything.'

'What do I do while I'm waiting?'

Guardedly Turbeville said, 'Somebody's got to do their share of paper work. What about three months on a desk job? Change of pace?'

'Oh no!' I groaned.

'Could be interesting.' Turbeville seemed to be enjoying a kind of private joke. 'And it's only three months.' As he noticed my look of dejection he added, as though musing to himself, 'After all, you've got the rank. People do have to go on leave.'

'You're not going to make me an instructor!' It was the hidden fear of everyone in S.O.E.

'Good Lord no!' I hardly knew Turbeville, so I was totally unprepared for his next remarks. 'No,' he repeated. 'But we do have a couple of problems. The first is how to keep you occupied for three months. The second is that the O.S.S. has asked if we can replace a man who's gone on sick leave – needs three months off. An American. Washington knows all about your future plans, and they thought it might be a good idea if you could help out. And in three months you'll be all set for Champagne.'

'I suppose I'll have to.' I could hardly conceal my disappointment. 'Where?'

'As an assistant military attaché,' said Turbeville, 'with a little undercover work. We'll lend you to the Americans for three months.'

'Where?' I repeated.

'Berne,' said Turbeville blandly. 'Or as you Americans would say, "Berne Switzerland".'

45

It was more than two years since I had said goodbye to Sonia, and I was thinking of that farewell in Rolle as my car bowled along the wide, sunny road southwards from Berne, past fields hazy with heat, the lazily chewing cows looking as though they had been scrubbed each day, and the country chalets, red and white flags everywhere. Soon after I skirted Fribourg I was dropping down to the lakeside where I reached Lausanne, then Morges, past the clinic where Anna had stayed to recuperate. A few minutes later I was approaching Rolle, past the old castle on the left then, almost opposite the cake shop, I saw the fountain on the main street. It was decked with petunias. I swung right up the country lane, under the bridge, and there, swinging gently over the white gate, was the wooden sign, 'Three Circles Farm'. As I drove through the open gate, hooting, I caught a glimpse of the low white house and heard the soft splash of water from the drinking trough, almost hidden under the canopy of the plane tree.

There was a rush to open the front door, cries of excitement as the two girls ran out to greet me – Sonia, to me unchanged as she threw her arms around me, and Anna, more reserved perhaps, a little plumper but with a smile and a kiss and, like Sonia, bubbling with excitement.

I carried my overnight bag into the house, up the old stone stairs and along the corridor to the end room where we had spent our last night together – the same four-poster on the raised dais, the same flimsy white curtains at each corner.

'Oh Larry! It's been so long,' Sonia said, when we were alone. She stood on tiptoe to reach me. 'Just forget everything and kiss me – then later we'll sit down together just like an old married couple and fill in the years apart.'

'You mean – we're bored with each other?' I teased her.

'Ass!' How long was it since she and Anna used to regard 'ass' as their favourite word? 'If you show one sign of boredom in bed I'll know you've got a new girl.' And, typically female, she asked suspiciously, 'Have you? Honestly?'

I shook my head. 'Not me. I've never wanted to. Must be something wrong with my hormones or genes – undersexed. The British have a saying that all us Americans are oversexed and overpaid.'

'The British? You were in England?'

I nodded. 'Two years there, except for trips – well, you can guess where.'

'You never told me.' There was a hint of reproach.

'I couldn't, darling. Imagine if I'd written you a postcard – you, an enemy – saying that I was off to France at the weekend.'

'All these long years of separation.' Her eyes looked troubled and glistened with unshed tears. 'And I've been thankful you were safe in America – while all the time . . .'

'If I'd written to you, the censors would have thrown the letter away.'

'It must have been terribly dangerous.'

I smiled and kissed her. 'Don't worry. I'm fine. Thriving!'

'For how long?' she asked almost bitterly.

'For ever. With you. And now this bonus, plucked out of the war, thrown into peace – I don't know how to behave! Weren't you surprised when the embassy in Berne let you know I was coming?'

'I thought it was a dream,' she said simply while I looked out of the bedroom window. It was warm, with the dappled evening sunlight moving across the ceiling of the room each time puffs of cloud chased the sun away. Once in bed, we lay in each other's arms, just as we had always done, enjoying the joys of anticipation, yet our love-making, after the long absence, was quiet, in a way more beautiful, tender, just as happy, yet without the savage desire which in the past had sometimes made the physical act into a frantic fight.

'Do you think we're growing old?' I asked afterwards. 'Loving quietly like this?'

'Not old. Mature.'

'I know,' I said. 'All the suffering we see around us, it's helped to change both of us. And the hell that's going to break out soon.'

'Hell?'

'It's no secret,' I said. 'The Allies are going to launch an invasion of Europe; they'll have to. Otherwise the war would go on for ever. Like stalemate in a chess game.'

'When?'

'I haven't the faintest idea. But they can't delay it much longer. I'm not telling you military secrets. I don't know any details, but that doesn't mean that everyone in England – and France and Germany – doesn't know that an invasion is being planned. So I'm not talking out of turn.'

I explained that though I could tell her that I had been smuggled into Europe I wasn't really breaking secrets, so long as I didn't say what I was doing. Each trip had been a separate secret – but it was a secret I didn't know about until each operation started. Nobody could betray me before I left – only if I was denounced by a traitor pretending to work with the Resistance.

'I shouldn't be telling you *anything*. But even if you were an Italian spy and told the enemy that Major Astell was a spy operating in France, it wouldn't make any difference. Nobody would know where I was going, when, what I was called. My name changes on every visit. I must hand it to the British: they produce a watertight way of protecting their men – and they'd do anything to rescue any of us who get into trouble.'

If Sonia and I had both changed, Italy had changed too; it now hardly existed as an entity, but had reverted to the warring factions of barely a hundred years previously when a city like Florence had been an enemy of a republic like Venice.

'Ciano was murdered early this year, wasn't he?' I asked.

She nodded. 'In January. Poor Galeazzo! He was pretty awful, but he did help us, because when he saw that the Italians were on the point of surrender he very smartly had himself appointed ambassador to the Vatican. And it was then that he helped Francesco push forward his plan for an annulment. It's odd, isn't it – that you never met Ciano, yet he was not only responsible for getting Anna her freedom but will enable you in the end to marry me?'

I let the remark pass. Any retort would have been barbed, for I still felt angry at the mention of his name.

Instead I asked, 'Americans in Britain knew nothing really

of what happened, where you all stand today. Can you fill me
in? Give me a picture?'

'I don't really know myself, except that by the end of
1942 – after the Italian defeats, especially in North Africa –
anti-Fascists set up a committee of different parties in Turin.
All north Italy – big firms like Fiat – went on strike. Thank
God I wasn't there.'

'The luckiest thing you ever did in your life was to get a
permanent residence in Switzerland,' I said. 'But you still
haven't explained how in the middle of a war you could
manage to get rid of a dictator as powerful as Mussolini.'

'I do know that Francesco played a part in searching for a
peaceful way out of the war. Then in July last year – and,
believe me, to everyone in Italy 1943 will be a year never to be
forgotten – it was decided to get rid of Mussolini.'

What fascinated me, as I listened to Sonia's explanation, was
that anyone as powerful as *Il Duce* could ever be kicked
out – short of being assassinated, that is. But people in
Britain, and no doubt in America too, couldn't possibly
imagine the utter lack of morale and fighting spirit that must
have followed the catastrophic defeats inflicted on the Italian
armed forces.

On 24 July 1943, Mussolini – just back from a meeting with
Hitler – was confronted by his Italian opponents, the Grand
Council. Count Dino Grandi, former ambassador to London,
invited the king to assume command of the armed forces and
exercise his constitutional powers. Grandi told Mussolini to
his face, 'You believe you have the devotion of the people.
You lost it the day you tied Italy to Germany.' That afternoon,
when Mussolini's resignation was accepted, King Victor
Emmanuel told him, 'You are the most hated man in Italy.'

I still didn't know what happened then. According to Sonia,
Mussolini was bundled out of the meeting in an ambulance
and driven to Ponza where he was held in custody. Marshal
Pietro Badoglio formed a new government. She only discovered what really happened through Francesco before he
quietly slipped out of the scene.

'The next forty-five days, leading to the armistice, was a
mixture of farce and tragedy,' explained Sonia. It seems that
Badoglio was one of the most monstrous double-crossers in

recent history. After all, he had led the campaign against Ethiopia; now he dissolved the Fascist party. But he kept on pro-German soldiers and officers and promised Ribbentrop there would be no change in Italian foreign policy. At the same time Badoglio was negotiating with Eisenhower. In the end, according to Sonia, he lost all credibility, and Hitler lost patience and sent in German troops who crossed the Alps. And when the Allied troops landed in Italy, Badoglio surrendered to them. This left southern Italy as a government under Badoglio. But in the north, German glider troops had freed Mussolini who immediately reformed his Fascist party. Apparently there followed a chaotic winter with Italy under three masters – Badoglio working for the Allies in the south, Mussolini hoping for the re-emergence of power in the north, and the Germans in control of large sections where, in effect, they were the occupying power.

'It was soon after this,' said Sonia, 'early this year, that Ciano was captured by the Germans and handed over to Mussolini. He put Ciano on trial in Verona and had him shot for treason.'

'And what happened to Francesco?'

'He was arrested with Ciano – I do know that – and sentenced to death, but he and several others escaped. I'm very worried about him. I had one message saying that he was safe a few months ago. I know we can talk as though he's just a good friend – he never has been any more than that – but the truth is, he's vanished.'

'Killed? You can't just vanish.'

'You can,' she said sadly. 'I don't think he's dead. If Mussolini had him prisoner at the time Ciano was murdered he would certainly have been included in the trial at Verona. But I saw a list of everyone who had been tried. Francesco wasn't among them.'

'Perhaps he's in hiding.'

'I hope so. He knows I'm here. He's always kept in touch.'

But now, as she explained, Italy was in such disorder that nobody knew where anyone was. And, as she added with a wry smile, that also concerned her annulment which had almost come through before Ciano was arrested.

'But now,' she shrugged, suddenly despondent, 'just as our freedom is in sight, Italy's in such a mess that we may never be able to trace the papers. I may even be free by now – or next month – and then we could be married. But for all I know, we'll never find out.'

That evening, forgetting that back in London you went to endless trouble and bribery to acquire an occasional bottle of Scotch, here in Rolle a bottle of my favourite Old Rarity awaited me, and we sat talking before dinner.

I was delighted to see how normally Anna behaved. She was eager to be told everything she could about my life, though I had warned Sonia not to share the information about myself with anyone – not Anna, not even Guy if he happened to come down to Rolle as he did occasionally. So to Anna I talked about my 'desk job'; and I did say that I had been to Britain; almost every American had been there or North Africa, but I didn't enlighten her about the secret nature of my work. It was a natural caution, I suppose. I knew that by rights I should not have told a single soul about my work, but then – I justified myself – Sonia and I were a single soul.

We had so much to talk about that there seemed no end – or rather so many loose ends that we didn't have time to tie them all up. Guy, for instance, had the previous month been to Rolle for a day but no one had heard a word from him since.

'I think he feels more at home when he's in France than he does in Switzerland. He's bored here.' It was Anna who spoke. She didn't talk a great deal, but she had an uncanny habit of striking any verbal nail right in the middle. I could just imagine how bored Guy *would* find Switzerland – whereas to me, perhaps as a change from action, or simply because Sonia was there, I began to feel more and more as though I never wanted to leave the country.

We all had our worries, of course. Anna was concerned about Papa. No one had had any news for months; on the three brief and highly secret trips I had made to France I hadn't dared to telephone him. But I was able to quiet some of Anna's fears – our fears – by asking the embassy in Berne if they could find out anything from the U.S. Embassy in Vichy. A few days later I received a signal from Vichy which read laconically, 'Subject under investigation is alive and kicking.'

One thing was puzzling: Anna's complete lack of interest in

our mother. Mama's letters to me in London, always addressed 'c/o the Army Post Office' were non-committal, perhaps because she knew they would be censored by the military. But she did write more openly to Sonia, possibly because letters to neutral countries were censored by civilians.

'As far as I'm concerned,' I laughed when discussing the censorship problem with Anna and Sonia, 'I'm sure Mama thinks that if my letters are censored by the U.S. Army they'll probably be deliberately handled by my closest friends who are snooping to see what I've got to say. She just won't believe that censorship is an impersonal affair.'

To Sonia, and thus to Anna, Mama had even confided that she was thinking – only thinking; she underlined the word three times – that she might not return to Douzy after the war. She didn't write openly about divorce, but she sometimes hinted at separation, that she was in love with someone in New York.

'She'll never come back to poor Papa,' said Anna bitterly. 'She's having too good a time.'

The three months of early 1944 slipped past in perfect bliss. I could never quite fathom the underlying reason why we seemed happier in that period than ever before, excepting the first year of innocence. Was it the years of separation? Perhaps the forced parting was a test: if you failed, your love split up, as Mama's seemed in danger of doing; if (without trying, that is) you succeeded, then the bonds of love were more strongly bound together than ever before. That's how it seemed to me anyway. In those three months I went to the office at Berne with very little work to do, and drove off at lunch time each Friday to Rolle, returning on the Monday morning. And on two occasions Sonia spent the week at Berne in the apartment which I had taken over from the man on sick leave.

'All we want is Marcel's and dinner in the rue Jacob,' said Sonia happily.

'You're asking too much. We'll have to wait for that. Meanwhile,' I added with a laugh, 'you'll have all the Swiss cheese you can swallow.' It was said as a joke because I had fallen in love with Swiss regional cheese dishes – an appetite sharpened by the knowledge that as soon as I returned to

England I'd be lucky to get one thin slice a week of what the British called 'mousetrap cheese'.

'When I go back to England,' I laughed again, 'I'll take all my luggage allowance in cheese.'

'Don't talk about leaving.' She kissed me – this was back in the living room at Rolle and Anna had gone to bed. 'Let's hang on to what we've got.'

If we had been worried from time to time about Papa, I could understand that Sonia must be worried about Francesco. After all, even though a husband in name only he was close to her. And then news of him came from a startling and totally unexpected source. At first I couldn't believe my eyes. On the last day of the second week we spent together in Berne, Sonia and I were walking hand in hand through the main street with its gaily coloured, elaborate fountains, arcades in streets jutting off, and Berne's famous sixteenth-century clock on the Gate Tower. We stopped to watch its figures striking the hour under the shadow of the beautiful old-fashioned gabled houses when a voice in cultured French said, 'Good morning, Countess – and good morning, Herr Astell.'

I spun round. I knew that voice anywhere.

'And,' it added silkily, 'so pleased to see two people so much in love after all these years.'

'Herr Abetz!' I blurted out. 'What are you doing here?'

As Sonia clutched my arm and said, 'Good day,' Abetz replied, 'Well, Mr. Astell, I am an ambassador, if you don't mind, and I have the right to visit our embassy in Berne if I feel like a change.'

'Of course,' I muttered.

'More to the point,' he added as we stood in the warm sunshine under the clocktower, 'If it's not an impertinent question, what are you doing here? I thought all you young Americans were in khaki helping to save the British from defeat.'

'I'm attached to the embassy here for a few months,' I said shortly.

'Ah! One of us! Welcome to the club – even if you are only a temporary member.' Then, as I was wondering how to get away, he added two things: 'Strange, running into you both, because' – with a nod to Sonia – 'I have news of your husband.'

'Francesco?'

'Ah! I see you remember his name. Well' – looking straight at our linked arms – 'he seems to be your husband only in – er – name.'

'Where is Francesco?' asked Sonia almost hoarsely. 'Please! We're all very worried – no news . . .'

'He's safe – for the moment. And I'm trying to help him. But I'm afraid' – again that silky voice, the deprecating shrug of the shoulders under the pink face, ice-blue eyes, the reddish blond hair – 'you Italians are giving us in Germany a great deal of trouble. So *volatile.*'

I squeezed Sonia's arm to stop her from getting angry. It was true that the Germans despised the Italians, but I didn't want to be dragged into a battle of words. He would tell us all he wanted to when he felt like it. But there was no need to give him the satisfaction of letting Sonia beg for news.

And in the end what he told us was simple but reassuring. Francesco, unable to get into Switzerland, let alone telephone Sonia, had been in danger of arrest ever since Ciano had been arrested. He had managed to escape to Lisbon with the help of Abetz. 'After all, we worked together in Germany and in France,' said Abetz. 'It was the least I could do as one gentleman to another.'

I let the first 'gentleman' pass without comment. 'And I regret to say that there's a price on your husband's head – as a very senior member of Ciano's staff,' said Abetz. 'Mussolini wanted him first – and almost had him shot. Now the anti-*Fascisti* want him dead or alive. Stupid people. I arranged for him to be issued with the necessary papers – for a new life, if you like – and he's waiting now for transport to Argentina. Yes, there are more than a million Italians living in that country and most Argentines are a pretty rotten lot, so any man like your husband is bound to succeed. Buenos Aires is, I am told, a paradise. Francesco will fit in there perfectly. A very elegant figure, especially as he will be able to keep his title once he has arrived in South America.'

'Well, thank God he's safe,' said Sonia. She almost had to drag out the words, though she did sound immensely relieved.

'This war,' Abetz waved an airy hand, 'will soon be over – when we've won it.'

'How can you ever think that?' I retorted. 'You can never win the war against America and Britain.'

'My dear Astell,' he said, 'once the British and Americans start to invade France – if they are stupid enough to commit suicide – the Allied losses will be so appalling that in a few months the Third Reich and America will arrange a negotiated peace. And then we can join up to get rid of the communists. You wait and see. *Auf wiedersehen!*'

That was our last complete week in what we eventually called nostalgically 'the Swiss interlude'. We didn't see Abetz again, and when I drove Sonia to Rolle on the Friday I left my usual weekend address and phone number at the embassy. It was our eleventh weekend together so I knew that peace, for us, was running out. But I was unprepared for the news that awaited me at Rolle on the Friday evening: an urgent request, left with Anna, to telephone the embassy as soon as possible.

I called the duty officer the moment I entered the house.

'Thank God you arrived in time,' he said. 'I've a message for you. There's apparently a plane leaving Zurich tomorrow morning at 5.00 a.m. – and you've got to be on it, to catch a connection from Lisbon to London.'

In a way it was better that way. I dreaded long partings, and our life together over the years seemed to have been brutally interrupted so many times that it was less painful to have a quick farewell imposed on us by others.

'Don't worry,' I said during that last dinner in the old farmhouse dining room. 'Despite what Mr. Abetz says, I reckon I'll be back by the end of the summer. And free too.'

'Don't tempt providence by saying things like that,' begged Sonia.

'I won't,' I laughed, and then, thinking of the imminent parting, I asked, a little troubled, 'What about Anna?'

'Don't worry,' Sonia reassured me. 'She's getting better every day. She'll stay with me as long as she likes. You know how close Anna and I have been all our lives. And she reminds me of you.'

'But the future?'

'After the war – who knows, she might go to America. Your mother has already suggested it. We'll see. The most important thing is for her to relax – and there's no better place than Switzerland for that.'

As she was speaking, Anna came into the room. 'I forgot to tell you,' she said to Sonia, 'but there are a dozen letters which arrived while you were away. I left them on the desk in the sitting-room.'

'Bills, I'm sure,' laughed Sonia, but one of them at least was not a bill. I saw Sonia handle the envelope, saw its thick square shape, rather like an envelope concerning an official invitation.

Sonia, I could tell, knew who had sent it. And I could sense her mounting excitement as she ripped open the envelope, then read the contents. When she turned to me her eyes were swimming.

'It's from my lawyer in the Vatican,' she cried. 'It's come through! The annulment! It's been granted! Oh darling! The lawyer says there'll be a short delay until the official documents arrive by registered post, but then – well . . .'

'And then,' I said gently, 'then nothing will stop you being called Sonia Astell for the rest of your life.'

46

The summons from F section came the day after I arrived back in England. I could tell from the tone of Turbeville's voice when he spoke to me on the phone that this was a call to action. I felt a flutter of excitement – I actually felt the pounding of my heart like a hammer – when I was ushered into his modest office in Harley Street.

'Have a good time in Berne?' he asked by way of starting the conversation.

'Very enjoyable,' I replied. 'And not too much work.'

'Plenty of time to visit Rolle,' he almost chuckled. Seeing my embarrassment, he added, 'Don't worry, Astell, we're all human. I'm told she's absolutely stunning. And that you're going to get married after the war. Wonderful.'

'Spies spying on spies!' I said angrily.

'Not at all,' he replied. 'Just perfectly routine checks.'

I knew he was right.

'Don't worry,' Turbeville said. 'Make yourself comfortable.' He led me to a couple of deep leather armchairs. 'And to put you out of your misery – you'll be leaving right away.'

The hammering of excitement increased with every word he spoke.

'It's tricky – very dangerous. And – don't panic – it involves your own home, the Château de Douzy.'

'What do you mean?'

'That's why we chose you. You *know* it, but it may be too close to you. So close that at first we ruled you out for the operation.'

I felt a sudden surge of anger but managed to contain it.

'Yes, we did have the feeling that personal problems might interfere with the logic of the task you have to perform. But we decided you were experienced enough to overcome this. The local Resistance is very good in the Reims area.' I had a sudden flashback to that last day in France, so long ago it seemed, and wondered what had happened to Gaston – and for that matter to Olivia.

'It might help, Major Astell, if you paid attention,' said Turbeville mildly.

'I'm sorry – but the shock of what you've told me – and I was friends with one or two of the Resistance people . . .'

'I know,' he said not unkindly. 'Who knows – you may run across some more of your friends soon,' adding like a cold douche, 'those who weren't killed as reprisals after the death of Hoess. Now' – rather abruptly – 'I'd like to ask you a few questions about your local territory. What do you know about the village of Rilly?'

I told him all I did know – that the Germans had blocked the southern end of the tunnel, that the R.A.F. had bombed it inefficiently, adding, 'My belief is that the Germans are using the tunnel as a sort of storehouse.'

'Right. Storing what?'

'I have no idea.'

'I'll come to that later,' said Turbeville. 'Now, what about the Douzy pyramid – your family pyramid, right?'

I nodded, and explained that the Germans had closed the pyramid long before Pearl Harbour.

'You're sure it's closed?'

'Absolutely. I mean, it was closed when I last saw it. There's only one real way into Douzy pyramid and that's through the main entrance, cut into the side of the hill – it was all boarded up when I last saw it.'

'What about the back entrance through the *celliers* – the underground passages through the farm near the château?'

'They were boarded up too. Of course it might have been opened up by the Germans – I wouldn't know.'

'No, they haven't opened it up. I don't know whether you are aware of this, but the Château de Douzy was requisitioned by the Germans – that means your family home. It's now an officers' mess.'

I was staggered. I should have thought of it, of course – obviously Douzy was now German-held property. But the Germans, strutting round our house! 'I wonder . . .' I began.

'Your grandmother is still running the vineyards.' Turbeville anticipated my question. 'Because of her age – and her French birth – she's not been interned. She's living in the cottage that you used to rent to a couple of old ladies.'

The Misses B and B! So Grandma was living there.

'And my father?'

'He's fine. Helping the French.' And then, obviously enjoying a moment of quiet drama, he added in an elaborately casual tone, 'In fact I had lunch with your father at Berlinguets three weeks ago.'

'You *what?*'

'I thought that would amuse you.'

'But you . . .' Perhaps inadvertently I had thought of him as an armchair officer. Now he added even more drily, 'When we are on to a critical operation, the Chief believes in checking the preliminary steps *sur place*. Your father is well. He's been allowed freedom to continue his work, using his French passport.'

'I don't suppose – I haven't seen him since before Pearl Harbour . . .'

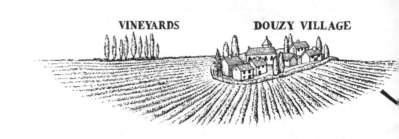

VINEYARDS   DOUZY VILLAGE

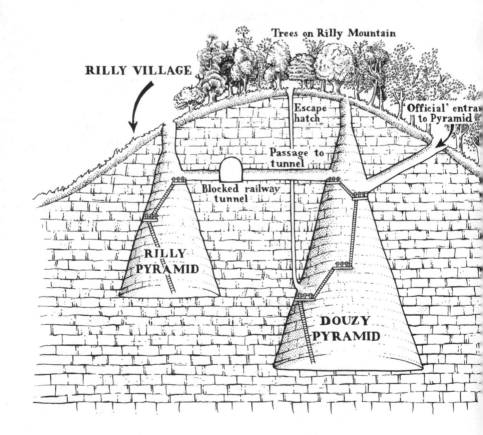

Trees on Rilly Mountain

RILLY VILLAGE

Escape hatch

'Official' entrance to Pyramid

Passage to tunnel

Blocked railway tunnel

RILLY PYRAMID

DOUZY PYRAMID

UNDERGROUND PYRAMIDS AT DOUZY & RILLY

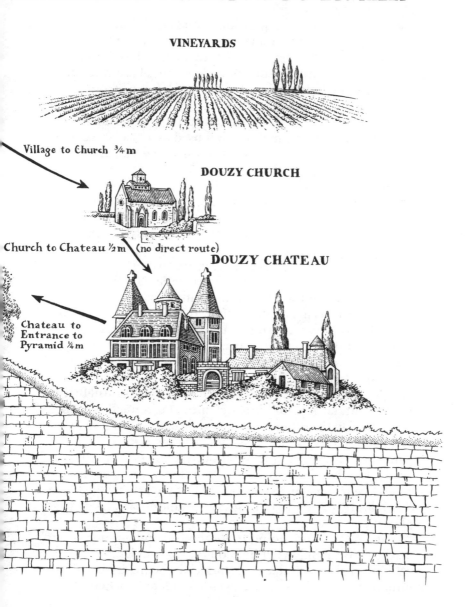

VINEYARDS

Village to Church ¾ m

DOUZY CHURCH

Church to Chateau ½ m (no direct route)

DOUZY CHATEAU

Chateau to
Entrance to
Pyramid ¼ m

'I couldn't say anything, of course. I went on business. But I told one of our local Resistance executives to tip your father off – after I had returned to England. Just to say that you were well and living in America.'

I knew I shouldn't ask questions, but I couldn't refrain from this one: 'How did you manage to meet my father?'

'Easy,' replied Turbeville. 'Before the war I used to manufacture bottles in my factory outside Lyons. I went to see if I could get your father to persuade the Germans to give us a permit to increase production of bottles for champagne. And now' – once again he switched abruptly – 'to business. You are right. The Rilly tunnel is being used as a vast storehouse. But as far as the Douzy pyramid is concerned you are wrong. It has never – I repeat never – been closed.'

'Before Pearl Harbour it was,' I said.

'Not even then.' Turbeville shook his head. 'It looked closed. It was meant to look closed. But there is a third entrance to both the Rilly and Douzy pyramids. Or there was until it was bricked up.'

'Of course! Hardly an entrance, more an exit.'

'Yes, you've got it,' agreed Turbeville. 'In the old days corridors led from the Douzy and Rilly pyramids straight to loading platforms inside the railway tunnel. The original idea, as you know, was to ship champagne straight on to the railway. But the idea never came to anything.'

'But they were never used,' I said. 'And surely they were all bricked up years ago?'

'Right. We believe the Rilly exit to the tunnel is still bricked up. So your father couldn't get into the tunnel even if he wanted to. On the other hand, we've been told that the Douzy wall blocking the way into the tunnel has been knocked down. It's now the entrance to the pyramid, and can of course be used secretly by the Germans because nobody can get into the tunnel except German personnel. In fact we believe the Douzy pyramid is being used as a huge secret laboratory.'

'I don't believe it!'

'That's why you're going to Reims. To find out if it's true.'

I asked Turbeville what he thought was hidden.

'We're fairly sure that the tunnel is being used to store components for V2 rockets, even completed rockets. It's an ideal place – it can't be bombed. Also, we know that in Germany new tunnels are being prepared in an old potassium mine at Bleicherode, ten miles or so from the Kohnstein mountains. Some of them go five hundred feet below the surface. The main objective is to prepare sites for V2 rockets that can't be bombed if the Allies start a second front. The Rilly tunnel fits the bill perfectly. High-level photo reconnaissance shows that they're planning to store a liquid oxygen plant as well as other detailed material.'

'But isn't Rilly too far from the coast?'

'It doesn't really matter.' As Turbeville explained, the V2 needed no sophisticated site works, unlike the V1 which required a distinctive ski-ramp to launch it and which was easily identified by Allied aerial photography. A V2 needed only road access to flat ground with a metal or concrete slab for the launching pad. It was invisible from the air, and a V2 could be launched by mobile teams capable of setting up the weapon, arming and fuelling it, and then firing it, all within four hours.

He explained in some detail the mechanics of the V2s. I asked him, 'What about the secret work that's supposed to be going on inside Douzy? What does that consist of?'

He hesitated and his voice was suddenly invested with an entirely new note of gravity. 'It's dynamite. No, it's worse than dynamite.' Turbeville hesitated again, then said, 'I want to put one question to you before I tell you any more – off the record. Knowing that your family and friends may be involved in the Reims area – especially if there are reprisals – you can opt to be sent somewhere else on another mission. We need you in France, but you don't have to be sent to Douzy – for I'm afraid everything may centre on the pyramid – your pyramid. I'm not sure, but if our fears are correct . . .'

'You should know me better than that,' I said almost harshly.

'I do. I knew your answer before I asked the question, but we have an understanding in F section. If we send anyone – especially a Frenchman – behind the lines to organise sabotage, which means automatic reprisals in his own area, among his old friends, we feel it our duty to point that out before he agrees to undertake the mission.'

'I understand. But what's so special about Douzy?'

'I think you'd better have a word with one of our tame boffins,' said Turbeville. 'He's waiting outside to see you.' Boffin – a slang word for what the Americans called an egghead – was one of dozens of English words introduced during the war. This one was a grey-haired Dr Chisholm. He started by saying, almost jovially, 'I'm going to ask you a question to which I know you won't be able to give me any answer.'

He roared with laughter, and I couldn't help smiling, though. I hadn't the faintest idea what he was talking about.

'Ever heard of isopropylmethyl phosphoro-fluoridate?'

He had such an impish look that I was almost tempted to ask, 'How do you spell it?'

'Don't worry.' He almost choked with laughter at his own sense of fun. 'We'll use its more common name: Sarin. Ever hear of *that*?'

I shook my head.

'At this stage I'll just say that Sarin is the deadliest chemical killer the world has ever known. One fiftieth of one drop of concentrated Sarin will kill a man in sixty seconds. And our information is that Hitler is manufacturing Sarin – in your pyramid at Douzy.'

A long unmeasurable span of silence seemed to kill the air I was breathing as the two of us faced each other across the bare wooden desk. It was the sort of silence that lasted perhaps a minute, perhaps a lifetime, for I was not thinking of clouds of death sprayed from the skies, of hateful Germans, of the beastliness of war; I was thinking simply with an agony I couldn't put into words of – my father.

I found it hard to concentrate, and finally Dr. Chisholm said, 'It must be a blow to you – your own estate, your home. But, remember, we don't know for certain. So let's take heart. First things first.'

He went on, 'This may all be a rumour, but we've got to know. And unless things change, the mission on which we would like to send you will fall into three parts. The easiest one will be to check on the contents of the tunnel – are there any V2s there? Second, you've got to find out if the Germans are manufacturing Sarin in Douzy. And thirdly, and *only if you're absolutely certain*, and only after specific instructions from London, you'll have to' − he hesitated − 'neutralise the plant. Even if it means blowing up, or sealing the pyramid up for ever.'

My brain was racing overtime. The problems of finding out didn't worry me − well, they wouldn't have done except for the one overwhelming thought that haunted me: Papa. Did he know? Was he aware of the monstrous evil in the next pyramid? If what Chisholm said was true, it would have to be blown up. And even if my father didn't know − and I knew in my heart that he couldn't know − what would happen if I was ordered to blow up Douzy? For, though the entrance to Douzy and Rilly pyramids were apart at the apex, the bases of both pyramids were adjacent by the very nature of the Roman excavations and construction. The holes were tiny at the top but huge at the bottom, and as they both came inwards towards each other, they met. If I had to blow up Douzy, the explosion would certainly blow up Rilly as well. Unless I could warn my father? But no, that sort of private consideration was against all the rules of S.O.E. The very factor which, according to Turbeville, had made S.O.E. hesitate before choosing me for the mission. But perhaps it would never come to that.

'This Sarin,' I said to Dr. Chisholm finally. 'Do *you* think the Germans are really making it?'

'A German chemist − I'll let you read all the details later on − discovered Tabun, an earlier nerve gas, in 1936 and then he discovered Sarin while he was engaged in further research. It's interesting to know that the German plant, which is situated on the river Oder where some Sarin is now being manufactured, is ten storeys high. It seems that apparently the height is needed to start the process at the top end of the building so that the mixture goes downwards through miles and miles of pipes by gravitation until the product comes out on the ground floor. I mention that because it's an interesting added reason for using a pyramid a hundred feet tall like Douzy. It's also important, of course, because Douzy is so much safer. All the dangerous work is being done underground in virtually bombproof surroundings. Sarin is so deadly that they can't risk having the plant bombed. So – almost by accident – General Hermann Ochsner, the head of the Nazi Chemical Division, thought of the champagne cellars. It seems he had visited them before the war.'

'But why Douzy? Why not Rilly?'

Turbeville, who was listening to the conversation, sighed. 'Let me make it clear that there has never been been a word uttered against your father. He has saved scores of lives – but you must appreciate that all this is a blind. The Germans wish to make the entire area more – content – so that no one will stir up any trouble. There is an understanding officer in charge. He keeps up very good relations with the champagne producers, and that means work for all the people in the area. Your father is honest, loyal, and would be horrified if he knew what was really happening. But the entire operation – allowing your father the liberty he has achieved to increase production – is a plot to lull the people of the area into a sense of false security.'

I had often wondered as much. Poor Papa! So honest, as Turbeville had said. Such a *gentleman*, never in his wildest dreams imagining that anyone would be capable of such madness, such deceit, even in warfare.

'This German general – Ochsner?' I asked. 'Does he really have any power?'

'He does,' said Dr. Chisholm, 'and we have a copy of a secret memorandum which Ochsner drafted for Hitler as far back as 1939 in which he cited several reasons why Germany should use chemical warfare, as he put in the memorandum, "In the coming European war". Here, read this; it's a copy of the Ochsner report.'

He handed it to me and I read, 'Thanks to the unique position which our chemical industry enjoys in the world, we are in a position to achieve and hold our lead over all countries – if we show the necessary determination.' But it was the last reason that made me break out into a cold sweat: 'We must never forget the importance of terror in the civilian population,' wrote Ochsner; 'the impact of the air force using chemicals in fairly substantial quantities against the enemy hinterland, in particular against industrial concentrations and large cities, could have a very great effect on morale. There is no doubt that a city like London would be plunged into a state of unbearable turmoil which would bring enormous pressure to bear on the enemy government.'

I looked at Dr. Chisholm, handing him back the piece of paper. I found my hand was shaking.

'Is it really as bad as that?' I asked.

He nodded. 'Tabun and Sarin are colourless, they have virtually no smell, and microscopic quantities can kill thousands in under a minute.'

'How?'

'They're absorbed through the skin or the lungs. They work very simply – by blocking an enzyme in the body which controls the movement of muscles. Death results almost immediately.'

'I should explain,' added Turbeville, 'that our information – which is admittedly very sketchy in parts – leads us to believe that it's possible the V2s hidden in the Rilly tunnel are being fitted with special warheads which could carry chemical gases. We've heard – no proof yet – that German scientists have discovered how to detonate warheads hundreds of feet above the ground. If that happened over, let's say London, you'd have clouds of invisible, odourless Sarin over the capital. It would virtually kill the entire population of the city. And then, of course, Britain would have to sue for peace – simply because a new and terrifying dimension would have been added to conventional warfare, one against which there would be absolutely no defence. It's as though America suddenly realised the dream on which she's been working for ten years – we know what that is – to split the atom and contain it in a bomb. Imagine one atom bomb destroying an entire city: the other side would have to give in.'

Dr. Chisholm handed over a buff folder. 'I know the technicalities won't mean much to you,' he said, 'but glance through this memorandum on Sarin. I think it's the sort of information you'll be able to digest more easily in print than if I tried to explain it. I'll leave you now, but please read it before you leave this room.'

The folder was marked 'Top Secret' and I sat there, trying to understand the fearsome details.

'Don't worry about remembering anything,' said

Chisholm. 'When you get your real orders we'll go through this all again – a dozen times if necessary. This is just background. Ring this' – he indicated a bell on the table – 'when you're through and I'll collect it. I'm afraid you'll have to be locked in while you read it.'

The document was not very long, typed on foolscap paper and divided into sections. I settled down to try to absorb the details. The first part read:

DEVELOPMENT AND PROPERTIES OF SARIN
AS MANUFACTURED IN GERMANY

Sarin is the trade name given to isopropylmethyl phosphorofluoridate which was first discovered by Dr. Gebhardt Schrader of I.G. Farbenindustrie in Leverskusen, Germany, during the same time that Tabun, the name for Ethyldimethylamidophosphorocyanidate was being manufactured. (Cases of Tabun incidentally when shipped to storage places early in the war were always labelled 'Trilon', a popular German soap.)

Sarin, however, is difficult to manufacture, but is more deadly than any of the other chemical agents developed by Germany. The lethal dose is one milligram – that is to say, one-fiftieth of one drop. It works with a devastating speed, acting on a key enzyme. This enzyme is called acetylcholinesterase commonly known as 'acat'. This enzyme in the body controls muscular activity.

CAUSE OF DEATH

The body includes millions of junctions in the nervous system in which the chemical acetylcholine (which is body-produced) sends out automatic nerve signals of which we are unaware. If the nerve signals overreact the body automatically counterbalances the danger by releasing acetylcholinesterase thus neutralising the dangers of acetylcholine.

If a minute particle of Sarin enters the body through the skin or lungs it immediately stops the production of acetylcholinesterase, causing the body to lose control. The muscles begin to vibrate; this in turn is followed almost immediately by paralysis. The involuntary muscles which normally help to regulate blood vessels and internal organs no longer function properly.

The pupils of the eyes constrict, the heart slows, the bladder and alimentary canal are also constricted. The penis invariably stiffens into an erection. Death follows within sixty seconds, whether the poison enters the body by injection, is absorbed through the skin or is inhaled. Insofar as it is possible to label a cause of death, it is generally caused by asphyxia following paralysis of the muscles of the respiratory system.

LAUNCHING METHODS

Almost everything we know is subject to confirmation so far as launching methods are concerned and is the result of information supplied to us by undercover agents and a study of R.A.F. P.R.U. (photographic reconnaissance unit). It is believed that warheads have been specially constructed for use with V2 rockets which can now be aimed with a large degree of accuracy to fall within a rectangle sixteen miles by thirteen miles at a target 183 miles from the launching site. The V2s can be assembled and launched within four hours, and if the preparatory work is done by night the cumbersome machinery would not be seen by P.R.U. By day, if aircraft are in the vicinity, it is comparatively easy to take action because, though the V2s can be assembled and fired quickly, each one needs a large convoy of ancillary machinery. (See below.) The V2 is a short name for the second *vergeltungswaffen* (Vengeance) weapon but is always known to the German army as the A4. It is Mark IV in the series of 'A' rockets developed by the German scientist von Braun. It weighs approximately 13.6 tons at launch, and carries a warhead that can be loaded with one ton of H.E. or else with small quantities of Sarin. It is estimated that the rocket motor, using liquid oxygen and alcohol, would burn for seventy seconds.

One of the reasons that leads us to suppose that rockets are being stored in the Rilly tunnel is that the P.R.U. show an increasing amount of specialised vehicle traffic in the vicinity. For, even though it may be possible to mount and fire a rocket in four hours, an enormous convoy is required. For each battery there are three special tractors, each carrying a rocket, and drawn by a half-track which also carries the firing crew. Three tankers, up to sixty feet long, are required – one for alcohol, one for liquid oxygen, one for auxiliary fuel. In addition, there must be a generator truck for electric power and a firing control truck, as well as staff cars for officers.

The standard warhead fuse operates by an electrical contact system which allows the warhead to explode three feet below the ground before detonation. We understand that for use with Sarin the Germans are experimenting with a new proximity fuse which would release gas seven hundred feet above ground. Information suggests that the Germans are endeavouring to modify the Zunder 19 (fuse 19) designed originally for a two-hundred-and-fifty-kilogram bomb with a burst height of around 115 yards.

PRODUCTION LOCALITIES

A statement by Albert Speer, Hitler's Minister of Production, a copy of which has reached London, reads as follows: 'I know from various associates that they are discussing the question of using our two new combat gases, Tabun and Sarin. They believe these gases would be of particular efficacy and they have in fact produced the most frightful results. For the manufacture of this gas we have about three factories, all of which are undamaged.'

We also have unconfirmed information, however, that Sarin is being manufactured in France, where General Ochsner, as a result of his visit to the Champagne region, decided the caverns or deep cellars surrounding the area would be an ideal bomb-proof site. The deepest underground chalk cave in this area is situated at the village of Douzy, just south of Reims, and we understand that old disused tunnels link the underground pyramid with the bomb-proof tunnel outside the neighbouring village of Rilly.

Earlier information on the manufacturing processes in Dyhernfurth on the river Oder near Breslau, based on information reaching us from German Jewish chemists fleeing from Germany, say that a maze of piping is required before the original raw material can be transformed into the finished product.

Aerial photographs taken in the Champagne region by P.R.U. indicate the import of a large quantity of steel drums, usually eight feet long and two feet wide. In the judgment of those evaluating the photographs, these drums are of three-quarter-inch steel. They are painted silver, with a paint which is known to erode in the case of a phosphate leak.

Other P.R.U. evidence gives clear indications of the material being shipped for use with rockets.

CONCLUSIONS

All the evidence points to the manufacture and/or storage of Sarin liquid in one or more chalk pyramids south of Reims. Before any decisions can be made as to the bombing or sealing up of the storage spaces, it is suggested that an agent be sent to the area to penetrate the above-mentioned pyramid and advise, after which S.O.E. H.Q. can determine what action should be taken.

As I closed the buff folder I sat back, hand stretched out to ring the bell, then paused. Jumbled thoughts, fears, danced round my brain, all in the end revolving not so much round the diabolical witches' brew being manufactured in Douzy pyramid – though that was fearful enough – but the more selfish, more terrifying worry of the part played by my father. Oh yes, it was innocent enough, it was laudable, no danger on that score. But the secret thought that all of us had been hoodwinked by the Germans was something I found impossible to believe. The smooth Major Kissling and his explanation that Douzy pyramid had been closed to save my gullible father from any embarrassment! All false, all lies, to cover up the fact that probably it had never been closed at all. The Germans had entered through the old, long-forgotten bricked-up passages linking the pyramid with the Rilly tunnel. To the world, Douzy was closed – and there was evidence of that in barred and shuttered gates at the grandiose front entrance while the original Roman apex entrance, long since covered with a thick plate of glass the size of a dining room table, was covered and surrounded with German barbed wire. There were even, so the warnings read, landmines near the vicinity.

I knew that my father was a patriot, who would rather die than betray France, the country he really loved above all others. He had a curious innocence – which made him unsuspecting of anything devious. He took everyone at his or her face value. He had found Major Kissling a 'gentleman', and when Kissling suggested closing the pyramid my father had agreed because he genuinely believed that Kissling had closed it to protect my father and the family from embarrassment. It was the same with my father's attitude to the workers in Rilly. He was saving lives! Major Kissling was a humanitarian – this, I could see, was how my father's thoughts were running – one of hundreds of Germans forced to fight for Hitler, but doing his best to alleviate any suffering. Maybe Kissling was innocent. Maybe he *didn't* know what was going on in the tunnel under the pyramid? Maybe the German army's Chemical Warfare Division kept its secrets away from the ordinary German officers? And maybe there was nothing in the Douzy pyramid after all?

Waiting to press the bell, I remembered the time when I had voiced my doubts on Papa's work to Gaston. He had laughed in my face. He had actually told me that after the war the French would erect a statue to my father for all the wonderful work he had done to save Frenchmen.

Maybe it was all nonsense. Wouldn't that be wonderful, like

a huge weight which had been crushing my shoulders suddenly being taken away by a miracle. But as I pressed the bell, heard the key turn in the lock and Turbeville walked in and picked up the file, I knew it was all true.

47

'Right,' said Major Turbeville briskly, 'here are your latest orders. Your fourth mission, eh? Well, you leave in four days.'

It was now the beginning of May 1944 and he handed me a copy of the official orders. It was headed 'Operation Instruction F103a'. Under that I read, 'Operation: Pedlar; field name: Johnnie; name on papers: Jean Vivier.'

Pedlar was, I knew, the code name of the circuit operating around Reims. Until a few months previously the circuit in the area had been *Professor*. I did not know why it had been changed. Its nearest neighbour was *Silversmith*, the circuit operating between Reims and Châlons. So that meant that I was going home at last!

'I don't need to tell you that things are on the move,' said Turbeville, 'It's any day now.'

He was, of course, referring to the invasion plans for Europe. Everything pointed to a massive action in the near future. 'And then,' added Turbeville, 'if our suspicions are right, Hitler, who's absolutely mad, may well decide to bring the world down with him. You know, like Wotan at Valhalla. To kill not only his enemies but his own people. Because there's increasing evidence that Hitler's now convinced the German people have let him down and deserve to be punished.'

'Thanks for the cheerful news.' I tried to match Turbeville's dry sense of humour. 'Who's coming with me as radio op?'

Normally an agent such as myself travelled with a radio operator, for though I had learned the groundwork of Morse and how to operate a set if I had to, the sending of cyphered

messages was so vital – usually nothing to do with the operation – that it tended to be treated separately. And it was a rule
of S.O.E. that though the agent had full responsibility in the
field the W.T. operator, as he was known, was allowed a great
deal of latitude because of the high risk of discovery when he
was tapping a message on the air. My eye caught a paragraph
addressed, 'Notes for liaison with W.T. Security: The W.T.
operator assigned to you will be under your command and
will take his instructions from you, but he will be the ultimate
judge as regards technicalities and security.'

I had practised W.T. with several operators, some of them
back in England after a spell in occupied territory, others new
to the job and ready to set off on their first mission. I liked to
know who my W.T. operator was; so much depended on his
character.

'Who's coming with me?' I repeated the question almost
casually.

'She's already there – waiting for you.'

'*She!*'

Turbeville nodded. 'She's very good, a French woman; but
remember – keep your messages short, shorter than ever
now. When the balloon goes up it's going to be hell for
everyone. You blokes *do* bear charmed lives – in comparison
with W.T. operators. With the sophisticated methods of
tracking down transmissions by direction finders the average
life expectancy of a radio operator in the field is now just under
seven months.'

'I hope she's good!'

'She's the best. Code name Portia. She'd better be good.
Your information could make all the difference to the outcome
of the war – if it's what we think it is.'

Turbeville had a mass of instructions for me. First of all, he
wanted me to take with me a new radio set. The one in the
Champagne area was giving trouble, and S.O.E. had per-
fected a new, later set. Agents had no speech radios, but
S.O.E.'s new machine was the short wave Morse transceiver
– a combined transmitter and receiver, B Mark II, which
weighed thirty pounds and was fitted in a suitcase two feet
long. The signal was weak and needed seventy feet of aerial
which didn't have to be fixed. It could trail along the ground –

providing it wasn't seen. The frequency it worked on was determined by removable crystals, small enough to lie in the palm of the hand. Every operator needed at least two to vary the frequencies, but they were delicate and easily broken.

'So take care of it,' Turbeville begged me, and using the nickname by which all radio operators were known, added, 'The pianist is looking forward to getting her new toy.'

There were other details to be worked out. My cover as Jean Vivier, code name Johnnie, was as a vigneron, a disguise I could wear without even trying. The S.O.E. wardrobe department, in a warehouse behind Lord's cricket ground, fitted me out with peasant's clothes. All this was fairly simple. So were the basic orders – to identify the contents of the tunnel and the pyramid. No problem there. I was given the sum of 200,000 francs, and with it a prim warning: 'Please account for all expenditure when possible.'

As usual I was also given the code name of the operator who would help me locally. Each operator in charge of major missions worked with one of the leaders of the Resistance in his particular area. Often the man – or woman – would work with him. All that Turbeville told me was that my contact – who would contact *me* – was codenamed Hamlet.

Codes and passwords were vital, for they had to be memorised and if you forgot the magic words you would never be able to make contact. Some codes, or false names and addresses, were needed in case something went wrong with an operation. I was supposed to be met by Hamlet, but if he didn't turn up, if the French reception committee failed to keep the rendezvous, then I had to telephone Madame Ronson, at 205 rue de France in Reims, and give the password which was based on a simple inversion so that I could be sure the coast was clear in a safe house. I would ask Madame Ronson if I could come and see her. If she replied, 'By all means, do come,' that would be a warning *not* to come, as the Germans would be either in her house or in the vicinity. If, on the other hand, she said, 'It's not really convenient,' that meant it was safe.

S.O.E. had spent a great deal of time devising types of passwords that were not too difficult for uneducated people to remember and use; and experience had shown that the inversion system was the safest.

'As you're working in the vicinity – and even with the beard you may be recognised – you face an added danger. Yet you're the only man in the world who has any chance of getting into Douzy and finding out what's happened. But you *are* known. One of the problems you'll face' – all this from Turbeville – 'is knowing who your real friends are. I mean fellow members of the Resistance. Your number two, Hamlet, will give you the latest general recognition passwords. At the moment the one we use in Pedlar is, "*Où peut-on trouver de l'essence à briquet?*" and the correct answer to this request for lighter fuel is, "*Du carbonant, vous voulez dire?*"

As far as my messages to London were concerned, I would code them all myself before passing them on to Portia. Earlier, the commonest cypher had been based on a line from a poem chosen by the agent so he or she was certain to remember it. But now I was issued with a 'one-time pad'. This was a pad of ultra thin silk slips on which columns of random letters and figures were printed. I would use them in the order they were on the pad and burn each one after use. There was only one duplicate – at S.O.E. in London.

'The one-time pad is useful for another reason,' said Turbeville. 'There's no way your radio operator can decode it under torture, and what's more, once you've burned the silk slip, you can't decode it either, whatever the torture. Damned clever, these boffins.'

Among other problems which I had to memorise was the address of a *cachette*. If I ran into serious trouble I was to go to the *cachette* in a safe house in Paris and tell London by means of a guarded postcard sent to a name and address in Lisbon. 'And remember, the French spell it differently – "Lisbonne" – so if we get a card from you in Lisbon,' explained Turbeville, 'you will be contacted at the *cachette* and we can then try to get you out of the country. But we hope it won't come to that.'

When I had been told that I would be picked up by car and taken to an airfield 'somewhere in England', I said almost without thinking, 'I hope you pack up the radio well. It would be a tragedy if I parachuted in and then we broke the radio after a bad landing.'

'You're not parachuting in,' said Turbeville blandly.

'Didn't I tell you? God! I must have forgotten. You're going in by Lysander. Don't worry, it can land on a sixpence. Here's your exact destination. It's a grass field near a tiny village called Trois-Puits, just south of Reims. It's easily picked out because a small river called the Rouillat crosses the main road just south of Reims. It's moderately hilly country, with small valleys where the pilot will be able to land without any trouble. The Lysander – as usual – will be on the ground for a maximum of two minutes before taking off. They don't like to waste time.'

'I know the place well,' I said.

'By the way,' said Turbeville when discussing last-minute details. 'What about your next of kin?' With a suitable look of apology, for he couldn't quite conceal his cynicism, Turbeville added, 'I know it won't be necessary, of course, but on every op I have to put the same question.'

'It's a bit difficult,' I hesitated. 'I do have a mother.'

'Are mothers difficult?'

I shook my head. 'My fiancée lives in Switzerland. I would like her to know I'm – well, in the land of the living.'

'That can be managed. A monthly message from your old friends in the British Embassy in Berne. Fill in the papers here' – he handed me a form – 'and,' with a touch of mockery, 'don't worry about phoney excuses to hide the fact that she's an Italian. Married to someone else.'

'You knew?'

'Of course. We *try* to know everything.'

I had flown familiarisation missions over England in Lysanders several times, and I was delighted, even relieved, that I was being landed rather than parachuted into France. The captain of the aircraft was the same squadron leader, a man called Dobson, who had taken me on the previous short trips.

We made our way to an airfield which bore no name, but which I guessed was at West Malling in Kent, where we had a final briefing. The Lysander was a small, sturdy, single-engined, high-winged monoplane with a cruising speed of about 165 miles an hour, and if fitted with an extra tank it could fly to Champagne and back and land in five or six hundred yards of grass or clover.

I was flying alone with the pilot, so at 11 p.m. when the moon was full and we prepared to depart I was given the best meal I had ever eaten in England – bacon and eggs and fried bread. At the last minute a Scotland Yard detective gave me a friendly search to check that I didn't have any incriminating documents – such as laundry marks, spare dollars, odd bus tickets or whatever. As usual all my English money and a few odds and ends such as keys were put in an envelope and labelled with my name, then sealed in front of me. Only then was I given the final items of equipment. First my money so it could be worn round the waist in a special money belt which I put on before I put my clothes back after the search. Then a syringe of morphia, a compass disguised as a button, a .45 Browning, a flick-knife, and finally my L pill – which would end my life in less than a minute if I fell into the hands of the Gestapo.

'All set?' asked the briefing officer.

'Fine by me,' I agreed.

The heaviest luggage – the radio – was packed under the front seat nearest the centre of gravity of the plane which weighed less than five tons. My suitcase was strapped on to a shelf behind the back seat. I was placing it and other packages below the shelf – it seemed easier that way – when Dobson, who was supervising everything from his maps to his petrol gauge, said, 'Better put it back on the shelf, old boy. Anything stowed underneath has a tendency to slide down the tail of the fuselage when we climb – and we don't want to waste time on the ground when we get there with you crawling inside looking for something.'

There were two other heavy packages. 'Machine guns for the lads,' explained Dobson briefly.

We crossed the enemy coast at eight thousand feet, with nothing but a little desultory flak to interrupt the steady drone of the single motor. The coast of France lay below, etched as clearly as a pictorial map. Through my intercom Dobson shouted, 'Calais!' and pointed to a large black smudge on the right – a big city. I was not in the Lysander to map-read – a highly technical job requiring one to translate the lie of

streams, railways and roads from a map to the limited visi-
bility of a place far below where people were trying to shoot
me down.

I had been too excited to experience any sensation of fear
during the flight – and during previous flights – but once we
approached the target area I began to feel a little different. As
we crossed into 'home country' Dobson yelled, 'About fifteen
minutes.' He opened up a flask of hot coffee and handed me
some in a tin mug.

'Watch out for the recognition signals,' he shouted.
'Tonight it's the letter "R". It should be repeated three times.
Don't get mixed up with the ground landing lights.' He
waited for a few minutes then suddenly shouted, 'There it is!' I
had never even seen the tiny pinpoint of light, a dot, a larger
dash dash, another dot. Then blackness before the message
was repeated.

'We're ready to land!' He returned the signal out of the side
of the plane. 'As soon as they see our signal they'll switch on
the landing lights.'

Only three such lights were needed for a Lysander pick-up.
They were arranged in the form of an upside-down L or, to
put it another way, the top and left hand sides of a square. I
could see the top line – indicated simply by two tiny torch
lights; this was the crossbar at the upwind end, so that we
would land on the field facing this line.

But where from? What side of this two-lamp line was the
end of the field? We had to know which direction to make our
approach otherwise we wouldn't be flying into the wind as we
had to.

'Okay!' cried Dobson, pointing out the faint twinkle of a
third light. This was the suggested actual 'start' of the airfield,
the landing point on the 'strip'. There was no strip really, of
course, just the field, but the Lysander was easy to handle, easy
to land slowly, and with the two flashlights marking the 'bar'
at the end of the field Dobson knew he could land on any part
of it just before he reached the twin lights – preferably near the
third light, which in a sense was the control tower of the
operation.

There was no problem. We bumped down within fifty
yards of the pick-up flash. The other two faint lights dis-

appeared – until Dobson was ready to fly again, then the markers would indicate the lie of the land, and the direction of the wind for take-off.

The night was warm and smelt good, and as I tumbled out the pilot shouted above the sound of the propeller, 'Cheerio! Good hunting!' and without a moment's hesitation he lumbered round and made his way to the far end of the field. As he revved up the small single engine he seemed to rush past me, balance and wobble for a few minutes in the night air, then start to climb and vanish until I was alone.

Suddenly I shivered – half from cold, half frightened. I had been told to remain where the plane had actually landed because of the heavy packages, including the radio and my deliberately cheap cardboard case, kept closed with an old piece of rope and containing my spare clothes as a vigneron. Anyway, I couldn't possibly haul everything to the edge of the field where I would have had a spurious feeling of being safer.

I was not alone. Soon I could hear whispers, then *smell* a horse, hear the rumblings of old wheels. The pinpoint of light had vanished. A dark figure lumbered up, said, 'You're Johnnie? Jean Vivier? Good. Come with me. Here, let me carry this.' He knew which was the suitcase radio, for he said – and I could almost feel the grin on his face – 'Our pianist can hardly wait to play with her new toy.' He had a young laugh, and was obviously enjoying himself.

With the familiarity of one used to handling heavy loads he picked up the packages of guns and put them in an old farm cart which I had hardly seen in the dark. It was very dark, but the moon eerily etched in the scene at certain times. 'Delivery is a dangerous business,' he said. Another man arrived, a dark shadow, shook hands with me but said nothing, then led the horse away. 'They'll be looked after, but it's better if we split – so that if one lot gets caught the other might be lucky.'

As we crouched, half loping towards the corner of the field, I reflected suddenly, hugging my suitcase, that I didn't know who in the hell the man was; I had been taught to memorise passwords, but when I said, 'You haven't identified yourself. Where's Hamlet?' he just laughed cheerfully and said, 'I'm taking you to him. I go under the name of Oscar. Don't worry, I'm not a German. I was one of the men who helped to surround Lisette's house when we killed the Gestapo man. That was a night! Here, this way. It's a two-mile walk. Yes, I know who you are. I work for Moët et Chandon.'

So much for security! For secret passwords and double checking! A moment later, as we almost reached the gate, I got another shock. Near the corner two figures converged from the far end of the field. Both were women. Both were cycling over the grass. Even the dark could not mask something familiar about one of them. As I made out the figures in the moonlight, wobbling across the rough field, I knew that figure: nothing could disguise it. She cycled past the gate in the distance and into the nearest lane, and then was gone.

'Yes,' admitted Oscar with a laugh, 'I thought you'd recognise her. No one on earth can disguise La Châtelaine. She and Hamlet's sister run our airfield. It's her field; she goes up and lights the torches when a drop is expected.'

I might have known it! Nothing could stop La Châtelaine from fighting the Germans. Not even age. Even so it was damned stupid for anyone to allow an old woman like that to come out in the middle of the night and play at soldiers. I wondered if Papa knew. I was sure he didn't.

No one had told me the identity of Hamlet, but even in London I had guessed – and hoped – that it might be Gaston. Now, due to careless talk on the part of my reception committee, I was virtually certain, for Oscar had said that Hamlet's sister was La Châtelaine's assistant at the airfield. And La Châtelaine didn't encourage strangers to work with her; she would automatically choose someone from the family – and who better than Aubergine, Gaston's sister? The need for security had been drilled into me so remorselessly at S.O.E. that I was appalled at the casual way the man had leaked the secret.

The safe house was in old Pagniez's cottage – as I had expected. Oscar tapped a signal on the heavy oak door. It was instantly opened, and though the room inside was dark and I could see nothing for the moment, I knew it was Gaston. We threw our arms round each other. Oscar slid away. Gaston closed the door and switched on the single light bulb. Though thinner, he looked just the same. So did the living room of his father's cottage.

As he brought out a bottle of *marc*, I asked, 'How long is it, Gaston?'

'Must be eighteen months. That was a day to remember when we all said goodbye.'

'As long ago as that?'

'Even longer.'

'See my father?' I asked.

'Often. He's doing a fine job as usual in the Rilly pyramid. But he keeps himself to himself.'

'And what about La Châtelaine?' I tossed back the tiny drink in one gulp and held out my glass for another. 'I couldn't believe my eyes. I hope she didn't see me.'

'I'll tell you all about it later. And don't blame me!'

'And your father?' I changed the subject. 'He must be getting on now.'

'He's dead,' said Gaston briefly. 'Nearly a year ago. Old age — and he never really got over the shock of that terrible day at Douzy.'

'I'm sorry,' I said awkwardly.

'It's a long time ago now,' Gaston sighed. 'And a lot more people have died since then. Yes, it's getting on for two years. You'll find a lot of changes have taken place. We heard vague rumours about you — nothing tangible — that you were in America.'

'I was.' I stretched my legs and leaned back in the worn old chair. 'Did my preliminary training there.'

'And now?'

'It's a long story. Let's sleep on it.'

In fact S.O.E. had instructed me not to reveal *all* my suspicions, but to work with Hamlet step by step. First things first. And that meant a check on the tunnel without even discussing the next step — not the contents of the Douzy pyramid, but to check first on whether or not it was being used.

'You're sure this is a safe house?' I asked.

'Absolutely. As far as the Germans are concerned, I'm a veteran who became a respected vigneron. There's nothing — absolutely nothing — to link me with the activities of Hamlet.

In fact, since that day I've never really done anything of any importance. We've been told to lie low – I don't know why, but they're orders. That and answering radio questions from London.'

'And the house?' Again I persisted. 'You're sure it's safe?'

'The Germans occasionally pop in for a drink, but most of them are Alsatians; many of them worked in the German vineyards across the border before the war, so in a way they're understanding and never suspicious.'

'And if they do come? Any searches?'

'No, never. But just in case, there *is* a loft. I'll show you where later on.'

'And my cover? Jean Vivier?'

'Perfect – because Jean Vivier exists – yes, he's alive and well . . .'

'And . . .'

'In England.' Gaston almost grinned. 'Vivier is Free French and he's been staying with me as a vigneron for six months. He's been registered, probably had his identity card checked. Even had a beard like you. Now he's joined de Gaulle's staff in London, but nobody on the register here knows he's even left the area. So *you* are Jean Vivier. You can use his room, work on the land – when you need to. I more or less run the vineyards when La Châtelaine isn't here.'

'And La Châtelaine? That does worry me, Gaston. She's an old lady; I'd have thought you'd have tried to keep her out of this sort of thing. I was horrified when I saw that old figure wobbling around on a bicycle.'

Gaston voice was almost sharp, 'You *thought*! Since when did La Châtelaine allow her workers to think? She *acts*. She held us all to ransom. Yes, she *forced* us to let her join the Resistance.'

I asked how, and it was a story quickly told. The indefatigable Grandma had, it seems, casually mentioned her frustrations to Madame Robert at the Home Farm, saying she wished she could do something to help beat the Germans. Madame Robert told Gaston. And there was a way that Grandma could help – by allowing the Resistance to use a lonely field beyond the vineyard as a secret airstrip. Grandma owned the field, it was true, but the Resistance didn't want to use it without her permission in case of discovery by the Germans. So when she asked if she could help it seemed a perfect way to solve the problem.

'Of course La Châtelaine jumped at the idea,' said Gaston. 'But dammit, she made conditions. It was her land, she said, so it would be her airfield, and we could use it if we let her run it. Well,' Gaston almost grinned, 'you can't argue with La Châtelaine. So we got an airfield – and a ground staff. Couldn't ask for a better team. And your grandmother looks ten years younger.'

The questions were tumbling over each other as I sought to fill in the gaps of lost years. 'And the Germans are using the château,' I said. 'I did hear that.'

Gaston nodded again. 'They just marched in one day, nearly a year ago it must have been, and took the place over as an officers' mess.'

'And La Châtelaine lives in the old Misses B and B house?'

'Yes,' said Gaston. 'She was furious at the time. But in a way it's better. Jean, the old butler, has been forced to work for the Germans, but that means he can keep an eye on the place. La Châtelaine hasn't got the labour needed to keep up a place like the château, so she's better off living quietly with one maid – your Aubergine.'

'It seems so awful – life so disrupted, poor Grandma and your father – so bloody terrible, this war.'

'And it's lasting so long,' Gaston sighed.

'It might start moving a bit quicker soon,' I said. 'And maybe we can help to make it shorter still.'

'Your mission?'

'Yes. But let's give "Hamlet" and "Johnnie" a few hours off! Let's pretend we're Gaston and Larry – until we've finished off this bottle. And tomorrow we'll get to work.'

We stayed up half the night just talking – about the good old days, the happiness that was Douzy, about Willi, Anna, Sonia, Mama – carefully! – and how it had all started: the war and then the terrible things that had happened to the family. Since this was like a twenty-four-hour leave pass, we were talking about real people, so there was no way I could ignore Olivia – and no way in which I could force Gaston to lie if I asked how she was. So I had to go straight to the point.

'I know we said we wouldn't talk business tonight,' I smiled, 'but how's Portia? No, I've already guessed – a woman. It must be Olivia.'

He shrugged his shoulders. 'No point in denying it. You'll know the moment you hand her a message for transmission. She's the best in France. Takes the craziest risks – or did until I ordered her – yes, ordered her – to take life more easily.'

'I'd like to see her as soon as I could. Is her safe house a secret?'

'It's supposed to be. Because she's a Jewess – involved in a murder case – there's no way she can ever go out, even leave the place where she lives.'

'Christ! What a life.'

'Well, she does go for walks at night. And often I join her. But she's got to be kept hidden – and it's selfish, I know, but in a way the more she's hidden the safer the signal.'

'But where?'

'In the belfry at Douzy church. You remember? It's not only safe, it has the advantage that she can trail her aerial down the side, just pay it out like a fishing line, and then when she's transmitted pull it in.'

'But to *live* there . . .'

'I've begged her to go. I even contacted London to suggest they might fly her out. But nothing doing – she just won't budge.'

'I'd love to see her soon,' I said.

'Of course. It's all so long ago that sometimes I forget that in a way she was part of your family.'

It gave me a peculiar feeling to think that Olivia was barely half a mile away from the place I was sitting – and there was no way that I could ever go to see her unless it was behind the back of the enemy.

The next morning we started work in the vineyards. It was the best cover – the simplest way of being able to exchange information without exciting any curiosity, especially from the occasional German patrols which I was told passed our way from time to time. There was plenty to do in the vineyards at this time of year. In high summer the soil had not only to be harrowed; the vines were receiving their second trimming, a careful, tricky operation to reduce foliage just where it would allow more sunlight to filter into the clusters of grapes.

'No chance of any of our neighbours recognising me?' I asked.

'Eventually you're bound to be seen. But not yet. Apart from the beard, some of the civilians are new, we're so short of workers, so there's rarely more than two or three men to a plot of land. I can arrange that we work together and make plans as we talk.'

Bending over side by side, I explained to Gaston my 'stage one' orders. Someone had to penetrate the Rilly tunnel and discover what the Germans were storing there. Or rather confirm my suspicions.

'London's certain the Germans are keeping components for V2s there – or even completed rockets. It's up to us to find out before any action is taken.'

Gaston listened, but I found it hard to concentrate on what we were talking about. It was not only the beautiful summer sun after English weather; it was the feeling I was *home*, working in our own vineyards, that opposite as I looked up I could see the stark outline of Douzy church – the church where the entire family had been christened, had gone to first Communion. It gave me a singular feeling to be living here – and yet not living here. It was Monsieur Jean Vivier who was squatting down where I was working; it wasn't me.

'It won't be easy;' Gaston interrupted my thoughts. 'We've thought once or twice of taking a look – there must be something suspicious about that R.A.F. bombing – even though it was ineffectual. But getting past the German guard – and the gates into the tunnel – it needs a bit of thought.'

'London's anxious to know quickly,' I said. 'They've got other jobs lined up after this one.'

'Won't be easy,' he repeated. 'We'll talk about it tonight.'

His voice was interrupted by a roar of anger. La Châtelaine, bicycle thrown down at the corner of the field, charged towards us shouting, '*Merde! Crétins! Imbéciles!*'

'That's torn it,' whispered Gaston as he stood up. 'But keep calm.'

'What the devil do you think you're doing tearing off all

those leaves?' shouted La Châtelaine furiously to the bearded man, whose eyes were still on the ground. 'Don't you know how to prune vines?' And with added anger at my downcast eyes, she shouted, 'Get up, man, when I speak to you. Look at that!' I *had* done a poor job of the second trimming, and there was nothing for it now but to stand up. Despite the beard, there could be no way a woman couldn't recognise her own grandson. '*Idiot!*' she cried – and stopped dead, eyes narrowing at recognition.

'You remember Jean Vivier?' said Gaston tactfully as a few other workers in nearby vineyards stopped to listen to the tirade.

I must hand it to La Châtelaine. She took what seemed to be a deep breath, and then pointing downwards shouted, 'Look! Like this!' She dropped to her knees, those nimble fingers of hers stroking the vines. There was the beginning of a tear – the first I think I can ever remember seeing from her weather-beaten face – as she said, 'God bless you, Larry,' then straightening up, as she cried to Gaston in a voice loud enough for everyone in the vicinity to hear, 'I'd fire this dolt on the spot if you weren't so short-handed! For God's sake, get your workers to learn their business properly.'

Then she stalked away, without a glance backwards, to the corner of the field. I had a picture of her, her long green skirt, small hat, picking up her old bike and setting off for the next vineyard.

48

I did not see Olivia for four days, though Gaston arranged to deliver a coded message telling London the day after my arrival that I had landed safely. But this was a 'courtesy' visit. Normally most radio operators landed with the agent whose messages they would transmit, so they knew each other, however slightly. I hadn't met my operator – not officially, anyway. And as the whole success of our plan would be nullified if she didn't get the message through to base, everything in the end depended on her.

I made my way to the church, walking, an old hoe across my left shoulder, like any scruffy, bearded vigneron on the way home after a day's work.

A hundred yards from the church a workman stood by the edge of the ochre path, leaning on his rake as though resting from hard work. He wiped his forehead.

'Good afternoon,' I said, one workman greeting another. 'Is that the village of Douzy over there?' This was a simple inversion password. I knew that this was Douzy, everyone in the area knew. If the workman nodded agreement, that meant he was not a member of the Resistance. No suggestion that he was a potential enemy, but he wasn't a watchman, looking out for anyone suspicious. However, the man replied, with Douzy in full view, 'But no! Douzy's straight down the hill.'

He had completed the password. I could trust him. We shook hands, as the French do on the slightest pretext, and then I whispered, 'You're sure the coast is clear at the church? And the belfry?'

'Clean as a whistle,' he replied. 'The good father has gone to the village – he always does, every evening; he asks no questions, just goes, visiting the people, sometimes stopping for a *vin rouge* at the Café des Sports. He's a good sort. Doesn't necessarily want to get involved, but he thinks we use the church for secret meetings. He's no idea about' – he hesitated – 'the pianist.'

He was inclined to be talkative, but I put him off as politely as I could, with a 'See you again soon, I hope.' Then I walked to the church – where we had been ordered as children to attend every Sunday with Mlle Lisette, where we had been washed and scrubbed for our Communions. I pushed open the heavy door leading directly to the nave. Even in summer the church had a feeling of cold; it seemed vaguely inhospitable, offering nothing of the warm welcome one felt a church should offer. But perhaps, I thought, as my boots rang on the flagstones, it was the lack of a congregation that gave it its cold, unlived-in atmosphere.

The staircase to the belfry was concealed behind the door

near the back of the modest choir stalls. It was not deliberately hidden; it was such an ugly narrow staircase, and in such bad repair, that years previously a separation wall with a door had been built to hide the rear section of the church. Because the stairs were dangerous – unless you watched out for the ones to miss – the door was always locked. The key was kept on a lintel above. Anyone wanting to use the stairs would warn Olivia – who also had a key – by giving the Beethoven signal – three sharp knocks, followed by a pause and one which somehow seemed longer, the unmistakable V for Victory signal.

I heard a faint reply, not far above, and only then unlocked the door to the musty, dirty stairway and started to climb up.

'Hamlet?' asked a soft voice.

'Portia?' I whispered.

She was very changed. Nothing could hide the beautiful soft eyes, not the size, not the shape; but even though they sparkled a welcome as I reached the wooden floor of the belfry, her eyes had a certain wariness. They reminded me of the eyes of a cat, always on the look-out for the unexpected. Yet, despite a certain shyness, those same eyes were filled with pleasure – after all, wasn't I the one who had 'officially' welcomed Olivia as a member of the family? She was one of us, and always would be.

'You look healthier and younger than ever,' she laughed.

'You too.' I scrambled off the top rung and sat down on a wooden chair, one of three which had somehow reached the rooftop eyrie.

'Oh no,' she said sadly. '*You* look marvellous, but me, no. I'm a very old lady now – in experience, anyway – and no longer a very pretty one.'

Though nothing would ever be able to iron out the wrinkles that lined her, I was even more shocked to see that her hair had gone completely grey. The fact that it looked unkempt, even dirty, couldn't be helped. But grey! Neither could the lines be helped. But what had happened to the beautiful creamy pallor we had all so admired in Olivia? Her skin was as grey as her hair.

'I know.' Instinctively she patted her hair when she realised I was looking at her. 'The only place I can wash is in the bathroom behind the vestry,' she said, adding with a laugh more like her old self, 'The water's very cold in winter, and though Gaston does his best to keep me supplied with soap, at times we run out.'

'You're really a prisoner here.' I felt awful watching her.

'I am,' she admitted frankly, 'but it has to be like this for several reasons. After I took the W.T. training in Morse, I had to find a safe place where the chances of a radio detector were minimal. The power of the W.T. transmitter is so bad that they must have an aerial – even a trailing aerial. What better place than to hang it out over the edge of the belfry when I'm on the air? Obviously the height helps to give me better reception as well.'

'But you *live* here, Olivia. What about eating and . . .?'

'The boys bring in more than I can eat. And there's always a bottle of wine to spare. And a Thermos of soup. There's a loo at the bottom of the stairs next to the vestry. It's not too bad . . .'

A sudden thought struck me. 'The bell? The sound must break your eardrums.'

'There is no bell. The Germans melted it down for scrap. Otherwise I couldn't have stayed here.'

I looked round as she poured out a glass of wine. 'Douzy *blanc*,' she promised me. The belfry was perhaps ten feet square, with the steps coming up through a hole in one corner. There were three wooden chairs, a camp bed, blankets, pillows. For washing an old-fashioned jug or pitcher stood in a basin. There was a bucket on the floor below the rudimentary dressing table. 'One of the boys brings up a new pitcher of water every day, and I throw the dirty water out of the window.' My eye caught an old-fashioned chamber pot below the bed. 'At night I can go down,' she laughed, 'but I daren't in the day time, so if I need to . . .' She shrugged her shoulders.

'And that?' I pointed to the machine pistol hanging on the wall. 'Where did you get that?'

'You don't remember? It's one of the machine pistols the boys took when they shot all the S.S. men at Lisette's – or rather you did. They took everything, remember? Uniforms, guns, S.S. caps – everything. My Schmeisser machine pistol is my last line of defence. Nobody can get up to my place. *Nobody*. I can shoot down every single man who tries. They'd have to burn the place down to get me out.'

Later, when it came to despatching the message, she was intensely professional. 'The new piano is a joy,' she cried as she opened the narrow window by the bed and paid out her aerial down the side of the church wall. She inserted the right crystals to get the correct frequency, and, when she had made contact, tapped out the short message I had sent in code, then waited for the acknowledgment or instructions. After London signed off, she pulled up the aerial, twisting the wire round her left hand like a ball of wool, then tucked it into the appropriate place in the corner of the set. 'That's that until the next transmission,' she said, and closed down the dowdy-looking suitcase.

'It's a rough life,' I said to her.

'It is. But Larry, if my messages can help to get one more German killed then I feel the same sense of achievement of anyone who's been successful.'

As I prepared to climb down the rickety stairs I said, 'I'll be back in a couple of days. Maybe I'll come at night and we can go out for a walk, for a breath of air.' I added with a laugh, 'We can take a walk round the churchyard!'

'That would be very nice,' she said quietly.

I reached up to kiss her cheeks – a purely family kiss, the kind to celebrate a reunion; nothing more than that. To my surprise she skilfully moved the cheek away.

'I'm sorry.' I didn't quite know what to say or do.

'Don't be sorry. I'm not much for kissing anyone. Maybe when we're all free again – and I've got my looks back,' she said bitterly.

'That's all right,' I said awkwardly. 'But your beauty is inside you, Olivia. It's got nothing to do with whether or not you've had your hair waved. You're Olivia – the one and only Olivia. Remember?'

'Am I? Do I?' Her voice was forlorn.

We spent many hours discussing how best to get into the Rilly tunnel. At first, without involving anyone in direct consultation, Gaston talked over possibilities with individual members of the Resistance. Many were French civilian workers who had access to the general area of the tunnel entrance which was near Rilly railway station. In the old days the train service linking Reims with Épernay had entered the tunnel a few yards after leaving Rilly station. But after the Germans blocked the tunnel people had been forced to use a slow train which meandered through a dozen villages before linking up with the main train and then going on to Épernay. The junction from the main line to this branch line was actually in Rilly station.

From time to time the Resistance gleaned odd snippets of information, snippets which made more sense to me than they did to the villagers, for I was able to interpret them — London had told me what to look out for. And several things I did learn. Every now and then trains manned by Germans drove into Rilly itself — and stopped there. It seemed absurd for a train to puff its way all the distance from Germany to Rilly — and then, after unloading, to return to the Fatherland. Ridiculous, unless the train was transporting vital raw materials to a place like Rilly where nothing ever happened.

In the end I would still have to get into the tunnel to see for myself, but it was important to know that some of the trains arriving from Germany included double-length flat-bed trucks. The machines on them were under wraps, and the imagination of the locals was limited to the possibilities of large field guns. I thought differently. Later, some inquisitive Resistance members discovered that one train was carrying three huge transformers. They did not have the faintest idea what they might be used for, but I knew that mobile transformers were needed to take any rockets to possible launching pads. There were other snippets of information that I was able to piece together, like parts of a jigsaw puzzle. One *cheminot* — the French railway workers were among the forefront of the Resistance movement — noted a German goods train arriving at Rilly and then noted it when, five days later, it left on the branch line. It was eight double-length wagons shorter. They had just vanished. Of course they hadn't really. Despite R.A.F. bombing, the tracks of the main railway line still continued into the mouth of the tunnel. Obviously the flat bed railway wagons had been shunted inside the mouth of the tunnel which was guarded by a twenty-four-hour sentry patrol behind specially built grilled iron gates twenty feet tall, with only a small doorway in the grille through which Germans could enter on production of special passes.

There was another intriguing point. Nobody could hide the arrival by road of three convoys of extra-long Mercedes trucks – huge eight-wheelers which arrived near Rilly and were promptly driven into a nearby field and wrapped in tarpaulin – as though they were never going to be used. I knew from London briefings that however quickly a V2 could be fired it needed a large convoy of ancillary equipment – containers of liquid oxygen, transformers, and so on. It seemed clear to me, in view of London's suspicions, that all this apparently unrelated movement of *matériel* indicated V2s – either for assembly or to be stored. I asked one or two *cheminots* if Europe's railway system included any simple method of being able to transfer extremely heavy and unwieldy loads from goods trains to road haulage. Apparently it was a fairly simple operation provided you had the right machinery. Specially constructed chassis trucks only a few inches lower than railway trucks could be backed up against a train and the machinery could be transferred to the lower level by a system of rollers. The truck would then drive off to a parking lot, fully laden, and the empty railway wagons shunted to a siding.

Yet how could I ever get into the tunnel? And stay there for, say, twenty minutes? For though I had only told Gaston that I wanted to check on the contents of the tunnel and its state of readiness, it was also vital to find out if the old, never-used subway linking the railway tunnel with the Douzy pyramid had been re-opened by the Germans, as London suggested. That subway was large enough to have accommodated in the old days a primitive form of tram on which the champagne could be pushed in bulk from the pyramid to the railway siding inside the tunnel. The idea had come to nothing, but the linking subway still existed, and I wanted, if I could get into the Rilly tunnel, to see if a way had been opened up by the Germans to get into the pyramid when ostensibly it was closed.

So: how to get in? I asked Gaston to arrange for me to meet one of the leading *cheminot* Resistance men whose work was a legend. His code name was Drax and he was only twenty-two, but he had helped to derail several trains. He had even orga-nised one head-on collision between two trains on the Paris–Lille line. One was filled with German troops on the way to the Channel ports, the other with Panzers destined for the Russian front. Drax arranged for the switches to be manipu-lated and over a hundred and fifty Germans were killed.

He was a likeable young man with a frank face, almost innocent. He looked as though he'd never shaved, as remotely different from a professional train-wrecker as a killer from a bank clerk.

'I'm just ready to create a big bang,' he said. 'I don't want to get out of practice.'

Expertly he rolled a cigarette, running the thin edge of the paper along his lips, then asked me, 'Can you wait five days?'

'As long as you like – up to a point. But why five days?'

'We've got a German train due here on 31 May – that's a Wednesday. Don't ask me how we found out, it's too compli-cated, but basically the Germans have to give advance warning to the French railways of a German goods train coming through, simply because everything has to be sorted out and preparations made in case some of the tracks are on different gauges. It's not as complicated as it sounds, but it takes a lot of time to prepare. And the Germans have to tell us what to expect. Otherwise they'd have to run all the railways them-selves and they couldn't possibly do that.'

'And this train's a big one?' I asked.

He nodded, picking a piece of loose tobacco from the tip of his tongue. 'I saw a copy of the manifest – forty-two double length flat-beds. And – this is interesting – a *wagon-lit* for the big shots, led by a general, no less, on a tour of inspection. Named something like Hocher.'

'General Hermann Ochsner?'

'That's the man. You know him?'

'Not personally, but I know all about him. He *is* a big shot.' I didn't bother to tell him that he was the head of Hitler's chemical corps. 'But if you could blow that train up!'

'I will, if you give the orders.'

'You think you could?'

'Drax can do anything,' said Gaston. 'But there's always

one thing that has to be weighed up – is it worth it? In terms of reprisals, deaths and so on?'

'If Drax can blow up the train at Rilly and cause enough commotion to give me the chance to get into the tunnel – yes, I hate to think of the reprisals, but I have to say one thing to you, Hamlet, and you, Drax – it must be obvious to you that I'm on to a very big thing. It may sound pompous, but it's something which, if I'm successful, could make all the difference to the outcome of the war. It could shorten it, it could do anything. I'd put it as high as that.'

'That's good enough for me,' said Drax, rolling another cigarette. 'What about you, Gaston?'

'I'm with you, if. . .'

'If we can get into the tunnel?' I finished his question.

Gaston nodded. 'The Germans aren't fools – and they don't scare easily. They *might* think that we derailed the Ochsner train just because it's an attack on a big shot, but some Germans would begin to wonder if it's a trap to draw attention from those guarding the tunnel. We could get the disturbance laid on – in theory, anyway – but still we don't know how to get into the tunnel during the panic.'

I was puzzling over the problem when I had a curious feeling that I *knew* there was a way to solve it, to get into the tunnel, but somehow I had missed it. It was as though someone had dropped a hint and I had thrust it aside unthinkingly.

We discussed whether during the hiatus that ensued it would be possible for any one of us to scale the iron gates.

'Impossible,' said Gaston. 'Forget it.'

'But the small inner gate is open?'

'Always – but with a heavy guard. It's open because technicians keep on going in and out. But security is watertight.'

We even wondered whether it would be possible to climb to the top of the Rilly mountain – which was more of a thickly wooded hill, anyway – and then for some of us to drop the others by a rope.

'It's too far. And you'd be seen – a sniper could pick you off as easily as hitting a fly on a wall.'

Still, I was plagued by the fact that there *was* a way – and I knew it, or ought to know it. Somewhere a link was missing. I sat there smoking and drinking with Drax and Gaston.

'You've got a gun, of course?' asked Drax.

'A .45,' I nodded. 'Not the biggest in the world, but . . .'

'Not as big as Olivia's machine pistol,' laughed Gaston. 'One of those we pinched . . .'

'I've got it!' I cried. 'Olivia!'

Gaston looked baffled.

'No, I'm not going to involve her. But it's what she *said*.' What had she said when she was showing me the machine pistol? Thinking back to the days when we had freed her, she had almost laughingly said, 'We took everything, remember? Uniforms, caps . . .'

'Where are the S.S. uniforms?' I asked Gaston almost hoarsely. 'The ones we stripped from the bodies that day?'

Gaston looked doubtful. 'They were distributed to other circuits and used several times. One British P.O.W. reached the coast in one of those uniforms.'

I felt a great let-down. 'You haven't got any left?'

He shook his head. I suddenly realised, of course, that it was a long time since we had stolen those uniforms, and a lot of things had happened – and yet I also realised that wearing German uniforms offered us the best chance we would ever get of entering the tunnel: we'd wait for the derailment at the station, almost in the centre of Rilly, and then in the terrible smash-up Gaston and I, dressed in S.S. uniforms, could shout to the guards at the iron grille, 'Help! Come quickly!' or something like that. In S.S. uniforms nobody would dare to question anyone. I could picture it. All the Germans would be terrified – a high-ranking officer ambushed, perhaps even killed, forty or fifty wagons derailed, smashed up – in uniform we could almost *walk* into the tunnel!

And now, dammit, I thought despondently, I had remembered the S.S. uniforms, but I had forgotten that we had acquired them nearly two years ago; and no Frenchman was going to keep German uniforms in a drawer as a souvenir.

'Shit!' I said it in English. 'I thought I'd found a way out.'

'That means *merde, non?*' asked a sympathetic Gaston. 'I know how you feel.'

'Anyway, it's too late now. We must think of a new plan.'

Drax hadn't been following the conversation, no doubt because it referred to previous actions which we had taken together.

'You want some uniforms, is that what you mean?' he asked.

'It was an idea.'

'Maybe I can help.'

'You've got some uniforms?' I asked incredulously.

'Not military uniforms. But maybe better. I've got a different idea – but basically it's the same. The *cheminots* killed four German railway workers on our last derailment. A driver and some guards. We could use their uniforms.'

I must have looked doubtful.

'No, wait,' he explained. 'Rilly station, where we're going to blow up the train, is barely two hundred yards from the entrance of the tunnel. Am I right?'

I nodded.

'Well, we'll make *two* explosions. One half-way along the train, a second five minutes later, when all hell's broken loose, in the front section of the train. Not too far front, but when that goes up, and everyone's panicking, I'll be dressed as a German engine driver, you two as guards or whatever we can find for you. At the critical moment – remember, we're only two hundred yards from the tunnel entrance – the engine driver will either get out of his cab or I'll come in and kick him out. You jump in. Then, with the power of the locomotive – tough enough to carry over forty full-laden wagons – I'll pull the engine to full steam ahead. The engine should have enough force to tear itself away from the wrecked carriages near it – for a while. I'll be screaming that I can't stop the thing. I don't know much German, but enough to know how to shout out that I'm scared. It'll look just as though it's a runaway engine. And before anyone realises what's happening, it'll be on the rails heading straight for the grilled iron gates. It'll smash right through them. That'll be a nasty moment – maybe we can jump off in time. Then I'll bolt for it – I'll vanish. You two can get into the tunnel, throw away the jackets if you don't want to be recognised – you can get away with German issue trousers for a while – and take a quick look round, and then' – he shrugged his shoulders –

'it's up to you to make yourselves scarce. How's that for an idea?'

I stood in awe of this remarkable young man with his baby face.

'There's no flaw anywhere,' I said softly. 'Thanks, my friend.' In actual fact I used the word *copain*, which means you are closer than a friend; in English you might say 'a pal'.

'It's going to be exciting,' he said with a laugh.

'It's all set then.' I looked around for confirmation. 'I'm going to report to London, then all we have to do is wait − until 31 May.'

49

Two days before the train was due, when Drax was deciding where to lay explosive charges, two of the Resistance *cheminots* were caught by the Germans and never seen again. No one knew what had happened, why or how they had been caught, because they were hustled off to jail. But Drax did know they had been checking on locations for him. The Resistants had been posing as members of one of the innumerable repair gangs needed to keep the tracks in good repair. So many were needed that Frenchmen had to be employed from time to time. For some reason they had been suspected. Immediately, all French workers were cleared from the tracks for several miles north of Rilly, and replaced by German army engineers checking against possible sabotage.

'Explosives are out,' said Drax, anger at the hitch in his plans darkening his baby face. 'We'll have to derail instead.'

I must have looked puzzled. We were meeting as usual in Gaston's house.

'We did it on the Paris−Lille train. We'll switch points outside Douzy.' He explained more simply by spreading out a large-scale map of the type used by professional railwaymen. It showed no roads, but took note of signal posts, points, dangerous curves where speed had to be reduced; it even showed the location of sidings, and of course the secondary line used since the tunnel was blocked.

'And there are two points of importance.' Drax pointed to his map. 'The train will automatically slow down as it approaches Rilly – after all, it is the end of a long journey. But once it gets the green signal at the Rilly signal box before the station it will carry on slowly. The points are always kept in the same position, so that every south-bound train automatically goes round the mouth of the tunnel. The only exceptions occur when wagons have to be shunted into the tunnel. Then the points are switched over.'

Drax's alternative scheme was simple. Resistants would overpower the signalmen in their box after dark, set the Rilly signal at red – in those days unexplained delays were always occurring – and when the engine driver stopped and leaned out of the cab he, too, would be overpowered. At that moment – before anyone on the train had time to wonder what was happening – the signal would turn back to green. Drax would take the place of the engine driver. As the train blew steam and started to move, the signalmen would switch the points over and the train would go straight past Rilly station and carry on until it smashed into the gates at the mouth of the tunnel.

'It's the same ending we planned, only the methods have had to be changed. But in actual fact it's simpler this way. Better make sure your gun works. You'll be needing it.' To Gaston he asked, 'What plans are you making for a getaway?'

Gaston explained that Oscar – he was the young man who had met me the night I had landed in France – would spend the evening at the Café Moderne at the edge of Rilly, ostensibly drinking, with his horse and cart waiting outside.

I was thinking about what Drax had said – that I might need my gun. I had never shot a man in cold blood – I wasn't even present when Guy had shot Hoess – but my training as a potential killer had been so thorough that I knew that I would never be interested in feeling pity for the men at the receiving end of my American .45 automatic Browning, known as the M1911A1. It was often used – in preference to revolvers because saboteurs preferred it. It was not only less bulky than the old-fashioned 'six-shooter' but flatter, about nine inches overall length, and could be fitted with a silencer whereas the revolver couldn't.

I oiled it carefully, pushed the catch to eject the magazine, loaded it with a clip of seven bullets, then pushed the magazine into the butt until it clicked, after which I pulled back the slide which compressed the spring with my left hand and cocked the weapon ready for use. Then I put on the safety catch and fitted the silencer, basically a set of flanged 'sleeves' which fitted over the barrel, lengthening it. The .45 could only be fitted with the Welrod silencer, or, in more technical terms, the Mark I Hand-Firing Device.

The moment to reveal the tunnel's secrets had arrived. Preparing the Browning, loading the magazine, had helped me to overcome the tension of the long wait. I hated anxious preparations, but now anxiety was replaced by a new emotion. I grasped Gaston's hand and said, 'I'm ready!' And dread of danger now was a shared one. I suddenly felt younger – how absurd, I thought – but I did. Razor sharp with anticipation. The preliminaries were over; the job was on.

Almost on the point of leaving I explained to Gaston the importance of accuracy if or when we got into the tunnel. I had to drill the fact into him, even though with his knowledge of car mechanics he would be able to view anything with a more technical eye than even I could, especially if any rockets were fitted with warheads.

'I know I'm a bore, but it is vital to remember the technical details, to be able to recognise a V2 rocket *instantly*. We may have less than a minute inside the tunnel – that's if we ever get in. Or get out! And we daren't make a mistake. That's why I'm asking you to come along with me. In case one of us can't get away, the other can radio London.'

Details of the rocket had been drilled into me even before the R.A.F. bombed its first site at Peenemünde. What we expected to find was a monster of a rocket, forty-six feet long, five feet in diameter and weighing around fourteen tons, able to be fired from a mobile launching pad, at a speed faster than sound, so that it would in theory reach London from the Channel coast and explode in less than six minutes.

'It's a terrifying thought,' I said to Gaston.

663

By 11 p.m. – with the train due at 11.30 – Drax, Gaston and I were hidden under some of the tarpaulins covering trucks in the big field used as a carpark outside the station. We wore our ill-fitting German railway uniforms. My .45 with its silencer seemed bulky. I also felt for my flick-knife. We had to wait until the very last minute before overpowering the three men in the signal box – two German operators and one soldier as a guard. But we knew exactly what to do when the moment did arrive.

And it would all have to be over in five minutes – not a second longer. At 11.25 we slithered silently across the grass of the parking lot until we reached the edge of the railway and the signal box. It was lit up; we could hear talking and laughing from inside, for it was a warm night and the door was open at the top of the steps.

Drax had to go first because he was the only one who spoke a little German. But it was important that I went second, for I had a specific job to do as I was the only man with a silencer on his gun, so that when the first surprise turned to suspicion I could handle the soldier, for he would probably be the only man who was armed.

Heart pounding, I followed Drax up the wooden steps to the signal box, flooded with light. At the one moment in my life when I craved darkness, obscurity, I was bathed in light as bright as stage footlights. It was intriguing how, in moments of tension – and in this moment I knew I would soon have to kill a man I had never seen – odd thoughts chased across my mind. It wasn't fear, nor the prospect of being an executioner. Breathless with fear, heart constricted, I found myself thinking, that bloody man Turbeville never told me I might have to work under arc lamps!

Drax appeared in the doorway and cried in his passable German 'Guten Abend. I've been told to report for the return journey.' The German uniform gave the three men in the glass cabin a second of spurious confidence that all was well, while I heard in the distance the sound of the approaching train. I could see outside on the darkness of the track the bright light of the signal showing green, like a green halo.

The second of hesitation was enough. The German soldier, suspicious, started to say, 'You're a bit early, aren't you? The train hasn't arrived. What's the password for tonight?' He half levelled his Tommy gun, not sure how to react. I gave him no chance to think. Standing behind Drax I shot the German straight in the face – higher than I had expected: I had aimed for the heart, but had forgotten the upward kick. I heard the hiss of my gun with its baffles to silence the noise, then sound and vision fused as the German's face seemed to splash out in scarlet as if someone had hurled a tin of red paint across the room, covering the wall.

One signal operator started to scream but it was stillborn as I wheeled round and shot him in the back before the sound left the signal box. The third man I covered. He was terrified. His mouth was slack with fear and he started blubbering and begging for mercy. Then suddenly, standing there, he put his right hand to the back of his trousers. He wasn't reaching for a gun. He had just emptied his bowels and was suddenly embarrassed.

Gaston stood at the top of the steps; the rhythmic puff of the approaching train was growing louder.

'Where's the lever that operates the points switch?' rapped Drax.

The man hesitated. He moved to the stack of old-fashioned levers with a curious ungainly walk, as though trying to stop the contents of his trousers from seeping out over his shoes. 'And the signal – switch it to red!' shouted Drax. 'Come on! Unless you want to be shot too.'

I took in the scene. The soldier's head had been almost blown off; half of it remained on his neck. The bleeding had slowed down; I could actually see inside his head, where it had been blown off, leaving a cross-section. The German signal-man had died more cleanly, one hole through the back. I had remembered the upward kick of the .45 and allowed for it. He had slumped into the side of the instrument panel, almost sitting on the floor, eyes open and staring, not even a trace of blood showing through the dark green jacket.

The terrified man pointed to a lever.

'Pull it!' shouted Drax. 'Or you'll get the same treatment.' The man hesitated. Drax pulled a knife. 'Pull it, damn you!'

'Yes, sir,' gasped the man. 'This one.'

With a savage jerk Drax pulled the lever himself. It was

extraordinary, as though the stage had suddenly changed its spotlight. The vague greenish tinge up the line gave way suddenly to a reddish glow.

'Now,' cried Drax. 'The points.' He knew there could only be one alternative point on the track ahead so there was only one lever to be pulled to switch over the points. Drax tugged away.

'On to the train!' he cried. 'The two of us,' he said to me. 'Come on! You've got your gun with a silencer, Johnnie' – he used my code name. 'We'll take care of the driver and his mate, one way or another.' Then, he explained, the signal must be pulled back to green. 'We'll start the train. It'll be slow – we can't even get to fifteen miles an hour by the time we go through the station. You can jump on, Hamlet.'

As he started to run down the steps he turned to Gaston and with a look at the terrified man said, 'You know what to do.'

We ran along the side of the track. The chug-chug of the train had turned into a louder, more impatient noise, but almost as we reached the red signal we heard the rhythm slow down. There was a squeal of brakes and the great black shadow groaned, the wheels seemed to cry almost plaintively, and then with a hiss the engine stopped by the red signal light. I heard the engine driver shout out, asking what the hell had happened, and Drax's reply, *'Es hat einen Unfall gegeben!'*

'What kind of an accident?'

'This way,' cried Drax as though making off.

In a matter of seconds, but swearing furiously, the driver climbed down the rung of iron steps. As he tried to peer into Drax's face, ignoring me – I was only a fireman – he turned his back to me. From point blank range I shot him through the neck. He never knew what ended his life as he slumped on the track without a sound. I heard nothing but the swoosh, but the shot was so close I could smell the singeing, the burning, of his hair.

'What the hell's happened?' asked the driver's mate.

For a moment I caught sight of his face, a kid of perhaps eighteen, round-faced under a mop of blond hair, a pudding basin haircut. But they were sometimes the most fanatic, these blond super-Aryans. This was no time to threaten. As he saw my automatic he started to beg, but if I had argued he might have killed me. As it was I cut him off for ever before anyone had a chance to cut me off.

'*Vous êtes vraiment professionel!*' said an admiring Drax, as he blinked the torch in the direction of the signal box. All the same, I felt slightly sick at the thought that in the space of two or three minutes I had abruptly ended the life of four unknown men who had probably never done any of us any harm.

'Come on!' I was climbing up the steps. 'We've got no time to waste.'

Gaston had seen the flashlight and changed the signal back to green. He was running towards us. With professional skill Drax pulled the complicated levers inside the engine cab and the great beast, straining to pull its massive load from a standing start, grunted and heaved and squealed almost like a living animal, with a hiss of steam and groaning of effort. As it increased speed Gaston jumped on the bottom rung and hauled himself up, gasping, 'Made it!'

'Great!' cried Drax. 'Now you're on, prepare to jump – or we'll all be killed.' It was an eerie sight, unforgettable. To the right of the engine was Rilly station, a few chinks of light in the waiting room peeping out from a badly arranged blackout. Some people stood on the platform – soldiers, engineers, guards, I suppose. Suddenly they realised that something was wrong – I could hear it from the shouts – and what I couldn't hear I could see, gesticulations, and raised arms. They must have realised that the slowing moving train should have gone right automatically, taking the fork that led past the main railway and round the side of the mountain. I could hear the screams, almost drowning the roar inside the cab of the engine. Then as the train didn't stop the screams increased in harshness, fear, the edge of pandemonium. I could hear this, but all I could see was the black outline of the mountain looming in front of me, and the ring of lights in its centre – the inside of the tunnel – as the monster grunted on relentlessly towards catastrophe.

As the lights inside the tunnel increased Drax shouted above the din, 'Ready to jump! You've got three seconds. Then we go.'

Without warning, I suddenly saw in front of us the huge bars of the twenty-foot iron gates. Gaston and I jumped to the left – hurling ourselves out as far as we could in case the engine toppled over. Drax jumped to the right.

Then everything was engulfed in a great roaring, grinding of metal on metal, with escaping steam, with the cries of men on every side, screams of panic or pain. The engine was too tough to fall over – Drax had known that. As it hit the gates, I saw a terrifying, almost human dragon gushing steam from its nostrils, the engine not flat any more, but at rest with its front wheels raised like a praying mantis.

'All right?' I shouted to Gaston. He patted my shoulder and a crowd raced along towards us. Back on the train itself I could hear and vaguely see the doors of sleeping cars open, people clamber down. It didn't look as if anyone had received more than a severe shaking, the train had been going too slowly. But there was shouting everywhere. Anxious hands helped to lift me up, to see if I was hurt. They all spoke German – any French villagers had obviously not been allowed so near the tunnel. I took refuge in what they would expect – a sense of shock, bewilderment, a lot of head nodding. My uniform helped, and I was treated with respect. I stumbled to my feet. So did Gaston. I knew just enough German to shout, 'Explosion! Beware!'

Realising that I was an 'experienced' – if slightly bemused – engine driver or assistant, they opened a way for me to clamber over the twisted girders and make my way to the front of the engine, beckoning Gaston to follow me. I had one objective – and one word left in my vocabulary. Clambering over the wrecked girders of the gates until I was standing right at the entrance to the tunnel – stretching ahead, all its lights blazing – I shouted, trying to make myself heard above the hissing, '*Aus!*' 'Out!' My voice rang with a simulated mixture of authority and fear, and I hoped that my gestures looked like those of an expert on the verge of panic, urging everyone to escape while there was still time. I didn't realise it until later, but when falling I had cut my head – only a slight graze, but enough to give me a convincing and heroic trickle of blood.

Men from inside the tunnel scrambled across the twisted metal in their anxiety to run. I think almost everyone in the world has a horror of being buried alive, and perhaps they thought that a violent explosion – if the engine blew up in the mouth of the tunnel – might bring about a rock fall that would block the tunnel for ever. Anyway, they bolted.

From inside the tunnel I saw a couple of men silhouetted against the arc lights, and started to wave to them. Then, as though impatient with a couple of idiots who did not realise the danger, I ran along the inside of the tunnel, warning them to get out. The uniform helped. To the onlookers, I was still dazed with shock, but I was the only man around who *knew* the dangers. Drax had told me that there was little likelihood of the engine blowing up, but the soldiers and German civilian workers didn't know that. In any event most of them had drawn back fifty yards or so. Several German sentries had not escaped before the crash. Their bodies lay strewn across the tangled wreckage as though pinned there, arms and legs outstretched and twisted like some grotesque display of butterflies.

Two sentries who hadn't been hurt shouted incomprehensible words as Gaston and I started to climb into the actual tunnel.

'*Nein, nein!*' one cried. '*Verboten!*'

'*Aus, aus!*' I pointed to the figures in the distance.

One German ran out of the tunnel to force the crowd to keep away. He tried to push them back. The other soldier hesitated. I thought the uniform had won, but he still said, '*Verboten!*'

I *had* to get into the tunnel. In a matter of minutes someone would stumble on the bodies by the signal box. Even apart from that, no doubt some officials clearly suspected sabotage, so they hardly needed the proof that would confirm suspicion. There was a hell of a lot of noise, not only from men shouting, but from others trying to force open doors that had jammed. Two of the flat-bed trucks just behind the engine had overturned – a gigantic piece of machinery which I didn't recognise lay smashed by the side of the track. Apart from the bodies, a dozen or so men – and, I noticed, two women – were receiving medical treatment. One man had a leg trapped by fallen masonry and was screaming.

Finally I realised the only way to get rid of the sentry was to beg him to come with us. Luckily the din was so terrific it was easier to pretend to shout and not be heard. So, as I mouthed noiseless sounds, I beckoned him to join me. That – and my uniform – satisfied his doubts.

Almost gratefully, it seemed, he followed me as I loped in, still shouting, for effect, '*Aus! aus!*' and keeping with him his submachine gun.

I don't suppose I had been in Rilly tunnel since I was a child and then I had only peered into it from the subway that linked the tunnel with the pyramid before it was blocked up. What astonished me was the filth on the walls. Most chalk passages in Champagne retained some of their original colour, and in places like the pyramids they give the effect of a blinding whiteness. But over the years hundreds, thousands of trains had puffed their way through the tunnel, belching filthy smoke which had long since covered the walls with a black deposit, absent from the miles of corridors underneath Reims where the air suffered no such pollution.

We were running along the left-hand side of the tunnel, along the two lines of track, when I was suddenly faced with the huge bulk of a rocket. There was no doubt about it: I didn't need my technical training. I must, without thinking, have hesitated as I looked at it, for the soldier jerked up his submachine gun and shouted, '*Verboten!*'

'*Ja, ja!*' I cried, but Gaston knew as well as I did that we couldn't keep up the deception, based on a vocabulary limited to two or three words, much longer. Gaston was walking behind me, and knew what to do. As I stumbled forward, suddenly realising that the figures ahead had mysteriously vanished, that the tunnel as far as I could see was empty, Gaston put his left arm around the neck of the guard, jerked it back, and at the same time as the German cursed and struggled plunged his knife straight into the man's back, just between the shoulder blades. As the man sagged – I wasn't sure if he was dead – Gaston gave a sharp jerk back and I heard the neck crack as it snapped. Gaston grabbed the German's machine gun and whispered, 'Seen enough?'

'No. Not yet.' I was taking in every detail I could remember – not only four V2s assembled on flat-beds and ready to be towed out to be fired, but also generators, massive lumps of machinery which I didn't understand, obviously crates of spares. The awesome sight was staggering. The entrance to the tunnel might have been only a few yards away, but the noise, the fearsome pandemonium of the crash, the twisted heap of metal, had been exchanged as abruptly as though an operator had inserted a new slide to illustrate a lecture. The evidence of chaos had been substituted for the silent evidence of a secret engineering machine shop.

Only one thing puzzled me. Where was everyone? The tunnel was deserted. I could understand that those near the mouth of the tunnel must have emerged – to help, out of curiosity, out of fear, for a dozen reasons – but I had seen shadowy figures further back. Where were they? They couldn't be *hiding*. Who from? What for? It didn't make sense. And therefore they had left the tunnel by another exit.

'There's only one way they could have gone,' I whispered to Gaston. 'Into Douzy pyramid. You go back – in case I run into trouble. I'm going in to see. But it's imperative that you get away, just in case I can't get out. Then you can contact London and tell them there are four V2s.'

It had to be done that way because in my bones I had always believed what London had told me – that the way into Douzy pyramid, which to the outside world was closed, lay through the subway connecting it to the railway tunnel.

I knew that the entrance from the tunnel to the subway had long since been bricked up, but it would have been easy to knock it down, open up the subway – and provide a secret entrance to Douzy pyramid.

'I'll hang on for a bit longer,' Gaston whispered.

'*Please* – go. As they say in the movies, "That's an order." Your going is a routine precaution, but absolutely vital – to keep the boys in London informed if I'm delayed. Nothing's going to happen, but that's the drill.'

'I hope you'll be okay. But if it's an order . . .' He squeezed my shoulder. How crazily life changed! Once a kid with whom I played, then father's driver, then my mother's lover, now my closest friend. He slid away quietly.

I wanted one thing: confirmation that the old bricked-up subway linking the pyramid with the tunnel had been opened – and what lay before it. I crept towards it carefully under the arc lamps, which were swinging directly overhead on flexes. When the subway had been built we had also erected a narrow platform in order to lower champagne directly on to the railway – grandiose plans that had never been used.

I climbed up the platform – and there, as I had known all along, was the subway. Open.

One thought struck me. Rilly had also built a subway like ours linking their pyramid with the tunnel. It had been sealed off at the same time. Had the Germans opened that too? If so, not even a moron could fail to see what was happening in the tunnel. Somebody would have been curious enough to investigate. And my father was in charge of operations in the Rilly pyramid. I began to sweat – at the thought that just a few yards away my own father, who did not even know I was in France, worked every day. Did he know what was happening on the other side of the brick wall in the tunnel? I had to find out. I had to make sure that the tunnel was closed off. A monster V2 on a flat-bed blocked any view. But I crawled under the wheels, wriggling along the track; then, lying on my stomach, I peered at the opposite wall, hoping, praying, that one look would be enough. It was. A jet-black soot encrusted every inch of brick, bricks undisturbed for years since the entrance to both subways had been bricked up. At least there was no way my father could know what the Germans were doing in Rilly tunnel. Or for that matter in Douzy pyramid.

Innocent or naïve, he was quietly getting on with his job of helping – and, to be fair, saving – Frenchmen, without the faintest suspicion that anything so close to him was unusual, that he was being duped, all but cosseted by the Germans with a few titbits in the way of saved French lives.

I crawled backwards to the lighted hole in the wall, until my feet touched the small raised platform. Then I was able to slither sideways. I *had* to go into the subway for a look. I knew that I had accomplished stage one. I had identified the V2s, would be able to report on a mass of machinery which was obviously ancillary *matériel* to be used for launching. So, in theory, I should chase Gaston, try to escape in the dislocation. For all this action – the penetration of the tunnel, the killing of the soldiers, had only taken minutes. I had no doubt that back at the entrance to the tunnel the scene, with the dead and wounded, the danger of explosion, the hissing of steam, would be one of uproar. If I threw away my railwayman's uniform, I could probably escape, trousers unnoticed, and reach the Café Moderne.

Yet I couldn't do it. I might never again have such a golden opportunity to examine the pyramid. I wouldn't wait – the subway wasn't very long – but what if I could already report back that it was being used? Suspicions, though, weren't enough to Turbeville; I had to report what I saw with my own eyes. Not the details, just a picture, just proof that it *was* being used, when the Germans had gone to such lengths to let the local people believe it was closed, and would remain empty until the end of the war.

The old tramlines still existed in the subway though the light inside was not as bright as in the tunnel proper, so I almost fell over the line. I held on to the damp brick on the wall – the wall paler, lighter, uncontaminated by soot. I could smell the slightly sour smell of champagne cellars, just as I had when a child.

I felt my way along carefully. The subway was perhaps a hundred feet long, possibly a little longer. As I approached the pyramid the semicircle of light at the far end grew into a startlingly bright, white light, of an intensity that I had never seen before.

And then I was there, huddled against the damp wall, staring out at the scene which my reason told me *must* be our Douzy pyramid, but which the same reason told me could not be the same place, it was so completely unrecognisable. It had to be Douzy, and yet it couldn't be. Yet it *was*. The white walls of the past and present were the only common factor. As for the rest of this new world I gazed on, I might as well have been on Mars. The dim light so necessary for storing champagne had been replaced by arc lamps so bright I couldn't look directly into one. That was not all. The eerie drama of Douzy had lain not only in its whiteness, but in the strange emptiness of its echoing, pointed vaults. Now, not only had the dim light been replaced by vivid lighting, but the emptiness had vanished too. In its place I saw a vision of some future planet of terrifying platforms and tubes that filled the pyramid almost from its apex to the ground far below. It not only looked like some insane magician's cave, but like a giant's Meccano set. And in the middle, rising from the floor as I watched, a

673

modern lift whined upwards – high above my head, carrying two men and a long silver-coloured tube. What had Chisholm said back in London? 'The steel canisters are painted with a special silver coating which changes colour if any of the gas escapes.' Without any question I was looking at one of the canisters which the R.A.F. had photographed above ground, and which Chisholm had warned me about. And what else could that canister contain but Sarin?

Suddenly I shivered with fear. I felt rather than saw the presence of another man watching me and wheeled round, automatic flashing up and firing without stopping to think. I hadn't *seen* anything. And it all happened before I did see anything, long before I was able to adjust from staring into the blinding light of the pyramid into the gloom of the subway behind me – perhaps two seconds, which is a lifetime or a flash of lightning, a compound of time. An arm with something in it, an extension of metal, a gun perhaps, swiped across the side of my face, tearing it open, and as I screamed the unknown assailant struck again, this time aiming for the back of my skull. I ducked.

Dimly, automatically, I could hear my old sergeant-major in the S.O.E. training camp at Arisaig say in his Scottish accent, 'It's easy to learn how to fight if you fight dirty.' I slid to one side as I felt his breath and then, almost blinded by blood, I hit him, a short punch like a piston, straight into his kidneys. As he half fell my knee drove into his groin. He still wasn't out, but neither was I. I knew that if I was caught by someone who had seen my inspection of Douzy I would be tortured for years. If it came to that, I must grab my L-pill. But I wasn't caught yet, though neither was he defeated. As he tried to hit me again across my face, I slipped deliberately on the damp chalk subway, then as I fell against him I jabbed the fingers of my right hand into his eyes. The sergeant-major had taught me that trick too, long after Guy had deliberately blinded Hoess.

No man could stand that pain without instinctively moving his hands to protect himself. As I felt my fingers go into the softness of the eye, he screamed and raised his hands. I reckoned I had perhaps thirty seconds to get out of the tunnel before he raised the alarm – if he was able to. I didn't wait to find out. Without a moment's hesitation I jumped on the man's face as he fell. Heavy peasant's hob nailed boots splintered bone, teeth, jaw, skin; and what was left of his eyes.

Wiping the blood from my face, I staggered, crouching, along the subway to the tunnel. Once at the entrance I hoped I could pass as a man who had been injured in the derailment. I never quite lost consciousness, but nor was I aware exactly what was happening. I reached the exit to the tunnel, struggling to stop my body from leaving my brain, which wanted to stand in mute defiance of what my body wanted to do. To help keep myself moving I grabbed anything I could, including shards of razor-sharp glass which my bloodied eyes couldn't see.

I never knew until later that, in the brief moments before I was attacked, Gaston had been waiting outside, lost in the panic of the crowds surrounding the wrecked train, dozens of men still searching for bodies or trying to extricate those who had been trapped by the giant gates. Somehow Gaston had reached me, wiped my face and helped me away. Dimly I remember falling, then being dragged by my feet. I learned later that Gaston had finally had to carry me like a sack to the outskirts of Rilly and then to the Café Moderne. Oscar seemed to have vanished, but the horse and trap were outside, and Gaston dumped me in it, covered me with straw and set off. I knew nothing until I woke up: three days later.

50

So far as time was concerned I lost two weeks of my life, recovering slowly from the injuries I received in the subway. Drifting in and out of consciousness, I had no idea of the momentous news that the Allies had landed in Europe during the first week of June. I did not even know where I was. I had assumed I would seek refuge in Gaston's house, but only later I learned that after the train crash his house was being watched.

So instead Gaston took me to another safe house – an extra-ordinary old mill standing on the ridge of a small rise not far from Verzenay. In the First World War the Germans had constructed a concrete blockhouse on the ground floor of the mill, from which they could direct machine-gun fire over a wide area. After the war the blockhouse had been virtually closed, but the mill still operated. It was about eight or ten miles from Douzy – far enough away not to excite German anger at the 'outrage' at Rilly. But the miller was an active member of the Resistance and the mill had the advantage that a fugitive could be hidden high up – providing he could make the stairs.

My most urgent need was for medical attention, but my most immediate fear was that I would be found in the hue and cry that followed the derailment of the train. This was the second time in two years that the Resistance had struck savagely against the Germans – first the murder and obvious torture of Hoess and his bodyguards, all killed; and now a full-scale attack on a train, carried out with all the hallmarks of professional expertise. We couldn't tell what the Germans were thinking, but General Ochsner, who had escaped injury, must have realised that the thorough preparations to derail a train at an unknown village smacked of secret knowledge on the part of the Resistance or agents sent to France by the Allied High Command. The exploits of the S.O.E. were already legendary and the murders in the signal box, and in the cab of the engine, all had a professional stamp.

The reprisals were swift and savage. Without any trial ten men and women were publicly shot outside the small *hôtel de ville* at Rilly. Others, uncounted, were indiscriminately snatched from their homes and despatched, like cattle being rounded up, to concentration camps.

Such random slaughter was a classic German method of waging war through terror. It was hard for the local people to derive any consolation from the knowledge that they were suffering for what might look like an act of bravado in derailing the train. How could they ever realise that the casualties among civilians in Rilly was a modest price to pay for preventing the enemy use of Sarin, which could exterminate entire cities?

Many Resistants – and they must have included men like my father – faced a terrible moral dilemma when weighing Resistance killings against the revenge taken by the Germans. I myself found some refuge from twinges of conscience in the anonymity of the innocent victims. But once I knew the identity of a victim – once I could picture his or her face – everything changed. Six days after we had escaped, when I was just emerging from a kind of delirium, I heard that Oscar had been tortured, then executed.

Poor Oscar! Twenty years old and so full of life. In a way, I suppose, every death in war is the same – the brutal ending of a life. But it somehow seemed more wicked when it happened to a young man rather than an old one. The old had been through a life, had something to remember in the last moments of death. But youngsters – what did they know about living? Men like Jean-Pierre who had been cut off before his life had really started. With his bashful schoolboy crush on Anna, his life had been limited to a couple of blushes. It was the same with Oscar, laughing as he cried, 'I love this life! I'm living for the first time.' Lying in the stifling heat of my old mill hide-out, wounded – not necessarily, though in some pain – I recalled the cheerful way Oscar had hidden the canisters of arms in the old farm cart the night when I landed, laughing on his way to the edge of the field. I caught myself thinking of him and in my half dreams mixing his face with that of Sonia, of all the life that Sonia had given to me, while poor Oscar had never known his 'Sonia', never had an experience which truly meant that life had been worth living. Even at thirty-two, I could not really complain, whatever happened to me.

Gaston kept me fed with the latest news via London or on a battery radio which we had hidden in the mill. The news of the Europe-wide advances was the finest tonic I could have been given. The fighting was tough, but the bridgehead in Europe had been securely established. Fascinated – lying in the comparative safety of the mill, everything shrouded in fine white dust, the silence of the countryside broken by the grinding stone wheels of the mill itself or the sound of horses and carts as presumably sacks of flour were loaded up – I listened to the details – those which were released: more than a thousand warships taking part, four thousand landing craft, more than eighty-three thousand British and Canadian troops, another seventy thousand Americans.

'It's incredible!' That was all I could say to Gaston – until I got a message from London on 17 June saying that the first V1 rockets had landed on London four days previously, and that in the following twenty-four hours the Germans had launched two hundred and forty-four V1s.

Then I got the message I had really been waiting for. It read: 'It may soon be time to strike are you OK please acknowledge?'

I wasn't really 'OK' but I wasn't going to be left out of the biggest climax of my S.O.E. career. 'Ready for action,' I signalled back via Olivia and received in return a laconic 'Stand by.'

A local Reims doctor who was in the Resistance had come to visit me on his bicycle twice a week, usually at night. His name was Claude Benoit, and on the first evening he had had to stitch me up without any anaesthetic. To stop me jerking with the sudden pain as I hovered between agony and merciful oblivion, Gaston held my arms, while Dr. Benoit said, as though I were a child, 'There, there. Only three more and you'll look as beautiful as new.' He put in eleven stitches. Luckily my jaw, though badly bruised, hadn't been broken, but two back teeth had been smashed and would have to be extracted, though a visit to the dentist would have to wait.

At first my nose was so large I could never stop seeing it in front of my eyes. It had been slightly broken – a hairline fracture – but Dr. Benoit assured me it would give me no permanent catarrh.

I wouldn't admit it at first but what really hastened my cure, especially the gash across my face and the cuts from broken glass, was Dr. Benoit's insistence on using an old wives' medicine, one familiar to every single vigneron living in Champagne. It consisted of a rather unpleasant kind of fungus or mould which seemed to appear on the slightly damp chalk walls of every cellar. On each visit Dr. Benoit smeared every cut with it, every gash. Only years later did I realise the fungus was a pure form of penicillin.

By the middle of July I was walking again, and receiving

regular coded messages from London, mostly concerned with scientific procedures to be followed when the time came to blow up Douzy. I knew that S.O.E. had charts of most of the underground cellars – not only in Reims but places like the sewers of Paris – and they were anxious that I should understand where exactly to place any explosive charges in order to collapse the walls in the pyramid. As Dr. Chisholm had said in London, 'The only safe way to neutralise Sarin is to bury it alive – for ever.' That meant collapsing the pyramid.

By now it was clear that S.O.E. regarded my evidence as proof that Douzy must be 'neutralised' – a favourite word at S.O.E. – but though the liberation of Europe was proceeding magnificently it had not yet reached the point where Hitler would despair. The operation had to be timed exactly – by others who knew more than I. Only one worry nagged me during the period of waiting. What was going to happen to my father when I faced the moment for action? Sometimes at night, tossing on my straw mattress after a supper of thin, watery and often cold soup, I would dream of my father – wild dreams, that he was executed by the Germans, that in the tangled skein of the nightmare world he had taken my place and was secretly plotting against the Germans. Sometimes I woke up sweating – from weakness as much as from the stifling heat of the blockhouse. I was praying that he would denounce the Germans, but I knew that in fact my father didn't have the faintest inkling of what was happening under his nose, next to the office where he was working. Yet there was no way I could tell him.

'I don't know what the hell to do,' I sighed to Gaston. 'It's the height of bloody irony. Here's my own father convinced he's helping the French when in fact he's helping the Germans – in his own pyramid, in Douzy. And here am I planning to blow it all sky-high.'

By now I appeared more like my old self, or at any rate like Jean Vivier. I was able to help in the mill and also to work in the Douzy vineyards a couple of days a week, for Vivier's papers were in order. I was even able to exchange the occasional word with La Châtelaine when working. Gaston had, of course, warned her right at the start that on no account must she share any of her news with my father. It wasn't that we distrusted him, but even Gaston was now beginning to realise that though my father's intentions were strictly honourable, they were not turning out to be as heroic as Gaston had at first thought.

One day I was harrowing some hard soil round the roots of the vines when simultaneously I saw the shadow and felt the presence of Grandma looking down on me. She pointed to some vines, asked an aggressive question, even moved behind Gaston to show him something, and then, amidst the disguise of her words and actions – always in case of collaborators – she suddenly hissed in my ear, 'I've got a message from Olivia. London says you've got to keep clear of Douzy.'

'What on earth do you mean?' I was almost angry at the way La Châtelaine was – as usual – giving me orders. 'Why haven't I got the message through the usual channels?'

'Because Douzy church is under suspicion. Germans are searching there regularly. Gaston – you ought to get out right away. And someone has to find a way of getting Olivia out.'

I dropped my hoe in confusion. Grandma had the wit to shout, 'Clumsy fool! You almost snapped the root of that vine.'

'What do you mean? Is Olivia really in danger?'

'I don't know.' Quickly, squatting as though showing me how to do better work, she said, 'I've arranged to find out. No one questions me. The Germans all know me – they know who I am.'

With an angry toss of her head for the benefit of other workers, Grandma disappeared. She had hardly left the vineyard and cycled away out of sight when I saw a small armoured vehicle appear at the far end of the field. Three German soldiers jumped out, brandishing sub-machine guns. I saw gesticulations, then one of the vignerons pointing in our direction. We were some distance away.

'I'm running for it,' I gasped. 'I daren't risk being questioned. And until this scar on my face is healed . . .' Gaston realised as well as I that anyone who had been 'wounded' was *always* suspect when the Germans wanted to arrest someone.

'Run along the ditch at the back,' he whispered urgently. 'Then to the woods. Better make for Verzenay. It's not Reims, but it's easier to get lost, even in a small town. I'll find you through the bookshop.'

We both knew the address of the 'cut-out' bookshop at Verzenay, a system which helped to eliminate betrayal by traitors or even by loyal men and women who had revealed secrets under torture.

'Look after yourself, Gaston,' I panted.

'You too;' he started to run in the opposite direction. At the far end of the vineyard was a large ditch which had been dug many years previously to mark the boundary between our vines and those of Mumm. But it had been constructed by someone with a passion for English gardens, and so the ditch was similar to an English ha-ha, invented by the British landscape gardeners in the nineteenth century to keep cows from straying without disfiguring the view by unsightly fences. In fact, because of the slight dip in the hillside, it was impossible for the German soldiers to know there was a ditch at all, it was so cunningly disguised, even though they were only two fields away.

As I ran, crouching, towards a belt of woodland, I heard the stutter of machine-gun fire and warning shots. They couldn't see me. I stumbled on. Gaston had vanished. The ditch led straight as an arrow to a small copse. I was sure I could make it, and then – if hidden for only minutes – I could set off in a new direction.

Certainly it was no longer safe either to return to the mill or to Gaston's house or the vineyard. Once you saw a couple of German soldiers asking to point you out, it meant that you and the place where you lived were under surveillance. And with the traces of facial wounds difficult to explain away, I had no doubt that the Germans would ask me a great many questions – and not very politely.

I decided to make for Verzenay. It would not take long to reach, especially if I could steal a bicycle. And it was unlikely that the entire German army had been alerted just to question Jean Vivier. At Verzenay both Gaston and I had the address of the safe house, and the password. And I had to be doubly careful, now I had received the news that the operation was going to be undertaken soon. Apart from any personal consideration, it meant that I had to take the greatest possible care not

681

to fall into enemy hands before we cut off Germany's supplies of Sarin. I knew that the actual go-ahead message, giving me an approximate date for action, would depend on when the Allies reached the critical point at which Hitler would be faced with the need to try the gambler's last throw – to force Britain to capitulate by the use of a new and terrible weapon, at which moment he could magnanimously offer a 'just' peace to the Americans. Now that critical point was almost reached.

I was wondering how best to steal an old bicycle, then hide in the ditch and wait for dark, when burst after burst of machine-gun fire tore into the still afternoon. The noise was horrific, and couldn't have been more than a mile away, one rat-a-tat running into another, so that it sounded as though a hundred men had opened fire. I had no idea what had happened. Because I was in the ditch the noise seemed to come first from one direction, then another. I stumbled to the point where the ditch ended at the small copse. Cautiously I peered over, almost expecting bullets to send up spurts of dirt as I was spotted. But I had been forgotten; the attack was somewhere else. But where? I had lost my bearings, but once I had crashed – all thoughts of silence forgotten – through the tangled thicket and brambles, I knew where the German attack was being launched.

A dozen men with machine guns had surrounded the church at Douzy, and were firing indiscriminately – but always pointing to the sky – to the belfry on the top of the squat church tower. At Olivia! She must have been discovered – or betrayed – and now she was trapped, trapped at the top of a flight of rickety steps so narrow she had once boasted that, with her machine pistol, no one would ever be able to take her alive.

My first thought was that I – and Gaston who must be somewhere around – had to save her, not only because she was Olivia, but because, with the training that had been drilled into me, I had to protect my wireless operator; until I made alternative arrangements, she was my only way of keeping in contact with London – at a vital moment.

I had my .45, but I was too far away to risk using it. I had to get closer. It was strange, but even as I crept nearer I could sense the beginning of panic in the Germans. The shooting became more sporadic, and I realised they were taking casualties. I saw two bodies being pulled out of the church, then heard a single shot from inside, followed by a scream – a man's scream. Olivia was still at the top of the belfry, shooting anyone who tried to mount the stairs.

Hiding in the undergrowth not a hundred yards behind the church, I could see four or five Germans in the churchyard. There might be others inside the church. Then, on the road beyond the opposite side of the churchyard, I saw Gaston. He was walking unconcernedly towards the lane that led to the village, almost as though he were making for the Café des Sports to slake his thirst with a Slavia at the end of a hard day's work.

A crowd of men and women on the fringe of the village watched uncertainly, attracted by the noise of heavy firing. A German who was near warned them to return to their homes, and most scuttled away after he had fired a burst above their heads.

Gaston seemed not to notice what was going on. The soldier ran towards him, shouting to him to follow the others, to go away, gesticulating with his sub-machine gun. Gaston pretended not to understand, even made a gesture with his right hand to indicate he was going for a drink, then pointed to the Café des Sports in the village. The German waved him on. I had no idea what Gaston would do – or what I would do.

Then suddenly, before I even saw what had happened, I smelt it: the smell of burning in the church. Almost immediately I saw the first greedy tongues of flame. Gaston must have had the same instantaneous reaction as me, but he was closer to the nearest German, and as I drew my automatic and ran crouching towards the churchyard from one direction I caught a glimpse of Gaston suddenly spring forward, hurl himself at the nearest unsuspecting German and, as they fell together, grab the German's Tommy gun. Holding the barrel, he hit the German across the head with the metal butt. The soldier fell back, not yet unconscious, but Gaston had no time to deal with him. Dead or alive, nothing mattered in those desperate moments except one thing: to save Olivia before the flames burned down the ancient, tinder-dry steps to the belfry.

The flames had so far been contained. Perhaps it was the

heavy stonework of the old church. At least there were no flames leaping out of the church windows or roof, nor yet the sound of crackling, that most ominous tell-tale sign of fire. But smoke billowed from everywhere, and it could only be minutes before the entire church – or the wood inside the heavy stone walls – became a raging inferno. And then there would be no hope for Olivia.

I reached the churchyard first, shot once into the back of a German who never even saw me, he was so entranced gazing at the smoke. Almost immediately Gaston seemed to change, ignoring all danger, every vestige of prudence, crying almost like a man demented. I don't suppose I actually had the time to realise at that moment that I had never seen Gaston behave like this before. Legs apart, the German machine gun at his hip, he stood there spraying bullets at the three or four remaining Germans until not one was left alive.

Inside we both started choking, but the choir at the back of the church, though filled with smoke, wasn't crackling. Gaston shouted, 'Olivia! Come down! It's safe!' The first flames were beginning to lick their way round the feet of the steps.

'You can handle this,' I shouted to Gaston. 'I'm going to drag the bodies in from outside. If the church burns down, and the bodies are all inside it might be put down as an accident. At least we won't be blamed.'

I saw Gaston start to climb the steps, but at first he was impeded by the bodies of men who had fallen to Olivia's Schmeisser. He pushed them down with his feet. I dashed out, escaping for a few moments from the acrid smoke, retching as I pulled the bodies in by their heels and laid them in the nave. After I'd pulled the last one in I dashed across to the choir stalls and the belfry steps. The wooden floor had long since gone, while the broken steps had almost disappeared, enveloped in the beginnings of flames. I heard Gaston cry out above me for Olivia to be careful in case the steps gave way. She came round the corner of the steps, eyes red, face blackened.

'You'll have to jump for it,' cried Gaston, now half-way up the steps. 'Larry will catch you when you fall.'

'No, this first!' cried Olivia, and with only one word she shouted, 'Catch!' and threw the radio, in its suitcase, into my arms. Only when I had safely caught it did she accept the help from Gaston. The last four or five steps were well alight by now, but Gaston lowered her down, and as she jumped I broke her fall and we both landed together on the floor of the nave.

Gaston jumped next. Almost at the same moment the roof of the nave collapsed and the flames, as though angry at being robbed, moved inwards, turning the choir into a furnace.

'Christ! That was just in time,' Gaston grinned. 'Is all the evidence inside the church?'

I nodded. 'You all right, Olivia?'

'Yes,' she gasped. 'But some air – I'm choking. And I've got a message for you.' Surrounded by the flat gravestones all three of us drew in huge mouthfuls of air until our lungs would hold no more.

'Look at that!' Gaston showed me the bottom of his trousers. They had actually caught alight as he jumped.

Still finding it difficult to speak, Olivia turned to Gaston and said, 'Just give me a moment, darling, to get my breath back.'

The tone of her voice – the use of the word 'darling' – made me look at her and then at Gaston.

'I wasn't going to tell you,' said Gaston awkwardly when he saw me staring. 'Not until we could celebrate – the three of us. But Olivia and I hope to get married when all this is over.'

'Gaston! Congratulations! I'm so glad. And for you, Olivia. So happy. Oh! Really happy.'

A small patch of grass edged the graveyard, and we lay on it ready to move as soon as we could get our breath back. Olivia was still breathing hard, as though the air was rationed, and her supply might be cut off at any moment.

'A minute more, then we must run for it,' Gaston warned us. But I was looking at the flames and the smoke and thinking how long Douzy church had been part of our lives, long before we had even thought that one day we would be killing people inside it.

'Let's go;' we were still retching, but I turned to Olivia and said, 'Didn't you mention something about a message?'

Olivia nodded, getting off the ground with difficulty. 'I lost the text in the scramble to escape. Sorry,' she apologised. 'But I can remember the text as it was in plain language. It just said, "Neutralise objective urgentest."'

51

Now we had to implement the plan within hours, not days. Our method of contact had been arranged, but getting to Verzenay didn't prove easy because for the next forty-eight hours the countryside was filled with avenging Germans – and at the same time the sultry August weather suddenly erupted into the most violent thunderstorms that locals in the area could remember. As far as I was concerned, it meant that I spent two nights soaked to the skin in ditches, often flooded. I had nothing to eat for three days except for some fruit, and on one occasion the remnants of a loaf which I stole from a farmhouse kitchen.

On the fourth day I set out on my way, the most be-draggled, scruffy peasant in Verzenay, and made my first stop at the bookshop run by Monsieur Dufy – no relation of the painter.

He looked me up and down – until I asked him if he had a copy of a first edition of Alexander Dumas.

'I'm afraid not, sir,' he said, ignoring my wet and dirty trousers, 'but I'm told that one has arrived at the wholesalers.'

Dufy's bookstore, in the rue de Tremoille, was a cut-out rendezvous. No one knew who passed on a message or to whom. It was used not only to contact people – in this case the reply meant that Gaston had arrived – but for W.T. messages to be handed to operators. The cut-out acted as a double guard against betrayal. So many good men – loyal Frenchmen, eager Britons, brave Poles – had volunteered to help France, only to be betrayed by traitors, so that when they knocked at a safe house they were greeted by members of the Gestapo. Dufy's bookstore helped to stop this. By the use of simple codes, intelligent to anyone who didn't even know them, hundreds of men had been forewarned. Dufy only needed to say in answer to a query about Alexander Dumas, 'Sorry I'm afraid the supply has dried up.' You were then warned.

Now I knew Gaston had arrived, I made my way to the safe

house. There I was given some dry clothes, a bowl of soup – and the chance to find out from Gaston what was happening.

'Olivia's all right,' said Gaston. 'She's staying with La Châtelaine.'

'I'm so glad about you two,' I said a little awkwardly. 'I never really thought Olivia and Guy would get married. He's not really her type. Never was.'

'I don't know about that, though I knew what happened at the château. But we all forget,' said Gaston, 'that I've been looking after Olivia – virtually a prisoner – for two years. You're bound to feel something for each other.' He added with his infectious grin, 'After all, she's only human – and most of the time I've been the only man available.'

What a significant choice of words! 'I've been the only man available.' For there must have been a time long ago when Mama, looking hungrily at Gaston, had harboured the same thoughts in the same village, 'He is the only man available.' And how ironic that Gaston should fall in love with a wonderful, intelligent and loyal girl – but still a girl with whom both my brother and I had been to bed. It was, I thought wryly, just one happy family.

For two days Gaston and I shared a room in Verzenay. The bookstore was our lifeline to London, for we used it as the cut-out station between ourselves and Olivia. Olivia, of course, could never appear personally – she was high on the Nazi wanted list as a 'Jewish murderess' – and nor was it possible, or wise, for either of us to make regular trips to the B and B house to check on messages when the circuit with London was opened at regular, pre-determined hours. So La Châtelaine stepped into the breach. It was natural, really, a kind of evolution in her progressive and bloodthirsty determination to kill as many Germans as she could.

There were very few messages for London, for when I acknowledged the 'go ahead' signal I told London I would observe radio silence until after the action had been taken. That, however, wouldn't stop London sending any urgent messages to me, so a daily check had to be made. This was La Châtelaine's job. In her trap she paid regular visits to Dufy's bookstore, on her way (deliberately) to the Boulingrin, because she had always gone there and everyone knew she had. Late in the day I would ask politely, but regularly, if Monsieur Dufy had received any copies of Alexander Dumas first editions. If he had, he beamed and handed me a message which I read and destroyed. If he said that no books had arrived, then I knew that there had been no word from London.

When I explained to Gaston the full gravity of the stakes we were playing for, and that somehow we had to neutralise the stocks of Sarin, we both thought at first that the only way to enter the pyramid would be through the old blocked-up entrance from the *cellier*, the above-ground workshops and presses behind the Home Farm. The Germans had not only covered the main entrance to the pyramid with barbed wire, they had also bricked up one particular gallery leading from the *cellerie* directly to the pyramid. Obviously underground passages branched off in several directions to different cellars, but only the one leading to the pyramid had been blocked off.

Fortunately, none of the Germans who had blocked up this entrance had the faintest idea that not far away the Astells had bricked up another cellar – more than a tunnel, an entire wall, to hide the Hisp. and its precious stocks of petrol. I knew that the wall which Papa had built was thin and could be easily smashed open. But behind it tunnels led out to dozens of cellars and passages and I felt sure that if we could quickly break into the hidden cache of petrol we might be able eventually to find our way into the pyramid.

The *cellier* was never guarded. The Germans didn't have a large enough garrison in the Champagne area to have a man at every entrance to every cellar. And besides, Champagne was 'at peace' with her enemies, attempting to live with them as harmoniously as possible. Yet the plans presented many difficulties, and the need for action was growing more urgent, especially after I received a message at Dufy's bookstore, terse and to the point: 'Informatively Pétain arrested. Resistance uprising in Paris now control all main buildings. De Gaulle enters Cherbourg 20th. When are you ready?'

I burned the message, but only after reading its contents to Gaston who whistled, 'They really want their pint of blood.'

'This time it's really death or glory!' I replied as cheerfully as I could. 'But with a time limit.'

Certainly I hoped we had found the simplest of all ways to reach the pyramid; but I felt that first we should check.

'And there's only one person who knows every passage leading to every cellar,' I said to Gaston. 'It's La Châtelaine. We've got to meet her.'

'Isn't that dangerous?'

'It's necessary,' I insisted. 'We'd look bloody stupid if we got into the Hisp. cellar and found it led nowhere.'

'I still say it's risky.'

'It's the only way,' I said. 'La Châtelaine is involved now, like it or not. And she's in the most powerful position a secret agent could be in – the boss, respected and feared even by the Germans. Her word is law. If we break into the Hisp. cellar and she wants to cover up the hole in the wall which we make to get in, say by stacking up some empty barrels – or even by putting the bricks back – nobody will dare ask her why, let alone argue with her.'

'That's true,' agreed Gaston. 'I'll make the arrangements to meet her.'

Using the cut-out at Dufy's bookstore, we met the following day in the village house at Verzenay where we had taken refuge. I explained that I must get into the Douzy pyramid. 'And please don't ask me why, Grandma,' I said as firmly as possible. 'It's top secret. And London has ordered me in.'

I told her about the bricked-up wall hiding the cellar where the car had been stored, together with petrol, on the outbreak of war.

'Well, that's news to me,' she almost chuckled. 'I always supposed the Germans had stolen the Hisp., taken it away or something.'

She thought for a long time.

'You see;' I was instinctively trying to persuade her. 'Once inside the Hisp. cellar we could use plastic explosives to break into any tunnel leading to the pyramid. The noise would be muffled. But it's vital to choose the right place for the explosion among the honeycomb of tunnels. That's where you can help.'

'I'm sorry, Larry,' she said finally, 'but it's impossible. I know the cellars where the Hisp. was hidden. They lead down to a dead end. There's no way through. You can take my word for it.'

I must have looked crestfallen.

'Don't worry,' she said. 'There's a much easier way into the pyramid. I could show you right away how to get in.'

'But how?' I found it hard to believe.

'Did you know that when my father was alive there had been an explosion in one of the neighbouring pyramids?' asked Grandma. 'No one ever discovered the reason why, but ten people died simply because there was no way any of them could get out. My father's immediate reaction was to make sure a similar tragedy could never happen in his pyramid. So he built what the sailors in submarines call an escape hatch.'

'But Grandma, I never heard of it!' I exclaimed. 'I never knew it existed.'

'There's no reason why you should. It's been forgotten – after all, it was built before you were born. There's never been another explosion in any of the pyramids in the Champagne area and there probably never will be. We found out later that the original tragedy had been caused not by an accident but because someone with a grudge – a crank – had blown up the pyramid on purpose. But your great-grandfather took no chances, and decided to build his escape hatch.'

She explained the details, unknown, fascinating, all taking place many years previously. In effect the hatch consisted of a narrow sloping shaft with iron rungs fixed into the chalk walls on either side from a point on the Rilly mountain. It ran right down to the base of the Douzy pyramid, almost to the point where it was adjacent to the Rilly pyramid. The shaft contained an exit so that people could escape from the base, and another exit at the half-way mark near the subway leading to the tunnel.

'But I've never seen the exits – or heard of them. Have you, Gaston?' He shook his head. 'And anyway,' I continued, 'how could anyone construct such a shaft – years ago, when there was no modern machinery?'

'They dug down on a slope,' said Grandma. 'And though I've never been down I'm told that when the work started the chalk was pulled up from the beginning of the shaft by what the Americans call banana sledges.'

According to Grandma, the excavations would, when they reached a certain stage, branch outwards – just like the Romans did, but on a much smaller scale, and the engineers constructed small cellars into which they piled the chalk they were excavating from the shaft, so that they never really had to carry the load of chalk which they were digging out any great distance. And sometimes, it seemed, they actually came across old disused cellars or galleries, opened them up and used them to get rid of the chalk they were extracting.

It seemed, too, that though the escape hatch had impressed my great-grandfather and his cronies it was valueless, not only because there was no likelihood of any explosion but, as Grandma explained tartly, 'The general opinion has always been that anyone trapped at the foot of Douzy would have died of a heart attack trying to climb about a hundred and fifty rungs of that ladder!'

'What I don't understand,' I repeated to Grandma, 'is why I never *saw* anything.'

'I think I could find the entrance and show it to you. It's on the hillside. It must be about half-way between Douzy and Rilly. It must be overgrown, of course, and it might take a bit of finding.'

'But I never saw any exits *inside* the pyramid.'

My great-grandfather, it appeared, didn't like the exit to be too obvious. He knew where it was, but both exits from inside the pyramid were invisible from inside. They could be broken down by pushing. Either from inside or outside the shaft.

This news opened up an entirely new avenue of planning. Providing we could find the shaft entrance on the Rilly mountain, we might be able to reach both the railway tunnel and the base of the pyramid. To Gaston I called it a miracle because I was so staggered that none of us had even heard of the escape hatch. Looking back, it is understandable. No one remembered it any more. It had never figured in any of our plans, our discussions, our talks. The entrance itself wasn't really on Douzy land, but on the hillside above the Rilly tunnel. It must have sloped down towards the base of both pyramids at quite an angle. I don't suppose anyone had given the long-forgotten – and highly impractical – escape hatch a single thought since before we were born. And now that old Pagniez was dead, La Châtelaine was probably the only person who would be able to find it.

We had two objectives: the Rilly tunnel had to be blown up with P.E., using delayed action fuses to give us time to escape. However, the pyramid needed a different treatment, details of which had previously been carefully explained to me – even with diagrams produced in London. For we did not want to blow *up* Douzy pyramid, we wanted to blow it *down*. It was no good blowing up the pyramid and in the process releasing all the Sarin.

Our task was to prepare a series of explosions which would cause the walls of the pyramid to collapse inwards and bury the lethal contents. According to the explosives experts in London, the simplest method was to mine the walls round the base of the pyramid so that they would dislodge huge blocks of chalk and weaken any overhang. P.E. charges, carefully placed, half-way up the pyramid, could also be used. The explosives experts in S.O.E., who superintended my crash course, had insisted that the shock of the detonations would dislodge huge quantities of overhang. Five thousand tons of chalk would probably bury the secrets of Sarin for ever. The only explosion factor that I *didn't* need to learn was that the explosions laid at the base, where both pyramids were ad-jacent, would surely dislodge the chalk at the base of the Rilly side of the pyramid as well. What if those detonations dis-lodged huge lumps of chalk high up the Rilly pyramid, and it, too, started to fall and crumble inwards?

Grandma must have realised vaguely the dangers of what we planned to do, for, sitting at the village house at Verzenay, she asked one question in, for her, a very quiet voice: 'What about your father?'

Most of the Rilly mountain, as the glorified hill through which the tunnel ran was known, consisted of rough untended 'mountain land', too difficult for farmers to reach; nor was the soil good. A few clumps of trees clothed the uneven landscape, together with acres of scrub and gorse, bright yellow in June, but now just a mass of sharp, prickly bushes. A few narrow paths criss-crossed the countryside, produced by the repeated tread over the decades of walkers. It was not very pretty, too rough, too neglected, and even the Germans found it too boring to police it with any regularity.

Early the following morning, Grandma cycled to the foot of the Rilly mountain and climbed a quarter of the way up, so as not to be seen arriving there with us. Her energy was amazing. She was dressed in a long skirt, thinner than usual because of the heat, and a pair of stout shoes, with a bandeau holding her wispy grey hair in place. Her heaviest items of 'clothing' consisted of gold bangles round her skinny, pockmarked wrists, gold chains hanging from her scrawny neck, and half a dozen rings – one a magnificent diamond solitaire – on her bony fingers.

Slowly, knees bent as we climbed, we followed the forgotten footpaths up the modest hillside. We met no one – nor had we expected to. Peasants do not as a rule waste their time on land they do not use profitably. And with waist-high scrub or gorse and the occasional clumps of trees, together with the angle of the ground, it was virtually impossible to be overseen by anyone except by an aeroplane from above.

Gaston had brought with him two implements only – a crowbar and a heavy hammer, together with two powerful English-made torches, standard S.O.E. issue. I had complete faith that Grandma – a walking geographer in her own area – would find the place, but I was not so sure that it would be quite as easy to force open any entry into an underground shaft that hadn't been used for fifty years or more. So it proved to be. The entrance took some finding, simply because it lay beneath a mass of tangled undergrowth. Too late I realised I should have brought a spade or hoe, but we hacked away with the crowbar until we had dislodged the main roots, tearing them out with our hands. Finally we cleared away the circle of cast iron. I could read part of the raised inscription, presumably the name of the maker, '*Établissements Gérard et Fils*', but the date of the manufacture and the address of the maker were undecipherable.

'It's going to take hours to force this open,' I said after a quick examination. 'It's jammed solid. We can do it, but . . .'

'Yes, I know,' said Grandma. 'All the same, I'll have to leave you here. I must go to the *cellier* and then to Douzy to see if there are any messages. Here' – she pulled out a paper bag from her capacious pockets – 'some cheese from the Home Farm. I'll check tomorrow at Dufy's to see what's happened.'

Her last words as she set off down the hill were, 'Remember your father. Better give it some thought.'

It took us four hours of backbreaking work to undo the manhole cover. It had rusted solid into the rim of the escape hatch and we faced two alternatives: to return to Verzenay and organise, through the Resistance, tools more suited to our task, and even possibly a blow-lamp if we could find one; or else alternatively just hack away, taking hours to do the job ourselves. We chose the latter way, and stayed where we were. I didn't want to go down the hill unless I had to. Though we were moderately safe when working in the vineyard, I always felt a stab of fear if I was anywhere unusual – in other words, walking down the Rilly mountain. The catastrophe of Rilly had rocked the Germans in the entire area, and when it was followed by the disastrous fire at Douzy church the Germans became even more nervy and even more savage in their determination to find out who had been responsible – and why. So any 'simple' French peasant walking near Rilly – even on the hill above – might be brusquely told to produce his papers, and count himself lucky if he didn't end up being arrested for questioning. So the fewer unnecessary journeys, the better.

Finally, we got the manhole cover freed of rust and dirt. It lay on the supporting rim, but it took the two of us all our strength to open. It occurred to me that, in the event of an explosion, workers who climbed the shaft would find at the top that they hadn't got the strength to push open the manhole cover – so they'd never have escaped anyway.

'We'll leave the cover slightly off centre, when we climb down,' said Gaston – even he was panting with the effort of hauling it away.

'When *I* go down,' I corrected him. 'I'm trying it out first – and alone. God knows whether the iron rungs will hold in the chalk or what I'll find. And' – with a smile – 'I might need you to get me out.'

Gaston knew better than to waste energy on argument. In the Resistance, internal squabbling, jockeying for power, especially among rival political factions, caused untold delays, sometimes resulting in death through negligence or, worse, betrayal. One of the strengths of S.O.E. was its clearly stated power to lead. When the S.O.E. organised Resistance groups, or helped to arm them, any local Resistants who believed they knew better (but had no idea of the long-term planning behind specific incidents) would be discarded quickly; and if disloyalty were proved, they just vanished – equally quickly.

'I'm going in for a look-see,' I explained. 'I want to discover if there's any way I can tell from inside the shaft when we reach the subway leading to the Rilly tunnel. Somehow we'll have to break into the tunnel when the time comes – probably on the way *back* from the base, but God knows how.'

The first rung was barely two feet above the lip of the shaft and I stepped on it gingerly, half expecting that with rust and old age it might fall out of the side of the shaft, which was very narrow at the entrance. But the rung held without the slightest looseness. Slowly I climbed down. I was in a slanting position, face to the rungs, and it was inky black. The circle of light above me grew smaller with each fumbling, faltering downward step. I couldn't help reflecting that really Great-grandpa had been responsible for a remarkable engineering achievement. I knew that this must be a copy of the many French escape shafts used for emergency in coal mines; but they had been made with all the money, expertise and engineering paraphernalia of huge government organisations. For one man to sink a shaft like this was a remarkable – if unnecessary – achievement.

The darkness was impenetrable. Not one speck of light, reflected, direct, even imagined, showed beyond the pinprick far above. I had my torch – and the S.O.E. had taken a leaf out of the German practice by devising torches, like the German ones, with a specially designed clip: mine could be fixed either on to a belt or on to the top of a pair of trousers or even the outside of a breast pocket. This meant that I could use both hands on the rung above. The narrowness of the shaft had another advantage. As climbers do when climbing a narrow rock staircase, the shaft was in places narrow enough for me to use my back. It was useful now to rest my arms, for I was employing muscles in a new way, so that on the upward climb I would have even more need of a backrest.

I had not been worried by the physical effort required, but I had not reckoned on one thing: the foul air inside. There had been no fresh air in that shaft for decades, and I gagged with every step I took down. I was breathing used-up air and at times I had to struggle not to vomit.

I kept careful count of the steps and after I had gone down fifty-eight of them I nearly jumped out of my skin – and I would have done had there been room in the narrow, airless, chalky shaft. For suddenly, without warning, I heard voices. Two Germans were talking, laughing, so loudly that for the first impossible moment of fear I thought they were in the shaft below me. Of course it couldn't be. Then I realised that I must have reached the subway. There could be no other explanation. The two Germans must be in the subway, separated from me, from the shaft, by a wall no thicker than a piece of three-ply wood.

It was obviously disguised. I wondered why in the first place the precautions had been taken. Perhaps Great-grandpa didn't want anyone using the subway to the tunnel – to know that, in effect, the shaft provided a secret *entrance* into the pyramid. The existence of the shaft must have been a nine days' wonder when it was first built, and no doubt there were plenty of daredevil youngsters anxious to explore it.

The garrulous Germans kept talking, loud enough for me to hear some words distinctly, though I hadn't the faintest idea what they were talking about. The voices seemed to come from all around me; no sense of sound direction, not even up or down. They were like reverberating echoes sometimes used in the movies to create an eerie effect.

I was so scared I rested without moving a muscle, hardly daring to breathe. In fact I could actually hear one of them give a sudden cough and then spit. If I could hear *them* talking so clearly, what would happen if *I* sneezed or coughed? The conversation seemed to last an age and I began to feel nauseous; then an attack of cramp in the calf of one leg almost made me scream. All I could do was move the ankle in an up and down motion then press hard with my instep on the rung of the step below me. But the illusion of nearness – not an illusion really, but I felt as though I were separated by a sheet of glass – was so overpowering that I experienced a sense of danger even just by pressing the sole of my foot against the iron bar.

Finally the voices grew less raucous. I heard the sound of footsteps moving away. They must be walking along the subway towards the Rilly tunnel – or perhaps in the other direction, into the pyramid proper. I waited a few more minutes – or seconds, I hadn't the faintest idea – then pulled my torch, which had been switched off, from my belt, and, leaning my back against the shaft to take the strain, I shone the torch on the side of the shaft. There was nothing in front, for the rungs could only be embedded in the solid material facing me. But where had the voices come from?

Almost panicking, I realised that the weak wall – the wall containing the 'secret' exit – must be behind me, the one I was leaning against. With a sudden surge of fear I was terrified that if I pressed too hard I would fall into the subway. Instinctively I held myself flat against the rungs. It was impossible to turn myself round; the shaft was too tight a fit. I did manage to half twist round, but I was so frightened of dropping my torch that before I did so I clipped it again on to my belt. If that fell to the bottom of the shaft I would not only be sightless, but the noise would be bound to raise an alarm.

Finally, by holding on to the rung with one hand and switching the torch round to pinpoint sections of the wall, I was able to make out some dusty, dirty thin lines – obviously invisible unless you were looking specially for them.

Very, very gently I pressed the wall. It gave slightly. Nothing to worry about – unless I was rough – but I knew then that this small section of the shaft, the exit from and into the subway, wasn't chalk at all. It had been made, I guessed, of thin wood, plastered over on the other side so that the join would be invisible.

The first thing I did now was to identify the crack so that each of us could spot the place immediately when we returned. I didn't want to spend precious seconds, in this foetid atmosphere, looking for it – especially as I knew that the next time we would be festooned with P.E. and fuses, to say nothing of guns and grenades. I would have been grateful for anything – a piece of chalk to give an 'X-marks-the-spot' identification. But I hadn't any. I tried to rub away the dust, but it was so thickly encrusted that it would have taken a chisel to scrape a mark. Finally I did the simplest thing of all. I tied my handkerchief to the nearest rung. Then I started my climb again – this time down to the bottom.

52

We decided to blow up the tunnel and the Douzy pyramid around 1.15 p.m. on 24 August. By then I was fighting fit again – and I needed to be, for the trial run down the shaft had taught me that I would need every ounce of my strength. I let London know, in code, using my silk pad.

I knew just what I would have to do after kicking our way into both the tunnel and the pyramid. I was sure that we could get in fairly easily, by pushing the weak section of the wall away, but I didn't want to rush in, firing at random, a target for any Germans who would certainly be armed with sub-machine guns. No; wearing gas masks as we pushed in, we would roll in canisters of tear gas which Gaston had saved from previous raids. Two would go into the gallery joining the pyramid with the tunnel, while I descended to the base, broke open the false wall, and rolled in three more. The Resistance had been collecting German tear gas for months.

Instinct – or training – told me that a sudden outbreak of gas – any gas – in a lethal store of Sarin would cause instant panic.

'What I plan,' I explained to Gaston, 'is to fall down as I break in, roll or hurl in the first canisters, crying in German, "Gas! Sarin gas leaking!" or something like that. Then pretend to faint. It'll panic even the strongest nerve – specially among troops who know that the Germans are on the run and that gas is stored in the pyramid.'

'And me?'

'When you break into the gallery door, you do the same thing – throw one canister, crying, "Gas Leak!" and run like hell – as though trying to escape the gas, to the Rilly tunnel. Then you open up another canister. It'll start a panic, I'm certain of it. After all, everyone working at Douzy and in the tunnel must know the danger they run of a leak from a lethal gas.'

We would have our gas masks, of course – the French had issued them at the start of the war. And that, I argued, would also help, in the first panic, to make us less noticeable.

'But surely the people working on dangerous gases in Douzy will be issued with protective suits and gas masks?'

'They will, I agree,' I replied. 'But we've chosen to start the attack at midday – quarter past one – because we know that the main body of methodically minded Germans in the tunnel go for lunch at one o'clock, leaving temporary guards on duty. Remember three things, Gaston – their instinct, even as they grab their gas masks, will be to climb upwards – away from the clouds of gas hugging the floor. Second, I'll be so damn quick – and so damn scared – that I'll lay those charges before they know what's happening, and then be away as they're already climbing up the stairs to escape. And three – most important – no one is going to believe that anyone can push open the wall of the pyramid. It's like' – I hesitated, searching for the right metaphor – 'like pushing down the walls of Jericho.'

Our preliminary plans were simple. Gas masks presented no problem. We both had Schmeisser machine pistols which we had stolen from the Germans, plus our automatics. We each carried a couple of grenades, our P.E. and detonators in separate haversacks – old French army issue; everyone used them since the end of the first war.

The plastic explosives were harmless, until the detonator was inserted and primed. We would each insert the detonators, with a 'pencil' time fuse set for thirty minutes, at the very last moment before bursting in and rolling the canisters into the room. I reckoned that, with the fuse set beforehand, I could be inside the pyramid, stick in four lots of P.E. and be out and start climbing up the shaft in about three minutes.

Even though Gaston, stopping at the gallery, would be in position before me, he would synchronise his attack with mine so that all the clouds of tear gas would seep into all areas at the same time.

We would both have our torches, and Gaston would carry a coil of rope, wound round one shoulder like a mountaineer. 'In case one of us needs to help the other if anything goes wrong,' I explained.

I gave my last instructions personally to Grandma at our final meeting before we left for the hill. 'There'll be no problems,' I assured her. 'But I'll need to get a message away urgently – from the top of Rilly hill. Do you think you can make it? Then collect it?'

'Of course,' she snorted, as though to say, 'How dare you!' Then she added, 'So you're going down?'

For the first time I could remember, her voice held doubts. I had noticed slight traces before, the old angry authority being subdued. Not that I minded. La Châtelaine had for so long been 'a character' that maybe a few doubts would mellow her! Or perhaps she was just getting tired and older.

'I must,' I said to her. 'A great deal depends on it.'

'I don't understand why you have to do this,' she said. 'And it's not my place to ask. But Douzy pyramid is a part of us – part of our lives.'

'But Grandma,' I tried to explain, 'in one way you're right, but in another you're wrong. You talk about "Our lives" – but they're not our lives, they haven't been for years. They belong to the Germans – all of us do.'

'Never!' she cried with a flash of her old spirit.

'Soon it'll be all over,' I said gently. 'But you're the one who always said that we had to kill every German we could. Well . . .'

'It all seems so senseless. Here, give me a *marc*' – she asked for her favourite drink. 'I can hardly remember the times when all of us were so happy,' she said bitterly. 'And now, what happens?' She held out her blue-veined hands for the small glass of fiery drink. 'Anna, living in Switzerland. Your mother in America. And where's Guy?'

'He's all right. Sonia saw him not long ago. He's fine – working with the Resistance near the Swiss border.'

'And Sonia? Fancy Sonia. Like one of the family — and now an enemy.'

'Not for long,' I promised her.

'And your father?' She looked at me suspiciously. 'Tell me — is he involved in this? Your father?'

'No, Grandma. I promise you. That's the reason why I've never let him even know I'm in France — I don't want him to be involved.' It was true, though I didn't think it necessary to tell Grandma that I had been ordered by London not to let my father know that I was in the area. Or that I was worried about the danger of blowing up Rilly as well as Douzy.

With an almost uncanny touch of suspicion, La Châtelaine said slowly, 'So long as nothing happens to your father — he's a very precious man. And a very loyal Frenchman. And don't forget that he's my son as well as your father.'

As she left, after making arrangements to meet on the mountain, I had the uncomfortable feeling that she wasn't just expressing a hope; she was warning me obliquely where the responsibility would lie in the event of any tragedy.

Everything went according to plan. We reached the top of the hill early in the morning, and waited in the scrub until after midday, when laboriously we started to pull the rusted old manhole cover aside. Before we were ready to climb down, we tore out a few big branches of gorse and small branches of trees to try, as we balanced just inside the shaft, to cover up as much of the hole as we could. We weren't very successful, though we did manage to pull across some of the larger broken branches. Anyway, we expected to be back on the hill without much delay.

I climbed down first. Because of the slope it was comparatively easy, though the stinking air still made me gag with every step I took. But with our faces to the rungs I experienced none of the tension I would have felt had I been climbing vertically downwards for such a long stretch of ladder. Every step could have been missed so much more easily if it had been vertical. And I would have gone hurtling down into the black unknown pit below.

I went first, mainly because I would be able to feel, with my hands, the rung on which I had tied my handkerchief to mark the entrance to the gallery leading to the Rilly tunnel. And of course I had to go further down than Gaston, so it was obvious I should go down first to be able to point to him above me where to break in when the right time came.

As soon as I felt the handkerchief I reached one arm above me and gently tugged Gaston's trouser leg. He knew then that silence was imperative, for we were separated by a false wall almost paper-thin. I climbed down a couple more rungs. Then, holding on to one rung with my right hand, I was able to shine the torch on to the dusty, chalky surface of the shaft and indicate the rough outline of the false exit. Gaston gave the thumbs-up signal. He could see it clearly, and he knew just what to do – give me time to get to the bottom of the shaft, set the timed pencil fuses embedded in the P.E., then wait for our synchronised watches to read 1.15.

I knew I could get the timing exactly right, for I had asked London to parachute (with other supplies) some standard R.A.F. issue chromium-plated Rolex watches, of the kind R.A.F. navigators used when they had to reach a specific target a thousand miles distant, and were only permitted a fifteen-second discrepancy in their E.T.A. – estimated time of arrival.

I had warned Gaston that, worse even than the heat on the descent, would be the stench of stale air, so foul that it would take all his efforts not to vomit. So far, of course, we had not worn our gas masks, but now I began to wonder if we wouldn't be better off wearing them, and at least breathing filtered air.

Leaving Gaston to await the synchronised time, I made my way down to the base. I had my two grenades, my P.E. ready, when I reached the bottom. The time pencils, with their delayed action fuses, were ingenious and they came in various sizes – or rather time zones. Mine were half-hour fuses, timed to blow up the P.E. thirty minutes after they were inserted and primed. They were light and easy to handle. By the light of my torch I checked on the time: 1.04. It was the moment to insert the time pencils. Each one consisted of thin wire sticking out of a small tube. In my last few minutes I stuck one wire deep into each of the pieces of P.E. At this stage the fuse was still safe. At the very last moment before I thrust open the 'door' and rolled out the cans of gas, I would squeeze each tube on the fuse. This forced out acid which would burn its way along the thin wire until it dissolved – in exactly thirty minutes, when the charge would blow up.

As I stuck the wires in, I knew it was a sticky moment. I had either to hold or to handle, at the same moment, four clumps of explosive, primed to blow up; two grenades; three canisters of gas; and a torch, so that I could see – amongst other things where to burst into the pyramid.

By 1.14 I was wearing my gas mask and all was set, torch hanging by my pocket. The lumps of P.E. were cradled in my left arm. I carried one canister of tear gas in my right hand, two more in my haversack. I suddenly thought, with a slightly sick feeling, 'Goddammit! This is *our* pyramid. It belongs to us! I hope to Christ I don't end my days in here.'

Then I charged in.

The phoney door gave way like rotten matchwood. After all, it was nearly a hundred years old. I had, for safety's sake, smashed it open with my bottom; it was safer than the other way round. I was terrified that the P.E. would go off if I messed around with it too much. As the door gave, I swivelled round, pulled the pin out of the canister of tear gas, and immediately the gas seeped out. I screamed, holding my mouth open for a second, 'Gas! Sarin!' The words were the same in German as in English. Then I pulled my gas mask over my face, and fell down as though I was dying, but I fell down very, very gingerly – still grabbing the P.E.

The effect was electric. I had known it would be; even in London, S.O.E. had regarded the actual blowing up of the pyramid as comparatively easy, and nothing to worry about in the panic. They had been much more concerned with how I would get into it. Well, I'd done *that*.

Even I, though, was astounded. Screams, shouts, filled the air. I couldn't tell what anyone was saying, but I could see that the lunchtime skeleton staff was gripped by a total panic. Some were not even carrying their gas masks – like so many of us in the war who regarded them as an unnecessary encumbrance. Without hesitation, but still screaming, 'Gas! Gas!' I rolled open another can, then, still on my back, I hurled the third can as far as I could into the middle of the ground area. Up the steps a panic-stricken group of twenty or thirty men were trying to scramble to safety. In the centre of the pyramid was the lift, specially constructed, and made of steel, which at first had reminded me of a huge Meccano set. Amongst those scrambling to safety I only caught a glimpse of them because I now had to stick the P.E. where it would do most harm. S.O.E. had explained how to place it in cracks where it would weaken the lower sides of the pyramid, forcing the walls above to crumble inwards through lack of support.

I reckoned I could spare sixty seconds – perhaps two minutes at the most. The base of the pyramid had miraculously become half empty. I found one group trying to escape into the steel elevator which the Germans had installed. It was not supposed to take men, but machinery. However, gas was everywhere and a thick spreading cloud of it was engulfing the few men left on the ground floor. I ran across to the other side of the base to spread the P.E. around the entire area, and as I was running back, and passing the lift, a German shouted at me.

For a moment, hardly able to see through my gas mask, I almost shot the vague shadow half hidden in the mist. But then I realised that I was stumbling, that he was trying to help me get into the lift, that he must have mistaken me for a German. I could do only one thing. With a groan and a muffled shout of 'Sarin!' I slid to the ground as though dying. It was enough. The German forced his way into the lift and left me for dead.

No one could see me. I knew, though, that I must not let the lift ascend, for – gas or no gas – it would lead to the gallery and escape via the tunnel.

Even though Gaston must have used gas in the gallery, I couldn't risk the other men escaping from inside the pyramid. As I reached the false door, perhaps twenty feet from the lift, I grabbed one of my two grenades and pulled the pin with my teeth. Then I hurled it with all my strength straight at the strange-looking open steel construction of the lift. I barely managed to duck behind the foot of the escape hatch – the other side of the wall – before the lift seemed to erupt in an almighty crash. A blinding flash lit up my narrow entrance, mingled with screams and groans and curses. I didn't dare spare even a second to look. Apart from the urgency I was not an explosives expert. All I knew was that the acid was burning into the fuse of the explosives, and if the walls of the pyramid collapsed so, too, would the base of our escape hatch. I was also afraid that the explosion in the lift might set off a chain reaction that would blow up the P.E. as well – before it was due to be exploded.

Somehow I reached the half-way stage of the upward climb. Panting, almost invisible in the haze of gas, Gaston grabbed me under the arms and helped me on to the solid ground of the opening next to the gallery, which Gaston had forced open – as easily, I could see, as I had done below. He had already set the fuses for the V2s and was back at the escape hatch. As I joined him, ready to clamber up, two Germans in gas masks arrived. Gaston shot one and then, as the German tore off his mask in a gesture of terror, Gaston shot the second.

'There's more on the steps coming up inside the pyramid,' I shouted, though I wasn't sure whether he could hear me.

He must have done, for he cried, 'We can't wait for long!'

'Leave it to me.' I was retching with the foetid air. I rolled my second grenade down the chalky steps; on the other side I saw a German standing on the ledge opposite – the very ledge where Papa used to invite guests to see the wonder that was Douzy, the very ledge where I had first met Willi. I saw the German hesitate and pull out a gun. He never had time to use it. Gaston shot him with his Schmeisser, and I saw the man tumble over the edge and into the tangled mass of wreckage of the lift below.

'Let's go!' I shouted. 'Time's short!'

'All laid?' asked Gaston.

'Everything. Four explosives at the base,' and looking at the luminous hands of my watch, I added, 'Twenty minutes until the bang.'

'Same here,' said Gaston. 'Let's get out of this place before it collapses.'

'Okay in the tunnel?'

'Sure,' said Gaston who was able to take his gas mask off as soon as we got up a couple of steps. He was breathing heavily and he too was retching. 'Two charges under each of the four V2s, one extra near the first rocket. Then I laid three charges just inside the half platform, to bring down the sides of the pyramid above us.'

I had my foot on a rung of the ladder to start the last ascent up to the hilltop – my hands had actually gripped the rung above me – when I stopped.

'Come on!' cried Gaston desperately. 'We've only got nineteen minutes left.'

'I can't.' I opened the mouth of the gas mask for a second and gasped, 'You go on, Gaston. I've got a job to do.'

'Your father?'

I nodded, short of words, short of breath. I stood there, then, holding my breath, eyes closed tightly, just for the moment I pressed my face to the cool, damp walls of the gallery as though to rid myself of the hideous gas and the equally hideous dilemma.

'For Christ's sake, put it on!' Gaston must have thought I had lost my reason. I hadn't – I pulled my mask on before I opened my eyes. But I knew that this was no longer a simple matter of our survival.

'You go,' I shouted hoarsely. 'I'm going to warn my father. I *have* to. I'll follow you up.'

'How?' shouted Gaston. 'How can you?'

It was difficult to shout clearly through the mask, even though I could sense that the gas was beginning to thin out.

'This!' I held out my last small piece of P.E. 'The wall to the Rilly pyramid.'

Gaston would know what I meant. In the old days a gallery had connected Rilly pyramid with the Rilly tunnel – just like our gallery. And though the entrance linking the Rilly tunnel to the pyramid had been blocked up by the Germans, it could only be the thickness of a brick, even of plaster. One tiny explosion would blow a hole in it without any problem.

'I'm coming with you,' Gaston's muffled voice shouted. 'But for Chrissake let's make it quick – I'm so scared I've just pissed in my pants.'

We couldn't waste a second – not even in argument. Nor did I want to tell Gaston to make his way up the shaft, because I knew he would refuse.

We ran along the gallery, every step sounding hollow on the damp chalk, with the occasional clink as boots struck the old tram lines. The inside of the tunnel, arc lamps still lit, like giant eyes suspended from the ceiling over the low-lying clouds of gas, made an eerie backdrop.

'Careful of the P.E.,' warned Gaston. 'Go between the rockets.' He wriggled ahead. The tunnel was eerily deserted. But I knew that, before the explosions were timed to go off, the first panic would subside and men with gas masks would return to investigate.

On the other side of the giant V2s, opposite the gallery leading to Douzy, I could see the bricked-up entrance to the Rilly gallery. I started to fumble with my plastic explosive – no danger until I had inserted a pencil fuse – when Gaston seemed to emerge from nowhere like a shadow, wielding a huge hammer.

'This is quicker!' he shouted, his voice deadened and stifled by the mask, then swung the hammer into the centre of the brick wall. Only it wasn't brick. It was ordinary lath and plaster. I barely believed it. It had been erected as a real 'show wall' to keep the French from prying into the Rilly tunnel.

'Wait.' My dampened voice sounded odd. Then to save time I just hurled myself bottom first into the lath and plaster wall and almost fell into the gallery.

Time, I knew, was running out. I didn't have to look at my watch to know that we had perhaps fifteen minutes left before Douzy and the tunnel were blown up. At least the air on the other side of the gaping hole through which I had fallen must be purer, fresher. And there had been no gas there. I pulled the mask upwards, leaving it over my forehead so that I could pull it over my face quickly, and switching on my torch stumbled forward towards a circle of light at the far end of the gallery. I heard Gaston clumping after me. Even though this gallery had been unused for two or three years the air there tasted like nectar after the gas mask.

As I reached the circle of light, the end of the tunnel, the platform – just like ours – looking down on the floor of the pyramid, a startled German soldier barred my way. Terrified by my appearance from nowhere, my gas mask worn like a hat, he began to shout, '*Was is . . .?*'

I had no time – not even five seconds to spare. I hit him across the chest with my machine pistol, grabbed him as he stumbled, and hurled him over the railings of the platform, to lie sprawled out on the floor below.

The cries from fifty people or more gave way to silence as I stood by the railings of the platform, arms spread out and upwards like a prophet or a messiah, and shouted in French, 'Everyone run for it! Run like hell! Go now! The pyramid is going to be blown up!'

I heard a shot from the ground. A bullet whizzed past me, but I shouted again, 'Run! You will all die if you don't. You have ten minutes!' The seconds it took to throw the man overboard, to cry a warning, took effect before I had a chance to look for my father. I had to find him.

I had no need to. He found *me* – without knowing who I was. Completely fearless – for after all I had just thrown a man to his death – my father grabbed me by the shoulders, wheeled me round, and shouted angrily, 'What the hell do you mean by bursting into my office!'

He must have had his desk behind the balcony where I had been confronted by the German, and he tore at the strange bearded interloper livid with fury. 'What the devil . . .?'

Human reaction is difficult to measure. I was so concerned with warning my father – and the people, some of whom were beginning to stream up the stairs to safety – that all I did at first was to beg him, 'Be quick. You have only ten minutes.' With my own life hanging by a few minutes, it never entered my head that he wouldn't recognise me, that I would have to identify myself.

'We're blowing the Douzy pyramid up in ten minutes!'

'How dare you?' He peered at me, his mouth open with astonishment.

'Yes, it's Larry!'

'My God!' he whispered. 'What are you doing here?'

'I've been living here for months. *Please* Papa, please, leave now! We're blowing up Douzy in a matter of minutes.' I looked at my watch. 'Eleven minutes exactly. Nothing can stop it. The explosives are all laid. The fuses are working. It'll blow up. Rilly as well.'

'But why are you here? Dressed as a peasant? And you – that's Gaston, isn't it?'

'Yes, sir' – the words slipped out involuntarily.

'That gun!' He seemed stupefied. 'Are you in the army?'

'Yes, but that doesn't matter. I joined up in America, I've been trained in Britain. I was landed in France to blow up Douzy – so get out – *now* . . .'

'But why? We've had such good relations . . .'

'It's all a blind. All *this*, Father' – with a sweep I indicated the Rilly pyramid – 'you've been kept quiet – anaesthetised, if you like, to stop you finding out what's been going on in Douzy.'

'But,' still bewildered, 'Douzy's been closed for years.'

'It *hasn't*, Papa.' I couldn't help adding bitterly, 'Thanks to the policy of keeping everyone happy the Germans have been able to divert suspicion from anything that's happening in Douzy.'

'But what? Why blow it up?'

'You never thought to check?'

'Why should I? Check what?'

'It's *your* pyramid, Papa. The Germans hoodwinked you by . . .'

'Nine minutes to go!' cried Gaston.

'But *what*?' cried my father.

'Douzy has enough stocks of German chemical gas to destroy London – and enough rockets in the tunnel at Rilly to see that they can reach London. Now, Father, will you go?' Turning to the edge of the gallery, I shouted, 'Run, everyone – you've only got a few minutes left before this place goes up in smoke.' My father had turned whiter than the chalk walls around him. He looked at me uncomprehendingly. His face had aged – not by wrinkles but by the realisation of truth.

'What have I done?' he asked hoarsely. 'Why didn't you warn me, tell me?'

'I couldn't. Everything I was doing was too secret. I was under orders. Run for it, Papa. I can't come out with you.' I knew that all workmen at Rilly wore identification tags and somebody like myself would never pass the main gate – especially as nothing had happened yet. To all intents and purposes the exit and entrance into both pyramids were perfectly normal. 'I'll make my own way,' I explained.

'What have I done? My God, what have I done?' he asked over and over again. 'If I'm to blame . . .' His face crumpled almost into tears. 'You could have warned me,' he cried.

'I couldn't.'

'You could.'

'Eight minutes,' said Gaston. 'Come on!'

Then in a split second I grabbed my father's shoulder and in the old French way I kissed him on the cheeks and cried, 'Good luck, Papa! Run. *Now*. Run as you've never run before.'

I might have been kissing a statue. He looked at me – through me – as though he didn't recognise me, didn't *want* to recognise me. As though I was an unwelcome interloper, the bearer of bad news. As I crouched and started off to run towards the tunnel, across it, then up to the steps in the shaft, I looked back at him. He was standing there, refusing to budge, just moaning over and over again, 'What have I done? What have I done?'

'Seven minutes! We'll just make it if we run like hell!'

Once near the end of the Rilly gallery we put on gas masks and then squirmed underneath the V2s and into the second gallery. As we crossed the tunnel I saw four men in gas masks run towards me. Because I was also in a gas mask they didn't know who I was. Gaston gave them one burst and we ran on.

'You first!' I shouted to Gaston and he didn't have the strength to argue further.

I had no time to take a last look into Douzy pyramid, no time even to give more than a fleeting thought to the times we had spent there. For no reason I remembered the visit of Mr. Vance, the owner of the *Globe*. Why have I thought of him? I wondered, my immediate horizon bounded by the feet of the panting Gaston climbing above me. I heard him shout, 'Safe to take off our masks!' And of course the tear gas was below us by now. I pulled mine off, dropping it as I did so. The torch gave me a welcome light and then far up – hidden at first because the steps were on a slanting shaft – I saw the welcome circle of distant light.

Neither of us could talk, we were so exhausted – by retching as much as by climbing. Then ten or fifteen rungs from the top I almost fell. The rung ahead of me, on which I depended to haul my feet up from below, parted in my hands. I started to fall right down the shaft, arms and legs scrabbling for a rung to grasp. Vainly I tried to use my back to gain a purchase. My flashlamp was wrenched from its hook. I lost my grip on my Schmeisser, and it clattered below, hitting rung after rung.

'Gaston!' I screamed as a red hot pain shot through my left arm and shoulder. Until then he didn't even realise what had happened.

I must have had barely three minutes left to live. And the pain shot through my arm so that I could hardly bend it.

'Gaston!' I cried again, but he was already clattering down the iron rungs until he was directly above me.

'I've twisted my shoulder and arm, and lost my torch. Shine yours down and I think I might make it.'

But I wasn't sure I could. I had fallen five rungs and was badly bruised. It's true that as we neared the end of the shaft the air was a little better, and that made breathing easier; but it required enormous physical strength to pull myself up with only one arm.

'Here,' said Gaston, 'hang on to this.' He threw down his length of rope, one end tied round his waist, then said, 'Can you tie the other end round your waist? Then I can help to take the strain.'

It was impossible with one arm – and, however much I wanted to, I just couldn't use the left arm and shoulder.

'You'd better get up top,' I said. 'We can't have more than one minute left.'

'Shut up,' he said. Holding on with one hand, he hauled the other end of the rope up, made a loop, then cried, 'Try and get it over your shoulders and under your arms. Then I'll help to pull you up.'

Somehow I managed to wriggle the loop underneath my armpits. 'Good,' he cried. 'Now let's try it.'

Laboriously I used one hand. Certainly Gaston was taking most of the weight, so that I was able to make slow, if agonisingly painful, progress.

'But we'll never make it,' I gasped.

We didn't.

Ten rungs from the top, the whole of Rilly mountain seemed to tremble. Deep, deep below us was a terrible thunder. Then the earth shuddered as though in an earthquake, so that all around us was a temporary feeling of impotence. Another clap of thunder – much nearer this time – was heralded with more violent shuddering; flakes off the side walls disintegrated and though nothing happened above me I could hear the noise of falling rocks below us. One of the rungs above me suddenly loosened. I yelled to Gaston, 'It's all coming out!' And as he helped to pull me up, the rungs underneath me gave way, falling to the ground with an ugly ringing noise as they hit each rung below. Worse, I was left dangling, held only by one arm and Gaston's lifeline. Trying to synchronise our movements, he yelled, 'Try to move with me! Now! Up!'

Slowly, with agonizing pain, one useless arm and shoulder dangling beside me, I pushed with my feet against the opposite wall of the shaft so that I was able to make one superhuman effort and put a foot on to the rung above the one that had given way.

Again I had to repeat the twisting manoeuvre in order to raise myself just one rung at a time. And always I could hear vague rumblings of rocks below, falling into the shaft; once I vomited – with foul air or fear, I don't know which. I felt as though I was going to keel over; I grabbed the rungs with my one good arm as though my hand was welded to the iron step.

The moment passed. Miraculously I made one more step up the ladder, and each rung meant one step nearer purer air. It was as though I was managing to surface when drowning and finally found my head above water. The separation of bad air and good air was finally as clearly divisible as water from air.

After that everything seemed easier. Not only was the air purer, the shaft was narrower, so that I was able to use my back more and more against the rungs, and this helped to take the strain. Finally Gaston scrambled out of the hole, grabbed the rope and hauled me up on to dry land.

'We made it, thanks to you.' We both lay gasping on the hilltop.

'How's the shoulder?' He lit two cigarettes, one for me.

'Hell – but not broken. God, I was scared in that bloody shaft.'

'Me too!'

'What do you think happened?'

'There was an explosion all right,' said Gaston. 'No doubt

about that. When I felt that first shudder I thought we were both going to slide down.'

'I believe it's the slant in the safety shaft that saved us from being blown up,' I said, and engineering experts later proved this theory to be correct. Because the shaft was slanting from the top of Rilly mountain it meant that the nearer we got to the top of the shaft the further away we were from the Douzy pyramid.

'But what about the Rilly tunnel?'

'That's different. We've blown the *contents* up, not collapsed the tunnel. Which you couldn't have done anyway.'

'How's your shoulder?' he asked again.

'Absolute hell,' I repeated.

'More work for Dr. Benoit;' he sighed with mock despair. 'You certainly keep him busy.'

The shoulder wasn't a bad injury. It might have been a collar bone dislocated, I couldn't tell.

'I'll make some sort of sling to keep it tight to the chest,' said Gaston. 'That'll save the pain.'

We had no means of telling what had happened, apart from the sound of the explosion. I said to Gaston, 'Hope my father got away.'

'I hope so.'

'You sound doubtful.'

'I don't know;' he hesitated. 'I had an awful feeling as we rushed off that he didn't *want* to leave.'

'Funny – I thought that too. Oh God! What a bloody awful life this is!'

Only four days later did we get back to the base of the mountain.

I had arranged with La Châtelaine – in her role as courier for Olivia's messages – to climb the hill if she could, or else send another member of the Resistance, at 3 p.m., for it was essential that I let London know as soon as possible. Yet both of us were afraid to go down the hill too quickly in case we were challenged. Though the hilltop at Rilly seemed quiet enough on that warm August afternoon, we knew that all hell must have been let loose among the Germans down below if the V2s and Rilly had been blown up.

Yet on the surface nothing had apparently happened. Unlike the derailment at Rilly station or the fire at the church, both of which had produced chaos visible to all, the violent explosions in the pyramid and the tunnel had been shrouded in secrecy. Many Germans might well have thought they had been caused by gas. Those who had escaped from Rilly would soon be spreading rumours all over the area. Yet even to them everything on the surface seemed tranquil. It was so quiet that even Gaston and I found it difficult to recapture the seconds – those fearful seconds – when we were all but trapped in the shaft. The earth had literally trembled at that moment.

'But we're out now,' said Gaston. We were still filling our lungs with deep breaths as though to make up for lost time. And it was thus that La Châtelaine found us.

Even she was puffing when she strode over the brow of the hill, barely a quarter of an hour behind the rendezvous time. Of course she didn't know what had happened. She had no idea of the magnitude of the operation we had been told to undertake. Nor could she yet know whether my father had escaped or perished or was even involved. How could she? Escape from what? Possibly she didn't even know that an explosion had taken place – or why.

'All I can say is that something big has happened;' she sat down on a patch of scrub, surrounded by bramble and gorse, a remarkable figure to look at: heavy boots peeping out of her 'working' corduroy trousers; her green felt hat, hiding wispy hair; and a *cabochon* star sapphire ring the size of a pigeon's egg.

'I don't know what's happened, but the Germans are running round in circles as though the bottom's dropped out of their world. They're arresting anyone they can find.'

'Any news of Papa?' I ventured.

'Oh, they won't arrest *him*,' said Grandma firmly. 'But you two – I knew since the day you landed in our field that you'd be engaged in a big project – apart from the train – and I'm proud of you both. But' – with an almost severe glare, as though to act the part she had always been determined to play, she added – 'don't spoil everything by getting caught.' Looking at my bad shoulder, she asked almost gruffly, 'Hurt yourself?'

'I twisted my shoulder. It's okay – nothing broken – but it hurts like hell.'

'Look after yourself,' was her way of expressing her fondness for me. 'And you'll want something to eat. Here.' She opened a brown khaki haversack, often used by women to carry their gas masks. 'I've brought some sandwiches. A couple of *baguettes*, straight from the Home Farm, and a couple of bottles of red wine. I'll take the message to Olivia right away. But promise me one thing, Larry – and you, Gaston – to stay here, in hiding, till I come to fetch you, till we know it's safe.'

'Unless I get orders from London,' I promised her, 'I will.'

'That's understood then. *Bon! A bientôt!*'

'Let me know if,' I hesitated, 'you have any news of Papa.'

She looked at me suspiciously, but she refrained from questioning me, and just said quietly, 'I will.'

With that Grandma strode down the hill and out of sight. Purposely I had not given her a written message to transmit. I knew that behind the apparent quiet the Germans must be going frantic – and that was just the time to pick up all the Frenchmen and search them. So I told her the message verbally – it was safer that way. And it was only two words anyway – 'Mission accomplished'. She could remember that.

When we saw her sturdy figure disappear below the rim of the hill we opened the wine, drinking from the bottle. It was extraordinary, really, how, now that it was all over I was suddenly hungry and the earth smelt good as I seized a *baguette*. In the heat of the high afternoon, birds were darting among the bushes, even some wasps came buzzing suspiciously close to us. It was as though the war below was being enacted on another planet. Here we were at peace – having a picnic, just as Sonia and I had planned on that day when we drove from Rolle.

We stayed on the mountain for four days and nights. My shoulder gave me hell, but there was no way I could get to a doctor. On the other hand, I was able to rest it. We made a rough sling out of a length of the rope, wrapped the part where the arm would lie in an old pullover, then pulled the sling tight so that my shoulder couldn't move. There was no break, of that I was sure, and the best cure for a sprain or a bad twist or even a dislocation is not to use the injured limb at all.

Throughout those four days we had no news. We had hoped that by venturing to the edge of the hill overlooking Rilly and the entrance to the tunnel we might be able to see something of what was happening, but it didn't work out that way. The tunnel didn't enter Rilly mountain in a way that enabled us to look down the face of a cliffside. Rilly sloped down from the top of the hill, and it was covered with scrub, trees which effectively blocked any view, even parts of the village itself. Had we climbed half-way down it might have been possible, but with my bad shoulder – and the danger of a nationwide search – that was too risky, especially as curiosity would have been our only motive.

It was cold at night, but we did the only thing possible – made quilts of dried brushwood. Anyway, both of us were used to sleeping rough. Nothing could have been worse than the days I spent sleeping in a Scottish ditch. And though we weren't exactly living off the fat of the land, Grandma had provided enough bread and ham to last us a few days. We were a little short of wine, but that was our own fault – after Grandma had gone down the hill we had drunk a bottle between us to celebrate. We felt we deserved it.

Around 3.30 on what I now know to be the fourth day on the hill, we ate the last of the bread and ham and drank the last of the wine. We were not quite sure of the date; Gaston reckoned it was 27 August. I thought it was the 28th, but it was by no means certain, for the days and nights on the mountain seemed to fuse into one long day. Sometimes – out of boredom or exhaustion? – we slept in the afternoons. Sometimes we stayed awake with cold during the night. The measurement of time had in a few hours been eroded so that we could only guess what day it was. Our situation was made more bizarre because we were blanketed in complete silence. We might have expected the sound of distant gunfire, even rifle shots. Nothing!

Then on this day we did hear distant sounds, nothing we could distinguish, but, far below, the sounds were masked by trees as well as distance. Then we heard shouting and noise as though the Germans were rounding up hostages or taking prisoners for work camps. It was impossible to identify the sound, it was so vague.

There was nothing vague about the next sound. We had been straining our ears in vain, even behind bushes and trees where we had made our rough shelter, when my breath seemed to stop as our own silence was broken by a sinister, unexpected noise – that of feet approaching: big feet, men's feet, more than one man, feet crackling on dry wood just behind the trees. Then the most frightening sound of all – German guttural accents, '*Ja!*' '*Das ist sehr gut!*' and phrases I couldn't understand. Gaston had silently picked up his German machine pistol. I, of course, had dropped mine in the shaft, but I still had my .45 and had loaded it with a full clip of bullets, plus one in the breech. Now I slipped back the safety catch, and froze behind a tree. Maybe they would pass us by unnoticed. I saw ahead of them – and us – our empty wine bottles, our litter, some paper. It wouldn't mean anything to them – at least I hoped it wouldn't. I couldn't tell how many Germans there were, but if they spotted us, well, we would kill as many as we could before they killed one or both of us.

What, I wondered, had brought this patrol up to the top of the normally uninhabited Rilly mountain? Why so suddenly, so unexpectedly? Frozen immobile, there was nothing to do but wait.

In my imagination the stamp of approaching footsteps sounded like death knells, as my twisted shoulder, imprisoned in one position, became knotted with cramp brought on by fear. 'I'm a prisoner of fear,' I thought for no reason. My right hand still gripped my automatic, but for a moment panic struck, as I realised that my right hand had now also become locked with cramp; locked in a grip nothing could prise open. I couldn't say anything, but my pleading eyes, turned first to Gaston, then down to my right hand, made my agony plain. Without moving his feet, cradling his machine pistol in one arm as carefully as a baby, he quietly prised open my fingers. The pain was excruciating – but he did open the fingers, gently. The only thing neither of us thought of was that the hand, bereft of its clasping fingers, was for a few seconds as useless as a dummy's. Without warning my snub-nosed automatic crashed on to the brushwood. 'Crash' may sound like a big word for a small steel implement, but it sounded like that to me – and to the Germans. I heard a hoarse cry, '*Was ist das?*' and then, as I could imagine German sub-machine guns going up to the 'ready' position to fire, Gaston opened up at the unseen target behind the woods. Figures – how many? What arms? Hidden on the other side of the screen of trees, I waited for the sound of anguished wounded, the reply of massive German firepower which could butcher us, the unseen target behind the trees. It didn't come. Instead, as I was thinking that Gaston had missed them, and as I managed to bend down and – cramp forgotten – picked up my automatic, there was a totally unexpected cry.

'*Kamerad!*' shouted voices, and one in French added, 'We have no guns!'

'It's a trap,' I whispered. 'It must be.'

'Don't worry.' Gaston pushed a new magazine into his Schmeisser. 'One move out of those bastards and I'll fire.'

'*Kamerad!*' cried the Germans, and then as we waited behind the trees, our position identified to them by the pattern of Gaston's firing, I saw a sight I never thought I would see. Through the trees five Germans approached, arms and hands held high, shrieking as though in unison, '*Kamerad! Kamerad!*'

'They're not fooling,' I whispered, and stepped out into the open, motioning them with my automatic to keep their hands up.

'You check that they've got no guns, Gaston, and watch it – there's still five of them to two of us.'

Yet, despite my instinct for preservation, and to kill immediately, I knew instantly that they meant no harm. They couldn't be deserters – a German *never* deserted. Yet why were they shouting '*Kamerad!*' – and unarmed?

An unexpected thought trickled into a brain dulled by the pain and inactivity of the four empty days and nights. *What had happened during those last four days?* In the world? In France? At Rilly? Our last radio news had told us that de Gaulle had landed in France, that the Resistance had taken over the main government offices in Paris. Could it be that the Allies had already taken Paris? It's so hard, when you have been apparently losing a war for so long, to believe any good news.

I dismissed the idea. It was impossible to have reached Paris so quickly. Yet why were these Germans wandering around a lonely mountain, unarmed, surrendering?

'Anyone speak French?' I demanded, signalling to the men to lower their arms.

'*Oui, monsieur,*' said one eagerly.

'What's happened? Why this – this "*Kamerad*"?'

He looked at me in astonishment. 'But sir – you didn't know?'

'Know *what*, for God's sake?'

'Your American General Patton has marched into Reims. This morning. The fighting in this sector is over.'

I couldn't believe it. Gaston looked, open-mouthed.

'And that's not all, sir.' The German was eager to tell us everything. 'Two days ago de Gaulle entered Paris. In Italy the Allies have taken Florence – and Mussolini has been executed.'

'But the war – that's still going on? Germany is still fighting?'

'Yes, sir,' he said, nodding. 'But I speak for every one of hundreds of German troops in this area who have already been sent east in case the Americans arrive. We don't want to be sent to the Russian front – so, will you accept our surrender? *Please, sir!*'

All at once I couldn't stop laughing. Nervous reaction, I suppose, to the hell of that trip to blow up Douzy. They laughed too – with relief. One of them offered us a piece of sausage – a sort of peace offering.

I did want to ask one question: 'Did anything happen in Rilly? In the pyramid?'

'Many dead,' answered the German soberly, almost guiltily. 'I don't know what happened, but the tunnel has been blown up. I do know that, and I heard that the pyramid at Douzy – I'm not sure, I always thought it was empty – but there was an explosion there too. At least, that's what I heard.'

For a few moments we all looked at each other, enemies, yes, still . . .

'Monsieur Gaston Pagniez will accept your surrender,' I said, pointing gravely to Gaston. 'Now, if you say it's safe, we can go down the hill.'

There was, however, one more visitor to the top of Rilly mountain. She came into view a section at a time, because the last few steps of the path she had taken were steep, so that Olivia's face appeared first, then her blouse, then a dark coloured skirt, legs, finally shoes.

As she waved, ignoring the Germans, Gaston ran forward to greet her, and he took her in his arms and kissed her gently. The Germans stood huddled together, as though gaining strength from each other, apart, as next I kissed Olivia on both cheeks and said smiling, 'How does it feel to be free? To walk outside?'

'Wonderful,' she said. But there was no smile in her voice.

'Is Grandma all right?'

'She is' – still the grave warning tone in her voice – 'but she didn't feel up to the task of coming to see you . . .'

'Task?'

'Yes, Larry dear.' Olivia was never one to spar with words, she was too forthright. 'Your father – perhaps you've already guessed – and we sometimes forget, you know, he was La Châtelaine's son. He died very bravely. We only heard yesterday.'

I sighed. He *was* my father, but distance, time, events, war, had in a curious way separated us, made him a stranger to me. I don't mean that cruelly: we both loved each other as much as we had always done; but – it was almost as though I was being told bad news of a distant relative I hardly knew. It was unfair of me to think thus, but in those first moments it was perhaps better; at least it helped to exorcise any of the guilt I felt at having helped to cause his death. And to exorcise, too, the last few seconds of our only meeting since Pearl Harbour – the look of anguish in his face when I confronted him, the near sob in his voice when he cried, 'What have I done?'

'Do we know any of the details?' I asked heavily.

'Most of the men escaped from the Rilly pyramid. And they all said the same thing, that your father – in a way my father too, he was so wonderful to me – he refused to move until the others had gone first. The last few were too late, it seems. About a dozen men, your father and his close friends, were there when the pyramid blew up at the base. Apparently it wasn't a very big explosion, but it rocked the sides and the whole thing fell inwards.'

'Thanks, Olivia, for coming to tell me. Did Grandma take it very badly?'

'Yes. We forget she's an old lady. She's been sustained in a way by all the excitement – it's pumped adrenalin into her day after day – but now it's virtually over. She's still in the Misses B and B house. Aubergine is with her. La Châtelaine is spending a few days in bed, but she'll be all right when she gets over the shock.'

'I'll go to see her as soon as I can. But first of all I must get into Reims and check in with the colonel in command of the U.S. unit.'

'I thought – S.O.E. . . .?' asked Gaston.

'That's true,' I said. 'But as Americans – and as a last hope in case I was caught – I was also attached to Com.Z., the American communications section. I must get a lift there as soon as I can and report in.'

'I'll come with you,' said Gaston. Awkwardly he added, 'I'm so sorry about your father. He was such a fine man, Larry. I don't know what to say . . .'

'Thanks,' I cut him off. 'There's nothing anyone can say. It had to be, I suppose. Something else to live with. Let's go.' And sadly, if victoriously, we made our way down the hillside, a strange assorted party: a Frenchman, the man who had been my father's chauffeur and my mother's lover; a wonderful Jewish girl, betrayed by another Frenchwoman; a handful of Germans; and an American.

'It takes all sorts to fight a war,' I said, but I said it to myself.

53

Reims was like a new world, one we had forgotten, the dreary twilight world of subdued people, hardly daring to speak, every guarded word or furtive action couched in fear. The French had for so long been oppressed, *suppressed*, that at first they had been almost afraid to shout their joy, even talk aloud. Then, as we reached the capital of Champagne, and handed over our prisoners to an American patrol, the bubble burst.

The Germans had gone! Run away! The Tricolour flew everywhere, appearing so quickly it was almost as though the flags and bunting had been kept hidden by men and women of faith and hope, to be brought out when the nightmare was over.

At first I felt ill at ease as Gaston and I walked along the streets towards the market place behind the boulevard Lundy. Some pretty girls rushed forward with flowers, and when one tried to kiss me I drew back, suddenly aware that I hadn't brushed my teeth for four days. I'm sure I looked filthy, but so did many people after a day's honest toil. The difference was that I *felt* dirty.

We went into a small bar and ordered two draught beers. After the waiter had sliced off the froth with his wooden slat, we both drank our half pints in one gulp. It was so cold, so beautifully tangy and sharp, that we both smacked our lips at the same time – loudly.

The barman looked up, laughed at the sound and said, 'Tastes good, eh?'

'Nectar!' I cried, and the words broke the spell of reserve. The barman hadn't noticed that I looked dirty, that I must smell, that my beard was untrimmed.

'Come on,' I cried to Gaston. 'I'm going to shave off my beard. You could do with a shave too.'

We both went into a small barber's shop and I felt a new man when we emerged.

'Let's see if we can get a square meal at the Boulingrin.'

'Like this?' Gaston might have shaved, but he still looked dubiously at our old clothes. We hadn't been able to change *them*.

'Sure. The Astells regard it as our local bistro.'

'I'm not an Astell.'

'You are now.' I put an arm on his shoulder. 'In all but name – just as much a member of the family as Olivia has always been. Come on.'

Monsieur Leleu was delighted to see us and, perfect gentleman that he was, found a table for us with a whispered,

'Steaks — beautiful ones — for you both? With *pommes frites?*'

As we nodded, he added, 'I was so sorry to hear about your father. So many fine men and women have died for our country. But it's good to see *you* back — and alive.'

Sitting at our corner table, a dish of *pommes frites* dusted with salt in front of us, we tucked into a couple of the largest steaks I had seen for years.

'Not bad, eh?' I looked at Gaston.

He laughed. 'I'd forgotten about steaks. I'd forgotten what they looked like, never mind what they tasted like.'

We washed the meal down with a bottle of Bouzy *rouge*.

'I kept it specially for old friends,' said Leleu. 'Just a few bottles.' And later, 'No, no, Monsieur Astell. I wouldn't hear of it. This is on the house — to celebrate.'

As I thanked Monsieur Leleu, he apologised for not having any good coffee, so we skipped the ersatz substitute and were starting on large glasses of the finest *marc de Champagne* when suddenly I heard a yell, 'Larry! Larry!'

I almost knocked down the small square table with its red and white checked cloth as I tried to swivel round. I knew that voice anywhere.

'Uncle Oregon!'

And there he was, not only my uncle, but my mentor, the man who had founded the *Paris Weekly*, who had given me my first job as a junior reporter, who had guided my footsteps from there to the *Globe*.

Gaston dragged a chair from the nearest table. Oregon looked as though he would prefer to sit down — and for that matter, so did we. After all, we had spent four days and nights on a hilltop.

'I'd no idea you were here,' I said. 'I heard a couple of years ago from Mama in New York that you'd been interned in Fresnes, and that you'd managed to get one letter through to New York. After that, not a word. It's wonderful to see you. And looking so fit . . .'

He wasn't that fit really. The twinkle in his eyes was still there, but dulled. The halo of curly white hair had thinned down and what was left was more straggly than curly. And he had lost a great deal of weight.

'But you're still a chainsmoker,' I laughed.

'Started the day I was released. The Resistance took us to Paris. I only stopped to buy some Gauloises, then I bummed a lift here as soon as it was safe. Yes, I will have a *marc*,' he said as Monsieur Lelcu produced the bottle. 'Tell me – how did *you* get back here so quickly?'

'It's a long story,' I laughed. 'Actually, I've been here for weeks. I'm in the U.S. army. I joined up after Pearl Harbour.'

He must have looked puzzled, for he asked, 'Odd sort of uniform you're wearing – farmer's clothes!'

'Let's just say I'm on leave. I'll tell you the whole tale one day soon.'

'And the *Globe*?'

'Not a word since I joined up. Have you seen Grandma?'

'Have I! I had a job finding her, but eventually I tracked her down. Larry, I hear she's been running an airfield for the Resistance.'

I nodded. 'But how is she now?'

He lit another cigarette, stubbing the first one out on the ashtray. 'Very depressed, as you can imagine. She must have taken a hard knock when she heard about your father – especially as she hadn't the faintest idea whether or not *I* was alive.'

'But you are,' I cried. 'And what do you plan to do next? Take over the running of the vineyards?'

'Me a vigneron?' His face crinkled into that special smile I remembered so well. 'Never! I'd make a balls of it. I know as much about grapes as about balls. They're all vaguely spherical but of different sizes and have different uses. No. Besides, La Châtelaine tells me that Gaston here has been running the vineyards better than any of us ever did.'

Gaston was hardly the blushing type, but he did look pleased and said 'Thank you,' as we poured out a final glass.

'Well,' I asked, 'what *are* you going to do?'

He looked at me with genuine astonishment.

'I'm off to Paris, of course – to reopen the *Paris Weekly*. What else? It'll sell like hot cakes to the American troops.' With a grin he added, 'Want to rejoin the old firm?'

I shook my head. 'Thanks for the offer, but before anything else I've got some unfinished business to attend to.'

'Such as?'

'Getting married. Remember Sonia?'

'Ah! Darling Sonia. But she is married.' It was more of a statement than a question.

'Annulled. It's an old Vatican trick – if you've got enough money. We're free – both of us. As soon as I get permission from the army brass I'm off to spend my leave in Switzerland and get married.'

'Bully for you! Your father . . .' He paused, suddenly embarrassed at the unthinking use of the word, then hurried on. 'Well, I've always thought that when you two were caught in what must have been very delectable *flagrante delecto* you should have been allowed to marry. It's a pity when parents stand in the way of young love.'

'And do you remember Olivia?'

'Of course. That beautiful creamy complexion. Is she all right?'

'She certainly is. She's been working in the Resistance as a radio operator. She's getting married soon.'

'Seems to be catching.'

'To Gaston.'

'Well, I never!' Oregon sounded really surprised. 'I thought – well, what about Guy?'

I explained the ways that all our lives had been divided. It was the first time that Oregon knew of Guy's activities or that Anna had been living in Switzerland with Sonia.

Just before Oregon got up to leave, he said, 'I'll be staying here for two or three days. But what about *your* future? Now that your father has died, will you be taking over the business?'

'I don't think so. In theory my job on the *Globe* has been kept on for me, but I've also got an idea for a book. I can't really decide anything until I've seen Sonia, had time to think things out.'

Oregon was thinking. 'Maybe Guy would like the job?'

'Working with Gaston's wife? Come off it, uncle!'

'Hadn't thought of that.'

'I was only joking,' I explained. 'In fact Guy's married to the secret service. His immediate boss in Switzerland, Allan Dulles, has been doing undercover work – brilliant man, lots of guts, and Guy has been working with him.'

'But that's going to stop now.'

'It seems that Allan Dulles – who has a brother, Foster – is being tipped to head a new organisation, hasn't even got a name yet, though it might be called the C.I.A. – stands for Central Intelligence Agency. Guy's been offered a big job with Dulles. He loves that line of business.'

'Isn't it sad,' Oregon sighed. 'Our beautiful, wonderful Douzy – and nobody really wants it.'

'That includes you,' I couldn't help saying.

'I know. I was the first. Ah well! Where are you staying?'

'Nowhere. We've been living rough. Probably I'll spend a couple of nights in the B.O.Q.'

'What on earth's that?'

'Bachelor Officers' Quarters.'

'Why does everything have to be in initials?'

'It's habit,' I laughed. 'And after the B.O.Q.' I added, 'It's Switzerland . . .'

'So that' – though he looked older, Oregon still had his infectious laughter – 'so that you can finally make an honest woman of Sonia.'

Later that day, after Gaston went to meet Olivia, I stopped an American M.P. who looked twice at my dishevelled, unkempt appearance, until I used the magic formula, 'Section Q.J.', the code name used by both the O.S.S. and the S.O.E. men reporting after finishing a project. It gave them the highest priority and came under Com. Z., which ran the communications network.

The officer who greeted me was a Colonel Nolan, very agreeable and anxious to help; and after fitting me out with a uniform, took me up to the château to see Douzy. He was very impressed with the fact that an American family produced such a famous champagne, and though the war was not yet over he promised to arrange leave for me as soon as I had been debriefed. He was a bit shattered when I said I wanted to visit Switzerland, but once I explained that I had a car and lots of petrol, he readily agreed.

The Château de Douzy was a shambles. I was horrified, almost sick, as I took the colonel on a conducted tour of the lovely old place. The German vandals who had been billeted there had behaved like pigs. 'Officers and gentlemen – in

726

theory,' I commented bitterly to Nolan, who immediately ordered a detail of men to be sent from Reims to help clear up the mess. Plates and glasses had been smashed. Remnants of old food had been strewn in the living room, on the floor, even on the chairs, and of course there were empty champagne bottles by the dozen.

When Nolan discovered that my family actually produced their own champagne as a way of earning a living – 'And a famous champagne too,' he added – I had to open a couple of bottles, and, despite the ghost of Papa haunting the house, I welcomed the colonel in the traditional manner.

'Astell champagne;' he tasted it reverently. 'I never thought . . .'

'*Pardon, monsieur.*' The voice was quavering as Jean, the old butler, materialised from nowhere, to offer the colonel more champagne and then, when I embraced him, promptly burst into tears. I remembered that Jean had remained at the château when the Germans commandeered it – a sensible move, for at least it meant he had been able to keep an eye on the place. But a sudden reunion, the relief, the death of my father a few days previously, and then the sight of me in uniform – it had all been too much for the old man.

Tearfully – but still professionally – he opened another bottle, then Madame Robert, the farmer's wife from the Home Farm, arrived carrying two hams. Soon Monsieur Roland, the *patron* of the Café des Sports in the village, came to pay his respects, and after that, so it seemed, almost the entire village streamed in. Gaston and Olivia turned up. Everyone was excited at the thought of their newfound freedom – nothing could dim that – yet while Colonel Nolan stood smiling and drinking amid the 'foreign' throng of villagers, Roland tapped on the glass with a pencil for silence and then, in a polite but muted toast, cried, 'To *Messieurs Astell – père, frère et fils.*'

Father, brother and son!

They were welcoming me back, of course. But they were also paying their last respects to Papa, with a mention too for Oregon. Colonel Nolan, who could barely stop showing his admiration for the house – even in its filthy state – was standing in the conservatory, where the geraniums still bloomed, climbing up the back wall.

'Lovely, isn't it?' I pointed towards the dell and, below it, the orchard.

'Breathtaking!' Then he saw on the other side of the horizon a pile of blackened masonry, the sharp edges of ruins jutting out like decayed teeth.

'Douzy church,' I said. 'And you see that girl over there?' I pointed her out. 'She's a French girl who suffered terribly at the hands of the Gestapo, but do you know, she escaped, we helped her, and then she spent *two years* hidden in the belfry of the church, sending radio messages to S.O.E. in London. That's *real* bravery. Finally, the Germans set fire to the church to try and burn her out.'

Nolan looked at Olivia with admiration. Then his eye caught a movement half-way up the dell. 'There's an old gal cycling towards us,' he said. 'Another villager?'

'Only one woman in Champagne cycles like that,' I answered, amused. 'That's my grandmother. She's quite a character, and known all over the Champagne area as "La Châtelaine". She's around eighty, and cycles everywhere; everyone, including the Germans, is terrified of her.'

'She does look a little' – politely – 'unusual.'

'She is. She's a hundred-per-cent French. My grandfather, who died long ago, was American, but it's always been Grandma who runs the show.'

'Are *you* frightened of her?' asked Nolan with a laugh.

'Terrified!' I laughed back. 'Or was. She's beginning to mellow a bit, and though I haven't seen her since my father died, I imagine she took it hard.'

A few minutes later La Châtelaine arrived and, after leaning her ancient bike against the stable doors, marched in followed by Aubergine. Colonel Nolan stared in wonder when I introduced her to him. She was dressed in her corduroy trousers, her usual green felt hat, and on her blouse she boasted an enormous emerald brooch. Her knotted, gnarled fingers were covered with rings.

As she kissed me, I said gently, 'I'm so sorry, Grandma . . .'

'I know, Larry.' She was more emotional than I had ever seen her. 'It's war. It's horrible. But he died bravely – my son died a hero – and you have a father you can be proud of. At least that's something.'

'My respects, Ma'am.' Colonel Nolan, who had a pleasant smile, took her hand. 'And I'm arranging for my boys to come and clean up your place.'

'Thank you, Colonel. *Salles Boches!* I want to get the smell of Germans out of the house.' To me she added, 'I'm very selfish, Larry. I know how you must be feeling.'

'I understand, Grandma.' I didn't want to elaborate on the events which had taken place at Douzy and Rilly. They would soon be buried with honours in legend. 'You know what Oregon said? That if all Frenchmen had been as loyal as Papa, France would never have lost the war.'

I turned to Colonel Nolan and said, 'You did promise me I could go on leave if I provided my own transport?'

'Sure. You'll have to be debriefed, but that won't take long, will it?'

I didn't think so. Department Q.J. would handle it, but I did ask if there was any chance of getting a phone call through from the military switchboard at Reims to Switzerland. Nolan didn't seem to think there would be any problem.

I made a suggestion: I would return with him right away to Reims, make my report to Q.J., then phone through to Rolle. 'And tomorrow,' I said, 'I'm going to show you the sight of a lifetime – if you can spare an hour or two. We're going to have an official unveiling of the Hisp.'

'Hisp?'

'Short for Hispano-Suiza, the finest car of its kind in the world when it was built. More than a car. A twelve-cylinder battleship. Then we'll have lunch.' I turned to Jean. 'Can you and Madame Robert prepare a scratch meal?'

'Easily, sir,' Jean said eagerly. 'And if we knock down the wall before lunch, I could get some of the '33 vintage.'

'You have to knock down a wall to get at it?' Nolan was baffled.

'It's the finest vintage since the early twenties – and my father not only walled up and hid his favourite car, he walled up ten thousand bottles of '33 to stop the Germans drinking it. They never discovered where it was. We'll crack some bottles tomorrow.'

That evening – it was still Monday, 28th, the day Reims was

729

liberated – I spoke to Sonia, asking my very first question, 'Has the completion of the annulment come through?'

'Yes, it has. But when shall I see you? I wouldn't be allowed to visit France – not now. But you? I can hardly wait.'

'On Thursday,' I promised. 'Tomorrow I'm going to get the Hisp. from the cellars. I'll have to give Gaston the day after that to tune it up. And then, darling Sonia, at dawn on Thursday morning, I'll be on my way. And tell me – how long will it take us to get married? The formalities, the paperwork?'

'I'll be round at the town hall in Rolle tomorrow morning first thing.' Her voice was not only laughing, it was singing with happiness. 'Oh! darling, is it *really* over – is it really possible?'

'It is. And soon I'll be introducing you to all our friends – and this time for ever – as Mrs. Larry Astell.'

The re-emergence of the Hisp from its hiding place had all the overtones of pomp usually associated with the launching of a ship. A score of villagers arrived at 10 a.m. and were offered free champagne – though not the '33. With Gaston in charge, one bottle of non-vintage was ceremoniously hurled at the wall my father had built. It smashed against it in a shower of froth. Then Gaston and three or four helpers armed with sledge hammers started to break down the wall.

When there was a hole large enough to scramble through, Jean crept in with a torch to find the '33, and emerged with a couple of bottles. Soon the wall – hated symbol of Nazi domination – had been demolished, and the Hisp. stood like a ghost wrapped in dust sheets.

We tore it off. Some dust had slipped in through the years, that was inevitable, but even so the black monster with its silver fittings would need only a feather brush and a little polish to restore it to its former magnificence.

'Quite an automobile,' said the colonel.

'She is. And she does a hundred miles an hour. By tomorrow night Gaston will have her tuned to perfection. He's worked on that car since he was a boy.'

★   ★   ★

We drank quite a few bottles of the '33, more than we had intended to, because La Châtelaine joined Colonel Nolan for lunch, together with Oregon, who was leaving the following day for Paris. Then Gaston and Olivia arrived after he had interrupted work on the Hisp. I was delighted when Grandma invited Gaston to lunch, asking Nolan, 'I believe you've met? Gaston is the head of our vineyard production.' How Gaston had changed his life since the time when he used to tinker with cars, or drive Papa – and Mama – in his chauffeur's uniform. I could not have asked for a better friend, a more staunch comrade. He deserved everything – including Olivia, already changing for the better. Nothing would ever erase the wrinkles caused by suffering, nothing could obliterate the memories, but at least she had had her hair waved, touched up, and her nails manicured. She was, in short, a woman again. I raised my glass to her in a silent toast. A wonderful girl.

Then I drank another silent toast – to Anna. Sonia had told me on the phone that she had virtually recovered – enough to be planning a trip to America as soon as she could find a passage. Wonderful news! I wasn't all that sure how a very much changed Mama would get on with her daughter, but the fact that Anna was well enough to want to travel meant that the terrible scars had all but healed.

As the meal ended, Grandma drank a toast to her son, then turned to me, glass raised, and said, 'All of us here send our love to Sonia. It's like a bridal party. But it's more than that. We're saying farewell to the France we knew, for we know it can never be the same again. So off you go, and get married. And God speed you. But come back – soon. We need you. We need all the friends we can muster to help rebuild our new France all over again.'

Within a few hours I was on my way to Sonia. It was a warm, sunny day, and the streets of country villages were lined with flags. The elegant black and silver car purred along silently with hardly more than an engine whisper. Sometimes in a village street men and women turned and clapped at the sight of her, so rare was such an emblem of luxury.

I stopped at the roadside to drink some wine and eat some *baguettes* which Madame Robert had packed for me, then set off again towards Dôle. Nearly there! And I was thinking not only of the meeting with Sonia in only a few hours, but the very first time I had driven to Rolle – then in my beloved M.G. – and of that journey back, and how everything had started when we lay in a bed of golden corn flecked with red poppies.

How much had happened since then! Not only war, but life itself – those first entrancing months in the rue de l'Université when I worked all day in the rue du Sentier, learning to be a newspaperman, then danced or made love all night till the first streaks of dawn touched the Champs-Élysées as we walked home. And then the arrival of Sonia's parents, Signor Riccardi and his friendship with the sinister Otto Abetz, of the way they used their hidden powers to murder two Italians, and later to force Sonia to leave France. And then her marriage to Francesco – but even that didn't stop us loving each other. It led us to the mad journey through roads choked with traffic in a vain bid to help Sonia escape before France fell – until I lost her after the air raid.

Then war – with Mama almost drowned in the *Athenia* – and the saving of her attaché case, with its tell-tale photo of Mama and Gaston. I would never tell him that I knew about them. It was after that, after I stumbled into the flat in Germany to find Willi beaten up, almost dying, when the worst of all terrible tortures happened to the Astells. Anna and Olivia were captured by the Gestapo, and suffered the fate of the damned until, with the help of Sonia, we rescued them.

Now it was all over. I couldn't remember the number of men Gaston and I had killed in cold blood – face-to-face killings, not the impersonal load of death dropped by a bomber pilot. I never would remember. I wanted only to forget it all.

I drove carefully through the twisting streets of Dôle, and headed for the Juras and Pontarlier. That was where we had stopped on the first journey, pausing at the 'frontier' town for a glass of beer, then tearing off to find the cornfield.

That was what I wanted to remember. The war had been an interlude, fought by others. Life had really started – for me anyway – on that first trip to Rolle, and now, after all the agonies that life and fate had laid before us, like tests to be surmounted on the road to happiness, we had come full circle.

Once again – a day later, a year later, a lifetime later? – I was driving through the sunshine to the lakeside at Switzerland to meet a beautiful girl. The same beautiful girl, dressed in pink on that day so long ago, the only girl I had ever loved, and ever would.

Afterword

Abetz, Otto was jailed by the French in 1949 for 20 years, but was pardoned and released in 1954. He and his wife died in 1958 when their car, driven by Suzanne, was in a crash on a German autobahn.

Portes, the Countess Hélène de was ironically also killed in a car accident, but within a few weeks of the fall of France in 1940. She and Reynaud had lunched near the Mediterranean town of Seté when he set off, driving the car, with Madame de Portes a passenger. He lost control, the car hit a tree head on and she was killed instantly. Reynaud lay critically ill for several weeks in a hospital at Montpellier.

Reynaud, Paul, after recovering from his accident, was jailed by the Germans for much of the war. After 1945 he married again, returned to politics and died in 1966.

Bullitt, William C, having served as U.S. ambassador to France from 1936 to 1941, became Roosevelt's special representative in the Near East and a special assistant secretary of the Navy. He died in the United States in 1967.

Gaulle, General Charles de returned from virtual retirement in 1958 during the Algerian troubles to become prime minister again and, later in the year, first president of the Fifth Republic. He died in 1970.